The Broken Eye

Lightbringer: Book 3

BRENT WEEKS

orbit

www.orbitbooks.net

ORBIT

First published in Great Britain in 2015 by Orbit

5 7 9 10 8 6

Maps by Chad Roberts Design

A CIP catalogue record for this book
is available from the British Library.

ISBN 978-1-84149-911-6

Typeset in Sabon by Palimpsest Book Production Limited,
Falkirk, Stirlingshire
Printed and bound by CPI Group (UK) Ltd, Croydon CR0 4YY

Papers used by Orbit are from well-managed forests
and other responsible sources.

MIX
Paper from
responsible sources
FSC® C104740

Orbit
An imprint of
Little, Brown Book Group
Carmelite House
50 Victoria Embankment
London EC4Y 0DZ

An Hachette UK Company
www.hachette.co.uk

www.orbitbooks.net

For Kristi, who gets better all the time – and makes me want to do likewise,

and for Mom, who took a seven-year-old kid who hated reading and kindled a lifelong love.

Contents

The Seven Satrapies

Hellmount

IDOSS

The Red Cliffs

The Cracked Lands

Atash

Ru

Ruic Head

The Chromeria

Big Jasper

Little Jasper

Rath

Green Haven

THE FLOATING CITY

Blood Forest

The Great River

VERIT

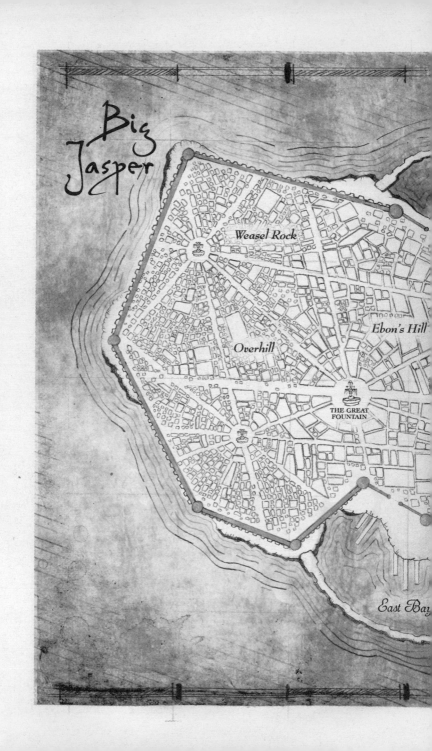

The man who is content to live alone is either a beast or a god.

– Aristotle

Chapter 1

The two Blackguards approached the White's door, the younger rhythmically cracking the knuckles of his right fist nervously. The Greyling brothers stopped in front of the door, hesitated. *Pop, pop, pop. Pop, pop, pop.*

The elder brother, Gill, looked at his little brother, as if trying to emulate their commander's sledge-gaze. Gavin hated it when Gill did that, but he quit popping his knuckles.

'We gain nothing by waiting,' Gill said. 'Put that fist to use.'

It was early morning. The White usually didn't emerge from her chambers for at least another two hours. With her declining health, the Blackguard were doing all they could to make the old woman's last months easy.

'How come it's always me who—' Gavin asked. At nineteen, Gill was two years older, but they were the same rank, and they'd been elevated to full Blackguard status at the same time.

'If you make her miss it because you're arguing with me . . .' Gill let the threat hang. 'Fist,' he said. It was an order.

Scowling, Gavin Greyling knocked on the door. After waiting the customary five seconds, he opened the door. The brothers stepped inside.

The White wasn't in her bed. She and her room slave were praying, prostrate on the floor despite their age, facing the rising sun through the open doors to the balcony. Cold wind blew in around the two old women.

'High Mistress,' Gill said. 'Your pardon. There's something you must see.'

She looked at them, recognizing them immediately. Some of the nobles and luxlords didn't treat the youngest of the full Blackguards seriously. It was a judgment that cut because it was partly deserved. Gavin knew that even a year ago, he wouldn't have been promoted to full Blackguard at seventeen. But the White never treated him like he was beneath anyone.

1

He would gladly die for her, even if someone told him that she'd die the next day of old age.

She broke off her prayers, and they helped her into her wheeled chair, but when the old room slave waddled over to close the balcony doors on bad hips, Gill stopped her.

'She needs to look from the balcony, *caleen*,' Gavin said.

Gavin wrapped the White in her blankets gently but efficiently. They'd learned exactly how much delicacy her pride would stand, and how much pain her body could. He pushed her out onto the balcony. She didn't complain that she could do it herself. She would have, not long ago.

'In the bay,' Gill said.

Little Jasper Bay was resplendent below them. Today was the Feast of Light and Darkness, the equinox, and it was turning into one of those autumn days one hopes for: the air chilly, but the sky blindingly blue, the waters calm instead of their normal chop. The bay itself was conspicuously underpopulated. The fleet was still gone to fight the Color Prince at Ru and stop his advance. Gavin should have been there. Instead, he and three others had been sent back by skimmer on the eve of battle to report the fleet's disposition and plans.

Surely by now, the battle had taken place, and all that remained was to wait to hear whether they should rejoice in their victory or brace for a war that would tear the Seven Satrapies apart. Thus the White's prayers, Gavin supposed. Can you pray about the outcome of an event after the fact? Do they do anything then?

Do they do anything, ever?

The White waited silently, staring at the bay. Staring at nothing, Gavin was afraid. Had they interrupted her too late? But the White trusted them; she asked nothing, simply waited as the minutes stretched out.

And then, finally, a shape came around the bend of Big Jasper. At first, it was hard to get a sense of the size of the thing. It surfaced a hundred paces from the high walls ringing the entirety of Big Jasper, which were lined with people jostling one another to see. The sea demon was visible at first only by the wake it left, plowing waters to the left and the right.

As the sea demon came closer, it sped up. Its cruciform

mouth, half open, swallowing the seas with its ring-shaped maw and jetting them out through its gills along the whole of its body, now opened full. With each big gulping pulse, its mouth opening wide now, water splashed out to the sides and back in great fans every fifty or so paces, then, as the massive muscles contracted, the water behind it hissed with churned air and water.

The sea demon was approaching the seawall that protected West Bay. One galley was making a run for a gap in the seawall, trying to get out. With how fast the sea demon moved, the captain couldn't have known it was precisely the wrong direction to go.

'The poor fool,' Gill muttered.

'Depends on if this is a coincidence or an attack,' the White said, eerily calm. 'If it gets inside the seawall, they might be the only ones to escape.'

The galley slaves lifted their oars out of the water as one, trying to make as little disturbance on the seas as possible. Sea demons were territorial, but not predators.

The sea demon passed the galley and kept going. Gavin Greyling expelled a relieved breath and heard the others do the same. But then the sea demon dove, disappearing in a sudden cloud of mist.

When it reappeared, it was red-hot. The waters were boiling around it. It veered out to sea.

There was nothing they could do. The sea demon went out to sea, then it doubled back, accelerating. It aimed directly at the prow of the galley, as if it wanted the head-to-head collision with this challenger.

Someone swore under their breath.

The sea demon rammed the galley with tremendous speed. Several sailors flew off the deck: some into the sea, one flying until he crunched against the sea demon's knobby, spiky head.

For an instant it looked like the ship would somehow hold together, and then the prow crumpled. Wood exploded in shards to every side. The masts snapped.

The entire galley – the half of it that was left – was pushed backward, ten paces, twenty, thirty, slapping huge fans of spray into the air. The sea demon's forward progress was only briefly slowed. Then the galley was pushed down into the waves as that great hammerhead rose even higher out of the water and kept pushing. Abruptly, the ship's fire-hardened wood hull shattered like a clay pot thrown against a wall.

The sea demon dove, and attached to that great spiky head by a hundred lines, the wreckage was dragged down with it.

A hundred paces away, a huge bubble of air surfaced as the last of the decks gave way underwater. But the ship never rose. Flotsam was all that remained, and not nearly as much of that as one would expect. The ship was simply gone. Perhaps half a dozen men out of a crew of hundreds were flailing in the waves. Most of them couldn't swim. Gavin Greyling had learned to swim as part of his Blackguard training, and that most sailors couldn't had always struck him as insanity.

'There,' Gill said, pointing. 'You can see the trail of bubbles.'

The sea demon hadn't gotten trapped inside the seawall, thank Orholam. But what it seemed to be heading for was worse.

'High Mistress,' a voice broke in behind them. It was Luxlord Carver Black, the man responsible for all the mundane details of running the Chromeria that didn't fall under the White's purview. He was a tall balding man in Ilytian hose and doublet, with olive skin. What remained of his long dark hair was streaked liberally with white. Gavin hadn't noticed him. A Blackguard, and he hadn't noticed. 'Your pardon, I knocked but got no response. The beast has been circling the Jaspers, five times now. I've given orders for the guns on Cannon Island not to fire unless it attacked. They want to know if they should consider this an attack.' The defense of Little Jasper was technically in his portfolio, but Luxlord Black was a cautious administrator, and he liked to avoid blame wherever possible.

What could a cannonball do against such a beast?

'Tell them to wait,' she said.

'You heard her!' the Black bellowed, cupping a hand adorned with many rings to his mouth. There was a secretary on the roof, one floor above the White's balcony, holding a polished mirror a pace wide, leaning out over the edge to listen.

'Yes, High Lord!' The man hurried to flash the signal, and

a younger woman replaced him at the edge, trying to listen without appearing to be listening to the wrong things.

The sea demon was now hugging the coast, swimming through waters so shallow its back was visible. It rammed through the portmaster's dock without even appearing to notice it. Then it reached the far northern tip of Big Jasper.

'Oh shit.' The thought was everyone's, but the voice was the White's. The White? Cursing? Gavin Greyling hadn't thought she even knew curses.

The people on the Lily's Stem had lost sight of the beast as it had come in close to Big Jasper, and the sea demon was bearing down on the bridge before any of them could react.

The bridge floated at exactly the height of the waves. Without supports, the yellow and blue luxin formed a lattice that looked green. It had withstood battering seas for hundreds of years, the chromaturgy required to make such a thing now beyond perhaps even Gavin Guile himself. More than once it had served as a wavebreak for ships trapped outside the seawalls during storms and had saved hundreds of lives. The sea demon's first, incidental contact with the bridge rocked the entire structure. It threw hundreds of people off their feet.

The vast shape slid along the smooth luxin for ten, twenty paces, then slowed, seeming confused by the contact. Its confusion lasted only an instant, though, as fresh billows of steam rose around it. The sea demon's head plunged into the waves and it sped out to sea, its vast tail slapping the water beside the Lily's Stem and sending geysers over almost the whole length.

Then, out at sea, it turned back again.

'Tell Cannon Island to fire!' the White shouted.

Cannon Island sat in the bay opposite the Lily's Stem. The likelihood of the gunners there making the shot was remote.

But a slim chance at distraction was better than none.

The first culverin fired immediately; the men must have been waiting for the order. The shot was at least a thousand paces, though. They missed by at least a hundred. The island's other five guns facing the right way each spoke in turn, the sound of their fire lagging behind the bright flash of it, the roar reaching the tower at about the same time they saw the splash.

5

Each missed. The closest splash was more than fifty paces off target. None deterred the sea demon.

The crews began reloading with the speed and efficiency that could be only imparted with relentless training. But they wouldn't get off another volley in time. The sea demon was simply too fast.

The Lily's Stem had become chaos. A team of horses had fallen, panicked, and turned sideways with their cart within the confines of the bridge itself, blocking all but a trickle of men and women from getting out onto Big Jasper. People were climbing over and under the flailing, biting horses.

A stampede flowed out of the other side of the bridge, people falling, being trampled. Some few would make it in time.

'Carver,' the White said, her voice clipped. 'Go now and organize care for the dead and wounded. You're faster than I, and I need to see how this ends.'

Luxlord Black was out the door before she was done speaking.

Four hundred paces out. Three hundred.

The White reached a hand out, as if she could ward off the sea demon by will alone. She was whispering prayers urgently under her breath.

Two hundred paces. One hundred.

A second dark shape suddenly streaked under the bridge from the opposite side, and a colossal collision with the sea demon sent jets of water a hundred feet into the air. The sea demon was launched into the air, bent sideways. A black shape, massive itself but dwarfed by the sea demon, had hit it from below. Both crashed back into the water, not twenty paces from the Lily's Stem.

The sea demon's superior mass carried its body all the way into the bridge itself, shooting a wall of water at the tube and over it. The whole edifice was rocked by the force of the wave – but not shattered.

In a spray of water and expelled breath, flukes and a black tail surfaced. That tail smashed down on the sea demon's body, and then the whale darted into Little Jasper Bay. Out, away from the bridge.

'A whale,' the White breathed. 'Was that . . .'

'A sperm whale, High Mistress,' Gill said. He'd loved stories

6

of the sea's pugilists. 'A black giant. At least thirty paces long, head like a battering ram. I've never heard of one that big.'

'There haven't been sperm whales in the Cerulean Sea for—'

'Four hundred years. Since the Everdark Gates closed. Though some persisted for another hundred or— Your pardon,' Gill said.

She didn't notice. They were all too engrossed. The sea demon was obviously stunned. Its red-hot body had turned blue and sunk beneath the waves, but even as the sea calmed from the aftershocks of the collision, they could see the red glow begin again. The waters hissed.

A swell of that big body underneath the waves, and it turned and began to move – chasing after the whale.

The White said, 'That kind of whale is supposed to be quite aggress—'

Four hundred paces out from shore, another eruption of water as the two leviathans collided again.

Sperm whales had been the only natural enemies of sea demons in the Cerulean Sea. But the sea demons had killed them all, long ago. Supposedly.

They watched, and again the giants collided, this time farther out. They watched, in silence, while the rescue operations below worked to clear the Lily's Stem.

'I thought those whales were usually . . . blue?' the White asked Gill, not turning from the sea.

'Dark blue or gray. There are mentions of white ones, possibly mythical.'

'This one looked black, did it not? Or is that my failing eyes?'

The brothers looked at each other.

'Black,' Gill said.

'Definitely black,' Gavin said.

'Bilhah,' the White said, addressing her room slave by name for the first time that Gavin remembered. 'What day is today?'

''Tis the Feast of Light and Darkness, Mistress. The day when light and dark war over who will own the sky.'

The White still didn't turn. Quietly, she said, 'And on this equinox, when we know the light must die, when there is no

7

victory possible, we're saved – not by a white whale, but by a black one.'

The others nodded sagely, and Gavin felt like a significant moment was passing him by. He looked from one to another. 'Well?' he asked. 'What does it mean?'

Gill slapped the back of his head. 'Well, that's the question, ain't it?'

Chapter 2

Gavin Guile's palms bled a warm, thick gray around the slick oar in his hands. He'd thought he had respectable calluses for a man who worked mainly with words, but nothing prepared you for ten hours a day on the oar.

'Strap!' Number Seven said, raising his voice for the foreman. 'More bandages for *His Holiness*.'

That elicited a few pale grins, but the galley slaves didn't slow. The big calfskin drums were thumping out a cetaceous pulse. It was a pace the experienced men could maintain all day, though with difficulty. Each bench held three men, and two could keep this pace for long enough to allow their oarmate to drink or eat or use the bucket.

Strap came over with a roll of cloth. She motioned for Gavin to present his hands. Strap was the burliest woman he had ever seen, and he'd known every female Blackguard for twenty years. He pulled his bloody claws off the oars. He couldn't open or close his fingers, and it wasn't even noon yet. They would row until dark; five more hours, this time of year. She unrolled the cloth. It seemed crusty.

Gavin supposed there were worse things to worry about than infection. But as she wrapped his hands with efficient motions, albeit without gentleness, he smelled something vibrant, resin overlaid with something like cloves, and heard the tiny shivering splintering of breaking superviolet luxin.

For a moment, the old Gavin was back, his mind reaching for how he could take advantage of their foolishness. It was difficult to draft directly from luxin breaking down, but difficult was nothing for Gavin Guile. He was the Prism; there was nothing he couldn't—

There was nothing he *could* do. Not now. Now, he was blind to colors. He couldn't draft anything. In the threadbare light of the slowly swinging lanterns, the world swam in shades of gray.

Strap finished tying the knots at the back of his hands and growled. Gavin took that as his sign and lifted weary arms back to the oar.

'F-f-fights infection,' said one of his oarmates, Number Eight, but some of the men called him Fukkelot. Gavin had no idea why. There was a loose community here with their own slang and inside jokes, and he wasn't part of it. 'Down here in the belly, infection'll kill you quick as a kick.'

Superviolet luxin fighting infection? The Chromeria didn't teach that, but that didn't make it wrong. Or maybe it was simply a new discovery since the war and no one had told him. But his thoughts were drawn instead to his brother, Dazen, who had slashed his own chest open. How had Dazen not succumbed to infection down in the hell Gavin had made him?

Had the madness that had convinced Gavin he had to kill his imprisoned brother not been madness at all, but only a fever?

Too late now. He remembered again the blood and brains blowing out of Dazen's skull, painting the wall of his cell after Gavin had shot him.

Gavin put his bandaged hands back on the well-worn oar, the grip lacquered with sweat and blood and the oil of many hands.

'Back straight, Six,' Number Eight said. 'The lumbago'll kill ya if you do it all with your back.' Now, that many words with no cursing was just a miracle.

Eight had somehow adopted Gavin. Gavin knew it wasn't pure charity that led the wiry Angari to help him. Gavin was the third man on their oar. The less work Gavin did, the more Seven and Eight would have to do to keep time, and Captain Gunner wasn't taking it easy on the speed. He wasn't keen on staying close to the site of the fall of Ru.

In another week, the Chromeria would have pirate hunters out: privateers given writs to hunt the slave takers who'd swept in upon the wrecks of the invasion fleet, saving men in order to press-gang them. They'd look to ransom those who had relatives with means, but many would doubtless head straight back to the great slave yards of Ilyta, where they could offload their human cargo with impunity. Others would seek out nearer slave markets, where unscrupulous officials would forge the documents saying these slaves were taken legally in far distant ports. Many a slave would lose his tongue so he couldn't tell the tale.

This is what I led my people to, Karris. Slavery and death.

Gavin had killed a god, and still lost the battle. When the bane had risen from the depths, it had smashed the Chromeria's fleet, their hopes thrown overboard like so much jetsam.

If I had been declared promachos, it wouldn't have happened.

The truth was, Gavin shouldn't have only killed his brother; he should have killed his father, too. Even up to the end, if he'd helped Kip stab Andross Guile instead of trying to separate them, Andross would be dead, and Gavin would be in his wife's arms right now.

'You ever think that you weren't hard enough?' Gavin asked Seven.

The man rowed three big sweeps before he finally answered. 'You know what they call me?'

'Guess I heard someone call you Orholam? Because you're seat number seven?' As six was the number of man, so was seven Orholam's number.

'That ain't why.'

Friendly sort. 'Why then?'

'You don't get answers to your questions because you don't wait for 'em,' Orholam said.

'I've done my share of waiting, old man,' Gavin said.

Two more long sweeps, and Orholam said, 'No. To all three. That's three times no. Some men pay attention when things come in threes.'

Not me. Go to hell, Orholam. And the one you're named after, too.

Gavin grimaced against the familiar agony of rowing and

settled back into the tempo, sweep and stretch and brace against the footboard and pull. The *Bitter Cob* had a hundred and fifty rowers, eighty men in this deck and seventy above. Openings between decks allowed the sounds of drums and shouted orders to pass between the upper and lower galley decks.

But not only sound passed between the upper and lower decks. Gavin had thought his sense of smell was deadened after a few days, but there always seemed some new scent to assail him. The Angari fancied themselves a clean people, and maybe they were – Gavin hadn't seen any signs of dysentery or sweating sickness among the galley slaves, and each night, buckets made the rounds of the slaves, the first full of soapy water for them to slop on themselves and the second full of clean seawater to rinse. Whatever slopped free, of course, dribbled down on the slaves in the lower hold and, dirtied further, into the bilge. The decks were always slippery, the hold hot and damp, the sweat constant, the portholes providing inadequate ventilation unless the wind was high, the dribbles of liquid from the deck above that dripped onto Gavin's head and back suspiciously malodorous.

Footsteps pattered down the stairs, the light step of a veteran sailor. Fingers snapped near Gavin, but he didn't even look over. He was a slave now; he needed to act the part or be beaten for his insolence. But he didn't need to cower. On the other hand, he *did* still need to row, and that took all his strength.

Strap took Gavin's hands off the oar, unlocked the manacles, whistled to Number Two. Numbers One and Two were at the top of the fluid slave hierarchy, allowed to sit up front and rest, trusted to run errands without chains on, and only required to row when another slave got sick or fainted from exhaustion.

After Strap manacled his hands behind his back, Gavin looked at Captain Gunner, who was standing at the top of the stairs out of the hold. Gunner was Ilytian, with midnight black skin, a wild curly beard, a fine brocaded doublet worn open over his naked torso, loose sailor's pants. He had the handsome intensity of madmen and prophets. He talked to himself. He talked to the sea. He admitted no equal on heaven or earth – and in the firing of guns of any size, he was justified in that.

Not long ago, Gunner had been jumping off a ship Gavin had lit on fire and poked full of holes. Gavin had spared Gunner's life on a whim.

The good you do is what kills you.

'Come on up, little Guile,' Captain Gunner said. 'I'm running out of reasons to keep you alive.'

Chapter 3

Kip's palms bled vibrant crimson around the slick oar in his hands. His palms had blistered. The blisters had filled with colorless plasma. The tender skin beneath had torn. Blood had swirled into the plasma like red luxin. Chafed ceaselessly against the oar, the blisters broke, bled. He shifted his grip. New blisters formed, colorless. Filled with crimson. Burst.

He didn't see the color, though. Couldn't see anything. He could only imagine the colors waiting for him as soon as he shed the blindfold Zymun had put on him to keep him from drafting. Zymun, the polychrome who'd followed the Color Prince. Zymun, who'd tried to kill Kip in Rekton, and tried to assassinate Gavin at Garriston. Zymun, who held a pistol pointed at Kip's head even now. Zymun, his half brother.

Zymun, whom he would kill.

'What are you smiling about?' Zymun asked.

The rowboat bobbed and lurched on the waves as it had for the last two days. Without the use of his eyes, Kip couldn't thread his way through the chaos of the waves, rowing at the right time, pausing when appropriate. From time to time, he'd pull on one oar and feel it slip free of the water. He'd flounder until Zymun barked a direction. Two days they'd been doing this. Two agonizing days.

The blindfold was overkill the first day: Kip's eyes had swollen shut. During the battle he'd accidentally hit himself, and then Zymun had punched him in the face. He had a dozen small cuts on the left side of his face and down his left arm from when the merlon of the green bane had been hit by a cannonball and exploded into shrapnel. Andross Guile had stabbed him in the shoulder and gashed him along his ribs.

If it hadn't been for his Blackguard training for the last months and the fact he had a gun leveled at his head, Kip wouldn't have been able to move. As it was, the unfamiliar exercise reduced his muscles to quivering clumsiness. His back was agony. The fronts of his legs, kept constantly flexed as he tried to keep his balance in the bobbing boat, were murder. His arms and shoulders were somehow worse. And his hands! Dear Orholam, it was like he'd dipped them in misery. His burned left hand that had been slowly healing was now a claw. It hurt to tighten, it hurt to loosen, it hurt to leave it alone.

Kip was fat and frightened and finished.

'More to port,' Zymun said, bored. He didn't think enough of Kip to pursue why Kip had smiled. He was too canny to come close at a slight provocation, and the waves were too heavy today for him to risk putting himself off balance for a momentary pleasure.

He'd never offered to take a turn at the oars.

The only thing that kept Kip going was fear. It was exhausting to be afraid for two days straight, and it was starting to make Kip a bit furious.

But what can I do? I'm blind and reduced to such weakness I couldn't win a fight with a kitten, muscles sure to clamp or collapse at any move I make. Zymun has set the field. He has the cards: six colors and a gun.

But as soon as Kip saw it as a game of Nine Kings, his terror eased. He imagined analyzing the game with the patience of a blue. Could Zymun be nearly as frightening an opponent as Andross Guile? No. But if you have a terrible hand you can still lose to a bad opponent.

Zymun could kill Kip at any moment, easily and without fear of justice or repercussions, because no one would ever know.

Yes, yes, we've established that, but so what?

Kip's best card was Zymun's laziness. Zymun knew they needed to row or they could fall prey to pirates and be enslaved. Zymun didn't want to row himself, so Kip was safe until he irritated Zymun enough to overcome his laziness, or until Zymun didn't need him any longer.

Zymun had great cards, but a great card that you never play is a worthless card.

Zymun had a ludicrously inflated opinion of himself – he'd already spoken at length about all the things he would do once he reached the Chromeria. Kip didn't appear in those stories, which told Kip all he needed to know about his own future. But Zymun's inflated opinion of himself meant he had a proportionally deflated opinion of others. Kip acted beaten, and Zymun believed it. Of course he was superior. Of course Kip would be devastated by that fact and realize that he was helpless.

'I really expected the sharks to get you at Garriston,' Kip said, threading a grudging admiration through his tone.

Zymun wasn't an idiot, despite his arrogance. Once the sun went down, he lost his luxin advantage. Then he only had three cards: the pistol, Kip's injuries, and that his own muscles weren't devastated from a dozen hours of grueling labor. Anytime Kip had turned over last night in his sleep as he lay in the front of their little boat, under the bench, Zymun had woken instantly, the flintlock already cocked and pointed at him.

Kip's odds of getting accidentally shot if Zymun twitched in his sleep were depressingly high.

'Wasn't a pleasant swim,' Zymun said. After a silence, he said, 'I expected that waterfall to get you back at Rekton.'

Peeved, Kip the Lip almost brought up their next meeting – in the rebel camp, when Zymun hadn't recognized him. But taunting a man with a dozen sure ways to kill you wasn't the height of good sense.

'Guess we've something else in common then,' Kip said. 'Hard to kill.' He shouldn't have bothered trying to draw them together with some illusory common bonds. Zymun was pure reptile. Kip thought the boy must try to hide it most of the time. With Kip, he didn't. Another sign of how Kip's time was limited.

'We're the blood of Guile,' Zymun said. 'But you'll forever be a bastard. I'll prove myself to grandfather, and be an heir. The heir.'

Kip rowed. 'You're sure?' he asked. 'About Karris being your mother? I never heard so much as a whisper.' He hated being

14

blindfolded, having to sift Zymun's tones of voice rather than look for the momentary grimaces or twitches that might betray the truth.

'She was betrothed to the Prism when they conceived me. That makes me legitimate, to most people. When he broke their betrothal, she went and stayed with relations.'

'In *Tyrea*?' Kip asked. That was where he'd first seen Zymun, defying his master, throwing fireballs at Kip, and forcing Kip to jump off the waterfall.

'Blood Forest. Little town called Apple Grove. I went to Tyrea later. It was the only place to go to learn drafting that wasn't the Chromeria.'

'Grandfather's idea?' Kip asked. It sounded like Andross Guile. Have the boy educated, trained, and kept off the table. A perfect hidden card. While being honed into the perfect weapon, Zymun would also be kept from developing his own allies at the Chromeria. He would be perfect for Andross's use against Gavin or the Spectrum, but he wouldn't be a threat to Andross himself. The boy didn't even realize how cynically Andross was using him.

Guess I've become a little cynical myself, to see it so clearly. Or maybe I'm only cynical where Andross Guile is concerned.

Regardless, Zymun didn't answer. Or perhaps he answered by nodding.

In two days, Zymun had never asked about Karris. He seemed to think her position on the Blackguard made her acceptable to have as a mother, but not intrinsically powerful, and therefore not interesting. He saved his questions to arm himself for his meeting with Andross Guile. Kip wished he could be there to see that.

The next time Kip's oar slipped off a wave, he coughed hard. He wheezed into his hand and pushed the blindfold up his nose fractionally. Coughing, even fake coughing, hurt like hell. He'd inhaled a lot of seawater after he'd jumped into the Cerulean Sea to save Gavin Guile.

He'd once thought of himself as the turtle-bear, made with a special gift for absorbing punishment. He was really going to have to come up with some other special gift. This one was terrible.

He went back to rowing. Zymun had made him strip off his shirt, both so he could see if Kip tried to pack luxin, and to keep himself warm. With the cloud cover and the autumn wind, it was chilly for much of the morning and evening. Rowing and sweating, Kip didn't notice the lack so much.

At the end of each stroke, his head naturally tilting back, Kip took a tiny sip of blue under the blindfold. In the weak, gray, cloud-filtered light, the sea was soup, and his eyelashes and the blindfold blotted out most color, but he didn't need much. Couldn't take much at once, or Zymun might see it. With only a little at a time, Kip's skin was dark enough to camouflage the luxin as it traveled from his eyes, through his face hidden by the blindfold, down his back, and was packed beneath the skin of his legs and butt, out of sight. Zymun had checked his scalp and the skin hidden by the blindfold a few times, so an abundance of caution was in order.

Now, certain that Kip wouldn't draft, Zymun expected him to attack at night, when his own powers were weakest. But as a full-spectrum polychrome, Kip knew weakness wasn't measured in colors. There was no difference between Zymun having a dozen sure ways to kill him and only having one, if time was limited enough. In fact, if Zymun could be more easily surprised because he had a dozen ways to kill Kip than if he'd had only one, then those extra ways actually made him weaker.

Some people think that you play Nine Kings against the man, not the cards. It sounds clever, but it's rarely true.

By late afternoon, Kip had enough luxin. It took all of his concentration to row and push his pain aside and slowly thread the luxin up his back, up the back of his neck, up into his scalp. To draft luxin, it had to be connected to blood. Most drafters chose to tear open the skin at their wrists or under their fingernails. After a while, scar tissue formed; the body adjusted. But you didn't *have* to push the luxin through a spot where you'd done it before, and Kip didn't intend to. Every fraction of a second lost made death more likely.

The sips of blue made it all seem so logical. Kip's senses were acute, filtering out the wind and his own heaving breath. He divined that Zymun was seated facing him. Kip knew where the bench was, could tell that Zymun was seated in the middle of it from how the rowboat sat even in the water. He could hear Zymun shift from time to time, looking behind them or to shore.

The blue couldn't mute sounds, though, only sift them. The irregular wind obliterated much of the information Kip could have used. Nor did blue mute all his body's agony. Kip had husbanded his dwindling resources as carefully as possible, acting slightly more exhausted than he was so that he could grab a moment of rest between each oar stroke – balancing Zymun's laziness against his own life.

It had to be today. It had to be soon. He didn't have much strength left.

Kip hunched, grunted in pain, and released the oars, faking a leg cramp. The move was sudden enough it probably almost earned him a musket ball between the eyes. He massaged his leg with both hands, evaluating, testing, stretching not just his legs, but his hands and arms, too.

There was a sudden snort and a small cry.

Planting his legs wider than he had before, making them less helpful for rowing, but hopefully more helpful for a sudden leap, Kip settled back into his place, groped blindly for the oars. He pretended he hadn't noticed, but he died a little.

Zymun must have just dozed off. Kip had woken his enemy. With blue sharpening his senses, if Kip had waited even a few moments . . .

He hadn't. That was no use. Commander Ironfist had told them, 'Looking back doesn't help. Dwell on your mistakes when you're in safety. *Get* to safety first.'

'If you think I'm going to help you, you're insane,' Zymun said.

Kip groaned from the pain of moving his arms. He didn't know if he would have the strength even to lurch across the boat. He groped around blindly, missing the oars that he'd released. He said, 'Longer I fumble around for the oars, the longer I get to rest.'

'Right hand. Up and forward. Up more. Use the chain, stupid.'

The oar, held in its oar lock, bobbed and swayed with the action of the waves. It smacked Kip's fingernails. Kip grunted. He bent his wrist to reach the manacle, and followed the chain to the oar. He hadn't forgotten about it. But it was better to look stupid.

It was better not to look like he was calculating exactly how long that chain was. Kip grabbed the oar. Then he repeated with his left hand, and he started rowing again.

'More to port,' Zymun said, bored. 'That's it.'

There was only one way this could work. Kip had to knock Zymun into the water and not fall in himself. Once Zymun fell in the water, his pistol would be useless. He would only have time to throw one burst of something at Kip. Because all luxin had weight, that action – regardless of which color of luxin he chose to throw – would cause the reaction of pushing Zymun deep under the waves.

If Zymun missed with that first strike, Kip had a chance. He would have to row like mad. When he was able to see how far from shore they were, he could decide whether to risk going back and killing Zymun, or leaving him to his fate in the sea. After Zymun's impossible escape through shark-filled waters last time, Kip planned to kill him and be sure.

If Kip was too slow, though, he'd get shot. With no idea what direction to row, and as weak as he was, he would die. If he knocked them both into the water, he would die. Zymun was the better swimmer even when Kip was healthy.

There would be only one slim chance. Kip would be ready for it. His eyes, shielded from the light under the blindfold, were naturally wide, dilated. He tried to narrow them consciously, a trick any experienced drafter could do instantly. If he was dazzled by the light, he'd miss. If—

Zymun's weight shifted. 'Orholam,' he said.

The moment was on him so suddenly, Kip almost missed it.

'A galley,' Zymun said. The blue luxin Kip was holding told him that Zymun's voice was muted by being turned to the side, looking. 'I think it's pirates.'

Now! Blue luxin tore through Kip's skin at his temples. With fingers of blue luxin, he flipped the blindfold off his head – and leapt.

Chapter 4

'I smell so much as a resiny fart, and I paints my deck chunky, little Guile. Red and gray and bony, you elucidate? I know luxinly smells,' Gunner said as he led him onto the deck of the *Bitter Cob*. 'Or more like, I paint it all in brown and squashy, right, right?'

Gavin walked into the light with a lead heart.

'Right,' he said. Because he had feces for brains. Funny.

'Luxinly? Luxic? Luxinic?' Gunner asked. The man loved language the way a wife beater loves his wife.

'Luxiny, but I like your way better.'

'Bah.'

It was close to noon, choppy seas tossing the light galley more than he expected. These Angari ships were different. But what had been the most salient fact of his whole life – the light – struck him as insignificant. It was an overcast day, but with lots of light for a Prism. But this light kissed his skin like a lingering lover leaving. The hues of gray and white and black gave him despair where before the scintillant spectra had given him inconceivable power. He'd thought he'd adjusted to the loss of his colors, but it was one thing to face his loss in the darkness of a prison, another thing altogether to see that his prison was the whole world. And Gunner knew it. He had taken one look at Gavin's eyes the night he'd captured him and he'd known.

So why is Gunner paranoid now?

Because he's Gunner.

'On yer knobbies,' Gunner said.

Gavin got on his knees, planting them wide on the deck so the rolling motion wouldn't knock him down. He couldn't tell if the stretching hurt good or hurt bad, but as long as he didn't lose his head or any other limb more important to him, any break from the oars was a good thing.

Gunner looked at him. 'What happened to Gavin Guile, levering the world on the fulcrum of his wantings?'

On one level, this was the clearest thing Gunner had said to him yet, but Gavin had told Gunner he wasn't Gavin. It was probably one of the dumber things he'd done in the last year, though there were a lot of contenders for that crown. 'He died.' That ought to work, regardless of which Gavin Gunner meant.

'Tragical. How?'

The trick to working with the insane was never to profess surprise. Nor to expect it. Opacity was a dagger Gavin could wield, too. 'I ran out of mercies until I had only the musket-ball mercy left. Clickety-clack, clickety-clack. Boom boom. Meatsack mercy. Yellow cell red, liver made dead.'

Gunner folded his arms. He looked at Gavin like he was very puzzling. 'You rave.'

'I crave.'

'You knave.'

'I slave.'

'I save.'

'From waves?'

'And you gave,' Gunner said. He gestured to his big white musket, propped against a doorframe some paces away.

Gavin stopped to let Gunner win. He did want to get a better look at that odd thing, but Gunner alternately wanted to show it off and looked paranoid that someone was going to steal it. Gavin couldn't pay too much attention to what Gunner treasured. Nor too little.

Gunner laughed, sealing his win, taking Gavin's hesitation to be a concession of defeat. They'd played this game before. Years and years ago now. If Gavin weren't utterly in the man's power, and Gunner utterly insane, Gavin thought he might like him. Gunner said, 'I don't take men who've been in Ceres's bosom too sincere. Them watery kisses make men crazy, and ain't no Guile started out overmuch sane. Tell it straight as shooting. Are you Dazen Guile, back from the dead? You tell me this, and not half the tale.'

Which didn't mean what the words meant. Gunner's patience was shorter than his fuses. So Gavin gave it in brief: 'Never died. Captured my brother at Sundered Rock, and took his place. His friends looked better than mine, so I took my brother's clothes, and I took his place. But not a month back, I decided my imprisoned brother had gone frothing mad, and I killed him.'

It was so simple to say the words. Gavin had thought it would be impossible to tell the truth he'd worked so hard to hide for so long. But he felt nothing. He should feel something, shouldn't he?

'The sea she sends me mysteries to invigorate,' Gunner said.

Gavin was sure, this time, that Gunner had used the wrong word on purpose. 'You're quite an invigorator. No wonder you're Ceres's favorite.'

Gunner spat into the water, but Gavin could tell he was pleased. 'You're *Dazen*? Straight bull's-eye?'

'I been shootin' in the dark so long I ain't sure what I am, now. I *was* Dazen, though. Straight shootin'.' Gavin wasn't sure why he did that, dropping into patter when he spoke with others who did so. He'd always done it, though, copying accents and odd phrasing when he spent too long in any one place.

'You say this because you know Gunner worked for Dazen,' Gunner said. 'You're lying. Hoping to edge with me.'

Hoping to edge? – oh, hoping to gain an edge. 'Sure. And before I killed my brother, he told me your birth name was Uluch Assan. You were so very important to him, those were his last words.'

Gunner's eyes glittered dangerously. 'Not impossible for a Prism to learn an old name.'

'Before you agreed to work for me – me Dazen – all those years ago, you told me lies about how you killed that sea demon as we sat in the slaves' quarters drinking that foul peach liquor. And when you professed to believe that there was no such thing as superviolet luxin, we played a little game with a feather to quell your doubts.'

A worried look crossed the pirate captain's face. 'Took Gunner three shots to hit that damned dancing feather. Was an eagle feather, though, not quail.'

There was no point correcting him, so Gavin continued, 'I feared I'd made you so furious that you wouldn't work for me. I let you hit it . . . on the sixth shot, ya damned liar.'

Gunner went rigid. Shit. The man told lies to aggrandize himself so often, he might think that his version was the truth.

Not the battle to pick, Gavin. Gunner strode away suddenly, heading to midship.

Gavin stayed where he was, on his aching knees. It was bad stretching now, he was certain of it. The two sailors who'd accompanied him looked confused as to what they were expected to do.

'Free his grabbies!' Gunner shouted. He was rummaging in a barrel.

The sailors unlocked the manacles, but kept Gavin on his knees.

Gunner grabbed something from a barrel and threw it at Gavin. He bobbled it in his bandaged, stiff hands, and it bounced on the deck. A sailor fetched it and gave it back to him. A big, wrinkled apple.

'Take him to the beakhead,' Gunner said. 'Watch him close as Aborneans groats. A Guile in a corner is a sea demon in your washtub.'

Here I didn't think you bathed. Gavin didn't say it, though. There was little to be gained by mocking his captor, his master, and much else to be retained. Teeth, for instance.

The sailors pulled him to his feet and pulled to him to the prow. They turned him around, forced him to his knees again. Gunner was forty paces away, at the farthest point astern. He held a gleaming white musket. Or a musket-sword? It had a single blade with twin black whorls crisscrossing up the blade, bracketing shining jewels. The blade had a small musket inset in much of the spine except for the last hand's breadth, which was pure blade.

Gavin had a dim recollection of the thing, but it slipped away from him. Something about that night, and a clash with his father and Grinwoody and Kip. He had suffered great violence before and lost hours of time to it, and he'd certainly known men in the war who'd lost memories of injuries. But there was something about Gunner fishing him out of the waves, and then beating him with the flat of the blade? It could only be that. Gavin was still recovering from his bruises, but he didn't have any stab wounds or he probably would be dead by now.

Still, what a terrible idea. To make a musket barrel thick

enough to deal with the power of exploding powder was to make a weapon far too thick and heavy to be an effective sword. Was this some sort of odd jest?

'If you're Dazen, you'll remember our little demonstration,' Gunner shouted.

It was, of course, the part of Dazen and Gavin's meeting that Gavin Guile – the real Gavin Guile – *would* have heard about. 'Recalling' the demonstration would prove nothing. But apparently Gunner didn't realize that.

'The seas were calm that day, and you were only twenty paces back,' Gavin said.

That day, the cabin boy had wet himself, holding an apple in his trembling outstretched hand above his head. Later, Gavin had heard the story that the boy had held the apple on his head. No one explained how a boy would balance an apple on his head on a rocking boat. But it did make a better story.

Twenty paces made a good story. Forty was suicide. Gunner might be the best shot in the world. It didn't matter. Even with an identical charge of powder, and wadding tamped down to exactly the same pressure, and a perfectly round musket ball with no flaws from its casting – even with no wind, and no lurching deck, a musket was only accurate to within a space maybe as large as Gavin's head at forty paces. Some men liked to believe differently, but the truth was that if you hit a smaller target at that range, it was purely luck. Gavin knew how good of a shot Gunner was. He didn't believe the man's story of killing a sea demon, but if anyone in the world *could* have done such a thing through accuracy alone, it would have been Gunner.

And there's the problem with arrogance wed with excellence and insanity – a marriage with three partners is already over-full. Reality's intrusions were unwelcome. Gunner had spent the last twenty years convincing others that he was unable to miss; now he seemed to have convinced himself, too.

'Gunner got given a gooder gun than, than, than . . .' The pirate devolved into curses, angry at not coming up with an alliterative way to say 'than he had twenty years ago.'

It wasn't full-on rage, merely frustration, but Gavin had seen Gunner shoot a man because he was hungry. Gunner was going to go through with this.

23

Gavin's stomach sank. What could he do without drafting? Maybe knock out each of the two sailors next to him – and what? Jump off the ship? There was no shore in sight. They'd simply turn around and pick him up. And trusting his body to be strong enough to take out these two sailors and jump before Gunner could shoot him was optimistic at best. He might not even be able to swim with how much abuse his body had taken recently.

He was overcome with a weariness more than physical. This? This was to be his end?

Gavin had been in too many battles to believe that there was some force that protected the men who should live. One of the greatest swordsmen in the world had been killed next to him, while out of sight of the enemy – a freak ricocheting bullet had caught his kidney. A stallion worth satrapies had stumbled on a body after the battle was done, and broke his leg. A general got dysentery because he'd shared his men's water and meat, rather than eat at his high table. A thousand indignities, a thousand tales that ended without moral or meaning, merely mortality.

War is cause, all else is effect.

Gavin took a bite of the apple. It was sweet and tart. The best apple he'd tasted in his entire life.

Pride, you wanted some little piece of me? Here. Take the whole fucking thing. Gavin spoke in his orator's voice: 'Captain Gunner, I don't think anyone in the world can make this shot. You think you're this good? I don't. I think you're better. You make this shot, and you'll be a legend forever. You miss it, and you're just another pirate who talks big.' Gavin put the apple in his mouth, held it in his teeth, and turned his head to the side, giving Gunner only a profile view.

All activity on the deck stopped.

So I die with an apple in my mouth. My father would have some words about this, no doubt. And Karris will be rightly furious.

Because he'd turned, Gavin couldn't see how Gunner responded, if he was furious or amused. Gavin couldn't see any of the other sailors' reactions. He only saw gray sea and gray sky. The only light granted to him was ugliness. He was

24

only beginning to regret that he'd wasted his last words taunting a pirate when something wet splattered across his face.

He wondered if it was his teeth. There was that momentary delay, when you're hurt badly and you're not sure what's happened. Was he dead? That flash perhaps the spark of his cranium exploding? He didn't hear the musket bark, but that happened sometimes.

Cheers erupted around the deck. The apple was gone.

One of the sailors picked up a few chunks from the deck. He fit them back together. Held them up. He shouted, 'Cap'n Gunner cored it perfect!'

Gunner seemed oblivious to the cheers. He set the white gun-sword across his shoulder and swaggered over to Gavin. That swagger scared Gavin more than Gunner's normal insanity. It meant Gunner was surprised he'd made the shot, too. Orholam's balls. 'Not one man in the world could make that shot,' Gunner announced. 'Cap'n Gunner made that shot!'

'Cap'n Gunner!' the crew roared.

Gunner stood over Gavin, triumphant. He twisted a bit of his ratty beard and chewed on it. 'Manacles!' he barked to the sailors beside Gavin.

They slapped Gavin in chains once more, but he was barely aware of it.

Thank Orholam, if he'd gotten himself killed Karris would never have forgiven him. In fact, when he got free, this was going to be one story he wouldn't be telling her.

Gunner laid the musket-sword across his palms. Showing it off, now, so Gavin supposed it was safe – advisable even – to show appreciation. The blade was a thing of beauty, covered with some kind of white lacquer, Gavin guessed, and adorned with gems so large they had to be semi-precious stones. Gavin was no expert at swordsmithing, but it looked like a parade piece rather than a warrior's tool. The gems appeared to go all the way through the blade – weakening the structure – and painting the blade white with black whorls? You'd have to keep an artisan on hand to repaint it constantly. A single cutout in the blade gave a hand rest to steady the gun when firing, weakening the blade further. But Gavin saw no frizzen, no pan, no hammer, no way to balance the butt to achieve any sort of accuracy or to absorb the kick. Was this a jest? It was too thin to be a credible musket anyway.

'I don't even load it,' Gunner said. He knew that Dazen had shared his appreciation for masterwork firearms. 'It makes its own bullets, and they're more accurate than – well, you saw. Trigger pops down here when it's loaded.'

'How . . . how?' Gavin asked. It was an impossibility, of course. But he'd just had an apple shot out of his mouth at forty paces on the deck of a rolling ship. He found himself quite credulous at the moment.

Gunner grabbed the pommel, twisted, pulled it back. A small, smoky chamber was revealed. Gunner poured black powder into it from a powder horn, pushed it back in, and then pulled the pommel back out. It unfolded to make a small buttstock. He grinned like a first-year discipulus who'd gotten away with a prank.

And there it was again, that hint that the crazy was at least half for show. Gunner had spoken without a hitch. It made sense immediately, once Gavin thought about it. Gunner was eccentric. He'd always chosen words wrong. Being thought eccentric or stupid would mean being the target of ridicule among the hard men he led, so instead he had to be absolutely crazy. Men get nervous around insanity, wonder if it's catching, and keep their distance. Perfect for a new captain who not only wanted to continue being a captain, but wanted to become a legend.

'How accurate?' Gavin said.

'Hit a scrogger at four hundred paces. Ball don't wobble. It's better magic than all the magic you once called yours, Giggly Guile.' Gunner lifted the musket to his shoulder and tracked a seagull on the wing two hundred paces out. He fired, just as it swooped lower – and missed. ''Course, she still won't do it all for you. Makes me respect her the more. She demands excellence, like the sea.'

Gavin hadn't watched the shot, though. He was studying the musket. There appeared to be knobs and small dials in the space revealed by the extended stock, marked with tiny runes. That Gunner didn't call attention to them made Gavin believe that the pirate hadn't yet figured out what they did.

'May I?' Gavin said.

Gunner looked at him. He laughed. 'Former Prism though you be, Gunner's no fool enough to put magic in your hands.' He spat into the sea, then took a rag and began cleaning the black powder residue off the blade. 'Have to hold her real careful. Dangerous as Ceres, this one.' He sank into thought, and Gavin wondered if he'd been brought onto deck simply for Gunner to show off.

Not that he minded. Any rest from the oars was rest. Of course, he'd rather not have muskets discharged in his general direction while he was resting, but beggars and choosers and all that.

'What ransom should I ask for you?' Gunner asked.

Ah, so he brought me up to talk? And couldn't help but shoot at my head, though he had a ransom in mind? Maybe the madness wasn't *all* for show. 'My father believes me dead. Hell, Gunner, I believed me dead.' And like that the memory was back, hot and sharp: Grinwoody crashing into them, two blades and four men, and Gavin had seen that there was no way to save Kip from the tangle of hands and odd angles – except to divert the blade into his own chest.

Whatever possessed me? Oh, Karris, did I do it just to do one thing that might make you proud of me?

But thoughts of Karris were too painful. She was all color in a world gone gray.

And his own father had only wanted the dagger. Musket-sword now, Gavin supposed. The Blinder's Knife, Andross had called it. It was one thing to wonder if your father cares more about gold or status than he does about you. Every son of every rich and powerful man must fear that, but that his father would kill him for a dagger? His own father?

'The boy,' Gavin said. 'Where is he?'

'Threw him overboard for Ceres. As thanks. Ceres and me is square now.' Gunner grinned unpleasantly. 'How much, little Guile? Five hells, what do I call you? Dazen? Feels like talking to a ghost.'

'You can call me Gavin. It's easier. You can ask any ransom you like. The more ridiculous, the better. He'll stall you until he can get spies to confirm you have me. Truth is, he'll botch it so that you kill me and he can hunt you down afterward. He'll make it look like you're bloodthirsty and he had no blame in making you kill me. He doesn't want me, Gunner.'

Gunner grinned like he liked a challenge, and the mask was back. 'So's long as he wants you as much as a pants pox, why should Gunner keep you resting tidy next to his own joyful jewels?'

Oops. But Gavin's golden tongue was already moving. 'If you kill me, he can give up his pretense that he wants to ransom me. That means he won't load up a treasure ship in the first place. He'll just bring the warships.'

Gunner scowled. He jumped up on the gunwale, squatted, one hand holding on to a rigging line, thinking. 'You're being turrable helpful.' Gunner spat in the ocean again. 'Funny thing about the Angari. Feed their galley slaves like they're freemen. You seen? Treat 'em real good. The best slaves on the crew get taken in to port, fed real food, even taked to a bosom house. They lose a man every so often doing that, but it makes the whole crew work hard. Feeding 'em good makes 'em strong. Cuts what cargo you can carry since ya has to carry so much food. But this little here galley can go two or three times as fast as most anything on the Cerulean Sea. A few galleasses could chase me down if the wind was right, but if I have room, I can cut against the wind and leave 'em behind. They shot the Everdark Gates in this ship. She's light as a cork and fast as a swallow. Perfect ship for a pirate, if you can snatch up enough cargoes. Beautiful little ship. And only the four swivel guns and one long tom. This is the best galley with the best crew on the whole sea—' Gunner dropped his voice to a whisper. 'And I hate her. One cannon! One. I should demand Pash Vecchio's great ship, what's her name?'

'The *Gargantua*?' Gavin asked.

'That's it!'

'That might be difficult—'

'Your father's the Red. He's richer than Orholam. You're the Prism. They'd revirginize old whores to get you back.'

'I sank the *Gargantua*. Before the battle at Ru Harbor.'

In a moment, Gunner had drawn a pistol from his belt, cocked it, stuck it over the hollow of Gavin's right eye. A killing rage lit his eyes. Whatever part of his madness was for show, this part wasn't that. With difficulty, he uncocked the pistol. 'This prisoner is exuberical,' Gunner said. 'Put him back on his oar until he works it off.'

Chapter 5

Teia and some of the Blackguards finished their morning calisthenics on the *Wanderer*'s rear castle as the sun climbed the horizon. She and Cruxer and five of the other top inductees were the only ones from their Blackguard trainee class on this ship. The others were on another ship with the other half of the remaining full Blackguards. Though they were constantly reminded that they hadn't taken full vows and were thus not full Blackguards yet, that didn't mean the Blackguards watered down the nunks' exercises. Cruxer had followed their example manfully, and they had followed Cruxer's as well as they could, muddling through complicated forms they'd seen but had not yet learned.

Commander Ironfist, leading them, took no notice of the stragglers. The legendary warrior had always been a cipher, but for the past week he'd been even more intense than usual. Teia didn't know if the exercises (and their horrible butchery of them) was another pedagogical technique, or if the leader of the Blackguard simply didn't see them. Regardless, the commander scrubbed his scalp with a wet cloth, cooling off. He had a stubble of wiry hair on his head now. He'd stopped shaving it bald and anointing it with oil after the Battle of Ru, more specifically, after the Miracle Shot – a prayer and six thousand paces and a direct hit on a newborn god. He glanced at the rising sun, its disk not yet fully clear of the horizon, glowered, and wrapped his ghotra around his head and headed down the steep steps to midships.

Working the soreness out of an ankle she'd twisted when she'd stumbled on a rope – er, *line*, on a ship, apparently – during an unfamiliar form, Teia walked over to the gunwale where Kip and Gavin Guile had plunged into the sea a week ago.

'Hard to believe, isn't it?' Cruxer asked, coming up beside her at the railing. Little Daelos, the shade to Cruxer's sunshine, came with him.

Cruxer could have been talking about a hundred things. Hard to believe that they'd fought in a battle? That they'd lost? That they'd fought a real god? Hard to believe that Gavin Guile was dead? But he wasn't talking about any of those, and Teia knew it. 'Impossible,' she said flatly.

'How are you doing with it?' he asked.

Her elbows resting on the railing, she turned and looked at him, disbelieving. Sometimes Cruxer could be the most excellent human being she'd ever met. Other times, he was a moron. 'It's a lie, Cruxer. It's all lies.'

'But the Red wouldn't lie,' Cruxer said weakly. Maybe it wasn't his fault. Cruxer had grown up with good people in authority over him, and he was scrupulously moral himself, so he didn't have the reflexive disrespect and suspicion toward those in power a slave girl did.

'Go on, Teia,' Daelos said. 'You know that Breaker blamed Andross Guile for trying to block him from joining the Blackguard. And we know Breaker got drunk that night. With how rash he always was, I don't see what's so hard—'

'Is,' Teia interjected.

'What?' Daelos asked.

'How dare you give up on Kip. Go away, the both of you. I'm sick of you.'

Daelos rolled his eyes like she was being an unreasonable woman. It made her want to show him what she would do if she were actually unreasonable. On the other hand, Cruxer simply paled. He pushed back from the railing. Teia knew he'd only come over to check up on her, like a good commander does. But good intentions don't cover everything. They left without saying a word.

You're being rude and unfair and you should apologize, T. But she didn't.

Andross Guile said he'd mocked Kip that night, as he always did. He had no love for the boy, he'd admitted. Perhaps he

30

shouldn't have said anything in the aftermath of a battle. But how was he to know Kip was drunk? He'd never imagined Kip would attack him.

Gavin Guile and Andross's slave had tried to intervene. Kip had stabbed Gavin accidentally, and when Gavin Guile fell overboard, Kip had been so distraught, he jumped in after him.

And there the matter rested. Watch Captain Karris White Oak – or was it Watch Captain Guile now that she'd married Gavin? – had gone insane, shouting that they must be wrong, that Andross was lying. Teia thought the woman was going to attack Andross physically until Commander Ironfist had intervened and literally carried Karris off the deck. She'd not emerged since.

No one else contradicted the Red. There had been more than a few tense conversations between Commander Ironfist and the Blackguards who had been assigned to protect Gavin that night. The Prism had ordered the men to bed, and who would have thought he would be in danger on the very night he'd proven his heroism once again? He'd killed a god!

No, Teia had tried to say, Kip did that.

It seemed somehow small to set the record straight with the Prism lost, and they looked at her like she was spitting on his grave. The man had been adored, and everyone remaining in the fleet had proven their loyalty to him that very day by fighting at his side.

That didn't lessen the burden of guilt on the Blackguards. They'd failed. They were coming home, while their charge was dead. It was a blot they would never erase.

The murmur of voices below her chased out any further thoughts. Teia glanced around at the sailors. Mostly men, the sailors were careful to be discreet about their ogling of the female Blackguards – or had grown careful since Essel had broken one's nose – but they still did it. But they didn't ogle Teia. Hipless, breastless, short, and with short hair, when she wasn't invisible, the most Teia could aspire to was being a mascot taken under the rough men's wings. Nine out of ten of whom she could beat to a pulp, but they didn't know that. Right now, though, she was thankful to be ignored.

The cabin right below her was Andross Guile's. She'd been

eavesdropping here every chance she got for the past week. She interspersed her spying with clambering up the rigging and taking pointers from the sailors, learning a bit of their work. She'd also pretended to pray here, sitting very still. She'd pretended to mourn, too. This was where Kip had jumped or been pushed into the sea. The pretense at tears had turned to real tears, once. She'd liked Kip more than she'd thought.

As she was sitting on deck, Commander Ironfist approached her. She moved to get up, but he motioned for her to stay in place.

He stood with her for a long minute, and she would have appreciated his silent companionship if she hadn't been worried that he would figure out exactly why she'd chosen this spot.

Finally, he said, 'Kip – Breaker – asked me to make sure your manumission papers go through. And I will. You know you're one of the best inductees. You know the Blackguard is hurting for good people. But it's your choice. When I was your age, I took an oath because I was expected to, not because I wanted to or thought it was right. I won't do that to you, Teia.'

And then he left.

She folded her legs and thought about taking her manumission – and what? Going home? Getting married to a shopkeeper? Learning a trade? What trade? It was too strange, too much of a leap after what she'd been experiencing in the last months. She put it off to think about later, and strained to hear Andross Guile's voice. At first, he'd never had his window open, but in the last few days it had been open every time. In the mornings were her best chances to hear anything at all. Once the wind kicked up, it was impossible. But so far she'd heard nothing in seven days. Mostly it had been innocuous orders to his room slave, Grinwoody, the old Parian whom it seemed Andross Guile trusted deeply.

But it was another wasted day. Teia heard little. Andross and Grinwoody had worked together so long that their speech was lacunic, full of understood ellipses.

'Any evidence he's not deluding himself?'

'None. Of course, when we get evidence, it will be too late for one of us.'

'And too late for us, either way. Damn,' Andross said. His voice was louder. He was standing at the porthole. 'It was that close, Grinwoody. Its hilt almost in my hands.'

'It was my failure, my lord.'

'No, you saved my life, again.'

'My strength is not that which once it was, my lord. I allowed myself to be surprised.'

Teia scowled and drew her gray inductee's cloak close about her for warmth. Grinwoody allowed himself to be surprised? By Kip? So Kip *had* attacked them? Was it possible? Kip wouldn't have done something so foolish, would he?

Yes, of course he would. But attempt murder? No, not Kip. He might lash out to hurt, but not to cripple, not to kill, and she'd seen him furious.

'Look on the bright side, my lord. You won't be Freed this year.' Grinwoody's tone was whimsical, but it chilled Teia. Was Andross Guile planning on breaking the halo? Why would Grinwoody announce it so blithely?

A hand emerged from the porthole and a homing pigeon sprang into the air in a rush of feathers, startling Teia, but no one appeared to pay attention either to her surprise or to the bird – there had been many of the latter sent in the last few days.

Then the voices faded as Andross closed the porthole. Teia wanted to get up and leave immediately, but she was well aware that she was sitting on the deck immediately above Andross's room. Even with her slight weight, the wood might groan from her weight shifting. She waited a few more minutes, pretending to meditate. Kip had been her training partner. He'd gambled something – she still didn't know what – to win her papers from Andross Guile. And then he'd promptly tried to free her. He'd listened to her when they'd talked about strategy, made her feel like she, a slave, might have something smart to contribute for the first time in her life.

Teia realized her fist was closed over the little vial of olive oil she wore, squeezing it in a death grip. She loosened her fingers from the symbol of her slavery. The gift had been a threat and a reminder from Aglaia Crassos: olive oil, ostensibly to ease her work in the slave brothels. Olive oil, to keep her alive through thirty to fifty men a day. Whenever Teia thought she didn't have any strength left, she touched that little reminder of slavery. Of what could be. Of what Kip had promised to put behind her, forever.

In the short months they'd trained together, Kip had become more than just her partner, he'd become her best friend.

And she hadn't realized it until now. She hadn't been there when he needed her. He couldn't really be dead. If he hadn't panicked, he could have floated until morning. Teia hadn't heard any stories of sharks – not that that meant much. The survivors didn't want to dwell on what could have so easily happened to them, too.

If he'd made it until dawn, he'd probably been picked up by a slaver. After how much Kip had drafted the day before, he'd be lightsick even if he wasn't otherwise injured. He'd even left his spectacles case in his bunk. He'd be helpless.

If Kip was even alive, he was probably chained to an oar, right now.

And there was nothing Teia or anyone else could do for him.

Chapter 6

Zymun was standing, shading his eyes with one hand, the heavy pistol pointed straight down at the deck. Kip launched himself forward, popping the oars up through the open oarlocks. The sudden slap of an oar against the water attracted Zymun's attention first. He looked toward the sound instead of toward Kip.

Kip's arms were too weak to throw in front of him with the full weight of the oars in them. But he didn't care about making it pretty. His hands dropped and he threw his shoulder into Zymun's side. He caught the smaller young man at elbow level, crushing his gun hand back down, and as both of them were rising at the moment of impact, Kip's big frame said, "Here's all my momentum, brother. A gift."

Zymun popped up into the air. His ankles hit the gunwale and he flipped upside down in a most gratifying manner. As the splash resounded, some distance from the boat, Kip fell. He smacked his cheek on the deck. With his arms behind him, anchored by the weight of the oars, there was no catching himself.

But he fell into the boat, and that was all that mattered.

With strength he didn't know he had, Kip levered himself upright. He was already drawing in blue luxin, and in the rush of pleasure at drafting and at seeing his tormentor splashing in the water, he almost missed it: the boat was ringed with luxin. Red luxin and yellow. There was a long leash to all that luxin attached to Zymun.

Zymun surfaced and Kip saw the mouth of the pistol in his hand loom large. It was pointed straight at Kip. The hammer snapped down on the frizzen as Zymun pulled the trigger. And nothing happened. The gun was waterlogged. Zymun disappeared behind a wave.

Hurriedly drafting blue blades in each hand, Kip slashed through the green luxin manacles holding his wrists onto the oars.

Zymun swept a hand in a big, splashing circle. Kip knew he was reaching for the leash.

Kip dove off the opposite side of the rowboat.

Even as he hit the waves, he knew he'd done the wrong thing. Instead of drafting to cut himself free of the boat, why hadn't he drafted to cut Zymun's leash?

Stupid, Kip, stupid.

He was still underwater, kicking and putting as much room as possible between himself and Zymun, when it felt like a sea demon slapped the sea. Kip surfaced and saw a rising tower of black smoke and red-orange flames where the boat had been. He couldn't see Zymun; the boat was between them.

Zymun would be the better swimmer, even if Kip had been hale and whole. There would be no vengeance for Kip today. If Zymun saw him, Zymun would come after him. If Zymun came after him, Zymun would drown him.

Kip bobbed in the water for a few more moments. He couldn't swim. His arms were lead weights, and though his legs weren't yet dead, they would be soon. His fat would make him float if he didn't panic, but floating wasn't going to get him away from Zymun, much less the pirate galley. Kip looked around for it, but from the water, he couldn't see the ship.

And it wasn't going to have any problem finding them, not with the bonfire Zymun had made of their boat.

Oh. Simple.

Kip drew in as much blue as he could hold and drafted reeds around his hands. The reeds let water stream past his fingers, then he shot luxin through the reeds, pushing the water out. Like the kick of a musket, by pushing water back, it pushed you forward. Kip drafted the reeds to brace under his armpits, took a deep gulp of air, and pointed his head for shore.

Best of all, Zymun had never seen it.

He moved far more slowly than Gavin Guile had when he'd fought the sea demon. Kip knew he was doing something wrong, but he didn't know what. But the speed was still three or four times faster than he would have been able to swim. And soon, he realized his relative lack of speed was a blessing. He wasn't cutting a wake in the water that would mark his location for the pirates.

An hour later – or maybe it only felt so long – Kip staggered onto shore. He had to get to the cover of the trees. If he collapsed in sight of the galley and fell asleep, it would all be for nothing. So he walked, shoeless feet making the sun-bright sand squeak. The Atashian coast was littered with beautiful beaches like this. Palm trees swayed silently. He made his way to the shade and finally turned to look back for Zymun.

The burning boat was gone, sunk, even the black smoke dissipating. The galley had reached the spot where it had been, though. Kip didn't know much about galleys, but this one was small. Perhaps thirty paces long. Hard to tell at this distance, though. They flew no flag. Not Gunner's galley.

They had stopped, though, and Kip saw men throwing a line into the water on the far side of the boat.

So Zymun was alive. Kip's heart sank. If Kip had been captured by pirates – or even regular sailors – he would have been worried about being pressed into slavery. He would have thought he only had the slimmest of chances. For Zymun, he had no such fears or hopes. Zymun would probably be captain of that galley before the week was out.

Orholam strike him. Orholam blind him. Orholam take the light from him in life and in death.

Kip was safe, though, for the moment. He needed water. Then food. Then a way home. But nothing would stand in his way. These were trifles. His life was a trifle. But his message was not. The men and women on the ship that night had seen Gavin Guile plunge overboard after being run through with a sword. They had to believe him dead. Kip knew better, and only Kip knew that Gunner had him.

And should the gods themselves stand against him, Kip was going to get his father back.

Chapter 7

The pistol was useless. Worse, Zymun had thrown it away in a fit of pique in the water. He floated, watching the pirate ship bear down on him. They thought they'd make him a slave, no doubt. They'd try, no doubt.

He couldn't help but smile. There are so few real chances in life to kill without consequences.

He would have liked to have access to more colors, but blue would have to suffice. He packed the blue luxin into his shoulders and back where it would be covered by the sleeves of his tunic. He wasn't good at packing luxin. It was uncomfortable, and he never fully cleared his skin; he always retained a pale blue hue, like he was freezing to death. He could do a thousand things excellently, but hiding his excellence wasn't one of them.

The burning rowboat finally had enough of its hull consumed that it dipped the last smoldering beam in the waves with a hiss. He hoped the pirates wouldn't wonder how a rowboat could produce so much smoke. Maybe they'd think he'd been carrying tar or black powder.

At least it looked like Kip was dead. Zymun had never heard

or seen him after the boat exploded, and he didn't think the boy had gotten clear. He himself had ducked under the water to avoid the force and shrapnel from the blast. Sad to have lost his boat. He should have known Kip would try something. Slippery, and quicker than you'd think a blindfolded big kid could move.

It didn't matter. The pirates would scoop him out of the water, and would have whether he'd been in the boat or not. He had only to wait. The swimming was no problem; in Apple Grove where he'd grown up, every boy and girl swam for fun, jumping off the big rope swing or riding the smooth stones of the waterfall.

In minutes, the galley arrived. They threw a line to him, then tossed webbing over the side and a toothless sailor shouted at him to climb.

What else am I going to do, you cretin? Stay in the water?

Zymun climbed. He hopped over the railing, spry, ignoring the drawn swords four men held pointed at him. No one had drawn a musket. Good. He kept his eyes down, though, waiting to see who would speak.

'Young,' the mate said. He was the toothless man, and as ugly as a day at the oar was long. 'Skinny, but not too soft. And at his age, he'll toughen up fast. He'll do nicely. Trench was coughing blood yesterday. Give us a chance to rest him. Orholam smiles on us.'

'You're going to enslave me?' Zymun asked, his tone that of a scared boy's.

The captain spoke up. He was a braided-beard Atashian, though with brown eyes rather than that people's usual blue. 'Enslave is such a hard term. We all work here. Doesn't Orholam say all men are brothers? You'll work beside your brothers on an oar.'

'And if I refuse?' Zymun asked. He let the blue luxin travel down the underside of his arm. With his hands at his side, it would be all but invisible.

'We all work,' the captain said flatly. 'My ship, my world.'

Zymun could make his proposal now. Could reveal that he was a polychrome. This captain didn't seem terribly belligerent. He hadn't struck Zymun, despite chances to do so.

'I have a better idea,' Zymun said. 'How about—' He shot

a spike of blue luxin through the face of the man nearest him. The sharp luxin went straight through the man's aquiline nose and into his brain. Zymun spun with the kick of having shot so much mass, using the spin to flick out another blade of blue luxin. He lopped off the other man's hand at the wrist. He shot a blunt rock of blue luxin into that man's chest, knocking him off his feet. In an instant, Zymun had another seething spike spinning slowly in his left hand, pointing it at the captain.

His actions, so sudden and swift, and so swiftly stopped, stunned the slavers. They didn't react, and Zymun didn't move. If he did, he'd spook them. If the whole ship attacked him, he might be able to kill everyone, but he couldn't command this ship. He didn't know how it worked. He took advantage of the pause to replenish his luxin.

'How about,' Zymun repeated, 'I join your crew for a time? I'm a polychrome, Captain. This, this was me using one color. I can use six. You give me the mate's room, and I'll fight with you for three months, or three battles, whichever is first. My magic will make all the difference. Three battles that you're guaranteed to win. Then, when I've paid you in full, you take me to Big Jasper and let me debark with the share of the treasure that you think I've earned. You'll still be the captain, and I won't take a thing from you. We'll part as friends.'

'Or?' the captain asked. His hand was twitching toward the pistol in the bag at his belt.

'Or I kill you and offer the same deal to your first mate. Maybe he'll not be so fast to leap to defend you, knowing that by doing nothing, he gets rich himself.'

'Barrick was a good man,' the captain said, looking at the dead man. The other, handless, had already passed out from blood loss. He could still be saved.

'So you know,' Zymun said, ignoring that, 'I'll be the most important man in the Seven Satrapies soon, and I could use a man of your talents in the future.'

The captain looked from Zymun to his mate, who was stony-faced. The captain dipped his fingers into a pouch and pulled out some tobacco. He tucked it under his lip. He stared at the man, still bleeding on the deck. 'Rawl, bind him up.'

The mate, apparently named Rawl, did as he was bid. The captain still said nothing to Zymun.

Zymun let it sit, the captain's death still spinning slowly in his hand.

The captain spit brown juice onto the deck. It landed in blood. He scowled. 'Deal,' he said finally. 'I got a few grudges you might help me with. If you can help me take one pirate in particular, I'll let you go after one battle, on my honor as son of a slattern and a sailor.' He extended his hand, a bit gingerly. That flash of fear comforted Zymun to no end. A man who feared him this much, having barely seen what Zymun could do, wouldn't attempt treachery soon. Perfect.

'Who's this pirate?' Zymun asked.

'Fancies himself a bit of a cannoneer. Calls himself Cap'n Gunner.'

Chapter 8

When the *Wanderer* came in to the pier, Teia was already waiting at her spot on the railing. In addition to the normal crush of sailors and longshoremen and merchants and fishermen and scattered noblemen, the piers of Big Jasper were crammed full of small folk desperate to find out if their loved ones had made it home.

At the same time, there was a crush of Ruthgari soldiers, loading ships to go join the fight that Teia and her friends were just returning from.

The ship's passengers crowded around midships where the plank would be lowered. Teia hopped up on the railing, one hand holding a rigging line to keep her balance. She stepped outside the railing, grabbed the hemp webbing in both hands, and rolled down. It was a brief flash of joy that she even remembered how. Her early lessons had included acrobatics daily, but since she'd started practicing with the Blackguard, there had been none.

Clinging to the webbing, Teia could already see their pier

was lined with people desperate to hear more news. Andross Guile's flagship was the first of the mangled fleet to make it home. Word of the defeat had already reached the Jaspers by homing pigeon, but the people were hungry for details. The ship came to rest against the pier with a bump. A sailor balanced next to Teia on the webbing grinned at her and hopped off first, running to secure the lines on massive cleats. Teia hopped off a moment later, not able to jump quite so far with her short stature, and plunged into the surging crowd of gossips, friends, and families, and food vendors and wine sellers eager to find those eager to cleanse their palates of hardtack and stale water.

Being swallowed by an uncaring crowd was an odd relief. Teia was short enough that she disappeared. Her acrobatics and fighting teacher back in Abornea had been only a little taller than Teia, and she'd encouraged her to explore crowds, to get to know their moods, from the angry crowd streaming out of a hippodrome after a horse race where their favorite had lost, to the eager crowd meeting the arriving dancers and menageries of exotic animals for the Odess Sun Day Festivals.

There was an awareness you could cultivate only in the claws of such a beast. A thousand or ten thousand bodies might move, but you could only be aware of perhaps a dozen immediately around you, especially if you were small. And you had to be most aware of your own movement. There's a mesh point, a fuzzy line where your movement can be assertive, even rude, without being taken as aggressive. There was a timing: a momentary sharp annoyance could be ignored if you were gone by the time the person you'd jostled hard turned to find you. Teia ducked and pushed and surged and slithered through the bodies, her form fluid, her mind submersed fully in her body.

Her trainer, Magister Lillyfield, with a body like a young woman's and her face craggy as the Red Cliffs, had even wanted to take Teia and her master's daughter to experience a crowd in riot in the Darks, the wretchedly poor Angari ghetto that had persisted for centuries in Odess, but Teia's master would never let her.

The familiar beauty of the Chromeria's seven towers gleaming in the sun brought no joy to Teia today. Teia had nowhere to be. Commander Ironfist had said only to his Blackguards, 'Take the day. Tomorrow, dawn at the field, as usual.'

A restless energy filled Teia. She needed to wander. It was good practice. The better she knew the city, the easier her Blackguard training would be. But today there was something she needed to do. She felt herself clutching at that damned vial again, using up a precious hand that could help her maneuver through the crowd.

Too much thinking, T.

She was just making it out of the docks area when a man bumped into her. She'd moved enough to merely brush past him. It could only be deliberate.

But he was gone, and there was something in her hand.

Teia turned and, stationary, lost her momentum, lost her rhythm. The crowd spit her out into the bazaar adjacent to the docks. She hadn't even see the man. Had seen a dark cloak, maybe a grayish tunic . . . Damn, it was gone. Like she was an amateur. She moved out of the stream of people and looked at what was in her hand. A note.

She knew immediately she wasn't going to like what was written there.

'Teia, look in paryl. Now.'

Teia's formal lessons in her special color had been brief, but Magister Marta Martaens had pounded into her that seeing a woman's pupils grow until the whites of her eyes disappeared was not merely disconcerting for others, it was terrifying. That manipulation of the eyes was what had to be done to see paryl, which sat on the spectrum as far below sub-red as sub-red was below visible red. In the past, she'd dilated then constricted her pupils quickly, but it was tiring. Now Teia put on the darkened spectacles Commander Ironfist had given her and relaxed her eyes, farther, farther.

The first place she saw paryl was written across the chest of a broad-shouldered Chromeria guard. The words, shimmery, floating, lighter than air and delicate, glowed: 'Bribed.'

Her chest tightened. What? Why? She was suddenly passive, standing like a mark, agape, like a new arrival to the Jaspers, gawking rather than moving, working, planning.

'Help you, miss?' the guard asked, noticing her gaze.

Teia shook her head and ducked past him. She strode into the market where a herald standing on his small box looked at her. Floating above his head was one word: 'Ours.' Had he stared at her?

Who were they? What were they doing? Why were they showing her this? It obviously meant they had a paryl drafter. A skilled one. More skilled than Teia, to make words that persisted. Or one very nearby, who was placing these beacons mere moments before she arrived.

On a wall down an alley, the words: 'This way, Teia.'

She froze.

On another wall: 'We won't hurt you.'

On another wall, there was a puff of released light as a man leaned a hand against a wall where the ephemeral words had been placed: 'Only we can—' the rest was gone, and even those tore and disappeared as the man shifted his hand, unseeing.

Teia's heart pounded. Breathe, Teia. This is how people go lunar. Seeing things no one else sees, imagining conspiracies.

But madmen are mad because what they see isn't there.

Teia had only seen two other paryl drafters in her life. Magister Martaens, who'd given her a handful of lessons at her former owner Aglaia Crassos's behest, and a man who stabbed paryl into a woman's neck and left her seizing to death.

The alley was right there: 'This way, Teia.'

That man, that assassin, had used solid paryl to kill, like in the stories. Magister Martaens had sworn that solid paryl was impossible. Or at least that she couldn't do it. If Teia could learn to draft solid paryl, she could defend against it, right? Perhaps these people could teach her.

Paralyzed, indecisive, passive and hating herself for it, Teia looked down the alley. Paryl's greatest strength was that no one could see it except a handful of people in the world. If someone else could see their murders, those assassins lost their greatest weapon.

Which made Teia a threat to their power. Teia had seen an assassination. Perhaps they feared she'd seen the assassin, too.

So, Teia, do you isolate yourself with a man you know has

murdered an innocent before, and who is threatened by your very existence?

Putting the matter that way made what remained of Teia's curiosity shrivel from a big succulent grape to a nasty little raisin. Teia hated raisins. Loved grapes. They weren't the same thing at all, no matter what people said.

If the man had wanted to simply murder her, he could have done it already. With his paryl messages, he'd proven that he could move nearby without her noticing him. So he wanted to get her alone first. Why?

It couldn't be for something good. The man was a murderer. If your enemy wants it, don't let him have it.

She ran.

Teia got a few startled looks as she bolted, but she didn't care. As long as no one shouted 'Thief!' no one was going to care much about a young girl running. She hit the next busy intersection and slipped through the crowd there as fast as humanly possible. She slid between a yoke of oxen and the cart piled high with hay they were pulling before the man driving the team could even squawk. She ran along the lip of the little fountain at the center of the intersection and dodged through the line gathered for the water. She ran toward the next street, then stopped, backtracked a few paces, and dodged into an alley. She ran down that alley, nearly slipping on the garbage and slops, turned the opposite way down the next street, and turned up the next alley.

It started misting rain. Teia hadn't even noticed the clouds gathering. She took off the dark spectacles, dropped her pack at her feet, flipped her cloak around so its muted blue side was out, put the pack back on, but in the front, and pulled the cloak on over that. She pulled up the hood and joined the streams of people hurrying in the rain. It was harder to modify your gait when you were rushing. Throwing your hips around to mimic a curvier woman was easy for her at a walk, she could merely bring her steps together as if walking a rope. Doing that while half jogging as if to get out of the rain? She wasn't that good.

She began rummaging through the pack as she walked. She hadn't brought much she could use for disguises to wear, but she did have a bright yellow shawl and a scarf. At the next intersection, she ducked into a merchant's stall as if using it to cut a corner into another alley. She dropped the hood, pulled out a red scarf – or maybe it was green, the squad liked to play its little jokes on each other, and knowing her problem with colors, none of them would tell her straight.

She bound the scarf around her hair, and threw the shawl around her shoulders, tying it quickly. She ducked her chin and then walked back out the way she had come, holding the cloak shut and using the bulk of her pack on her front to make it look like she was pregnant. She put a hand on her belly to complement the disguise.

Teia hated slow disguises. Hated not making a speedy exit. But so did everyone else, and that was why this kind of disguise could be so effective when fleeing. She walked right by a tall man in a gray cloak who cut through the shop and headed into the alley. Maybe it was a coincidence. Maybe he was just a man hurrying home in the rain.

After two agonizing blocks at a slow deliberate place with a hand on her swollen belly but not too much waddle, Teia ran again – but not home. She ran to the brewery where Marta Martaens had said she'd taken a room.

The brewery, the Maiden's Kiss, was housed in a squat, square building. It was whitewashed like almost all the buildings on Big Jasper, with a domed roof. This one was a shocking pink, the wooden doors were plain except for a stylized maiden in profile, offering a kiss. There was no text. Teia knocked firmly on the door.

An apprentice opened the door, a young girl not past ten years. 'Is this where Marta Martaens takes a room?' Teia asked.

The girl's big brown eyes went bigger. She hesitated. 'Can you wait here? Back in two shakes of a lamb's tail?'

Odd one. And Teia didn't like people acting odd when her life was on the line. Her throat was still tight. But she moved that tension to her body, readying herself for attack. She knew being aware but loose was faster, but there no way she could find that calm right now.

She looked around in the rain, measuring everyone, but there were few people on the streets now, and the rain was coming down harder. Teia's last talk with Magister Martaens hadn't gone well. The older woman thought that even talking about the possibility of the paryl assassination would invite all paryl drafters to be hunted down. And Teia had lost the magister's tutorship briefly thereafter when Andross Guile had somehow gotten Aglaia Crassos to sign over Teia's slave papers, and she hadn't seen Magister Martaens since then.

The door opened again, and a wiry woman in an apron gestured Teia in. 'Bel!' the woman barked. 'Leaving a visitor out in the rain? Where's your manners, girl?'

Little Bel's face fell. She bolted.

'Weeper, she is,' the brewer said. She sighed. She wore a headscarf not unlike a man's ghotra to hold back an impressively large crown of brown hair while she worked. And she was obviously working: her skin shiny with perspiration, the veins on her thready forearms popping out. 'I got wort to watch, so apologies for being abrupt, but what's your name and what do you want?'

'Teia. Adrasteia. I came to see if my old magister Marta Martaens is here.' Teia had pulled her own wet scarf off her head and shook out her cloak, revealing the pack over her stomach.

'Huh, thought you six months on, and I figgered she'd have told me if that was so,' the brewer said, nodding to Teia's fake belly. 'Marta's gone. And you're not the first to come asking for her. I'll tell you what I told him, because it's the truth. Good tenant. A bit tetchy, but a good woman. I don't know where she went. She lost her position at the Chromeria, and that was the only reason she was here, so I din't see nothing amiss in her leaving.' The brewer walked to a counter and reached underneath it. 'But I'll also tell you this. She left a note that I was only to give to a girl named Teia. Just so you know, the man who came asking after her offered me money if I'd detain you.'

Teia was ready to fight. She shifted her gaze from the woman's face to her midsection. Motion comes from the core, let your peripheral vision see everything else.

'I didn't take it. I'm not a savage, and there was something funny about him. Red hair in a fringe, balding, odd necklace.

Barely saw it, but my papa used to pull teeth. That necklace was all human teeth. Something nasty about that I'd rather not know. Read your letter quick and go. I wouldn't put it past him to be watching even now. Oh, and don't fold the note. Marta was particular about that. You can use the back exit if you want.'

To reach the back exit would require Teia to walk through an unfamiliar building, away from the public, isolated and vulnerable. Maybe the woman was being as helpful as she seemed. After all, she didn't have to announce that the man had been here. But Teia had been a slave too long. She wouldn't put herself at anyone's mercy.

She took the letter carefully and opened it slowly, keeping an eye on the brewer.

'You can burn it in the fire if you like,' the brewer said. 'I got wort on. Orholam watch ya, girl.' The brewer turned her back and went back into the shop.

'Teia,' the letter read, 'my work with you is done. I've learned of my brother falling very ill, so I'm heading back to my family farm in Maelans. My apologies for leaving so abruptly, but I'm sure our mistress will take care of you. Orholam's blessings on you.' That was all, it was signed with her name and carefully folded. So far as Teia knew, Marta Martaens didn't even have a brother. She immediately widened her eyes full to paryl.

Fraying apart now that it was exposed, there was something written in paryl. No wonder Marta hadn't wanted the letter folded. It would have destroyed the secret message. 'It's all true. The killings, everything. The Order of the Broken Eye is real, and now they're after you. Orholam forgive me for leaving you alone in this, but there's no fighting these people. Run, Teia. – Marta Martaens.'

Chapter 9

Karris Guile, born Karris White Oak, trudged up the steps from the top floor of the Prism's Tower to the roof. She had come directly from the docks, and had barely so much as thrown her bags onto the floor of her new room – Gavin's room – when his room slave Marissia had demurely handed Karris the note. It was odd that the White should summon her to the roof in the rain.

Poking her head out of the door, Karris saw the White tucked in many blankets, seated in her wheeled chair, turned to face the wind and the lashing rain. She was enjoying herself. Flanking her were two large young men, Gill and Gavin Greyling. They, like Karris, were Blackguards, sworn to protect and defend the White and the Prism. The difference was that these men had fulfilled their duty. Each was holding up a waxed fabric parasol – an umbrella – over the White to shield her from the rain. But the old woman seemed to be enjoying the way the wind whipped the rain into her face despite the Blackguards' best efforts.

'Watch Captain,' the brothers said, nodding to her in place of a salute, given that their hands were occupied.

'You may go,' the White told them. 'Please wait for me at the stairs. Inside. Karris will guard me now.'

Gill gave Karris his umbrella, and the men retreated. Karris held it with both hands, protecting the White as much as possible. The old woman had a childlike glee on her face, though. Every drafter's eyes took on the color they used, but the pattern by which it did so was unique to each. Karris had red stars on a green field. Orea Pullawr's light gray eyes had filled in two arcs: blue on top, and green below. In recent years, as she'd stopped drafting for so long to extend her own life, those colors had become washed out, desaturated. But in the wake of the assassination attempt on her in her own chambers, the blue arc was vibrant once more, and straining at the very edges of her retinas. *That*, Karris had expected. But the green was vibrant as well, telling Karris that the White had been drafting green, too. She didn't have much time left.

'I hoped it would bring the influences back into balance again,' the White said, 'as green's wildness so often balanced the ponderous logic of blue for me for so many years. I found after the attack, I was content to sit and watch and wait. It is no longer the time to sit and watch and wait, is it, child?'

'Please don't leave me,' Karris said. Her stomach convulsed, but she held the sob down. She took a deep breath, surprised. She thought she had more control than that.

'But that is the way of this world, is it not?' the White asked. 'We go ahead alone, or we stay behind bereft. All of my dear friends from my youth are dead already. Only my one old foe abides. I almost don't know what I would do without him.

'Karris, it is in carrying heavier burdens than we think we can bear that we become stronger. Are you ready?'

'You cannot give up and die,' Karris said angrily. 'You're the best there is. No one can replace you.'

Unexpectedly, the White chuckled. 'Words every megalomaniac longs to hear. But true only of the truly bad and the monumentally great. I am neither, Karris. I am merely competent, my failures significant and sadly frequent. That I am not bad perhaps makes me better than many a White before me, but the good and the great are two disparate camps that rarely overlap.'

Karris sighed, not certain she could speak of Gavin without dissolving. She looked away, unable to take the compassion in the White's eyes. 'I feel so betrayed.'

'By Gavin? For dying?' The Chromeria didn't say that, not yet, not with what Gavin had meant to everyone. And they didn't know that he was dead. But the White spoke of fear and anger, and such things weren't bound by evidence and the blue virtues.

'The Third Eye. She said if Gavin made it through the battle, that he would live at least until the day before Sun Day. I thought . . . I thought we'd made it. The battle was over, wasn't it? I went to bed believing I'd be wakened with kisses.' Instead it was screams, and death. Kip had tried to kill Andross Guile, they said; Gavin had intervened, been wounded accidentally, fell overboard. Then Kip had jumped in after him. The ship hadn't been able to find Kip or Gavin's body in the darkness.

'Even if she sees the truth infallibly, which I'm not convinced of, there's nothing that says the Third Eye must say truthfully what she sees,' the White said. 'Perhaps by lying to you, she helped the world avoid a greater tragedy.'

'I believed her,' Karris said simply. She felt so empty. She was trapped. She wanted to hold on to hope because she hadn't actually seen him die, and because it felt like she was betraying him if she gave up on him. But on the other side, she could see resignation reflected in every face. He was dead, and there was work to do. There was a terrifying power vacuum, and parties eager to fill it, and heretics to fight, and, and, and. She couldn't grieve until she knew. But she knew she might never know.

'I heard there were portents here, too,' Karris said. 'Something about a sea demon fighting a whale?'

'Two weeks ago now. The very day of the battle.' She didn't expand on it. She knew when Karris was trying to change the subject.

The rain lashed them. It was getting chilly.

'I should take you inside,' Karris said. Avoid it. Put it away. Face it later, alone.

'No.' The White's one word was a leash. She spoke and expected full obedience. 'Let me see your eyes, girl.'

Karris locked gazes with the old woman. Where once she had been proud of her eyes, now she was ashamed. She'd been proud of their beauty, ruby stars blooming on an emerald field, the colors pure and bright and powerful. Now the stars dominated, and her eyes showed her as a woman with only a few years left. A woman who lacked the self-control to make it to forty.

'You're to stop drafting. Entirely and immediately,' the White said.

It was like being told to stop breathing.

'I know what I'm asking,' the White said. Of course she did: she'd done it herself. But that didn't make it any easier for Karris. 'And I'm not asking. It's an order.'

'Yes, High Mistress,' Karris said stiffly. She'd thought that the White might give her some sympathy for the death of her husband. Apparently there was no softness to be had here. Karris's jaw was clamped tight shut, but she kept her face as blank as she could. 'If I may be excused,' she said, and turned her back.

'You may not,' the White said sharply.

Karris stopped. She was a Blackguard; she knew all about hard obedience. She kept her back turned, mastering herself.

'You married Gavin Guile, the Prism,' the White said. 'You're hereby relieved of all your duties as a Blackguard. You will return your commission, effective immediately.'

Karris stopped breathing. Her knees weakened. A gust of wind tore the umbrella from her limp fingers and threw it off the roof before she could so much as blink. She stood, accepting the rain's stinging lash. Cold outside and in. All she was, since she'd put away that fool girl who'd enjoyed boys fighting over her, all she'd made of herself, was a Blackguard. She'd barely been allowed to try to get in to the elite unit, and she'd risen to watch captain, and found that there she was content.

For two days, she'd had everything: the man and the work she loved, a hard purpose and a way to accomplish it, surrounded by those she admired – loved. Sisters and new brothers to replace those who'd died in the fire in her youth. And then she'd lost Gavin, and thought nothing could get worse. And now the White – of all people, the White! – was kicking the last leg out from the stool.

'I'm not sure why this is a shock,' the White said calmly. 'A Blackguard, married to a Prism? You had to know that this would be the most likely outcome. Were you so wrapped up in your passions that you didn't think at all?'

'You said . . . you said that my case was the exception that proved the rule!' Karris said.

'That was in allowing you to pursue your love and letting you resign honorably, rather than expelling you in disgrace.'

'What's the difference?!' Karris shouted.

Gill Greyling poked his head out the door, and he and Gavin came outside, but stayed where they were at the White's gesture. They stood impassively in the rain, but Karris knew that stance, like a leashed hound, ready to attack at a word.

'One is shame, and one is honor, and if you can't tell the difference, you have greater problems than we can address,' the White said.

'But, but, he's gone! Dead! It's a moot point. I . . . I thought that . . .' Karris had thought that the rules didn't apply to Gavin, and that by marrying him, he would stand up for her and the rules would bypass her this once, too. She'd thought perhaps she deserved this slice of happiness, that in the end, Orholam had taken pity on her.

'He's lost. It's not the same thing. Not yet, not for my purposes. Some on the Spectrum will want to declare him dead immediately, of course, but we will have other problems in naming a new Prism. But at the least a new Prism-elect must be named by Sun Day. We must find him before then.' She turned back to the rain, enjoying its wetness on her face, seeming to have dismissed Karris already.

'That's it?' Karris demanded. 'Now that I've served my purpose, I'm to be cast off?'

'In this life, we are not garments which may be washed and worn again, Karris. We are candles, giving light and heat until we are consumed. You burned more brightly than most. It has a cost. Mediocrities like me? Dim flames burn longer.'

'I'm not *finished*,' Karris said angrily.

'Perhaps then you are not so delicate a flower as you have believed,' the White said.

She said nothing more, and didn't look at Karris. Karris thought of storming off, of swearing, of crying. Instead, she stood in the rain, letting it cool her anger, tame her wildness as it soaked her hair, pushing strands in front of her eyes. It took her two tries to speak. 'For the longest time, I was just going to let it go, but . . . Why did you send me – *me* – to infiltrate Rask Garadul's army?'

'Back in Tyrea?'

'It wasn't *that* long ago,' Karris said. 'Rask was in love with me. I had no idea. You sent me into a situation with no warning. I was captured. Could have been killed.'

The White's eyes weighed Karris. 'Have you ever picked up a weapon in the middle of battle? Perhaps after you'd lost your own?'

'A musket once, in Garriston. When I tried to use it, it didn't fire.'

'Mm. It happens.' The White said no more.

'Me? I was a weapon you picked up? Not knowing how I'd serve? That is . . . that's *horseshit*. You know me! I'm hardly an unknown for you. And hardly a battlefield necessity. You could have sent any of the Blackguard, and any of a hundred other soldiers or slaves. Half of them could have done as well as I.'

'My purpose wasn't to win a fight; it was to test a weapon.'

'What?' Karris demanded.

'You've many strengths, Karris Guile, but you return to the same ones over and over again. You're afraid to stretch yourself. I'd given you chances to accomplish other tasks that could easily have been done through a bit of flattery or bribery, and you always took the direct path, relying on authority and hierarchy. But then, when I would prepare myself to cut you loose, you'd do something brilliant that showed me you were capable of thinking for yourself. You simply *like* to have others give the orders. So I put you in a situation where there was a vital task, but no direction on how to accomplish it. I knew you might die, and I'd have carried your death heavily for misjudging you. Instead you passed, and now I've gained something even better than me trusting you.'

Karris scowled. 'And that is?'

'You trust yourself. A little more, at least.'

Karris shook her head. 'Then why take me out of my position? I understand Andross Guile wanting to take away something I love, but you? Why wouldn't you fight for me?' And there it was again, the hot tears threatening. Her throat tightened.

The White blinked, and her face transformed in a moment with an intensity that breathed fresh youth into her face. 'You listen to me, Karris Guile. I will never *stop* fighting for you!' She sat back, and looked abruptly old once more. 'I grow cold in this rain. Take me inside. But before we go, I have a new assignment for you, Karris Guile. One befitting your new status.'

'My new status? As a widow? As a former Blackguard?'

'As a woman with no work and ample time on her hands.'

It was a slap in the face. Karris's anger flared. 'Am I to knit sweaters and darn socks, High Lady?'

'I've lost my mobility. It makes it far too easy to track with whom I meet. You, Karris, are to manage my spies.'

Chapter 10

Teia didn't cross the Lily's Stem to the Chromeria until she saw a group of young Blackguards heading back. They were from her ship. Had she really been gone so short a time that the other nunks were only reaching the bridge now? She checked the alleys again and, despite the rain, put on her darkened spectacles again for a moment. She opened her eyes wide, wider, until her eyes were all pupil. She looked left and right and deeper into the intersection. She looked behind herself, deeper into the alley, searching for any sign of paryl, or of the assassin. Nothing.

She grabbed her spectacles and tucked them into a pocket and hurried into the main stream of traffic ever flowing across the bridge, past the Chromeria's guards, standing in mirrored armor in the usually empty sentry boxes. The war. The war was real now, and they were prepared for an attack. Here. Surreal.

'Is it true?' one of the guards asked the Blackguards. 'Is the Prism dead?'

'Lost,' one of them said.

'Lost? What? Like he's a penny? Lost at sea ain't just lost. I heard you combed the shores for days, looking for him. Ain't you lot supposed to keep him from being lost?'

One of the Blackguard nunks, Ferkudi, snarled and leapt at the guard. But the others pulled him back and toward the tower.

'You lot let our Prism die!' the guard shouted. 'What good are you if you let a Prism drown on your watch? None of you even jumped after him?'

Ferkudi cursed, and Cruxer got right in the guard's face. He said something Teia couldn't hear, but made no move. The guard said nothing more, but he had tears streaking down his face.

These people loved Gavin. They barely knew him, and they weep.

No, maybe that wasn't right. They didn't know him personally, but Gavin had been everywhere visible for longer than Teia had been alive. And he'd been a good Prism. The rumors had to be flying everywhere on the Jaspers, with the official word being so pitifully incomplete – not a position at all, really. 'Lost.'

'Lost.' Not a word you want to toss around lightly at the beginning of a war whose two battles had both been . . . setbacks for the Chromeria.

Gavin had been nigh unto a god to these people, and they'd lost two battles despite having him fight on their side. How would they do without him?

It had been a question the Blackguards had been asking themselves for days. And their failure had not passed their notice, either.

Teia said nothing, though, and walked past with her head down.

Despite that the Lily's Stem was covered in a dome of blue and yellow luxin, translucent and insanely strong, Teia walked for twenty or thirty paces before she took off her hood. The tide was rising, and the wind was causing whitecaps. The Lily's Stem crossed the waterline, so now the waves were smashing against the bridge, which didn't so much as shudder. It was a symbol of the Chromeria itself. All the tumult and the roar of the world crested and smashed against it, and it stood, unchanged, unmoved, impervious.

It was always eerie, though, walking through the light-tunnel, watching bursts of water flare high over your head, sometimes crashing all the way over the tube. There had been attempts to blow the bridge before with barrels of black powder. At least three attempts had been stopped. One wagon had made it, the Tellari separatist inside bleeding, dying from his wounds even as he maniacally set fire to his cargo.

The explosion, confined to the tube, had blasted out both sides like a musket firing two directions. Dozens had died, and yet the bridge held. Ahhana the Dextrous had been the superchromat yellow drafter who'd been the lead drafter creating the bridge, more than two hundred years ago. There were engineers even now who claimed succession down a line of tutors to the woman, so famous had she been.

Teia tried to remind herself of that strength when a wave smashed against the side and washed all the way over the top.

She avoided the others: Ferkudi and some of his friends from the earlier Blackguard classes. For a moment as they laughed, though, happy, not two minutes after grieving and being ready to fight, Teia saw them as her instructors must: children, sixteen and seventeen years old, laughing about someone's awkward attempts at kissing, and yet warriors at the same moment, lethal and lazy, implacable and silly, man and child.

Too much thinking, T.

She somehow made it into the lift without them noticing her among the others. It was a good thing about being slight. Sometimes you wanted to be overlooked. She didn't feel like talking, but she wondered if they'd think her unfriendly. No, they were too involved with themselves.

Staying on the lift when the inductees got out, Teia left instead at the level of Kip's room. The clerks had been too busy in the days immediately before the fleet left to do any normal business. That had meant Teia and Kip couldn't file her paperwork. It meant she was still, technically, a slave. With Kip gone, she needed to file that paperwork immediately. If old Andross Guile remembered her, he would surely seize her as his grandson's property, if only to spite Kip.

You idiot, Kip, why'd you attack Andross Guile? Of all people, you attack *him*?

And where was Kip now? Would he ever come home?

Come home? To where Andross Guile and a noose are waiting for him?

Kip could be alive, but Teia would still probably never see him again. He'd been her partner for only a few months, but their time together had been intense. They'd been outcasts together, and fought together, both figuratively and literally. Teia's heart ached.

She tugged on the vial of olive oil she still wore at her neck. She would wear it until she got the confirmation from the secretaries that her manumission papers had gone through fully, irrevocably. Then she would smash it. Soon, she hoped.

The key turned easily in the lock, and Teia opened the door and stepped inside quickly.

'Hello, little dove,' a man said from the darkness. 'Turn around.'

Teia froze up for a moment, then turned, keeping a hand on the latch. 'Who are you?' she asked. 'What are you doing here?'

'Two . . . excellent . . . questions,' the man said. He had fair skin, freckles, a fringe of orange hair brushed over in a vain attempt to conceal a knobby bald pate. He wore a rich trader's garb with a thin black cloak, and held a velvet-brimmed petasos in one hand, but most striking were his eyes. They were amber-colored. Not from drafting yellow or orange luxin, but naturally amber. He smiled, showing stark white teeth. 'When we're in public, you shall call me Master Sharp.'

Which prompted the obvious question, 'But in pri—'

'Murder.'

'Excuse me?' Teia asked. Fear shot through her, and she hated it.

'Murder. More of a title. Murder Sharp. Had a real name, once. Gave it up.'

Which prompted more obvious questions. But to hell with him. 'What are you doing in here?' she demanded.

'Recruiting.'

'You fail. Now get out.' Recruiting?

He made no move to leave. 'You made a good decision back there at the docks, though it made my life more difficult. Bright girl, aren't you? Seeing the paryl but ignoring it? You saw an enemy with unknown abilities asking you to meet on ground of their choosing – and you chose not to come into that fight. That was . . . wiser than your years. It makes me want you more. I have a job for you. And if you do it, I will give you your papers.'

'What papers?' Teia asked, playing stupid.

'Indeed?' he asked archly. 'After I've complimented your intelligence? You are a child, aren't you? An uncut gem, though. If you perform my task today, I will give you your papers, I swear by my very soul and my hope of illumination. If you do not, I will give them to Andross Guile, for whom I have worked in the past. A little reminder to him of who and what you are will be sufficient to make your life difficult, don't you think? Do you think these manumission papers will ever see the light of day if I take them to High Luxlord Guile?'

The answer was obvious. 'How do I know you'll give them to me?'

'I hold oaths holy. If, however, you attempt to circumvent my plans again by going to some other authority—'

Teia attacked him, jabbing a fist at his throat.

And promptly fell, nerveless, into his arms. He lifted her easily and laid her on Kip's bed as gently as a lover. She couldn't feel anything. Her body was simply gone, a blank in her senses. She smelled the odd man named Murder. He smelled of orange peel and ginger and mint, invigorating, appealing even. She hated him for that.

He smiled toothily with the whitest, most perfect teeth she'd ever seen, and arranged her limbs for her. He put two fingers against her upper lip, not shushing her but instead feeling her breath, and withdrew when he did, seeming content. 'Can you speak?' he asked.

She opened her mouth, but there was no control of her air to scream, she couldn't even whisper. Something was very, very wrong. Confusion threatened to break into panic.

'The body is such a mystery, don't you agree? The sheer number of things that must go right from moment to moment to keep this meat operating.' He picked up her limp arm and dropped it. It fell, lifeless. 'Let me tell you the most interesting thing: the more you know, the greater you realize the mystery is. The wisest chirurgeons in the satrapies still believe blood sits static in our limbs, that it ebbs and flows like tides, perhaps even tied to the moon. My people, on the other hand, have known for centuries that blood circles the body, that the heart is a pump. We know because we can see it. And yet even to us, we who see plainly what a hundred generations of chirurgeons have not yet discovered, there are mysteries. We are not so much greater than they are, after all. Different in degree, but not in kind. I know that a pinch here or a crystal there will, if I'm lucky, produce this and this. You moved so fast. So fast. Do you feel any tingling in your feet yet? Blink once for yes, twice for no.'

Teia felt nothing. Nothing. She was a prisoner, trapped in

her own unresponsive flesh. She felt tears forming. Then, tingling, one foot and then the other. She blinked, almost involuntarily.

'Good. Tingling should begin in your fingers any moment.'

He was right. For all his supposed ignorance, he was exactly right. That didn't make it less terrifying, just differently so.

Murder said, 'Stop thinking about your fear. Your feeling will all come back. I'm very good at what I do. By the time you're able to speak, I want you to guess how I did it.'

Teia hated being easily biddable, but there was something intoxicating about the man. Further, he was right. She took a deep breath, and realized she could feel it in her chest when she did so. Thank Orholam.

It took a few more breaths and frustration before she could relax enough to open her eyes full to see paryl. What she saw took her breath away.

The entire room was filled with paryl. A gaseous, luminous cloud of the stuff filled every nook and cranny. More than that, the paryl appeared to suffuse both her and Murder's bodies. It went *through* them. Murder had used that property to reach inside her body and tweak something. Her Blackguard training had only begun to delve into what kinds of wounds resulted in what kinds of damage. She knew that was something the full Blackguards studied. And her own experiences of battle, of watching the dead and the dying and the injured, were still too raw for her to take them apart and think about what kind of wound produced what. But she had seen animals slaughtered at Lady Lucigari's estate growing up. Goats and pigs and cattle. The cook preferred a deep slash across the throat to bleed the animal, but her husband Amos had liked to use his ax.

He was one of those men who'd never been to war, but liked to talk about how great he would have been if he had. Butchering an animal was as close as he could get. Teia had seen his wood ax fall, and an ox fell lifeless and limp when the ax bit through its spine. She'd seen him make a mistake while drunk, and only crush a vertebra with a clumsy stroke, seen the cow's back legs drop limp while the front still stood.

'You pinched my spine,' Teia said.

Murder brushed her cheek tenderly. 'Smart. True, as far as

it goes. But I don't recommend you go around pinching spines randomly to figure it out. Do it wrong and you stop the heart or lungs. It took me six tries before I got it right. And then after I thought I'd mastered it, I paralyzed a boy permanently. Had to arrange it so it looked like he fell down a well. He lived for six months until someone forgot to give him water and he slipped away.'

'How many of you are there?' Teia asked.

'Few enough we're always looking for more. Enough so we don't take those unfit for duty. Can you move now?'

'Yes. May I?' Teia hated herself for asking, but Murder was like a wild animal. Any sudden move might set him off.

'Open your mouth,' he said. She did. 'Good girl.'

With a wide finger and thumb, he pushed her lips back like she was a horse. She pulled back. 'Be still!' he hissed.

She froze.

He pushed her lips up and down, manipulating them to give himself a better look in her mouth. Then he stuck a long, delicate finger in her mouth, feeling her teeth one by one, seeking out every imperfection, moving from the front of her mouth to the back. There was odd pleasure in his eyes.

Teia had the sudden, wild impulse to bite his finger off. She had no idea why his touching her like that felt like such a violation, but he made her feel dirty, his eyes wide with desire, not magic.

And then he was done. He pulled his finger out of her mouth. It was wet. He smelled it, then held it under her nose.

'Parsley,' he said. 'Chew parsley, and your breath won't be so foul.' Then he sucked his finger. 'Smell.' He put his finger back under her nose.

She smelled. It smelled like spit to her. Ugh. Why had she obeyed him?

'So much better, don't you think?' Master Sharp asked.

Teia said nothing. Her stomach was in knots, and she didn't trust her voice. She was suddenly sure that he'd been tempting her to bite him. What would he have done if she'd given him that excuse? It was like a nightmare she couldn't wake from.

He stood. 'Smart. And young. You'll be formidable, Adrasteia. If you live. If you're not given to an owner who decides to break that spirit in that most effective way a young woman's spirit can be broken. I know you think you're so strong nothing can break you. It's a comforting lie, but don't test it.

'Believe me, no one is that strong. But I don't ask you to live in fear, Adrasteia. I merely suggest you use that wisdom you've shown before. Think not just about the fallout for you if you tell someone. Consider what happens to Commander Ironfist if he takes up your cause. Perhaps it would go well if I were to give your papers to any ordinary slaveholder. But if you pit Commander Ironfist against Andross Guile? Who do you think would win in that kind of fight? Ironfist is a good man, and he'll go to his destruction for you, if you tell him.'

Teia wanted to kill him. How dare he threaten Ironfist?

'Or perhaps you can go to Karris? You have trained with her, after all.'

Teia hadn't even thought of that, though now that he said it, she was sure she would have. Karris was a woman in the Blackguard, an Archer who knew their special burdens, and she was a good woman. But that Master Sharp had thought of it made her heart sink. He knew everything, and he was fast, faster than he had any right to be. Of course, he'd been preparing for this meeting, too.

There was a thought that was important behind that fact, but Teia couldn't get to it past her fear. 'What would happen to her?'

'Maybe nothing. High Luxlord Guile already hates her. Of course, now that she's Gavin's wife – or widow – they *are* family now. So I imagine the White will be pressing Karris to make peace with the old man. Karris might not be too eager to take up another cause that puts her in direct opposition to one of the most notorious grudge-holders in the Seven Satrapies. How well does she really like you? Or perhaps she will take up your case, and you'll not only cost her her chance at peace, but he will win. The law is on his side, so he will win. And then what will he do to you to spite her?'

Teia licked her lips. 'He might want peace, too, you know. He could give me up as a gesture of goodwill.'

'Goodwill?' He chuckled, as if it were droll. 'Andross Guile is full of will, I grant, but little of it is *good*.'

The whims of the great crushed the lives of those who labored beneath them. Bringing yourself to their attention was always risky. Teia was doomed.

'Of course, you're right,' Murder Sharp said. 'Logically, that *is* a possibility. I suppose you'll have to weigh the odds. In the meantime, I advise you to keep your head down. We'll give you orders soon. One simple assignment, and you're free. Pardon, let me amend that. One simple assignment, and one meeting afterward if you do well, for my masters would like to take their own roll of the die at recruiting you.' He walked to the door. 'Think carefully of all the costs of acting rashly. You have so much potential, Adrasteia.' He slipped out and closed the door. Her last glimpse of him was of the sigil across the back of his cloak, the silent-winged night hunter, the owl, wings flared, claws extended, nearly invisible, stitched in gray thread on gray fabric.

Teia jumped to her feet and ran to the door, snatching up a dagger on her way from its hook on the wall. She put her hand on the latch to throw it open – stopped.

Seconds drained past. Open the door, Teia. Go after him and stick this dagger straight into his back!

She locked the door. Sat heavily on the bed. The weight of her tiny olive oil vial was like an anchor dragging her down, down. A slave again, after freedom had been this close. It was worse than death. She crawled under the covers and curled into a ball. But she didn't cry.

Her eyes were leaking, but she didn't cry. Damn it.

Chapter 11

Rowing. The pain had become either bearable or so familiar that it couldn't keep his attention.

Ten days after Gunner cored the apple in Gavin's mouth with a musket ball, the drummers rattled an odd tattoo in response to some order the slaves couldn't hear. Gavin looked over at his oarmates. He didn't expect anything from the man

next to him, Orholam. The nickname was for his number –
Seven – but Gavin had slowly realized the Angari slaves had
a darker sense of humor in their naming. Seven radiated kindness, but he almost never said anything, and when he did, it
was rarely helpful. That these very qualities were why he'd
been named Orholam was a sentiment so profane and dis-
respectful that the Highest Luxiat and head of Orholam's
worship on earth had laughed for a good ten minutes when
he finally understood.

He'd almost recovered from his laughter when Fukkelot had
cursed at him, and he finally understood that name, too, sending
him into fresh gales of laughter.

The foreman, Strap, had eventually used her own much more
obvious namesake to shut him up.

Rowing. The pain could be catalogued, but even the catalogue was tedious. His fellows were more interesting than the
chafing, the blisters, the cramps, the knots.

Fukkelot was more helpful than Orholam, and more verbal.
Gavin had heard of sailors swearing constantly, but that was
usually a figure of speech. Fukkelot wasn't right in the head
somehow, swearing a stream of curses without willing it, day
and night.

Now he grinned at Gavin. 'Battle,' he said. He grunted. His
jaw and neck twitched repeatedly. 'They let us know so we
use our strength when we need to.' Then he went back to
whispering curses, as if it were a relief.

'Do they unchain us?' Gavin asked, rowing, rowing. 'You
know, in case we sink?' He was joking. Mostly.

'Win or die,' Strap shouted.

'Row to hell!' the slaves shouted in response.

'Scratch the back of Shadow Jack!' she shouted.

'Row to hell!'

'Row right back!' she shouted.

They pulled faster, in tempo with the drums.

'Pull!' she shouted in time with their pulling.

'To hell and back!'

'Pull!'

In less than a minute, they were flying across the waves. The
foreman ducked upstairs. She came back. 'We've closed to a

league. Wind's bad. Twenty minutes, if they never stop running.' She chortled. 'Three, Four, Five, if you don't get that oar fully stowed before the crunch this time, it's five stripes each.'

'You gotta give us enough warning,' Three complained.

Gavin expected him to get the strap for that, but the foreman was in a good mood.

'Kind of ship is she?' Three asked.

'Abornean galley.'

Murmurs. Bad news. 'How loaded?' someone asked.

'Sitting high.'

Curses. If their captain were competent, the chase would all come down to which slaves were in better condition – or could be motivated more. The motivation came by whip, mostly. Sitting high in the water meant it would be faster than usual and that it didn't have a full cargo to plunder if they did catch her. It was the worst of all worlds for a crew.

'Little fishies, you ready to swim?' Strap shouted out.

'Straight to hell, straight back again!' they shouted, but there was clearly less excitement in their tone.

'Pull!' she shouted. At some signal, the drummers increased the tempo.

Gavin strained against his oar. At each sweep, the rowers stood up as they pulled, sat on the backsweep and did it again. This Angari ship had added a wrinkle that one of the men who'd been a galley slave on a Ruthgari ship before said was unheard of on the Cerulean Sea – a footboard at an incline that allowed the slaves to more easily put the full strength of their legs into the sweep. Made it easier, he said. Made them faster, Gavin thought.

'They're runners!' Strap shouted gleefully. 'Let's see if they can race us, boys!'

They maintained their speed.

Two minutes later, she came down again. 'We're gaining on 'em. No way they can lose us!'

A small cheer ran through the slaves.

'Uh, uh, two, uh measures of, uh, strong wine for the first, uh, six benches tonight!' Fukkelot said. He cursed twelve times, loudly, as if he'd been holding back the tide simply to get a full sentence out. 'Or death!' He laughed.

Only for the first six benches – so the men farther back would have a reason to behave well and hope they got promoted. It was just one among many Angari traditions Gunner had kept after taking the ship and its crew. They had all sorts of ways to motivate their slaves. Gavin wondered if the Angari were more decent, more clever, or just slave-poor.

Karris, I labor among madmen and murderers.

Not so different from back home, then? she asked in his mind's eye.

How he loved her.

Karris, could you spell me for a bit on the oar?

Wish I could, love.

He saw her face twist with pity, and it cut through him. What was he now? Dirty, sweaty, stinking, bearded, hair shorn short, serving slavers. He blinked it away. Focused on his oar.

Strap said, 'Leonus, water. Don't need anyone passing out in the stretch.'

Leonus was a twisted-back, perpetually sneering sailor with the dark black skin of an Ilytian, though he had nothing of their accent. He shaved his wiry hair at the sides of his head and let it grow in a knotted crown above. He thought the slaves hated him for his deformity, and he took it out on them at every opportunity, giving them plenty of real reasons to hate him. He moved among them with a cup on a long handle. The task actually took considerable dexterity – giving water to a man who's constantly standing, sitting, moving moving moving, with a long oar and numerous arms intermittently in the way. Leonus took every advantage when he thought the foreman wasn't looking to swing the cup into slaves' faces, smashing lips and breaking teeth from time to time. They were so desperate for water, though, that they took it rather than turn away. Leonus was the kind of scum that enjoyed that most of all.

Back in Gavin's past life, one of the biggest burdens of leadership had been finding and removing such men from every command. Any short-term results they got from the fear their men held them in was ultimately spoiled by how they ruined morale and stopped men from taking initiative.

Gavin heard the crack of a whip, and heard Leonus cry out behind him. Strap shouted, 'Don't fuck with them, Leonus!

You keep my boys from rowing, and I'll wipe your ass with hull barnacles. You hear me?'

Even Orholam grinned at that, though when Leonus made it to their bench, each slave kept his face carefully composed. Strap was as wide as the sea, foul as a latrine, and had more tattoos than any four other sailors combined, and Leonus rightly feared her. The malformed man gave them each water quietly, hatefully.

At their increased pace, the slaves sweated freely, and the always hot, always humid cabin got hotter and wetter. One slave cried out with a muscle cramp in his leg and went down. His oarmates struggled to maintain the pace without him.

In an instant, Strap was on top of him, beating him mercilessly with the whip. After six or eight strokes, she unlocked the slave's manacles and bodily hurled the man back down the aisle. Number Two was hustled into place.

The foreman looked pleased that they hadn't slowed their pace. She walked up and down the aisle, checking the men for signs of exhaustion, then walked to the back. Gavin heard the slave's cries and the snapping of leather, the thudding of fists and feet on flesh. It was insanity to beat a man for what he couldn't control – and for a few long strokes of the oars, Gavin wondered why the otherwise sensible woman would do it.

Ah, preventative brutality. Beat the man who can't help his cramp so that others don't fake a cramp to get a rest.

Unjust, but probably effective. Gavin wasn't sure if he admired or hated Strap more for it.

The door to the main deck two flights up cracked open, letting midday light down the sweat-slick stairs. The foreman went up the steps, and Leonus took her place at the bottom to repeat any orders she might shout.

'One hundred paces! Ain't turning!' the foreman shouted.

'One hundred paces!' Leonus shouted. 'Drummers, places!'

No one had explained what Gavin was supposed to do, or what happened in what order, but another drummer joined the first, pounding a big, hollow-sounding drum to add to the first. He beat at exactly the same tempo, though, standing in front of the slaves on the port side.

'Uh, fuck fuck fuck fuck, listen to our drummer, not theirs,' Fukkelot said. 'Last—' He dissolved into curses and grunts for a while, getting more and more frustrated that he couldn't speak clearly. Finally, he managed, 'Last second, we stow the oars. After uh, uh, uh, a sprint, though.'

'Turning to port, seventy paces!' the foreman shouted.

A muffled report resounded from the long tom mounted on the prow of the *Bitter Cob* and shook the deck like a punch in the chest. Shouting abovedecks. Pounding feet. A musket fired above, followed by Gunner's shout. He wouldn't want anyone on deck shooting out at that range. He wouldn't trust anyone but himself to hit a target that far away.

Gavin gritted his teeth, his legs quivering, arms burning, sweat dripping into his eyes. The slaves were barely touching their butts to the wood benches at this pace.

A high, loud crack sounded from some musket that Gavin couldn't place, but that sounded very different than – oh, that could only be Gunner's musket.

The *Bitter Cob* veered to starboard. Gavin figured they must be trying to cut directly behind the other ship, to keep them from getting a broadside. It would only work if their own ship were significantly faster.

'Starboard side, battle speed!' Strap shouted.

'Starboard side, battle speed!' Leonus shouted.

The drummer on the starboard side picked up his pace, beating triple beats in the space of two beats on the port side. It made the *Bitter Cob* cut to port, while losing almost no speed.

'Battle speed, all!' Strap shouted.

'Battle speed, all!' Leonus shouted.

They sprinted across the waves, throwing their whole weight into every stroke. There were no chants now. The men had no breath to spare. The heat was unbearable. Gavin heard the slapping of a whip, but his world was constricted to the pain in his shoulders and lungs and legs and back and calves and arms—

'On my mark, stow portside oars!' the foreman shouted. Before Leonus could even finish repeating the order, the foreman shouted, 'Mark!'

The drummers pounded three great wallops, and stopped abruptly.

The slaves heaved their oars down, lifting the blades out of the water, and then pulled them into the hold, hand over hand, pulling them all the way inside so they wouldn't be snapped off in a collision.

For one moment, as the drums fell silent, as the slaves gasped for breath, as the men above braced for impact, there was no sound but the peaceful hissing of the waves.

Then hell broke loose.

Chapter 12

Kip walked shoeless on the beach for an hour before his feet blistered. He walked on blistered feet for half an hour before the blisters cracked and bled. He walked on bleeding feet for less than a minute before the obvious occurred to him.

He sat heavily on the sand and sighed. How many months had he been drafting now? The Chromeria taught that you weren't supposed to think of drafting first to solve your problems, but they had it exactly backwards.

Magic was useful for *everything*. It just killed you. You should always think of it first. Then you should decide if a little dram of death was worth it.

Functionally, perhaps, the same thing. Provided you thought of it before you were bleeding to death on a beach in some distant corner of the satrapies because you were so damn dumb.

Using the green of the jungle canopy as his source, he drafted a green, flexible sole to walk on, thought about it for a minute, and then drafted entire boots of green luxin. Because his feet were already bloody, he left an open connection between his feet and the bottom-most layer of the sole so that he would be able to adjust the grip of his shoes immediately. It flirted with the line of using magic in ways that became part of your own body – incarnitive. But there were no magisters here. Kip walked, adjusting his boots until he was happy with them and trying to lock that design in his mind in case he ever needed this again.

Every drafter did this, he realized. They came up with useful designs and memorized them to be used quickly again. It was just that simpletons designed shoes while savants designed skimmers. The number of designs you could make as your colors expanded had to be an exponential curve. Had Gavin Guile memorized a thousand thousand designs, or did he just understand magic so deeply that he didn't have to memorize designs? He merely created what made sense. Like you don't have to think how to walk up stairs that are slightly steeper than the stairs you're used to. You just do.

It seemed the more Kip learned about magic, the more impressed he was with those who used it artfully.

Then again, he'd gone green golem once, purely on instinct.

You got potential, Kip.

And you know what potential means? he replied.

'Ain't done nothing yet.'

It was actually kind of comforting to hear the sound of his own voice.

He kept walking. Whether under oar or sail, galleys could travel twelve to fifteen leagues a day. Most galleys only had a range of four days before they needed fresh provisions. As galleys became less prevalent – being replaced by ships with longer ranges – many of the coastal towns that lived on the galley traffic were struggling. They would die in another generation or two, but they weren't gone yet. So at the maximum, there had to be a town within sixty leagues.

Assuming he hadn't been dropped precisely in between two towns, Kip would obviously find one closer if he walked the right direction. But he'd been blindfolded. The nearest town could only be a league or two south, while he was heading north.

Of course, there should be little towns in between, too, like that little fishing town so close to Ruic Head where the whales had gone crazy, and the people, too.

That was, if all the towns hadn't been abandoned by people fearful of the advancing army of color wights, in which case, he could walk until he died and—

Not helping, Kip.

He was hungry. No, don't think about that. Anything else. At worst, if Kip could walk eight leagues a day, he should make it to a town in seven days. At worst. He could do that. All he needed was water. He could live on his fat for plenty long enough, theoretically, though he would walk slower as he became weaker. He found himself moving imaginary abacus beads as he did the figures. Funny, that helped.

That is, it helped him with the arithmetic. A smarter person would probably shut off his brain and walk. Kip had always been about as good at shutting off his brain as he was at shutting off his mouth.

Straight pipe between the two, mother used to say.

He was assuming he could walk eight leagues a day. Here, on the clear beaches, that seemed entirely plausible, but Kip knew there were other areas of the coastline that were rocky, where cliffs bordered the sea, or jungles abutted the waves almost directly. Points protruded full leagues out into the sea. If Kip followed the coastline exactly, he would have to travel much more than the sixty leagues a ship would travel between towns. If he didn't follow the coastline exactly, he'd risk getting lost in an unfamiliar jungle or forest.

For a few minutes, he had to concentrate on breathing, his throat constricted, his chest tight, trying to throttle him.

But he didn't stop walking. His mind clamped down on that refusal like a bulldog's jaw locking. He was the turtle-bear, and the turtle-bear can't be stopped. What was the worst that could happen? He could fail? He'd failed before, plenty. He could die? He'd almost died plenty of times now. Sometimes it was scary, sometimes it was terrifying, sometimes it was exhilarating, often it was uncontrollable no matter what you did, right or wrong. You don't stop and make death a sure thing just because going on *might* result in death. Kip was a fat miserable disappointment, but he wasn't a quitter.

He grinned suddenly. A fat miserable disappointment – who had, albeit with lots of qualifiers, killed a king, saved the Prism, and killed a god. Not bad for a fatty. Hell, he'd even outsmarted Andross Guile once.

Odd that he thought of outsmarting Andross Guile as more impressive than killing a god.

The god thing felt like luck, though, or like Orholam had surveyed the field for a suitable tool to keep his Prism alive, and finding none suitable, had picked up Kip because he was closest.

Kip paused.

I treat myself pretty shitty, he thought. I'd never let anyone treat a friend of mine this way.

An hour later, he found a stream. He drank, hoping the water was good. Truth was, he didn't have much choice. He slowly drank more, waiting to make sure it didn't make him throw up, and then sipping more. He stood, wishing he had a waterskin.

He caught sight of his green luxin boots. Golly, if only I had some way to make a waterskin!

With a sigh, he drafted a green bag. Magic first, magic always, Kip. He scooped up a great volume of water, then bent the green until it fit comfortably across his back. Drafted straps that fit his shoulders, drafted a belt.

Magic. So useful, it's like . . . magic.

'Talking to this madman is making me crazy!' Kip said.

Funny. You'll know you're almost finished when you forget it's supposed to be ironic.

He decided while he was walking, he could catch up on all the *practica* he'd missed. Unfortunately, at his level, the Blackguard training had consisted almost purely of hand-to-hand combat, the idea being that such was the foundation for all their future training. On the ships traveling to Ruic Head, they'd been taught proper grips and basic handling of swords and how to reload muskets. The other new Blackguard inductees already knew it all. Some of them had been training with weapons for years. Some were proficient with bows and other weapons that Kip had barely even picked up. He was way, way behind.

But I can go green golem.

Fat lot of good that does me now.

He felt like the coast was swooping out to a point, but looking at the sun alone wasn't enough to confirm his suspicions.

His classmate Ben-hadad had once said that he'd learned to draft a sextant so he would never be lost. Of course, you still needed a compass, too, and while you could draft a housing and a medium on which to float a bit of philosopher's stone, there was no such thing as lodestone luxin. Some things still had to be done the hard way.

And easy or hard, Kip didn't have any of the skills that would have saved him. This was what losing one game of Nine Kings had cost him – his grandfather had forbidden Kip to attend *practica*.

Kip was trying to intuit what others had studied for generations. Well? Am I a genius of magic, or not?

Wait! Why am I messing about thinking about sextants and compasses and waterskins? I should be making a skimmer. He'd seen it done. He'd even helped propel one.

But a failure with a complicated device like the skimmer would leave him in the middle of the sea, with no way to get out. Kip could float, but it wasn't like he was going to drift to Big Jasper, and if he tried Gavin's jetting trick to swim, he'd break the halo before he got halfway there.

I can draft all these colors. It's as if I've got a toolbox full of every imaginable tool, and I'm too stupid to use them.

Too ignorant, perhaps, a kinder voice answered him.

It was true. You wouldn't blame a savage for the fact that he can't read.

But you wouldn't trust him with reading you letters, either.

The light began to fade, and Kip turned his mind to different problems. He found a clean area of the beach, just at the edge, where the palm trees gave him shelter. He took off his water pack. Staring at the darkening sky, he gathered enough blue to draft a blue luxin box with a single hole in the top, and sealed it. Then, standing on the beach facing the sinking sun, he gathered as much red as he could, patiently, slowly. The passions of red flooded through him, but he ignored them and simply filled the blue box. He filled the box full with the version of red luxin called pyrejelly.

He hadn't been thinking clearly, and by the time the box was full there wasn't enough heat coming from the sun to give Kip sub-red. He'd need to light his fire manually. It took him half an hour in the fading light to find a rock that looked like flint.

He banged rocks together for another half hour. Nothing sparked. He wanted to scream. He hitched his pants up and sat, rubbing his face. He tightened his belt, and saw that he was past the last, tightest hole. Not six months ago, he'd been at the loosest hole on the belt, praying he didn't get any fatter because he didn't know where he'd get the money or the leather for a new belt. All the rest of his clothing had been replaced at the Chromeria, but it had seemed wasteful to get rid of his belt. Besides, his mother had given it to him, during one of her rare sober spells.

Kip pulled the belt off. One of the flints had a sharp point that he could use to scratch out a new hole.

He looked at the buckle. The *metal* buckle. If he could punch himself in the stupid, he would knock it to Sun Day. Kip scratched the buckle against the flint he'd found, and wonder of wonders, it sparked. He lit the pyrejelly with no problem. It burned nicely. Kip sat and pulled his water pack to himself as the stars came out. Maybe some water would take the edge off his hunger.

The green luxin pack was sealed. Kip hadn't drafted any way to open it. If it had been light out, he could have drafted more green and simply opened the green luxin and re-drafted it shut. Instead, he had to treat it as a purely physical object.

He wanted to cry. Or scream. Or throw a fit. Instead, eventually, Kip dug a hole in a weak part of the water bag with the sharp flint. Holding the pack over his head, he was able to drink from the warm stream of water until he filled himself.

Kip's lamp guttered as the pyrejelly burned below the level of the hole. With no wick to pull the jelly up to the air, the fire starved and went out. Kip looked at it like it had personally betrayed him. He could smash the blue lamp holding the jelly, of course. He'd not made it very thick. But then the pyrejelly would burn off in perhaps a half an hour. If Kip had his spectacles, he could use that firelight to – he didn't. Those were back on the ship. He'd not been wearing the lens holster the night Gavin had almost been killed.

He took that dagger for me. Kip had thought that Gavin liked him, approved of him like you approve of a well-trained pet. A sane man might risk danger to save his dog, but only an idiot would die for a dog, right? Gavin Guile was no idiot. He knew his worth in the scheme of things, and things couldn't have been going better for him – he'd just married Karris, just turned a decisive defeat at the hands of the Color Prince into a narrow victory. Kip had seen it in his eyes, as Kip had revealed Andross was a red wight and attacked him. Gavin had known. Known about his father, for one. He'd shown no surprise. He'd been keeping that card in his hand, to play at the right time. And Kip had shouted it out to the world – Kip the Lip, saying exactly what he thought, speaking without thinking, endangering plans he couldn't even fathom.

But Gavin had also known – in that moment, Kip had seen it – as they scrambled, four men, fighting over two blades, that Kip didn't have the leverage to stop Andross and Grinwoody from burying the knife in his chest. What Kip hadn't seen then, but knew now, was that with how their hands were interlaced, the only direction Gavin could pull the blade that wouldn't be blocked was toward himself. He'd done it on purpose. He hadn't stabbed himself, of course – he wasn't suicidal – but once the blade's direction had changed, Grinwoody and Andross had pushed hard instantly, not knowing, or not being able to stop, or not caring.

Why would Gavin save me, knowing the cost was his own life?

Gavin gave his life for me. The Prism himself, the best Prism in centuries, maybe ever. What did that mean? What did that say about Kip's worth?

The thought was too big. The emotions welling up behind it too frightening. Kip was that lost kid whose mother had forgotten him in a closet full of rats. He wasn't . . .

A tear dropped from his cheek and hit his protruding stomach. Where had that come from?

He rubbed the tears away with a grubby paw, bear once more.

And what the hell had happened with that knife anyway? The Blinder's Knife, Andross Guile had called it. A knife that didn't kill Gavin, but grew inside him instead. And how did my mother get such a thing?

That was better, safer, cerebral. Kip could think about that. But not, it turned out, for long. He was exhausted. He hadn't drafted a pallet to sleep on, a blanket – could you make a blanket out of luxin? – or any kind of shirt. He hadn't prepped any of the mundane bedding that might have made his sleep more comfortable, either. He broke the top of the blue luxin lamp and scraped a spark into it.

My father loves me. Of all men, Gavin Guile thinks I'm worth saving.

The luxin lit with a whoosh, and Kip felt waves of warmth beating back the night's cold. The fire would not last long, but Kip figured he'd be asleep by then.

He was right. No sooner had his bare shoulder touched the sand than he began to dream of beasts and gods.

Chapter 13

~The Ex-Priest~

'War is always an excuse for the monstrous,' Auria tells me. We've climbed high enough we can't see the raiders' torches anymore. The light filtering through the fog on the headland is weak, but rising.

'Anyone who kills Angari is doing Orholam's work,' I say.

'Darjan, all are his children, even the disobedient, and what you're planning is forbidden,' Auria says. Her dark curls are matted with blood, her face blanched from its usual mahogany – from the bad light, I hope, and not from blood loss. I know it isn't fear. Auria has never been afraid in her life. There are a hundred good reasons why I should listen to her. Karris Shadowblinder herself – Lucidonius's own widow and heir – put Auria over me in our training. She's older than me. Wiser, too.

But I'm stronger.

'I hate waiting for the light,' I say. I have a pair of Lucidonius's marvelous spectacles, crafted by his own hand. Since he's passed, you'd think they're holy relics with how everyone treats them. Well made, though, anyone would admit. And utterly revolutionary. It hadn't been that no one had thought of melting metal ores into molten glass for their color, it was that they couldn't get the fires hot enough, couldn't get the ores pure enough. Lucidonius had solved that, too, showing himself to be a mundane genius as well as a magical one. He'd been infuriating that way, but those lenses had changed everything, for drafters everywhere. A lens grinder, their mighty Lucidonius. In addition to everything else. Changing our lives in a thousand ways. Drawing us along behind him like leaves in a gale.

And leaving a terrible mess when the storm passed.

'As Pride is the first sin, so Power is the first temptation,' I intone. Lucidonius preached that, and became powerful, more powerful than the pagan priests and prophets. Pagan priests like me. I begin drafting.

I was a *kaptan* of the *aḥdar qassis gwardjan*. Lucidonius's words had somehow changed my heart, but I still wonder if they ever changed my mind. Or maybe it was the other way around. His words were enough to make me give up my comfort, my position, my place, my prestige, but now as I look down toward my new home, where doubtless the streets run red with the blood of my new neighbors and only friends, I think perhaps Orholam didn't change me enough.

Every color is from Orholam, Lucidonius had said, holding a prism above his head as he preached peace and brotherhood between colors and countries. It had made sense to many, but perhaps especially to those like me, who can draw more than one color. In my land, my mastery of green had always been praised, but my use of blue condemned by my brother qassisin. Even though it made me a better gwardjan.

Maybe none of it made sense. Maybe Lucidonius was merely more right than those who'd come before him. Maybe what I'm about to do isn't a sin against Orholam, that odd desert god who lives in the sky and everywhere, invisibly, rather than walking the earth like a proper god. Maybe it is. He'll have to forgive me, for though I am no longer an aḥdar qassis gwardjan, I cannot stop being a gwardjan. It is who I am. Who Orholam made me, if Lucidonius spake true.

I draw on the light, and my green *jinnı-yah* is there, familiar to me as my dead wives' faces – my beloved wives, forced into the orgiasts' flames to expiate the shame and crime of my apostasy.

'I've missed you,' Aeshma whispers along my skin, her touch caresses.

I've missed her, too. Of course I have. But she knows that.

I expect her to be angry, haughty, to punish me for turning my back on her. But she's more canny than that. First she'll get her hooks into me. Later, she'll punish. Nor does she go to my libido, once so potent, now seemingly dead since my 'Annaiah and Siana burned. Instead, she waits. Perhaps she sees from my face that the only pleasure I seek is the pleasure of battle, of red vengeance. Perhaps even after all this time she feels me directly.

'I would have made you the next Atirat,' she says, mournfully. She puts her hand on my wrist as I start to pour luxin forth from my skin there. 'You were to be a god.'

'The daemon's in your eyes,' Auria says. 'Do you see her true, or do you see how she wants you to see?'

I remember when Lucidonius bent the prism toward me as my jinnı-yah stood in front of my eyes, shouting blasphemies in my ears. The sudden wash of other colors had shown me what the priests of the other colors saw when they looked at her. In every other color, Aeshma was a horror. No wonder the other *qassisin kuluri* warred with us, called us daemon-worshippers. And then Lucidonius had flipped a mirror out, and in that full-spectrum light, I'd seen that even the green was a thin mask.

Aeshma was no beauty. She was all disease and ugliness.

I'd shattered the prism, shattered the mirror, swearing Lucidonius had ensorcelled it, that he'd tricked me, shown me lies. But I was wrong. Later, I'd done the same trick when I found other djinn foolish enough to manifest themselves in their priests' eyes. The prism we used was a mundane prism, the mirror plain silver and glass. Eventually the Two Hundred had learned that we could expose them. They came up with elaborate lies to those they snared to explain why they no longer would appear at all – blamed it on the stain Lucidonius had brought to the world. Truth was, they didn't want to be so easily unmasked.

Aeshma says nothing more. I know she was one of the foremost of the Two Hundred, nearly one of the Nine. A new Atirat is not born solely of one man's conquering all human contenders. His partner jinni-yah must conquer all of her rivals as well.

The armor wraps around my body. I hold open only points at each joint. It's not as efficient or flexible or reactive as how I had once done it – with every pore, every sweat gland, every hair a point of contact. Back then, I'd let my jinni-yah control the armor, shifting it, reacting to dangers I couldn't even see, her immortal will complementing my mortal will. The two of us had been one in a way I couldn't share even with my wives.

I draw on blue, looking above the frames of my green spectacles at the lightening sky. Blue is safe, for me. I never bound my will to blue's. To me, it is only a tool, albeit one that cools my passions. My jinni-yah would never let me draft much blue. She was too jealous. I'd thought it was simply her nature, but now I see that she needed me all to herself if she was to win her fights with the other djinn. An Atirat who was not a pure green? Impossible.

As Pride is the first sin, so Power is the first temptation.

Funny how Lucidonius put that in the present tense, though telling a creation story. Not, Pride *was* the first sin. It made the thing applicable to us, as much as to the First Light. Good trick.

'My heart is yours, Darjan, but I cannot save you if you don't let me help,' Aeshma says. Her voice is so like my dead 'Annaiah's that I know she's stolen even that. Clever, clever wench.

'You can't listen to what she says, Darjan,' Auria says in the mundane world, voice weakening. 'You know she lies.'

I know.

'Show me I can trust you,' I say aloud. I hope Auria thinks I'm speaking to her; I hope my jinni-yah thinks I'm speaking to her.

The light is good now. I start running toward the village. Another color might sneak in, hoping to find the raiders asleep, exhausted from a long night of murder and worse. That isn't the way of green. My jinni-yah sings battle rage and bloodlust, and I know that she knows me too well.

Rage is not only red's. I draft enough blue to make sharp edges for the thorn swords that sprout from my hands. My legs are sheathed in luxin, protecting my knees, adding springiness to each step, adding the power of my will to my movement, allowing me to jump farther than any mortal, to land safely, to run faster than a charging grizzly. I am become a beast.

I see the dead: a young woman, Luzia Martaenus, lying on her side with her head cracked like an egg, her baby-swollen belly run through half a dozen times. Her younger sister is dead, cut down closer to town. They'd tried to escape together. Ruy Garos lies facing town, his pitchfork lying in the sticky pool of his blood. Perhaps he'd tried to cover Luzia's escape. He'd always loved that girl, though she'd married the town drunk instead.

Usually, the Angari raiders treated the people of Atan's Town like a crop. Weed out the men who can fight, cut off the thumb of the right hand of the young men so they can still work, still breed, and take the prettiest women for slaves and concubines. Then the Angari would come back years later, long enough that the people could have built up a little wealth, but not long enough that they could build up enough strength to give the raiders much trouble. Of course, the raiders killed those who irritated them, too. Sometimes they killed for sport. Sometimes they maimed for fun. But this . . . this was something else. This was pure punishment, a massacre.

Everyone is dead. I see little Gonzalo, the farrier's simpleton son. He's been impaled on a pike, sodomized, the point of the pike sticking out of his gaping mouth up at the sky.

I howl, waking the whole goddam camp, and my Aeshma comes back over me, putrid and beautiful, a diseased whore. She is as ugly as what I plan to do, and my soul is a small price to pay for vengeance. It makes me monstrous. I am become a beast. I am become a god. Vengeance is mine.

Chapter 14

The galleys collided with a tremendous shock that sent half the slaves tumbling backward over their benches. A slave screamed as the manacle on his wrist tore his arm out of its socket. The *Bitter Cob* sank in the waves, having hit below the other galley's center, then it lifted both ships and began to slide along the opposing galley's side.

The other galley's oars, fouled and crossed and yanked from their rowers' hands, snapped like kindling as the *Bitter Cob* scraped along her hull. Falconets discharged from the main decks of both ships, and muskets punctuated screams of rage and screams of fear and screams of pain.

Heaving himself to his feet on the overhead oar, Gavin thought his part in the battle was done, but the Angari did things differently.

'Up!' Strap shouted. She had a splinter of wood thicker than Gavin's thumb all the way through one shoulder. She didn't even seem to notice. Orholam's beard, she was fierce. 'Man the oars! Knock those—'

A roar and an explosion of timber cut her off. The woman disappeared in sudden sharp light as the enemy's cannon blasted a hole in the deck, followed instantly by a thick billow of black smoke, choking everything with sulfur and sunlight diffused with smoke. The sound deafened Gavin. He was only aware of the oar moving in his hands.

Blinking, gasping, coughing on burning fumes, he helped his oarmates, only slowly figuring out what they were doing. They stabbed the oar out repeatedly, Fukkelot guiding it, Orholam giving the lift, Gavin mostly interfering.

Through the smoke, not five paces away from them across the waves, he saw the bobbing forms of sailors on the other galley, trying to right their cannons from the collision. Loaded cannons. Aimed straight for the slaves' benches. Gavin's fellow slaves—at least those who'd fought before and weren't injured

– were using their oars to keep the sailors from lighting the cannons, to keep them from spewing death through the *Bitter Cob*.

Gavin helped Orholam and Fukkelot, stabbing their oar straight into an Abornean face that appeared in the smoke. It was a cabin boy, not twelve years old. The boy went down, face smashed, a slow match spinning out of his hand.

Fukkelot was trying to shout orders, but in the pressure of the situation, he was seized up with cursing. Orholam had the best view, so Gavin stabbed and stabbed, trying to figure out what Orholam wanted from his actions, throwing his whole, waning strength into the effort. Every so often, he felt the crunch of oar smashing against something softer than wood.

The wind blew the smoke clear enough that Gavin saw boarding nets thrown over the gap between the ships, saw men scrambling across. He thought he heard Gunner laughing somewhere, battle-mad.

The other galley was taller than the *Bitter Cob*, and Gavin could see the rowers over there huddled beneath their benches, cowering, hoping the pirates boarding their vessel passed them by. Some did. Some slashed at the helpless slaves as they passed, laying open heads, splitting shoulders, hacking off skinny, starvation-frail arms. Because they could. Because man loves to kill.

'Fuck,' Fukkelot said.

'Fuck,' Gavin agreed.

As the smoke slowly cleared, Gavin saw a girl burst from one of the cabins of the opposing galley. She was dressed in men's trousers and a vest, but her long dark hair bobbed and streamed as she fled. A moment later, a pursuer appeared. It was one of Gunner's men. He was holding his trousers up with one hand. She must have just escaped him.

Fighting, petite, fierce, and underestimated – the girl reminded him of Karris when they'd first fallen in love. It was intolerable that anyone should—

'You with me?' Gavin asked his oarmates.

He didn't have time to see if they were. The young woman ran past, running for a hole where the traders' galley had been stove in. Gavin and Fukkelot pushed on the oar. Orholam guided it. It caught the pursuing pirate in the jaw. He flopped down, twisting, in a spray of sweat and teeth.

The young woman ran past. A sailor appeared out of nowhere as she headed for the gap, and the sea. She didn't slow, didn't dodge. Instead, she accelerated right into the skinny man. They collided and her momentum carried them both into the water. And out of sight.

Gavin looked to Orholam. He craned his head out as far as he could, but then shrugged. He couldn't see anything.

The fighting continued for a few more minutes, but it seemed their part was done. The fight was confined to the other galley, and the exhausted rowers on the *Bitter Cob* began collapsing to their benches. Some vomited. Gavin looked for Strap. There was nothing but blood, and an entire bench of slaves blown to pieces on the port side, along with one slave across the aisle, and a hole in the starboard side where the cannonball had exited. He saw a tattooed arm that might have been Strap's.

The hunched form of Leonus limped over toward the splattered remains. 'The gods are kind,' he said. He chuckled. 'To some of us.' He leaned over painfully and picked up something. It was Strap's whip, with her hand still clamped on it in death. Leonus pried her grip open and tossed her tattooed arm into the sea. 'Looks like you pretty boys have a new foreman. Unless you want to follow the old one?'

Chapter 15

Kip dulled the edge of sharp hours with drafting. The emotional rush of drafting different colors as the sun limped to the top of heaven's dome distracted him for a while. A few hours. A day. But hunger is sharper than luxin.

Will is a knife of lead. In the end, the body always wins.

That second day with no food, he drafted only what was necessary. He'd already fixed his pack, fixed his boots, drafted a shade for his sun-scorched skin after deciding he couldn't figure out how to draft luxin clothing.

On the third day, he had to stop following the beach as he reached a rocky point of crags and cliffs. He cut through the jungle. Climbing over mounds of roots, angling up hills, trying to compensate for compensations made hours earlier, he got lost, the canopy blocking out the sun, his own stupidity and heat exhaustion keeping him from doing much but finding a stream and lying down in it.

He woke to the brush of something on his hand. A tiny black-and-orange frog sat there. His skin burned where its stomach rested against skin, acidic slime scorching him. He flinched and it hopped away. Then he looked down, his vision following his gaze like a slow landslide.

He was covered in leeches. Dozens of leeches. He was dizzy. He rolled to all fours and vomited water and stomach acid all over his hands. He stood and staggered into the jungle, gear forgotten, tearing off his trousers, falling. The world was hot fog. He puked again. Lost himself, not unconscious, but unaware, animal, a beast.

Found himself some time later, naked, sitting in a shifting patch of sunlight. He was staring at the cloudless, merciless sky. Couldn't bear to look at himself, couldn't bear to see those wriggling fat black leeches attached to him, sucking his blood into their bloated bellies. Drafting his blood for their blood magic.

Shhhhhh, the wind blew through the branches. *Shhh*.

He sucked in blue light, the blue blood of creation. Light is life. He sipped blue until it filled him, until he was only thought.

His racing heart slowed. He closed his eyes and let the blue course through him. It filled him with awareness. Thirty-one pairs of jaws, attached at the front and back of the leeches' bloated bodies to his skin. Four singles who'd had one half or the other knocked free of Kip's skin by his movement. With the blue in him, Kip remembered some long-forgotten advice on how to remove leeches. Not with fire or alcohol or the juice of lemons, else they'd retract angrily, vomiting foulness back into their bites as they recoiled. Instead, a fingernail to break the seal of their mouth on your skin, front and back. A fingernail and patience.

Kip's gorge rose once more, but he stared at the sky again

until his mind was a placid, still pond. He couldn't bear it. Not sixty-some times. He lost the blue completely and was almost a beast again, trapped, trapped in his skin with leeches like he was trapped in a closet full of rats—

Like this.

Calm. Gentle. He took in blue, and more blue. He barely had the will to open himself, barely understood what the swirling color was doing almost of its own accord. It filled his body, found every tooth, every Y-shaped incision.

Gather your will.

He had no will. He reached toward sub-red for passion, toward green for wildness.

No, your will. Luxin is your tool; you are not its tool. Stand.

Kip still hadn't gathered any will, but he stood, feeling persecuted. He knew what to do, but knowing what to do here was like knowing that all you had to do to climb a mountain is to walk. Orholam give me strength.

He already has. Use it.

Arms and legs outstretched, Kip clenched his fists, bowed his head. The power didn't course through him in a scream of rage and omnipotence, but instead in drops of silent tears. It followed his blood, finding tiny mouths, shutting them, rejecting them, sealing the poisoned blood away from him, and forcing it out, too.

One by one, the leeches dropped off. Dropped off his arms. Dropped off his legs. Dropped off his chest. Dropped off his back. Dropped off his butt. Dear Orholam—dropped off his groin. Dropped off his face.

Kip was streaming blood from sixty-two tiny wounds. The leeches' poison made blood run free. Kip wondered how much blood he'd lost. Several of the leeches nuzzled his feet, looking for a new spot to feed. He stepped away. He had no revulsion left. There were only problems, and fixing them.

Oh, simple. He drafted blue caps over every cut. As soon as he took a step, he dislodged a quarter of the blue caps. Of course. Blue was too stiff; if he moved, he would lose his bandages.

He leaned against a tree, sat, drafted a blue cocoon around himself, sealed it, sealed his wounds, and slept.

He woke twice to vomit, wasn't sure if he remembered to draft his bandages or his cage anew.

He dreamt or he had visions or he did things barely aware. A quietly weeping woman, in the gray morning light, hair in a great kinky halo. 'Why are you crying?' Kip heard the voice asking, only realized it was his own after the words were out.

'I weep because you suffer, and only the second sons of Am are entitled to feel pity without passion. And even then, not in life.' She stood and her aspect changed suddenly, flickering between this dignified woman and something entirely other. 'Sleep,' she said, quietly radiant. 'You won't die on my watch.'

All faded into fever and nightmares and sweat and shivering cold and thunder and cool water. He heard the sounds of birds screeching, monkeys howling, something like a dog barking at him, but all of it fast, too fast, skipping along the surface of time as if he were in his father's skimmer, light flashing across his face and disappearing like it was happening in seconds, when he knew it must be days. He had some recollection of holding a broad leaf to his face, funneling water to his lips as a mighty downpour shook heaven and earth.

When he woke again, he was himself.

He felt clear, but weak. He dissolved his blue cocoon, and almost vomited again from the touch of luxin, lightsick. There were paw prints in the mud around his cocoon, big ones, not wolves, though, he knew wolf prints from growing up in Tyrea. There were no human prints, though, not even his own. The woman had been a hallucination, a fever dream.

How much had been dream or delusion? He took a deep breath, checking himself, checking his surroundings. No leeches, no frogs, no storms. Not now anyway.

Kip stood on wobbly legs. He couldn't tell how long he'd been here. The only indication of passing time was his cuts, scabbed over. So the leeches had been real. He examined the cuts. Leech bites usually heal more slowly than most wounds, but with the blue luxin helping, Kip guessed he'd been in his barely conscious state for less than a week.

The hunger had lost its urgency. Kip felt an odd purity, the serenity of saints and ascetics and the batshit insane. The clarity of a soul detaching itself from its flesh home, perhaps. He walked for an hour before he realized he was naked. His first thought when he became aware of it wasn't embarrassment; it was protection. His skin was a poor barrier for the rigors of jungle travel.

He began drafting while he walked. He tried green first. It was so abundant, it was the most obvious choice. But he gave it up soon. Too heavy, too coarse to wear against his skin. When he came across a clump of trumpet-shaped dazzlingly yellow flowers, he stopped. He tried to weave cloth of yellow, but he always lost that perfect, fine mesh point where yellow would hold its solidity before he could get a sizable chunk. The smaller the amount of yellow he tried to make solid, the easier it was.

The declining sun lit up a spiderweb, and Kip was mesmerized by the beauty of it. A tiny moth flew into the web and stuck. The spider moved in to make its kill, but Kip was entranced by the web itself. He extended superviolet luxin toward the web – finer fingers than his fingers could ever be. The anchor lines were like steel cables, but the trap lines had little dots of goo in which more line was spooled. Sticky there, but it also kept the line initially tight, while keeping slack so that the webs didn't snap when fought directly, they would yield and pull and entangle.

Superviolet. Superviolet was the answer. Not to that, but—

It felt like the pieces to the problem were swirling around his head, just out of reach. The sun sank, leaving Kip cold. He hadn't even drafted his shelter. He sat in a torpor all night. When the sun rose again, he had it.

He wove superviolet into tiny links, like a single chain, though instead of pounding each link shut like armorers did, he could simply draft them into perfect loops one after the other, thereby depriving the chain of any weak areas. Then he flooded that form with yellow luxin, his will having to touch each tiny link to seal it. It took half an hour. No problem.

The second chain was much harder; he had to thread each loop through two other loops of the first chain. In an hour, he had two connected strands of yellow luxin chain-mail cloth. Two connected, impossibly short strands of yellow luxin. He almost gave up then. Instead, he sat, staring. Barely even thinking. The water of a stream rushed past on its way to the sea, and Kip watched. Open luxin still streaming in his fingertips, he touched the water like it was open luxin flowing past, the blood of the earth.

For a moment, he felt Orholam himself, the creator larger than this earth, this creation, but acting through it, like all the universe was luxin held open in His hands. A flash, blindingly bright white light, the sensation of life, light, as Kip was pulled through the water to the sea to every water that touched the sea, flashing out to a thousand veins, river-arteries aglow with power. Everywhere, all at once, not just a tracery of lines on a map, but with depth. Water following the sun's call and breaking into mist, rising, becoming clouds. Water, lying on the deeps, its belly scratching sunken cities. Whales and sea demons barely large enough to touch his consciousness, giants like minnows darting everywhere, life too small for a human eye, basking in Orholam's light, their mindless life itself singing his praise by *being*.

Kip lost consciousness.

When he woke, the strand of cloth was in his lap, twenty links wide. He straightened his legs, worked the cramps out of them from his cross-legged pose. He stared at the strands as if they were mocking him. He hadn't drafted those extra strands, had he? He'd not been himself, but he thought he remembered all that he had done.

Kip stared at the water, and touched it again, his will open. But now it was only water. 'I want to save my father,' he whispered.

Silence.

'I'd pay anything,' he said.

But light abides not a lie. He heard nothing.

There was a part of Kip that had felt destined for greatness from the time he was young. Maybe everyone felt that way. It hadn't mattered how he looked on the outside, that his mother was mindless in addiction, that he was fat and ugly. No matter how much he despised himself, some part of him thought that someday, *someday* he would shake the pillars of the earth. That something amazing inside him would be let out. That he had a destiny.

Every stone they'd cast at him, he'd accepted, and he'd used them to construct a little altar to himself. Andross Guile laughing, telling him about the Lightbringer. 'The old word that says he'll be a "great" man from his youth could be a pun in the original Parian – another meaning of the word "great" is "rotund." Which . . . *well.*'

He's supposed to kill gods and kings.

I've done that.

He's supposed to be a genius of magic.

What if I am that?

Gavin had said, 'Don't ruin yourself on this foolishness, boy, there is no Lightbringer.'

And yet Kip believed. He wanted to believe. Needed to.

'I keep trying to draw you as the next Prism, and I can't,' the Mirror Janus Borig had told him. And then as she died, she'd said, 'I know who the Lightbringer is now.'

She meant me. She had to mean me.

But there was only silence.

Kip stood. He followed the stream to the shore, turned north. At sunset, he found a lone farmhouse. An older woman in a simple farmer's dress was standing outside, singing a song to the setting sun in a language Kip didn't recognize. She saw him from afar, smiled, and beckoned him to come with one hand as she continued singing. The sound was like the rivers and the winds and the deeps of the sea, and the warmth and light of a fire against a child's fears of the darkness. It held the promise of the morning and the comfort of a mother's heartbeat.

For Kip, who hadn't heard a word spoken in days, the euphonious rise and fall of foreign syllables unencumbered with translation were a perfect, gentle transition from the raw terrors of the jungle into the sparse, hard-earned comforts of this frontier farm.

'So you're it,' she said, voice low and calm, moving slowly as if he were a wild animal, speaking softly as her song faded, settling into Kip's heart. She smiled. 'Was thinking I heard wrong. "Clad in light"?' she asked, addressing the sky. She laughed heartily and that perfectly human sound made Kip wake as if from a dream.

But not all at once.

He realized he was still naked. He draped the cloth in front of him, but without urgency, without embarrassment. He had a thought and knew it was strange at the same time: the locals have a custom, this clothing custom, though here there are no thorns to snatch and tear your skin; I should go along.

The locals? You mean *humans*, Kip?

Ah, there he was. He himself, Kip the Lip. Some part of him was glad that that Kip wasn't gone for good.

She studied his eyes, seeing him come to himself, and her leathery, freckled skin wrinkled merrily. 'He told me to expect something today. Been on tenterhooks through all my washing and weaving. Had that little phrase, "clad in light," pop in my head.' She shook her head. 'Convinced myself it was "lightly clad." Well, you are that, aren't you? Good thing the Good One sent you now, young sir. I fainted the first time I saw my husband naked. No *wyrthig*, swear. Took the shine right off the rose for him, I tell you, and I didn't do much better for years. The Lord of Light loves to give me a gentle elbow about all that from time to time. But come. Let's take care of you.'

And so she did. She took Kip in, fed him from the soup she'd already had on, though she only gave him the broth, then she bathed him, tended his wounds, and put him to bed. When he woke, two days later, she fed him again. Coreen was a widow, but several of her sons and daughters lived within easy walking distance and one at least visited each day, so when Kip told her he needed to go to the Chromeria, she found out that a trader was due to leave in two days and would make room for Kip – for free. Kip spent one more day abed, and then was up.

They developed an easy rapport, joking and teasing as if they'd known each other for years. She reminded him of Sanson's mother back in Rekton. The woman had always made extra cakes or sweetmeats or pastries, and they'd played an informal game of Kip trying to steal one or two without her noticing. He almost never got away clean, and when he did, she'd ask him some question that he would try to answer around a mouthful of whatever.

She took care of me, knowing my mother wasn't doing so,

and she did it in a way that never made me ashamed. She made it a game, for me. Kip had seen the fun in it before, but he'd never seen the kindness of it until now.

And she's dead. Like all of them.

Maybe Coreen's jokes and laughter were a kindness, too. She'd seen that Kip was barely sane; she'd heard him wake sweating and screaming from another of the dreams, and she treated him like a mother would treat an incorrigible friend of her son. Kip found out that her late husband had been a renowned veteran of the Prisms' War, though she never said on which side and Kip didn't ask, and that made more sense of it. She had some of a warrior's sense of humor: black and light, irreverent to death as death was irreverent to all else.

But she had a warmth, too, that was hugely appealing, and part of Kip wanted to stay here forever.

On his last full day, dressed in the widow's husband's clothes, which fit well due to Coreen's labors with a needle and thread, Kip fixed what he could around her cabin. He drafted a few yellow lux torches, made some fire rocks to help start a blaze easily, tried his hand at drafting green to fertilize the vegetable gardens of her two daughters, and fixed a broken axle on a haycart by sheathing it in solid yellow luxin – something useful he'd actually learned during his lectures. Imagine that.

The morning he left, Coreen said, 'I can't let you go without saying my piece. Have I earned that?'

'Of course.'

She took a deep breath. 'Kip, the Lord doesn't want you to think you're worthless, but he may want you to think you're worth less than you presently think. He wants your eyes to be whole, so you have an accurate view of *you*. It's done in love, you understand? When you surrender what isn't under your control, you're not giving up a crown, you're giving up a yoke. I told you about my prudery in my youth. I was a beautiful girl, and though I never would have said it, I thought I was more virtuous than Orholam. My false virtue – not modesty, pride – took the joy out of my marriage bed. I'd fought to maintain a virtue, and I thought that because I'd had to fight so hard, it must be the highest good. Giving up my claim to look down on those I didn't approve of was like losing a limb. But do you know what it's like to try to walk with three legs?'

It was getting uncomfortably close, and Kip was afraid of what she would say next. 'You've seen me naked, you know I do,' he said. He grinned.

She shook her head like she knew she'd walked into that. She leveled her soup ladle at Kip's nose. 'Kip, scrious hat on, or I make comments about your manhood that you'll never forget.'

Kip swallowed. 'Yes, ma'am. Sorry, ma'am.'

'Taking correction was like losing a limb to me, but it was worth it. A good father doesn't let his children stay stuck. Orholam is a good father, Kip.'

'Right now, I'm more worried about being a good son.' Deflect, deflect, don't let her ask what I should give up.

'Then you are wiser than your years,' she said, and he wondered if he'd been nervous for nothing or if she was letting him off easy. Then she got a twinkle in her eye. 'Oh, and Kip . . .'

'Don't. Please don't. Please?'

'That's no *limb*. A good strong sapling, maybe. Now my husband . . . *That* was a limb. Let's just say maybe modesty wasn't the only reason I fainted.'

'I said I was sorry,' Kip whinged.

She pinched his cheek. 'I know, but you deserved it. Don't worry. You've got more than ample to satisfy. Bigger than my own sons', and if my daughters speak true, bigger than their husbands', too.'

'Ah! I have to see these people!'

Chapter 16

Karris sipped her kopi quietly in the Crossroads. The stimulant was a poor choice for her anxiety. She was seated in the clerestory, facing the big, gorgeous stained-glass windows that had once been the pride of the Tyrean embassy. She wondered how the owner of the Crossroads had been able to purchase this building, and what it had cost. In the years since the fall of Tyrea, it had become the city's most fashionable kopi house, restaurant, brewery, smokehouse, and – downstairs, out of sight of those with tender sensibilities – the foremost brothel in the city.

For that matter, she wondered who the owner was.

Kind of thing that a spymistress should be able to learn, isn't it?

She wasn't kept waiting long. She supposed that was one of the perquisites of her new position. She was the White's right hand, and no one would keep the White waiting. The man who sat across from her was an Ilytian banker, the scion of one of the great merchant banking families, the Onestos, twenty-five years old, and probably just now being treated as an adult, brought home from learning his trade in one of the satrapies and now entrusted with meeting the Prism's bride – or widow. At twenty-five, he could be treated as barely an adult because he still had another fifty years left in his mortal span. How different the lives of munds.

Turgal Onesto was dressed in his Sun Day best, and smelled of some fine perfume Karris would have been able to place if she'd been a lady instead of a warrior these blighted sixteen years. He sat, gulping. It had been a long time since he'd been asked to report. The White had recruited him as a boy. For her part, Karris didn't feel much better. She hadn't worn a dress since that bastard King Garadul had captured her and forced her to. She'd wanted to wear her Blackguard clothes, but those had been seized and forbidden her. Karris still wasn't sure whether they'd been taken on Commander Ironfist's orders or the White's. Neither would say, which told her that whichever had done it had done it with the approval of the other.

So here she was, sending a very public message by the garb she had chosen to wear. Because her husband was the Prism, she would wear garb drawn from each of the satrapies, to show she didn't favor any over the others. Today, that meant wearing a loose-fitting white silk abaya, subtly embroidered with murex purple thread, but she wore the jilbab down – modesty was not prized on the Jaspers as it was in the Parian inland and highlands. Along with the traditional white of mourning, for Parians believed that death was a procession into light, and not into darkness, Karris had chosen some few hints of bright color, not pure funerary white. She wore a bright scarf, white and blue and red and purple and green, though she had bleached her hair white.

My husband is lost, and for this I grieve, her clothing said, but he is not dead. The richness of it said that she expected to be taken seriously, that she was taking her place as a woman of means and influence. She even had a Blackguard bodyguard. That it was her squat friend Samite made that marginally better, but the woman treated her duties seriously, standing beside the table, watching everyone and everything, treating Karris as if she were just another ward who would doubtless be blind, deaf, and dumb to danger.

'It's to free you to pay attention fully to the task at hand,' the White had told her.

Karris crossed her legs as the banker sat. It was a thobe, not a dress, she told herself. Still, it made her feel naked and vulnerable. Worse, she hadn't even been able to pick it out for herself. Marissia had helped her, last night, asking the parameters she wished to fulfill. Karris did, though she didn't tell the slave her task. The slave had accepted her silence on that and simply told Karris she could go to bed; it would be taken care of.

When Karris woke, this awaited. The fit was perfect. 'How . . . ?' she asked Marissia as the slave woman had tied the laces.

'The tailor still had your measurements.'

Karris looked at her. 'I haven't been to a tailor's shop in years.'

'And I noticed you'd lost some weight since then, so I suggested a few alterations,' Marissia said, her voice level.

The eye for detail and the memory – the sheer bloody competence – was infuriating. So Gavin hadn't kept the woman purely for warming his bed. Perhaps she wasn't good at that, at least. Perhaps he'd merely—

What delusions are you filling your head with, Karris? She's beautiful, she's competent, she's been Gavin's room slave for years. Karris had told herself she wasn't going to be jealous of what Gavin had done during the time she'd no claim on him. It wasn't fair. It wasn't right . . . and it wasn't going away. She should be happy that he'd only slept with his room slave, and not every woman who would have been happy to have him.

But seeing that Marissia was eminently competent roused something ugly in Karris. She should appreciate the woman. For Orholam's sake, was she looking at a slave as a rival? Ridiculous! She could put the woman out at a moment's notice. But that wasn't fair, either, was it? Marissia was trying to serve well and unobtrusively – she was even hiding how well she served so as to remain beneath Karris's notice. Probably in case Karris was as petty as . . . as petty as she was.

I would ruin a woman's livelihood and steal her purpose from her for what, exactly? For serving Gavin well?

Serving him well all night long, no doubt.

And what of it? That is her life, her duty. Would I be happier with her if she had served her master poorly in petty rebellion, as other slaves do? Has Gavin said a word about Param or Naelos, whom you took to your bed mostly to spite him? She'd made Param make love to her in total darkness, so she could imagine he was Dazen. But at least both of them were gone.

And what, like I didn't know about Marissia?

He's gone, Karris. He's gone.

The wave of grief came out of nowhere. Karris's throat tightened; her eyes filled.

She let out a breath like a hiss, looked away, got control of herself. Turgal blinked, and repeated, 'Are we to have a privacy shield?'

'Yes, yes, of course.' Karris gestured to the beautiful woman who served as a greeter. Turgal's eyes were all over her. Not very discreet, for a banker. For a moment, Karris felt old and overlooked. Turgal looked at the greeter like that, and not at—

She silently cursed herself. She'd dressed modestly, specifically so she *would* seem respectable, and now . . . Back on keel, Karris.

She gestured for the greeter to draft them a privacy shield.

Karris handed the woman her payment. 'May I bring you more kopi, my lady? And my lord, would you like something?'

Karris acquiesced to more kopi, and the banker ordered ale. The greeter disappeared into the kitchens and reappeared almost immediately. She put down Turgal's ale and Karris's kopi and saucer, drafted the invisible superviolet bubble that would block their conversation from others, and drafted the fans that allowed some airflow. She gave a big, perfect smile at the young banker, bowed low enough to both of them to display cleavage, and went back to her station.

Probably works nights downstairs.

And since when did I get so prudish? Like my Blackguard brothers were pure as heaven's rain?

After Turgal Onesto had a sip of his ale, Karris said, 'I need to assume control of my husband's accounts.'

'As you doubtless know, the Onestos never comment on the status or existence of accounts. Which accounts did you have in mind?' He smiled unconvincingly.

'What do you mean, which accounts? All of them,' Karris said. She'd known this wasn't going to be easy. The proximate cause for this meeting was, of course, to take control of Gavin's accounts. What else would one meet with a banker for? That Turgal Onesto was also one of the White's spies merely made this meeting potentially doubly productive.

'I'm afraid that we don't keep accounts by name, only by number. It keeps hostile nobles and kings and parents and others from seizing accounts that have been opened privately,' Turgal said. He smiled pleasantly. Fop he might be, but this was a conversation he had clearly had before.

More, it was a lie. Karris was certain of it. There was no way the Onestos wouldn't keep track of the account holders' names.

'What happens when account holders die?' Karris asked.

'Nothing. The Onestos don't even have knowledge of when that happens. We have no way of knowing that. As I said, we don't link names to accounts.'

'What happens to the *money*?'

'It remains in the account, of course.'

'Uh-huh, for how long?'

'If an account has had no activity for a generation – defined by old tradition as forty years' time – the monies therein are made available for other loans.'

Which was doubly a lie, and a subtle pair of lies at that. The money was never put aside in the first place. The moment money was deposited, it was loaned elsewhere. And when he said 'made available,' he meant that it then moved into his family's personal coffers. It wasn't completely unfair, Karris supposed. If an entire family was extinguished, as had doubtless happened many times in the various wars that had wracked the Seven Satrapies since the Onestos had entered the business, and if no heirs stepped forward, what else should they do with the money? Give it away? It was a perquisite of taking the risks of bad loans.

Of course, if they were less than diligent in their pursuit of finding heirs, it would also be a quick way to pad their own accounts. Too much of that, though, would hurt their reputation. A bank was only as good as its reputation. So the appearance of punctilious virtue had to be of the utmost import. Of course, generations of the Onestos now long dead had built that reputation to such a height, it was quite possible Turgal and his compeers felt they could coast on it to enrich themselves.

And if they thought that, they probably thought right. Their children and grandchildren would pay for it, of course, but Karris wouldn't be there to feel vindicated.

'Before you came here,' Karris said, 'you looked up all of my husband's accounts to see what I would be talking to you about. Did you bring them?'

He blinked. 'I can't comment on the existence or status—'

'Which is a yes. And you brought them. You wrote them down.' It would, the White had guessed, be quite a few different numbers, and Turgal Onesto didn't have his ancestors' head for numbers. The White said writing down the account numbers would be a direct violation of family policy. They believed in memorizing everything. What was in your head couldn't be stolen, at least not without your knowledge of the theft.

Karris was surprised that the White would know so much about a mere merchant family, but the White believed in

96

knowing as much as possible about those who had any kind of power. In a hundred years, she said, the Onestos would probably be more respected and more titled than most of the remaining eighty-seven and a half out of a hundred noble houses in the Seven Satrapies.

It had been a joke, and Karris hadn't caught the punch line. Twelve and a half percent was the typical rate of interest the Onestos charged. Twelve and a half, out of a hundred left . . . Ah. Then she got it. Here she'd been wondering if there really were exactly one hundred noble families in the satrapies. Even the jokes told Karris how much she had to learn.

He reached for the slender scroll case he kept slung across his back.

But in addition to being given a network of eyes and ears, the White had also been directing Karris to some fingers as well. Some of which were very light.

Turgal Onesto reached in the scroll case and found nothing. He upended it. Nothing. Empty. His face lost all color, then went green.

'Tell me you at least wrote it in code. Your family must have a dozen ciphers.'

'Of course. Of course. Setback, not a disaster. It's right . . .' He reached into the satchel he'd brought. Groped. Blanched once more.

'You brought the key to the cipher along with the message?' Karris rubbed her forehead. 'You're not making some very poor jest, are you?'

Turgal's wide eyes told the tale.

'Your grandfather is going to be so very displeased.'

'Most people don't even know it's a cipher!' Turgal said. 'It's just a piece of wood, a cone. If you don't have exactly the same . . .' He trailed off. 'You! You did it.'

'Turgal, listen to me.'

The veins on his neck were standing out. A temper, huh? Well, let him try something, please. She'd see just how much freedom of movement she had in this thobe after all. And for however embarrassing a man might find it to have his bung packed by an Archer, how much more embarrassing would it be to be humiliated by a woman in a thobe?

But then again, the Blackguard clothes were an armor that kept Karris out of fights. Bullies didn't want to fight and lose. New garb, new rules.

She realized then that his lack of cooperation in the first place might have something to do with her choice of Parian garb. The Onestos were originally Ilytian, and there had long been strife between them and Paria. Especially among the rich, who felt unfairly taxed when they used Parian overland routes for trade during the winters.

Many nobles who were raised on Big Jasper prided themselves on putting those petty struggles in the past, but Turgal hadn't been raised here. He looked like another young rich urban fop, but he had the biases of his elders.

Karris suddenly wondered if Marissia had dressed her like this on purpose. But Karris hadn't said anything about meeting with an Ilytian, had she? Had she let something slip, and this was Marissia sabotaging her, or had she not said anything and Marissia would have helped her avoid it if she had?

'Turgal, I could have played this a dozen different ways. I could have delayed our meeting and showed up in front of your father with all the correct numbers. I could now expose you and destroy you. Instead, this.' Karris fished the cone out of her bag, along with paper. She handed both back, and pulled out a third paper, with the cipher correctly translated and put on flat paper. All done in the time that he'd taken to walk to this meeting. 'I don't wish to destroy you,' Karris said. 'But I will have your respect.'

The spine went right out of him. 'You have it. Please, I'm on my last leg with my grandfather. He'll disown me. If he does that, I can't be any use to you, right? Right?'

'I have no intention of destroying you, Turgal. I want you to take all these monies and transfer them to a new account – just in case someone else also has these numbers. This will happen today.'

'I can do that,' he said.

'High Luxlord Andross Guile might come after this money.'

'My grandfather always deals with him personally. But if the monies are in a new account, even Andross Guile won't get them out.'

Smart of the grandfather, then. Turgal wouldn't last two minutes with the old man. 'Good,' Karris said. 'Now, as a gesture of goodwill: your old rivals, the Adini family, have been planning to move their main Abornean warehouses from the Darks to Eastland. They need more storage and the harbor there is better. They've found exactly the area they need, and have been quietly buying up the deeds. There are a few hold-outs, whom they've begun harassing. If your family wishes, you can buy these properties simply by telling the owners, "The sun shines on the obedient." The White expects that you will still allow each of them a fair profit, because they will sell to you. You, in turn, can sell those properties at a huge profit to the Adini – or if you so desire, deny the sale in order to hurt them. Tell your grandfather that he must protect the families who sell to him from Adini retribution and that he ought to send his fastest ship, whatever he decides. This matter is three weeks old already.'

Turgal's eyes lit up. 'If this is true, this will make me look indispensable to my grandfather. This is . . .'

'Very gracious of us. You're in business with us, Turgal Onesto, and you will find us good partners. It is in our interest that you rise, but only so long as we help each other.'

'Yes,' he said. 'That makes complete sense.'

'Please understand me, Turgal. Some interpret kindness like this as a lack of will. If there is one thing that we at the Chromeria have in abundance, it is will. If you cross us . . . but that need never happen. We won't ask of you more than you can bear to give. Do you understand?'

He did. She saw in his eyes that he had gone from scared to saved to vassal, in the space of minutes. Karris only wished that she had been able to do any of this on her own. Instead, every pressure point and bribe had been the White's suggestion.

But then, that is how masters teach apprentices, isn't it?

Karris gestured to the greeter that they were done, and would like the privacy shield to be withdrawn. The woman came over immediately. Karris said her goodbyes to Turgal Onesto, and passed a hefty tip to the greeter. The greeter discreetly palmed Karris a bundle of rice paper documents: her reports.

The entire conversation with Turgal Onesto – as well as it had all turned out for Karris – was a sideshow for the White; it was the development of a future possible source, and a way to secure Karris's independence. He had actually held out on one of the largest accounts, which he either didn't know about or actually had memorized. It didn't matter, leave him his victory, the White had said. It would be leverage they could use later if they needed to bring him to heel. The real source here was the beautiful greeter and superviolet drafter, Mahshid Roshan, who saw everyone, and knew everyone, and heard everything either directly or through the other servers and slaves here. She was one of the White's best spies, and Karris needed her.

Karris got up, careful not to gaze too closely at the woman who should be just another servant to her, and went on her way. At the door, she dismissed Samite, who pursed her lips but went.

At least the next part of her day would use some of her old Blackguard training – she had to make sure that between meetings, she wasn't followed.

It was almost a relief to her when she was.

Chapter 17

In spite of the fact that many of the Blackguard inductees had just returned from actual war, their training resumed immediately, and their trainers still treated them like they barely knew anything. It might have been true, but it still irritated Teia no end. The weeks passed, and the trainers acted like nothing had happened, like nothing had changed.

'It's meant to give you normalcy,' Ben-hadad said to her after another practice had left them all breathless, and not a few of them puking. The others had dispersed. For the new Blackguards, there was always somewhere to be, work and studying that needed to be done yesterday. 'The order of it. You've been off where things are crazy and chaotic. You come back, and it's all under control. It's supposed to be comforting. The world's changed overnight. Prism's gone, probably dead. Chromeria's lost two major battles in a war we all thought would be one little skirmish. Everything's gone to hell, and everyone's scared. Normalcy? It's a mercy. And it's worse for the rest of us, you know.'

'Huh?' Teia asked.

'Those of us who didn't go to Ru. They crack down and make us all train twice as hard, and we know it's mostly for your benefit. You come back like war heroes. You're barely an inductee, Teia, and we've all already heard how you led the assault on Ruic Head.'

'Led it?' she asked, incredulous. 'I just took point for a while.'

'You impersonated a Blood Robe soldier and led their patrol into an ambush, saving an entire unit and preserving the mission that ended up killing a god. Without you, none of that would have happened.'

'It wasn't like that,' Teia said.

'So which do you prefer?' Ben-hadad asked.

'Huh?'

'That everyone ignore what happened except for a few whispers, or that everyone walk in awe of you, when you know what happened was less glorious than the stories?'

Teia scowled. 'Oh.' Dammit.

'It's not the first time the Blackguard has dealt with young fighters,' Ben-hadad said.

'Since when did you get all wise?' she asked. 'We're gone for less than a month, and even your spectacles work now!'

Ben-hadad grinned. 'I got my third recognized,' he said.

'What?! Your third color?' Teia asked. Ben-hadad had been a bichrome who'd arrived in spring – too late for the school lectures, but he had gotten into an earlier Blackguard class. As his dual-lensed spectacles attested, flipping down one lens at a time, he had always been able to draft blue and yellow, and had been on the verge of green. 'But . . .' They'd been worried that if he were acknowledged as a polychrome he would be forced out of the Blackguard. Polychromes were too valuable to endanger.

'War changes everything. You know how far down the Blackguard's numbers are. They're not going to let a Blackguard go, not one who's already in training. Even if I am a polychrome. Barely.'

'How long have you known?' Teia asked. It wasn't unheard of for a person's abilities to expand in their teens; most bichromes and polychromes started with one color and expanded gradually, but there was something odd about how Ben-hadad said it.

'I've been able to draft credible green for three months now.'

'You shit!' she said. 'You didn't tell me?'

'You were busy with Kip. All the time, on duty and off.'

'He's my partner.'

'Was.' Ben-hadad's eyes widened, like he'd given something away.

'What's that supposed to mean?' Teia asked.

Ben-hadad's jaw clenched, and he scowled, then said, 'War changes everything. I thought maybe it could change that. You know.'

'Know what?'

'Kip's dead, Teia. It's been weeks. If a loyalist had picked him up, we'd have heard by now. If a slaver had picked him up, they'd have asked for a ransom. They don't hold on to prizes like a nobleman's son.'

'He's not dead.'

'Even if you're right, he's dead to us. Even if he survived, he attacked the Red, Teia. He can't be a Blackguard.'

'The Red is lying. There's no way Kip—'

'Because Kip never acted on a mad impulse before, right? He's so levelheaded. Orholam's balls, Teia. It doesn't even matter what really happened. The Red is the Red. And he's the head of his family. And he's Andross Fucking Guile. If Kip comes back here, it's suicide. He's out of your life. I just thought . . .' He blew out a breath, seeming to deflate. 'Look, I'm sorry I said anything. This was not . . .'

'Not what? Not *what*?' Teia demanded.

'Look, I – dammit! Forget it!' He stormed off.

Asshole! Teia turned her glower on a little slave girl who was staring at her.

'Pardon me, Mistress,' the girl said. She gulped. She couldn't have been more than ten, hair in tails. There hadn't been any wars recently enough that she could have been seized in them, which meant the girl had been sold by her parents. Betrayed.

Teia made her face a calm mask. No need to frighten a helpless girl with fury that had nothing to do with her. 'Yes, caleen?'

'A man sent me to tell you he must meet with you immediately. He's in your room.'

'A man? What did he look like?' Teia said.

'Tall, Mistress. Red hair? Smiled a lot?'

Teia cursed loudly, scaring the slave girl. 'I'm sorry. You may go. Thank you.'

It was time. Master Sharp had her job. One job, and she'd be free. Right. Teia knew how that worked. One job, to get you in deeper. How dumb did he think she was? On the other hand, what choice did she have?

How awful could it be?

She didn't want to think about that. She went to her room – Kip's room – quickly. She hesitated in front of the door, then, figuring that Master Sharp could kill her quickly, invisibly, and without leaving a trace no matter what she did, she opened the door.

Master Sharp was seated on her bed, legs crossed daintily, hands folded in his lap. He favored her with a large, beautiful, false smile. 'There's a ship docking within an hour. It's called the *Red Gull*, from Green Haven. There's a man aboard, a mund, Dravus Weir, distinctive red and yellow and green hat. He'll be carrying a bundle of papers. Maybe in a messenger case, silver scrollwork on the ends. But maybe not.'

'You know I'm red-green color-blind. And if the papers aren't in a case, I won't be able to see them regardless,' Teia said. 'You know—'

'I'm well aware of your limitations. I'm trying to figure out your abilities,' Master Sharp said. 'You'll be expected to . . . relieve him of those papers before he makes it to the Blood Forest ambassador's residence. Dravus Weir is a spy, so he'll be on his guard. Whatever happens, you are not to let him identify you. I'll trade you those papers for your papers. You understand? Your freedom, for one little theft.'

Of course she did. She'd been dreading this task for – 'Did you say one hour?' she asked. It would take her that long just to get there.

He smiled his selachian smile.

'Get out,' she ordered.

'Pardon?'

'I have to change. I'm not going in nunk's clothes. Now. I don't have time for your nonsense.'

He slapped her heavily, knocking her down. 'Remember who gives the orders here, caleen. You can show respect, or you can be taught it.'

Teia stood on shaky legs, fists clenched. Time's wasting, Teia.

She shucked off her gray inductee's trousers and tunic and stared death and vengeance at Master Sharp as she pulled on her discipula's garb. It would stand out less than the inductee's clothes, but still more than she would have liked. Unfortunately, she wasn't rich enough to have more than two changes of clothes.

Master Sharp merely watched her passively. 'What's the vial you wear? Oil? Perfume?'

'It's nothing.'

He let her get away with it. 'I'll be in front of the Crossroads tavern. Two hours.'

In minutes, Adrasteia was moving quickly through the crowded afternoon streets of Big Jasper, blotting out fear with action. Once there was a gang that saw her, but she managed to lose them. It took another few minutes from her, though. Once she thought she saw Kip, stepping out of a tiny shop in a cross alley, but it was just her imagination – or her guilty conscience.

This one thing, and she was free.

It wouldn't be real freedom, of course. She'd be snared in something worse. But getting her papers would mean that ownership of her couldn't be passed around. She'd be a slave still, but only informally a slave to Master Sharp. Freeing herself from one man would be a hundred times easier than freeing herself from all the laws of the satrapies.

I'm a slave, not a fool.

But would she rather be tied to Master Sharp, or to Mistress

Aglaia Crassos? Murder Sharp was brutal, but Aglaia was respectable. He hid in the shadows; she hid in the light. Teia would take her chances with shadows. Do the job, Teia. You'll need all your wits for this one.

It was impossible. She had no time to access her tools, her disguises. She hadn't studied the man she was supposed to rob. There was more going on here. It could be that Murder Sharp simply didn't know that he was asking the impossible, or it could be more.

It was more. Teia was sure of it. But if it was more, what could it be? Was he setting her up to fail? Why?

Still thinking. Time for that later. The first thing Teia needed to do was make sure she succeeded. While the drab white dress of a Chromeria student with her hair pulled back by her gold-colored scarf was less conspicuous than her inductee's garb, it still wasn't good enough.

It was ten blocks before she found what she was looking for: a boy, perhaps twelve years old – younger was important – out in front of a shop, sweeping the area clean, alone, hard-working, wearing an apprentice's clothing and a hat with a wide brim, plain.

She put a little sway into her walk. He glanced up, stared at her, looked away shyly, then glanced again.

'Hi, handsome,' she said, walking straight up to him.

'Who?' he said, looking left and right. He blushed. 'Me? Uh—'

She kissed him on the mouth, pulled his hat off, and slid her body up against him. His entire body locked up. She released him. 'Thanks,' she said, putting his hat on her head.

His mouth hung open, but he was speechless.

She glanced back before she went around the corner, and blew him a kiss. He was holding one finger up, but he didn't move. The broom had fallen to the paving stones at his feet, forgotten.

For the next two blocks, she jogged, just in case he came to his senses. Then she started scouting the laundry lines, looking for something her size. Laundry was supposed to only be dried in the heat of the day, so that the beams of light from the Thousand Stars wouldn't be blocked if they were needed in the late afternoon or evening, but of course not everyone followed the rules. She had flexibility for what she stole, of course. She had a belt if the trousers she ended up taking were too large, and as long as the shirt or tunic wasn't enormous, it could work. But baggy clothes could be sloppy, and if she had to run, she didn't want trousers that would fall down around her ankles.

She slowed as she saw what she wanted. A boy's trousers, and a tunic, together on a line, one story up, with a cart parked right underneath them. A girl perhaps six years old was holding the pony, keeping the cart while her father or mother was inside.

Teia broke into a jog and jumped up onto the back of the cart, then stepped up onto the edge of the bed like a cat walking a fence. She snatched the trousers and tunic, dropped to plant one foot on the driver's seat, and rolled as she hit the street.

She rolled to her feet not five paces from the little girl.

Teia winked at her and smiled. Then she bowed. The child looked so shocked that Teia thought she might not say anything at all.

Then the little girl burst into tears.

Walking as quickly as she could, Teia hadn't quite made the first corner when the little girl's mother ran out to her. Mercifully, the child was so distraught she couldn't explain that a woman had fallen from the sky. Teia made it away cleanly.

She avoided the main streets, preferring the slight possibility of crime to crowds. Then she ducked into a bakery's doorway. This late in the day, they were closed, lanterns extinguished.

Teia pulled on the trousers under her dress, glanced up and down the street, and only saw a few women who didn't seem to be paying attention, and shucked off her dress. She pulled on the tunic, folded the dress quickly, belted trousers and tunic, bloused everything so it was baggy. Put on the hat, tucked her hair up into it, then stuffed the folded dress down to her stomach inside the tunic. The belt held it in place, and it helped flatten out what little curves she had.

It was depressing how little she had to do to make herself look like a boy.

She was back at the docks ten minutes later. When you came

in to port, all your awe was taken by the city's domes and stars and the Chromeria's seven gleaming towers. Coming to it from the city was different altogether. To call the docks extensive was an understatement. Big Jasper was one of the largest cities in the world, and almost all of its supplies had to be brought in by ship. The system looked like chaos to the uninitiated, though Teia had once heard a fellow student whose father was a stevedore wax poetical about the symmetry and art of it all. To her, it looked like an ant swarm. Thousands of people crisscrossing, a snarl of ships of every size, carts streaming in and out, queues of burly men going in one way, and women with abacuses ticking off beads for purposes Teia couldn't even guess at.

Teia walked straight up to a man who was answering laborers' questions, directing them this way and that. 'The *Red Gull*?' she asked, lowering her voice an octave.

'Pier Twelve, green side.'

Telling him that 'green side' didn't help a color-blind person would just draw more attention to her, so Teia kept her mouth shut and walked.

The *Red Gull* was already docked, and before she even got onto Pier Twelve she saw a dandy in a wide hat of a couple different shades and yellow. Her man. Amazing luck.

He looked slightly the worse for wear from his time on the ship, relieved to have solid ground underfoot again. He was whistling.

Teia drew in paryl, cupped loosely in her hand, drafted off center so it decayed rapidly back into its spectrum of light, but now focused in a beam. Relaxed her eyes and ducked her head so the hat's brim shielded her eyes as much as possible. She had to do it quickly. There was no way she could put on spectacles – which only the wealthy could afford – and maintain her disguise, but if anyone saw her pupils, they'd likely shout.

The light cut through his garments, through his hair, though it wasn't powerful enough from this distance to go through his heavy leather gloves or boots. She watched him as he went past.

Belt buckle, sword, coins tucked in a breast pocket. All these

107

lit up, white in her vision. But no silver scrollwork document case.

If he had the documents on him, they were either tucked into his boots or gloves or lengthwise beneath his belt – or made of thin enough paper that the paryl went right through them. No matter what, she was darked.

She fell in behind him, following thirty or forty paces back. If he was delivering papers to the Blood Forest embassy, she had about fifteen minutes to make the grab. She knew Big Jasper well, but she didn't know how well this spy knew it. Neighborhoods between the docks and the embassy district weren't nearly as bad as those farther north.

The spy walked confidently, though he did check behind himself once in a while. He never looked at a map or asked for directions. So he knew the city.

Teia couldn't follow him and close the distance while he was being this careful. Disguised as a skinny poor boy in a hat, she could blend in well, but the man was a spy. Surely he'd notice her before she could catch up and steal from him.

If he knew the city, and if he was heading directly to the embassy, there were two alleys between main thoroughfares that he would cut through at different spots.

It was a gamble, but it was the best Teia had.

The spy brushed his left glove, as if reassuring himself that something was still there. That was it. Luck!

Teia peeled off and turned left where two roads diverged. After half a block, she began jogging. It drew attention, but not too much. Apprentices often had to run when performing chores for their masters.

She circled several blocks, jogging fast. The crowds thinned out, and she turned down the street that should intercept the spy. Too late. He was already there, heading across the road, crossing in front of her. Teia cursed quietly, and doubled back.

One last chance. This time, she ran full out to make it to the last alley. She was small enough that she might still have looked like a boy playing. She tried not to let her panic show in her face. She'd only have one chance.

She turned down the cross street and made it to the alley entrance.

Heaving a few deep breaths and trying to calm her nerves and steady her hands, she ducked her head low so her face would be hidden and headed into the alley. He was at the far end, coming toward her. Her heart was pounding so hard it shook her whole frame. There was no one else in the alley. If she were quick, she could intercept him as he passed through a narrow spot. Perfect.

Teia kept her head tilted, hat down, shielding her eyes. There wouldn't be a whole lot of grace in this one. She would do a bump and grab, and if he didn't notice immediately, he probably would within a few seconds. There was no crowd here, no distractions. She'd just have to hope she was fast enough to get away. She was already plotting escape routes – but let that be. Pay attention. First thing's the grab.

She stepped through the narrow spot just as the spy did. She pretended a stumble. He brought his hands up and pushed her away. She grabbed the notes, but it wasn't clean. She tugged a bit of sleeve, too, and the spy turned as she yanked the letters free. Shit!

And then something happened too fast for her to follow. The shadow of that narrow spot in the alley came alive, detached itself from the very wall it had been part of, and imprisoned her arm.

It whiplashed her back toward the spy. Something warm splattered against her lips and neck. The spy raised his hands, panicked – his throat slashed open, his jugular fountaining blood all over Teia.

Teia pushed the spy away and he fell, gasping like a fish. The shadowed assassin put something into her hand. A bloody knife.

She recognized him by his size and stature and eyes, because he was completely covered otherwise, his cloak drawn tight over his head, the side of the hood hooked closed to make a mask over his face, only his eyes uncovered. Murder Sharp.

He released her, stepped back quickly, stepping over the spy dying at his feet as if there were nothing noteworthy in having murdered a man.

'You're a murderer now,' he said. 'Run, or you're fucked.' His cloak shimmered, starting around his eyes, and in trails like smoke that raced in spirals down his body, light twinkled and then disappeared.

She heard the scrape of his boot in the alley, but there was nothing there to see. She tried to look in paryl, but she couldn't control it. She was frozen. She looked at herself – covered in blood, bloody knife in her hand, dying man at her feet.

A sharp sailor's whistle blew in the air, the three-tone call for help. Unmistakable for anything else. 'Good luck,' the air said. She could hear Murder Sharp's wide grin, even if she couldn't see it.

Teia stood, paralyzed, for one moment more. She saw a watchman two hundred paces down the alley. He saw her, too, bloody blade in hand, standing over a dead man. She ran.

Chapter 18

Gavin hoped that the ship going in to port would give him a chance to escape. If not that, at least a chance to send a message. And if not that, he hoped that the sailors' natural braggadocio would serve to get word to the Chromeria for him. But though Gunner might have been half crazy, he wasn't stupid. After he'd taken the Ilytian galley, they'd headed directly to port. The Ilytian sailors who had survived the attack had been chained to their own oars, replacing the dead slaves, given fresh oars from the supplies on the *Bitter Cob*, and kept strictly away from the *Cob*'s crew.

Away from Gavin.

The *Bitter Cob* had dropped anchor a fair distance from whatever the nearest town was. The slaves thought it was Corrath Springs, though more than half the slaves were Angari and therefore strangers to the Cerulean Sea, so Gavin figured everyone was guessing, putting a name on a place to try to give themselves some illusion of control over it. The other galley, *Rage of the Seas* – a grandiose title, but the Ilytians didn't have much use for modesty – had been manned by

Gunner's first mate and the third mate, who hated the first mate, and Leonus, who hated everyone.

Gavin thought it was a smart move. Men who hated each other were much less likely to collude. If the officers came back with wildly different stories of how much they got paid for the galley and cargo, you could ask Leonus. Not a foolproof design, but reasonably good, especially if the next time you sent different men.

The crew who'd stayed behind were unhappy about not getting a chance for shore leave, but Gunner silenced that in short order with a few beatings.

The mates and Leonus came back the next morning, having sold the *Rage of the Seas* and the slaves – and doubtless spent the night being entertained at a brothel, but that was a tax any wise captain was willing to pay. They hoisted anchor and headed out immediately. The only supplies the men had brought back were barrels of hardtack and barrels of brandy. The galley slaves all got a measure, with a double for those in the first six rows. Leonus shorted them all, though, setting aside enough for himself that he got thoroughly sick.

It was also thoroughly stupid. If he'd only shorted a few of them, or those in the back, he could have stolen the same amount of drink. Instead, he was uniting the slaves against him.

Once they'd been under way for a couple of hours, Gavin was chained, released from his oar, and bundled upstairs. He was taken to the poop, where Gunner was waiting.

Gavin was forced to kneel again, and his chains locked to a ring on deck. He didn't fight, didn't grimace.

'You're a problem,' Gunner said. He dismissed Leonus and the other sailor who'd brought Gavin up. He had his curious white gun-sword hoisted over his shoulders, and was hanging his hands off it like it was a yoke.

'My apologies,' Gavin said. In quick glances, he studied the blade again: white and black, seven lambent gems. If he'd been able to see colors, it probably would have been even more impressive.

'How long until they name your replacement?' Gunner asked.

'Men like you and me can't be replaced, Gunner, only followed.'

A quick flash of a grin. But then, 'Answer the question, Six.'

'Prisms and Prisms-elect are traditionally only named on Sun Day. If he or she dies before Sun Day, most of the duties are deferred, and the balancing is accomplished through manual means – that is, drafters around the world being told not to draft as much of one color, but more of another.'

'Good news at last,' Gunner said. Then he spat over the deck. ''Traditionally'?'

'During wars, four times Prisms have been named early, with the final ceremonies put off until Sun Day.'

'So you could already be replaced?' Gunner said. 'Good thing you're good on an oar, I guess.'

Oh, Gunner was worried that if he didn't ransom Gavin before another Prism was named, Gavin's value would go down. Orholam's sweet saggies, like Gavin was property. The thought clanged, dissonant, the vibrations shaking sand from surfaces that had been smooth, revealing rusty nails beneath the surface. It was one thing to be forced to row. Even to be beaten was hard and infuriating, but nothing more than Gavin had dealt with in training. Sore muscles? He'd had those for five hundred days straight as he'd designed the skimmer. He'd had men and women try to kill him, he'd been hated and feared everywhere he went. But to *be* a slave?

No, this was an unpleasant land he was visiting. It wasn't his new home. Good on an oar? He would escape or be rescued, there was no question of it. He wasn't a rower; he was simply rowing for a time.

Gavin owned slaves. When he saw stray looks on their faces, fear or despair or disgust, he judged whether it was an assassination attempt – and if it wasn't, he dismissed it. Dismissed them. Because they were beneath his notice.

The only slave he'd treated like she was human was Marissia. He'd been good to her, at least. More than good. He'd been an excellent owner to the slave closest to himself. That had to count for something.

'You're certain your father doesn't want you back?' Gunner asked.

'You saw where that sword was, didn't you?' Gavin asked. He meant when Gunner had fished him out of the water. He

112

didn't remember it himself, but he'd been told he'd been impaled on the damn thing. 'My father put it there.'

That was true, as far as it went. Gavin had taken the dagger into his own chest when he saw it was him or Kip. An odd touch of mad heroics. And now Kip was drowned. Which showed all the good heroics do.

'What do you want?' Gavin asked.

Gunner spread his arms, soaking up the sun. His jacket parted over his sinewy bare chest, and he held the ivory and ebony musket-sword easily. 'Gunner wants a legend,' he said.

'You've got two. The Sea Demon Slayer? You've been a legend since you were six and ten. And you captured me, a legend if there ever was one.'

'If you says so yourself,' Gunner said, grinning.

'I figgered Gunner wouldn't be one for false modesty,' Gavin shot back.

Gunner paused. 'Indeed, no.' He got pensive. Finally, he gestured to his ship, his crew, even his miraculous sword. 'It ain't enough. You understand? Of all of 'em, you understand, don't you? I was a boy when I did that other. That can't be the pineapple of my life, can it?'

Gavin didn't grin at the malapropism. Gunner wouldn't take even a hint of well-meant mockery, not now.

'It was half luck,' Gunner said. He shook his head. 'A man's more than one act, ain't he?' But he didn't wait for Gavin to answer. He pointed to the horizon with grim amusement. 'There, you see it?'

Gavin couldn't see it.

Gunner grunted, looking at Gavin's chains, but decided to keep him in them. 'We're being followed by a galley. Belongs to one Mongalt Shales. He's sworn vengeance on me. Two years ago, I was gunner for the famous Captain Giles Tanner. You know him?'

Gavin had to shake his head.

Gunner grunted, like it was a loss, but a digression too far to fill Gavin in. 'Pirate, 'course. We found a galley and gave chase, and I made a shot from the long tom. Didn't just blow the first mate off the wheel – I blew off the wheel. From three hundred paces. Bit of luck to that shot, I admit. Without her

113

bein' able to turn, fight was over like that. No one else even died.'

'The mate blown off the wheel was Shales's kin?' Gavin guessed.

'Sister. He's been following me since. Found me at a bunk-house in Wiwurgh. Started a fight. I busted out half his teeth. Found me at a whorehouse in Smussato. Challenged me to a duel. I suggested pistols. He said swords. I left him with a dozen cuts and a broken hand. Found me at a tavern in Odess. Challenged me to a duel again. I stickulated that we fire pistols from forty paces. He missed. I shot him in the groin. Winged him, but never heard if I unmanned him or not. He lived, so it can't have been bad, but I saw blood. Thought that would put him off finally.'

You thought castrating a man would *stop* his quest for vengeance?

'He follows me now. I keep enough distance to taunt him. To let him think he'll catch me, if he just gets the wind right, or if I make one mistake. Not sure how he motivates his crew. Imagine they'll mutiny someday.'

'So you're letting a lethal problem fester because . . . why? Because you're bored?' That Gunner hadn't killed his pursuer either said Gunner was a better man than Gavin had thought, or a far, far worse one.

'Gunner likes that word. What's that mean?'

Which . . . oh, fester. 'Get worse. Like a wound that gets gangrene or leaks pus.'

'Knew it was a good one. You're a smart man, Prism. Festure.'

'Fester,' Gavin said before he could stop himself.

Murder passed across Gunner's face in half a second, then departed. 'Fester,' he said carefully. 'What would your father do if I sent him your eyes?'

Gavin suppressed a quick stab of revulsion and fear. 'That depends.'

'Pray tell.'

'He would doubtless make some public expression of grief. That would be a mummer's show I should be sorry to miss. He'll come after you regardless, but you tell me, are my eyes still prismatic?'

114

Gunner's fist came out of nowhere, crushing the side of Gavin's face. Unable to defend himself in his chains, on his knees, Gavin crashed heavily to the deck. He heard a mechanical sound and looked up, blood filling his mouth, to see Gunner had the musket-sword loaded, cocked, and pointed at Gavin's head.

'You mock me?' Gunner asked.

What? 'My eyes,' Gavin said. 'Do they look like prisms? Do they reflect light anymore?'

'No, plain blue,' Gunner said, staring down the barrel. 'Ah, prismic. Right. 'Pologies.' He hoisted up the gun. 'Prismic?'

'That's right,' Gavin said.

'Prismic?'

'Prismatic,' Gavin admitted.

'Prismatic. That's right. Your eyes did used to be all prismatic. If Gunner popped 'em and sent 'em to Papa, he'd think that I don't have his boy after all. Looks like you keeps your peepers. 'Course, I could pop one out. Just because.'

Karris, could you please come and save my ass? While there's ass left to save, please? 'You know, Gunner, I like you a lot. But you frighten me.'

Gunner smiled big, and the danger passed. He looked out at the sea again.

Gavin thought to speak, then thought better of it. Gunner was pensive. Let him think.

'A great musket and an impossible task,' he said after a long minute.

'Hmm?'

'That's what I want. That's all.' He looked at the musket-sword he'd pulled from Gavin's side, somehow without killing him. 'I used to want to make the perfect musket. This destroyed that for me. I can never make one this good. I used to want to shoot the Everdark Gates. This ship has destroyed that for me. It's all been done.' He stomped on the deck. 'Gunner was born too late. The last impossible task in this world, he accomplished in his youth.'

He sank into himself, the bright sun no longer penetrating his darkness.

'I don't think that's true,' Gavin said. 'There are a dozen challenges worthy—'

The butt of the musket flashed out, slamming into Gavin's stomach and knocking his wind away.

'Do not think to placard me, Guile. I'm no child to be twisted round your twosies. Take him below!' he roared. 'Now! Before Gunner blows off the head of our prize!'

Chapter 19

Even as Teia's feet beat the paving stones, her mind locked up. She was like an animal. She got to a narrow intersection in the alley, and realized she had the bloody knife still in her hands. She skidded to a stop, turned, and flung the knife down the alley, then turned and went the other direction. The ringing of the steel on the stones felt like another alarum bell. She scrubbed her face with a sleeve. It came away bloody.

She was *covered* in blood. Dear Orholam save her. Teia sprinted down the block, slowed to a walk at the corner, entered the main street, and moved toward the first shop. It was a wool carders' and weavers' store, broad shutters open, some of their wares displayed on the street. Seeing an old, toothless woman at the counter inside, Teia squatted down between a rack of woven goat wool ghotras and the wall outside. If the woman came out, the opening door would shield Teia from her.

There was only long enough to wonder if she'd made a terrible decision; then the whistles started. Teia heard men running, not ten paces away. The watchmen, blowing their whistles, high and angry. Running toward the murder, though, not away from it. Trying to figure out what had happened, right now, not yet trying to catch who'd done it.

It was agony not to be able to see anything, but Teia kept down, and in a few more seconds, the door squeaked open and not just the old woman but another woman as well walked out of the shop past Teia.

'What you figure they're on about this time?' the younger woman asked.

Teia vaulted through an open window into the shop and with light, quick steps, darted up the heavy stairs. The large room upstairs was packed to the rafters with raw wool, but the door to the roof was bolted and locked.

'Jofez?' a man's voice called out, apparently having heard her steps. 'You up here?'

Oh, blackest hell!

She heard footsteps on the stairs and moved behind one of the stacks of wool. The man hadn't brought a lantern with him, but neither had she, and her eyes weren't accustomed to the darkness. She'd frozen up before and let fear stop her from dilating her pupils consciously. What if she always did that? What if she was destined to fail when it really mattered? What if—

Teia closed her eyes, let out one breath, and opened them again. She felt the stretching as her eyes dilated open, wider, wider to good night vision and into sub-red.

The warm blob of a man standing on the landing at the top of the steps came into the soft focus that was the best you could get from sub-red. Hottest at the face, hot everywhere skin was bare, duller everywhere clothes covered skin, except groin and armpits.

She tried to circle opposite the man, but in staring at him rather than paying attention to the darkness around her, she stubbed her foot against the wooden base beneath a stack of raw wool. It made a dull thunk.

'Jofez?' the man repeated, stepping closer.

Sub-red wasn't good enough here. With speed she didn't know she had, Teia relaxed her eyes further and drafted a paryl torch, but the paryl light didn't cut all the way through the heavy wool. Useless.

Come on! Her desperation lent her will, and the paryl light sharpened and stabbed the way through edges of the wool stacks. It illuminated them only dimly, but it was enough for her to make out the figure stepping forward mere feet away from her. She wended her way through the stacks carefully, able to make out every detail of the ground easily, not making a sound now.

'Melina, if that's your damned cat again, I'm gonna kill it.

Scares the hell out me all the time, doesn't even catch rats.' He continued grumbling and made his way down the stairs. 'What the hell is going on out there?' he asked, finally hearing the whistles.

Then he was gone.

Adrasteia breathed. She was almost out of paryl, so she let the light die out.

She didn't have much time. This was a dead end, so she had to move. She navigated her way through the stacks until she found washed and bleached wool by smell and touch, and then grabbed some and scrubbed her hands. She had no mirror, and no idea of exactly where she had blood on her, but she'd have to do the best she could quickly. She tucked what she'd used deep into the pile – maybe they'd blame the cat and think it had killed a rat here. Sorry, folks.

Then she stripped off the boys' clothing she'd stolen and rubbed her face and chest and arms with the clean back of the tunic, hoping she was cleaning off all the blood. She pulled on her dress in the darkness, fumbled with the laces.

Hurry up, Teia. Get moving.

She debated leaving the bloody clothes here, but it might only be minutes before someone came upstairs with a lantern, and if they put things together, the guardsmen would immediately start asking if anyone unusual had been seen leaving the shop. Someone in the neighborhood would say they'd seen a discipula, and the search would be quickly narrowed.

So she was going to have to carry bloody clothes – damnation! – right under their noses. She folded the clothes as tightly as she could, pulled off her hat, stuffed the clothes inside it, and walked downstairs, trying not to give away the riot inside her chest.

No one was in the shop, but quite a few other shopkeepers and passersby were walking toward the alley to see what had happened. Teia scanned herself for blood. It looked like the dress was clean – she'd worried that blood soaking her shift might have wicked through the dress, but as far as she could tell she'd been lucky. She glanced around for a mirror. There was none in the shop.

With her heart in her throat, she stepped back over the

window frame and caught a glimpse of her hand – there was blood under her fingernails, and rimming every cuticle. Both hands.

Oh hell.

She stepped out into the street, slipping behind the old woman. The younger man and woman had already walked into the alley and left her to mind her shop.

Glancing over her shoulder, Teia almost bumped into another store owner who was standing in the street, looking torn between minding his shop and going to see for himself. 'They say it's a murder,' he told Teia.

'Orholam bless, that's awful,' she said. She meant it. A wave of emotion rose up from the depths. She swallowed hard, clenched her fists and jaw.

Not now, Teia. Not. Now.

'That sort of thing doesn't happen up here,' he said. 'We're good people here.'

She made a sound of agreement and kept moving. He barely noticed her go.

It was terror to walk against the flow of the curious, knowing that looking over her shoulder would make her look guilty. She heard someone running. 'Make way! Make way! Watch coming!'

She kept walking. A sharp whistle blew twenty paces behind her.

Don't run. You look like a helpless little girl. He won't tackle you; he'll grab your arm. Then you counterattack. If you run, he tackles you. With his weight against yours, you're dead.

The whistle sounded again, almost right in her ear. When he grabs your arm, turn with it, bring your elbow to his head to stun him. Then run. Two blocks to an underground gutter. Figure it out from there.

Then, from the pounding footsteps, she realized there wasn't one guardsman, there were two. Two? Her plan wasn't going to work for two.

She froze.

The two guardsmen ran right by her.

'Watch coming! Make way!' one of them bellowed. They ran on, and were swallowed by the evening crowds.

Within another block, everything resumed as normal, the crowds unaware of the death so nearby. Teia made her way to a fountain in a market, where some of the vendors were already closing up. She sat on the edge and trailed her fingers in the water as if idly. She sat up, looked around for anyone watching, and rubbed her fingernails on the folded tunic.

'Whatcha doing?' a little boy asked her. He was irritatingly cute. One of the merchants' boys, no doubt.

'I'm a drafter,' she said. 'Begone or I'll set you on fire.'

The boy's eyes widened. She faked a lunge toward him, and he bolted. She rubbed her other hand quickly and stood. She had to keep moving, had to get rid of the bloody clothes.

A few blocks away, she found a large mud puddle. She pretended to stumble and pitched the folded clothes into the middle of the puddle, then stepped on them. Mud stains over bloodstains. She pulled the caked, dripping clothes out and put them back into the hat distastefully.

It didn't look like anyone even noticed.

A block later, she threw away the clothes and hat in a rubbish heap. She circled a few more blocks to make sure she wasn't being followed, stopped at another fountain and scrubbed her face and hands. Satisfied, she finally headed back for the Chromeria.

No one stopped her. No one knew. She'd gotten away with it. She even still had the letters. Her mind wasn't ready to start wrestling with what had just happened, though.

Coming back to the Chromeria was like entering another world. A world without murder, without shadows that sprang to life. A safe world. She crossed the Lily's Stem and headed toward the entrance of the Prism's Tower, where her room was.

She was almost to the door when she saw a man who looked a lot like Kip, leaning against the wall, flipping through playing cards as if memorizing them. As if there was nothing strange about it.

He didn't look up.

'Kip?' she said. 'Kip!' She ran over to him and threw her arms around him. 'You're alive!'

He didn't return her embrace, and for one moment she had the terrible thought that this wasn't Kip after all. She let go of him, stepped back. He did look different: he'd dropped probably another three sevs, his broad shoulders emerging more and more as his fat receded. His jawline more pronounced, face harder without the baby fat to soften it. But it was Kip. Something else was different about him, too. She'd thought she'd seen him in town – and she had. And suddenly fear took her by the throat.

'I just arrived. I was so excited to see you,' he said. There was no joy in his tone. 'This isn't how I pictured this.'

A weight dropped into her stomach. It was hard to breathe. Guilt raced all over her face. Kip saw it.

'Kip.' The word came out barely above a whisper. It was hard to breathe. 'Kip, I'm a slave. You don't understand what that means.'

'You're not a slave.'

'How long did you follow me?' she asked. He couldn't have followed her for long without her noticing, could he?

Kip's expression flickered from looking like a puppy you'd kicked and a hard man, hiding his wounds. 'You should probably change that bloody shift before anyone else notices it.'

She panicked, and set off rapidly, but his long gait kept him with her easily. When had he gotten so tall? Of course he hadn't been able to follow her all the way from the city. What had he seen? Maybe he'd followed long enough to see her steal the clothes. Bad but not damning, and he'd seen the blood, worse, but still not damning.

On the other hand, if he had seen everything – from a clear vantage – he would know she wasn't a killer. If he'd seen *almost* everything, he might think she was.

And what was the cost of telling him? You're a slave Teia, not a fool. What does it mean? Think!

She got in the lift, where there was another discipulus with them, so Teia was spared having to come up with more lies.

The question wasn't, what am *I* doing, the question is, what are *they* doing? There wasn't one thread here, there were two.

As she and Kip stepped off the lift, her breath caught. So simple. Everything she'd stolen for Lady Verangheti – actually for Lady Aglaia Crassos, though she hadn't known that then – had been metal so she could see it. But everything had also been easily identifiable. She'd thought it was so she would know what to steal. It wasn't.

They'd been keeping everything she stole so they could blackmail her later – it was all proof that she was a thief.

Kip grabbed her arm painfully and pulled her around. She was suddenly aware of how big he'd gotten. Muscle was filling in everywhere the fat had been, but so slowly that none of them had noticed, until now, when he must have been starved for weeks to lose so much weight.

'Teia, dammit, tell me the truth!'

It wasn't fair, she thought, how boys do that. How one second they're big children, and the next second they can tear your arm off.

Looking up into her friend's face – no, her master's face, still, despite everything, still her master until those papers went through – she felt something inside break, but it was sweet; it was honey dripping from a broken honeycomb. He knew. She had to tell him everything and hope for the best. Even if he recoiled, even if he ran away, she wouldn't be alone with this burden anymore. The very prospect was light and hope.

Kip seemed to realize how hard he was holding her arm, and he dropped it. 'You get in a fight or something?' he asked.

Teia's heart started beating again. He didn't know. Relief rushed through her in waves.

He scowled, and she saw that he knew he'd botched it.

'I need to change, and we need to have this conversation somewhere where we can't be overheard,' she said. In control once more, buying time, getting a little space to think.

Surely she wasn't the only one who would be interested to learn that Kip was back. Surely spies would be reporting to everyone in power that he was here. Surely at least the White and the Red and the commander of the Blackguard would hustle as soon as they learned Kip was here. How long did it take the spies around here, anyway?

Then again, it would be best for Teia if she made it to the lavatories before meeting any of the servants of the most powerful and interested people in the Seven Satrapies.

'This will go better for both of us if I can get cleaned up first, Kip,' she said as she hurried.

She saw Gavin's room slave Marissia coming from the direction of Kip's room just as they reached the girls' barracks. Teia kept her head down. 'I'll be five minutes,' she said as she ducked inside. 'Maybe ten.'

There were no girls in the barracks. Thank Orholam for small mercies. Most were out studying or working or at dinner – which reminded Teia that she hadn't eaten since breakfast. She closed the door behind her, and then waited, listening.

'Kip,' Marissia said, her tone constrained. 'I'm delighted to see you alive. You're needed upstairs, immediately—'

'I'm sorry, but I'm busy—'

'—at an emergency meeting of the Spectrum. It's not a request, Kip. You can come with me and we might straighten this out, or you'll be seized by the Black's watchmen and probably beaten, and the Red will get what he wants. What are you doing wasting time with a slave? You should have reported to the White immediately. Pray Orholam your foolishness does not cost us lives.'

'I just got here not ten—'

'Now, Kip.'

For one stupid moment, Teia wanted to go out there and slap Marissia's face. How dare she talk to her friend like that? Slave? Slave? You're a slave yourself, you stupid—

Teia leaned close to hear how Kip would respond. The opening door smacked her in the cheek, stunning her, though it didn't hit hard.

'Don't think you've escaped notice, caleen,' Marissia said quietly through the crack in the door. 'Why haven't you filed your manumission papers? What game are you playing? For whom?'

The door shut, and footsteps receded, and Teia was left alone swimming with an anvil.

One thing at a time, she told her panic. You're still covered with blood, stupid. That first. She went to her bed and opened her chest and grabbed a clean shift. She went to the lavatory, poured water into a basin, and looked at herself in one of the mirrors.

Checking quickly to see that no one was coming, she stripped off her dress. Seeing the splash of blood across the front of her shift, darker where it had dried, but still livid up at her neck where her warmth and sweat had kept the gore liquid, she had the sudden urge to tear it off, to weep, to vomit. That man, the look in his eyes, that knowledge that he was dying and there was nothing he could do—

She took a deep breath, steadied herself against the basin.

Careful not to smear blood against her face, she pulled the shift off. She stopped her first instinct: to plunge the shift into the water and try to clean it. It was blood. The stains wouldn't come out, and it would leave the water a bloody mess. Instead, she looked at herself for any evidence of blood on her own body. She dipped the hem into the water and cleaned her neck, between her breasts.

Orholam have mercy, she had blood in her *ear*. She couldn't get it off.

Her stomach convulsed, but she held back the vomit. Slowly, meticulously, she dipped another clean portion of cloth into the water and cleaned her ear, behind her ear, her cheek. She checked her hands once more. Cleaned under two fingernails. She folded the ruined shift carefully so that none of the blood-stained parts were visible, toweled off with the hand towel, and pulled on her fresh shift.

She tried to smile at the mirror. Weak.

It was the best she could do.

Now to dispose of the shift – the last direct evidence of a murder that could be tied to her. The shifts were numbered on the back so the laundry slaves could return them to the appropriate girls. Teia tore the shift and ripped out the number, which was harder than she expected. Just a small square of cloth, not even as wide across as her thumb, and thin. She popped it in her mouth and swallowed it.

She stuffed the shift into the bag for menstrual rags and headed to Kip's room. She opened the door carefully, her eyes wide to paryl, certain she would find that damned man inside again. There was no one, no traps, but there was a folded square of paper on Kip's dresser. Teia approached it slowly, certain it hadn't been here when she left.

It read: 'T., As promised. – M.S.'

Had this been here when Marissia had checked the room?

Teia's throat tightened again. Orholam, what would she have done if Kip had been with her when she came in and found this? The weight of the secrets was suffocating.

Opening a letter from Murder Sharp was like handling serpents. Teia picked it up carefully, saw that there was only paper inside, and leaned back as she opened it.

It was her papers, the deed to her very body. Signed, everything in order. Ready to be filed.

Teia walked downstairs, waited in a line for a few minutes, and handed her papers to the clerk. He checked and double-checked everything, and then talked with an older clerk, who gave him a key. The man came out with several fat coin sticks. He counted them out for Teia, and had her sign a document stating she intended to join the Blackguard, then handed the coin sticks to her.

'Congratulations,' he said. 'You are hereby released from all oaths of loyalty to any other than the Blackguard and the Chromeria.' He smiled at her and patted her hand. 'Perk up, why don't you? You're *free*.'

Teia had achieved what she'd yearned for above all else, what she'd sought for years, and she was richer than she'd ever dreamed, but she'd never felt less free in her life.

Chapter 20

Karris took the spy following her on a merry chase through the worst neighborhoods of Big Jasper. She'd walked through the poverty a thousand times, and never felt nervous, but today was different. Without the aegis of her Blackguard garb, she felt oddly vulnerable. She didn't like it. In fact, she hated it. She nodded to shopkeepers she'd known for a dozen years, and they barely responded. They didn't recognize her when she was wearing a thobe.

Worse, their heavy-browed sons didn't, either. She could beat any five of them, of course, depending. But the skirts of a thobe were too easy to snag, and her own experience with getting beaten in that alley not two months ago was too fresh for her to be haughty. She felt a stab of that same feeling of helplessness she'd spent her whole life fleeing.

Someone whistled at her. Her fists clenched. Dammit, all her instincts were wrong here. It was like the world had changed, and no one had bothered to tell her – all because she was wearing a thobe. Going and punching the whistler in the face wasn't going to get the same cowed reaction that it would have when she was wearing her Blackguard garb. Neighborhoods that should have been dangerous for her prey were instead dangerous for her.

It felt like a failure when she put on her green spectacles to let them know she was a drafter. Thank Orholam she had that at least. At a single disapproving raised eyebrow above those spectacles, the men gathering blanched and disbursed.

It made her wonder. Other women dealt with this kind of thing every day, without bloodshed, without incident – and without a drafter's spectacles. Karris literally didn't know how they did it. She wondered if that didn't make her weaker, somehow, in her strength. Another woman would have defused the situation before it became a situation. Karris only knew how to intimidate, to evince superior power one way or another. She'd had drafting for so long, she wasn't sure how she would deal with life if she didn't have it. Humbling thought.

And now, she didn't have drafting. Not really. She could wear the spectacles, but if she drafted, the White would know. Even if she didn't know, if she asked, would Karris lie to her?

No. Not to the White.

She was still being followed.

She took off the spectacles and walked straight until she found the alley she'd been waiting for – long, without any other entrances, nor other alleys running parallel to it. If she were to be followed at all, her tail would have to follow down this alley. She stepped into the weaver's shop on the alley corner. 'Scarves?' she asked. 'Silk if possible? I'm a wedding guest.' She smiled blandly, and the delighted woman disappeared into the back of the shop, as Karris knew she would, leaving her undisturbed. Karris put a danar on the counter to pay for the deceit and the ambush place, and hid among the free-flowing bolts of cloth hanging from the ceiling.

Her tail passed the doorway blithely.

Karris was on top of him in a moment, side kick – left foot behind her right, power gathered in her hips, and right foot shooting out sideways into the man's passing shoulder with the force of a horse's kick. Petite as she was, it didn't matter, with all her power applied so perfectly. The man shot up to his tiptoes and was thrown sideways. He hit the wall of the alley, three paces away, with a crunch. Before he could even crumple all the way to the ground, Karris was on top of him, fingers locked around his windpipe, pinning him to the wall, fist drawn back.

The man was caught in an awkward half crouch. He groaned. He'd been wearing a hat, and now it lay at his feet. He was perhaps forty, greasy, had sun-dark skin, a messy semblance of an Atashian's beaded beard.

He grunted. 'Tol' me you might hit me. Thought to myself, little woman like that, how hard can she hit?'

'Who sent you?' Karris asked.

'He's too careful for that, girl. He told me to tell you, this could have been another rough lesson like the last time. This is mercy.'

'What? Another lesson?'

'When you got beat to hell. And I didn't have anything to do with that, so don't take it out on me. Hey, you mind letting me sit down or stand up?'

Karris let the man go.

'My thanks.' He looked at her, and blanched. 'Nine hells. You're the white Blackguard, aren't you? The girl, changes her hair. That bastard. Sending me after you. You didn't even draft.'

'Tell me something that convinces me not to hurt you.'

'Fine, hell with him. Didn't pay me that much. He told me to string you out, make this take as long as possible. He didn't even set up a time for me to meet up with him again and tell him what I'd learned. You got somewhere else you're supposed to be?'

Karris didn't think so. But she didn't let the man's words

distract her. He could be talking so that his friends could take her unawares. But there was no one else in the alley.

'What's your name?' she asked.

He grimaced. Gave up. 'Dayan Dakan.'

'You owe me, Dayan Dakan.'

'Ah, balls.'

If whoever had hired him wanted this to take as long as possible, she needed to reclaim as much time as she could. She ran, arriving back at the Chromeria sweating in a very unlady-like fashion. She'd considered hiring a horse, but figured it would have actually been slower. Not all streets were open to riders, and with the time it would take to hire a horse in the first place, running was faster, even awkward as it was in a thobe. She hopped into the lift, and took it as high as she could.

'News?' she asked the Blackguards at the top of the lift. One was the new boy, Gill Greyling, the other was the tall eunuch Lytos.

They looked at each other. Neither said anything.

'Where's your escort?' Lytos asked.

Dismissing Samite after going to the Crossroads might not have been the best idea, but she wasn't going to talk to Lytos about that.

'Gill, you owe me,' she said. 'And this won't even be close to setting us even.'

He sighed. He clearly would have preferred to forget letting that strumpet into Gavin's room. He cleared his throat and said, 'There's an emergency meeting of the Spectrum. Was supposed to start an hour ago, but Yellow and Sub-red couldn't make it then. They're just getting started.'

Lytos looked at the young man.

'What?' Gill asked. 'She's one of us.'

Lytos glowered at him.

'What?'

'Thank you, you're both lovely,' Karris said. She ducked into Gavin's room – it was still too strange to think of it as her own room – and tried to decide if she needed to change, or if she could just use some powder to combat the sweat. She looked around for Marissia. For a room slave, the woman didn't spend much time in her room.

Now I *want* Marissia to be here. Not very consistent, are we, Karris?

She mopped her face with a cloth and then slapped powder on quickly, fought with her hair for half a minute, and decided history belongs to those who show up. She headed to the lift.

'Wow, that was quick. You look f—' Gill started to say.

'Not a word, boy. Not. A. Word.' Had she really just called a nineteen-year-old a boy?

She approached the Spectrum's Chamber and the Blackguards standing outside it, and suddenly wished she looked a little more glamorous.

'Lady Guile,' the ranking Blackguard said. It was her old counterpart.

'Watch Captain Blademan. Good afternoon.'

'The Spectrum meetings are only for the Spectrum, Karris, you know that,' he said, stepping in front of the door.

'I'm my husband's representative here.' It was weak, and they both knew it.

'Karris, please, don't make a scene.'

'It's Lady Guile, thank you, and a lady doesn't make a scene.'

Watch Captain Blademan was befuddled for a moment. And a moment was all Karris needed to thread her petite figure past him and open the door.

'Lady—' He stopped abruptly as the door swung open and Karris walked inside.

She walked over to Gavin's seat as insouciantly as if she herself were Gavin Guile. She sat. She didn't see how the rest of the Spectrum took her appearance, because all of her attention was on Andross Guile. He smiled behind his dark spectacles. The bastard. He didn't even look surprised. For a moment, it shook Karris's belief that the man who'd tailed her must have been sent by him. But if not Andross, then who?

'Hello, daughter, so good of you to join us,' Andross said. His shadow, Grinwoody, was standing at his elbow as always, whispering in his ear. 'I suppose that more than makes a quorum. Shall we get started?'

Karris knew they hadn't just started, but Andross liked to deadpan his jabs. It might not even have been aimed at her. She looked around the room and saw that only the Sub-red was absent. The woman was serially pregnant and usually nursing one of her brood, but she didn't usually let either get in the way of her duties.

'We can continue from where we were, Andross,' the White announced.

So it had been a jab. Well, to hell with him. Karris was here now. It was a victory, if a small one.

'For reasons we discussed before all the hangers-on were allowed into this hallowed chamber,' Andross said, 'certain, more drastic moves must wait. Our representatives are scouring the seas and the beaches as we speak. Until then, we have to play the hand dealt us, yes?'

Karris had no idea what he was talking about, but she could see tight-lipped nods among the Colors at the table. If they'd been talking just a few minutes ago even more privately than this, it must be something very secret. He'd said 'hangers-on,' plural. That meant that he wasn't just talking about Karris coming into the room. The Spectrum must have been meeting without slaves in attendance, even without the Blackguard. What was so secret that the Blackguard wasn't allowed to attend?

From the White's expression, Karris could see that the woman didn't like such secrets referred to even this obliquely.

'In the meantime, we're at war.'

Klytos Blue shifted in his seat, like he wanted to speak out, but daren't, not against Andross Guile.

But Andross Guile flared with anger. 'You'd deny it, Klytos? Still? How many of our ships must they sink? How many of our people must they kill? We face nothing less than the old gods, and those heretics who would bring them back. We will have a little respite this winter – but it is a respite that will help our enemies more. Few ships can traverse the Cerulean Sea in winter's storms, and our enemies are on foot. We will have only those few Ruthgari soldiers and the remnants of the Atashian forces, under that idiot General Azmith.'

'That's my cousin!' Delara Orange said. Her face was slack, flushed, eyes bloodshot.

'Then you've one idiot in your family. Or is it two?' Andross shot back.

She huffed and fell silent. It was an acquiescence, though, and Karris thought that if Delara admitted her cousin was stupid so easily, then Andross might actually be understating the case.

'You need to get word to him,' Andross said, 'that he is to fight delaying actions only. Under no circumstance is he to risk a large-scale conflict.'

'Have we not sent these orders already?' the White asked.

'We have.' Andross didn't elaborate, and for Karris, he didn't need to. She had seen how men intent on glory could get others killed. And Andross didn't like giving an order when he had not the means to enforce its obedience.

'Delaying actions?' the White asked. 'How much ground are we to give?'

Andross sighed. 'We will need to marshal our forces for the spring. Realistically, we won't be able to stop them from advancing into Blood Forest.'

'There are border towns. Ox Ford, Stony Field, Tanner's Turn, Mangrove Point. Are you proposing we just let them die?' the Orange asked quietly, horrified.

'How do you propose we save them?' Andross asked. 'Do you know of good options? Please. Elucidate.'

'I – I just can't believe . . .'

'We tell the people to get out, burn it all, starve the Color Prince's army as it invades. Satrap Willow Bough won't like it, but if they won't . . . we have to look at the possibility that we'll lose Blood Forest.'

'You want them to burn jungles? In the wet season?' the Orange asked.

'I want them to win this war in one decisive conflict with no losses on our side. I want none innocent to suffer. You're asking what I want? Don't be fools. We *need* to win. So we need the Blood Foresters to poison wells. We need them to slaughter animals. We need them to torch their fields and cut down swaths of jungle and force every last one of their red drafters to break the halo if necessary to put it to flame. We need them to win so that nine months from now we aren't talking about what villages we'll have to abandon in Ruthgar.'

He let that sit, and no one said anything.

'In the interim, we've lost the bulk of our fleet. We could begin to build and borrow a new one, but I propose that we don't even need to do that. We only need these new sea chariots that the Blackguards have developed—'

'That Gavin invented,' Karris said.

'Yes, of course. The Blackguards merely perfected them. Whatsoever you please, dear.'

She sat back, stung. How did the bastard do that? Make her look so small?

Andross continued, 'With the sea chariots, we can control the seas, without the cost of an entire fleet. We know this Color Prince has been working with Ilytian pirates, and this way we can keep him from being resupplied by sea.'

This Color Prince. My brother.

'We can save specific tactical discussions for later,' the White interjected.

'Fair,' the Red said. 'But this we can agree on: our last battle was a disaster. We can't direct a war from afar. We're going to need a promachos.'

Delara Orange laughed aloud. 'And you did such a good job directing our last battle we should choose you, huh?'

Andross snapped back without the least pause, 'You're a disgrace who couldn't even hold her satrapy against a petty raider from *Tyrea*. You allowed this to blossom from a small problem to a huge one. Your defense was so heinously weak, I wonder if we aren't in the presence of a traitor. I never had functional command over those incompetents you insisted on being our generals, unlike the command a promachos would have, so check your memory. Maybe it's in the bottom of a bottle.'

'You stopped us from defending ourselves!' Delara shouted. 'You refused to help! You came too late, and you knew it. You want us to make *you* promachos?'

'Enough,' the White said.

'I wasn't talking about *me*,' Andross said. 'I'm too old. That burden is too great and—'

'I've lost everyone I l—' Delara shouted.

'Enough!' the White barked. 'Delara, you have our sympathies, and you still have your vote, which you will lose if you're not present to use it. Do not give that up. What is it you propose, High Luxlord Guile?'

I'm too old? The old spider was admitting that? Karris could scarcely believe it. Who would he be proposing instead?

'You all know that I had my disagreements with my son at times, but none of us can deny the unifying effect he had on the Seven Satrapies. He was a figurehead, but he was a well-loved one. In losing him, we have lost one of the most important bonds that holds these disparate satrapies together. For reasons that we should all know all too well, there will be . . .' He paused, parsing his words carefully. 'Unless Orholam relents, it appears there will be no new Prism this Sun Day, but by ancient law we *must* name a Prism-elect. So we must all be on the lookout for Orholam's chosen. I'm sure we will all spend much time in prayer. We will have to survive as best we can for a year without one. That means the old orders. Every drafter working together, and offsetting those who have joined the enemy.'

Karris looked around the table and saw drawn, gray faces everywhere. 'You're not giving up on Gavin,' she said. 'He's not dead. You should be focusing your efforts on finding him.'

'Of course we will,' Andross said smoothly. He smiled apologetically, as if dealing with a hysterical woman who couldn't bear to acknowledge her husband's obvious death. 'This is merely contingency planning.'

Karris wanted to punch his face in.

'Why can't we name a new Prism?' Arys Sub-red asked.

Karris saw that at least of couple of the newer Colors wondered the same, but Andross said immediately, 'This is not a matter for an open meeting.'

'You're calling this an open meeting?'

'Only the Colors themselves and the High Magisterium may discuss these matters,' the White said, clearly not happy to concur, but doing so. 'And not the one without the other.'

Karris's jaw clenched. Andross was angling for something, and she couldn't see what it was.

Andross continued, 'We have worked together before through such trials, and we can do so again. We *shall* do so again. Regardless, our needs, our war, and our peoples cannot wait until even Sun Day to find unity. We must face two painful truths before we lose everything: my son is dead, and we need a promachos.'

'He's not dead,' Karris said.

'Daughter, it speaks well of your loyalty and your love that you hope against hope as you do, but prudence demands a harsher reckoning with truth. Gavin is—'

'Alive,' a voice interrupted from the door. 'He's been taken captive by an Ilytian pirate named Gunner.'

Everyone stopped talking at once. Karris caught a faint glimpse of Marissia as the door closed behind Kip, who had just spoken. Kip! Kip was alive?

And Gavin? Karris's heart surged. She felt tingles all the way down her arms. It was hope. Real hope, not stubbornness.

In the weeks since the battle, Kip had changed. For one thing, he must have been starved, because he now looked merely thick instead of fat. He looked a Guile. Strong chin, blue eyes bright with intelligence, ringed with green from drafting, broad shoulders, broad chest, thick though still shapeless arms. But the biggest change was in Kip's demeanor. There was nothing flippant or sarcastic or jokey about him, not in this moment. He was focused, quiet, unimpressed by this collection of the most powerful people in the world.

'So the bastard returns,' Andross Guile said.

'Enough of that nonsense, grandfather,' Kip said. 'My father established what I am once and for all.'

'He—'

'Look at me, grandfather,' Kip snapped. 'I am Guile. Body, blood, and will. Deny it.' If you dare, his attitude added.

The very air seemed to vibrate with the tension as the men locked gazes. No one said a word. Even Kip's dagger of a sentence wasn't a boy's complaint: he hadn't said, "I'm *a* Guile." He'd said, "I am Guile," as if he summed up everything that it was to be part of that family. As if he were the culmination of it, which was true in some ways, Karris supposed. He was the only Guile heir.

The only heir they knew about. There was still a Guile bastard out there they didn't know existed. Must never know. Her stomach knotted up.

The Blackguards standing outside guarding the room looked uncertain. Blackguards never look uncertain.

The air changed. Karris couldn't tell how she knew, but she knew that Andross had been convinced. Now he was holding the moment purely to buy time – or perhaps for his own perverse amusement, but Karris thought the former. He hadn't planned for Kip to return. He was turning cards in his brain, three rounds ahead of everyone else.

Finally, a hint of a smile touched his lips. He made a slight gesture of acquiescence. 'Please share this news with us, grandson.'

'What did Grinwoody tell you happened? On the ship, I mean? After all, you were wearing those spectacles, and it was dark.'

What was Kip doing? Why did he care what Grinwoody had said? Why offer the cover to Andross Guile, his enemy? Karris's stomach sank. Kip was offering an out to the old spider, offering to help him cover up. Cover up what?

There would be no cover-up necessary if Andross Guile hadn't done something wrong. That meant he was at fault for Gavin's disappearance. Orholam damn him.

'I don't think you telling us the truth should require any rehearsals of what others have said,' Andross Guile said. Not accepting the olive branch.

Kip shrugged. 'Grinwoody and I were quarreling. I'd come along with my father, whom you'd summoned to meet with you. Grinwoody didn't want me to be there. I'm sure he believed you didn't want me to be there. He – a slave – laid hands on me, so I pushed him down the steps. Uncouth of me, and I apologize for it, grandfather. I shouldn't manhandle your property so. With the strains of the battle that day . . . regardless, he ran back toward us, and . . .'

Kip hesitated. Grinwoody's eyes looked dead. The slave couldn't even speak for himself. He knew that when millstones like the Guiles came together, even the most trusted slave might be sacrificed without a thought, ground to meal in an instant if Andross thought that he might gain something by sacrificing him.

'And he stumbled into me. I stumbled into my father, there

was some scrambling as we all tried to save him from falling overboard. But he fell in the water. I jumped after him. I know Grinwoody doesn't swim, so though he offered, it would have been pointless. It was my father's own fault that he'd dismissed his Blackguards, insisted on them going to bed. Otherwise he might have been saved easily. Instead, I pulled my father out of the water, and tried to light a signal. But instead of being saved by you, we were pulled out by Captain Gunner. He said some prayers to the sea, and threw me back in afterward.'

'But you saw that my son was alive?' Andross was intense, seemingly honestly disbelieving.

'Yes, sir. I'm certain of it. I'm surprised you haven't gotten ransom demands. Gunner recognized the Prism, sir.'

The White nodded. 'Gavin has mentioned this pirate before. Said he's quite the character, but not quite sailing with a full crew, mentally, as it were.'

'Grinwoody,' Andross barked, turning around in his seat. 'I thought you said the Prism was unconscious when he plunged into the waves.'

Grinwoody fell prostrate. 'My lord, mercy. I – I thought he'd hit his head on the way down. I believed he had already sank before the boy went after him. My lord master, I am so sorry. I have shamed myself and you.'

A silence. Cards turning. 'No,' Andross said. 'The shame is mine. I should never have given up on my son. In this year when I have lost so much . . .' He trailed off as if overwhelmed with emotion. Then he put his hand to his heart and made the sign of the four and the three. 'Orholam be praised.' He actually sounded sincere. Perhaps the old man really did love Gavin in his own way.

The words were echoed around the table.

Andross continued before anyone could interject. 'I should never have taken a slave's word on something so important. I'll punish him appropriately later. Kip! You have saved my son twice, and brought me news of his life. You warm an old man's heart. I shall have to reward you properly.'

'He's my father. No reward is necessary,' Kip said.

'I insist. Come to my quarters later. Now you're excused,' Andross Guile said.

The rest of them just watched as Kip struggled with the dismissal. He didn't want to leave, but he clearly saw no way around it. He bowed after a moment, and left.

Karris was certain she'd just seen one or the other of them bought off, but she wasn't sure whom. Maybe both. The sheer gall of them to do it in front of the whole Spectrum. And the sheer brilliance, to be able to get away with it.

If it had thrown Andross Guile off, though, he didn't show it. 'Well, this is marvelous. There will be some real challenges in getting my son back before anyone else does, but I think we can overcome those difficulties.'

As Kip stepped out, Arys Sub-red came in the door, heavily pregnant and winded.

'What are we talking about?' she asked, moving past Karris to her seat. She didn't have her youngest child with her this time, but she did reek of luxin and sex. Karris was no naïf, everyone knew that greens, reds, and sub-reds most of all liked to mix drafting and sex. It heightened the sensations and the emotions. Karris didn't care who Arys bedded, but coming to a Spectrum meeting sex-flushed and stinking wasn't something Arys would have done when she was in full control of her faculties.

The strain of rule kills us all.

Karris had thought that Arys had at least two years left, but now she wasn't so sure. Sub-reds tended to get territorial and fiercely, passionately protective of those they loved as they reached the end of their natural spans. And, of course, libidinous, but a woman in Arys's position shouldn't be showing that. Not publicly.

Andross pointedly looked at Arys, and then ignored her.

Delara Orange said, 'If the Color Prince ransoms the Prism instead of us, we'll be destroyed. It will utterly cripple morale. They would hold him hostage as guarantee that we wouldn't attack, and then—'

'No, no, no,' Andross said. 'Do you not understand what the sea chariots mean?'

Blank looks. Andross smirked. He loved it when his superior intelligence found such undeniable expression.

'How is a pirate to hide for long from us? How is he to fight us? We dominate the seas, even if no one knows it yet.'

'If we can dominate the seas, why don't we go after the Color Prince directly?' Delara asked.

'Because he's on land,' Andross said.

'I'm not stupid, thank you very much. I mean, if the seas are ours, why not land our men in whatever place is most advantageous? Behind enemy lines, perhaps, and—'

'Have you even looked at the sea chariots? We'd burn out a thousand drafters trying to move a single transport ship. We can deny the seas to others; we can search the seas for my son, and with grenadoes and other arms, we can sink the Color Prince's pirate mercenaries, but until we rebuild our own fleets, our armies can only approach by land.'

'So they don't really change anything,' Klytos Blue said.

'Other than assuring that we can't be attacked unawares and that we will know exactly where the Color Prince is at all times weeks before he knows where our armies are, yes, I suppose they change *nothing*,' Andross said, dripping contempt. 'What matters for the moment is that Gavin will be ours before long. We can't guarantee we get him alive, of course. But no one else will get him instead.'

And there was the serpent in him. That what he said was true didn't make it any more comforting. The White would have said the same, but she would have spoken to the emotions of the fact first, the thought of losing Gavin through some accident or through some pirate's fury.

But then all of what she'd been hearing hit Karris. Gavin was alive. Gavin was *alive*. The tears of relief blindsided her, and then blinded her. She didn't want to cry in front of Andross Guile, didn't want to show weakness in front of the Spectrum, but a single sob escaped her lips.

Everyone on the Spectrum looked at her, and Karris had to bow her head and clamp her eyes shut to avoid breaking down entirely.

She should keep her eyes open. She was a spy now. She should be paying attention. She should be of use.

Alive. It was hope and light and life and mercy. It was Orholam himself, reaching through the gathering darkness.

For once, Andross Guile didn't bludgeon Karris for her weakness. Instead, he said, 'Let us all go and send out our scouts and our messages and report to our satraps about this news. But most of all, let us all pray. For without Orholam's hand, our situation is dire indeed. Let us meet again soon, but for today, I think we've seen and said enough. High Lady Pullawr?'

Let us pray? This was Andross Guile saying this? How shaken was he? The man made a mock of the faith at every chance.

The White made the sign of the four and the three, and the rest of the Spectrum followed her lead. They lay their hands, palms open, on the table in front of them, receptive, open to the light, open to truth. 'Father of Lights, Holy One, Orholam.' She aspirated the *h*, giving it the old pronunciation. 'Righteous Father, Strong Tower of Kalonne, All-Merciful One, Comforter of the Downtrodden, Guardian of Orphans, Good Teacher, Deliverer, Unfailing Defender, Savior, Warrior of Justice, Supreme Magistrate, Worthy of Honor, Mighty to Save, Bright Morning Star, Fire in the Night, Hope of the Last Tribe, Indefatigable Healer, Restorer of the Broken, Father, King, and God.'

That last sent a shiver through Karris, even through her tears. Even as Parian men covered their hair from respect, that their glory not compete with Orholam's, so were there ways one rarely addressed Orholam – that name itself was but a title, a euphemism to show supreme deference, to show how high above the pagan gods he was. In speaking that small word, huge in implications, the White was revealing just how dire she thought the situation was.

'God,' the White breathed.

The room fell utterly silent. Karris fancied she could feel the play of light across her face.

'God, you are God alone. God, please save us.'

After the long introduction, Karris expected more eloquence, more beseeching, more . . . words. The salutation had been longer than the letter.

Then she realized that was the White's point exactly. The eloquence, the focus, should be on Orholam. His was the beauty and majesty and the power. He knew their need. He knew how best to help them. This heresy was not only a threat to an earthly order, it was a threat to the worship of Orholam throughout the Seven Satrapies, it was a defiance and renunciation of him. The White was merely declaring her loyalty and begging the help of their lord, as loyal vassals. What else, in the end, was there to say?

It was a mirror to the very help that the Blood Foresters in those border towns would beg, and that the Spectrum had silently agreed to deny. You must die, they had agreed without so much as a vote: you must die so that our purposes can be accomplished.

Karris only hoped Orholam was not so callous and practical with them.

Chapter 21

Teia hesitated outside the door of the Prism's training room, deep under the Prism's Tower, looking at a band of blue light illuminating the floor. She had never seen the room illuminated with colored light before. She hadn't even known it did that.

She heard the unmistakable percussive action of someone punching combos against one of the dummies, and oddly, that violent sound eased her mind. Whoever was here was training – and thus, wasn't an enemy. Though she knew from how he moved that Murder Sharp must train often, it was somehow impossible to imagine him doing it. He was only the finality of action, not the preparation for it.

Opening the door with the key that Commander Ironfist had given her, Teia went inside. She was just in time to see Commander Ironfist burst into action. His fists snapped out, punching the fraying leather heavy bag full of sawdust: stomach, chin, kidneys, and back up and down, too fast to follow, then he darted off to the side, running toward an obstacle course. He drew two practice swords while he ran.

Maneuvering with even one sword in hand or at your belt was part of Blackguard training that Teia's class hadn't even started yet – and that she'd noticed immediately during her brief participation in the battle at Ruic Head: trying to run and fight while carrying even a scabbarded weapon was hard work. Corners you knew your body could slip around suddenly caught your hip, threw you off your step. Carrying a blade openly was even worse, because you had to maneuver it by hand – if your blade stopped on a doorframe and you kept moving into it . . . not good.

So watching Commander Ironfist move through an obstacle course with two full-length swords was an education in itself. The commander was shirtless, wearing only his tight black trousers and the boiled-rubber-tree-sap-soled boots full Blackguards were issued: sticky, and nearly silent. Watching him explode from a full standstill was like watching a lion pounce – a ripple of muscles, a flash of flesh, and he was off, near full speed in barely four steps.

He hurdled an obstacle that came up higher than Teia's chest, ran straight at a wall that had only a circular hole a pace across on it and leapt – diving, swords stabbing through, shoulders barely clearing the narrow opening, body not even nicking the edges. He rolled to his feet smoothly, blades flourishing.

He ran at another wall, barely losing speed, and ran up it. His momentum seemed to flow into the wall, all of it completely at his legs, his hands and swords coming into his chest, waist cocking. He leapt off the wall, twisting, the blades flashing out to hit a dummy on either side, each of them held in a box ten feet off the ground, everything below their necks protected.

The momentum of swinging both swords left-to-right meant Ironfist landed sideways. He tumbled, taking the fall, and popped back up to his feet. He looked irritated. Teia saw the problem. Without maintaining his speed, Ironfist had no way of leaping the chasm that was the next obstacle, at least not without stopping and backing up and losing precious time.

He saw Teia, of course, but he saw that she had no pressing business, so he said nothing. He went back to his starting spot and repeated it again.

This time, as he ran up the wall, he slapped the swords against the wall, each wrapped in blue luxin, released them, twisted his body, grabbed them with the opposite hands, and leapt straight from the wall, slashing in from both sides, cutting through the dummies, and landing flat. He charged the chasm, not losing any speed, and jumped it, skipping off a platform that was too small to stop on and then regaining speed, leaping for a rope that hung over the next chasm.

He lost a sword on that maneuver, but he spun down to the ground and laughed.

'The Prism's own obstacle course. Of course, he cheats outrageously with luxin at every turn. He challenged me to beat his time before he left. I think I may just.'

As he approached, Teia was suddenly aware again of the sheer size and physicality of the commander. Her glance at his naked, scarred chest seemed to make him aware of his own half-dressed state. Oddly, he seemed embarrassed, the old habits of Parian modesty not totally overcome even after many years in the Blackguard. He grabbed his tunic and pulled it on.

'Here to train?' he asked Teia. 'I can get you started on drills.'

Teia stared at him, somehow unable to speak. She thought of telling him everything. But Murder Sharp could be standing in this very room.

'Turned in your papers, did you?' he asked. He'd seen her coin sticks.

'Oh. Yes.'

'Are you going to leave?'

'Can I really?' Teia asked. It still seemed impossible.

'If you turn in the money to the Blackguard, you're free. You'll be able to make more money as a mercenary if you stay in and leave right before final vows, but some leave at your place. If you've grown up as a slave, sometimes the thought of real freedom is too sweet to put off for even one more day. Others just talk about it. I've known Blackguards who talked for fifteen years about buying their commission back – fifteen years *after* final vows, you understand – and traveling the world. Treg was in his last year before retirement and was still talking about buying that commission back.' Ironfist grinned, but then the grin faded. 'He didn't make it back from Garriston.'

'I want to be a Blackguard more than anything in my life, but . . .' Teia's nerve failed her.

Commander Ironfist said nothing, just folded his beefy arms and waited. It was a patient silence, though, not demanding. Here was a man so busy he rarely slept more than five hours a night, but when he dealt with his Blackguards – even the nunks – he had a way of being present, unhurried. Teia had never really noticed how generous he was with his precious time, but now that she was experiencing it, she realized how often she'd seen it before, and she added it to the long list of things she admired about the commander. But . . .

I'm not a slave. Not anymore. And I won't be made a victim. I won't sit and let it happen, even if by moving I die. 'I'm being blackmailed,' Teia said.

'What'd they get you for?'

She was so startled by his total lack of surprise that she simply said, 'Theft.'

'How?'

'I've been trained as a pickpocket for years. It wasn't really my choice, you understand? My master? With my paryl vision, I can see where coins and scroll cases and the like are hidden. Half the time, I've been stealing from trainers who worked for Aglaia Crassos – who I just learned was my real mistress all along. But I just figured out today that they were smarter than I'd given them credit for.'

'Uh-hmm.' Commander Ironfist's face was as placid as a lake at dawn. He gave no indication of what he was thinking. She was afraid some monster might burst from placidity though, so she sped up.

'They bet I'd get into the Blackguard, and they knew that once I was free, they wouldn't have any hold on me, so everything I've been stealing has been stuff that is recognizable. They've probably got it all stowed somewhere in a place that they can tie to me.'

'So that's how you knew how to disguise yourself at Ruic Head,' Ironfist said. 'How good are you?'

'At lifting things?' Teia asked. She hadn't thought this would be his first question. 'Better than I am at fighting.' Not that she liked the fact.

'What would you say if I told you I work for Aglaia Crassos, too?' he asked.

Her heart dropped. She looked at the door for an escape. The commander calmly stepped between her and it.

'No,' she whispered. Begged. 'No, please.'

There was no way she could make it. No way she could fight off Commander Ironfist if he wanted to stop her anyway. It was madness to even think to oppose him.

But what was her other option? To just give up?

Her only hope was paryl, and even that was a thin hope. During the battle at Ruic Head, she'd done something with paryl that made everyone within sight think they were being burned to a crisp, but it had actually done nothing. If she could remember exactly how she'd done that, maybe it would be enough.

'Relax,' Ironfist said. 'I don't. I'm just surprised that it didn't occur to you. Usually those being blackmailed become paranoid.'

A breath whooshed out of her. 'Sir, I'm so deep in my own problems that I can't even imagine how bad my life would be if she'd gotten to you.'

'Can you describe the items to me?'

'Yes, sir.'

'In writing?'

'Yes, sir.'

'Do so. I'll take care of it. If.'

'Sir?'

'If this is all of it. You understand?'

All of it? Confessing to stealing trinkets was one thing, but what about Teia's own brush with murder? Would they believe her? What was more plausible: that Teia had botched a theft and panicked and stabbed a man, or that she had crossed some cabal of invisible assassins?

Even if they believed her, somehow Master Sharp would find out. She would wake to find him in her room again. And he would know. The thought turned her knees to jelly.

'Is this all of it?' Commander Ironfist asked.

'Yes, sir,' Teia said.

'Then let's go talk to the White.'

Talk to the White?! Oh, no. No no no. Even the best liars could have a bad day. Teia couldn't afford for that to be today.

Chapter 22

Time was measured out with such perfect regularity that time lost meaning. Gavin's every day had a similar rhythm. *Pull. Twist. Push. Twist. Pull.* Up, down, life circumscribed in ovals of work and rest and transition from one to the other. Scrape off the inefficient edges of every moment. Breathe in, breathe out, try to make the motion of the one to the other as painless as possible. Wake, sleep, and spend no time in between. Up before dawn, eating gruel, more gruel at lunch, sometimes with a slice of fruit to fend off scurvy, beans most nights, meat when they'd been particularly good. The ship stopped at a port only once a week, though they stopped at other times, too, for freshwater and for the sailors to have a chance to hunt. But most days were a blur, the round of pumping blood, or of the whip striking, falling, being raised, hesitating in the air for one instant, striking again.

Up before dawn, eating gruel. A chance at the waste bucket. Then rowing. Gruel, then a chance at the wash bucket.

The tempo ate leagues, a perfect balance between speed and exertion. If some emergency came upon them – or if they were to be an emergency that came upon someone else – the slaves needed to have the push to escape doom or to bring it. But that didn't mean they rowed slowly, not with this crew, not with this captain, not with this accursed overseer Leonus.

It was measured, and it was the same when they hit bad weather, the light Angari ship bobbing like a cork on top of the waves, vomit and water washing past the slaves' hardened feet. As the weather grew so bad that other ships stayed in port, wintering, they never slowed. These men had shot the Everdark Gates. A storm was a frivolity to them; they had only contempt for it.

Gavin could hear the drums in his sleep. His breath as he

lay under his bench came in the same intervals it did when rowing. His hands healed, formed new calluses, ripped open, bled again, fresh agony every morning.

Leonus was a fool, but the slaves knew their business, and not even his mismanagement could impede them much.

Up before dawn, eating gruel, the other slaves rubbing liniment into aching knees and backs and hands, staving off the day when they were no more use on an oar. Leonus strangled one man whose oarmates finally called him out after a spat. He hadn't been pulling his weight in weeks, maybe months. One word, and he was murdered in front of their eyes. A warning to the rest of them, Gavin supposed. Gavin gathered that the usual way was to whip the offender to make sure he wasn't faking, and drop him off at the next stop, and sell him for a pittance to some other crew desperate enough to take on an old, broken slave. Other slaves became beggars, some few lucky ones taken in to the luxiats' houses of mercy.

Gavin didn't know how long it had been since he'd been taken. He didn't know where they were. They'd seized five ships, and doubled back, hunting or letting Mongalt Shales catch up, any number of times. They could be off the coast of Paria or Ilyta or Atash for all Gavin knew. His beard had grown out. His hair, like all the other slaves', had been shaved short with a razor so it wouldn't catch on things. A pirate haircut was no thing of beauty, but these Angari were at least miraculously free of lice. Clean people. Considered themselves advanced.

One night, after a particularly good week when they'd seized two rich galleys, Gunner was rewarding the slaves. Double measures of strongwine and letting slaves come up on deck at night, albeit chained, and in small groups.

Gavin was chained to Orholam. They sat on deck, the strongwine keeping them warm. They had it so rarely that on an empty stomach, it had quite a kick.

Idly, Gavin stared at the stars, trying to figure where they were from the constellations. Off the Ruthgari coast, perhaps?

'Do you know why they call me Orholam?' the old man asked.

'Because you're kind and kind of useless,' Gavin said, grinning.

But Orholam wasn't grinning.

'Please, no blasphemy, young Guile. Not with me. Not tonight.' He paused. 'I was a prophet of Elelyo-n in a little village on the Parian coast between the Everdark Gates. We were isolated there, of course. No ships in or out, all our trade having to wend through the mountain passes, even our names for Orholam odd to other Parians' ears.

'In my youth, my village was raided by an Angari ship that had somehow made it through the east gate. The village was burned, my mother killed in front of my eyes, my father killed in disgrace that doesn't bear repeating, my young brothers and sisters either taken for slaves or killed, I knew not which. I escaped. I lived through the winter night inside the corpse of one of our oxen they had slaughtered for fun. They didn't even carry the meat back with them. Young men, laughing. I had been serving as a prophet under Demistocles. You're not familiar? Then I will be brief. Orholam began to speak to me even as a child. Under Demistocles's tutelage, I learned to discern when it was the Most High's voice, and when it was my own desires. I grew arrogant. I called down miracles, and they happened. You think your chromaturgy is a wonder? It is mere science. Men moving bricks. But my power? Orholam's power, unleashed from the heavens themselves? Like lightning compared to candle. But – and this I will grant you – the latitude you drafters are given is much wider. You do so much yourselves. But to us all, drafter and prophet alike, Orholam giveth and Orholam taketh away. We call him the Lord of Light, but we forget that he is lord.'

A sermon. From a man they called Orholam. Just what Gavin needed. At least it was different, and a good wine kick in the head can make even religion bearable.

'One day, a year to the day after I'd lost all those I loved, the Most High told me to heal an Angari widow. Leprous. In the hardness of my heart and the stiffness of my neck, I turned away instead.

'The next morning, Elelyo-n told me to go prophesy to the Angari. I fled instead. Not because I was afraid I would die

147

shooting the Everdark Gates, but because I knew I wouldn't. I knew he is merciful. I was afraid that if I told them to repent, they would, and I wanted nothing of mercy for them. I wanted them to burn. Men, women, children, eunuchs and servants and slaves, foreigners visiting their shores, rabble and king, soldier and merchant. I wished fire for them all.' His aspect took on a fierceness Gavin had seen before, though not on this man's kind face. It was a visage etched by the acid thirst for vengeance.

Then it was followed by sorrow deeper than words. 'I wished the very name of the Angari to burn and be known no more. I ran as far as I could get the other way, and ended up seized by river pirates at the head of the Great River. I was sold and sold again until I was marched overland and eventually sold to the Angari. As if it could be anyone else. I have served for fifteen years, and for ten of it, I lived in hatred. I have been ever a slow learner, but Orholam is patient.

'Elelyo-n hasn't spoken to me in many years, but the day we fished you out of the waters, he did. And again last night telling me that now you are ready. Not to hear. Not yet. But to speak.'

'To speak?' Gavin asked. 'What an odd prophet you are, to go around *listening*.' He looked at the canopy of stars overhead. Beauty in black and white.

They had to be somewhere outside Melos, if Gavin remembered the star charts correctly, and of course, he did. To remember was his curse.

'I have nothing to say.'

Very quietly, very gently, Orholam said, 'He said you would speak blasphemy. That you would need to lance the boil, and let the poison seep out before all else.'

'If he already knows what I'm going to say, why don't we just consider it said?' Gavin said. He thought to say it wryly, but it came out worse.

'It's not that he needs to hear it. It's that you need to say it.'

Gavin turned away. 'I have no idea what you're talking about.'

'Liar.'

Gavin snarled, 'How dare you? Don't you know—'

Orholam looked at the sailors, who'd glanced over at Gavin's raised voice, but the men looked in no mood to break off from their own conversations unless the pair got into an actual fight. He said, 'Don't I know who you are? Heh. You know, that was part of what I loved about being a prophet. A prophet is a slave of the Most High. A slave, but having such an exalted master gives us the authority to speak in one voice to satrap, soldier, servant, or slave. I thought that made me as important as a satrap. Really, it's just that we are equally small before him, ants and flies arguing for precedence under the gaze of a giant.'

'Now that's more the kind of talk I'd expect from a prophet.'

A wounded silence, but then Orholam said, 'It is odd to me, o man in ruins, that you who have been the answer to so many prayers should have none of your own, not even now, trapped and awaiting death. I have had fifteen years to grow past my rage at *being*. You haven't that luxury.'

'Rage at being? Folly. Folly as much as calling fifteen years as a slave a luxury. I was the Prism. How could a Prism, of all men, complain?'

'Better an honest ingrate than a liar who is still an ingrate, after all.'

'Call me a liar one more time, and you'll be swallowing teeth.'

'Let me tell you something, o slave Prism. When Orholam asks your submission, you can submit now and find the way easy; or later, and find the way hard; or never, and find yourself crushed.'

'Because he is punitive and cruel.'

'Because he is King. And the longer you walk in the wrong direction, the farther you have to run to get back to where you should have been.'

'He is no king. He doesn't exist. He's a comforting tale, a candle held against the darkness of our fears. There is only nothingness. It is as little use to curse him as it is to pray to him. We are a man who, having tripped, blames the stone for grabbing his foot.'

'Why then the fear to talk to him again?'

'First you call me a liar, and now a coward?'

'You need more honest men in your life. Or better ears. Orholam knows that in spite of all the mirrors he gave you, you still couldn't see yourself, so he took your sight. Perhaps it will sharpen your other senses?'

'Go to hell,' Gavin said. But a part of that breathless, chest-seizing fear rose up in him again. Exposure. How did the old man know he couldn't see?

Oh, but of course. If Gavin could draft, he wouldn't be here. That the man knew about Gavin's loss of the colors, his blindness, was no supernatural insight, it was mere deduction.

Orholam laughed. 'No, better than hell waits for me. For I have finally bowed the knee. These, our excellent hosts, have power over my body only. Freedom, for me, is only a matter of time. These shackles cannot hold me. I could ask Orholam to take them off, and they would drop from my wrists.'

'Prove it,' Gavin sneered.

A fleeting irritation passed over the prophet's face. 'It's only fair, I suppose, that you should tempt me to do what got me here in the first place. No. I shall not abuse the power entrusted me. I've been put here for me, but I've also been put here for you, Prism.'

'Uh-huh,' Gavin said.

'Orholam doesn't make mistakes, o man of guile. You became Prism by his will. That wasn't an accident. There are things only you can do.'

'Not anymore,' Gavin said. A cloud on the horizon lit from within as lightning sparked in it.

Better that he hadn't been born. Better that he hadn't been born a Prism. If only he hadn't started light splitting, if only he hadn't been a full-spectrum polychrome, if only he hadn't told Gavin about his polychromacy, hoping to mend the rift that seemed to have sprung from nowhere when Gavin had been taken away and named the Prism-elect, everything would be well. His older brother had taken Dazen's gift as a betrayal, as Dazen taking away the one thing that made him special.

So the real Gavin had retaliated by betraying his younger brother's elopement with Karris.

Sitting on the rocking deck of the galley, the false Gavin

drained his strongwine to the lees. He hadn't realized that until this moment. He'd thought for years that Karris had lost her nerve. He'd blamed her maid. He'd blamed his own poor planning, thinking he must have let something slip.

In truth, his older brother had found out, and in vengeance, had shared the secret. The White Oaks had then intimidated Karris's maid into speaking. That explained the guilt on the woman's face that night – it had been real guilt he'd seen there, but it wasn't the guilt of betrayal; it was the guilt of being too weak to stand up to pressure. A pressure too great for anyone in her position to withstand.

That look, that partial, unjust guilt, had been why Dazen left her on the wrong side of a locked door to burn, to die, unknowingly condemning all the rest of them as well. A moment of guilt that wasn't even hers had led to the deaths of all those people. It had been Dazen's sin in falling in love with Karris, his petty betrayal: eloping with the woman his brother wanted but didn't love. That had led to Gavin's huge betrayal. Gavin's sin, and Dazen's wild vengefulness, the acid that had etched his soul. Each had visited vengeance upon the other in a circling spire until the satrapies burned.

'Your father chose Gavin to be Prism, but Orholam chose you. Does that tell you nothing?' Orholam asked.

For a moment, the use of the correct name took Gavin's breath, then he remembered that in his shock at being captured, in a moment of blind foolishness, he'd told Gunner that he was Dazen. No prophecy. Orholam was the next rower on the bench. He'd simply overheard.

But if he had, who else had, too?

Gavin chuckled. Kind of low on the list of things I should be worrying about, isn't it? Dammit. It took me fifteen years to get up the nerve to tell you who I am really am, Karris, and I told a ship full of pirates within minutes.

'My father chose him because he was older,' he said.

'Your father, the descendant of Iron Ataea Guile? Swayed by a tradition of primogeniture that your family has rarely observed? Your father, who was himself the younger brother?'

'He chose him because he saw will in him.'

'And clearly his second son didn't have that,' Orholam

mocked, but gently. 'What your father saw in you was what made him reject you, and that very thing is why Orholam chose you.'

'And what thing is that?'

Orholam smiled. 'You'll figure it out, eventually.'

'You got some balls, you know that? You sit up here and drink with me, and you tell me what a terrible person I am, and then you insult my brother and my father, and you smile. You fuck.'

Orholam shrugged sadly. 'This is why there are few prophets. We end up dead a lot. The truth is offensive to men who love darkness.' He looked at the sailors, still talking drunkenly and loudly on deck, some of them already passed out. 'I think they've forgotten about us.' He extended a hand and took the tin cup from Gavin. He waited a moment, looking at the pirates, then nonchalantly got to his knees and reached deep into the barrel to draw forth additional measures of strongwine. He handed them to Gavin, and flopped back to sitting.

That was some recompense, at least. More wine. 'Here's to the profit in listening to a prophet,' Gavin said. He clinked cups with the madman and drank.

'Should I make that storm come upon us with lightning and fire?' Orholam asked.

'I thought you weren't supposed to abuse your power,' Gavin said.

'Ah. True. I forgot.' He drank. 'Looks like it's coming this way anyway.'

At the prow, Gunner was drunkenly making bets on what shots he could or couldn't make. No one was willing to bet against him, though, so he was berating his men as cowards. It seemed good-natured, but he had just shot a tin cup out of the mouth of a drinking pirate, firing the musket with one hand while with his other he was waving his manhood proudly back and forth, urinating in great figures of eight into the sea.

'Is everyone on the sea mad?' Gavin asked.

'A little madness keeps you from going crazy,' Orholam said. 'That one, curses Ceres? Got married young. Girl named Ceres. They thought it was a funny coincidence when they learned Ceres was an old pagan goddess of the sea. His two great loves were one, they joked. She committed suicide when he was on one of his trips. Drowned herself. He blames himself. Wasn't his fault, really, crazy often comes out around age twenty. A cruel enemy told him that Ceres heard that Gunner was cheating on her.'

Gavin swore quietly. 'How do you know this?'

'Orholam told me.'

Gavin looked at him.

'Just yankin' ya. You been on ships long as I have, all the good gossip comes around. Got that bit from a man who knew him before he was even named Gunner. Can't remember what his birth name was, though. Didn't seem that interesting at the time. Say, you're a dreamer of dreams, aren't you?'

'I dream now and again,' Gavin said dismissively. 'Everyone does.' But his stomach knotted up. He preferred this prophet silent and sweetly smiling.

'Powerful dreams. Dreams that scare the hell out of you? You wake in a panic, your chest so tight you can't breathe, soaked in sweat?'

Absolutely. Gavin shrugged a maybe.

'You're going to have a dream, tonight, tomorrow, I'm not sure, but soon. Remember it. Pay attention.'

'You can't make me dream dreams,' Gavin said.

'*I* can't. It's a game Orholam and I played, back when. I say he'll do something that I think is in line with his will, and then he kind of has to do it, or he'll look bad, not me.'

'Great game.'

'That's only the half of it. Every time I do that, he throws me something to do that I think is impossible and that I'm too frightened or too awkward to do. It used to be simple things, but they were hard for me at the time. He'd say, "Go tell that woman her husband loves her." And I'd feel like a fool, a crazy man to approach a stranger and say such a thing, but I'd muster up the juice to do it – and this slip of a girl looks at me like I hit her with a hammer between the eyes, and she bursts into tears. I never hear the rest of the story, but a year later, I see her with him, and they're both beaming and she's got a babe in arms. She looks at me, and she winks. Later, it got harder. "Go tell the governor that if he puts his hands

on his brother's wife one more time, he'll be dead in a month.'
That one didn't make me terribly popular. That governor took
it, though. Didn't even say a word to me. The brother's wife,
on the other hand? She tried to kill me.'

The lightning approached, and the drunk pirates watched
it come.

'Lift anchor!' Gunner shouted drunkenly. 'Wake the slaves.
We ride the storm!'

A pirate saw Gavin and Orholam where they were chained
to the mast and came to hustle them down to their bench. The
last thing Gavin saw before he was pushed belowdecks was
Gunner standing on the railing, balancing with the rigging in
one hand and waving a gunsword with the other. Lightning
cracked, highlighting his figure.

'Ceres!' Gunner shouted, his cheeks shining with tears – or
perhaps only rain. 'Ceres, you bitch! Kill me if ya can! I defy
you! I—' And then the roar of thunder blotted out all else.

Chapter 23

'Sir? You don't seem surprised,' Teia said to Ironfist. 'Did – did
you know?'

'I look like a babe in the woods to you, nunk?'

'Sir?'

'The Blackguard is the best of the best. The houses try to
get their hooks into most of our students, one way or another.
They've been successful often enough that we've had to grow
canny ourselves.'

'So you knew?'

'Come with me,' he said.

He put his ghotra on carefully and they walked to the lift.
'When I look at you, ask me if I want you to stay at the
checkpoint,' he said. He set the weights and they took the lift
to the top, where the Blackguards greeted him at the checkpoint.

'The White in?' he asked.

'Yes, sir,' Samite answered.

Ironfist paused, looked at Teia.

'You want me to stay here, sir?' Teia asked. Ironfist was being this careful? With Samite? He was worried about his own Blackguards reporting . . . what? That Teia was accompanying him on a meeting with the White? Such a meeting would be innocuous enough, wouldn't it? But that he was being careful meant that he was protecting even this from betrayal – by Blackguards he'd worked with for his whole adult life. Part of Teia wilted. She wanted the Blackguards at least to be pure. Something had to be pure and good, even if she wasn't. It also made the guileless Blackguard commander seem more crafty than she'd ever considered.

'It'll be fast,' Ironfist said, as if weighing it and dismissing the thought without too much thinking. 'Come.'

They walked together to the White's room. The Blackguards there announced him and Teia both – Teia was surprised that they actually knew her name. One should never underestimate the Blackguard, she supposed.

The White dismissed her old room slave and her secretary as they came in. The old woman had been drafting since Teia saw her last. It made her look healthier, but Teia knew it was only a veneer of health. If the White had decided it was permissible to draft, it meant she was planning to join the Freeing come Sun Day.

The White studied Teia as Teia studied the White. Teia wondered what the old woman saw.

'Aglaia,' Commander Ironfist said without preamble, 'trained her in theft. Has probably been keeping the items for blackmail. Explains Teia's facility with disguises. She came to me. Unprompted.'

The White looked unperturbed by the revelation, or by how Ironfist had launched into it without warning. 'When did you find out that there was no Lady Verangheti?' she asked Teia.

'Just before we left – wait, you know about that, too?' Teia said. Lady Aglaia Crassos had said that concealing her own ownership of slaves under the pseudonym Lady Lucretia Verangheti had allowed her to place spies in all sorts of places.

'If one is to go to the trouble of having spies, it behooves a lady to have the best,' the White said. She gave a small smile. 'How did you figure out that she was going to blackmail you? Surely after Andross Guile forced her to sell you to him, you must have thought that you were free – free of her at least.'

'I did,' Teia said. The truth was more complicated. She'd thought she would be free until today.

Her first thought had been that Aglaia had sent Master Sharp to pull her back into her web. But why frame her for murder?

It wasn't how Lady Crassos usually played things. As Lady Verangheti, she had been disciplined, making Teia steal harder and harder things, making her enmesh herself more and more in the web so that she would be fully caught before she thought to struggle. Lady Verangheti would have taken the steps one at a time: give Teia harder jobs until she balked, then reveal that Teia had been damning herself all along, then make her continue doing worse things until Teia would do anything at all. Such a spy – especially if she made it onto the Blackguard itself – would be an excellent weapon. And Lady Crassos seemed clever enough not to do anything that might break Teia out of her web early.

Like the shock of witnessing a murder.

Seeing a murder, Teia might logically go straight to Commander Ironfist and tell him everything. Lady Crassos wouldn't risk that.

So why would she frame Teia for murder?

No reason. Literally. Lady Crassos hadn't done it.

Before the Battle of Ru, her handler had been uninterested in the assassination Teia had seen in the marketplace. There was no reason for her to pretend that if assassination was what she wanted Teia to do. It would have been a great motivator: 'If you disobey, Adrasteia, I can have you killed like that. No one can stop me.'

In fact, it was *still* a good motivator. A good motivator to not tell the White, or Commander Ironfist, or Kip, or anyone else, about Murder Sharp.

Teia realized her silence was getting suspiciously long. 'I couldn't really believe I was free, and I had this terrible feeling, and the more I thought about it, the more plausible it seemed that she would keep something of what I'd done to use against me. She's . . . frightening.' Which was understating. 'But how'd you know about this? Did you both know?'

Teia looked over at Ironfist. He stared back at her, silent. He said, 'Adrasteia, in this game, one must either be as wise as serpents, or trust implicitly someone who is. I've always opted for the latter.' He inclined his head to the White. Odd how only moments ago he'd seemed jaded, and now he seemed the old Ironfist, too straightforward to be political. Teia wondered if it had something to do with his highly public loss of faith – and highly public regaining of it.

'Come here, child,' the White said. When Teia approached, the old woman examined her closely, studying her eyes with a sharp gaze. 'Commander, is there a slight violet tinge to her eyes, or am I fooling myself?'

The commander stared at Teia's eyes. 'Could be. I wouldn't see it if I weren't looking for it, though.'

'Spectral bleed, then. Affects even the paryl drafters, apparently.' The White heaved a sigh. 'Oh, child, if only you could be two separate girls. I should love to study both of you. But studying precludes using, and there is but one of you. Orholam knows best, one supposes. Still.' She cast her eyes skyward, though there was only ceiling there, as if gently castigating the creator of the universe. 'Tell me, daughter, about your family.'

'That's none of your—' Teia bit off her words, realizing who she was talking to. She swallowed. It was a perfectly neutral question, even friendly, but Teia had hoarded up the knowledge and the shame of her family for so long that any inquiry felt hostile.

'High Lady, perhaps this isn't the time,' Commander Ironfist said. 'We have only minutes—'

The White didn't take her eyes off Teia, but her tone sharpened. 'I'm known to have a keen interest in young people. Age is allowed her eccentricities. When you leave, Commander, you'll shrug and say, "You know how she is with young people." Then smile and go about your business, and the spies will, too. Family, child.'

'Father's a trader. Was. Day laborer now. Two sisters, younger. My mother isn't worth speaking of.'

'Your shame says different.'

Teia clenched her jaw. She stared at the window. This was the White asking. That Teia was even thinking of *not* answering was practically irreligious; it was certainly insubordinate.

She answered, but her voice came out flat. 'My mother lost her sense for a while during one of my father's journeys. Brought home any man who would come bed her. Finally found one who liked her enough to stay for a while. She held parties we couldn't afford, hired dancers and musicians like the rich do. We weren't rich. She ruined us. And when my father came back, I think she thought he'd kill her. I think she hoped he would. She'd sold all of us into slavery to pay back the debts she ran up.

'My father sold everything he had left – his ship, mainly – and bought back my sisters. I'd shown my talent by then, and I was too valuable. He didn't have the money to redeem me and he couldn't borrow that much.'

'And what did he do to your mother?' the White asked.

'Nothing.' There was no hiding the bitterness. Father, why didn't you fight for me? Why did you choose the one who betrayed you?

'And how do you feel about that?'

'I despise him for his weakness.'

'Rather than admire him for his goodness. Interesting.'

'Is it goodness to do nothing when wronged?' Teia asked sharply.

'You have no idea what he did or didn't do. Parents often shield their children from the truth of their fights, and you were living elsewhere by then, a slave already. You judge too soon, and too sharply. Something you would do well to grow out of. Only a fool judges with the heart alone.'

Teia took the rebuke, unjust as it was. Her father had passively accepted that crazy whore, said something about love and forgiveness. 'Are we finished?' she asked.

'Do you know,' the White said, 'that I had two daughters? I remember their teenage years. It was hell.'

Teia smirked despite herself. I'm sure you deserved a bit of that. 'Where do they live now? They aren't on Big Jasper, are they?'

'They're dead. One during the Blood Wars, and one immediately afterward, killed by men who refused to accept that the Blood Wars were ended. They thought their side hadn't meted out sufficient vengeance yet. My daughters' children were killed or whisked away into illegal slavery somewhere. Perhaps out there still, suffering. Their grandmother is the White, one of the most powerful people in all the satrapies, and they are slaves, all my wealth and my thousand spies worth nothing, for who sees a slave?' Her eyes seemed lit with fire. 'Slavery is an evil without which our world cannot function, but it is an evil nonetheless.' She grimaced. 'Which is why I will not have those bound to me bound by that, at least insofar as I am able. Ironfist.'

The man picked up a note from the White's desk and handed it to Teia. It had copies of receipts that she couldn't even read, at least not in a glance, and then a letter in an old familiar hand that she knew immediately. Her father's:

'My debts have all been paid in your name, Adrasteia. I've already got investors lined up to buy one of the new caravels come spring. Putting together a crew now. I failed you, but you never failed me. As soon as I can, I'll come to Big Jasper or wherever you're posted. Sisters are well. Kallea married a butcher and is expecting her first in spring. Husband's good for naught, but at least she's close. Marae now hoping to marry an officer. Good man. Any news?' He must have been limited on the amount of paper he had to use, because the last sentences were cramped, even briefer than usual.

Her sister was expecting her first child? Kallea was fifteen years old. Many poor girls married that young, of course. But Teia wasn't putting it together. It was facts, notes about another life, not hers. This kind of thing didn't happen to Teia.

'Why?' Teia asked. There had to be some trap, some trick, some way it would be whisked away. It was too good. 'Why?'

'Because sometimes I can do good,' the White said. 'No strings, Teia. The tragedies that befell me have left me with some gifts. Money, for one. What use has a dying old woman for money? I can bless you as freely as Orholam has blessed me. Light, life, and freedom, my child.'

It rolled over Teia like a rushing quake-wave. She had to fight it, push back. 'How did you . . . ? Now?'

'We began work on it as soon as you tested into the Blackguard. We want all our people to choose us freely. It cannot always be so, but we always make the attempt. This was delivered while you were away at Ru. I've been meaning to send for you since. It's been a busy time.'

'You were going to . . . all along?'

'In the scheme of things, Teia, it was a small thing for us, and we knew how big it might be for you.'

It took Teia's breath. She would cry later, but in this moment, she could barely breathe, barely believe this dying woman's goodness, her father's steadfastness, her sisters' lives veering so far to one side that Teia couldn't even see them anymore from where she stood. Good done for people she would like as not never see again. In this moment of compassion, somehow, though, she felt more alone than she had in all her years training and thieving in shame, hiding who she was in more than just the disguises they taught her.

'She wasn't the only one blackmailing me,' Teia blurted out. 'There's another. Worse.'

And she told them about Master Sharp. And about the spy, and the murder, and the flight, and Kip seeing her, and the theft of her papers, and their return. And when she was done speaking, then, finally, she felt free. She could take a full breath.

Oddly, the White looked, if anything, younger and more alive than ever. Her eyes lit with a readiness to fight. 'Teia,' she said, 'how brave are you?'

Ten minutes later, Commander Ironfist ushered Teia out the door, saying he would follow her in a moment.

When the door closed, he turned a skeptical eye to the White. 'You planned that.'

'I hoped for it.'

'You knew about the other. This Murder Sharp.'

She didn't admit it. 'Kindness can break chains that cunning cannot.'

'Is that what you are? Kindness and cunning coiled?' he asked.

'Was not the caduceus once the White's symbol?' she asked. Then her whimsy disappeared. 'The Order of the Broken Eye, Harrdun. There have been pretenders before, but how many pretenders have had the shimmercloaks? We have a chance here.'

'To smash them?'

'Or bring them back into the fold. But yes, probably. Heresy is a horse that takes the bridle in its teeth and won't submit to any hand unless it is beaten.'

'A strange idiom, from you who'd beat a man, but not a horse.'

'A horse can't deserve it.'

'Well, I hope that narrow-shouldered filly can hold the weight you've saddled her with. She'll be a warhorse, if.'

'If I don't kill her first,' the White said grimly. 'I know. One loses men and horses both to training. Is that reason not to train?'

'This isn't training.'

She moved as if to quarrel further, then sat back in her wheeled chair. She took a chain from around her neck, produced a key she'd kept hidden beneath her neckline.

'The master key to all the restricted libraries. This is what you came for, isn't it? You were scheduled to see me before the girl came back from Big Jasper. What is it you're hunting?'

'A fantasy. A suspicion. Foolishness.'

'But I'll know first, if you find something?'

He took the key from her and tucked it away. It was acquiescence.

'Be ware, Harrdun. My defenses are stretched thin.'

He walked to the door.

'Harrdun,' she said.

He stopped.

'The ghotra. You're wearing it again.'

He grunted.

'It suits you.'

161

Chapter 24

Gavin dreamed after the storm, but knew this was no dream. It was memory. For a brief moment, he fought. No, not this. Orholam, have mercy on me, not—

It was his first Sun Day as Prism. He was in his own apartments atop what was now his tower. It was just after noon, and the dawn and noon rituals were finished. Now he had only to murder four hundred drafters.

There was a knock at his door, and his mother came in. Gavin had barely had time to get home, grab a quick meal, and bathe. His room slave Shala – a woman his mother's age, whom his mother had appointed in place of the original Gavin's room slave, apparently trying to keep her second son celibate for the rest of his days – had shaved his chest, and two of the High Luxiats, Daeron Utarkses and Camileas Malargos, had anointed his whole body with oil and myrrh. Having the sister of two men he'd betrayed lay hands on his naked body had not been an experience he was eager to repeat, for they'd anointed his entire body, and when choosing, who would you prefer to have oil your rod and stones: an old man, or an old woman who had reason to hate you, though she might not know it?

A Prism was not his own; a Prism belonged to the satrapies entire, and to Orholam, and to his family, and to peace, and whatever scraps he could collect after all had taken their bites, he might enjoy for himself.

His copper-colored hair was bound back and the High Luxiats placed a crown on his forehead with a single diamond the size of a robin's egg. He wore a ceremonial shirt of red silk and cloth-of-gold open down the front, with sleeves so short as to be vestigial. His trousers were red silk so tight he thought they'd tear if he moved too quickly. But he was Orholam's hand on earth; it behooved him to look potent, virile, even sexual. Orholam was, after all, a creative force, a generative being. How much the creative and the reproductive overlapped swung back and forth between which High Luxiats held sway at any particular time. Creation was meant to reflect creator, they argued. As above, so below.

That the worship guided by the Prism often turned into worship *of* the Prism seemed to bother no one. Or no one in power. To Gavin's understanding of theology, that seemed a problem, but he was an impostor, and to protest too loudly might expose him. He did what he was told.

Felia Guile dismissed Shala and a young glowering Blackguard named Ironfist. When they were gone, she said quietly, 'My son, if you can make it through this, you will be Prism for a thousand years. You've done magnificently all day, better than you did when . . . you were younger.' She meant he'd done better than the real Gavin had done.

'I've killed more than four hundred men before. It won't be a problem.' The dreaming Gavin suddenly separated from the remembered boy. Had he really thought that, or had he been trying to impress his mother? He had wanted so desperately not to fail her. She had been magnificent, and he had known some of what she must have risked to keep him alive. 'These ones won't even be fighting back,' he said with a lopsided grin.

Felia didn't smile. 'Take off your shirt, I need to anoint you.'

'I've been anointed.'

'Not with this.' She produced a small jar with a yellowish-orange paste or lotion in it. She began to rub in into his skin carefully, only touching the areas that wouldn't be covered by clothing, as if the paste were terribly precious.

'What is it?' he demanded.

She didn't answer the question, saying instead, 'Gavin, I know so far you haven't taken your duties as the Highest Luxiat seriously, but on this night . . . Your leadership of the satrapies, your balancing for all the world; these are necessities, but distant ones. This night is the one bloody pillar on which all your power rests. It matters not that only you and the sworn one are in each room. When a Prism takes his duties lightly, or enjoys them, or gets blind drunk to brace himself for this burden – word always gets out. Those Prisms never last more than their seven, and many don't last that long. Sun Day is the death of an entire community, of a whole convocation of peers. This is where our communal worship meets one intense and final personal experience of faith.'

'I wasn't intending to take it lightly, mother. Merely trying to break the tension.'

She ignored him. 'You'll have only two minutes with each. We prefer to give each five minutes with you, but the sheer number of drafters who've burned themselves out in the war precludes that.'

'We could have begun sooner.'

'The High Magisterium and the Spectrum agreed that drawing out this Freeing for days would only draw more attention to the war and all its wounds. They want us to move on. All the drafters understand. Most have already been shrived by the lesser luxiats. Some, however, fear that the luxiats keep lists of their sins to use against their families in the future—'

'That's strictly forbidden!'

Had he been that young? That naïve?

'Strictly. But it happens. We root such out as quietly as we can, but with so many luxiats coming from noble families, the temptation is often too great for them; they can't help but pass along some helpful tidbit. As I was saying, some of the shrived will keep their most serious sins to themselves to be revealed to the Prism alone. You will find yourself in possession of many dark secrets. With your memory, it will be a potent tool. That is as it should be. But don't share those secrets with anyone. Not your father. Not me. He will pressure you to do so. The Prism sharing such things with his own powerful family would undermine your power at a thousand times the rate a mere luxiat leaking such things would.'

'Of course,' Gavin said. He'd had a sudden insight: the kind that now he would not expect such a young man to have. 'Some die with sin on their souls, just to keep the Prism from knowing, don't they?' He'd been young, but not stupid.

'Doubtless. Prism Spreading Oak was worthless, but Prism Eirene Malargos before him had a way of showing mercy to such. She would, after shriving one who had been an enemy, ask if they had any silent sins for which they could together

164

beseech Orholam's forgiveness. It's outside of orthodoxy, you understand, for to speak sins is to let them be exposed to the light, and is theologically necessary, but it was also very merciful. Such things get out, you know. She was well loved.'

'Sounds like a good idea.'

'Prism Malargos lasted two terms, but perhaps only because the Spectrum never had reason to fear her. She never advanced her family, nor any of the goals she held dear. She was a figurehead, nothing more. Consider carefully whether you want that fate.'

He turned to look at the gentle woman who had so often tenderly nurtured him. This steel. Was steel her natural state, just hidden, or was it simply that she would do anything at all to protect her last living son? 'I've given the satrapies ample reason to fear me, mother. A little love might not go amiss.'

She bowed her head. 'As you wish, Father.' Ever the Orange, Felia Guile knew exactly when to tinge that religious title with a playful smirk.

This time she did not. She gave him the respect that he still, as a young man, craved from his own mother. The respect of tens of thousands of others was reinforced rather than hollowed, as only a mother could do.

He certainly didn't get any respect from his father.

She closed the jar. 'The lotion I've applied to you will be preserved until dawn by the other oils you were anointed with. It's a mix of tiny particles of imperfect yellow luxin dust and superviolet. You can use a little superviolet to make your entire body glow, even in a darkened room. It makes quite a sight. Use it sparingly, and don't get too close to the torches or it will break down. It is incredibly difficult for the yellows to make, and it's a closely guarded secret. If you like, all the gold in your clothing can be lit as well. These are the last and holiest moments of a drafter's life. Make them special, Gavin.'

No pressure. 'Trinkets and magic tricks?'

His mother took a deep breath. 'I seem to remember Dazen awarding his army's highest honor to a commander after the Battle of Blood Ridge who routed the enemy with illusions that, were those enemies thinking rationally, wouldn't have deceived them for two heartbeats.'

She waited. But he refused to give her the satisfaction of admitting she was right.

'But at certain moments, two heartbeats is an eternity,' she said, quoting him. 'I might suggest that at the moment you slide the knife home, you begin to glow, and shine brighter as the drafter dies, to give her a symbol of her eternal reward. But . . . you are the Prism, Father.'

She could be astonishingly cynical, his dear mother.

'I'm a fraud,' he whispered.

She slapped his face, fury breaking through a veneer so cool he hadn't even guessed it was there.

Then, instantly, it was gone again. She rubbed the lotion back into place on his slap-stung cheek. Her voice was quiet, but each word was considered, knife-edged: 'We are all of us frauds. We are all of us frauds, and we are all of us doing the best we can to hold up a tower of illusions and ill-placed hopes. Do not fail us, my beloved son.'

The dream skipped forward then, through the long walk to the yard, through the cheers and praises and the prayers of another of the High Luxiats, blessing him and his work. Choice foods and rare wines were laid out. In some cases, whole communities had made the pilgrimage to Little Jasper to say goodbye to a beloved drafter who had served particularly well. Which this year meant drafters who'd been particularly heroic in the war.

Though it was a feast, Blackguards wandered the crowds, keeping their eyes on all the drafters who were nearly wights. Every few years, there was an incident, and in the aftermath of bitter war, they were wise to be on edge.

And then Gavin was ushered into a room, a long, thin dagger pressed into his hand. The closing of the heavy door shut out the cheers of the crowd utterly. He would move from room to room. The rooms were arranged in a circle at the base of his tower. Each room was tiny, with only a few simple decorations, a pitcher of wine and a smaller one of poppy liquor for the fearful, and a cushioned kneeler. Some drafters liked to pass the night in prayer vigils. Others relaxed and talked with family and friends in larger rooms or outside until the luxiats summoned them. As Orholam's favored, all the female drafters were seen first.

The first one was a haggard drafter of perhaps forty-five. She knelt patiently on the kneeler at the front of the room. Her back was to the small door where the luxiats would take her body, her face to Gavin as he entered.

'Greetings, my daughter, may all the blessings of the light be on you,' Gavin said.

The woman made no reply, merely stared at Gavin.

Gavin moved forward, taking the seat in front of the kneeling woman. 'I've come to shrive you.'

No reply. Usually the luxiat who spoke to Gavin between rooms was supposed to tell him if there were any special circumstances – a mute, or a drafter who might be violent, whatever. The luxiats had said nothing other than the woman's name.

'Do you have a confession, Vell Parsham?' Gavin asked uncomfortably.

'This,' the woman said. 'This is wrong. This is not what Orholam wills. This is a travesty. This screams to me of men and women holding on to power by their fingertips, by making someone else pay.'

'It's normal to be afraid,' Gavin said.

'I'm not afraid for my life. I fear for your soul, High Lord Prism. Orholam forgive you, for what you do this night is murder.' She pulled the low collar of her blouse aside to give Gavin a straight shot at her heart. 'End me now, Lord Prism, but someday, may you end it all or be ended. Know that Orholam is just, and tremble.'

Gavin stood and wet his lips. So dry. He blinked, approaching in a daze. 'Bless you, my daughter.'

He looked the woman in the eye as he stabbed her in the heart. Held those un-angry eyes until the light went out of them. Then he pulled the bell string incorporated into the kneeler. Two luxiats entered and caught the kneeling body before it could fall. The side door opened.

'Perfect time, High Lord Prism. There will be water and figs after the next room. Name's Delilah Tae, a sub-red.'

And then he was in the next room.

The woman at the kneeler couldn't have been more than twenty-five years old. She'd been weeping.

'My daughter, may the blessings of the light be upon you.' She dissolved.

Gavin took his seat. 'I've come to shrive you, daughter, that you may walk clean and pure and unashamed in the light.'

'I have a daughter, High Lord Prism. She's three. Please tell me I'm not doing wrong by leaving her. I can't control the sub-red much longer, though. I know it. I—I shouldn't have used so much during the war. I should have been smarter.'

'What's your daughter's name?'

'Essel.'

'Essel will be taken care of, Delilah Tae. I'll see to it personally.'

'We don't have any family, not since the war. I grew up next to one of the homes for orphans. Some of the luxiats have good intentions, but . . . tell me she'll not go there, High Lord, please. I don't deserve to ask anything of you, but—'

'I'll take care of her. I promise.'

The bell rang to let Gavin know he'd spent too long.

She gulped nervously. 'I've got more to say. I'm so sorry, I know you've got others waiting.'

'I'm here. I'm with you. Tell me what you have to say,' Gavin said.

'It was my idea. Garriston. My husband was a red. He and I used to do a trick where he'd shoot a stream into the air and I'd ignite it. We showed our commander, and he took the idea up like it was his . . . but it was mine. Pollos told me not to tell them about it, that it would be used for ill, but I did it. All those people. The whole city burning. They said eighty thousand died in that city alone.'

She dissolved then, incapable of speech. That wasn't your fault, Gavin wanted to say. It was mine. My brother's. We commanded such things. We knew. We knew, and we left the burden on people like you.

The bell rang again, more insistently.

In silent fury, Gavin reached out with blue luxin and ripped the bell off the wall.

He knelt across from Delilah and took her hands in his. 'Lord of Light, Orholam, God, see your humble servant. We pray you search us and know us. We pray your healing light would purify us of sins of commission and omission. In the fire of war, we have done unspeakable things. The luxiats may say our commanders bear the weight of those crimes, but Orholam, Father, we feel that weight on our souls. We repent of our rage and our recklessness, of duties undone. Forgive your daughter, Orholam, take her guilt and shame, and let her walk with you, forever.'

Gavin made his countenance glow softly as he spoke, super-violet and will and yellow triggering the cream's broken crystals, so it appeared he glowed with Orholam's light. Delilah looked up at him with big, wet eyes full of wonder, but also full of peace. He smiled at her until she shared his smile. He stabbed her heart.

And his own went icy cold.

He had kept his word to her, though. Gavin's mother helped him find a family to raise the child. Essel was a Blackguard now.

High Luxiat Jorvis opened the door. 'Lord Prism. We're running behind. We'll have to put off your refreshment until—'

'No.'

'Very well. Your next penitent is waiting. Her name is—'

'No!'

And as soon as his voice was raised, Commander Anamar of the Blackguards was standing there, threatening, his attention and menace turned toward Gavin. Gavin would ruin him for that.

'It's not enough time,' Gavin said.

'There's no choice. The ceremony must be finished by dawn. We agreed—'

Furious, Gavin walked down the hallway, toward the revelers outside. Commander Anamar stepped in front of him, blocking the door.

'If you want to have the use of your knees ever again,' Gavin said, 'you'll get on them now, and get the hell out of my way.'

The man looked to High Luxiat Jorvis, then stepped aside. He didn't get on his knees.

Gavin went out past him and took the steps up the podium two at a time. He sent two jets of fire into the afternoon air to get everyone's attention.

He couldn't remember what words he'd summoned. Oratory had become second nature to him. Something about a momentous year, and a heartbreaking one. Something about Orholam's heaven becoming richer at the price of those who would miss these drafters. Something about special circumstances requiring special action. Some false humility and misdirection.

'I, who serve as your Prism, I covet the time I get with each penitent in Orholam's presence. These are the holiest moments I know, and for my sake, I have asked Orholam that he not be too harsh a master with me. And Orholam is merciful! He has given me a special dispensation! I will meet with and shrive each penitent to be Freed for as long as necessary, even if it takes three days! The parties here will continue, at my own personal expense, until we have honored our dear drafters appropriately!'

A roar went up at that. Two minutes, to be shrived? After giving up your life for the satrapies? No one had liked it. Not even the luxiats who'd insisted on it. By claiming this special dispensation was for him and his own weakness, Gavin had come across as humble. Everyone knew, or would figure out in the next two days, that meeting for longer with each meant he'd just doubled his own burden, if not more.

But if one is going to be a fraud, one ought to do it well.

He jumped off the stage and headed back inside, past agape managers and slave overseers and luxiats who had just seen the labors required of them also double, the logistical nightmare, the long hours they would have to put in so that Gavin would look good. 'Make it so,' Gavin said. 'I don't care how. Do it.'

Inside, he walked past Commander Anamar and toward the next room. He paused at the door and turned back to the frowning Blackguard. 'Oh, Commander, I almost forgot.' Gavin had draped invisible superviolet in nets around the commander's legs as he'd walked down the hall, and now he shot green luxin up and along those nets. The green luxin wrapped around the commander's knees before he could react. Gavin clenched a fist and the green luxin crushed both of the commander's knees.

The commander dropped to the floor, admirably without crying out.

Dear Orholam, Gavin had been brash, but it had worked. Now he would have thought through what friends the commander had, who would be offended, whether they would take vengeance – and in the time he would have taken the window for such an action would have closed. Gavin had gotten away with a lot on brute charisma.

'Have your replacement report to me by the time I finish,' he said.

But the dream didn't end there.

He walked into the little room and shrived an Atashian green, Prayan Navayed, who confessed to cheating her employer, and to sloth in service, and to frequent defiance, and to beating the other slaves unnecessarily harshly.

Then came Jaleh Rodrez. She was a red. Lust, pride, wrath.

Tahlia Blue. Wrath, envy, sabotaging her sister's marriage.

Khordad Cruzan. A blue/green. Pride. Hatred of most of her family, hatred of her employer, hatred of even Orholam.

Estefania Kamael. A red. Bitterness and hatred.

Nairi Patel. A green. So close to wight she couldn't articulate anything.

Belit Beraens. A blue. Pride.

Bilit Beraens. Her twin. A blue. Pride. Even proud she'd outlasted her older twin, if only by a few minutes. Gavin didn't point out that since Belit had been born a few minutes earlier, her dying a bit earlier meant they were really about equal.

Alondra Patel. A superviolet. So close to wight she had to be held down.

Ada Khan. Envy. Fear. She was a mess of tears. Couldn't find her bravery no matter how Gavin tried to inspire her. The luxiats had to hold her down.

Mahnaz. A red. Already confessed.

Ameretet. A blue. Already confessed.

Pelagia Phloraens. Heresy. Since had renounced it, but still harbored it secretly.

Ihsan the Tailor. Cheating her customers, claiming she'd used magic when she rarely did.

Niga Roe. Spying on her employer, who'd been good to her.

Nin-Ki-Gal Day. Green. Already confessed.

Yiska Thews. A green/yellow. One of the only drafters of Angari descent in the group. Envy. Pride. Disbelief.

And a short break for dinner. More prayers. Gavin didn't even hear them. Didn't taste the food in his mouth. Went back to work.

Hagnes. A green. Had gotten roaring drunk during the ceremony, and was too incoherent to confess. Gavin tried to cover all the bases in praying for her before he killed her.

Fidelia Door. A superviolet. Claimed she had no sins. But did have a litany of destroyed relationships. Couldn't see, even with gentle prodding, that she was the common element in all of them.

Li-Lit Ohwarea. A red/orange/yellow. Had secretly tried to go wight. Admitted she couldn't figure out the problems.

Mylitta Ali. A red. A warrior who had been captured, her tongue ripped out by a squad of the Blue-Eyed Demons who had served Dazen. She was illiterate, so Gavin had to use sign language and yes-and-no questions to shrive her. She seemed relieved. None of the luxiats she'd visited before had thought of it or had time when she'd attempted to confess to them. Assholes.

Ghila the Mason. A sub-red. Quiet woman. Attacked Gavin when she thought his guard was down.

Please let me wake.

Elpida Bowyer. A yellow. Confessed that she loved her children more than she loved Orholam. And meant it. She thought it a real sin. She had to encourage Gavin to kill her.

Nukimmut Rose. A blue. Said nothing. Eyes full of hatred, watched Gavin all the way. He expected her to attack, but she never did.

Zenana Zenamus. A red. Proudly filled every second of her time with him recounting her sins. There was cruelty, shocking things with animals, torture, cannibalism, numerous murders, blasphemies, defamation of altars with luxiats she'd seduced, anything to sow chaos and horror. 'And now,' she said, 'since

I go to my death shrived, I'll join Orholam in paradise.' She laughed.

Tahirith. A yellow. Had merely killed her husband who habitually beat her. It was a relief, after Zenana.

Kyriaka Kyraeus. A blue from a noble family. Had joined Dazen's rebels, and when they lost had bribed slavers to take all of her servants if only they would spare her. Had been looking for her slaves since to redeem them, but ran out of time.

Loida. A red. Had participated in a small massacre in some Atashian village during the war. Didn't, on the other hand, feel guilty for spraying red luxin into Garriston.

Tsul. A sub-red. She confessed a thousand small cruelties, which she realized sprang from a life of hatred. She'd hated and envied multitudes, and though it had never reached any pinnacle of expression in violence or sabotage, she'd wasted all her years and talents. Said she'd sinned most against Orholam, for wasting the gift he'd given her, life.

Sar-Rat Bibiana. A sub-red. She'd tried to go wight, and had been so heavily sedated that she couldn't confess.

Shala Smith. A red. Drunk and high on poppy. Couldn't confess.

Tasmituv. An orange. Lies, she confessed. Always lying and manipulating. Long ago, she'd confessed to a luxiat for cheating on her husband, but still felt guilt for that, too.

Edna. A blue. Said she couldn't speak her sins, they were so black. Not even to the Prism. No prodding would move her.

Illi Patel. A yellow. Attacked Gavin. Had hidden how much she'd gone wight.

Lemta. A red. Wight. Was bound to the kneeler when Gavin got there. Couldn't speak.

Meghighda. A blue. Wight. Was bound. Spoke, but couldn't be understood.

Tamayyurt. A superviolet. Too wounded from the war to speak, burn scars and seeping sores covering her body, but smiled at Gavin, fully aware, refusing the poppy, ready for release. Gavin had taken a full minute after that one, unable to go into the next room.

Parvin. A red. A thief.

Tamazzalt. A blue. Another with a litany of sins, but so outlandish Gavin suspected she was lying, ill in the head.

Dulceana Havid. A young sub-red, and an Atashian-born Ruthgari noble. She'd cheated on her husband with a young noblewoman named Eirene Malargos. Information to be remembered, and the first time of the night Gavin had used his position for selfish ends.

Tamment Tailor. A blue. Simply said, 'Envy, lust, hatred, greed, sloth. You've got lots to do tonight, so let's be efficient about this, shall we?'

Tazêllayt. Blue. And Gavin discovered the real reason they'd anointed his body with oil: it made it easier to wipe your skin clean when someone coughed blood all over you. A quick rub at the washbasin that stood between each room, and a quick change of ceremonial clothes that the luxiats kept on hand, and he was on to the next room as if nothing had happened.

Tinsin Khan . . .

Tinsin Khan he could never remember. He'd even looked her up, afterward. Tinsin Khan, green, of the Floating City, Blood Forest, in service to the satrap's steward. No memory of her. Something had broken in him when the luxiats had washed the blood from his face and put him in new garments, as if it were commonplace. Had broken his very memory, of which he was so proud.

And now, though he could call up their colors and stories and sins and attitudes if he tried, he saw each one of the drafters differently; he pushed them back, away. They became only a name and a sin to be shrived.

Illi Alexander. Gossip.

Loida Moss. Poisoner.

Tinsin. Rebellious.

Tahlia. Envy.

Bell Sparrow. Seductress.

Li-Li Solaens. Wight.

Xenia Delaen. Wight.

Myla Loros. Wight.

Pelagia Breeze. Spy.

Meghida Talor. Hatred.

Tahirith Khan. Greed.

Edna Wood. Sloth.

Tasmituv. Lust. Was it possible for a woman dying a virgin to have lust be her principal sin? Yes, Gavin learned.

But he soon settled back into the torpor. Jaleh Smith. Incitement to murder.

Nairi Many Waters. Lust.

Lemta. Hatred.

But then even the sins were starting to sound the same. 'My husband never understood me,' 'If only I'd had as much as my neighbor,' 'It wasn't fair that . . .' Gavin could paint on a face of full attention, empathy, the same stock phrases, the same words in the same prayers. He could sound so sincere, but he heard his own voice as from down a tunnel. Even with his excellent memory, the penitents became only a name and a single detail. As if it weren't worth the space to hold a sin for each, unless it was a really good one.

Titrit. A fatty.

A part of him was horrified at himself. A fatty? No, she'd been . . . a blue. A pious and earnest woman. Fearful but resolute. Quavering voice that made her fat little jowls shake, and utterly . . . utterly boring.

Alé Aribar. Tried to seduce him to escape. Wasn't even close to attractive enough to make it tempting.

Dianthe Knoll. Perfect golden hair.

Titaia Cox. Odd warts, all over. Washed his hands twice afterwards.

Hêbê Ali. Claimed a hundred affairs. Ugly as sin.

Melite Melaens. Big hands. Big, big hands.

Agata Mason. How did she get any work done with breasts that big?

Leilah Tree. The grimacer.

Nurit Hex. Birthmark on her face.

Beulah Blue. No eyebrows.

Livnah Smith. Buck teeth.

Naamiy. Kept clearing her throat. Orholam's balls, would she never stop clearing her throat?

Ora Orestes. Seemed nice. Gray hair. Looked like a grand-mother.

Penina Duraens. A coward.

Minu. A drunk.

Ercilia. Wight.

Gilberta Gonzala. Cursed more than any soldier or sailor he'd ever known.

Neva. So skinny she must have some eating illness.

Xenia. Ugly.

Sar-Ra Hesh. Deserter.

Bili Oak. Stumpy.

Khordad Ali. Gorgeous, with a flat affect. Smelled of shit constantly due to what had been done to her when she'd been captured in the war.

Titaia Brown. Farmer.

Elpida. Smelled of fresh sex.

Dianthe . . . something. Weeper.

Hagnes. Weeper.

Hêbê Brown. Chatterer.

Podarge. Odd name.

Parvin Nyssani. Gavin twisted his wrist when the knife hit a rib.

Ada Gil. Made a funny little 'eep' when he stabbed her.

Livnah Elo. Wet herself copiously as she died. Dammit, they were supposed to take them to the toilets a few minutes beforehand to avoid that.

Naamiy Patel. Vomited blood.

Ora Jon. Attacked, badly.

Yiska. Rambler.

Ameretet Ali. Amazing beauty. Tried to seduce him. Gavin actually thought about it until he realized she was simply afraid, and that she would do anything for a few more minutes of life. Even cheat on her husband as her last act, instead of going to Orholam clean.

Ihsan. Mediocre drafter, mediocre looks, mediocre sins.

Ercilia. Died proudly.

Evi Black. Nice name?

Dulcina Dulceana. He didn't want to remember Dulcina, but he couldn't forget her. By the time he got to her, he'd been killing for almost nine hours. The drafter in the room was standing, leaning at ease against the kneeler. She was only perhaps sixteen years old. A dark-haired beauty with halos stretched to bursting with red and orange and yellow and green. She smiled at him, a full and innocent smile, neither seductive nor afraid, simply happy to see him. He was instantly smitten.

'Greetings, daughter. May the light always shine upon you. Dulcina, if you would like to—'

'Shh,' she said, touching her lips with a finger. 'I've already confessed.'

'Then would you like me to lead us in some prayers or songs?'

She shook her head. 'My High Lord Prism, you've been doing Orholam's work all day, and will do so all night and through the morrow. Let me give you a gift. The only gift I have. The gift of my five minutes. You may speak or we can be silent. You can Free me first if you prefer solitude, or at the end if you prefer company. As you will.'

He didn't understand. There had to be some angle, some advantage. It was all she had. It was her last five minutes, whereas to him it would just be another grain in a full hourglass.

There was no angle. There was no deceit in her open eyes. He stared at her for ten seconds, thirty. And then he was furious for no reason he could understand.

And then he broke.

And he wept.

And she held him. And they wept together.

And after five minutes, the accursed bell jingled. And he stood. And he begged her forgiveness. And he kissed her lips.

And he slew her.

And with her died his faith in Orholam. It had survived war and abandonment and massacres and deceit, but it could not survive the holiest night of the year.

It was midnight. He had killed one hundred drafters.

Three hundred and twenty-seven to go.

Thirty hours later, Gavin killed the last man just before the sun rose. And he went to his chambers, and for the first time since he'd brought hell to earth, he drafted black luxin.

Chapter 25

Kip took the lift down to head out to the Blackguards' training yard, but when he got to the ground floor, he couldn't force himself to get out. He was overwhelmed with people, with having just faced down his grandfather. He was trembling.

He'd figured out in his weeks coming back to the Chromeria that with both Kip and Gavin being lost to the waves, the Red wasn't going to let the blame for it land on his own shoulders. Nor would he be deprived of the services of his favorite slave, Grinwoody. That meant whatever story he'd invented blamed Kip.

Knowing he would have to answer for the crime he had tried to prevent, Kip had prepared as well as he could, charting a course whereby he might find some rapprochement with the man who'd probably accused him of murder and treason.

When he got off the boat, he'd asked the first person he'd seen what had happened to Gavin.

Regardless, going into that meeting should have been the prelude to imprisonment and execution. Kip still wasn't sure why it hadn't been. Part of what he'd been betting on was that Andross was a wight. And he wasn't. Not anymore.

Andross still wore his hood. Still wore his dark spectacles, but Kip had known, instantly. There was something different about his voice, and he hadn't been wearing gloves.

Kip's best card had suddenly disappeared. He'd planned to threaten to reveal that. If nothing else, before they took him away to prison, he could yank back Andross Guile's hood to show the man for what he was.

In the chamber, Kip hadn't had a moment to think about the further implications: a man had gone wight, and was now a wight no longer? Impossible.

Kip had merely spoken, weaving lies with a facility he didn't know he had, so befuddled and intrigued by the puzzle that he'd forgotten to be befuddled and overwhelmed by addressing the entire Spectrum.

And it had worked. Somehow.

There had been a little spark of joy dancing at the corner of Andross Guile's mouth. Surprise, but then pleasure. Like he enjoyed playing against a worthy opponent. Maybe that was why he'd let Kip off the hook, simply so they could keep playing.

Kip felt suddenly ill. He was alive because of Andross Guile's mercy? No, not that. He was alive because Andross longed for entertainment. There. That was more in line with the old horror. That made sense.

But now, suddenly, the people he should most want to see – his Blackguard compatriots – he couldn't bear to see, and he couldn't have even said why. He took the lift down, and down. He got off at the level where the Prism had his private training room. Kip had lost the key Commander Ironfist gave him long ago, but the door had a superviolet panel next to it. Kip had never really noticed them before – they were flat black, and only a few thumbs wide. He'd dismissed them, not realizing what they were, but he realized they were made of the same stuff as the Prism's room controls.

After gathering some superviolet, Kip extended it into the panel. Ah, there was another lock inside, so that the door could be locked against superviolets as well, but it wasn't locked now. Kip pressed superviolet in, and the mundane lock popped open. He went inside.

The silence was a balm. He wrapped his hands in long strips of cloth the way Ironfist had taught him. The old widow Coreen had given him clothes, and while they weren't exactly good for exercise, Kip knew that they would be replaced soon with Blackguard garb and a Chromeria discipulus's clothes, so he set to work on the heavy bag.

He started slow. Seven to ten minutes, Ironfist said, to warm up your fists and joints to the shock of hitting. Kip bent his wrist on an errant punch. He grumbled. He'd done the wrappings wrong. But instead of untying the whole mess and trying again, he drafted a green luxin brace around his wrist. Then he went ahead and made a full glove out of it. He matched it on the other hand.

Much better. He punched the bag lightly for the seven minutes, his fists warming, the pain somehow welcome, the loss of thinking, thinking, thinking a relief.

He moved over to the stretch bag, a smaller target that when hit snapped back toward you, building reflexes. After he got used to its movement, he looked beyond it, using the periphery of his vision to react. Then he went to the chin-up bar, and found he could do three now. Three! It seemed both an impossible achievement and pathetic at the same time. Three. Then back to the heavy bag.

By some accident, he turned on the lights on the bag. It lit up sections to tell him his next target: right kidney, gut, left jaw. With each punch, the bag reacted to how hard Kip hit it by blossoming in color from his punches. Light touches lit the bag blue. Kip's hardest kicks reached up to orange.

It wasn't long before he was wheezing at the effort of trying to get the bag to turn red.

He braced his gloved hands on his knees. He was hitting the damned thing as hard as he could.

No, he was hitting as hard as he could muscularly. Magically, he should be able to hit it harder.

But he didn't want to shoot his little green bouncy balls of doom across the room. If he could add his will to his muscles with magical stuff he threw, why couldn't he add his will to his muscles?

He remembered the wights in Garriston, leapfrogging from roof to roof, shooting luxin downward as they jumped, using the back kick to extend their jumps. It was the same concept that worked for Gavin's skimmers and the sea chariots. But both of those interacted more externally. They didn't *have to*, did they?

Kip drafted a shinguard, then kicked off his shoes. This next part was going to hurt. It always did. He began kicking the heavy bag to warm up for it. He'd been shown how to put power into kicks a dozen times, but it hadn't settled into body knowledge until today somehow. Maybe losing some weight had helped. He swung both arms in a guard to the left, letting his body stretch, his left foot turning until it pointed backward, hips opening, then jerked his arms back in, the torsion providing power as his right leg came up and pounded the side of the bag and set it swinging. That bag weighed two sevens. Not bad. He repeated it, not quite as successfully, from the left.

Enough warm-up. He filled himself with green luxin, then stabbed a bit of it through the skin at the back of his right heel. He winced, cut it wider.

Here goes nothing. He stood with his right foot back, twisted, snapped, and as his right foot came up, he shot green luxin out of it.

The sudden transfer of weight from his body into the air, but this time not opposing his body but aiding it, threw Kip's foot forward at tremendous speed. He kicked the bag so hard that he lost traction on his left foot and fell heavily on his side.

Laughter burst out from the door.

Kip popped to his feet in an instant, mortified. It was half a dozen members of his Blackguard class, led by Cruxer, who was grinning big. If it was possible, it seemed like the young inductees had changed in the weeks Kip hadn't seen them. Cruxer was bulking up, his tall, lean frame looking more muscular by the day. His eyes, though, looked five years older, either from the death of the girl he'd loved, Lucia, or from being in the Battle of Ru. Affable Big Leo's arms of banded iron looked even bigger. Gross Goss wasn't picking his nose, but he was itching it with a big thumb. Tiny Daelos didn't look any bigger, but he was beginning to look reedy and not just skinny and small. Ben-hadad still had spectacles with flip-down lenses, but he'd reworked them. These didn't look thrown together with string and glue; they looked a masterwork, a perfect complement to the burning bright intelligence in his eyes. Only Ferkudi looked the same, the craggy-nosed dope. Actually, that was deeply reassuring.

'Good thing Breaker fights better than he . . . uh, kicks,' Ferkudi said. 'Kicking is part of fighting, though, isn't it? Ah, that's a real flesh protuberance.'

The kids laughed.

'Shut up, you nunks,' Cruxer said good-naturedly. He led as naturally as the first-place Blackguard in the class should. He bowed his head to Kip. 'Godslayer.' He delivered it flat, so it could have been teasing or not. Or knowing Cruxer, he meant those who wished to take it as teasing to be able to do so, but he really meant it.

Son of a . . . Kip thought that nickname had died when he nearly had on the ship. 'Crux. Wh—what are you doing here?'

'In the Prism's practice room, you mean? They got so many recruits for the war training out in the yards, we Blackguards have been pushed into storage rooms and side rooms everywhere half the time. Teia somehow got us permission to use this one when the yards are full. I was going to cut her from the squad before that. She's not so good, but after she got us *this* place—'

'Hey,' Teia said. Somehow she'd lifted a blue luxin dagger from Ferkudi and was now pressing the point to Cruxer's kidney, smiling sweetly.

Cruxer grinned. 'The insubordination around here.'

'I thought you'd – I thought you'd think I was a traitor,' Kip said. That was it, that was why he hadn't been able to bear going out to them. These were the only people in his life who had made him feel like he belonged, and he thought they would have looked at him as an outsider, a traitor.

'Breaker, you're impulsive, but you aren't stupid. We didn't believe for a heartbeat that you'd try to kill the Red. It's ridiculous! You're trying to become a Blackguard! Protecting Colors is part of what we do. You wouldn't throw all that away. But if your father fell overboard, you jumping in after him without a thought? That's you. Completely.'

Ouch. 'How'd you . . . how'd you hear so fast?'

'Teia. Big gossip.'

'Hey,' Teia said. For some reason, she'd been glowering at Daelos, but she said nothing more.

Cruxer grinned again. 'Commander Ironfist thought you'd be here. Said sometimes those who've been in battle are a little reticent when they first come back.'

'You weren't supposed to share that last part, you oaf,' Teia said. 'What were you doing there, Kip? With your foot?'

She looked eager to talk about training. Well she might, he supposed. She and Kip were going to talk about her being all bloody in town. But not now.

'You're bleeding,' Cruxer said.

'Just an experiment,' Kip said.

They gathered around him. 'Go on,' Ben-hadad said. He'd seemed uncharacteristically nervous until now, when his eyes lit up at the possibility of a new discovery.

So Kip explained, and then he kicked the bag again, showing them. When you used luxin from one site repeatedly, the body eventually adjusted and there was little blood. But the first few times, it acted like any mundane cut. A cloud of unsealed luxin and blood both shot out of his heel like smoke out of a gun barrel, and this time he didn't lose his footing. He did nearly wrench his knee, though. The power was incredible.

But the bag lit up. Red.

Everyone stopped and looked at Kip.

'You could, uh, use this lots of ways,' Kip said. 'You'd have to, um, figure out your own center of weight and everything, but if you shot some from your shoulders when you ran, you'd run faster. Or when you jumped, you could shoot some—'

'From your ass! You'd be the fart flyer!' Ferkudi shouted. He reminded Kip of an excitable puppy.

They laughed, but only briefly. They were all captivated by the thought of it.

'I was going to say from your hips,' Kip said. 'I mean, if you did it from your feet, you'd probably flip over and fall on your head.'

'But *you* could do it from your ass if you want to, Ferkudi,' Teia said. 'Might as well have a wide platform.'

They laughed again, then quieted.

Big Leo turned to Cruxer. 'I've never even heard of anything like this. Is it forbidden?'

Cruxer shook his head. 'It isn't incarnitive, so I don't see why it would be. On the other hand, if you were doing it all the time, you might burn through your life in no time.'

'But that's true of any drafting,' Teia said. 'Used judiciously, think of it. We'd be faster, stronger, jump farther.'

'This can't be the first time anyone's thought of this,' Kip said, suddenly embarrassed.

'Every brilliant discovery is obvious after someone's made it,' Ben-hadad said.

'Did you really just come up with this?' Cruxer asked. 'No one suggested it to you?'

Kip shrugged.

'He shall be a genius of magic,' Ben-hadad said quietly, as if quoting something. The rest of them stopped, looked at him, looked at each other. Kip could tell they'd talked about it among themselves before.

'Does this mean we're going to have to fill ourselves full of holes?' Ferkudi asked.

Chapter 26

Aliviana Danavis stood high on the Great Pyramid of Ru, wrapping up teaching the women who would replace her. The four superviolet drafters who had been learning from Liv for the last four months were joined by Liv's personal guards. That guard had been formed around the core of men who'd helped her seize this very structure during the liberation of Ru.

Phyros was Liv's rock. Over six feet tall, wide as the sea. When they'd infiltrated the city, he hadn't worn his lucky cape because it was too distinctive, but usually he didn't go anywhere without it. It was the skin of a lion, the roaring mouth forming a cap for his head, the mane bunching around his shoulders. Over an alligator-leather vest with many straps, he wore a jade-and-turquoise belt that hooked with great, curving giant javelina tusks. The sheath for his belt knife was a hollowed-out sabre-cat's fang. He claimed to have killed each of the beasts himself, armed only with that knife. He despised muskets and pistols, but otherwise didn't have a favorite among weapons. He had two axes that looked like halberds with their hafts cut short in special slings on his back. Someday, he would craft a weapon from sea demon tooth, he said.

From anyone else, Liv would have thought it empty boasting, but Phyros she believed. She'd seen him without a tunic on, and he bore scars from claws and fangs like a man who had done everything he claimed.

The rest of her guard were less conspicuous, but perhaps no less dangerous. Tychos was an orange drafter, one of the best hex casters in the Blood Robes. He was a small man, violent, and strangely direct for an orange. Magic is no match for man, as an old saying went. There were crafty sub-reds and reckless blues. But here, it was probably one of the main reasons why he wasn't in contention to become the prince's candidate for Molokh. With one of Tychos's hexes woven into her cloak, Liv could inspire awe in everyone who looked at it. Or dread. Simply being aware of the hex was usually enough to end the effect – it was an imposition of will and could be broken, but most people hadn't fought hexes in hundreds of years. Tychos was a khat chewer, his teeth stained red from his constant use of the stimulant. With red teeth and orange eyes, the man would have looked a demon to Liv a few months ago.

But she'd come a long way since she'd left the Chromeria.

She finished up teaching the superviolet drafters how to manipulate the great mirror atop the pyramid, answering their questions, guiding their rough efforts to reach their drafting into the controls and shift the mirror to shoot light into any corner of the city, immediately empowering the drafters there, even late in the day when the shadows were long. Ru would never be as light as Big Jasper, with its Thousand Stars, but this mirror was a wonder. The light from it was as thick and potent as anything Liv had ever seen. It had helped birth a god – a god immediately slain by Gavin Guile, but still.

Unfortunately, turning the mirror this way and that to illuminate the city meant surveying the city itself. Unlike Garriston, Ru hadn't accepted its liberation joyfully.

The Color Prince had bet it would. Ru had as many reasons to hate the Guiles as anyone: they mercilessly quashed rebellions that had been sponsored by the old royal family. The massacre of the Atashian nobility during the False Prism's War. Even two short-lived and small uprisings since then. The streets of Ru had run with blood, blood the Chromeria had spilled. Freed of their satrap, they should have been natural allies.

Instead, its subjects had fought fiercely. The prince had been furious. He'd issued an ultimatum for several of the leaders of the resistance to be surrendered to him for immediate execution. When they hadn't been, he'd gone insane with fury. He'd given his army leave to do whatever they wanted for three days to punish the city.

Liv's guards had urged her not to go out in the city – even as they had taken turns going out themselves. The advice was simultaneously wise and patronizing. She hadn't intended to go. But she wouldn't be stopped from going out by any man. The Chromeria liked to cloak unpleasantness in soft ritual. Liv would have her truths served in hard light, thank you.

Phyros had tried to object one last time, as all of them shifted uneasily and armed themselves: '*Eikona*' – it was the term for the preeminent drafter of her color. The Blood Robes would have new titles. 'Eikona, I understand you want to look. It's natural. But you're what? Seventeen years old? Pretty, and a woman.' He scowled. Like she hadn't noticed her gender.

'Eighteen,' she said, even though she wouldn't be eighteen for another ten days. 'Thank you for your concern, and *fuck you*.'

Still, when they went, they'd prominently displayed their Blood Robes.

It had been a nightmare tour. The sights were etched on her eyes. It didn't bear thinking about now, even though some of the many fires burning in the city below her now were funeral pyres. Huge pyramids of flame. And still it wasn't finished. There were places the patrols couldn't go to collect the bodies for burning. It was still too dangerous. So disease spread.

She couldn't leave too soon. She fingered the black jewel in her pocket. Black luxin, the prince claimed. She didn't really believe it. It was likely obsidian only, though threads of darkness seemed to swim in the jewel. She didn't know how the Color Prince had gotten it. Regardless, he believed that it was a means of control. She'd first thought that perhaps he spied through it, but simply seeing wouldn't be enough to stop a god, would it? Surely it was something more dangerous.

She didn't like to think about it. Didn't like to look at it. Didn't like the feel of it on her skin. But he'd forbidden her to go anywhere without it.

'You have my things?' she asked Phyros.

'Packed and on the galley.' Phyros's voice was a deep, satisfying rumble that practically made your lungs vibrate themselves, like a tuning fork rung. It was, for some reason, incredibly comforting. She'd heard him bellow in rage with that voice, and having it on her side soothed all sorts of fears. Not that she'd ever let him know it.

The Color Prince didn't have nearly the number of ships he needed, so Liv and her guard would be traveling in a cheap, poorly constructed galley. Of course, there were villages for the supply of galleys around the entire rim of the sea. Traveling by ship wouldn't be fast, especially not when they would have to find ports to wait out every winter storm, but it would be faster than walking or riding, and much less dangerous. Any pirates who waylaid them would be in for several unpleasant surprises – though usually, merely announcing the presence of a drafter was enough to convince pirates not to attack. A little blast of luxin into the sky would be enough to turn back all but the most foolhardy.

Most of the class left, including one middle-aged woman who hadn't even discovered she could draft superviolet until after the death of her husband. One of the Blood Robe drafters had stayed at her boarding house and had administered the test to her on a whim. Middle-aged drafters. It was odd to Liv, but the Color Prince's vision was for a day when drafting wasn't a death sentence. Perhaps that day would even come soon enough to make a difference for Liv.

She stepped up to the great mirror one last time. It was easy now. Whoever had built this had meant it to be used. Some long-dead master craftsman. She stopped musing and turned the mirror toward the horizon. Navigators and natural philosophers had known about the curvature of the earth for at least a millennium, but it was the first time Liv had ever had to worry about it. It was also, so far as she could guess, why each of the great mirrors had been constructed on the top of a tall building.

That curvature was why when you watched a departing ship, its hull disappeared first, and it appeared to sink as it got farther away. The natural philosophers had figured out that the rate of that drop was two feet per league. If 'drop' made any sense, on a surface that appeared to be flat. You'd think that the calculation of how tall a structure would have to be would be simple – just subtract the total curvature of the earth per league from the height of the structure. Easy. Given that the Great Pyramid was two hundred and eighty cubits tall, or four hundred and eighty feet, you should be able to cast light from the beam to a distance of two hundred and forty leagues. If the receiving tower was equally tall, you should be able to double that, right?

Wrong, she'd found out. She'd struggled with her calculations, talking through them aloud with her guards. She'd had to explain to Phyros about the curvature of the earth twice, but then he'd been the one who grasped her model better than she did. She'd drawn on a parchment, then bent it, showing him how it worked. He'd pointed out that she was treating the mirror towers as if they were standing straight up in relation to each other. They stood straight in relation to the ground, but the ground was bent. It was like measuring the height of a man when he was standing straight up versus when he was leaning against a doorframe. The man might still be six feet tall, but the top of his head wasn't going to be six feet from the ground.

She'd done more calculations, and finally figured it all out – and was still wrong. She had no idea why.

In the end, the Color Prince had sent Samila Sayeh to her. The blue drafter had fought in the Prisms' War and made herself a legend. She'd fought against the Color Prince at Garriston, but had broken the halo, was captured, imprisoned, and, by his mercy, forgiven. She now fought with them. If the Color Prince's armies could find the blue bane, the woman was one of the leading candidates to become the next Mot.

Samila Sayeh had begun the transition to full wight differently than any blue Liv knew. She was starting with her left hand only. She said if she could figure how to make hard, crystalline blue luxin work on a part of her body that required such dexterity and flexion first, the rest of her body would be simple. Given the woman's status and fierce intellect, Liv shouldn't have felt threatened by her. But something rankled. And Samila didn't care, if she even noticed.

Samila had looked at Liv's problem, figured out the correct equations to use, demanding whole lists of relevant and seemingly irrelevant numbers, and done the calculations in her head, only her hand twitching as if moving invisible abacus beads. She gave Liv the answers, not explaining what she'd done. And then she translated some ancient scratching below the mirror in some language Liv didn't even recognize. There were instructions for exactly how to set the mirrors for dozens of major points around the world.

Then she left without a word. Not even the bare minimum of a nodded head and the 'Eikona' that Liv's status demanded.

The Chromeria's lapdog luxiats preached that the sin of superviolet was pride. Maybe in this one thing they were on to something, because Liv could barely contain her fury at being made to look a fool.

Even with that help, it had taken Liv an embarrassing half hour to figure out what that meant for her. Finally, she'd been able to aim the mirror out to sweep the sea to search for the resonance points the Color Prince had directed her to. His intelligence had been good. There was one near the Everdark Gates – and hopefully not beyond them. That point was Liv's goal. The superviolet bane was there, somewhere, on land or in the sea.

It was still there today. Liv was sure of it. Her mission was simple: she and her guards were to find either what the Color Prince called a seed crystal or the bane that would form around it, and take it for him.

Bending her knee to him alone, Liv was to become goddess. Fealty to One, as the Danavis motto proclaimed. To one only.

'The prince is giving us a two-week lead before he sends out the next team. Let's not waste it,' Liv said. Dressed in her immaculate yellow silk dress, the trim dyed with murex purple, she handed her jacket to Phyros before she began her descent down the pyramid. He put it in the bulging pack that carried everything she might need.

A goddess-to-be had people for such things.

Chapter 27

Liv had barely reached the docks with her entourage when a young woman with nose rings attached by chains to her earrings came forward. She wore a beautiful flowing dress in sea foam green, edged with crimson. Wealthy. 'Lady, Lady Aliviana!' the woman said. 'Your Eminence. Uh, Eikona.' She lay prostrate on the road, heedless of the dust.

It was foolishness. Putting such garments in the dirt, for what? To show respect? To Liv? It was insane . . . and pleasing.

'A moment of your time, Lady Aliviana, please,' the woman said.

Phyros looked to Liv. In his bearskins and bulging muscles, he looked like a frowning barbarian colossus. '*Eikona?*' In Liv's case, earning that title had been almost embarrassingly easy. There were hundreds of green drafters, hundreds of blues, hundreds of reds. And ten superviolets. She knew she wasn't as elite as the *eikonos* of green or blue or red, but the Color Prince treated them all the same, and made everyone else do likewise. She owed him for that.

Liv nodded. Phyros walked to the woman and picked her up by her neck. He was so big, he was somehow able to do it without strangling her, his big hand – one hand – wrapping completely around her throat. He lifted her to her feet and, ignoring all propriety, searched her for weapons quickly. The woman looked horrified, but she said nothing. Last, he clamped his big hand around her jaw and angled her face up. She instinctively tried to pull away, but he waited until she met his eyes, and gazed carefully at each eye in turn.

Satisfied she wasn't a drafter or bearing any weapons, he still didn't let her come directly to Liv. Phyros believed in picking your own battlefield, regardless of how inconvenient. He marched the woman up into the beached galley. Liv followed to her quarters.

Phyros drew back the skin hanging over the door and held

it open for Liv. The woman followed her in, looking vexed. She pulled the skin to shut it behind her. Phyros held it firm, impassive. He looked at Liv. She nodded.

'Shout if,' Phyros said. Odd habit he had, not finishing common statements, accepting it for granted that you both knew how they ended, so there was no need to go through the effort of saying the whole thing.

The woman closed the skin tight, turned, and took a deep breath. 'Eikona, thank you for meeting with me. My message is secret, and important. First, please see that I am no threat.' She knelt gracefully and spread her hands, palms up.

'Go on, and hurry, the ship casts off in minutes.'

'Yes, lady, of course. I come from the Order of the Broken Eye. We mean you no harm. Indeed, quite the opposite.'

An unwilling shiver went through Liv. She'd wanted to believe that Mistress Helel trying to assassinate Kip was an aberration, a woman ill in the head, delusional. She'd wanted to believe, as Gavin and Ironfist had said, that the Order was a loose collection of thugs taking on an old legendary name in order to raise their prices. But this woman seemed calm, professional, not a braggart. And the use of Mistress Helel as an assassin was nothing short of brilliant. Who would suspect a heavy, middle-aged woman of being an assassin?

So it was possible the Order was real. It was no wonder this woman was being so careful to show she posed no threat.

Seeing that Liv wasn't going to speak, the woman hurried on. 'The prince gave you a necklace; on it, there is a chunk of living black luxin. That jewel is a death sentence. It is the way he believes he can control you.'

'What? How does it work?'

She paused, painfully. 'We don't know, except that he believes he's mastered it, and that it will compel obedience. He believes it enough that he's willing to make gods.'

'You speak dangerous words.'

'Does he seem a man content with others having greater power than he does? He wishes to be a god of gods.'

'What do you wish of me?' Liv demanded. 'You think to test my loyalty so easily?'

'The prince espouses freedom, does he not? How is a leash freedom?'

'Freedom doesn't mean a lack of responsibilities. It means a choice between them. He is to make me a god.'

'Forgive me, Eikona, but you will make yourself a god, or fail. On your own. And black luxin is not so easily tamed as the prince believes.'

A shout from outside drifted in. 'Casting off in two! Rowers to your places!'

'Black luxin,' Liv scoffed. 'It's merely obsidian.'

'How can you say so? You who have seen it?'

Liv turned away. The swirling jewel was in her pocket, ever in her pocket. And the prince's instructions were clear: she must put it on before she claimed the bane. 'It is . . . merely cunningly cut. Tricks of the light.'

'The stones are related, lady. The old stories aren't lies, but they've been corrupted. Obsidian is black luxin, dead black luxin. It is said that all the obsidian in the world is the last remnant of a great war, thousands of years before Lucidonius. A holocaust that devoured light and life for millennia, from which we are still recovering. The living stuff . . . Eikona, it has will. It is insanity given form. It is a hole of nothingness that can never be filled. If you put it to your neck to feed and the prince's control slips, it will kill you. It has will; it may have intellect, too. If it devours a goddess, who is to say what it would do next?'

So Liv had been right to be leery of having the thing next to her skin. If this girl was telling the truth. 'What does the Order want?'

'Most of our knowledge has been lost to time and bloody purges. We are a weak, wan thing. A shadow of a shadow. And I the least of our folk, in case I was captured and tortured. We're not your enemies, Eikona. Become Ferrilux. Serve the Color Prince. Do all that you wish, but do not put black luxin in the nexus of your power. Do not put it in the center of the bane. One slip, whether the prince's or yours, and who is to say but that it would eat all the magic in the world?'

Chapter 28

They needed to have this out. Teia was in some sort of trouble, and Kip was going to make her tell him what it was. During a rest at practice, he'd told the squad a little about his adventure and almost the whole truth about what had happened to Gavin.

'There was a fight, over a dagger. Grinwoody tried to grab it and I tangled with him. Andross joined in and Gavin intervened. Everyone tangled up. My father diverted the blade into himself so I wouldn't get stabbed.'

More than a few puzzled glances at that. Why was it harder to tell a partial truth than a complete lie? Kip rushed on. 'But that wasn't the amazing thing. I jumped in after him. I lit some red to make a beacon, and when we got pulled out by this pirate, the dagger was a dagger no longer. It was a full-length sword with seven jewels of each of the seven primes in the blade. And when they pulled it out, Gavin . . . Gavin was alive. He didn't even bleed.'

They asked him questions then, most of which he couldn't answer, and Cruxer swore them all to secrecy; then, because their break had already extended for half an hour, he called it a day.

Teia had slipped out of practice before he'd noticed, and he hadn't seen her at dinner, so now he was waiting up for her in their room.

He'd been waiting half an hour, getting more and more cross, when he had a thought. He went to the tiny desk and found no papers. He hadn't noticed before because they simply weren't there. His ownership papers of Teia, that he'd already signed over. She'd taken them from his room, thinking him dead, and turned them in.

Of course she had. He couldn't blame her for worrying that with him gone, anyone might take his signed transfer of title. That was why she wasn't here. No longer his slave, she'd moved into the barracks. Good for her.

193

She owed him nothing, and the bond of master to slave – unwelcome though it had been – was gone. But maybe that had been the only bond they'd shared, and it felt like she'd given up on him.

He'd wanted her to be free, but he'd still wanted her to owe him, to be eternally grateful, to be somehow therefore subordinate. He'd wanted her to be free, but he wanted to decide for her how she should use her freedom.

Kip swore aloud, and went to bed.

The next morning, he went to breakfast, then checked the lists. He wasn't on any work details. He supposed that meant he should go to class.

Class. Ugh. He stood in front of the lift with all the other students and withdrew into himself, carrying his black little storm cloud around with him.

Of course, there were a thousand things Kip still needed to learn. He had some experiential knowledge, but almost no other kind. It would hamper him eventually, he knew. Hell, it already had. The extent of his knowledge was the bouncy green balls of doom. Well, practically. It wasn't going to be enough to keep him alive in the coming war.

Plus he'd managed to lose the knife that he was now more and more afraid was Important. Andross Guile had called it the Blinder's Knife. It was only because he'd been vague with the squad about where it came from that they hadn't asked him more about it. He'd let them think that it was Gavin's.

And how did my mother come by that, anyway?

Kip walked in to Magister Kadah's classroom. It was hard to believe that he'd first walked in here only a few months ago. He felt like he was ten years older. He sat at the back of the room. Even in a discipulus's clothing again, he didn't think he'd be able to escape notice, but there was no reason to stick his thumb in Magister Kadah's eye.

More than he had to, anyway.

A voice whispered in his ear: 'I hear you've connived your way into being declared legitimate, little bastard. Don't think it changes anything. I know what you are.'

Kip turned. 'So nice to see you, Magister.' He said it like he meant it.

She gave him a nasty grin. Kip's training and fighting had changed him so much that perhaps he should have taken some solace in the fact that Magister Kadah looked exactly the same: shrunken like an old woman despite only being in her early thirties, disheveled with hair that hadn't seen a pick since the last time Kip had been in class, green spectacles on a gold chain around her neck. 'Should I get my switch ready?'

'I don't know,' Kip said. 'I'm just the ignoramus son of a whore.' He winced. Kip the Lip wasn't so far in the past, apparently.

'Any more language like that, Kip Guile, and it'll be knuckles. You remember, I believe?' Magister Kadah said.

Kip put his hands on the desk before him. The fingers of his left hand still bowed upward, stiff and stubborn, though he was working on them. The pain of getting that hand smashed with a switch would be excruciating. The whole hand still felt like one exposed nerve.

He looked up at the magister, puzzled. What? He was supposed to be afraid of getting his knuckles rapped?

Teia and Ben-hadad came in right before class was supposed to start. They saw Kip, and mirrored each other's surprise at seeing him there, looked at each other, and then sat next to him.

The magister went to the front of the class, cleared her throat, and waited the moment it took for the class to fall silent. 'Discipulae.'

'Magister,' the class answered. Kip joined them. A new start, Kip.

'Discipulae, today we're going to be discussing orange. Any orange drafters here today?'

A few discipulae raised their hands. Kip debated raising his, and raised a couple fingers.

'Orange is singularly useless,' Magister Kadah said. She grinned nastily. 'You'll spend your lives making lubrication for machines and for storing away metals so they don't rust. It is, however, a relatively easy life. Your patron may have you draft barrels of the stuff each day, which may take you from sunrise to noon, and then to keep you from dying early, you'll be done by noon every day. Some will, happily, have other duties for you to perform. Usually non-magical ones: cleaning stables, dusting furniture, mopping barracks. Yes, Ben-hadad?'

'Orange can be used for more than that,' Ben-hadad said. 'And with a war looming that could destroy all of us, I think we should start training oranges to live up to their full potential.'

'Their full potential?' Magister Kadah asked. Her tone was meant to be a warning, but Ben-hadad seemed to think it was a real question.

'Oranges can craft hexes. It's said that in Ru, orange spies infiltrating the city crafted fear hexes invisible to the naked eye but so potent that people avoided whole neighborhoods – allowing the heretics to tunnel under the walls unopposed. Oranges can spike food and drink. Fear-casting, tromoturgy. Pathomancy. Will-blunting.'

'Forbidden!' Magister Kadah snapped. 'And at your level, forbidden to even discuss!'

'We're at war!' Ben-hadad said. 'I just heard that the last fort below Ruic Neck fell. From there, there's nothing to stop the Color Prince until they reach the Ao River. Even if you won't teach the oranges to craft hexes, you should be teaching us all how to resist them, and certainly how to recognize them.'

'This Color Prince will doubtless be put down in weeks if he hasn't already been. None of you will have to face orange heretics.'

'There are people who have already faced the Blood Robes in this very room,' Ben-hadad said.

Thanks, Ben.

'I see. So you *are* friends now, is that it?' Magister Kadah asked Ben-hadad, looking from him to Kip. 'Trying to make the "Guile" look good? Quite the pair you make, huh? The ignoramus and the boy who can't even read? How'd you learn all this?'

'I can read,' Ben-hadad hissed.

'The words just get scrambled for him is all, Magister,' Teia said. 'He can read if he goes slow.'

'Slow is a nice way of saying stupid,' Magister Kadah said.

Kip sighed. He'd had the best intentions.

'Ben-hadad, you think being friends with this lordling will

help you?' Magister Kadah asked. The whole class was silent, expectant.

'I'm not his friend because he can do something for me,' Ben-hadad said. 'And I resent your implication. You dishonor me and you dishonor yourself by speaking such petty vileness.'

A wave of shock passed through the young teens. They looked like they didn't want to look away for a heartbeat, in case they missed Magister Kadah's head exploding.

Magister Kadah's eyes widened, fists balled. 'You think he can protect you?' she demanded. 'Report yourself immediately, Ben-hadad . . . for expulsion.'

There was a collective gasp.

'Expulsion?' Ben-hadad asked, disbelieving.

'For gross insubordination. I've not used my power to expel a discipulus in three years. Perhaps it is time. You're worthless as a drafter; you'll be useful as an example.'

The old Kip would have jumped out of his seat and started shouting furiously. He would have tapped into the well of hatred at injustice that he'd carried since growing up with his addled mother. Growing up, it had never felt safe to be furious with her on his own behalf, but when he'd seen others suffering injustice, it had been there, hot and ready, a powerful insanity he could put on and only take off when he was exhausted. Kip had been going green golem since long before he could draft. Even Ram had feared him when he'd been like that.

Kip stood slowly. Teia tried to grab him, tried to keep him in his seat.

'What do you think you're doing, Kip "Guile"? You think I can't expel you, too?'

Of course she couldn't. 'You can't even expel Ben-hadad,' Kip said. He spoke evenly, respectfully, even mournfully. He didn't raise his voice, but he spoke loudly enough for all to hear. 'He's a Blackguard inductee, and if you think Commander Ironfist is going to let you thin his already strained ranks in a time of war, I wish you luck in the conflagration that will be your own career.'

A profound silence fell over the room. The whispering teenagers weren't even whispering, and Kip's tone somehow defanged Magister Kadah.

Respectfully, regretfully, Kip continued. 'Magister, you weren't always like this. You don't like children, I understand that. It's a failing, but all Orholam's sons and daughters have failings. You've been assigned by an angry superior or perhaps through cruel chance to do work that has never fit you. You've served quietly in a difficult posting because you love Orholam and you love the Chromeria and you love the Seven Satrapies. But you hate your work, and I bet that you hate what you've become. You're better than this. You've been punished for something, or perhaps for nothing, and you've done a lot of damage in turn. Not least of all to yourself. I will do what I can to help you.'

Kip stepped into the aisle, and without waiting to see how the magister would react, walked out of the classroom. He walked directly to the lift and headed to the top floor. He got off and checked in with the Blackguards. He recognized them: Baya Niel, who had helped kill the green god with Kip, and a curvy woman who he thought was named Essel. Teia had liked her a lot. 'I'd like to speak with the White, if she has any time today,' Kip said. 'Please.'

Baya Niel said, 'We can ask her between her other meetings to squeeze you in. It may be a few hours, though. If you're late to Blackguard training this afternoon, you'll bear the consequences.'

Kip shrugged. Consequences.

He waited an hour before Baya Niel gestured to him, letting him through. Kip headed to the White's room, past the Blackguards at the checkpoint and more outside her door. There had been an assassination attempt while Kip had been gone, foiled by the Prism himself, they said. That meant more guards, and more attentive ones. Kip was frisked twice.

When he got into the White's office, he was surprised by how healthy she looked. She bade him come to stand in front of her desk, and for a long moment she studied him. She had secretaries and messenger slaves attending her while she saw to her daily business overseeing the Chromeria. Kip stood silent; he knew not to speak until spoken to.

'Do you know, I expected you to look more like Gavin. You look more like your grandfather and great-grandfather. Do you know you are exactly what so many of the great families were hoping for, treating their sons and daughters like stallions and mares to be bred for this trait or that? The Blood Wars made people who should have known better act like animals themselves, I'm afraid.'

'High Mistress?'

'Your eyes blue to gather light efficiently, your skin dark to hide when you draft, a muscular frame for war, and of course, above all, always and forever, your ability to draft seven colors. It's not so simple, of course, to breed humans. And while some traits can be guessed with a fair degree of accuracy, we know not nearly the complexity of ourselves. I've never seen a child with blue eyes who didn't have at least two parents or grand-parents with the same, but I've seen a girl darker than you who sprang from parents lighter than me. It almost got her mother killed by the father, jealous fool, who still suspected her patrimony until the girl was old enough he could see she had his nose and eyes both. The world is more marvelous than we know, Kip. But you're here for a reason. What would you have of me?'

'A favor,' Kip said. 'Actually, two.'

'I gathered. It's rare that people come simply for my excellent company.'

'I'm sorry, have I done something to offend? I don't know the protocol here,' Kip said. He still had a weight on his soul.

She shook her head. 'Please, go on.'

'There's a magister named Kadah. I think she's requested transfers to other duties. Probably multiple times. Maybe long ago, and she has since given up. I think her transfers were blocked by some enemy of hers. Would you grant her application?'

The White looked pensive. She lifted a hand and gave some rapid set of signals that a secretary understood. A slave quietly hurried out the door. 'An odd way to get rid of a magister you don't like,' the White said.

'It's not for me. It's for her. She's miserable, and she's bad at her work because of it.'

'I'll know the truth of it in an hour. I'll decide then. And the second thing?' the White asked.

I want you to tell me about the Lightbringer, Kip wanted to say. I want you to tell me about the Blinder's Knife.

'I need a tutor,' he said instead. 'I don't mean to sound arrogant, but I have so much to learn. I'm a full-spectrum polychrome, and I can't sit in a class where I'm only hearing things that I already know. Much less waste my time butting heads with a jealous magister.'

'You think I can find you a magister who *isn't* jealous of a full-spectrum polychrome son of a Prism who's being given preferential treatment?'

'I was hoping you would do it,' Kip said.

She laughed, truly surprised. 'Oh, Kip. I'd forgotten how audacious the young can be.'

'I'm . . . important,' Kip said.

She liked that less. Her smile faded, died.

'In a very narrow sense, is all I mean,' he continued. He struggled to find words. 'My importance isn't – I shouldn't be given preference because of who I am. I'm important in that I have a vital function to perform.'

'And that is?' she asked, wary, perturbed.

I am to save my father, he wanted to say. It was a good purpose. Maybe it was even the purpose to which Orholam had called him. But if he said that, he would be lying. 'I don't know,' he admitted. 'But the task is what's important. I am merely the tool by which it will be accomplished, and I ask you to prepare me for it. My audacity is to serve Orholam without fear, believing he will walk with me through fire.' He wanted to be that certain, thought that he should be that certain, so he didn't realize it was a lie until it was already out of his mouth.

'Kip, we are all people of will here. Every man and every woman who wrestles light has tasted godhood. We are all important, or Orholam wouldn't have given us these tools, wouldn't have trusted us with these powers.'

'Like he trusted the Color Prince.' The words were out of Kip's mouth before he could stop them. 'I am so sorry, High Lady.' He bowed his head.

'Don't you see, Kip, the Color Prince's insanity and grasping for godhood is no counter to what I said. Power is the ultimate test of a man. The more you're given, the more opportunities for corruption. That many fail the test doesn't mean Orholam is wrong; it means that men are free. And great souls succeed or fail spectacularly.'

'Like my father,' Kip said.

'Your father most of all.' She hesitated, then waved her secretaries back. They immediately got up and went to stand by the door. One pulled a curtain between them and Kip and the White. Only a Blackguard remained, watching.

And my grandfather, he should have said. It was a perfect segue to address what he had seen. But what did he have to tell her? *Andross was a wight, and then he wasn't? Oh, and I lied to you and the entire Spectrum about what happened on the ship.* Kip was pushing his luck as it was. He was like a novice Nine Kings player. On the boat, he'd prepared one move ahead, and the lies he had prepared had worked spectacularly with the Spectrum. But now he was simply playing whatever card came into his hand. The lies made a lattice, the old moves constrained the new ones.

How does Andross do it? Does he remember what lies he's told every player?

Of course he does. That's what the Guile memory is for, for him. Here Kip didn't even know who all the players were. The White liked him, but he didn't think she would find the lies of a sixteen-year-old amusing or masterful. She was old, and old people want to see young people as refreshingly direct, simple, sweet, and innocent.

He might be holding exactly the card she needed to play against Andross – for theirs was a game going on decades – but Kip couldn't give it to her.

Perhaps, in this great game, there is no giving of cards. Only trades.

The White rummaged in her desk. She pulled out a small framed picture. 'When I die, Kip, I want you to have this. And after you've used it, if he still lives, I want you to give it to Gavin.' She turned it around, and Kip saw that it was one of the new Nine Kings cards. 'This is the work of a dear old friend of mine—'

'Janus Borig,' Kip said. He recognized the handiwork. He

took the framed card from the White. It was called the Unbreakable. It was beautiful. Janus Borig had clearly lavished attention and time on this work. Where some of the cards were the product of haste and compulsion – though all showed her total mastery of her art – this card was as intricately painted as any Kip had seen. A young woman with fiery hair stood on a hill dominated by an oak, the smoking ruins of an estate to her left. To her right was an abyss. Tiny flecks of blue and green touched her gray eyes. Tears stood on each cheek, but her jaw was set, eyes fixed on some point in the distance.

'I'd just buried my youngest daughter,' the White said. 'Calling me the Unbreakable has felt sometimes like a cruel joke, and other times a promise. I chose to live, to fight, even when fighting meant to fight despair and the taunts of meaningless-ness that is the abyss. This card is not all pleasantness, but I should like to be understood, someday.'

'Damn, you were beautiful. And fierce! And – and I can't believe I just said that out loud,' Kip said. He'd slipped up in recognizing the art. If he pretended to slip up in another direc-tion, he might be able to distract her before she demanded to know how he knew Janus Borig's work.

The White laughed. 'Well, thank you. I think perhaps Janus was being kind.'

'Janus isn't kind. She's honest,' Kip said. 'That's what a Mirror . . .' does. Shit. Can't hold a thought in your head for six seconds, can you, Kip?

'Don't feel bad,' the White said. 'I know an artful dodge when I hear one. And I've dealt with your father and grand-father for far too long to underestimate you, Kip, even if you are young.'

'You send satraps out of here crying, don't you?'

'It's happened,' she said drily. 'Janus,' she said.

So Kip told her about his meetings with Janus Borig. He told her that the woman had been working on his card. He told her about the assassins with the shimmercloaks. He told her about Janus Borig dying in his arms.

He could see it was a blow to the White.

'Kip, this is vital. Did she save anything from the fire?'

Kip had been bracing himself for that question for the entire conversation. 'She wanted me to grab something, but the fire was so intense, and there were piles of gunpowder everywhere. I was only able to grab the shimmercloaks.'

The White studied his face. 'You're a good liar, Kip, but I've dealt with the best. The shimmercloaks are good for killing people, but the cards are good for a thousand purposes. Janus wouldn't have let you dawdle grabbing weapons while letting the truth burn. It was her whole life's work.'

'She wasn't conscious,' Kip said, not willing to let a good lie die.

I thought we were going to go with refreshingly direct. Dammit.

The White sighed. 'I won't ask more. I hope you've put them in a safe place. Don't check on them often, else spies may find them by luck. Be ware of using them alone. I don't know what all the new cards are, but I can imagine some of the events of recent history would flay your mind.'

With his own hand so recently burnt clean of skin, it was a metaphor with some resonance for Kip.

Kip moved to speak, but realized that correcting her to say that he didn't actually know where the cards were would be to admit he had been lying. Every way he moved, she gained something.

'How come when you do this to me, I don't hate you?' Kip asked.

'Box you in, you mean?'

'Yes.'

'Unlike when Andross does it,' she said.

'Yes.' Emphatically.

'Because you can tell I love you and want the best for you.'

'Love me?' Kip scoffed. 'You barely know me.'

'When you have lived either a very short time or a very long time – if you've lived well – you will be able to love easily, too. Broken hearts have fresh places to bond with new faces.'

Kip wasn't sure how to take that, wasn't sure he could believe it. He said, 'You had other daughters? I mean, other than the one . . . Er, sorry.'

'Had, yes. Grandchildren, too. Had.' She stared at him for a while, inscrutably. She put away the framed card. For a moment, Kip wondered if she'd forgotten what he'd come here asking. Then he saw a twitch of amusement in her eyes. She could tell he was wondering if she was old and senile, and she was letting him wonder. It was a game to her.

And this woman was preparing for her death of old age? She was brighter than the rest of the Spectrum combined!

Kip waited.

'I'm too busy to teach you myself, though you intrigue me, little Guile. I do hope you make it to full flower. You are a boy with such potential.' She closed her eyes for a moment, upbraiding herself. 'Your pardon, a young man. I'm afraid that all men under forty are boys to me now. No, I can't teach you. I will look into the matter of this magister, though. And . . . you do need a tutor; this much is plain. You will continue with those classes she cannot teach, but in all she can, Lady Guile will be your tutor.'

'Lady Guile?' Hadn't Felia Guile joined the Freeing in Garriston? Kip wondered about that sometimes. She'd been in Garriston at the same time he had, and she'd never even asked to see him, her only grandson. Maybe a bastard was too shameful. 'Oh! You mean Karris?!'

'Mmm,' the White said, with a little smirk.

'That's great!' Kip said. Even if he was a little scared of her. She clearly knew everything, and she had his total respect.

'Attend your lectures – your *other* lectures – as usual until I can speak to her. She may need some convincing.' The White's smirk faded. 'Kip, Orholam walks men through fires every day. I believe that. But before you walk through fire, make certain it's one he's asked you to walk through.'

Chapter 29

After three days, the storm abated. Gunner had the *Bitter Cob* drop anchor in the lee of some little island while he waited for the skies to clear so they could find their bearings. The pirates were good enough to feed the slaves before they slept.

Gunner was fastidious in keeping his goods performing at their highest potential.

Gavin slept like a stone, woke, and slept again. He dreamed again, and knew he was dreaming. He was a child, and everyone was gone. Mother and father were at the Chromeria: father for some ceremonies, and mother to be near him. Gavin got to go with them because he was older. Dazen and Sevastian had to stay home with the servants and house slaves. Dazen woke alone in his bed, and thought of calling for his nurse. He was eleven years old, almost. Too old to be afraid of the dark. He wasn't sure what he'd heard, but he lay in bed, listening, almost too scared to breathe.

He was eleven. Too old to be such a scaredy.

Throwing off the covers, he reached from his bed to where his child-sized sword had fallen, trying to pick it up without stepping out of bed. It was too far away. He took his blanket and threw it over the sword, holding on to one edge. He pulled it toward himself, and it dragged the sword a little. In three more tries, he had it.

Swallowing, he drew the sword out of the scabbard. He heard glass break. It sounded like it came from outside, but he knew that was a trick of how the Guile home was laid out. The doors were huge, thick. Breaking glass could only mean that one of the other windows had been smashed down the hall. Sevastian's room!

Dazen forgot his fear and jumped out of bed.

He threw his door open and ran. The hallway stretched longer and longer. He reached a full sprint, but the walls deformed. He was getting shorter and shorter, fading, fading.

When he reached Sevastian's door, his hand passed through the latch. He couldn't touch anything. Couldn't change anything. His hand passed through the wood, too.

He threw himself at the door – through the door.

The blue wight snarled, standing over Sevastian's bed, all blue skin and red blood. It jumped up to the window and disappeared into the night. Dazen only saw his little brother's bloodied, broken body. He screamed. The smell of blood washed over him as he picked up Sevastian.

He was dead. The little boy had been pierced, a sword stroke or a spear thrust right in the middle of his chest. Little Dazen, wailing inconsolably, had no space for any other thought, but the dreamer saw more than he remembered. That sword or spear thrust had hit Sevastian high in the chest and come out the middle of his back. Sevastian had stood to confront the intruder, and been slain where he stood. A single, sure stroke. Good-hearted little Sevastian hadn't even had time to dodge or fight, hadn't believed someone would come to murder him in the night.

His own hands smearing blood on Sevastian's perfect, angelic face, Dazen wailed. Lying there, eyes closed, Sevastian could have been sleeping. Dazen shook him.

'Wake up! Wake up!'

Gavin woke to Orholam shaking him.

It took Gavin long moments for rocking of the ship and the hardness of the wood under his back to sink in. One nightmare to another.

'These are the dreams you send me, Orholam?' he demanded. 'Go to hell!'

Chapter 30

'Sailing galley. Ilytian canvas,' Leonus said.

Gavin thought it was horrible news, but the slaves murmured like it was a good thing. 'What's that mean?' he asked.

'Ilytian canvas, uh, uh, means Ilytian ship, uh, most like. Fuck. Fuck,' Fukkelot said.

'Don't the Ilytians have the best cannons?' Gavin asked.

'Don't matter,' Bugs said, across the aisle from Gavin. The man had some sort of condition, made his eyes bulge. It was hard to look at him, even in shades of gray. 'Treat their slaves worse than they treat their dogs. Starve 'em, beat 'em so bad they can't barely row. Ilytian galley can't run as fast, can't turn as fast as we can. Not by a long sight.'

It made sense, Gavin supposed. Ilytians captured more slaves than anyone, refused to be bound by the laws on the taking of slaves that the Chromeria imposed on the other six satrapies. If slaves were cheap, there was no need to take special care of them. The dead could be easily replaced. Ilytians were real bastards.

Gunner was Ilytian.

Gavin had found the man amusing, before he was under his power. Thought it was funny to play with Gunner's mind by stoppering the man's musket rather than killing him back when he sank his ship near Garriston. If he'd killed him, he wouldn't be here now.

Funny how the mind can wander, even when rowing. Gavin's frequently bloodied hands were wrapped now in cotton. He had a new empathy for Kip, who'd burned his left hand falling into a fire before the Battle of Garriston. His hands were agony every day. He'd thought he had a man's hands before, rough and calloused. He'd given himself too much credit.

'Win or die,' Leonus shouted.

The slaves didn't shout the response. They hated Leonus.

'You worthless shit sacks! You shout back, or I'll keelhaul every last one of you! Boy!' he shouted to the young man who had taken his old job as foreman's second. 'Whip that line. Now!'

The boy hesitated.

'Now!'

The boy lashed the whip across the bare backs of one of the lower rows. They cried out in pain. More than necessary, Gavin thought, but the boy hadn't hit them as hard as Leonus liked.

'Win or die!' Leonus shouted.

'Row to hell!' the slaves replied.

'Never slack!'

'Row to hell!'

'Scratch the back of Shadow Jack!' Leonus shouted.

'Row to hell!'

'Row right back!' he shouted.

The drums began pounding out their tempo, and Leonus disappeared to the next slave deck.

'Don't think I'm going to make it through this one,' Nine said.

'You never think you're going to make it through, Itchy.'

'This time's different. I can feel it.'

As before, with scores of men sweating in the tight confines of the rowing deck, it got hot fast. It was a bright, calm day outside, which meant this would be a clean, simple race to the death.

The drums pounded their steady tempo, and Gavin rowed. And rowed. And rowed. Twenty minutes. The boy went around and gave them water. At least he didn't smash their lips with the long-handled cup. Not on purpose, anyway. Thirty minutes.

Finally, Leonus poked his ugly head belowdecks. 'Drums, *corso!*'

The drums picked up, and Gavin settled into the new tempo happily. Happily. How strange was that? There was something oddly freeing about having no decisions to make. Go when they say go. Stop when they say stop. Eat when they say eat. Avoid the lash. Take your double serving of strongwine.

What am I going to do if I get free anyway, Karris? I can't draft anymore. Will you still love me when you find out I'm not what I was?

He could imagine the looks in people's eyes, the pity. He had been respected, loved, and feared in every corner of the Seven Satrapies, but the foundation of his power had always been his drafting. He'd been so much better than everyone else – so effortlessly good – that he'd become nothing else. He wasn't a man; he was a drafter. You couldn't think about Gavin without knowing he was the Prism, that he *was* drafting. That he was the best. The best now, probably the best in hundreds of years. Without that, he was . . . what?

An arrogant figurehead who ritually murdered scores of drafters every year. A hothead who threw young women off his balcony when they displeased him. And got away with it.

Other drafters made the transition from magical power to political power with no problem. The White had done it gracefully, his father less so. But Gavin? It wasn't in him. And it was one thing to stop drafting because you believed you still had service to give; it was quite another to not be able to. A man might take an oath of celibacy and be respected; a man castrated was at best pitied.

And there was no hiding the loss. By this Sun Day, it would be over, for good or ill. He would either draft while performing the Sun Day rituals, or fail to do so, or if he didn't make it back to the Chromeria by then, someone else would be named Prism. It was that simple. How far away was that now? Four months?

Karris, my life will be over in four months. No matter what. I'm so sorry. I wasted so much time. I wanted us to have a life. I wanted us to have children, to see you holding new life in your hands, to be whole with you.

Gavin suddenly wanted to vomit, and it wasn't from the exertion.

The drummer sped the tempo again, and Gavin didn't care. And again, the last sprint, but his mind was still, impenetrable, the actions all at a long remove.

Then, a shouted order, and the slaves stowed their oars with unhurried precision.

With the crash, Gavin was thrown out of his reverie. Wood screaming on wood. Oars snapping like kindling. Men shouting in pain and fear and rage. Muskets rattling. A cannon booming. The stench of black powder and fear. Men thrown off their benches. Gavin found himself staring at a gap-toothed sailor in the other ship. The man was standing up, having been thrown down by the collision. He had a slow match in hand, and was right behind a charged cannon.

Gavin flung out a hand, willing a spike of blue to fly into the man's eyes.

Nothing.

The man looked at him quizzically, then an oar cracked his face. He dropped, but someone else grabbed the slowmatch.

The ships continued their slide past each other, and the cannon boomed. Wood exploded, tearing the steps off and filling the slaves' deck with burning hot blinding smoke. The *Bitter Cob*'s cabin boy staggered past Gavin's bench in the smoke, twisted metal protruding from his back.

Another cannon boomed, tearing a hole upward, letting dazzling sunlight in, illuminating the roiling black smoke. The very air seemed on fire. All the slaves were coughing, lying down, abandoning their task of stabbing their counterparts with the oars.

Gavin heard the clatter of the grappling hooks at the end of the boarding nets as they were thrown across the now widening gap between the ships. Pirates were shouting, and the distinctive crack of Captain Gunner's musket sounded with a frequency that shouldn't have been possible. Shouted orders, and the clatter of feet across the decks over their heads, and the pirates boarded the other ship.

Then, abruptly, the *Bitter Cob* was quiet. The wind blowing through the oar-holes and the two big holes from cannon fire began dispersing the smoke. The slaves began sitting up, assessing the damage, even as screams for mercy and shouts of rage sounded from the other ship just paces away.

The cabin boy was dead, or unconscious and on his way to dead, lying in the center aisle. A young kid, and not possessed of good looks or virtue, but not deserving this, regardless.

The stairs up to the second deck were half torn off. Half a row of slaves had been pulverized. Blood slicked the deck in the back rows.

Before Gavin could even complete an inventory, someone swung down from the boarding nets and dropped in through the hole the cannon had blasted. He clambered for a bit, almost losing his balance. Any of the slaves nearby could have knocked him into the sea, but they were all frozen with surprise. The man was light-skinned, blond, dressed richly. Gavin didn't recognize him immediately as one of the crew. Worse, it didn't look like any of the other slaves did, either. He wasn't one of the *Bitter Cob*'s sailors, and he had a sword.

'I'm not going to hurt you,' he said. 'If you'll row for me, I'll free you.' He let that sink in for a second, then said, 'I'll free you now if you'll help me throw off the boarding nets. But quick!'

With his voice, Gavin placed him immediately. The young man could only be Antonius Malargos, a cousin of Tisis Malargos, who had become the Green briefly, before Gavin had deposed her, and a nephew of Dervani Malargos, who had become a god briefly, before Gavin had killed him.

'Who's with me?' Antonius asked.

A slave raised his manacled hand, and Antonius's pale skin lit with red luxin. He filled the lock with red luxin and then set it alight, burning it out. It burned the slave's wrist, too, but he was free.

'Quickly! We have only moments,' Antonius said. 'Most of the pirates are on the other ship. We kill the few men still here, cut the boarding nets, and push off. I'll free you all, I swear it on Orholam's name.'

It was a decent plan, if a desperate one. The other galley didn't have any oars on one side. If Antonius could seize the *Bitter Cob* and throw off the boarding nets, he'd have a good chance. If he made it ten paces, he'd probably make it back to port.

And as a Malargos, he had no reason to make sure Gavin made it home alive. In his place, Gavin didn't think he'd bring Antonius home. His family's mortal enemy, delivered into his hand. Gavin's heart despaired.

He saw Leonus had fallen between two slaves' benches. The man had struggled to his hands and knees. He was bleeding a stream from his scalp. Looked worse than it was: scalp wounds bleed heavily. But he did look woozy. Should Gavin warn Antonius?

A slave behind Gavin raised manacled hands. Antonius sighed with relief that another slave was taking his offer. He began walking back toward him. His eyes fell on Gavin, then moved on. No recognition. The Prism was dead. This bearded creature in rags and filth was nothing.

Gavin felt sudden hope that he might live, and a sense of the most profound divorce from himself he'd ever known. Antonius had seen Gavin in person before, and seen his face reproduced in a thousand paintings, etchings, and mosaics. And he didn't *see* him. He saw a slave. Gavin had thought himself inseparable from his power, from his title, from his position. He wasn't even inseparable from his own face.

Antonius stopped. Looked at Gavin again quizzically. His eyes widened. Gavin missed whatever happened on the boy's face next because he was looking at the boy's raised sword. So much revenge for the Malargos family, that close.

Gavin knew death, and he watched it coming, unblinking.

Antonius dropped to his knees. 'Your Holiness? You live!'

Gavin's eyes snapped back to the boy's. Far from thirsty for vengeance, if anything, Antonius looked on the verge of tears. Tears of worship, adoration, hope.

A child, not bound by what his parents hated. An innocent, putting his faith in a man he'd never met.

'Your Holiness, let's get these chains off you!'

How long had it been since Gavin had seen such goodness? How long since he'd felt it himself? Too long, and now it was too—

Too late, Gavin saw the movement. Leonus lurched to his feet behind Antonius. Gavin's hand shot out to stop him – and was jerked short as he reached the end of his chain, the manacle biting into his wrist, bloodying it. Worse, stopping it. But all Gavin saw was Leonus, crashing into Antonius's back, blade first. He tackled the young man into Gavin, stabbing repeatedly. Gavin was carried off the back of his bench by their momentum, the bench cutting his knees out from under him. The oar overhead and his manacles kept him from falling all the way to the ground, as his oarmates first were caught unprepared, and then tried to help drag Gavin out of harm's way.

Gavin couldn't move fast enough. He pulled the bandages from his hands, unraveling them as fast as possible, and lashed out with a knee. He missed because he was held too far away, then he kicked out with one bare foot at Leonus. Somehow, he hit the man in the throat.

Leonus rolled back on his heels, gasping. It gave Gavin a split second, and he used it to drape his bandages down around Leonus's neck. Once, twice, Gavin wrapped them, and then he yanked. It pulled the man off balance toward him.

Instantly abandoning his plan to strangle the man, Gavin hugged Leonus's head against his chest. With his twisted spine, Leonus's neck had grown thick as a bull's with muscle. Gavin whipped his torso left and right, left and right. He couldn't hear any crack of the neck breaking, didn't feel it, so he whipped back and forth until he was certain Leonus wasn't moving. He was a beast, and the rage was all.

And he was too late.

He released Leonus, unwrapped the bandages, and heaved his foul body into the aisle. He looked at Antonius's body lying between the benches.

Lying between the benches . . . and blinking up at Gavin. 'I think I owe my aunt Eirene an apology,' the boy said, very much alive. He spread one of the cut gaps in his tunic, showing a coat of the finest Ilytian mesh-steel beneath it. 'She gave me this for my birthday. I asked for a racehorse. I complained.'

'F-fuck,' Fukkelot said, impressed.

Antonius jumped to his feet, shaking it off. He began patting his pockets, looking for something. 'My spectacles. My red spectacles! Where are they? I can't burn open your manacles without them!'

The slaves began looking around furiously. Suddenly, freedom was this close – and with Leonus dead, it suddenly seemed real.

'Ah!' someone cried out. He lifted a mangled frame, the red lenses shattered to dust and tiny bits nowhere near big enough to draft through. There was blood on the deck – could it be enough? No, there wasn't enough light. To Gavin's eyes, it was a black pool.

Then Orholam stood. He lifted a hand. He held the manacle key.

Chapter 31

Arys Greenveil rose from the bed where her new lover lay spent. She drew a silk robe around her heavily pregnant belly. Child number thirteen didn't seem to want to leave her womb yet. Stubborn, like his mother. Her own mother had taught her that lovemaking would help convince a child to come to the light, and Arys had no baseline to say her mother was wrong – she'd tried it with every pregnancy. With her third, Jalen, her climax agonies had melded directly to labor pains, and Jalen was the sweetest of her children by far.

But this boy, number thirteen – the number of Orholam added to the number of man – he was going to be special, she knew it. Just as she knew it was going to be a boy. She moved to her desk and began reading her correspondence.

The correspondence never ended for Arys Sub-red. Letters from her satrap, of course, but also letters from family begging favors, from family friends begging favors, from friends of family friends begging favors. There were people asking favors for things she couldn't control in a hundred years. Her secretary, mercifully, separated all the beggars into stacks, and usually did an excellent job of it, but there were things a woman had to do herself.

Arys kept her own lists of favors granted and favors owed, and when she could, she matched those back and forth, trading up favors so that the right people would owe her for times such as this. Her home satrapy, Blood Forest, was going to be invaded, perhaps within weeks. The news wasn't encouraging. Against orders, General Azmith was preparing to make a grand stand at a town named Ox Ford on the Ao River. Her sources didn't think much of the man, or of the plan.

Atash had fallen as fast as a bard's pants, barely slowing the Color Prince's advance. If this wild gamble at Ox Ford didn't work, her own people were next. Arys would do anything she had to do to save her people.

She looked at one of her personal letters. It was from her sister, Ela. Ela was at least as passionate as Arys, and not half as wise. Ela claimed that Gavin Guile had seduced and murdered her daughter, Ana. She begged, demanded, ordered, and begged again that Arys do everything in her power to avenge her niece.

Not that Arys had been sitting still. As soon as she'd heard Ana had died, she'd begun investigating. Of one thing she was certain: Gavin hadn't seduced Ana; Ana had been trying to seduce Gavin. According to her roommate, Ana had tried half a dozen times despite increasingly firm rebuffs. The roommate had also said that Ana had been under intense pressure from her mother Ela to seduce Gavin, though that had taken some prodding to get out of the frightened girl. Whatever had happened in that room, Ana, the damned fool girl, had gone there of her own accord, and she shouldn't have been there. The Blackguards on duty had sworn, at least three times, that Gavin had screamed in fury at the girl and she'd jumped off the balcony in terror.

Ana had been a pretty girl, and love her though she did,

Arys had thought she was spoiled horribly. When people had less than half a dozen children, they always spoiled them. Ana had probably never had a man scream at her in her life. And yet, jumping off a balcony?

Was Ana *that* stupid? Arys didn't think so, but there was no way to prove it, was there? There were three witnesses, and they all said the same thing. Arys had hired the most beautiful courtesan she could find, and paid the woman a ruinous sum to seduce one of the young Blackguards who'd been there, a Gill Greyling. The courtesan had seduced him, got him drunk, and asked him about the event. His story hadn't changed. The courtesan said she thought he was lying, but if a man wouldn't let go of a lie when drunk and blinded by lust, there was no shaking it from him. It was a dead end, a sadly literal one.

Damn you, sister. What was the worst that could be true of Gavin Guile here? That he got furious at the daughter that you'd sent to seduce him repeatedly, and when she'd succeeded in getting into his bed and nearly ruining his relationship with Karris White Oak, whom everyone knew he'd loved for fifteen years, Gavin threw her off the balcony? If that was what had happened, Ela was as responsible for it as anyone.

Not that Arys wouldn't make Gavin pay for it, too, if she ever found out that was true. Family was everything. The Greenveil motto was *Fásann Ár Gciorcal*, Our Circle Grows. 'Circle' was understood to be family, and territory, and friends, and influence. Orholam knew that Arys had done her part on that account, and more. But anyone shrinking that circle would pay – damn it, Ana. Arys had liked the girl, mostly, though Ana had tried her luck seducing men who had been interested in Arys herself. Shooting high, and sometimes artlessly. How, though, was one to object to will in a drafter? Ana had been pretty enough to mostly go unpunished.

And found punishment too great by far.

But Gavin Guile was out of reach for the time being. Someday, Arys would ask him herself. Certainly she would before she voted his way ever again – but it wouldn't affect her vote in the end. She was practical, eminently practical. As practical as any sub-red had ever been, she liked to think.

And knowing that she was always laid up for a few days

at least after a birth, she quite practically moved on to her stack of must-read letters.

Another from her satrap, Briun Willow Bough, telling her things she already knew. Urgent, help immediately, you serve for such a time as this, et cetera. What did he think Arys was doing here, anyway? At the end, the letter asked if she needed to be replaced because she was too pregnant. Arys saw red. Too pregnant? That upjumped son of a carter was questioning *her*? She'd rip his squinty right eye out, pound it flat with a meat hammer, pan fry and feed it to that slobbering stupid piece of—

She breathed slowly. Easy, Ary.

The sub-red was close, always close these days. Two more years, Arys. You can make two more years if you're careful.

She put that letter down in a different stack. She'd have to answer that when she was no longer furious. Sometimes she hated her work. She caught a glimpse of her lover stirring in her mirror.

The work did have its perquisites, though, she supposed.

With her unfashionable red-red straight hair and freckles, many other women of thirty-five years would find it difficult to procure lovers. She did what she could to darken her skin and hide the freckles and the worry-lines, and few would guess that she'd had twelve children (though, honestly, most would guess she'd had one or two), but even dressed well, Arys's beauty was not the type of beauty that was celebrated at the Chromeria. Her blue eyes were her best feature – everyone loved blue eyes. But she'd had a lover – in her younger days, before she figured out how to pick men who knew the proper use for their tongues – who, immediately after they'd made love, had told her that her freckles were a tragedy. That otherwise she would be a beauty men would praise to the stars.

She'd been young, and not so good with her impulses as now. She'd grabbed his stones and tried to rip them off. She'd broken all of her nails, but his scrotum had torn in her hand. And then he'd beaten her fiercely.

It was easy to forget when you had so much power that sometimes the only power that mattered was the power of muscles.

It had taken her a minute to even remember she could draft

216

while being battered and thrown against the wall by that screaming, terrified, furious man, holding his torn scrotum in one hand and making a fist with the other. And then, drafting at long last, she'd burnt him to a husk. She'd lost the baby she was pregnant with at the time, and had never known if it was from the beating or from the huge amounts of heat that she'd drafted. Either would have been sufficient, she supposed.

She was at peace with her relative good looks now. Power made up for it. Pretty men and boys sought her out. Mostly, though, she preferred those who were not too pretty, but were instead strong enough to bring good blood to the Greenveil family, either drafters, or intelligent, or charismatic – they had to have some excellence, when she was looking for a father. Her current lover was probably a short-termer, though. Elijah was terribly interesting with his amber eyes, and wonderfully willful, a skilled lover, intelligent, and there was something oddly dangerous about him. But she wasn't sure she wanted him to be the father of child fourteen. She doubted she would keep him for another six months. But in the meantime, she planned to enjoy herself.

Drafting a little sub-red, she inhaled deeply. The sub-red blew on the coals of her lust.

'Elijah?' she said.

He sat up on the bed. He was exactly what she liked at this point in her life. Lean and muscular, with some interesting scars on his arms and chest, he kept his orangey-red hair cut close to his skull, his freckles were faded on his face and arms, his skin was ruddy, and he had beautifully white teeth. He looked at her – pregnant as she was – with undisguised desire. Having a man who would worship your body when you were hugely pregnant and awkward was perhaps the greatest luxury a woman could have.

But as she stood to go to him, she felt the familiar tightening in her belly. She hesitated. She'd been having practice labor pains for months, and she wanted to be sure.

Elijah stood and walked over to her, naked. 'Is it time?' he asked. He held her from behind, kissing her neck and cupping her swollen breasts in his hands.

She couldn't breathe for a moment. Her stomach felt as tight as a drum.

'Yes,' she said finally, pushing his hands away. 'I have to prepare myself. If there's time between cramps, I may need you again. Get dressed.'

'Do you need me to summon your slaves?' Elijah asked.

She hesitated. The pain passed. 'Not yet. It may be hours yet. Maybe you can put on that cloak of yours and nothing underneath,' she said. Truth was, she couldn't imagine making love now that she'd actually started labor. But if it was false labor, she wanted him here. She could fuck out her frustration.

If she were honest with herself, she wanted him here regardless. If there was one thing she regretted about not having married just one man, it was in a few times like this, where she wanted someone to love her and worry about her and try to protect her foolishly from things he couldn't protect her from. She wanted to tell Elijah she needed him for that, but she couldn't.

She sat at her mirror, drew out her kohls, powders, paints in grease to withstand the sweat that would be her lot for the next hours. The Greenveils were from the deep forest, and they kept the old ways in this. New lands and new titles were well and good, but he who loses the center of his circle is lost. Like the pygmies from whom they were long ago descended, the Greenveil women prepared for childbirth as for battle. Arys was a good hand with the paints. Before she'd risen so high that it was unseemly for her to help other women with their makeup, she'd done it often. She missed it.

For her first few children, she'd planned elaborately what her paint would look like, believing it would be an omen for how the child's spirit would turn out. She'd given up on that, and drew as the whim took her when she sat. She bound her long red hair back in simple braids, and applied the nine black dots across her forehead symmetrically around what would become a drawing of a fire crystal, then she connected the dots with yellow paints, making wings sweeping out toward her temples. An inverted triangle under one eye, a tear under the other. She had barely touched the rouge to her lips when the next cramp hit her, taking her breath, sending lightning through her belly to her back.

She paused, eyes closed, for a full minute. Then, though the pain hadn't passed, she continued with her rouge. Lips full and red, exaggerated. Lines of gold paint to emphasize her cheekbones. The contraction eased and she worked more quickly. Thorns.

How could one forget this pain? How could anyone want to go through this more than once?

Arys drew black thorns on the back of each hand, down the fronts of her thighs, in the center of her chest, bracketing her breasts, bracketing her swollen belly.

It wasn't good enough for the perfectionist in her, but as the next contraction hit, Arys decided it was good enough. She reached for her bell.

And Elijah trapped her be-thorned hand.

'What are you doing?' she asked.

'I could ask the same,' he said. 'Nine points on your forehead? For nine gods you never knew?'

There was something odd in his amber eyes. His smile was a little too big, and so white. 'Elijah, this is not the time,' she said.

'Oh, Arys, but this is exactly the time. I need you to listen closely to me for a very few minutes, and then make the most important decision of your life.' He lifted her hand from the bell. 'Would you like me to help you with your paint? I've got quite a delicate hand for this sort of thing.'

'No!' she said. 'Take your hands off me or I'll scream.'

'If you scream, you and your baby both will die.'

He said the words in such a pleasantly neutral voice that she couldn't believe she'd heard him correctly. She froze.

'I seduced you so that I could be here at this very moment, Arys Greenveil. My name isn't Elijah, it's Murder Sharp, of the Order of the Broken Eye. But I do some sidework, too. And when I can satisfy two factions at once . . .' He smiled. 'I'm a very special kind of drafter. I can kill you without leaving a trace. And I can get away with it. Childbirth is so very dangerous, isn't it? Especially for an older woman like you. And before you try anything, please know that I can kill you very, very quickly and silently. If you say anything, you'll die. Your death would please one of my employers more than the other, but it would upset me greatly. Nonetheless, all are free in the light. Light cannot be chained, nor can the will of any drafter.'

The contraction eased enough for her to take another breath, and she felt utter dread. He'd betrayed her! Made her look a fool. Her fury gathered, and the sub-red that had become part of her, body and mind, blew on those flames.

Elijah slapped her. Not hard enough to leave a mark for long, but hard enough to stun her. 'Think of your child, you fool,' he said. 'I haven't even told you the deal yet. Listen.'

A sudden contraction seemed to tear her in half. She couldn't have spoken if she wanted to.

'I need your vote, and your silence. When the Spectrum next meets, they will take up the matter of voting to make Andross Guile the promachos. You will vote for him. In return, when it is time, Andross will help make one of your sons or daughters a Color, and he will send help immediately for your family and your country against the Color Prince. It's a generous offer. There will be no counter. He also buys your silence about this visit. If you ever break this silence, I will personally kill all of your children, your sisters, and your brother. I will be a plague that sweeps through your house. In fact, that will be the excuse we use for so many deaths in one family – a plague.'

By the time the pain passed, Arys had recovered her wits. 'Why would you do this? Are you not working with the heretics?'

'The Order of the Broken Eye is . . . practical. You should admire that. If working for Andross Guile helps us for now, why should we not? But killing a Color is something the Order loves.'

'Help me stand,' she said. 'I need to walk to the birthing stall.' She reached up. Suddenly, one of her arms dropped, swinging dead to her side and slamming into her chair.

'You don't need to go there yet. I'm not so ignorant. Nor should you be ignorant of my power. That is the smallest fraction of it,' Murder said. He made a flicking gesture, and her arm began tingling, feeling slowly suffusing the flesh once more. 'By the way, it's a boy. Do you want me to stop his heart? Is that what you need to be convinced?'

'You monster.'

'War makes monsters of us all, and Lucidonius started this war, not us.'

'Go to hell.'

'That's your answer? That's your vote?' Murder asked.

'You wouldn't kill the baby. I've looked into your eyes as we made love. I've seen your soul, Elijah.' She couldn't have been so wrong about him, could she? She'd looked to him for his body, his flattery, his willfulness, and his quick tongue. And she'd barely looked at him at all, past that. He'd been a diversion. She began to ease open the drawer with her knee.

'Elijah was my name, once,' he said. He sounded wistful. 'I gave it up when I took the blinkers off my eyes to see the glories of a world unchained. I liked it when you said my name. I still do. Arys,' he said, his tone sharp suddenly, 'I know you've got a pistol in that drawer. I unloaded it.'

She stopped moving.

'I enjoyed my time with you far more than I thought I would, High Lady Greenveil. You're beautiful and intelligent and wilder than any woman I've had in years. You can say no to Andross Guile, because to hell with him, right? I understand. I've wanted to say it a time or three myself. If you say no but keep your silence about me, I'll let the baby live. And I'll make your passing as painless as possible.'

'I could lie.'

'There are six of your children on Big Jasper. Do you think you can get them off the island without Andross knowing what ship they're on? Because if you lie, they die first. Then I go to Green Haven and work through your circle. It will not disappear altogether; my reach is not so great, nor my time infinite. But a plague can undo an entire life's work in days.'

'You're that kind of butcher?'

'I am a holy warrior. I do not always enjoy my orders, but I always obey them.' His voice was low, but filled with conviction.

'I should have seen it,' she said. When she'd been young, she'd looked into each of the many who tried to woo her with a paranoid focus. In recent years, she hadn't paid as much attention. Too much sub-red, too long with fading looks.

He didn't answer, didn't tell her that he was very good at

what he did. Of course he was. They would have only sent the best.

'Lunna Green?' she asked suddenly. The Color had died inexplicably a few months ago.

He nodded, acknowledging it was his work.

'Who was that for? Guile or your order or both?'

He shook his head. 'You don't need to know.'

'Help me to the birthing stall,' she said. She would die squatting, as many a woman in her line had done before her.

'You need not my help nor any man's,' Elijah said.

It was true. Her last gasp of hope – using some martial art against him – was ridiculous in her pregnant state anyway. Better not to lose her dignity.

Dignity. I think about dignity, on my way to the birthing stalls? I *am* getting old. She looked at Elijah as he donned his gray cloak. He pulled a golden choker attached to chains within the cloak out of a pocket along the neck and fastened it tight against his skin.

'That your idea of freedom?' she asked.

'I serve in chains that others may live without them,' Elijah said. But he wasn't her Elijah anymore.

'One day, in your perfect world?' she asked.

'One day,' he agreed.

She stood, on her own. 'You'll wait until after the babe is born?'

'I will.' He paused, suddenly awkward for the first time. 'I'm afraid I'll also need one of your teeth. I'll wait until after, though. I just thought you, you should know. Your third molar on the left is quite beautiful.'

'I suppose I shan't be needing it,' she said, genuinely puzzled.

He seemed relieved that she didn't panic or insult him.

'How do you intend to stay hid— Oh,' she said as he closed his cloak and, after a shimmery wave passed through his cloak, disappeared, every part of him becoming identical to the wall behind him except for his bright bright amber eyes, which appeared to hang in space. She opened her eyes to sub-red, and there he stood. Clever, some mist walker's cloak out of story. So that was how he intended to be in the room where no men were allowed. That was how he intended to know if she complied.

Some small part of her was outraged that her murderer should watch her in such intimate moments, moments meant only to be shared among women. But that part of her was small, and tired. She hurt, and it was enough that the hurting would end. Not just the hurting of pregnancy, but the hurt of healing again, of cracked nipples and sleepless nights – the Greenveils kept the old ways, and took care of their own, no nursemaids, no surrendering the pleasures and pains of parenting to another. Family roots must be nourished first if they are to bear much fruit later. She hurt from the drafting, and the wanting to draft. Every pregnancy, she had more trouble stopping, and she felt sub-red's grip redouble on her when she went back to it. She didn't know how much longer she'd make. She'd told herself two years. She'd been flattering herself.

But cowardice and treason was impossible. Another contraction came upon her, and when it passed, she knew she was willing for there to be an end. She had one more fight left in her. One last, precious fight, but not a fight to kill. She would war with her flesh to push one more child to the light, and then she would lay down her burdens and trust the circle she'd grown to take care of its own.

She reached for the bell to summon her slaves. 'May my curse live on you, Murder Sharp.'

'And my blessing on you, Arys. I will make it painless.'

'Tell Andross Guile to fuck himself,' she said. She rang the bell.

Chapter 32

Is this to be my life now? Meetings and spying and listening and posturing? The backstabbings that Karris had once had to worry about as a Blackguard had been literal ones. Here, you never saw the blood.

Though to be fair, a metaphorical backstabbing here could lead to the actual death of thousands, not just one. Hmm. That thought put a little extra urgency to the verbal fencing, didn't it? Especially when Karris looked around the Spectrum's chamber and wasn't terribly impressed by what she saw.

Colors were supposed to be chosen by their satrap for their excellence and their piety. In truth, as with all positions of great power, it was far more complicated. Family loyalties, outright bribes, and even mistakes by the contending families could have led to a Klytos Blue being selected. And depending on the strength of the satrap or satrapah who appointed the Color, the Color might be a puppet, a representative, a delegate, or a loose cannon.

It hadn't always been thus. The satraps had once been veritable kings, with the Spectrum having to wait weeks or months to vote on the simplest measures as the Colors waited for their satraps' commands. Successive Whites and Prisms and Colors had worked together – united in this – to concentrate power here, at the Chromeria, and here, in this very room.

And still it bored Karris. Boredom was dangerous. A Blackguard knew that. Boredom made you sloppy, careless, and dead. You couldn't get sloppy around Andross Guile. They were waiting for the arrival of a few of the Colors still. Andross had called the meeting. Karris studied the figure across the table.

There was something different about him. Something that had changed over the course of the last weeks. In her time as a Blackguard, Karris's identification of potential threats had always been intuitive. Her training had taught her to translate those gut feelings – not just seeing a holistic threat, but realizing that the man was sweating, twitchy, not paying attention to what others around him were. Since the Battle of Ru, Karris had felt more and more that Andross Guile was a threat.

She'd dismissed it as hypervigilance, paranoia, hatred. Now that she had married his wayward son, which he had opposed for almost two decades, he had more reason to hate her than ever. There were a thousand reasons to see Andross as a threat. But why did she now see him as the kind of threat that made her Blackguard intuitions tingle?

Andross had always been a threat, always had power close

at hand. But that power hadn't been physical in years. Now . . . something was different.

He wasn't slouching anymore. In fact, he'd stopped slouching immediately after Ru, hadn't he? He seemed stronger, had regained that Guile broadness of shoulders, perhaps simply from holding himself well again, but perhaps it was new musculature – or worse. And he walked faster. Why? He was older. He'd lost his last son. If anything, a normal man would be weakened by such things, would be hastened toward the grave. But not Andross Guile.

Orholam have mercy, he'd gone red wight. Right under their noses. He'd been aggressive and willful for so long that no one had noticed his transition. Red to red wight.

Karris felt short of breath. She knew wights. Had hunted them with Gavin. Some could maintain the mask of sanity for months. They were a walking blasphemy, but they could speak of Orholam. They could hide almost anything – but they couldn't hide their eyes.

And Andross Guile had been hiding his eyes for years. Blocking the light, blocking temptation, he said. What if, instead, he was blocking everyone else from discovering what he was?

Karris reached to her hip unconsciously, but there was no ataghan there, no bich'hwa on the other side. Her own breath was harsh in her ears as her pulse picked up, as the battle juice began to flow. He would see her, he would take one look at her face, and he would know.

Indeed, these spectacles were different from the black lenses he'd worn before Ru. These were merely dark. He was no longer blind. No longer needed to be, because he wasn't afraid of the temptations to draft – he'd already given in to them.

And now her rational mind picked up those details she should have seen before – Andross looking straight at people, noticing visual details that he shouldn't have seen if he'd been blinded by blackened lenses. Mistakes, sloppy mistakes for a man keeping a secret. Perhaps understandable mistakes for a red wight, though. They were not known for their discretion.

Part of Karris was terrified – but part of her rejoiced. If he was a wight, he could be unmasked. Unmasked, he would be Freed immediately, Color or no Color. And then he would be gone. Dear Orholam, she could finally be rid of him.

She knew that a better woman would mourn losing her father-in-law to a violent death, would mourn even more that he had embraced madness and blasphemy rather than taking a dignified exit – but Karris wasn't that woman. She wanted Andross Guile dead, dead, dead. And if he were shamed and denounced in the process, so much the better.

As Delara Orange came in, reeking of brandy, Karris started scheming how she would unveil Andross, and how she would get a weapon beforehand. Wights who were unmasked were often devastatingly fast in their response, and people facing a wight who'd thought the person was their loved one were often tragically slow. Even Blackguards.

And it was the Blackguards who had the only weapons in this room.

Perhaps, then, magic was the way. She would have to watch Andross's skin – but the wily old goat was covered from head to toe, even wearing gloves.

Proof, then.

Karris had sworn not to draft, but she wasn't going to take that obedience – intended to keep her alive for longer – to be an order to die. She wondered if she could fill herself with green luxin without any of these drafters or Blackguards noticing. Out of all the people in the world, these people would be the hardest to hide such a thing from.

And yet there was no other way.

Karris leaned over, putting her elbows on the tabletop, scooting her chair back, in a most unladylike but thoughtful pose. She looked from person to person at the table, but it was all a show. She wasn't thinking; she was hoping.

The White was wheeled in slowly, and she appeared drawn and defeated. Karris sat up, and as if realizing that her chair was blocking the White's wheeled chair's path, she stood, bumping the young Blackguard Gavin Greyling. She scooted her chair in with an apology and moved out of the way, then sat, dropping the dagger she'd lifted into a pocket.

A dagger, against a red wight. Not the odds she'd want, but

it was good to have a backup if she weren't able to draft before he attacked.

'Before we bring this meeting to order,' the White said, 'I'm afraid I bear sad tidings. Our friend and colleague Arys Greenveil has passed away in childbirth this afternoon.'

'Orholam have mercy,' Orange said. She put her hand to her mouth.

'No, no, no,' Jia Tolver said. The Sub-red was her cousin.

'What happened?' Andross Guile asked.

The White shook her head. 'Her chirurgeons said that she seemed unusually tense, that she knew something was wrong, but she wouldn't say what. She only cared about her babe, Ben-Oni, she named him, Son of my Agony. After she heard his first cries, she hugged him, looked into the distance, and lost consciousness. She never woke.'

'Damn her,' Delara Orange said with real grief, 'I told her she couldn't keep having children forever.'

'We each serve as best we know,' Andross said quietly. It was meant to be comforting, and for a moment, Karris believed him. She'd forgotten that before he'd become the spider, he'd been a man of charisma almost as great as his son's.

She looked at him now, wondering. Could a red wight maintain such a façade? Perhaps grief was a passion, too.

The Spectrum joined the White in a prayer for the deceased, and Karris found some peace in the cadences, rising and falling. Dead during childbirth. She remembered her own childbirth. The pain. She'd thought she was dying herself. She had wanted to die, for a time. And then she'd realized she didn't hate herself, she hated her weakness. She'd come back, remade herself, joined the Blackguard, become brave.

And yet she'd run from that child. Was still running. Still felt sick at the very thought of it. She hadn't told Gavin about it, when he'd exposed all of his shameful secrets to her. He'd bared his throat to her, and she'd held him and listened, as if she were pure.

Her child – her son, for they'd told her the gender of her child by accident, though she'd begged them not to – was out there now, deep in the woods of Blood Forest, right in the path of an army of wights. It turned her stomach.

You can't run forever, Karris.

'I'm sorry to intrude on our grief,' Andross Guile said, finally, when the prayers were finished. 'But as we all know, these present crises give us little respite, no matter how much we need it.'

'Oh, for fuck's sake, Andross,' Delara said. 'Bring your business.'

Karris grabbed for the dagger in her pocket. A red wight, rudely contradicted? Powder, meet sparks. But . . .

Andross Guile smiled sadly. 'Delara, I'm sorry,' he said. 'I've been rude to you. Unfeeling. You've endured much in these last months, and I've added to your burdens, not eased them. I beg your forgiveness.' At first, Karris thought he must be mocking her, a snide, stone-cold deadpan sarcasm. But his gestures were placating, his tone sincere.

Someone leaned back in her chair, and when it creaked, the whole room could hear it, loud as a musket shot.

Andross Guile looked down at his lap, as if ashamed. 'These last years have been hard for me. I have seen my own power shrink. I stopped drafting to retain my sanity, and it was like shutting off the tap to Orholam's majesty for me. I have lived in darkness. The physical darkness made me sick, and became moral darkness as well. I have only thought of myself. I mistreated you, my fellow Colors, and I abused those closest to me: my last remaining son and my wife. Now both of those have been taken from me. My wife took the Freeing against my wishes. Slipped away because she feared – rightly – that I wouldn't give her my permission. When I lost my last son—' He stopped, a hitch in his voice.

He raised his head and turned his bespectacled eyes toward the White. 'You and I have jousted for years,' he said sadly. 'And for years, I have resisted your wisdom. For years, I have been on the very edge of the halo. I took to wearing gloves, and black spectacles, not just to shield myself from light, but to shield myself from your sight. So you wouldn't know how close to that fire I stood.' He heaved a sigh, and Karris gripped her dagger tightly, wondering if he would shoot out of his chair and start killing.

'It is time,' Andross said, 'for truth.'

Karris widened her stance, putting her feet on either side of her chair so she could jump.

Andross began tugging off his long gloves. 'At our last meeting, I am ashamed to confess it, but I was at the break point, and when we prayed for a miracle, I had only a mustard seed of faith that Orholam could do anything for us. For me.' He looked up, intensity writ in every line of his face. 'But I am here to tell you today that Orholam is *mighty*. And he is good. I fell asleep at prayer, believing nothing could save me, ready to suicide when I woke. I slept. I dreamed. In my dream, Orholam told me that old and frail as I am, he is greater than my frailties. He is magnified in my weakness. He is mighty to save. We are earthen vessels, but we can serve for his honor, and he will empower us to serve as he wills.' Andross took off his gloves and tossed them on the table. He threw back his hood. 'I prayed, I slept, I dreamed, I heard, and I am remade.' He opened his cloak and dropped it in his chair, and took off his darkened spectacles and dropped them on the table.

Karris had known that Andross Guile was in his mid-sixties – knowing they would die young, drafters usually married early, usually bore children as soon as possible – but in her mind she'd believed he must be ninety years old at least. He was old, he was decrepit, he had one foot in the grave.

But this Andross Guile wasn't the one she had known. She dropped her stolen dagger from nerveless fingers.

Andross Guile was bedecked in a luxin-red tunic with gold brocade that emphasized the broadness of his shoulders, the power of his straight back. His once-lank hair had been cut short, washed, combed. His skin seemed young, taut where it had been loose and flabby. But none of those were the real wonder. He laid his hands on the table, then turned them over.

Neither back nor palm was stained with red luxin. And as he turned his eyes on each Color in turn, finally coming to Karris, she saw the real miracle: Andross Guile's halos weren't even halfway through his irises. He looked like a man with ten more years of drafting in his eyes.

It was impossible. It had to be a hex, a phantasm of orange magic.

'Touch me,' he said. 'Look and see. Delara, is this a hex?'

'N-no,' she said. She didn't appear to be able to say anything else.

Jia Tolver did touch Andross. She touched his hand, his arm, in open wonder. The others needed no such proof.

'Orholam be praised,' Klytos said; and if nothing Andross had done or said for the last few minutes had seemed calculated, Klytos's invocation of Orholam certainly did. It snapped Karris back to reality. Andross Guile, whatever had happened to him, was still Andross Guile. She shouldn't lay down her wits simply because the impossible had happened. He was a Guile; the impossible always happened with that damned family.

Of course, I'm a Guile now, too. Dammit.

Andross let the silence stretch until it seemed someone else was about to fill it, and then he said, 'Orholam has charged me with a task, and has equipped me for it, and today, I ask the Spectrum to concur with his will. I am to put down this heresy, this blasphemous Color Prince, and to do so, I must be made promachos.'

It was a little rushed, but perhaps Andross Guile didn't see any benefit in waiting.

'I nominate Andross Guile to be promachos,' Klytos Blue said.

'I second my nomination,' Andross said.

'Point of order!' Delara said. 'Do we even have a quorum? Green is gone with no replacement yet named, the Prism is missing, and Arys has not yet been placed at rest.'

'The election of a promachos requires a majority of the currently serving Colors,' Andross said.

Carver Black nodded, confirming the truth of that. Everyone around the table quickly calculated what that meant. Black had no vote. White voted only in ties. With Sub-red dead and no replacement yet named for her, and Gavin missing along with the vote he carried as the representative for the exiled Tyreans who'd moved to Seers Island, a majority meant he only needed three of five.

He continued, 'It's a high hurdle, to be sure, but Orholam has given us a way to move forward despite that. You all have known me for many years, and you've known Orholam and how he works. You all know the crisis before us. I see no need for further deliberations. I call the question.'

Klytos voted yes, of course. Andross voted yes, saying that abstaining would be a false modesty. That left Jia Tolver Yellow and Delara Orange. He only needed one of them. If he lost both of them, the White would vote.

'I vote nay,' Delara Orange said, folding her arms. 'You have played me the fool for the last—'

'This is not the time for speeches,' Andross snapped. 'It's time for votes. Jia?'

Jia scowled, her unibrow squirming as her face went through a dozen expressions. 'I cannot stand in the way of Orholam. Our personal differences aside, this seems to me to be a very real miracle. I vote aye.'

A breath went out around the table.

'The ayes carry it,' the White said. Her tone and face both were inscrutable. 'We will administer the oaths of office tomorrow in the great hall. Acceptable, promachos-elect?' she asked.

'More than acceptable, High Lady.' Andross Guile smiled. He didn't even try to hide his triumph.

They were adjourned. Karris stood and walked out into the hall. She handed the dagger back to a confused Gavin Greyling as the young Blackguard stepped into the hall, but her chastising quip caught in her throat as she saw a familiar figure waddling down the hall.

'Caelia?' she asked. The little woman was not only a keen mind, she was also a drafter. Caelia had been the Third Eye's right hand, and had become indispensable to General Danavis – now Satrap Danavis – in ruling Seers Island, which Gavin had made a new satrapy. 'What are you doing— Oh no.'

'That's Caelia Green to you, appointed by Satrap Corvan Danavis of Tyrea,' the woman said with a grin. 'Boat just landed a few hours ago. Would have been here sooner, but there was some mix-up at the docks. I miss anything important?'

So that's why Andross had seemed rushed. He'd found out a dissenting vote was arriving. One vote would have been enough to ruin his plans. A mix-up at the docks? Andross's people had been stalling Caelia while the Spectrum met.

And on a difference of three minutes, all of history changes.

Chapter 33

Going back to the library after all that had happened to him since he'd been here last was eerie. Everything was exactly as it had been when Kip left. He walked past study tables with holes cut in the desktops for inkwells to rest, protecting them from being spilled. He passed down aisle after aisle of books, specially laid out to deal with the circular nature of this library, the bookcases themselves each slightly curved. This was only one of many libraries on Little Jasper, but it was the one that even first-year discipulae had access to, so it had been where he'd spent the bulk of his time.

A pang of nostalgia struck him, and he made his way to one of the desks. A stoop-shouldered nearsighted young scholar sat there. 'Excuse me,' Kip said. 'I'm looking for Rea Siluz.' The kind librarian had helped his studies of the cards and everything else. She'd also been the one who'd directed him to Janus Borig, the Mirror.

'Uh-huh,' the young man said. He turned back to his work. He had his own stacks of books and notes that he seemed deep in the middle of.

'Hey, I was—'

'There aren't any books on Rea Siluz. If you have a problem with that, lodge it with the Office of Doctrine.'

'Huh?' Kip asked. 'I'm not looking for a book on her, I'm looking for *her*. This tall, skinny, narrow face, dark hair? Usually works the late shifts?'

'Tell Timaeus very funny, and I hope his treatise rots in review.'

'I don't know anyone named T—'

'Shh!' The librarian turned back to his own work.

Kip gave up. Maybe someone in one of the later shifts would know her. Weird, though. 'I need access to the upstairs library,' Kip said.

'What year are you?' the librarian asked, peeved.

'I'm a Blackguard inductee.'

'Prove it,' the librarian said.

'Step out here for a bit,' Kip said. He cradled a fist in his other hand.

The man didn't look intimidated in the least. 'Accosting a librarian will get you banned from all libraries for a year.'

The cards spread in Kip's hand:

Ram, the bully. 'A year? Doesn't sound so bad.' A little looming, a little violence threatened. A little bit of taking a young man's physical weakness and rubbing his nose in it like dogshit. Smart Ram. 'A year?' Kip said. 'During war? And me a Blackguard, who might need this knowledge to fight? I don't think so.' Lord Ram: 'I'm a Guile. You think anyone's going to punish a Guile for breaking your face? I could throw you off a balcony, and no one would say a word.'

And he actually considered playing each, or all. He stopped, disgusted.

Come a long way since Rekton, haven't I? From powerless weakling to slaveholding bully. He had long known he was changing, but to this? Was this what he wanted to be?

'I'm sorry,' Kip said. 'It was a jest, and a poor one, unworthy of me and unfair to you. I beg your pardon.'

The librarian looked at him as if a Blackguard apologizing was the oddest sight he'd ever seen. 'Given,' he said. He shrugged. 'Name?' he asked, fishing through his piles for a list.

'Kip Guile.'

The librarian coughed. 'The Godsl— Ahem!' He shuffled his papers. Stopped. 'Uh, you can go straight up, Master Guile,' he said.

But Kip had no joy in it. Godslayer. It was another burden, another expectation, like he'd done it once, so surely he'd do it again.

'Uh, question,' Kip said. He turned on a chagrined, charming smile. 'Could I have just gone up without asking?'

'Of course. But if anyone is discovered in those libraries who is not allowed there, the penalties are severe. But we don't guard the door or anything. I mean, it's *books*.'

Good old Kip, ready to bash down doors – that were unlocked.

The first person Kip saw in the restricted library was Commander Ironfist. What?

'Commander! It's great to see you!' Kip said. 'I was kind of intimidated by the whole "restricted library"—'

The commander looked up sharply. 'I'm working, Breaker.'

'What are you working on?' Kip asked eagerly.

'Breaker. Move on.'

Kip craned his head to see the title, and read aloud, '*Mothers of Kings: An Unconventional Inquiry into Abornean Bloodlines*? What's that about? And all these others?'

'How far do you think you can run in twenty-four hours?' Ironfist asked flatly.

A dim light bloomed in Kip's tiny, tiny brain: *Warning, stupid!* 'Yes, sir!' he said, and retreated before he could hear any more words, which could only spell pain.

Kip moved to a desk where another luxiat five or six years older than him was studying. 'Pardon me, can you tell me where the genealogies are kept?'

The young luxiat looked up. His eye twitched guiltily, like he was reading something he shouldn't be. It was in some language Kip didn't know, though, so he had no idea what it was. The young luxiat scowled and said, 'You walked past it. Where that huge Blackguard is.'

Huge Blackguard? Commander Ironfist was legitimately famous. People on Big Jasper stopped and stared when they saw him, and not just because he was huge and handsome.

But the Chromeria was an enormous community, and to some, the famous people here were scholars or luxiats – people Kip had barely even seen. This young man would probably be as stunned that Kip couldn't identify the six High Luxiats as Kip was that this luxiat didn't know Ironfist. It was a little dose of humility.

Usually I need those more directly.

Anyway, much as Kip wanted to see the genealogies and family histories – how much time and blood had he spent getting access to those? It had been his original purpose in joining the Blackguard – he couldn't go and sit down by Ironfist, not now. 'Black cards,' he found himself saying. It just slipped out.

The young luxiat just looked at him. He looked somehow familiar, but it was probably just that everyone looked the same in those goofy robes.

'The heresy decks,' Kip said. Digging deeper, Kip.

'You young ones. You get access earlier than everyone else, and you still push it.' The young luxiat shook his head. 'Those books are in the restricted library.'

'*This* is the restricted library,' Kip said. 'Isn't it?'

'You think there's only one?'

'I did until just now.'

'Smarter than you look.'

'Huh?'

'But not by much, apparently.' The luxiat closed his book. He still looked tense. 'Sorry. Look, you're a Blackguard inductee, I can see that. That doesn't give you access to everything. Heretical materials and forbidden magics are off-limits to everyone except the Colors and those they've given special permission. The black cards are black because they're heretical, ergo . . .'

'Ergo, books about them are in the heresy section.'

'In the restricted libraries, but close enough.'

Kip saw that this wasn't going anywhere. More permissions? He'd just been talking to the White. He could have asked her. She would understand his interest in the black cards, at least, but that was no guarantee that she would think he should have access to them. And what was he doing here anyway? Trying to find scandals to destroy Klytos Blue? Who knew if his father even needed that done anymore? Too late, Kip. Again.

Gavin was being held on a pirate ship. Doubtless the pirates would be treating him well – he was the Prism, after all – though Kip figured they'd have to be keeping him blindfolded or something to keep him from ripping them all to pieces with his power. Still, who knew when he would be back?

'What's your name?' Kip asked.

'Quentin. Sorry. Quentin Naheed.' Nervous type, Quentin was. Seemed to have a hard time looking Kip in the eye. Oh well, scholars.

'Nice to meet you, Quentin. How do I show that I have permission?' Kip asked.

'You're just going to go get permission?' Quentin asked, smiling as if he thought it was kind of cute that Kip thought it would be so easy.

Kip didn't answer. Didn't much like grinning condescension.

Quentin shook his head, giving up. 'I'll be right back.' He walked to one of the librarians' desks and rummaged through a drawer, making small talk with the woman there. He came back and handed Kip a small square of red parchment.

Kip quickly filled in the relevant blanks, and as Quentin watched him, perplexed, he walked over to Commander Ironfist. 'Can you sign this for me, sir?' He handed him the quill, already dipped in ink.

'Breaker, do you know how many ways I could disable you with this quill?'

'No, sir.'

'Do you want to find out?'

'Only if that knowledge is academic rather than experiential, sir.'

The corner of Ironfist's mouth twitched, but it might have been Kip's imagination.

'This will make you go away,' Ironfist said. It wasn't a question.

'Instantly, sir.'

Ironfist signed it, barely glancing at it. 'Breaker, fortune favors the bold . . . but don't be bold with me again.'

'Yes, sir.'

Kip went back to grab his things and ask for directions to the forbidden libraries. Quentin answered, seeming stunned that it had been so easy for him. 'Hey, uhm, Quentin, thanks. You've been a big help.'

'My, uh, my – I can't believe you just—'

'I know, it's not fair. Try not to hate me. My family is kind of a bunch of . . . Well, we've got it better than we deserve. Hey, what do you study? Can I grab a book for you while I'm in there that might help you? I couldn't let you leave the library with it, of course, so I'd have to be here while you used it, but if I can help . . .'

'That sounds really danger – fantastic! I'd really appreciate that. I, I study all sorts of things. I'm, I'm a polymath.' He blushed. His eyes flicked up to Kip's, then away, and he spoke in a rush. 'Sorry, I've been working on getting over false humility, but it's really – anyway, I've studied first-century saints; I've memorized everything on Alban and Strang, and their commentaries. Transitional rituals from the time of Karris Shadowblinder. A little on alternate histories. Your eyes are glazing. The memorization of all those commentaries usually gets some res – it's five volumes – no? Doesn't matter.'

He'd studied all sorts of things? That sounded potentially useful. 'Anything modern? Or is that too danger-fantastic?' Kip smirked, though, to show he was teasing.

'By modern you mean contemporary?' It was a real question, though, and Quentin seemed to forget his awkwardness as their conversation moved to his territory.

'I didn't realize there was a—'

'Sorry, pedantic. Structures of persistent tribal hierarchies in Abornea? Um, modern martyrs? Kind of thought my own path might take a missional turn for a while there, not to mention martyrical. Temple construction techniques?'

'I don't suppose you know anything on modern genealogies? Noble families from now and during the False Prism's War?'

'No.'

'Mm.' It had been too much to hope, Kip figured. Like Orholam would simply send him exactly the one scholar who knew everything he wanted to know. He was more surprised how easily he'd called it the False Prism's War. Growing up in Tyrea, they'd called it the Prisms' War. Kip hadn't chosen to call it the False Prism's War to fit in; it hadn't even been a choice. This place was changing him. 'You seem familiar. Have we met?' he asked.

Quentin shook his head, blinked, froze, suddenly shy again. What a strange boy. 'I don't know. It's possible. Please don't take offense, but I don't really pay attention to Blackguards.'

That was fair. Kip didn't think he'd really looked a luxiat in the face in all the time he'd been at the Chromeria. He had a thought. Quentin had said that he'd memorized impressive amounts, and he'd clearly been given permission to study whatever he pleased. That had to be unusual, so he must be highly favored. Perhaps not so unlike Kip – though Quentin had earned what privilege he had. 'Tell me, Quentin, you're probably famous in your circles, right?'

'I wouldn't call it famous – blight and rot! There it is again. False humility.' He sighed. 'In my limited circles, yes.' He flushed again. 'And sorry for swearing.'

'How long did it take for them to try to sweep you up into their politics?'

'What? Who? Sorry, I don't understand.'

'The luxiats. Whoever's over you.' Kip could tell Quentin knew exactly what he was talking about, though.

'The magisterium is Orholam's hand on earth. It's not politicized like other institutions,' Quentin said. Nervous. Defensive.

For a moment, there was a choice. To Kip the Lip, or not. And then Kip said, 'A liar. Huh. That's too bad. You seemed like you could have been a friend. Good life to you, Brother Naheed.'

Chapter 34

Kip didn't have time to go to the restricted library immediately, and Karris still hadn't contacted him, so he headed to his next lecture. The magister was Tawenza Goldeneyes. She was ancient for a drafter, perhaps sixty, and with a ferocious reputation. They said she only took three discipulae a year – yellow superchromats, all. Kip, of course, would be joining the class after it had been meeting for months.

He headed for the yellow tower, crossing through the elevated walk with only a single gulp at the heights, and arrived minutes later at the door of a small lecture hall. He paused at the closed door. There was a sign on it. 'No Men Allowed.' He stopped. Scowled.

Kip Guile, kills gods and kings, afraid to knock on a door.

Totally different things. This is like walking into a women's privy.

He looked down at his burn-scarred left hand that was so quick to curl into a fist. C'mon, fist.

He knocked, a firm but gentle triple tap.

The door opened before he rapped for the third time.

'What are you doing?' an older woman with golden eyes and luminous skin asked him. It wasn't much of a guess who she was.

'Greetings, Magister Goldeneyes, I saw the sign—'

'But didn't read it? Can't read? Begone.' She swung the door closed.

Kip stuck his foot in without thinking. The door hit his shoe and rebounded open. Magister Goldeneyes already had her back turned, and she stiffened at the sound.

The two young women beyond her in the room, seated, necks craned to see Kip, looked suddenly aghast.

'Your pardon,' Kip said. 'I'm your new discipulus, Kip. I figured the sign was a mistake. Surely it means "superchromats only."'

'And?' she asked, turning. She looked at him like he was an insect.

Kip paused, not sure what she was doing. He said, 'I'm a superchromat.'

'A superchromat boy is like a dog that can bark "I love you." It's a novelty, not a precedent.' She slammed the door.

Kip took it. Just when he'd been feeling like he was Little Lord Guile Gets His Way. In the scheme of things, he probably was way past deserving it. Besides, it let him go to a forbidden library before Andross Guile could figure out some way to screw him out of it.

He realized he was blocking the door and a homely Abornean discipula of about twenty with faint yellow halos was trying to get past. He moved. As she slipped inside, she smiled apologetically and said, 'Some things the Lightbringer alone will set aright.'

She closed the door behind her.

In minutes, Kip was back in the Prism's Tower, approaching one of the rooms that Quentin had told him about. There was a librarian sitting in a chair in front of the door, reading. He looked excited to actually see someone. 'Oh, greetings!' he said. He pulled a key out of a pocket and extended his hand.

Kip handed the man his red parchment.

'Kip Guile?' the librarian asked. He could obviously read, so Kip wasn't sure how to parse the deeper question in the voice.

'That's right.'

'You were there.' The librarian licked his lips. 'Is he alive? Truly? They say he is, but that's what they would say, isn't it? To make us keep hope until Sun Day, wouldn't they? Is the Prism really alive?'

'I swear it,' Kip said. 'I helped pull him out of the water. He was breathing. It'd take more than a few pirates to put an end to Gavin Guile.'

The librarian nodded, heartened, his whole mien getting lighter. 'That's right, that's right. After all he's done.' The librarian scowled down at the red parchment and said, 'Thank you, and I wish I could let you in for giving me that news alone. But I'm sorry, sir. New rules. Your grandfather has decreed that only those with his personally written permission will be allowed access to this special section.'

'What?' Did he even have the authority to do that?

The librarian said, 'Just came down this morning, not two hours ago.'

Two hours ago. Before Kip had even come up with his brilliant plan to get Ironfist's signature. Kip didn't know whether to feel better because this meant that his grandfather's spies weren't *that* good, or to feel worse because his grandfather had foiled Kip's plan before Kip had even come up with it.

Little Lord Gets His Way, huh?

It took the wind from his sails. He only ended up going to one lecture. It was engineering, and the lecture covered angles of incidence: mirror armor quality and the refraction of luxin. The class easily had the best demonstrations, with armorers and war drafters standing up and talking about why this quality of mirror armor would perform against a missile of blue luxin at this angle, but not that one, and how keeping the armor clean was one of the biggest problems, dirt making them less reflective.

Some Mirrormen – usually either the elite infantry of any satrapy or simply the richest – took to wearing very thin cotton coverings over their armor so that they would constantly be buffing their armor to a high shine, either shedding it as they went into battle or keeping it on throughout. It was less impressive, one armorer said, but there was no reason not to let the luxin weapons attacking you do the work of cutting the covering. Most Mirrormen, though, wanted the mental advantage that their shining armor had on drafters. Or, more likely, Kip thought, they thought that if they had to do all the work to keep mirror armor shining bright, they were for damn sure going to show it off when they got the chance.

They only gave an overview and talked about one color today: blue. The series would be ongoing, and Kip hoped to make it to all of them.

Suddenly, though, the classes all seemed optional. He certainly wasn't going to go to the basic class with Magister Kadah, but that was the only class he technically had permission to skip. But there was too much else to do with war looming to waste on histories and hagiographies not directly related to the war.

'Uses of Luxin in Art'? Now? Who were they joking?

Other than the engineers, it didn't seem anyone else had broken out of their denial that the war was real – and that they might lose.

After that lecture, Kip went to lunch. None of the Blackguard inductees were there. Most were on a staggered schedule to allow them to make it to lectures and still go to practice. Kip saw the reject table where he'd sat just a few months ago. The group was gutted now. Teia and Ben-hadad had left, subsumed into the greater culture of the Blackguard. Kip had barely belonged at all, and the girl with the birthmark, Tiziri, had been sent home because of Kip's failure, stakes in a game of Nine Kings with Andross Guile. That left only Aras.

The boy was sitting alone. Kip hesitated, and then went toward him.

Aras looked up before Kip could sit. 'What are you doing?' he demanded.

'I was . . . going to eat,' Kip said. 'Can I join—'

'I don't need your pity.'

'Only people who need pity say that,' Kip said, the words crossing his lips before he could call them back.

'Never speak to me again.'

Kip gave up. He went and sat alone and ate his food in silence.

Not knowing what else to do with himself, Kip went downstairs. He'd still have Blackguard training later today, but he couldn't bear to sit and do nothing. Hurry up and start training me, Karris.

He found his father's training room almost exactly as he had left it, except the obstacle course had been rearranged. But Kip was drawn to the pull-up bar.

Before the Battle of Ru, that damned bar had been his daily humiliation. He'd come here alone so the others wouldn't see how pathetic he was.

He jumped up and did a pull-up easily. Well, that had been a bit of a cheat. He'd had some momentum from jumping. He did another. And four more. Six?

Six!

He dropped to the ground, and for the first time, the burning in his muscles felt like proof of progress, rather than punishment for failure. He wrapped his hands and moved over to the old punching bag, activating the lights with some superviolet. For a half an hour, perhaps an hour, he sank into the simplicity of hitting. Condemnations and memories of mockery rose to the surface like dross in the heat of the exercises, and he hammered them away one by one. Mother's sneering quips, Ram's teasing, General Danavis's disappointment, Aras's bitterness, punch by punch. He went from hitting the bag with sloppy fury to punching with passionless precision.

The body mechanics were beginning to sink in, too. He was hitting faster, more precisely, and harder, lines of force tracing up from his planted feet, through his hips, his tight abdomen, to uncurl like a whipcrack as he drove his fist into the bag. It felt . . . glorious.

There was a slight tear in the leather seam high on the bag, and Kip fantasized about punching the bag so hard he tore it open. It didn't happen, of course, but the fantasy kept him working.

He was just finishing up, unwrapping his hands, when the door cracked open. It was Teia.

'Thought I might find you here,' she said shyly. 'You big dope, you're going to be useless at practice. We'll probably both have to run.' She grimaced. 'Sorry, that came out all wrong.'

Kip grinned. 'It's good to see you, Teia.'

'You, too.' She hesitated. 'I'm sorry I wasn't there. Up on deck, I mean. You're my partner, and I wasn't there when you needed me. I've been feeling pretty awful about it. And then you came back, and it – it wasn't really the reunion I'd been hoping for.'

'About that . . .'

'Kip, I, I need to keep some secrets. Even from you. Can you trust me?'

When Kip thought of Teia, he thought of the petite girl whom he'd mistaken for a boy, months ago. A young slave, uncertain, in over her head. But also a girl who could accurately rank each of the Blackguard hopefuls and estimate that she was the fourth best of them, but somehow didn't realize quite how excellent that made her against everyone else, or how smart she was to estimate so accurately.

This Teia wasn't that Teia. Kip realized that while he was growing and changing through all the fights and all the old messages he'd told himself that he was realizing were lies, he had somehow thought that everyone else would stay the same. And it was a fool's thought.

Teia was little, but that didn't make her a child. She was being more mature than Kip had probably ever been in his life.

'I heard you saved the raid on Ruic Head,' Kip said.

Teia shrugged.

'Watch Captain Tempus said Commander Ironfist wanted to give you a medal.'

'What?'

'It got overruled by someone higher up, apparently.'

'In something regarding the Blackguards? Who could overrule – oh, don't tell me.'

'That's right,' Kip said. 'So as long as you're not working for that old cancer, sure, Teia, I trust you. You're still on our side, right?'

She laughed, but there was something uncertain in it.

'Teia, you're not . . . you're not working for my grandfather, are you?'

'Kip – Breaker, I can't tell you *anything*. But I will never betray you. You're my best friend.'

'I am?'

She looked away awkwardly. Kip could have hit himself. Not the right response.

'I mean, I just thought that being my slave—'

'What?!' Her face flashed to angry.

'Wait wait wait!' He took a breath. 'I wanted to be your friend, Teia. I was always afraid that when I – when I won your papers that it meant we couldn't be friends. And I didn't know how much of that stuck around. Even afterward, you know. I didn't know if I'd always remind you of that. You're my best friend, too.'

She looked mollified but still upset. 'I'm more than my slavery, Kip.'

'And I'm more than a Guile, but it's still there, like it or not.'

She pursed her lips, then nodded. She reached up and put a hand to a necklace she had, and Kip wanted to ask about it, but he could tell it was personal. A present from an old master, perhaps? Her face brightened, though her mouth twisted with chagrin. 'I didn't mean to put you on the spot. You know, calling you my best friend, like saying – like saying . . .' She grimaced.

'I didn't take it wrong,' Kip said, rescuing her.

'You didn't say it back because I – never mind. Can we go hit something?' She was blushing.

He had the sudden desire to grab her hand, but he didn't. Why did he feel so awkward and young all of the sudden?

Teia said, 'And you have to keep this from the squad.'

'No one will hear we're friends from me,' Kip said gravely.

'Breaker!'

He grinned, sketched a quick sign of the three and the four, promising. She grinned back.

She moved to speak again, to explain more about not explaining about coming back to the Chromeria bloody, to defend herself somehow, but she let it go, and he credited it to her as maturity. The immature Teia would have checked and double-checked. Or should he think, 'the slave Teia would have checked and double-checked'? Maybe this is who she always was, only held back by her slavery?

Well, I did one thing right, in my whole life.

'I missed you, Kip.' She grinned, and threw a towel to him.

He caught it, and his smile felt like it was going to break his cheeks.

'You ready to head up?' she asked.

He mopped his face. Good thing about going to Blackguard practice, he supposed – it was fine to go there sweaty.

The door cracked open behind them, and Grinwoody stepped in. Kip's smile dropped.

'Good afternoon, young master . . . Guile,' the old slave said. As always, he was dressed carefully, looked wrinkled as an old apple, and had a demeanor as pleasant as a night of diarrhea.

'Grinwoody, you're looking well!' Kip said with false cheer, deliberately invoking the familiarity of using the slave's name. How long had Grinwoody been there? Dear Orholam.

'Your grandfather requires you.'

'For Nine Kings?' Kip asked.

'I believe so.'

'I've got Blackguard training,' Kip said. 'I don't want to play him now.'

'Your desires are irrelevant. The promachos has summoned you. You will come with me. Immediately.' The old man seemed to enjoy making Kip furious.

The promachos? Dear Orholam, no. So that's how he had the authority to shut down access to the libraries. Dammit!

'Or what?' Kip said. He just couldn't help himself, could he?

The Parian slave turned to Teia. 'Or your friend here will be expelled.'

'Excuse me?' Teia said.

'You've not been addressed, slave. Be silent,' the old slave told her. Asshole.

'I'm not a slave,' Teia snapped.

'My mistake,' Grinwoody said. It clearly hadn't been a mistake.

Well, that answered one question. Teia wasn't working for Andross. He wouldn't threaten one of his own, would he? Or would he, so secure in his belief that Kip wouldn't let harm come to her?

Was Andross so good that he was comfortable playing against his own cards, knowing someone else would save them?

Kip felt ill, and he felt afraid. He was trying to match wits against this? Andross Guile was godlike in his intellect, and in his ruthlessness. Kip had called Magister Kadah's bluff, saying she could never expel someone who was nearly a Blackguard. But Andross could expel anyone he wanted. He was now the promachos. It was a calamity.

'I'm not ready,' Kip said.

'He doesn't require your readiness, he requires your presence.'

Kip cursed under his breath. 'I really hate you, Grinwoody,' he said.

Grinwoody gave a thin-lipped grin. 'The heart breaks, sir.'

Chapter 35

A few of the galley slaves whooped at the discovery of the key. The others were more wary, more frightened, maybe more cynical. Orholam took the key and ran around the galley, unshackling slaves.

'Grab ten of us to free so we can cut the boarding nets,' Gavin said. 'We need the rest of them still on the oars.'

'Free us all!' a slave near the front shouted.

'In time!' Gavin said.

'You're lying to us! Freedom now or never!' the man shouted back.

Gavin couldn't believe it. They were going to jeopardize the escape attempt. They had no time for this. 'Some of us are going to risk death cutting the ship free. If we don't get separation from that ship as fast as possible, they'll just come right back across the neto, or they'll load the cannons over there and kill us all. If you don't like it, don't row. Go ahead, kill us all.'

With that, Gavin dashed toward the stairs. They'd been ripped halfway off in a cannon blast. He grabbed a length of wood that had been torn away, and leapt up to the remaining stairs. Antonius Malargos followed him unquestioningly. The stairs led past the puzzled slaves on the next deck and to a cramped landing.

The hatch was concealed around two half-turns of the stairs, and closed. Gavin, Antonius, and half a dozen slaves stacked up at the door. It was locked.

Gavin threw his shoulder into the hatch. It was an awkward maneuver to attempt, given that it was almost directly above him.

'Orholam have mercy, what do we do now?' Antonius asked.

One of the slaves reached over Antonius's shoulder and found a latch hidden in the darkness. He slid it open, grinning, nothing but his teeth showing in the darkness. Gavin had hoped that perhaps his monotone vision would help him see better in the dark. So far as he could tell, it didn't. It was purely handicap. Unlike the wild stories he'd heard about blind men having preternaturally acute hearing or sense of smell, he had no counterbalancing ability.

It was, perhaps, just. When he'd been Prism, he'd had no handicaps. He'd moved from strength to strength. Now he had no strength at all.

'We need blades,' he said. 'Anyone have a knife? A sword? Anyone know how the boarding nets are attached? Is it grapnels, or are they tied on this side?'

Gavin prided himself on his memory, but he'd been unconscious when he was brought aboard. 'Doesn't matter,' he said, thinking aloud. 'We won't be able to untie them if they're under tension. We'll need to cut them regardless.'

Someone handed up one knife. One.

Gavin handed it back. He had training, and a piece of wood. 'Boarding nets first,' he said. 'Our only advantage is our numbers. We gain nothing if they get reinforcements. Nets off, get some separation. Kill men to get their blades, and cut those nets. Ready?'

He didn't wait for an answer. He threw the hatch open and jumped onto the deck.

The sudden, harsh light nearly blinded him, and being free of the confines of the ship let a flood of sound wash over him. A musket cracked fifteen paces away, but the pirate was shooting at a marksman in the rigging of the other galley. Gavin ran at him.

The pirate didn't even see Gavin coming. He swiveled to start reloading, and that move turned his back to Gavin. Gavin's makeshift club swept into the pirate's head like an oar cutting the sea. The man went flying in a spray of blood, and Gavin was on him in a second, ripping a knife from his belt.

Then he was up again, running. Speed and surprise were the slaves' only advantages. One pirate with a sword would be able to cut through half a dozen of the unarmed slaves and end their escape before it began.

There was one more pirate stationed at the nets at the stern of the ship, and this one saw Gavin coming. Through stupidity or shock, the man didn't shout an alarm, but he did ready his saber.

Gavin barely slowed. He lifted the knife and whipped it forward as if he were throwing it. The man flinched, bringing the point of his saber in as his muscles tightened. Gavin brought the knife down to parry the saber and threw his torso to one side as he closed the distance. Knife and saber slid against each other, the cheap metal throwing sparks. Gavin's club, wielded left-handed, only struck a glancing blow to the pirate's forehead.

But it was enough to stun him. Gavin followed the first with a full backhand swing. Teeth sprayed, and the man dropped. Gavin knelt on the man's back and jabbed his knife through the base of the pirate's skull. He rose with the saber, and threw the knife handle-first to whoever had followed him. It was Antonius, and for a second he looked like he thought he was being attacked himself, a victim of friendly attack.

Antonius dodged out of the way of the knife, and it clattered to the deck. He bent over to pick it up, and a musket ball whistled right over his head, scoring the deck ten feet behind him.

The other galley was taller than the *Bitter Cob*, and that could be good or bad news, depending on how enraged and careless the pirates were. If they wanted to get across the gap fast, they could sheathe their swords and simply roll down the boarding nets and be across in seconds. No man in his right mind who felt threatened would do that, though, and climbing down a declined rope net wasn't easy.

Of course, betting that pirates who followed Gunner were in their right minds might be a poor gamble.

Reaching the gunwale, Gavin found that the boarding nets weren't simply held grapnel to wood, which would have allowed him to pull the grapnel off and let the net drop. Instead, the grapnels were looped around the railing and tied back to themselves, then anchored to the wood railing. Bad news. But that loop held the hemp rope tight against the gunwale. Gavin slashed the rope, and it yielded on the second stroke. He looked down the length of the ship. There were four more grapnels. Four widths of hemp between him and freedom.

Four galley slaves had tackled a pirate at midships and were pummeling him to death with fists and feet. Antonius was charging for the farthest rope – smart boy – leaving Gavin to face another sword-wielding pirate. Out of the corner of his eye, Gavin saw a pirate with a musket taking aim at him as he ran, so he did a running slide, dropping to one hip to skim along the deck and then popping up with the sword wielder between him and the musket man.

Even as Gavin engaged with the swordsman, he saw other pirates jumping onto the nets, coming back to the *Bitter Cob*. He was running out of time. His saber and the pirate's thinner forward-curving ataghan clanged together, and Gavin was aware how long it had been since he'd practiced fencing. How long it had been since he needed it. But a pirate was really merely a sailor willing to kill. That wasn't the same as a trained warrior. Gavin saw two wide opportunities for deadly thrusts go by – and he was too slow to take advantage, too cautious to press an advantage.

But a third came. Riposte and kill, the saber slipping into

his opponent's chest only deep enough to open his heart, and then pulling back. Gavin stepped back to avoid the possible counterstroke – just because a man was going to die within seconds didn't mean he couldn't kill you in the meantime.

He realized that by stepping back, he was clearing the shot for the musket man, and he slapped the swordsman's blade aside once more and grabbed the man under the armpits even as he heard the musket fire. The man jerked, taking the ball in the shoulder right between Gavin's fingers. At least, he *hoped* it was between his fingers. All he could tell for the moment was that his index finger of his right hand felt hot.

He dropped the still-twitching body, found his finger bleeding, but still there, and slashed the rope where it crossed the gunwale.

A pirate was coming down the boarding rope more nimbly than Gavin would have believed, walking upright, stepping from rope to rope with the agility of a dancer – and *fast*. But the rope parted on the first cut, and the boarding net sagged suddenly. The man jumped, hands stretching to reach the gunwale and – just making it. The shock of colliding with the hull didn't shake the man loose, either.

Gavin slapped his blade down on the gunwale and eight fingers popped up in response.

A short scream and a satisfying splash signaled success.

'Row!' Gavin shouted as he crossed over the gap that had been blown in the deck by the cannon fire. But they were already on it, oars rattling out, first pushing off the ship, stretching the boarding net.

There were two grapnels left – and with a snap, the slaves aft freed one. It left only one at midships. Gavin ran for it.

Wood shrapnel exploded around him from musket balls. A pirate leapt off the boarding net, and Gavin slashed his groin open, not even slowing. He saw a pirate finish loading a swivel gun on the deck of the other ship and turn it toward him. He dove as it spewed death onto the lower ship.

Gavin rolled to his feet, groped to find the saber he'd lost in his dive.

'Guile! Guile!' a familiar voice shouted. Gunner.

Gavin looked up, already knowing what he would see. Gunner

stood, not twenty paces away, that magnificent black-and-white musket leveled at Gavin's face. From that distance, Gunner couldn't miss.

The oars dipped into the waves, but the inertia of the loaded *Bitter Cob* meant it would be seconds before they moved with any speed.

The saber was in Gavin's hand. If Gunner shot him in the head, he wouldn't be able to complete the stroke. He would die for nothing. But if Gunner shot him in the chest – the safer shot – Gavin could trade his life for the slaves' freedom.

What was the value of a few slaves compared to a Prism? What was the value of a thousand slaves compared to a Prism? What would the world gain if Gavin chose to make this sacrifice?

Nothing.

'You do what you have to,' Gavin said, to himself as much as to Gunner.

He slashed the rope, expecting a musket ball to tear through his body. It didn't. He'd braced so much for the impact that he didn't cut the rope on the first stroke. He slashed again, and it parted. The boarding net dropped into the water, scattering pirates.

Gavin looked at Gunner. The man still had his musket leveled, as if unsure himself why he hadn't fired. Gunner looked to the horizon. Gavin followed his eyes.

The ship that had been pursuing Gunner for years was there. In the fight, the *Bitter Cob* had sheared off all the oars on one full side of the galley Gunner was now on.

Gunner wouldn't be able to flee from the vengeful captain hunting him. And with his pirates decimated and probably out of ammunition, there was no way his crew could win the fight.

Not killing Gavin meant Gunner would die himself. What the hell? The man was bordering on insane, but all his insanity went toward serving himself, didn't it?

With an oath Gavin couldn't hear, Gunner lowered his musket. His head bobbed as he swore a dozen expletives in succession. His eyes were darting back and forth, but Gavin couldn't guess what he was doing. Then something arced out over the water – a spear? Gavin jumped backward as the musket-sword fell from the sky in a streak and clattered to the deck not far from him.

What?

The *Bitter Cob*'s slaves dipped their oars again, and the boat began moving at a decent rate, opening the gap between the boats, leaving pirates without any more powder at the gunwales of the other ship, cursing and looking baffled.

A wave tilted the galley and the musket-sword started sliding toward a gap where the gunwale had been shot off.

Gavin dove and grabbed the musket before it could fall into the sea. He stood.

Then he saw a disturbance on the other boat. A pirate was jostled so hard he fell off the side as someone – not *someone*, Gunner – sprinted along its side. As the boats separated, the waves shifted them so they sat nearly stern to prow, and Gunner ran straight toward the prow of the crippled ship, launched off the gunwale and leapt into the air, shouting something that may have been, 'Fuck you, Ceres!'

For an instant, Gavin thought the crazy pirate was actually going to clear the gap. He soared through the air, arms and legs wheeling – and plunged into the sea with a splash.

Gavin ran to the stern. The galley slaves didn't pause in their long sweeps, and the gap widened, and widened. When Gavin got to the stern, he saw several pirates in the water, but none of them was Gunner. Then he looked down.

Pulled along in the water by a rope trailing from the *Bitter Cob*'s deck, Gunner was climbing hand over hand. He reached a loading ladder at the back and climbed up deftly. Gavin waited at the top, musket-sword nearly forgotten.

Gunner reached the top of the ladder, shook his head to clear his beard and eyes of seawater, and extended a hand to Gavin. 'What are you waiting for?' he asked. 'Help Gunner up. He spared your life.' And he grinned his mad, mad grin.

Chapter 36

Following Grinwoody, Kip walked toward Andross Guile's apartments with a familiar sense of foreboding. Whenever Kip had tangled with the old man, it seemed he'd gotten the worst of the bargain.

Grinwoody took them past where the entry hall to the Guiles' apartments used to be. Now that hallway was walled over. Andross Guile had incorporated his wife's apartments into his own, making one, much larger set of rooms. For some reason, Kip had thought that Andross would keep Felia's rooms as a shrine to her, untouched.

Apparently he'd given the old spider too much credit.

They walked past Blackguards keeping watch outside the outer doors – and looking none too pleased to be kept so far away – and went inside. Felia Guile's main room had been converted into an antechamber for supplicants to wait for the promachos to see them.

There were eight noble drafters seated around the room, some chatting, others eyeing the rest with open hostility. Kip recognized them as some of the foremost drafters of each color, though he could only put names to a few. The oldest was gray-haired Lord Spreading Oak, who was calmly reading a scroll of prayers – or, knowing the Chromoria, pretending to read prayers while concealing notes from spies. The rest were in their thirties. There was a dwarf woman whom he'd heard was the new Color for Tyrea. He recognized a Crassos – sister or cousin to the disgraced and executed governor of Garriston – and Akensis Azmith and Jason Jorvis, whose sister had leapt to her death from Gavin's balcony in scandalous circumstances the night Gavin had married Karris. The Jorvises were alleging that Gavin was somehow responsible for Ana's death and were demanding recompense. Kip thought they were disgusting. Denial was understandable, but using a suicide to advance your family?

Kip only knew one of the others: Tisis Malargos, the beautiful young fiery Green who'd tried to make him believe failing the Threshing would mean dying, and then had made him fail by handing him back the rope. Not his favorite person. Kip had rejoiced none too quietly when he'd heard his father had fooled her into voting herself off the Spectrum.

Once when Kip had come out of Andross Guile's presence nearly throwing up, Ironfist had told him that he'd seen satraps coming out of that room looking worse.

No matter how bad Kip's interactions with Andross Guile, at least Tisis was going to have to interact with him, too. Enjoy that, darling.

He nodded to her pleasantly.

She looked perplexed, and that, too, was sweetness to him.

Grinwoody had already disappeared in front of him, and another slave, dismissed, came out. Kip paused, his bravado leaking out like urine down a coward's leg.

He braced himself for the smell in that room. And the darkness.

He glanced back at Tisis – because she was easy on the eyes, not because he was worried what she thought of him – and saw a nasty little smile on her face at his fear.

Kip blew out, puffing his cheeks. He'd deserved that. He drafted a torch of superviolet light. Grinwoody opened the way with his perpetual sneer, and Kip stepped forward through the heavy curtains.

Into light.

For a moment, Kip thought Grinwoody must have led them to the wrong place. But as soon as he thought that, he knew he was wrong. He remembered this room, albeit dimly. Literally dimly. That chair, that table, that painting over the mantel, they'd all looked different in the harsh, superfine light of the superviolet torches Kip had drafted, but they were the same ones. That lush carpet, that was where Kip had fallen when the old man slapped the hell out of him in the darkness.

Andross Guile was propped on the edge of his desk, half sitting on it, half standing. It was the pose of a much younger man, but it seemed to fit Andross now. Kip stood, dumbstruck.

Andross looked like he'd lost a decade or two. He looked like, perhaps, a tough old farmer or carpenter. He still had a bit of the paunch Kip had noted long ago, but it looked like it was shrinking fast. He looked powerful, his broad Guile shoulders and strong Guile chin no longer hidden under layer upon layer of clothing. He smiled pleasantly, but though that face was Gavin's face, just older, the smile wasn't the same. There was some warmth lacking there. Gavin would grin recklessly, knowing he was getting away with things because he was handsome and powerful, but you always got the sense that he was amused by it all. You got the sense that underneath it, Gavin really liked people. Andross Guile saw *through* you, to his objective.

'When they told me you were back,' Andross said, 'they didn't tell me how little of you had returned.' He smirked. Of course he'd seen Kip at the meeting of the Spectrum. He must have meant his spies had told him Kip was back before that.

'I see I'm not the only one who's lost something,' Kip said.

'I meant that as a compliment.'

'Me, too. You were a wight.'

'Kip, a man only gets so many chances to start over in a life, or in a conversation. Don't miss an important one.'

Beast or not, it was good advice. Kip held his tongue.

Hey! Second time in my life!

'Nine Kings?' Andross asked.

'I'd be glad to, but I don't have my decks.' Wait, had Andross just asked that as a question? As if Kip could say no?

'I'm short a couple myself,' Andross said. 'But I've got plenty. You can borrow whichever you like.'

'What are the stakes this time?' Kip asked. He was a little rusty on the game, but if he had enough time to look through decks, he could at least still tell a strong deck from a weak one.

'So you didn't steal it,' Andross said.

'Huh?'

'Someone broke into my apartments and stole a few valuables. They also grabbed one of my favorite decks. It seemed like the kind of thing you might do.'

255

And he'd learned from Kip's expression alone that Kip wasn't the culprit.

They sat, and Andross put forward two pairs of decks. 'I thought we might try one of the old duels: the Twins, or Gods and Beasts.' They were classic pairings. In such games, the decks had equal relative strengths, though very different strategies. Each player was expected to have memorized all the cards in each deck. Luck still played a part, but a player with a sharp head for numbers could judge the probabilities that their opponent would draw a card to counter any particular strategy. It was the kind of game where Kip would get slaughtered, even though he knew most of the cards in each.

'Gods and Beasts,' Kip said.

'Interesting choice,' Andross said. And Kip saw that Andross thought Kip was making a comment even in this. Of course, they had just faced both gods and beasts.

Kip had chosen it because he thought it was more fun.

Now I'm being overestimated.

He wasn't sure if that was better, or worse.

'Which deck do you want, grandson?' Andross asked.

Now that Kip knew his grandfather thought Kip was making a point by which one he chose, he thought about it differently. 'Odd that they're on opposite sides, isn't it? In my experience, the gods and beasts have fought together.'

'Not odd at all,' Andross said. 'What can oppose a god but a beast?'

'Is that how you justify it?' Kip asked. No filter.

'When soft men sit in peace and criticize my choices ages hence, that they live to do so will be all the proof necessary that I did right,' Andross said. He picked up a deck. 'A man who hesitates could never become a god, so you'll be beasts.' He shuffled each deck as Kip watched, then dealt the cards. 'No timers. I wish to have a leisurely match, and we've seen what mistakes you make under pressure.'

Kip didn't touch his cards, didn't turn around. 'Tell Grinwoody not to stand behind me.'

Andross laughed. 'You make me wonder, Kip, if I posed such dilemmas for my father Draccos. So smart sometimes, so clever, so adult, and then the next minute an utter belligerent child, striking out and destroying things more good for him than for anyone else, simply because he's been vexed.' He waved to Grinwoody, who moved away from his cheater's perch over Kip's shoulder.

'Who starts?' Kip asked. He picked up his hand.

'I will. Privilege of age.'

Kip threw down his hand. 'You dealt me eight.' It was one card too many.

'Did I? Age dulls us all, I suppose.' He grinned, and this time there was real playfulness in it. So said the man who, just a few months ago, had looked twenty years older than he did now.

Kip couldn't help but grin. A little.

'Wasn't a good hand anyway, huh?' Andross asked. He picked up Kip's hand and shuffled again quickly, then dealt him out seven.

'Lousy,' Kip said.

Andross laughed, and Kip remembered how the man had said that he liked Kip – a little. He realized then that Andross had been testing him, seeing if he'd cheat. Or perhaps Andross wouldn't have thought of it as cheating. Maybe he would have thought of it as taking advantage of an opponent's error. But it had been a bad hand, which was why Kip had thrown the whole hand down for a re-deal rather than extend the deck and have Andross take out one card to bring him down to seven.

The promachos set the sun counter to predawn, and played his first card. 'So, grandson,' Andross said. 'The Chromeria finds itself about to enter a fight for its life, and most of them still don't realize the fact. What do you see that needs fixing?'

Kip cocked his head to the side. 'Are you serious? You really want my ideas?'

'Is it so surprising?'

'Yes, it is.'

'There are many things you can learn from slaves and spies, and I have learned them all. But some things can only be seen with one's own eyes. My eyes have been—'

'Broken?' Kip couldn't help but get in the little jab about Andross hiring that assassin from the Order, Mistress Helel, Kip saw Grinwoody tense, but Andross didn't miss a beat.

'Unavailable. I may have missed things.' But he was examining Kip sharply. 'Boy, I am ferocious when crossed, I don't deny it. I find being led by fools intolerable. But I am magnanimous in victory. I do what needs to be done to win and without putting on a false display of sorrow or reluctance; you think that makes me hideous? Others pay homage to common pieties with their lips but betray them by their actions. I am simply more forthright. Orholam needs even honest men, does he not?'

His eyes twinkled. That inversion, so typical of this family. Gavin would hint at irreligiosity and flirt with the line. Andross would breeze right past it, but if his approach saved them all regardless, who was to say that Orholam wasn't using him? Their ends were the same.

He was the promachos. Surely, if only to preserve his own power, he would fight the Color Prince.

So Kip told him about the classes, how the magisters were lecturing on topics that had nothing to do with the conflict at hand, that only the engineers seemed to grasp the problems. He also thought that they should have a whole contingent of battle drafters, not only the Blackguard and a few isolated drafters who learned the arts of war for their sponsors. He thought that they should open all the books of forbidden magics, and start teaching them – or at the least how to defend against them.

'And who's to teach all these new battle drafters?' Andross asked.

'The Blackguard,' Kip said. 'At least, those not directly involved with recovering my father. If they're not busy protecting the Prism and the Colors, might as well put them to use until spring. They'll complain, but training others is sometimes even better than being trained. And speaking of the Blackguard, there's a slave who scrubbed out. You should put him in with my initiate cohort.'

'What's his story?'

'Winsen was one of the best scrubs, but his master was a

258

horror. He was also deeply in debt, and he needed to sell Winsen into the Blackguard to avoid being ruined. Winsen failed on purpose.'

'And you wish to reward treachery?'

'I think what made him a bad slave will make him a great Blackguard. And we need Blackguards.'

The game proceeded to noon on the sun counter – the time when the most powerful cards could be easily played. Kip got a sea demon. As long as there were other cards on the table, the sea demon had to attack, but if only you had another card on the table, the sea demon would attack your own card. Like all the best daggers, it was double-edged.

'They say Gunner killed a sea demon,' Andross said.

'I've heard that,' Kip said. 'Do you think it's true?'

'I think it's possible. Carcasses have floated to shore before, so the beasts are not immortal.'

'How was Gunner supposed to have done it?' Kip asked.

'They say he filled a raft full of the ship's whole store of powder and floated it behind the *Aved Barayah* five hundred paces. Something about that little raft irritated the sea demon, I've never heard exactly what – apparently this Gunner has a penchant for irritating those more powerful than he. He waited until the sea demon surfaced and shot the raft with a cannon-ball just as the sea demon swallowed it. In heavy seas, if the tales be believed.'

Kip made a moue of appreciation.

Andross said, 'I'd wager it was more like two hundred paces. Regardless, impressive. Another version says he rode on the raft himself, singing sea shanties and howling curses at some whore he'd loved, and lit the fuse himself, jumping out of the way at the last moment. But sailors and a straight-told tale have but passing acquaintance.'

'I'd believe five hundred paces,' Kip said. 'I've seen the man shoot.'

Andross had a veritable army of wights on his side of the table. Plenty of fodder for Kip's sea demon, so Kip played his heavy galleon to be able to sail past Andross's defenses and attack him directly on the next round.

'I want something of you, Kip,' Andross said.

'Other than learning if I stole from you and crushing me in a few games?'

'Hard as it may be to believe, I want more than even your excellent company.' He said it flat, like he might have been mocking, or might have meant the compliment.

Kip found himself grinning despite himself. This was the man who'd tried to have him killed, who'd tried to kill him, who had lost Gavin for all of them. And yet Kip grinned.

And Andross grinned back. God or beast, the man appreciated when someone appreciated his sense of humor.

'Well . . .' Kip prompted. He couldn't take the suspense.

Andross looked up from the cards. 'I want to know where my other grandson is.'

A kick in the groin. 'Other?' Kip asked. Had he hesitated too long?

His face must have blanched, because Andross grinned wolfishly. 'I love surprising people. It was really one of the greatest losses of my seclusion. So much more satisfying when I can see your face.'

'Let's talk about that seclusion,' Kip said, suddenly ready to do combat. To hell with this old man and his tricks. 'Grinwoody, get away.' He didn't turn to look at the slave. 'Grinwoody, we both know I could have had you put out with forty lashes or worse when I spoke to the Spectrum, if I'd wanted to. I spared you. Get the hell out of here. Your betters are speaking.'

A moment passed. Kip saw Andross nod his head.

Grinwoody left, and Kip felt a little stab of pleasure.

So it begins. The opiate of power. Command and obedience, in a dance until you climb the greased pole high enough that all must obey you, and you must obey none.

'Thinking deep thoughts?' Andross asked.

'Am I so easy to read?' Kip asked.

'In your unguarded moments. You are young yet, trapped in that twilight of having adult thoughts and insights quite beyond what others think you should have, and being utterly, wildly out of control of your self. At your age, the emotions have a power greater than the intellect can tame. Slowly, slowly, they will become yours. Yours to master or at least to hide. If you survive so long.'

260

Kip looked at the cards, but he didn't see them. 'At moments, you sound so like my father that I despair.'

'At moments, you sound so like him that I rejoice,' Andross said. 'I have hope for you, Kip. But there are hard lessons between where you now sit and feel, and where you shall stand and act. You must become master to that within you, not its puppet. In the meantime, your mouth is a loose cannon, Kip the Lip.'

'I know. I'm trying to—'

'Shut up and listen. You react exactly the wrong way. You say startling things, often rude things, but sometimes with stunning insight. Someday, you will control that tongue. In the meantime, when you say something that shocks your inter-locutor, instead of being embarrassed and turning your eyes inward, pay attention! When you drop an explosive truth, don't look at yourself. Package away your feeble blushes and your horror for later; in the moment, watch what others do.'

Instantly, Kip was embarrassed at his own feebleness and foolishness. Exactly what Andross was speaking about. So he blurted, 'Why are you acting like my friend?'

'Not your friend,' Andross answered instantly. 'Your grand-father, for all it costs us both.'

'You fear me,' Kip said.

The astonishment on Andross's face was priceless. Then he laughed. 'I see. You were trying it. No Kip. And yes. Not fear of you. Fear that you may put this family in danger, though for the nonce, if you do something horrific, everyone knows that you don't act for me. As you grow older and more refined, that perceived gap will close. So in order for you to be of use to me, you must grow faster than the conventional wisdom believes possible.'

Oh, no pressure then.

But Kip realized this was exactly what his father had been trying to protect him from when he'd suggested Kip enter the Chromeria under an assumed name. And Kip had blindly wanted to be thrust directly into the middle of all of it. Had demanded it, long before he was ready.

'What are your plans for me?' Kip asked.

'You asked that before.'

'You were a wight then.'

Andross Guile paused. Looked at the cards. 'Do you think, grandson, that all my rage was born of red luxin?' He affixed Kip with his many-colored eyes: a background of shocking natural blue making a canvas for sub-red, red, orange, and yellow entwined like serpents.

'I won't tell you anything for free,' Kip said. He swallowed. 'We trade. Like adults.'

'Playing an adult while playing an adult while playing an adult, fair enough,' Andross said. He played a Flawless Mirror.

It didn't make any sense. His deck had no Prisms, for one, and if he wanted to play a burning ray, it would take two turns. He'd be dead by then, killed by Kip's heavy galleon.

Was he deliberately giving Kip a victory in the game so Kip would feel good about something after this talk?

Kip said, 'I'll tell you about your other grandson . . . if you give me written permission to all the libraries in the Chromeria. All of them.'

Andross raised his eyebrows. 'There are things in some of those libraries that could put the whole Chromeria at risk.'

'All the more reason that those who defend her should know them.'

'A full accounting of your half brother,' Andross said. 'All you know.'

'Done,' Kip said.

'Not done. That's your opening bid. Here's my counter. I told you how I like surprises. I want to buy one from you.'

'What's that?' Kip asked. This didn't sound good.

'Don't tell Karris about Zymun.'

What, as if Kip *wanted* to tell Karris about Zymun? 'Hi, stepmother, I met your real son. The one you've apparently been trying to hide? The bastard? Oh, and he's the worst person I've ever met. He tried to kill me. Oh, he also tried to murder your husband, his father.'

'Done,' Kip said quickly. 'If.'

Andross didn't ask, 'If what?' Instead, he said, 'Of course, if you tell someone else who may tell her, that's an abrogation of our agreement.'

I'm a turtle-bear, not a weasel. 'Of course,' Kip said irritably.

'And the if?' Andross asked.

'You're going to send out Blackguard on skimmers, looking for my father.'

'Sea chariots,' Andross corrected. 'Yes, of course.'

Something about his tone told Kip it was half a lie. Andross hadn't been planning on sending the Blackguards out – or if he had, he'd been planning to send them to look for something else. But now, called on it, he would send them. So that was a victory, Kip guessed. 'I get to go with them.'

'You've too much to learn here. It's what your father would have demanded for you.'

'I won't be moved on this. If I have to, I'll make my own skimmer and search for him by myself.'

Andross pursed his lips. Kip was testing his patience. 'You may go once. On the time of my choosing.'

'And you swear they'll be looking for him?'

Pique flashed through Andross Guile's eyes. Kip had caught him. He'd already said he would do it, so holding back would expose the lie.

'Done. I so swear,' Andross Guile said.

'And done,' Kip said.

'Now, tell me what you know, and let me see how good of a deal I've made blind.'

'Zymun was alive, last I saw him,' Kip said. 'He captured me, after the Battle of Ru, after Gunner threw me back into the sea. Zymun found me on the beach and took me prisoner. He was fighting for the Color Prince, you know.'

'I do. I'll claim I sent him to spy, if it suits me.'

Kip already felt like he'd got the worse end of things. What if he didn't find anything in the libraries?

He told his grandfather the whole story of his capture and his time on the boat with Zymun. 'And he's a serpent. There is no human kindness in him. He mimics feelings as if he had them, but he is nothing inside. He is thinner than parchment, and more evil than—'

'Than?' Andross asked.

'Than an old spider bloated with poison,' Kip said flatly, as if it might or might not apply to Andross himself.

Andross gave him, surprisingly, no reaction to that at all.

Turning to the game, he set his cards attacking – all of them, abandoning any hope of defense. Kip moved his hand to his counters, hesitated.

'No,' Andross said. 'They attack each other.' And so, instead of attacking Kip to bring his life down to one counter, Andross's six wights tore each other to shreds.

'Oh hell,' Kip said.

'Your turn.'

Kip's sea demon attacked first, and lacking any opponents, had to attack Kip's heavy galleon. It sank it easily. Kip looked at his cards. He had nothing. But that didn't mean it was over. The card that Andross needed was Burning Focus to equip to the Flawless Mirror. That card was in the deck, and Andross was playing like he had it, but that didn't mean he did.

'Do you want to resign?' Andross said.

'Never.' Kip had just drawn Amun-Tep, but with the sun waning, it would take him two turns to draw the power needed to play the character. Damn! He played a hulking duelist in mirror armor instead: Grath Hrozak. From his studies, Kip knew the real man had murdered hundreds personally, not counting the deaths he'd ordered. He'd served the Tyrean Empire, long before Lucidonius. He'd been yanked in and out of command because he was so brutal. He'd never taken a city but that he'd killed most everyone in it through crucifixion or flaying or both.

It was Andross's turn. He looked at the cards and sighed. 'Take this lesson to heart, grandson.' He played Burning Focus, equipped it to the Flawless Mirror. With the sun counters still just off noon, it gave him enough damage to go through Grath Hrozak, absorb what little damage was reflected by the mirror armor, and kill Kip.

'And what lesson is that?' Kip asked, barely able to contain himself. That had been a lucky sequence. 'That you sometimes have to sacrifice all your men in order to win? That sometimes even a beast like Grath Hrozak can't save you? That I should never play the mighty Andross Guile in Nine Kings?'

'I'll bring your brother here, as soon as I can recover him. And recover him I shall. I can't do everything our family needs to do alone. I need a right hand. Other options . . . haven't panned out. There is only Zymun . . . and you. I will make one of you the next Prism. From what you've told me of Zymun, if I choose him instead, it will cost you your life. He will not want a rival at his back.'

Kip felt a chill. He remembered Janus Borig saying, 'I keep trying to draw you as the next Prism, and I can't. You won't be the Prism, Kip.' He lifted his chin, sneered. 'So, that's what this is? You expect me to curry your favor now? You think adding a lump of sugar to the whip is going to change everything? You've tried to kill me before.'

'Yes, yes, we've talked about that little misunderstanding—'

'—and *failed*. Don't forget that, old man.'

Andross Guile's lips were a tight white line. A dangerous silence followed. 'This warning was a courtesy. I gave it in part because of that misunderstanding. I'm not looking for a puppet or a sniveling lackey, Kip. For the most part, I was deeply satisfied with your father's leadership. A weak man a poor Prism makes. To proffer me your respect is no sign of servility, grandson, it's a sign of wisdom.' Andross Guile walked to his desk, scribbled a note, and handed it to Kip. 'Make yourself strong, Kip. You have little time. You're dismissed. Give that to Grinwoody on your way out.'

'How do I convince you that I should be the next Prism?' Kip asked. Not that he cared. Not that he was afraid.

'I'll give you a task after you return my stolen cards—'

'I thought you believed me that I didn't—' Kip stopped as he saw the ugly look that passed across Andross Guile's face at being interrupted. 'Sorry.'

'I believe you didn't steal them. Probably the thief was my dear son. Unless you're a better liar than I think. Regardless, I want them back – and I want the new cards. Make it your mission. You have until Sun Day. Naming a Prism-elect will wait no longer. If you don't give me the cards – all of them – it won't be you.'

'You really have given up on my father.'

'A great strategist once said every military disaster could be summed up in two words: "Too late." When a plan fails, you don't wring your hands, you move to the next one.'

My father was merely a plan that failed?

Kip felt no rage, which surprised him. Instead, he thought: That's your son. That's your son, and that's all you can say? Was it so simple and cold for his grandfather, or was there a heart, somewhere deep inside him, hidden, broken?

Instead of speaking it now, he asked, 'What was the lesson? From the game, I mean.'

'Was there a lesson, or were there many?' Andross asked, as if to himself. 'Here's one: you back a man into a corner and show him no way out? When a man is utterly in your power but not yet dead? That's when you watch him closest.' Andross tugged several cards out of his sleeves and tossed them onto the table.

They were all the best cards in his deck. 'Now get out . . .' He turned his back before he finished the sentence. '. . . grandson. Send in that Malargos girl. Tisis? I'm going to see just how badly she wants to be the next White. If I don't miss my guess she'll be dressed to please.'

Chapter 37

Kip wasted little time going to the restricted library. His only stop on his way was to get his bag and blank papers, and to grab those of the squad who were in the barracks. The nunks had enforced study times, two hours a day. Each squad was generally required to be in the same place, though Cruxer could sign off for them if they had some excuse, which it seemed Teia often did.

But the rules never specified *where* the squad had to study, and if Kip was going to steal any hours from the day, those were about the only ones possible, unless he wanted to give up a meal.

Unthinkable.

Besides, the note was broadly worded: 'Kip is about my business in the libraries. Don't impede him. – Promachos Guile.' Kip was just sorry that it had mentioned 'in the libraries.'

If it hadn't, it would have been a writ to do whatever he wanted.

He gathered up the squad, though Teia was gone again. They were all eager for the prospect of seeing an area that was forbidden. Nor were they disappointed when they sailed past the librarian guarding the door. The man took one look at the note, paled, and let Kip and the squad in without a word.

This forbidden library took up almost half a floor of the blue tower. It was all gleaming hardwoods and burnished copper and arm chairs. Luxurious desks with comfortable chairs, and slaves to attend to every need – each had a copper necklace with two black stones pendent, carved with a Parian rune Kip didn't recognize. He asked about them.

'They're all illiterate and mute,' Ben-hahad said under his voice. 'So they can't spy on what you're reading.'

'Oh, I've heard about that,' Ferkudi said loudly, excited. 'Some slaves have their tongues cut out specifically so they can serve. Now *that* must be a real flesh protuberance.'

'They're not *deaf*, Ferk,' Ben-hadad muttered.

'Oh, sorry,' Ferkudi said, lowering his voice. 'Wait, why am I apologizing to slaves?'

He glowered at a slave, and when the others weren't looking, Kip saw the slave waggle a stub of a tongue at Ferkudi, who flinched. The next moment, when the others turned to see why Ferkudi had shrunk back, the slave was standing placidly, as if he'd never moved.

Ferkudi was cursing under his breath, but he made no move at retaliation.

Ben-hadad went over to a stack of books and looked at the titles. It took him a while, but no one intervened. Ben-hadad would accept help when he needed to absorb a lot of text, but could get angry otherwise. He said, 'This place looks like the High Luxiats have used it as their own private lounge. These books aren't forbidden. I think the venerable magisters simply don't like sitting on the same hard benches the rest of us do.'

'Does that slave have wine?' Daelos asked. 'You think I could . . .'

'No,' Ben-hahad, Kip, Cruxer, and Big Leo said.

Other than four slaves and the luxiat who was watching the door, this restricted library was empty. The squad drew together a couple of the desks, moving furniture with the impunity of the young, or of Blackguards, or of the friends of a young lord with a special writ from his grandfather. It felt great, but Kip clutched the writ close, certain someone was going to yell at them at any moment.

They'd settled down to study quickly, though. Cruxer wouldn't stand for less. Only Kip was released to browse the shelves. He grabbed books blindly, bound leather inscribed with faded runes and filled with delicate script that at first he didn't realize was in a language he could read. An account of some village he'd never heard of, filled with vocabulary that had to be of foreign origin. Another scroll that seemed to be about farming methods. Another entirely in Old Parian. Another in some language Kip had never laid eyes on. Another in runes.

An account of the pygmies – not of Blood Forest, nor of the archaic Blood Plains, but of Tyrea. Tyrea? Sounded fascinating, though the dates listed were some abbreviation that Kip hadn't seen, so he had no idea how long ago this had been written – and it was written about a time several hundred years before it?

He had no idea how this part of the library was organized, and picking up scrolls randomly was never going to help him find something useful. Kip headed to the front to find the guardian librarian standing out in the hall. As he got close, he heard urgent whispers. 'No!' someone said. Using the shelves to hide his approach, Kip crept closer until he saw the original librarian, speaking to some younger luxiats, '—and report to the High Luxiat that he can't send any more . . . I can let him know when these spies are gone, but—'

'Can't make us carry these all the way back. Can't the slaves—'

Kip stepped forward and saw four young luxiats-to-be flinch guiltily. Each was carrying a stack of scrolls or books. 'What's going on here?' Kip asked.

They all looked at the older luxiat, and Kip knew he was going to hear lies. 'Simply routine work, scrolls in need of mending being returned.' He turned to the young luxiats-in-training. 'Thank you, you may deposit those and go.'

'But before you go,' Kip said. 'You're to tell me your names.' They looked again at the librarian.

Kip sighed, putting on a pretty good pretense of exasperation. 'Who is the Highest Luxiat?' he asked. He didn't wait for the man to say, the Prism. 'That's my father. And who is in charge of all the Chromeria during his absence? The promachos. That's my grandfather. Who has told you to aid me as I go about his work. Do you think he sees not what you do?'

The librarian blanched. 'Tell him your names,' he said.

They did, and Kip said, 'Good, now I want each of you to go looking for a luxiat named Quentin Naheed. You are to demand that he attend me here, immediately. It's an order from the promachos's own hand. Understood?'

They scattered. It left Kip with a very uncomfortable librarian. Kip just stared at the man, trying to put some Andross Guile into his expression. The librarian looked away, and Kip broke out into a big grin. It worked!

He tried to recapture the fierceness, but even as the minutes passed, he could only get as close as dour.

'Hey, Kip! You feeling well? You look constipated,' Quentin Naheed said, coming into the library.

Kip winced.

'How'd you find— Oh, greetings, Brother Anir.'

The librarian scowled and moved to speak. 'Brother Anir,' Kip said, 'you're dismissed back to your post.'

The man went, and Quentin looked at Kip, surprised that he had power over a luxiat.

'I need your help,' Kip said. 'Not just today.' Kip showed him the writ.

'I would have helped without that,' Quentin said. 'I was thinking about before, and . . . you're right, I did lie to you, and that's beneath a luxiat of Orholam. It shall not happen again, not ever. This I swear in the light and by my hope of eternity. You will have the truth of me, no matter the cost.'

Kip raised an eyebrow. What a strange young man. But Quentin was deadly serious. Kip supposed that those who became luxiats had to be a bit peculiar by definition, though.

'Very well,' Kip said, feeling like he should react with some sort of sufficiently sober pronouncement, but he had nothing. 'These texts here. What are they?'

'I can look through each and tell you what each one is. Is that what you're looking for?' Quentin asked, puzzled.

'No, no. Some younger luxiats-to-be were tasked with bringing those books here, and I want to know why. Brother Anir said they'd been repaired? Is that true?'

Quentin went through the books and scrolls and scowled. 'I am loath to accuse anyone of falsehood, but . . . the condition of these books is not consistent with books coming up from the binderies. Mistress Takama would never let this work pass. Some of these haven't been repaired in decades. Nor do all of the books need repair, so this is not consistent with either going to or coming from the binderies.'

'Then what are they?' Kip asked.

'I don't *know*.'

But there was something in how he stressed that. 'Are you going to be honest, or only technically honest?' Kip asked.

Quentin hesitated. 'You're right. I . . . I'll have to pray about how reflexively I cover the truth where my peers are concerned. I should have said, "I don't know, but I can speculate." And as I'm sure you'll next ask what said speculation would be . . .' He blew out a breath. 'These are books from the other restricted libraries.'

'So?' Kip asked.

The rest of the squad had come over. Kip introduced them, and Quentin seemed to get more and more shy, but after introductions, Kip pressed him again. 'So?'

'So there are different permissions needed for the various libraries: you may get access to some libraries but not to others. This library is restricted at the highest level. I've actually never been here.'

'Oh, sneaky,' Ben-hadad said, shaking his head, understanding.

'What?' Ferkudi asked.

'I hate to say it, but I'm with Ferkudi on this,' Cruxer said.

'Promachos Guile opened almost all the restricted libraries

so that the forbidden magics could be studied – for defensive purposes only,' Ben-hadad said.

'The Magisterium was not pleased,' Quentin said.

'So the luxiats have been moving books out of the newly opened libraries into the libraries that are still closed,' Ben-hadad said.

'It's not technically disobedience,' Quentin said. 'I mean, the promachos's order was that the libraries be opened, not that all the books in those libraries should be open for study.'

'That's basically bullshit,' Kip said.

'Yes,' Quentin admitted. 'You have to understand, though, it's been a hard season for the luxiats. Half a dozen of the most respected scholars among us were made laughing stocks when it was discovered that the bane actually exist. Having the privilege of being the only ones allowed to study these forbidden materials stripped from us has been hard – and made harder when sometimes common drafters and Blackguards with no training have made discoveries we missed for many years. It's been a gushing well of humiliation.'

'You're going to be in big trouble for talking to us, aren't you?' Cruxer asked.

'Oh yes.'

'Well, you're in it now. Might be time to make new friends,' Ferkudi said. He grinned a big friendly grin and threw a meaty arm around Quentin's slim shoulders.

Quentin smiled uncertainly.

Chapter 38

For a city where light never dies, Big Jasper had a lot of dark places. And the Order seemed to know them all.

City and sky seemed to have conspired to bring darkness. Teia hunched her shoulders, determined not to be frightened. The moon had been strangled by dark clouds whose fingers thickened as they flexed and that celestial mirror expired. Fog billowed in off the water, hit the walls like an army in a suicide charge, and rolled right over them. For a few moments, Teia could see the fog massed above the walls, and then it came crashing down into the streets.

As it swamped her, blotting out sight, she heard a scream in a nearby street. No, not a scream. Just a cat, yowling in fury. Then it stopped.

The cobbles of the street were slickened with the damp. Teia saw a star bobbing along above her, and it took her imagination moments to calm and realize it was nothing more than a watchman's lantern. He passed directly above her on the wall, and he never even saw her. Teia brushed one hand along the wall, telling herself it wasn't for reassurance.

You're going to your death, the lantern seemed to whisper as it floated away into the distance. Find light!

I'm a slave, not a—

She stopped the thought. She wasn't a slave. She could leave at any time. She had money in her pocket. She had money in the barracks. She could buy a commission and go home. She could go and . . . what?

But she could figure it out. She'd have time. She'd have her family. She'd—

Fear makes you stupid. Look at what I've got here. Look at what I've done. Who back home would believe that I'd even spoken to the White, much less been given an assignment vital to all of the Seven Satrapies by her? Who would believe that I trained with Commander Ironfist, much less led him in an assault on the fortress of Ruic Head? Hell, with my color, who will even believe I'm a drafter?

Out in the wide world, what use is paryl? I can kill people secretly? Oh, lovely. Get lots of chances to use that in polite society. I can see through clothing? Oh, perfect, please tell me how well endowed Lord Fuddykins is! Ha.

You're not a slave anymore, Teia. So who are you going to be?

The Order isn't going to kill me. If they'd wanted to do that, they would have already done it. Right? But what if they changed their minds? If they wanted to kill her in the future, it wouldn't be that hard for them to find her, would it? Or her family.

Teia had to lean against the wall for a moment as her throat constricted. The darkness and fog were oppressive, heavy, clinging to her, making it hard to breathe, diving into her throat, invading her body. Her eyes widened and widened and she felt the tingle of paryl entering her.

Drafted it when I was scared. That's progress, right?

A lantern of the stuff bloomed on her fist and pierced the darkness in every direction. It cut through the haze as if it weren't even there and lent an odd metallic quality to the stones and the cobbles. She thought she heard something, and she looked behind her. Nothing.

When she turned around again, a hooded, cloaked man stood in front of her. Murder Sharp. He looked pleased with himself, or perhaps pleased to see her. 'Good color there. Tight spectrum, almost no bleed. You've got a knack. With paryls, we have to take what we get. Walk with me.'

'You look different,' Teia said. The last time she'd seen him, he'd had a fringe of orange hair around a bald scalp. Apparently it had been a ruse, because he wasn't bald. Now his hair had grown out, though it was still cropped short. It made him look quite a bit younger. He was growing out a beard, the scruff nicely delineated.

'I have the curse of being readily identifiable. I have to work harder for my disguises. I envy your bland prettiness.'

'Thanks?'

'It was a compliment. Do you have any idea how valuable it is to have a description of you be "slender, medium to dark skin, medium height, maybe a little on the short side, dark hair, fairly pretty"? Any distinguishing marks people will remember can be removable ones, like a beauty mark, or a wig – and with your skin tone, you can as easily seem to be a natural when wearing a wig of wavy dark blonde hair or black Parian curls. Being remembered or being forgotten is life and death in my work, so yes, I envy you. Here we are.'

He knocked an odd, syncopated beat on the door.

Great, I'm going to have to become a drummer on top of everything else.

The door opened, and with the light pouring out into the street, Teia constricted her eyes and let the paryl go.

Whoever had opened the door retreated back through another room beyond the entry. Murder Sharp handed her a white robe to put over her clothes. 'Don't identify yourself in any way. The others will be put in danger the more they know. Hearing your voice will be bad enough.' He gave her dark spectacles, too, and a white cloth veil. He dressed himself similarly, except he donned a mask with real white fur and yellow teeth, some snarling creature that looked like a cross between a weasel and a bear. Then he led her into the next room.

The building was a smithy. Lanterns provided cheery light and invaded the darkness outside. There were a dozen figures inside, chatting quietly. But all were cloaked and veiled. Only a few wore the weasel-bear masks. The veils were simple flaps of white cloth, hanging from each person's hat, leaving only their eyes revealed. Some of the veiled figures wore dark spectacles. Those must be drafters, making sure that no one would be able to recognize them by the luxin patterns in their eyes.

Of course, the disguises meant nothing to a paryl drafter. If Teia tried, she could see through their clothes, through their masks, through their silliness. She went from terrified to on the verge of derisive laughter in a second.

Fine, so maybe it was hysterical laughter she was on the verge of. Easy there, Teia. She followed Master Sharp into the smithy and looked from one figure to another in the red light of the forge fire.

'Order,' a man with a gruff voice said.

Order, as in come to order? or like, Hey, you all from the Order, come to order? Teia almost laughed again. Whoa, hold it together, T.

She tried to clear her throat, failed, and didn't dare try clear it again for fear of disturbing the newborn silence.

Though he was short, the others clearly deferred to the gruff one – and he was the only one who had two veils on. The one he wore under the white cloth veil appeared to be made of some kind of finely woven metal mail.

'If the Chromeria or its people find you here, or hear of it henceforth, you will be taken by the Office of Doctrine. You will be tortured. Your lands and titles will be seized. Your families will be punished. Your animals and houses will be burned, as if heresy could be purged with fire.' He paused. 'If you have not the courage to die in silence, go now, and be part of this company no more. The door stands there.'

The idea of being tortured by the very people she was serving was ice in Teia's stomach. Would the White claim her, if she were captured?

Only if it served her ends. And in such a war, claiming Teia might not be the White's best move. Every threat Teia heard was real. And that was if she were found by her friends. How much worse would it be if she were discovered by the Order? She looked at the door, and wondered if they meant it. Could she leave now?

'We've no cowards among us,' the man said. 'Good.'

Teia wanted to shout, Wait! I think I might be a coward! Can I think on it a bit longer?

But it was too late.

The members made a circle around the room, broken only on the side where the forge burned hot. Odd, at night. In the center stood a simple table. Teia felt a chill as she recognized the items piled there. They were all the things she had stolen for Aglaia Crassos – perfect blackmail materials to expose and ruin her, had she not already confessed all of it to the White.

'Hear the sermon of the first circle.'

'Hear, ye deceived,' the figures rumbled, as if invoking prayer.

'Everything you know about the Chromeria is lies,' the gruff man said.

'Hear, ye deceived,' the figures rumbled.

'Gavin and Dazen Guile ruined the world for their lust and pride. But out of the conflagration, out of the hundreds of thousands dead, some good came. Those of us who sided with Dazen Guile saw our hopes die when Gavin Guile came stumbling out of the smoke at Sundered Rock. The wiser of us ran. Most hid. But some were pursued by the vengeful, by murderers seeking to use the cover of war to hide their crimes, by assassins sent to silence us for what we knew.'

He stopped, and said nothing for a long time, as if reliving a memory. None of the others interjected, so Teia didn't move either.

'In our flight, many were lost. Good men, women who'd committed no crime but to lose. Others were dragged off into slavery, sold to the Ilytians in a trade the Chromeria condemned but did nothing to stop.'

'Hear, ye deceived.'

'But.' He raised a finger. 'In every darkness, there is hope for light. For light cannot be chained.'

'Light cannot be chained,' they intoned with him.

'A small group of us fled into the Atashian desert, across the Cracked Lands, pursued for more than a month into the wastes, until our pursuers gave up and we found ourselves without enough water to make the trip back home. So we pressed on. We found the Great Rift the day after we'd drank the last of our water. We climbed down it, losing two more brothers in the hike. And at the bottom, we found an ancient, abandoned city, carved into the faces of the cliffs themselves. We found great cisterns of water, renewed by a small stream, and we found wild goats to eat, and we found luxin the likes of which we couldn't believe, but most precious of all, we found truth.'

'Hear, ye deceived.'

'We were not the first wanderers to find this place. This was Braxos. A city thousands of years old. The pygmies of the darkest Blood Forest claim a common ancestry with the Braxians. We found the remains of a small, later community there – a scholar and his student, later his wife. They had come looking for the city, and had nearly died as we had, but two hundred years before. They stayed two years, tried to go home back to the Chromeria, and gave up and returned, certain the Cracked Lands were impassable. They stayed for the rest of their lives, had children. The community lasted three generations before it succumbed to the inbreeding that left them too feeble to survive those harsh lands.

'But what they did in those generations! They translated skins a thousand years old, and preserved them in script we could read. For the first time, we heard about the time before Lucidonius.' He looked at Teia, as if searching her soul. 'It is time for you to hear the truth, and to decide.'

'Hear the truth, ye deceived.'

'The Braxians always lived a tenuous existence there, though the lands then were not yet the Cracked Lands. It was, still, a desert, and life was hard. In those times, it was believed that each color was a god or goddess, and men clung to one or another. Drafters could never serve two colors because each was at war with each, or at best antipathic. Drafters flowed to those parts of the world where their color could be found, and in so doing, made the differences more profound. The fertile plains of Ruthgar gave plentiful green, so the world's greens left their own peoples and moved there, and the greens built their temple there, and fertilized the plains year after year, making them greener still. The Red Cliffs of Atash, likewise; the volcanoes of deep Tyrea, likewise. And so on.

'The Braxians had a different belief. To them, magic wasn't primarily about light; light was a trigger, the conduit for allowing your will to flow into the world, and into your community. Nor did they believe – as the Chromeria later would – that Will is finite. They didn't think they were using up their souls to make golems. They believed that Will is a muscle, and it is strengthened with every use, not depleted like sands from an hourglass.

'As gods rose and fell, all the nine kingdoms groaned under the weight of their struggles. When the reds gathered under Dagnu the Thirteenth's banner and went to war and wiped out the blues to the last child, they threw off the balance. For a generation, with no blues drafting, red ran amok, deserts spread, the lands cracked, the seas choked. Droughts spread everywhere, and the Braxians among them all were most vulnerable. Their brother tribes in the desert perished. It was no better when the blues had their revenge, two generations later: the waters rose and flooded the floors of the canyons. So much water it flushed the good soil away. The Braxians decided they must come up with some power that would give them a say in events in a world that ignored them, and crushed them in their wars, all unknowing. For our part, may—'

'—we listen and believe,' the figures joined in with him.

Teia got the sense that the exact words of the stories varied, but there were trigger phrases for their responses. It made the flesh on her neck crawl.

'This was the birth of the Order. First, there was only one: Ora'lem, the Hidden, the first Shadow. He wore a cloak which had been infused with the entire will of a polychromatic lightsplitter, a woman who had the talent that the Chromeria deceitfully swears is only known to Prisms. But Ora'lem was killed when he faced a sub-red – for his cloak only hid him from the visible spectrum. After his death, his cloak was recovered only with great difficulty, and the Order decided that Shadows should always work in a team of man and woman, for there are places shut to men and places shut to women, and the strengths of each should cover the weaknesses of the other. Over the generations, the Order amassed fourteen cloaks, some finer than others. Two, now lost, which had been owned by the mist walkers of old, worked in all spectra.

'Those fourteen warriors, the first Shadows, moved unseen among all peoples of the world. Fourteen righteous blades that brought justice. Fourteen mist walkers protected the people of Braxos, and the vulnerable everywhere. They traveled among every kind of drafter, and whispered in the ears of those whose power threatened the balance, telling them to desist. It worked, some few times. But most often, it did not, and the fourteen brought death to a few to sustain life for the many.'

Balancing, as a Prism did, but by force. By murder.

'Braxos flowered, and knew greater prosperity than ever. The very word that the Braxians wished the reds to calm their use of magic meant the reds did, controlling their own priests, without need for death. There was peace, and magic flourished. When others couldn't help and wights were terrorizing an area, it was the Shimmercloaks who intervened. The Order were the stern guardians of a harsh world.

'But the world is a spoiled child; it cannot long stand guardians, even when it needs them most.'

The figures said all together, 'We are the guardians. We are the hands of night. We are the walkers unseen. We are the sword of morning and the bludgeon of midnight. We stand ready. For war, for peace, for life, for death, we stand ready.'

My new friends, the insane vigilante drafter murderers.

'In this world perpetually on the brink, with only our hands to steady it, a young man came during a time of upheaval. New technologies were being discovered, and the balance was threatened on every side. He became a Shimmercloak, and he was, we soon could tell, among the greatest of us that had ever lived. Diakoptês, his name was.'

'Diakoptês, the Betrayer!'

'The Braxian lens-grinders were the finest in the world, and it was they who discovered how to melt metals into glass to make the lenses that would change the world. Pitchblende and lead for red, theion and calcium for yellow, cadmium and brimstone for orange, orpiment and iron for green, cobalt and theion for blue. These were to be our secrets, and our new power. No longer would we have only to rely on the seven teams, on trying to find new polychromatic light-splitters to make new shimmercloaks when the old ones were stolen or destroyed. Then came a young man. Diakoptês, his name was.'

'Diakoptês, the Betrayer!'

'Diakoptês the Shadow had killed for us in every one of the nine kingdoms. As famous for his temper as he was for his skill with blade and bludgeon. He began experimenting with black luxin, a color that can only be drafted by those with great evil in their hearts. He grew corrupt, and he lusted after power. We sent people to him, old friends to entreat with him. He slew them. He stole his people's designs, the very jewel of Braxian industry and two hundred years of innovation, and he equipped an army with it. And with his armies, he brought the bloodiest war the nine kingdoms had ever seen. He crushed them under his boot, and called himself a savior. He named free men heretics and brilliant women beasts. We know him by his true name: Diakoptês, his name was.'

'Diakoptês, the Betrayer!'

'But you may know him by his other name. The name he took for himself to make himself a god: Lucidonius, the Giver of Light.'

Teia shouldn't have been surprised that murderers and heretics should have blasphemous views of Lucidonius, but somehow, she was. Even the coarsest slave's complaints about how Lucidonius had overlooked the plight of the slave still assumed that Lucidonius, being mortal, had merely overlooked them, not that he was evil.

She bit her lip and said nothing, looking from hooded figure to hooded figure. Last, she looked at the pile of things she'd stolen, sitting on the stool off to one side.

'The Magisterium teaches that we have but one life, one judgment, and one eternity. There is in them no mercy for those born to low circumstances, to only bad choices, as if the daughter of nobility and the daughter of ignominy have the same chances at a life of virtue. The Braxians were kinder, more humane. We know that . . .'

They intoned, 'In death is the cleansing of sins. In rebirth is the hope for salvation.'

'He called himself the Second Eye of Orholam. And so it was that the Order to Break the Eye was born. So it was we slew our favorite son Diakoptês. Not in hatred, but in hope. Hope for his rebirth. Hope for salvation.'

Together, they said, 'We wait with hope and expectation. Breakers unbroken, our Long Vigil continues.'

'Thus ends the sermon of the first circle. May we all be worthy to learn more.'

They chanted something in a language that Teia didn't understand. Nor, it was clear, did some of them, from how they lagged behind the others with the unfamiliar syllables. Then, it seemed, they chanted a loose translation, not quite so rhythmic: 'True in darkness. True in light. True in daytime. True at night. Honest, fierce, loyal, strong, but hidden till we right the wrong.'

The gruff leader came close, and lowered his voice enough that the others would likely only hear pieces of it over the whoosh of the bellows one of them was working. 'You know what these are.' He picked up a silver bracelet, set it down.

'Things I stole on my mistress's orders.'

'Blackmail,' he said.

'Blackmail,' she agreed.

He lowered his voice further. 'Among the deceived, Adrasteia, you will always be a former slave. The highest you can rise is to be a Blackguard. It is a good position, for a former slave. Usually. Less good in wartime. Everyone knows that the

Blackguards' standards have slipped in order to replenish the ranks. You will be thrown at problems that the peacetime Blackguard would never accept. You will die for the White, perhaps, though this one is almost dead. She won't last two more years. And who will replace her? Someone you can love and respect? Will you be happy to give your life for the Red? Is that the life you want? A slave exalted, but a slave still. Is that the best you can do?'

He nodded to two of the masked figures and backed away.

Louder now, he said, 'We want you, initiate, but we won't blackmail you into service. The Order isn't looking for slaves. You can be a soldier to be used as cannon fodder for them, or for us you can be more. We're looking for Shadows. We're looking to give you a chance to make a difference. To change the course of all history. To pick up the pittance this world has given you and demand more, and in turn give more. There will be no work as hard as what we offer, but together we can remake the world.'

The figures stepped forward and set the silver items in a pitted bowl at the end of a paddle. They lifted it into the fire, and Teia watched as the silver wobbled, lost form, and melted, ready to be remade.

Chapter 39

'I want you to stab me,' Gavin said. He and the Malargos boy Antonius were standing on deck in the early morning light.

'Your pardon?'

'I've been stabbed by it before. Maybe twice.'

'Where?' Antonius asked.

'Off Garriston and off Ru. See? It's even been on boats both times.'

'I meant on your body.'

'Oh, in the back, here, and straight through my chest, here.' They were still short on clothing, so like the rest of the former slaves, Gavin went shirtless. It had scandalized the young lord, who had offered his own garments, but Gavin couldn't accept them, for reasons he couldn't have said. Regardless, it meant that when he gestured to where he'd been attacked, he was gesturing to skin.

Antonius leaned close. 'No scars. No scars?'

'I think that's part of the magic. Well, it has to be.'

Antonius hefted the sword and stabbed it down on the deck. Its point sank deeply into the polished, fire-hardened wood. He looked at Gavin skeptically.

'I think it's different, for me,' Gavin said.

He'd been doing a lot of thinking in the last day of freedom. First he'd thought of Karris, Karris, who had been so painful to think about when he was in the hell belowdecks. He could see her smile, the arch of her neck, her hair – blonde, now – and her tears of joy as they embraced once more. He could feel her fingers touching his face while he slept, assuring herself he was real. He could imagine nipping her fingers to startle her, and laughing together. He imagined her slim legs around his hips, her warm embraces – but then that, too, still hurt. His body had been hollowed out like a bowl for sorrows, and imagining pleasure filling it again was torture. He tried to imagine what she would say when she saw his eyes, instead. She had married a Prism. She had accepted the costs of being married to the most powerful man in the world, but she'd accepted the rewards, too.

He was that man no more. What he had promised was not what he was going to give her. What would she say to this withered husk?

I am not now that which once I was. What work of noble note might yet be done, by me? By this cripple?

That, too, was too cruel to countenance. So he'd thought about the musket-sword. It was the black in it that captivated him. It looked like obsidian. But no one could work obsidian into such delicate spirals; the stuff wasn't malleable. Obsidian fractured with hard, sharp edges. During the war, those who could afford obsidian had edged their arrowheads with the stuff, as it cut through luxin better than steel did. But few could afford it. That it interfered with drafting was known, though. Hellstone, drafters called it, thinking it darkness personified, a negation of light, and thereby a tool of the enemy.

Gavin had his – the real Gavin's – men collect all the weapons lined with hellstone and any gems or decorative pieces, put them in a few crates, and had them 'lost' when they got back to Big Jasper. It was war, albeit the end of the war, and things go missing. He'd used that treasure to line the tunnels of Gavin's prison beneath the Chromeria. He was very familiar with obsidian.

And this didn't make sense.

'Can we try a little bit at a time, rather than just run you through and hope for the best?' Antonius asked.

'When you put it like that,' Gavin said, 'that sort of makes sense.'

Antonius grimaced. He lofted the sword and extended it toward Gavin's chest. 'How about I hold the sword in place, and you can move forward as much as you want, and maybe the crew won't keelhaul me for killing you?'

'Fair.' Gavin held the tip of the white-and-black sword to his chest. He leaned in—

—and jumped back, cursing, blood dribbling down his chest.

Antonius jumped back, too, eyes wide. There was a moment of silence, while Gavin rubbed at the wound. 'So . . . that wasn't how it worked before?' Antonius asked.

Gavin cursed louder, swore at the heavens. There was no way he'd been imagining it. At least not the second time. The dagger had been a dagger when he'd fought his father and Grinwoody and Kip for it, and a sword thereafter. Gunner had admitted that he'd pulled it out of Gavin's chest – that Gavin had been fully impaled.

Maybe it only worked once. It took all your magic, and then it was done. But obsidian didn't do that. It could drain luxin from your blood, sure, but it didn't stop you from ever drafting again. Not even all obsidian did that.

'Can I try it on you?' Gavin asked.

'You said it took away your ability to draft,' Antonius said.

It wasn't as if Gavin had wanted to tell him, but there hadn't been any way to avoid it, either. The boy had asked him to draft some repair to the galley, and Gavin had no lie ready for why he wouldn't. 'That's right,' Gavin said. 'It's a guess, of course, but the events correlate.'

'So you want me to give up my ability to do magic to satisfy your curiosity?' Antonius asked. 'Don't get me wrong, I want to help, but . . . Maybe we could wait and try some other way?'

Gavin sighed. He couldn't exactly blame the boy. 'It's almost first watch. Time's up. We need to decide.'

Yesterday, in their initial exuberance and fear, they'd simply rowed until dark to get away. None of the slaves had thought to use sextant and compass to find their position, and it had been overcast. Antonius Malargos said they were between Rath and the Jaspers, two days out from Rath.

The crew gathered on deck. Many of them had slept on deck, not trusting that someone wouldn't come and lock them to an oar once again. In the growing light of the rosy-fingered dawn, they took their places.

Antonius spoke first. 'This day, we must decide our destination. We've food and water for what? Five days? I've heard tales of your rowing prowess, and I'm sure you could reach half the coast of Blood Forest and half the coast again of Ruthgar. But there are only two viable options: go to Big Jasper, or go to Rath.'

'Why would we go to Rath?' someone asked.

'You left out the third option,' someone else said. 'We can keep pirating. Sun Day's coming, all sorts of fat fish in the water for us to take.'

'Listen to me!' Antonius said. He was too fearful, too young. He thought he was losing the sailors' attention. He wasn't. They simply wanted to taste their freedom a bit. What could make a man feel more like a free man than interrupting his betters without consequence? For men who'd lived under the lash, it was fine wine.

'I'm offering you freedom, and more,' Antonius said. 'My cousin, Lady Eirene Malargos, is fair and rich and connected. If you land in the wrong city, you'll be seen as fugitive slaves, game for anyone to recapture. You land somewhere worse, and you're mutineers. You could be hanged or 'hauled. My cousin will give you papers, filed in every capital. Freedom. Never having to run again. It goes without saying that we split the cargo. Even shares for everyone. No share for me, though I rescued you. All that, and fifty danars each.'

'We want to keep the ship, too!' someone shouted out.

'The *Bitter Cob* will be sold and the profit divided up with the rest of the shares,' Antonius said. 'That's the only way everyone gets an even split. If some of you want to go in together and buy it, that's your business.'

Gavin stood up. 'Lord Antonius,' he said, inclining his head. 'I want you to know how much we all appreciate you and your actions. We'll make sure you're amply rewarded. However. I'm not really sure why you're even trying. We're going to Big Jasper, because whatever you offer, I'll double.'

The men cheered.

But Antonius held up his hand silent, waiting. Someone shouted, 'Shut yer yaps, ya rabble, let the lord drive the price up!' The men laughed, but eventually quieted.

'Two things,' Antonius said. 'One that you know, and one that you can't. First, you all know Eirene Malargos's reputation. She is a tough trader, but she always keeps her word, no matter what. Second, in normal times, Gavin Guile could indeed double whatever she and I could offer you. In normal times, I know Gavin Guile would honor his promise to us, though we all know that the Guiles have earned their surname anew a thousand times each generation.'

That was a bit too complicated a construction for the sailors. These were simple men. But Gavin didn't interrupt. Let the boy play his gambit. Gavin was ascendant once more. This was his game. He wasn't going to have a crew he'd served with for months be taken out from under him. He wouldn't allow it. He saw Orholam staring at him, his prophet eyes intent.

'But these are not normal times. As I heard from you all last night, Luxlord Andross Guile stabbed his own son and threw him overboard.' He paused. 'I tell you now that the luxlord has not been idle since his son has been gone.'

Men were looking at Gavin, and he felt dread rising in him.

'Andross Guile has been named promachos,' Antonius said. 'And he has consolidated power in a way that even Gavin

Guile couldn't do during the False Prism's War. He doesn't want the enemy son he thought he murdered to come back. For your own sakes and for Gavin's, the last place you want to go is Big Jasper.'

It took Gavin's breath. In that moment, he knew it was true.

And, too late, he realized that they had only Antonius's word on this. But these sailors, not schooled in oratory, many of them unable even to read, were able to read a face. Gavin's undisguised dread was a confirmation of everything Antonius said.

'But Gavin is the Prism. That's gotta count for—'

'Is he?' Antonius said. 'I know you believe he is. I believe he is, too. But if he came into Big Jasper and his father's men seized him, and he shouted, "I am the Prism!" would they not say, "Then draft, Prism, save yourself, prove yourself!"? He can't draft. He can't prove who he is. Gavin is our friend, and our Prism – aye, I believe it! But now, in wanting to go home, he is like a drunk friend who wants to swim across the sea. It is not a good friend who encourages that drunk to swim. Prove your friendship to Gavin, and your devotion to your Prism – by not letting him throw his life away.'

Gavin had no answer, no counter. His golden tongue was too heavy to make words. He hadn't thought it through, had been too busy thinking about the wrong things. He'd been outmaneuvered by a boy. He was slipping. He was lost.

'Tell me,' Antonius said, 'what happens to the simple sailor who comes between two warring giants? I tell you what doesn't happen. A simple sailor doesn't get paid double. He doesn't get rewarded. He gets killed outright. So tell me, who wants to head to Rath?'

Chapter 40

Kip didn't know why he was surprised. He'd thought once he got into the restricted libraries his problems would be solved. As if merely because you'd had to fight for something that meant it was good. The truth was harder to find. The books were filled with accounts the luxiats didn't want read, but finding exactly what Kip needed – when he didn't know what that was – was far harder.

The forbidden library had become the squad's second home. When Kip wasn't training with Karris or attending lectures or training with the Blackguards, he was here. If Andross Guile had been initially irritated that Kip had used his writ to get all of his friends access to the library as well, he'd been placated when Kip reported how the luxiats had been secretly defying the promachos.

Kip was sure there were some very unpleasant discussions between Andross and the High Luxiats after that, but of course he didn't get to see any of that. He was also glad to see that Andross had blocked any direct vengeance the luxiats might have wanted to take on Quentin. Not that the young scholar took much hope of that. 'Light never forgets,' he said.

'Huh?' Kip asked.

'It's how we say luxiats have long memories,' Quentin said, not even looking up from some boring tome of archaic theology. Quentin mostly filled his time doing his own research, exploiting the access Kip had given him to restricted materials for a treatise he was writing, but he'd also become a vital resource and good friend to the squad.

'Orholam have mercy,' Cruxer said. He'd finished his own studies for the day and had been helping Kip search for books on the black cards. He sat back from the scroll he had unrolled in front of him.

'What?' Ferkudi asked.

All of them were seated around a table. Ferkudi and Daelos – who had only learned to read in the last year and still read slowly – were agonizing over their own studies nearly as much as Ben-hadad, who'd known how to read for years, but still had trouble with the words swimming around the page.

All paused from their work. It had turned out there was a lot of boring material that the Magisterium had banned, but every once in a while they found a gem.

Big Leo said, 'You can't not tell us. I've been reading about flowering plants for two hours. Flowering plants, Cruxer.

Flowering. Plants.' Kip liked Big Leo a lot. His mother had been an acrobat and his father a strongman for a traveling circus. They'd been killed in the False Prism's War; Ferkudi had said it was because Leo's father didn't know how to fight, despite his enormous strength. Big Leo had vowed to become the best fighter he could, to never be vulnerable. But other than the intensity that sometimes came out when he was drafting red or sub-red, he was good-humored and wry.

Cruxer said, 'I sort of had this picture of the greens worship—' He looked around at them, suddenly embarrassed. 'Sorry, Teia.'

'Shut up,' she said. 'Go on.' The squad treated her like one of the boys most of the time, but neither the squad nor Teia was terribly consistent about when she wanted to *not* be treated like one of the boys.

He shook his head. 'It sounds like fun, right? Orgies and wild drunkenness and dancing and, uh, temple girls—'

'It wasn't only temple *girls*,' Teia said.

They looked at her.

'Don't even,' she said.

Cruxer cleared his throat. 'Uh, anyway. I just came across instructions for the planting ritual. It's, uh, it's instructions on how to prepare the infants for human sacrifice. It's not just how to remove the heart from such a small space, but also how to have musical instruments play loudly at the point when the infant starts wailing as they're cut open so that the worshippers don't . . . don't lose faith.'

The whole squad went silent for a moment. 'Orholam curse them,' Big Leo said.

'I could handle that. I mean, I'd heard they passed babies through the flames, and I . . .' Cruxer shrugged. 'It was just a story. But this . . . the worst part is it details how to choose the babies by lot, "due to the usual problem of there being many more infants offered by parents than the dozen needed." This wasn't some evil priest ripping a babe out of the arms of some young mother. They did it willingly. Our ancestors. Our people. How could they?'

Quentin said, 'If I may? There was a warrior-priest once named Darjan who they say saw and participated in all the worst of war: massacres and murders and torture and worse, and excelled at all of it. He was a leading pagan priest, but he became one of Lucidonius's personal converts, and after a lifetime of war around seven of the nine kingdoms, he put out one of his eyes, moved to Tyrea and lived out his days as an ascetic, climbing daily to the top of – well, a statue or what is now Sundered Rock or – there are arguments, and – not important. He spent the last thirty years of his life praying dawn to dusk, and – more not important stuff. He once said, "For most of our lives, that Orholam is just should fill us with fear, but there are moments when that truth is the only thing that can fill us with peace."'

Kip said, 'Are you telling me this is what I've been missing out on by skipping the "Lives of the Saints" lectures? Murderous warrior-priests who camped out back in Rekton? I climbed on that statue!'

'Way to miss the point, Breaker,' Teia said.

'You have to sit through a lot of lectures to get the good ones,' Quentin admitted. They all laughed a little, and they all knew it was only to cover over what they'd heard. But they were all ready to let it go.

'It's sort of a "Look inward first, but look outward, too"?' Teia asked Quentin. It was an old saying.

'Pretty much – the real quote was Ambrosius Abraxes, "Look ye first to thy innermost parts. Search and know them as does Orholam himself, and then may ye turn thy gaze to the deeds of those who persecute thee." Some of the saints had a real way with words, others . . .' He grinned.

Still serious, Cruxer said, 'This is who we're fighting. This wasn't an individual's guilt – one bad priest oppressing a community that feared him. It was the entire community, eager to participate in what they knew was evil.'

'There's no evidence that the Color Prince's people have done any of this,' Ben-hadad said uncomfortably.

'This is what they want us to go back to!'

'They probably don't even know about this,' Ben-hadad said. 'It's here, in this library. How would—'

'Are you on their side?' Cruxer asked. 'You read it, you tell me if such things don't go a long way to explaining why the Chromeria sent luxors out into the world.'

The table fell silent. Of all them, Quentin looked worst. 'That was a . . . dark chapter in the Magisterium's history. We don't even like to speak of it.'

Teia said, 'I've heard rumors that some of the High Luxiats themselves have been agitating to give the Office of Doctrine some of their old powers again.'

Quentin shook his head. 'Other luxiats have foolishly said such things, yes, but I don't think it goes that high.'

'They haven't squashed those rumors, though,' Kip said.

'They're scared,' Quentin said. 'But they're wiser than scared. We can trust them.'

'I'm sure people thought that the first time the luxors were established,' Ben-hadad said.

'Quentin's right, though,' Teia said. 'They're right to be scared. Every time we hear about the war, it's about a loss like at Ruic Neck. Even the victories don't make sense. A victory at Sitara's Wells? And then two weeks later a victory at Amitton? Our armies marched backward as fast as they could to reach the next "victory"? I think we're losing everywhere, and they're lying about it.'

'Enough about the war,' Cruxer said. 'I don't think we should be looking at these books anymore. These volumes were restricted for good reason. I think this knowledge deserves to be lost.'

'You can't be serious,' Ben-hadad said.

'Look at what I just read,' Cruxer said. 'I can't unlearn that! I didn't even read you all of it. It's worse. And I didn't even finish. What's wrong with saying that in some cases, other people know best?'

'I wouldn't trust anyone to know what's best for me,' Ben-hadad said.

'Then maybe you don't belong in the Blackguard,' Cruxer snapped, 'because that's what you agree to every time you take an order.'

'Enough!' Kip said. 'Cruxer, I'm sorry you had to read that. If you need to stop, stop. But I need to do this.'

'Do you? You don't even know what you're looking for.'

It was a sore spot. They'd looked through a mind-numbing number of genealogies: Klytos Blue was, like most nobles, related to nearly everyone, and though they'd found hints of dozens of scandals, none involved Klytos directly. It was getting harder not to conclude that they'd been wasting their time. Kip shot back, 'If you can't handle the horror of what man can do to man, maybe you're the one who shouldn't be in the Blackguard.'

The table fell silent.

Cruxer's ever-warm eyes chilled. 'Breaker, we're going to be part of this war, like it or not. It's going to kill some of us at this table. And it's going to change all of us. It doesn't mean we should be eager for those changes. Most of them aren't good.'

'These books could give us the edge we need to win,' Kip said.

'The best thing these books can do is to teach us forbidden magic.'

'For defense!' Teia said. 'How we can defend against what we don't even know?'

'Knowledge is a musket. You can use it only as a club, but will you? When your life is on the line? The miracle to me is that the luxiats were able to sequester this knowledge at all. Breaker, when I held Lucia in my arms as she was dying, in that moment, I would have damned myself with any magic known or unknown if it would have meant vengeance on her murderer.'

The faces around the table were somber. The young luxiat looked on the verge of fainting. Delicate sensibilities about damnation, Kip figured.

'There isn't only the danger to our souls,' Cruxer said. 'If we use these . . . the Color Prince's drafters will, too.'

'If they can figure it out. They don't have our books,' Teia said.

'They probably have their own books,' Ben-hadad said.

'But what if they learned it from fighting us,' Cruxer said. 'Then they'd think they have to use these magics because we are.'

'They're probably already working on all this,' Big Leo said. 'This stuff is forbidden by us – who they hate and wish to destroy. Let's be realistic; they're not going to be held back by beliefs they don't share.'

'We're talking about starting an arms race,' Cruxer said.

Teia said, 'We're not starting it; we're just starting to run before they cross the finish line.'

'The only way out of an arms race is to win,' Ben-hadad said.

'In such victories, all men lose,' Cruxer said.

'Better to lose your idealism than your life,' Kip said.

'You all agree with this?' Cruxer asked.

No one looked excited about it, but there were nods all around. 'Maybe we should listen to Kip on this, Captain,' Ferkudi said. 'I mean, he is the Li— Ow! What the hell, Teia?!' He rubbed his rib.

She stared at him. Around the table, smirks were being suppressed.

'Oh, right, we weren't going to talk about the Li . . . the li . . . littlest squad member?' Ferkudi said.

There were groans around the table. Big Leo buried his face in his hands.

'This again?' Kip said. He knew they'd speculated. Everyone wants to live at a pivotal time in history, right? And if you weren't arrogant enough to delude yourself into thinking *you* were the Lightbringer, surely the second best thing would be thinking you knew him. 'Not all of you, though?'

'Sooo,' Teia said, redirecting. 'Yes, Captain, we all agree.'

Cruxer blew out a breath. He looked from face to face. 'I can't lead where you won't follow, so I'm in. But I want you all to remember this. We had a choice here.'

Kip wanted to follow up about the Lightbringer silliness, but after the ominous gravity of that, it was too awkward.

They fell back to their studies. Gradually, they got back to their complaints about the archaic diction or how much work the magisters were expecting them to master or their Blackguard training or, in Quentin's case, with how he couldn't figure out the organization of the restricted library yet, which didn't follow any of the usual schema.

When they were getting up to leave, Cruxer pulled Ben-hadad aside. 'Ben. A word.'

Kip hung back.

'Ben, this squad is like a body. We've all got our different parts to play, but we need to work together. I need to know—'

'This is about me saying I don't trust anyone to know best for me?' Ben-hadad asked.

'That's right.'

'Crux,' Ben-hadad said. 'I don't trust you to know what's best for me. But I trust you to know what's best for the squad. For the Blackguard. And they matter more than I do. That's why I take your orders. And why I will. To the death.'

Cruxer's whole demeanor eased, and he was suddenly less worried leader and more happy young man, glad to have a friend back.

'Besides,' Ben-hadad said. 'Every body needs an asshole.'

Cruxer groaned.

'Did you hear that?' Kip said. 'He just volunteered to take all the squad's shit.'

'I didn't mean *I* was the asshole!' Ben-hadad said.

'It always comes back to poop jokes, doesn't it?' Cruxer said.

'In sailing, the poop by definition is at the—' Teia started.

'Don't.'

'Ah, just one crappy—'

'No.'

Chapter 41

It seemed that every time that Kip thought he'd seen all of the Chromeria, he found out that there was much, much more to it. Today, he was meeting Karris in the workshops beneath the blue tower. There were smelters and glass furnaces here, racks of tools lining every wall, and at least a hundred men and women swarming, drafters and non-drafters each at their appointed task.

Despite the furnaces burning along one wall, there was no smoke, and the temperature was only slightly elevated. Vents were everywhere – for air, but also for light. The purest lenses Kip had ever seen cast spotlights in perfect colors for drafting onto tables. This was where the work of light-crafting and research into practical applications for luxin was conducted. Everywhere, he saw people looking at papers or slates holding calculations they'd done in the study rooms above, checking them against what they were seeing in practice.

Kip saw his tutor standing next to a plain, fair-skinned woman with her blonde hair pulled in a severe ponytail, sleeves rolled up, skin stained faintly green and yellow, though she couldn't have been much more than thirty years old. Burning through her life fast.

Seeing Karris beckon him, Kip walked over. Since she'd started tutoring Kip, Karris had begun wearing the finest dresses and newest fashions. Kip had asked her about it once, and she said that with her short, lean figure, people constantly took her for younger than she was and questioned her – challenged her, in her eyes – far too often. By looking as rich as a Guile, Karris forestalled hassles. Kip knew she would have preferred to wear her blacks instead, but she only wore those when she and Kip trained together, and even then, despite the cost of clothing, her 'blacks' were red or green rather than black. That part of her life was dead, she said. And the even way she said it, never looking Kip in the eye, told him how much it grieved her.

'This is Lady Phoebe Kalligenaea,' Karris said. Her hair recently was a chestnut brown with lighter highlights, rich-looking and boring. She was also growing it out longer than she ever would have worn it as a Blackguard.

'She's got the finest control of any yellow superchromat known. Including Gavin. Lady Kalligenaea, this is my husband's son, Kip.'

'Mistress Phoebe will do,' the woman said. 'I'm a master crafter, and down here, that means more than a silly title passed down through accidents of birth.'

'Isn't being a yellow superchromat an accident of birth, too?' Kip asked.

Kip the Lip. But this time he didn't squint his eyes and sink into his embarrassment. He watched her instead.

'Aha! Maybe so, but I work to make the most of *this* accident. The other I avoid as much as possible.' She grinned, and revealed a big gap between her front teeth.

'So you're better than the Prism?' Kip asked.

She looked like she'd bit a lemon. 'At small things. I could never make Brightwater Wall, that's for sure.'

'What are you better at?'

Mistress Phoebe looked over at Karris. 'Direct, isn't he?'

'It's refreshing,' Karris said. 'At times.' She gave Kip the look. He understood.

'I've worked with the Prism, taught him,' Mistress Kalligenaea said. 'Luxin makes sense to him. Karris tells me you're same. His signature is magic that is beautiful and breathtaking in its sheer audacity – a whole wall of yellow luxin, who would dare such a thing? Much less dare it while an army was closing in? But . . . it lacks a certain elegance. Made of yellow, you could have a wall that still meets the requirements for strength – that is, capable of taking sustained cannon blasts – at maybe a third the thickness Gavin chose. When he isn't sure, he opts for more, always more, rather than to sit with paper and abacus.

'It's not a sharp criticism, mind you. If you have unlimited drafting potential, using more because it's quicker is a logical choice. The rest of us would burn out that way in days. We *must* opt for elegance over force. The other thing Gavin does well is that he remembers everything. It's sort of nauseating, to be quite frank. Once he gets a design right, I'll see him staring at it, turning it over in his hands, and then it's in his head. Ten years go by, and you ask him to reproduce the same cooling rack for bread, and he does it. It's a marvel. But! We aren't here to talk about Gavin Guile, we're here to teach you. They tell me you're a superchromat.'

The words of his testers echoed in his ears: freak. 'Some would say a superchromat boy is like a dog that can bark, "I love you"—'

'"A novelty, not a precedent"?' Her nose crinkled. 'Tawenza Goldeneyes is a gifted tutor, better than I. She's also a bitch. Karris told me she refused to tutor you. Even after Karris came down on her. Flat refused.'

'Called me a strumpet,' Karris said. She did not seem to find it humorous.

'Sorry?' Kip said.

'No matter. If she hadn't, Lady – Mistress Phoebe wouldn't have taken you on,' Karris said.

'You understand, if I take you on, and you ever get a chance to show up Goldeneye's discipulae, I want you to do it. Which means you have to be better than they are.'

Kip grinned. 'With pleasure. I'm at least that much like my father.'

'Can you draft a stable solid yellow?'

'On a good day,' Kip said.

'By the time I'm done with you, you'll have memorized how to make a yellow sword, from memory, within . . . eh, eight seconds.'

'Three,' Karris said. 'At most. By Sun Day.'

For a moment, Kip remembered scrabbling around on the old battlefield at Sundered Rock, looking for the telltale gleam of yellow luxin in the rising sunlight. Solid yellow luxin was the most valuable for resale. Picking through the mud, spitting on rocks and rubbing them clear with an already grubby sleeve, hoping against hope he could pay for dinner tonight instead of relying on charity again and hating himself, and hating his mother, and feeling guilty for it.

It was all different now. He wasn't sure why, with all the radical changes he'd been through, that somehow this little one struck him.

If I ever lose it all, I could still make a better living than I ever could have imagined back in Rekton, just by drafting bits of yellow luxin to sell.

All the inherited wealth and position were somehow external. But this tiny little thing was somehow his. He would never go back to who he'd been. Couldn't.

'Four months?' Mistress Phoebe was saying. 'Hmm. You have your father's memory? You as smart as he is?'

'No, and not even close,' Kip said, coming back to the moment, pushing all that self-indulgent nonsense away.

'More modest, at least, not that that's hard,' Mistress Phoebe said. 'Good. It'll make you work more than he ever did. Us mere mortals work for our bread and board. One hour a day, young Guile.'

'Every other day,' Karris said. 'He's got six other colors to practice, and Blackguard training.'

Kip groaned. Quietly. Karris would let him get away with that much.

'Sad,' Mistress Phoebe said. 'I had all sorts of onerous chores I was looking forward to him performing. Looks like it'll be study only instead.'

And so it had gone, with every color. Kip didn't know how Karris bullied, blackmailed, or begged, but she got him tutors in every color. She kept him in some of his classes – engineering and a basic history course – but had him skip others. The time for hagiographies would have to be later, she said, if he lived. Without exception, his tutors were excellent. Some of them were the best in their field, like Mistress Phoebe. Others were simply great teachers.

Karris taught him fighting herself, incorporating drafting with the purely mundane fighting that the Blackguard inductees mostly did. She said that once the rest of the nunks did start to incorporate drafting, Kip would either get much better than average or much worse: the others had only one or two types of luxin to figure out how to use in fighting. Kip had seven.

There was too much to learn in a man's lifetime, she said, and a woman would be weak in body by the time she learned it all. But she'd teach him as much as she could.

And she was a good teacher, despite the handicap of having to teach him drafting while being forbidden to draft herself. She had an uncanny instinct for knowing when he tried to ease up, but she wasn't cruel.

He could tell that she was figuring out her own new roles, too. When she walked with him from the blue tower workshops into the big practice field where the Blackguards met, he saw a flash of grief in her eyes.

Trainer Fisk saluted her, hand to heart. She moved to salute back, then stopped herself and nodded to him instead, a lady, not a Blackguard.

Kip had a thought before he jogged over to get in line, and blurted it out: 'He's coming back. I swear.'

She didn't try to deny she'd been thinking about it. 'The

world isn't always so merciful, Kip.' She turned and left abruptly, head held high. Something in the rigidity of it told Kip that it was that or collapse.

So unlike his own mother, for whom the least harsh word was an excuse to smoke more haze or drown in a bottle. He wished his mother had been half the woman Karris was.

And that thought led him to Zymun. Orholam's shit. Kip's oath, offered so readily, buying what he needed with the coin he didn't want to keep, was seeming more expensive by the day.

From Andross, who still played him regularly, Kip learned that Karris had disappeared after the war, only coming back to the Chromeria more than a year later.

That hadn't been uncommon. Families had been destroyed in any of a dozen ways by the war, and many of the old guard hadn't come back at all after Sundered Rock. Others had been gone for long periods simply trying to repair the damage done to their estates in their respective satrapies, having to hire and train new people to take over from those killed or exiled in the war. The old indolence so many families had been able to afford before the war was simply gone. An absence of a year for the scion of a once-great family had been unremarkable.

Andross said it had taken him a long time to find out what had happened. Karris had stayed with some distant relations in Blood Forest and left the child with them.

She still thought it a secret. But even if Kip were willing to risk Andross's wrath by breaking his word to him, how do you pull someone's secret shame out into the light, and then make it worse?

'That son you thought was secret? Andross knows all about it, and he's bringing him here. And your son may be more loyal to Andross than anyone. Oh, and he lacks all human decency and emotion except ambition.' Any way Kip played the conversation, it went downhill fast. And that was before Andross avenged himself.

I'm Kip the Lip, and in this, I'm *not* able to blurt out the truth.

Andross had looked at him during one of their games and

paused. Kip had been plying him for news of the war. The last he'd heard, the Chromeria had lost at Ruic Neck but had won – despite Teia's scoffing – at Sitara's Wells and a small town called Amitton. Andross naturally had all the most accurate and timely information available. Andross said, 'This is not for sharing, you understand?'

'Of course.'

'We're losing. We'll continue to lose for months. The winter storms could sink any ships with reinforcements or matériel we'd send. We're gathering what we can, and fighting delaying actions, slowing them. It will be after Sun Day before we can bring our full might to bear. We will lose all of Atash, and perhaps a third of Blood Forest, depending.'

'It's that bad?' Kip asked. Some people were still talking like they expected a quick victory now that the satrapies were united against the threat.

'Worse.' Then Andross had said nothing for a long time.

'What is a man's oath, Kip?'

He wasn't looking for an answer.

'What is a man's oath but his will put into words? If a man puts his words false, and sets will against word, are not both weakened?'

Kip's skepticism – not about the sentiment, but on the source of it – must have shown, because Andross said, 'You will notice, grandson, that though I often misdirect and manipulate—'

'Lie.'

'Yes, lie,' he said as if the difference were a trifle. 'But I almost never give an oath. When I do, I uphold it. Utterly. Every people from the moment Orholam gave man the light of reason has known and allowed the petty lies that are as natural as breathing, the words to which no will is attached. And every people has distinguished those from oaths. Vows. The moment of creation itself was a perfect word perfectly wedded to a perfect will.'

'You believe that?' Kip asked. 'I thought you were an atheist.'

The instant intensity came back to Andross's multicolored eyes. 'A word I hope you use not of me publicly, idly or otherwise.'

'Never,' Kip said.

He seemed placated. 'I have more . . . nuanced beliefs than most. Orholam is a lawgiver in a distant land. He is king of a thousand worlds. Such is enough for his majesty, and the actions of men are either mostly or entirely beneath his notice, their loves and hatreds, their triumphs and tragedies—'

'But not their lies?' Kip asked, pushing it by interrupting once again.

'Does the stone need to notice when you release it from your hand in order to fall? Orholam is lawgiver. When young lovers fornicate and sire a bastard, they aren't being punished. It's a natural consequence of the laws governing the system. Are you as dull as the luxiats that you cannot see the difference between this and atheism?'

'Orholam is a caring lord,' Kip said. Not so much because he believed it, but to see what Andross would say.

'Caring enough to give us rational and consistent laws, which is great care indeed. Laws that apply to the faithful, to apostates, to pagans, and to those in vast reaches beyond unknown oceans who have never even heard the word "Orholam." I find that infinitely more caring than some bearded giant who embraces some and smites others without reason.'

Kip had an intuition. What do you do with a fog of deceptions and misdirection? Drag that sonuvabitch into the light.

'I've really enjoyed training with Karris,' Kip said. It was a non sequitur if his grandfather weren't doing what Kip thought he was.

But Andross Guile clapped his hands once with real delight. 'Well played, boy!'

'All that about Orholam and laws, just to remind me to keep my oath about not telling her about Zymun?' Kip asked.

'Swords are dulled with constant use, wits, sharpened,' Andross said. But it was a stall. He played his Nine Kings card, and Kip had now played enough games that he realized Andross was almost certainly going to win in a few turns. Kip drew, needing Day of Darkness. He didn't get it.

Andross seemed to decide to expand. 'You want to break your oath, and you're looking for excuses to do so. But no. That's not all I'm doing. I'm teaching you how to be a man, Kip. One has duties to one's family. This, too, is Law. It was a task to which your mother was unequal, and now that you're an orphan, there is no one else'

A cold rage settled over Kip like the sheets of ice covering the Karsos Mountains' peaks, ice that lived through the hottest summer, frozen purity in the embrace of rock. The bluntness of brute certainty hit his faith like an iron hammer hitting ice, shattering and scattering it. Kip *had* to believe Gavin was alive, because without his protection, his possible vengeance against any who hurt Kip, Kip was naked and vulnerable and surrounded by enemies. He believed because he wanted to believe.

What do you do with a fog of self-deception?

Though the game wasn't finished, Kip silently gathered his cards, never looking his grandfather in the eye, and left.

Andross Guile didn't say anything until Kip reached the door. 'I should have known you weren't ready. I misjudged you. A boy you are, still.'

But Kip had kept his oath, which perhaps meant that Andross had gotten exactly what he wanted.

It was enough to keep him up late at night, wondering what he should have done or said instead – which made the training a welcome relief. It was a few hours of total absorption. The language of hand-to-hand combat was direct and simple, the deceptions revealed within seconds, and in Kip's case, spoken with a very limited vocabulary.

'Form up!' Trainer Fisk barked. 'Squads today. We're doing Specials.'

An appreciative mumble went through the inductees. Specials was the term for the quirky, dangerous assignments Trainer Fisk and Commander Ironfist came up with to challenge the inductees to think creatively. It was a change to the old way of doing things, but Commander Ironfist was fearless. He needed Blackguards immediately, so the old system of graduating in cohorts was out, too.

Now, he'd told them, as soon as they'd learned all the skills they needed and had proven that they had the character needed as well, they could be promoted. For some of them, that might be soon, he said.

Everyone assumed he meant Cruxer and a couple of other

boys from cohorts ahead of theirs, but everyone hoped it applied to them, too.

There was some grumbling among the senior cohorts, of course, but much of that was alleviated when Ironfist immediately took half of them for final vows. There were new scrubs, too, comprised of young men and women who gazed with awe at even the inductees. *That* felt odd.

By the Feast of the Longest Night, they'd gone on Specials a dozen times, and seen twenty inductees sworn in as full Blackguards.

But not all the changes had been instituted by Commander Ironfist. As promachos, Andross Guile had immediately set most of the full Blackguards to training the small army the Chromeria kept. In addition, every drafter on the Jaspers, whether enrolled at the school, or doing research there, or even civilians who had long ago left the school, was now required to attend combat classes led by Blackguards.

All of it had been done by Kip's suggestion to Andross – and he kept *that* a complete secret. The Blackguards would lynch him for it, though he was still convinced it was the right thing to do.

Though many of the squads experienced turnover, Kip's squad crystallized with Cruxer, Teia, Big Leo, goofy Ferkudi, mechanical-spectacled Ben-hadad, little Daelos, and Gross Goss, who was currently picking a scab.

'If you put that in your mouth, so help me,' Daelos said.

'I wasn't gonna,' Goss complained.

'Sure.'

'I don't see what's so terrible about it.'

'Form up, nunks,' Cruxer said. He was the undisputed leader of the squad, though challenges could be made every week. Cruxer was the toughest and the best leader. The squad left well enough alone.

'Squad Aleph!' Trainer Fisk barked. 'Swear to Orholam, you keep lagging, I'll bump you down to Yod next week. Asses to your lines. Now!'

Kip's squad, despite having him in it, was the best squad: they were Aleph – the first letter in the Old Parian alphabet. Kip had asked. Of course, the good squads kept getting members promoted into full Blackguards, so the chaos weakened their teamwork. Cruxer had been offered promotion, which would have made him one of the youngest full Blackguards ever, but he'd turned it down.

Ten squads of six, seven, and eight each lined up. The Specials were different every time, but they were always meant to re-inforce some lesson about the Blackguards' life. Sometimes the special task was simply watching a street corner – where nothing happened. The squads that got those tasks always complained bitterly, of course, because the other tasks were usually a lot more fun.

'Squad Yod! There's a jeweler off the embassies called Master Athanossos. He has received a ruby worth twenty thousand danars. Bring it here. Go! On the double!'

When they were out of earshot, already jogging up the ramp, he said, 'Squad Teth! Steal that ruby from Squad Yod before they get back. If they're not successful lifting it in the first place, I expect you to do it. No one injured. Use your wits. Go!'

And so it went. Squad Kheth was assigned to shadow a diplomat visiting his mistress on the other side of the city. They were to work in rotations so they weren't seen, and be ware of the man's bodyguards, who were mercenaries from the Cloven Shield Company. Squad Zayin was to watch an alley in the slums, and only if a Blackguard inductee came running through the alley were they to do anything – at that point, they were to take whatever it was he or she had and take it to a house in the slums. They didn't get to know what the item was. Squad Vav was to pick one merchant from one of the prosperous markets. Every member of the squad was to steal something from his stall or store. If they were even noticed – not just caught – they were all to pay him back double, out of their own wages. If they were not caught, they were to show their loot to a full Blackguard who would be in the market. Squad He was then to put it all back, again without the merchant noticing.

Squad Daleth was to find the leader of one of the criminal gangs gaining strength among the refugees, and beat up him and his top two lieutenants – and get out without losing anyone to injuries. After they left, Squad Gimel was assigned to take up a position where they could watch. They were to act as reinforcements if it looked like Daleth was in serious trouble. No killing, but anything short of that they would be allowed. If everyone in Squad Daleth swore they hadn't needed help, those squads would swap rankings.

Squad Beth was set on a fetch-the-item run. Those were the worst. Sometimes they were utterly straightforward, and other times the squad would be attacked by almost anything. It was, of course, a pretty good test for young Blackguards, who never knew when an assassination might be attempted, and had to learn to deal with boredom without losing their edge.

And that left Kip's squad.

Trainer Fisk grimaced at them. They fully expected to get the hardest assignment. They were the best, after all. 'You've got a new squaddie. Boy, form up!'

The squad looked at each other as a young mountain Parian came forward. He wasn't tall, and he had some baby fat, where his people were famed for their lean height. But they all recognized him. It was Winsen. He'd been part of their class, until he failed out, losing to Kip in the final testing – losing, only Kip had known, on purpose to spite his master.

'We get the bump-outs now?' Big Leo asked.

'How come he gets in?' Ferkudi asked. 'He came in twentieth. Why not let fifteen through nineteen first? Even those washouts would be better than him, right?'

Kip didn't point out that *he* was number fifteen, thanks.

'Breaker *was* fifteen,' Daelos said.

Thanks.

'Maybe the others were already gone? Recruited elsewhere or shipped home?' Big Leo asked.

'You don't think the Lightguard recruited 'em, do you?' Ferkudi asked.

'Lightguard,' Big Leo scoffed. 'That's a rumor.'

Cruxer stepped in. 'What's the word, Winsen?'

Winsen shot a look at Kip. 'Just lucky, I guess.'

'Are you ladies done with your kopi and chat time?' Trainer Fisk demanded.

'Ladies?' Teia complained. 'I was the only one not—'

'Are you interrupting me, nunk?!' Trainer Fisk shouted at her. He walked over and got right in her face. She swallowed and shook her head.

'Good! There's a man spouting heresy on a street corner, calls himself Lord Arias. Ain't no lord I ever heard of. He's one block south of Verrosh. Find him, and beat the hell out of him. Not in your Blackguard garb. Regular clothes.'

It was one thing to go beat up the leaders of a gang who were terrorizing the poor and frightened. Some crazy preacher? That was different.

'How many guards does he have?' Cruxer asked.

'None we know of.'

'So why are – I mean, why should it take all of us to beat him up?' Teia asked. Kip could tell she only narrowly avoided asking what she really wanted to ask: why are we beating up someone just for talking?

'It's an order,' Trainer Fisk said. 'You have a problem following orders?'

Chapter 42

'Soul poison,' Orholam said. 'You never told me about the soul poison. Why didn't you tell me about the soul poison?'

'Stop it,' Gavin said. 'Stop saying that.'

'Had you not been told it is death and evil and murder? It is eating you, destroying you!' Orholam said, eyes bright with fervor.

The *Bitter Cob* had made it to the edge of Rath Harbor last night before having to anchor. Once the sun rose, the portmaster would be out to assess taxes and to direct them to a berth. Gavin's options for escape were rapidly dwindling.

No, that wasn't true. There had never been many options. Once the portmaster came, Gavin had to go with the man or resign himself to Malargos custody. He would, doubtless, be their 'guest.' Without drafting, he would be helpless.

Well, overawing one portmaster. How hard could that be?

Gavin left Orholam and jumped up on the gunwale. He *could* swim. Sharks and crocodiles swarmed to the carrion that inevitably washed into the waters of a great city – not least of which was the dead people who were disposed of in that old favorite way: tossing them in the river. Fishermen armed with harpoons hunted the sharks and crocodiles in turn, harvesting fins and skin and teeth. It was a rather smaller circle of nature than Gavin was comfortable with. Set against the perennial battle of nature versus man, swimming in a harbor like this was a big bet on the men.

Even if he made it to shore, dripping wet, dirty, emerging from the shoreline muck, he would then have to escape. Without coin sticks, without friends, without drafting. Gavin had been naked before and felt less naked than he felt now. He looked at the tranquil, trashy water below him and realized for the first time that he could drown in that.

Vulnerability sat hand in hand with Mortality. They beckoned Gavin to come.

'Tell me about the black luxin,' Orholam said, quiet, tense. Gavin hadn't noticed his approach.

Losing my edge, to be startled like that.

'It's a myth to scare young drafters.'

'You wish to be unflinchingly honest with yourself. Yet here you fail. It must have scared you terribly. Terrified you. Made you piss yourself. Made you run. But there was nowhere to run, was there? Of a sudden, the world was not as you'd believed. Did you see them?'

'Them? I have no—'

'You were a better liar when first Gunner pulled you out of the sea. Or is it especially hard to lie to me?'

'One would hope that it would be especially hard to lie to Orholam, don't you think?' Gavin said lightly.

'Man's first recorded words to Orholam were a lie, so no. Men lie to Orholam as readily as they lie to their wives. Show me your hands.'

Gavin got down off the gunwale. The sky was lightening, but there were still few sailors awake. They had privacy. Not that he wanted it. He showed the man his hands.

'Remarkable,' Orholam said. 'As our mouths utter both blessings and curses, clean water and foul from the same well, so too your hands. You've drafted white luxin, too.'

'What the hell are you talking about?' Gavin said.

'Hoo-hoo! A puzzle you are indeed! You remember drafting the black, but not the white?!'

'Quiet, dammit!'

Gavin had seen men whose hamstrings had been cut who didn't fall so fast. The prophet simply dropped. Gavin bent over the man—

Who blinked up at him. Then stood, shaking his head. His eyes stuck on Gavin's, and he stood, transfixed. He swallowed. Tried to speak. 'You've come face to face with truth, and refused to see it. You've chosen cowardice when you had it in you to choose courage. You've chosen black instead of white. You've failed, Guile.'

'*I've* failed?! You sent me those dreams, didn't you? Through some magic I don't know, some kind of will-casting. You did this to me. You, and him.'

'Tread lightly, O Son of Am.'

'I'll tread how I please! I didn't fail. God failed.'

'Those two words cannot be put together in any way that makes sense.'

'God failed *me*.'

'Because an earnest prayer cannot be answered no?'

'Lies!' Gavin hissed.

'Then Orholam will give it to you plain: you keep up your lies, and you'll be stricken blind.'

It was such a bizarre threat that Gavin was taken aback. 'I already am blind.'

'Perhaps that much is true,' Orholam said. 'He who refuses to see is no better off than he who can't.' Then he hobbled away, carefully avoiding sleepers on deck.

Must have smacked his leg in his fall. Lucky I didn't smack more than that.

The boy would be up on deck any time. Then Antonius would follow Gavin like a puppy. Though he wasn't stupid – he'd certainly proved that in convincing the sailors to go to Rath – he was ignorant. He had no idea that his family hated Gavin. No idea that his uncle had become a god, that Gavin had killed him. No idea that Gavin had stymied his cousin Tisis's entry to the Spectrum. Either he had no idea about any of these, or he didn't care.

But hoping that Eirene Malargos would share her nephew's lack of concern was a bridge too far.

Might Eirene be turned into an ally? She was known to be fiercely protective of her family, prone to anger and jealousy, but scrupulously fair in her business dealings. Never broke her word, but went out of her way to crush those who broke their word to her, whether in business or in bed. She'd held her own family to bad business deals they'd made with others, even when she could have used her burgeoning power to overturn them. In short, a woman to be feared and admired. She was exactly the kind of person to remind Gavin that not all power was magical. If Gavin could survive her rage . . . no. He'd injured her family too many times.

If he were still a Prism, it would be one thing, but now? What exactly did he bring to an alliance?

'What were you talking with the godmonger about?' a voice asked, low. Gunner.

The crew had found a cage in the hold, last used to carry a cheetah from the edges of the Verdant Plains. They'd tied the cage down on deck and stuffed Gunner in there, after giving him a good beating. His eyes were swollen to slits. Gavin had stopped them before they killed him.

'Don't talk to me,' Gavin said. 'I've had enough with crazy men today, and the sun isn't up yet.'

'Gunner ain't crazy,' Gunner said. 'Gunner's mad! It's differnt.' He chuckled to himself, but quietly. He was obviously in pain.

Gavin looked to the city, aglow, catching the first rays of the rising sun. The city had grown around a massive fortress on the hill overlooking the Great River Delta. Long ago, Oakenshield Fortress had become Castle Guile for a single generation and then as the family's fortunes had waned, it became Corinth Castle, then Rath Skuld. Now it was simply known as the Castle. During Taya Oakenshield's time, it had extended two great walls like legs down to the harbor so that it couldn't be cut off from supplies. Later wars and lulls between wars had seen walls built out farther from those original walls, the original walls plundered for their stones, the new walls demolished by a Blood Forest army, and the original walls rebuilt.

The city's petitions to the Spectrum to rebuild the wider walls after the Blood War was finally over had been turned down time and again. Andross Guile had been at the center of that denial, preaching peace through mutual vulnerability – for others, as always. Of course, the army this city had to worry about now wasn't Blood Foresters but Blood Robes. The enforced vulnerability of the city was another thing that wasn't going to make a Guile popular with Eirene Malargos.

More worrying was how anyone in power felt about the way Gavin had ended the Blood War. It had been bold, bloody, and effective. To a younger Gavin, the only thing that mattered was that it had worked. He wasn't likely to find allies here.

Gavin looked around the ship. The *Bitter Cob* indeed.

'You give me that rifle, I'll punch a hole in that portmaster for you,' Gunner said. 'One shot, no tricks. From here, they wouldn't even think it came from us. They'll be looking on that ship for the shot's original.'

'Origin,' Gavin said. 'And what the hell's Rifle? Family name?' Men named weapons all the time, but that wasn't a language he was familiar with.

'A rifle. Not a name. It's the spirals inside the barrel. Knew me a smith was working on the idear. Worked real good, but you had to cast your musket balls perfect, file off the seams, make exact globes. Don't think this one shoots globes. That smith'd give his dick hand to see my girl here.'

He ignored Gunner. In the distance, the portmaster boarded another galley half a league west. The shore was half a league north. A long swim, the last few hundred paces covered in scum that was likely sewage. It wasn't simply gross. Gavin had known good swimmers during the war who'd gone through muck like that to return from scouting. A day later, they were fevered and shaking. Three days later, dead.

'That's half a league,' Gavin said. 'Gotta be close to two thousand paces. Those boys kicked whatever sense you had left outta you.'

'Two shots, maybe. No more'n three.'

Give Gunner this, the man never doubted himself. It had been something they'd had in common, once.

Gavin didn't have to make it all the way to shore here. There were river barges and the rowing galleys favored for transport up and down the Great River all throughout the delta. With the sun coming up and dazzling the eyes, it was possible Gavin might not be seen.

And there weren't only sharks and crocodiles in this water, right? Gavin recalled hearing something about friendly river dolphins. Maybe that had been a myth, though. He'd heard they were *pink*. Friendly pink dolphins?

Right, those sounded real.

''Ay. Fukkelot,' Gavin said. The man was waking, not far away. 'And the rest of you.' He didn't raise his voice, and he held a finger to his lips. He didn't want Antonius hearing. 'This here's my musket. As some of you know, I paid all my magic to get it. I got nothing now, nothing but this. Time was, I would have demanded your service. Now, I just ask. If I ever done you a good turn—' He couldn't help it. 'If I ever done you a good turn'? It was a formulation to make him seem more like them, to fit in. Dissembling was as natural to him as drafting had been. 'Hold on to it for me, would you? Don't want nothing else. No share. You know I pulled my weight when it was time to pull. You know that without me cutting those lines free, we'd still be on the oars. I can't compel you to do this thing, and I wouldn't if I could.' Well, there was another lie. Harmless, though. 'Hide this musket from the boy, and from the Malargos woman, and from my father, and from this one.' He nodded to Gunner. 'Time comes, if I can, I'll repay you a hundred times. But I can't carry it with me.'

'Wa-wa-why not?' Fukkelot asked.

'Because,' Gavin said, giving his best devil-may-care grin. He always gave that grin when he was terrified. 'I ain't a good enough swimmer to carry it with me.'

He tossed the rifle to Fukkelot while the sailor cursed in appreciation and Gunner cursed in frustration and Gavin's own throat swelled with trepidation.

It was stupid, but it was simple: stay and let what would happen happen, or risk crocodiles and sharks and sewage.

Sewage shouldn't be so bad during flood season, right? Or did that make it worse? Gavin stood on the gunwale, balancing without even touching the lines. He turned to the prophet, who was still watching him with burning eyes from across the deck.

'Orholam,' Gavin said, 'do I have your full attention?'

'Always.'

'Good.' He cracked his neck right and left. 'Because *fuck* you.'

He dove into the water.

Chapter 43

The water was warm and buoyant. That was Gavin's first warning. Now that he was in it, swimming a stroke that one of the Guile house slaves had taught him long ago in a different life, he remembered that the confluence of the Great River and the Cerulean Sea caused odd currents and warm spots throughout the Great Delta – and that the sharks didn't like the freshwater coming from the river. On the other hand, the crocodiles didn't like the saltwater. Crocodiles were much more likely closer in to shore. So Gavin would be giving both kinds of predators a chance at him.

And yet. There was something of that old blue peace here in the sea. Better, of course, to float on a narrow blue luxin skimmer. Better to feel the sun like a caress on the skin, the water a cool counterpoint. Better by far to be able to see the blue. He felt the briefest pang of loss, and then pure, unadulterated rage washed over him.

Limbs cutting smoothly through the waters, he suddenly wished that a shark would come. He wanted to fight. No, he wanted to kill. He wanted the terror of almost dying and the mastery of killing, of triumph.

Insanity.

He headed straight in, not pausing to look behind. He shed the encumbrance of his shredded tunic and trousers to give himself every chance at speed. He saw a river galley ahead and swam for it. He was a faster swimmer than he remembered. Perhaps the leaner muscles of rowing were better suited to the task than the bulk he'd developed from shooting a skimmer from a dead stop in the water to flying across the waves. That was a freedom he would never feel again.

The river galley started moving when he was still two hundred paces out. Its inertia should give him a chance. He kicked.

No damn sharks. Please no damn sharks.

Water was streaming through his beard, causing a drag he'd never felt in his clean-shaven past.

Let them be blind to me, just for a little longer.

But the galley began moving, and within moments, it was no longer perpendicular to him. He cut the angle, but ended up only even with the riverboat, and then behind it.

And then it pulled away, and left him exhausted.

But he'd come to some sort of channel. He saw buoys to either side. He trod water for a minute. When he looked back, the *Bitter Cob* was in the distance. But the oars were out, and it was turning toward him.

Oh, hells.

But another river galley was sweeping through the channel, from farther out. It would pass fifty paces south of him – so he swam back toward the *Bitter Cob*. In another minute, he saw he'd miscalculated, or the river galley was turning, because it was headed straight for him. It was going to hit him.

He started to swim off to the side, when he saw a fin and a dark shadow, that way. He turned, heart in his throat, and saw another to the other side.

It was too late to move either way now. The galley was on top of him, sending out little sprays to each side of the bow as it cut the water.

Gavin took the deepest breath he could, and flipped around, his feet pointing toward the hull, and dove backward. The hull slapped against his feet even as he sank, but he absorbed the shock and pushed off it, using the hull's force to propel himself deeper into the water.

He arched his back as he sank, hoping he'd made it deep enough not to be crushed by the rest of the hull or ripped to shreds against barnacles. He flipped over, opening his eyes, oars full of water, pressure on his chest. The monstrous shadow was passing above him. It was impossible to tell exactly how far away the hull was.

There was good news, if you could call it such. There were no barnacles on the hull. Of course, it must be a riverboat. Easier to keep clean and moving fast.

It meant he could surface, and if he misjudged, it wouldn't be his death by scraping and infection. Though if he shed blood in this water, the sharks were close.

He kicked, and felt his hand brush something rough and muscular. He barely saw the shape as the shark's shadow disappeared into the murk. He lost a bit of air. One chance at this.

A bank of oars went down on one side, agitating the water. A sharp turn. It slowed the boat at just the right moment. Lungs afire, Gavin swam hard for the surface, nearly cracking his skull against the last edge of the hull as it passed above him.

He shot out of the water and clawed for anything, blinded by the spray of water.

His fingers caught in something, but his left hand pulled free immediately. He held on by his right hand alone, body dangling and then pulled through the waves. He almost lost his grip before he was able to slap his left hand up into the net as well.

He blinked and coughed, trying to get his bearings. His legs were still dragging in the water and his hands were holding on to a thick net, the individual ropes cutting into his fingers as he tried to support his entire body's weight on their narrow cords.

The net wasn't empty. There was a tiger shark in it. Alive. One of Gavin's hands was right by a pectoral fin. The other was stuffed nearly into its gaping, gasping mouth. Gavin's weight was holding his hand away from those rows of razory teeth, but one thrash—

The shark thrashed.

Gavin dropped his hand and his body spun. With the motion of the boat dragging his body through the water, he couldn't stop his momentum. The other hand got twisted painfully into the net. He almost cried out.

Then, being dragged backward, he almost cried out again at what he saw. Four fins in the water – no, six. All following the boat. Being dragged like this, he was the bait. And the boat wasn't traveling nearly as fast as the sharks could swim.

He saw blood course down his extended arm. It wasn't his. The shark in the net above him had been harpooned. With Gavin at the net's lowest point, he became the path for the blood to course into the water. He was no expert on sharks, but he had seen them in frenzy – and it all started with blood.

'Blood's drawin' 'em, Kleos. See if you can get another before we get to the freshwater!' a voice called out above Gavin on the deck.

He heard the heavy breathing of a fat man on the deck above him, audible even above the hiss of the waves, and he could just see the tip of a harpoon bobbing in and out of sight.

Gavin almost called out to the man. But he knew how he looked. He looked like an escaped slave. Most mariners would claim him as the bounty of the sea, and immediately put him back on an oar. Without papers to prove he wasn't a slave, there would be nothing he could do except try to convince them to ransom him – to whom? Would Karris hear about his plight before his father would? Would the men believe that the Prism himself had come to their boat, or would they dismiss it as the ravings of a madman?

He wouldn't work an oar again. He would die first.

The net holding his hand shifted as the fat man stepped on it and heaved the harpoon into the waves. Gavin spun again, this time with the net releasing its grip on his hand. He couldn't even feel that hand, couldn't tell if his grip would hold. He scrambled, kicking in the waves, desperate to swim to steal the smallest moiety of assistance.

Two fingers of his other hand caught the net. Worn to scar and callus by his months on the oar, those blessed fingers held despite everything. And now he was being dragged straight backward, giving him a perfect view of the shark approaching. This would be no exploratory nuzzle, he could tell. It was going to strike.

Swinging slowly from left to right, Gavin got his fists full of net. He couldn't spare the time to look up and see if he was putting a hand in the captured shark's mouth above him; he couldn't take his eyes off the shark in the water.

He pulled his knees up to his chest as the shark struck. Jaws flashed past his feet – missed. The shark spun in the waves and swam off in a broad circle. They didn't like approaching the hull. Didn't like that they could only strike from directly behind.

At least Gavin hoped that was how they were thinking, and that none were swimming deep under the waves to strike him from below.

The man on deck had almost retrieved his harpoon now, and Gavin saw his chance. The weight of the harpoon meant that it would dangle within reach of him at the stern. When it came, he would grab it and yank hard. The sailor, not expecting any such thing, would be hurled overboard. For the sharks.

It meant killing a stranger. A man about whom Gavin knew nothing. An innocent.

Fuck him. Gavin would live, and he would live free, and he would be armed.

The rope stretched within reach for one heartbeat, but Gavin couldn't get his cramping hands to loosen in time to swing – and then the sailor pulled the harpoon off to the side so it wouldn't tangle in the net. Damn!

Gavin turned his eyes back to the sharks, but none of them came at him. And indeed, they began hanging back farther and farther. The sailor with the harpoon swore.

'Freshwater,' he said, grumbling to himself.

And now that Gavin's vision wasn't battle tight, he saw that they had entered the very mouth of the river, not far from the western shore. The river itself was vast, wider than any river in the world. But the western shore was close – and as dirty with the sluggish current as he'd feared. If the boat he was riding on docked somewhere nearby, at least its hull would cut the sludge, and a quay would give Gavin plenty of places to hide. If, instead, they went farther up the river, he would jump off at the Great Bridge.

In a few minutes, though, he realized that he was being

terrifically optimistic. He was hanging on the back of a boat, and though his arms didn't have to bear the full weight of his body since he was half immersed, he did have to fight against the waves trying to pluck him from the boat, and his hands were losing feeling again.

He decided to try to climb up the net, but as soon as he coaxed one hand into releasing its death grip, the other hand betrayed him. He fell into the water.

The pain in his unclenching fingers was excruciating at first, but as he flopped his way to the surface, the pain almost felt good, a promise that his hands would function again. Someday.

With the river galley pulling away from him, Gavin got his bearings again. In the mouth of the river, with the sun rising, he was far more visible than he had been before. If he could get far enough up the river, he would fall under the city's jurisdiction, and then at least he could hope to be turned over to a magistrate rather than directly enslaved. Depending on how law-fearing whatever captain picked him up was.

Best not to get captured at all.

By luck, he wasn't too far from the Great Bridge. If he could make it to its shadow, he would be far less visible. Swim to a huge pylon, climb up the scaffolding, and make it to shore.

He set off immediately. He'd not made it this far in life by hesitating.

When he was two hundred paces away from the bridge, he saw two things at the same time, both of which took his breath away, for opposite reasons. A Ruthgari war galley was emerging from the shadow of the Great Bridge, and the standard flying from its low mast – deliberately just a couple of feet shy of the height of the Great Bridge – was the proud bull of the Malargos family. At the same time, Gavin saw a dolphin coursing through the river toward him. It popped out of the waves, and though Gavin couldn't see the hue, he remembered the drawings, long-beaked and muscular. A river dolphin.

Please come here, you little miracle.

Gavin had heard of dolphins saving swimmers before. He'd heard of them letting men grab on to their backs and ride. The dolphin was his only hope to make it to the shadow of the bridge in time.

River dolphin. He couldn't tell if it was pink or not, of course. It could have been piss yellow for all Gavin cared: it was salvation.

Gavin kept swimming as the dolphin slipped right up to him. But at the last moment, it turned and stabbed its beak into his ribs. His breath shot out and he inhaled water. Before he could even cough it out, the dolphin emerged again from nowhere and hit him again, cracking a rib.

He flailed, gasping for breath. Then it hit him again, this time smacking his head. Dazed, he sucked up a lungful of water. He lost consciousness.

Chapter 44

'I can't do this,' Big Leo said. 'This Lord Arias is a twig.'

'What's hard about it?' Daelos asked. 'Go out there and lower the boom on him. I've seen you do it before.'

'The boom?' Ferkudi asked.

'I didn't mean I can't. I meant I can't,' Big Leo said.

'That doesn't make any sense,' Ferkudi said.

'I meant in good consc—' Big Leo said.

'Nah, I mean the boom. Aren't booms more dangerous when they're swinging around than—'

'Maybe that's the test, Leo,' Ben-hadad said, fiddling with his lenses. 'Maybe we're supposed to refuse an immoral order.'

'Or maybe we're supposed to follow an order when we can't see the bigger picture,' Ferkudi said.

The others looked at him. After the three-quarters of the time that Ferkudi was a clown, he'd come back and surprise them with some keen observation.

'What?' he asked. 'What?'

Kip's squad, dressed in street clothes, had scouted the broad corner at Verrosh and Harmonia. There was nothing particularly special about this corner that they could see. No one else was watching it. It wasn't particularly prosperous. It wasn't the busiest in the city. Perhaps, for a heretic, that meant fewer merchants' guards and house guards who might throw an elbow or a stone. Perhaps he was just moon mad and he'd picked this corner randomly.

Daelos and Goss were still out watching approaches to the corner, and Teia was ambling through the intersection itself, seeing what she could see, but the rest of them were huddled in a circle behind a store, trying to figure out what to do. They usually found a rendezvous point farther away, but there hadn't been any good spots.

'Hey! What are you boys doing? Get out of here, scram!' a hairy-armed store guard barked.

Cruxer gave a mild oath at himself. Kip knew the young man would see it as a personal failure that someone had noticed them clumped up. Cruxer gestured, and they all started walking away from the shop.

'Yeah, that's right. Scurry away, ya little vermin,' the store guard said.

They gritted their teeth and didn't reply. Knowing that you could win a fight wasn't a good enough reason to jeopardize a mission.

Tempting as it was.

The goon sneered. He obviously thought they were up to no good, but as long as they weren't threatening his employer's store, what did he care? He didn't follow.

'Feels like there's got to be some trick,' Kip said.

'There is,' Teia said, rejoining them silently. 'But not on us.'

'What is it?' Cruxer asked quietly.

'There's a woman watching the preacher from across the street. She's carrying bandages. And the preacher himself, he's the real thing. He's a Blood Robe. He's got sealed scroll cases that he's handing off to certain people as they pass. He's a handler of spies.'

'Oh, I can do this. This Lord Arias is a twig,' Big Leo said. He loosened up a shoulder that would have made a draft horse jealous.

'Hold,' Cruxer said. 'We don't know that he's alone. But I do feel better knowing there's some plan, even if I don't know what it is. Give me a second.'

And the insane thing with Cruxer was that it *was* only a

second. He scowled, looked at his team, and then started giving orders.

In moments, the team scattered, each to his or her appointed task. It left only Kip with nothing to do. 'Cruxer,' Kip said. 'Captain, I mean.' When they were on assignment, even the inductees were supposed to observe the official order scrupulously. 'You've done me nothing but good turns. We both know I wouldn't be in the Blackguard without you, but you can't keep me out of the action. Doing that will only make those who are already better than me get even farther ahead. I need to be in the thick of things.'

Cruxer's brown eyes, barely edged with green and yellow around the iris, fell on Kip like a sledge. 'I'm captain,' Cruxer said.

That was all there was to it. 'Yes, sir,' Kip said.

'There's a good vantage. But we're gonna have to climb,' Cruxer said. He took off.

A climb difficult enough that Cruxer found it worth mentioning? 'Wonderful,' Kip said. He jogged after the older boy.

They cut wide a few blocks, slowed as they crossed the main streets, and came eventually to a building on the opposite side of the intersection from the spy. They went around the back of the building, which had scaffolding up, as the dingy dome was being worked on. The ladder had been pulled away from the scaffolding – doubtless to keep young scoundrels from climbing it.

Cruxer rested his back against the wall, took a wide stance, and cupped his hands, waiting for Kip to use it to jump.

'I could draft a ladder,' Kip said.

'You'll jump,' Cruxer said.

'I'll jump.'

'Hand to shoulder, then pull yourself up.'

Easy for you to say. Kip rolled his shoulders, shook his head, and took a deep breath.

'Not got all day here, Breaker.' Cruxer leaned his one shoulder forward, to give Kip more space to step.

Kip charged with the grace of a drunken turtle-bear, stepped into Cruxer's cupped hand, onto his shoulder with the other foot even as Cruxer heaved his foot upward, and jumped. His hands slapped easily onto the edge of the wood platform, and he still had upward momentum. He pulled himself up and flopped onto the platform.

He spun around on his stomach and offered a hand down. Cruxer, standing in place, jumped straight up, grabbed Kip's hand, kicked off the wall, and landed – standing up, stepping carefully over Kip.

And *that's* why he's the captain.

The scaffolding extended around the front of the building, and there were piles of brick stacked on it, waiting to be put in place and whitewashed. Cruxer and Kip moved forward, keeping low. The intersection was forty paces or more wide here, and against the dingy dome and the bricks, the two of them should be virtually invisible. Close enough to watch, far enough away not to be seen, and close enough to help if it all went to hell.

'Breaker,' Cruxer said. 'It's time we acknowledge something.'

That doesn't sound so good. 'Mm?' Kip asked.

'You're never going to be a Blackguard.' Cruxer didn't say it as a threat. He said it as simple fact.

Kip's heart leapt into his throat. 'I'm getting better. I'll catch up, I swear.'

'It's not that.'

Then Kip understood. 'Look, I know the squad has this thing about me being the Lightbringer,' Kip said. 'But—'

'Doesn't matter.' Cruxer poked his head up over the edge. Big Leo was still making his way up Verrosh. Even hunched to seem smaller than he was, the young hulk was hard to miss. 'They'll never let you take final vows.'

'They?'

'Let's say you make full 'guard. And you get put on rotation to guard the Red, whom everyone knows you're feuding with. Hard to imagine, isn't it? Or maybe you've patched up your feud with him, and you get put on rotation to cover the White – whom everyone knows *he's* feuding with. Hard to imagine, isn't it? I'm sure your grandfather has plans for you. Becoming a Blackguard would give you all sorts of protections from him. There's no way he'd let that happen. That's if the White doesn't have her own plans for you.'

'Maybe her plans involve me getting those protections by staying in.' But Kip was only denying it because he wanted it to be wrong.

'Blackguards face the truth, Breaker. It'll be a miracle if she lives long enough for you to make it to final vows.'

Kip's stomach sank. Everyone knew the White had a year left, two at the most. Cruxer was right. There was no way Kip would be ready to be a full Blackguard in that time. Ironfist had bent the rules to get him this far.

'And if your father comes back in time to work his own particular magic, I'm sure he's got *his* own plans for you.'

He thought of his grandfather's view of oaths. If Andross Guile had meant what he'd told Kip, he definitely wouldn't want Kip to make an oath that might put Kip against him – which was precisely what taking the Blackguard oath might do. He threw his hands up. 'So why even have me in the squad?'

Cruxer body-slammed him with a disappointed look. 'Don't go back to being that whinging fat boy Kip. You're Breaker now.'

Ouch.

'You're in the squad because you deserve it,' Cruxer said. 'The question for you, knowing that your time with us is limited, is what are you going to accomplish here? Heads up. We're go.'

Big Leo walked as inconspicuously as possible through the thin crowd until he was about ten paces from the preacher, who was holding forth, though no one seemed to be paying him any attention. From their vantage, Kip couldn't decipher a word either said, but Leo had planned to allege that the heretics had been responsible for killing his sister.

Leo shouted something, and then jumped on the preacher before the man could flee.

Since his cover was as a simple laborer, Leo was careful not to fight like a trained fighter. He simply grabbed the preacher's hair in one hand and punched him rapidly in the face. If you've never been hit in the face, it's deeply shocking even if there isn't much power in it. Kip knew that Leo could have killed the man in a blow. Instead, he was pulling each punch, hitting the man in succession: cheek, eye, nose, mouth, cheek, eye. Blood poured freely, and the man was going to look and feel like he'd been beaten within a thumb of his life – without actually endangering him much. Big Leo hauled the man up, holding his entire weight by his hair as the man collapsed, and slugged him twice in the ribs, hard enough to break them.

Leo dropped the man and turned, and this time spoke loudly enough that Kip could hear him: 'Shame on all of you for tolerating this heresy in your midst! These people are monsters! Murderers! You let him walk free and spread his poison here? Shame!' Leo spat on the stones and turned to stomp off.

No one did anything. Not that the squad had expected them to, but it was nice to see something they'd planned work: by identifying the spy as a heretic, they'd hoped Leo could get out clean.

Unseen though, behind Leo, Lord Arias had risen on unsteady feet. He pulled out a knife. Leo's back was to him. The spy lurched toward him.

It was too far away for a shout to do any good. Worse, a shout might distract Leo from the sound of the spy approaching him.

The spy drew the blade up to bury it in Leo's back – and his arm dropped, limp. The sound of the blade tinging off the paving stones made Leo spin. He saw the knife and the staggering man at once, and his fist came up in a flash.

'Don't kill him!' Cruxer whispered, as if he could will Leo to inaction.

Big Leo unclenched his fist and grabbed the spy at the collar and the waistband. He spun in a rapid circle with the man and hurled him out into the street. He stood for a long moment, flexing his fists. Kip could see that the battle juice was on him. Big Leo had gone for a quick fistfight, and had almost ended up dead. It was hard to think rationally. Leo took a step toward the downed spy.

Teia darted out from the crowd. 'Brother!' she shouted. 'Thank Orholam!' Kip couldn't hear the rest of what she said, but she took Leo by the arm and pulled him away. He didn't resist. Her appearance had snapped him out of his rage.

She pulled him down Verrosh Street.

'What the hell was that?' Kip asked.

'Good luck?' Cruxer suggested. But he grinned. Kip could tell he knew exactly what had made that knife drop.

'I'm serious.'

'That was paryl. You're not the only one changing things around here. Teia's got a few tricks, too. That one doesn't usually work for her yet, though. Thus: good luck.'

Together, they watched. Teia was soon indistinguishable, but it took longer for Big Leo to blend with the crowds. Then Ferkudi and Ben-hadad came onto Verrosh, blocks down, almost out of sight, and began separately walking toward the square. They passed Big Leo with neither side acknowledging the other.

'You see anyone follow Leo?' Kip asked. He hadn't.

'One possible. We'll see in a moment.'

If the spy had an ally eager to exact a quick vengeance or even just to see where Leo had come from, it was vital that that friend fail.

Ferkudi stumbled into someone and they both went sprawling, Ferkudi taking by far the worse of it. He made a big show of it, crashing into a Parian headscarf seller's booth and sending scarves flying.

Only Ferkudi could lower the boom on himself.

A slender Parian woman dodged out of the booth instantly, shouting and waving her arms in big gestures.

'They get away?' Kip asked.

'If they didn't with *that*? I'll give them a thrashing myself,' Cruxer said.

Down in the intersection below them, though, another quieter drama was playing out. The woman Teia had seen had come to the downed spy and was tending to his wounds.

'Thoughts?' Cruxer asked.

Kip studied the woman. Teia said she'd already had bandages near to hand before anything had happened. 'A spy to spy on the spy,' Kip said. 'A better way to insinuate her into their ranks than just showing up and saying, "Hello, I hate the Chromeria, too! Can I join you?"'

'Good point. And see that one back there? Beaded beard, gold earrings?'

Kip grunted an assent. He hadn't seen him before now.

'That's the spy's actual handler. He almost came out of hiding when Leo struck, and then he almost ran away. Now he's just watching. I think we can call this mission a success.'

'As long as no one saw *us*,' Kip said.

'We'll wait here for a bit.' Cruxer sat with his back against the bricks. Kip sat beside him.

Minutes passed, and Kip had a thought that he'd had half a hundred times before. Now was as good a time as any. It seemed that he got in trouble for the times he didn't speak nearly as often as he got in trouble for speaking too fast. But he'd been a coward with inaction too many times.

'Captain . . .' Kip said. 'I just . . . about Lucia. The assassin – the assassin was aiming at me.' He could still remember Lucia with her back to the assassin, stepping into the line of fire at the last instant. He would never forget the look on Cruxer's face as the young man had pulled Lucia's bleeding body from Kip's stunned arms and into his own.

Cruxer stared into the distance. Then his mouth twitched into a sad smile, remembering Lucia. Then he was back. 'I know,' he said.

'You know?'

'I went back to that alley. Recreated the murder. The target could only be you.' He shrugged.

'You're . . . you're not mad?' Kip asked.

'I'm furious. But not at you. Breaker, if Lucia died saving your life, her death may still have been an accident, but it's no longer meaningless. Death for a purpose? What more could any of us ask? Lucia wasn't good enough to make it into the Blackguard. She knew it, and she was just beginning to grapple with the death of that dream. She was never going to make it into our ranks, but she still died serving our highest ideals. It's not for nothing.'

So this is why he wants me to be the Lightbringer so much. If I am, Lucia died for the most important person in history.

'But what if I'm not the Lightbringer?' It just slipped out, quiet and sad.

'Don't you take it away from her,' Cruxer said. 'It has nothing to do with that. All are equal in Orholam's eyes: she died for a friend, a squad mate. It is our earthly task as Blackguards to die for Colors and Prisms – but in Orholam's eyes, dying for a pauper means as much as dying for a prince.'

Kip sat there for a few more minutes. He knew Cruxer meant it. But Cruxer saw Orholam's hand everywhere. He believed that Orholam intervened in the world constantly. Commander Ironfist saw Orholam as a distant king who could intervene when he chose, but rarely chose to do so. Andross thought Orholam had set the world in order, but hadn't touched it since, allowing the whole system of the Chromeria and the Magisterium to become a swindle that the nobles and Chromeria had pulled over on the Seven Satrapies.

Oddly enough, the latter part seemed to be the Color Prince's view, too.

What Gavin's view was, Kip didn't know. Nor did he know what the truth was.

'Captain. I don't know if this is the time, but what do people really know about the Lightbringer? At worship that one time, Klytos Blue said we're all Lightbringers, and I've spent a few hours looking up prophecy interpretations in the libraries, but they all seem to contradict each other, so I gave it up. All I got is that he's going to restore true worship – whatever that is. He's going to comfort the afflicted, open the eyes of the blind, throw down the altars and high places, raise up the oppressed, and cast down the wicked.'

'And kill gods and kings,' Cruxer said. He smirked.

'Gods and kings, plural?' Kip asked uncomfortably.

'I can't remember. Of course, it depends which Seers you accept as canon. Those things are accepted by pretty much everyone. Some of the weirder Seers said, uh, can't remember the exact phrasing, something about killing his brother—'

'Well that's promising.' Zymun could use a good killing.

'—and dying twice.'

'I take that back,' Kip said.

'You did go overboard, and we thought you were dead, so that might count as one,' Cruxer said. 'And everyone dies at the end of their life, so that could be it.'

'Or . . . the pirates who rescued me threw me back overboard, so maybe *that's* twice,' Kip said. He didn't buy it, though.

'Great! Really helpful. Now I know I only need to die one, two, or zero more times. I may have to kill at least one more god and one more king. I do have to figure out how to heal blind people, and maybe pick up a bit about true worship.'

'Breaker, if it was easy, everyone would agree about it. A Seer sees a true vision, but they have to translate that into words, and that means into their own language, and into their own metaphors. And that's if she's a true Seer – there have been false ones. There are luxiats who make their life's work of this sort of thing. Luxiats who are much better scholars than Klytos Blue, I might mention.'

'But if it's all theological complexity and uncertainty, it's useless! I mean, if I can't figure out what it means, what's the point?'

'Maybe it's not for you.'

'I accept that, but if I *were* the Lightbringer wouldn't I need . . .'

'No, even then.'

Kip looked at him, puzzled. 'I'm . . . uh, not following.'

'The Lightbringer Prophecies may well not be for the Lightbringer's benefit. They're for everyone else. For the soldier who understands only a snippet, but it helps him hold the line. For the bereaved widow. For the young scholar, searching for meaning. What's it matter, anyway? You've done pretty well so far not knowing the prophecies,' Cruxer said.

'Deliberate ignorance. I like this idea,' Kip said. He thought for a moment. 'Everything we've said could be talking about my father. People thought he was dead when he fell into the water—' And somehow survived being stabbed with a knife that had morphed into a sword while it impaled him. Kip hadn't told *that* part to anyone. They had already disbelieved him when he'd simply said his father wasn't drowned. Who would believe the rest? Kip didn't believe it; half the time he was convinced his eyes must have been playing tricks on him. '—and we've already talked about how a god being killed on Gavin's command could well count even if he didn't land the final blow.'

'His childhood doesn't fit. Prophecy says the Lightbringer will come from the outside, outside the accepted or something.

It fits a bas— a person initially thought to be a bastard coming from Tyrea. Doesn't get much more outside the accepted than that. Gavin Guile is the son of Andross. He grew up here. He was groomed to take power. It doesn't get much more *inside* than that.'

'Well, you didn't tell me about that part!' Kip complained.

'I'm a Blackguard, not a luxiat. If you want to talk about prophecies, the people you should see are . . . well, actually they're the last people you should see. In fact, I'm not so sure we should be including Quentin in any of this.'

'Quentin? Why not?'

'Somehow I thought it would be obvious to you. I forget you grew up in Tyrea.'

'Why wouldn't I go to the luxiats?'

'Because if now is the time true worship needs to be restored, it means the luxiats are doing things so wrongly that Orholam himself is putting his hand in to make it right.'

'Well, shouldn't they *welcome* Orholam moving? I mean, they're luxiats.'

'Breaker . . . are you really that naïve?'

'They serve Orholam! That's their job!' Kip said.

'Voice down.'

'Sorry, Captain.'

'We Blackguards exist to stop assassinations. It doesn't mean we look forward to them.'

'Totally different,' Kip said.

'The more power you have, the more skeptical you're going to be about someone coming along who wants to take all of it away. There have been false Lightbringers before. If you show up out of nowhere without undeniable proof that you are who we suspect, you might find yourself standing right at the fissure line of a schism. There have already been attempts to kill you, Breaker. Where do you think those have come from?'

One came from my grandfather, but he denied the others.

'Who else would even know you were alive?' Cruxer asked. 'I don't think the Color Prince would think you were worth killing when you first came here. If anything, you did him a favor by killing King Garadul and putting him in power.'

'Thanks for reminding me.'

'So if not him, Breaker, who?'

The Order of the Broken Eye? But they were just assassins for hire, right?

So unless there were yet more unknown enemies out there, it had probably been luxiats who'd tried to kill Kip. But *luxiats*? Really?

'Hells,' Kip said. More enemies.

Then he was struck by the fact that of anyone, it should be Cruxer who had such a cynical view of the Magisterium. 'Captain? Doesn't it shake your faith, I mean, if it really was the luxiats who killed Lucia?'

Cruxer looked away. 'My faith isn't in men.'

Which didn't leave Kip with anything to say.

But that had never stopped him before. 'So,' Kip said. 'If I'm never going to be a Blackguard, what do you think I should be using this time for?'

'Learn to kill. Learn to lead. Learn who your friends are, and then draw them so close to you that *every* time someone shoots a musket ball at you, it hits one of your friends and not you.'

'That's . . . that's a horrible way to think about friends.'

'Breaker, if you become a Color or a Prism, and a thousand times more if you become the Lightbringer, you'll no longer be merely our friend. You'll be our lord first. It is right and proper that we should die for you. It is our purpose.'

Suddenly, Kip felt like he was locked in that closet again, covered by rats gnawing, gnawing, gnawing at him. But now the rats were cares, worries, burdens, people he could let down, people who would die if he failed, people who would die even if he succeeded. He felt sick and claustrophobic, hot and cold.

'Knowing I would die for you, how would you live if you were worthy of that sacrifice? Live that way,' Cruxer said.

'Simple, huh?' Kip asked sardonically.

'Simple. Not easy.'

They sat in silence for a few more minutes. Kip pretended to be thoughtful, but the idea was so big it couldn't bear the weight of someone looking at you and wondering how much of it you'd processed. So mostly, he sat there and pretended to think, and felt wretched and dumb.

When they got up to go, he said, 'Should we follow their route to the safe house and check up on them, or should we go direct?'

'Let's go direct. They got away clean.'

Chapter 45

Within three blocks, Teia realized she hadn't gotten away clean. As invisible as she'd thought she was, someone was following her. There were tricks to this, as there were tricks to everything, but figuring out if you're being followed was one of the things the Blackguard practiced. So Teia wended her way through the neighborhoods carefully. At first when she'd split from Big Leo, she'd moved at a fast pace. Not jogging, but clearly moving with purpose. At the fifth turn, she was certain: she was being followed.

It was odd. Big Leo would be a hundred times easier to follow. But maybe they figured Big Leo would be that much more careful. Or maybe they were afraid of him. Or maybe they'd followed him as well.

The man she suspected of tailing her was small. Laborer's clothes, dark hair pulled back tight, and ratty beard adorned with dull beads. He carried a petasos folded in his hand. He was alternating putting the hat on and taking it off to make himself harder to spot as a constant presence behind her. Not a bad trick.

He walked as if he knew the neighborhoods – not glancing around looking for landmarks. When Teia slowed and turned back toward the neighborhood they'd left as if her guard were now down, he followed. That was when she was sure he was following her.

And this is where working with a squad is beautiful.

Teia almost grinned as she headed toward their secondary ambush point. It had been Cruxer's idea, and Teia had been proud of his deviousness. He seemed so upright and good she'd worried he couldn't be sneaky. Goss and Winsen would be waiting to incapacitate her tail. Ferkudi would be following one minute back. Daelos would take care of helping Big Leo. Kip and Cruxer would follow Big Leo if it looked like he was being pursued.

It was the right division of labor. No enemy would be going to send a man who couldn't fight after Big Leo. Still, the two squad members who least inspired Teia's admiration—or in this case, confidence – had to be Goss and Winsen.

As usual when they worked in town, none of them were to draft unless it was life-or-death: they couldn't give away who they were.

Teia came around an alley and pulled her hood up. It was a brisk winter day, so it shouldn't be too alarming to her tail, but the hood was her sign to Goss and Winsen that she needed scrubbing. She winced, though. She'd ducked around that corner, hadn't she?

She walked down the alley, past Goss and Winsen's hiding places, whispering, 'Black hair, Atashian beard.' Then she kept walking.

Can't look back, Teia. Don't give it away. She took care not to duck around the next corner, but she did stop as soon as she was out of sight. She took a deep breath and drew a flat-bladed knife. She got down on her knees and extended the blade past the corner, trying to see in the reflection if a shadow darkened the entrance to the alley.

Nothing. Nothing she could see, anyway. She needed to buy a good little mirror for this.

She waited, certain she would hear the sounds of a scuffle, or a sharp yelp as Goss slammed the piece of wood against the man's shins as they'd planned. They would rob him if they could, too, to make it appear random, but stopping pursuit was their first worry.

Nothing. Where is he?

As soon as Teia thought the question, she knew she was in trouble. She rocked back onto her feet, taking a squatting position from the kneeling one she'd been in. She began leaping to her feet even as she felt the arms close around her.

The man yanked her backward, stopping her momentum with an arm across her chest. Her reaction was instant enough to make any Archer proud: when you're rarely as strong as those you fight against, you learn to change the rules. Instead of trying to pull against the man's grip, Teia pushed hard *into* it: he had pulled her backward, so she jumped backward, too.

Surprised, the man careened backward, and they slammed into the side of a building together, the man's body cushioning the blow for Teia. His grip relaxed, and she dove for the ground.

The last of his grip on her arm whipped her hand into the wall, though, and as they fell in opposite directions, they were suddenly both looking at her knife, dropped on the ground.

They both jumped for the knife that lay between them, and they both arrived at the same second. But where the man grabbed for the knife's grip as they slammed back together, Teia was already grabbing for the man's wrist. Not finding resistance where he expected it again, the man couldn't stop the blade as Teia helped its upward momentum – twisting the man's wrist at the last moment so he rammed the blade full into his own gut.

Shock lit his eyes as he felt the blade slide home, and that gave Teia the pause she needed to pluck the dagger from his fingers. Then they were pressed hard together. He reached around her back and embraced her. He grabbed a fistful of her hair and pulled hard. His breath was hot and stinky on her face.

'Adrasteia the Implacable indeed,' he said. 'Bless me, goddess. Bless me!' He laughed sickly, and held her tight.

What the— Where was Ferkudi? He was her backup. Where was he?

Teia was trapped. She panicked. Her knife hand was free, and she stabbed. Stabbed, stabbed, stabbed. Not artfully, not carefully finding the angles between ribs that she'd been taught through so many hours. She was flailing, flailing, screaming, barely aware of the sound of her own voice. Her vision went red, and all the world was close and hot and unbearable.

Someone was shouting. Shouting her name. She twisted, lashing out with elbows as the man slid down her body, grip weakening, but she hit nothing.

Someone ripped the little man off her. Ferkudi lifted the man in a hug, trapping his hands down at his sides. Then he ran at the opposite wall of the alley, lowering his shoulder at the last moment and crunching the man against the stones. The man dropped in a bloody smear, falling to the dirt.

Teia spun, crouched low, feral, knife in hand.

Goss and Winsen both stood there with their hands up. 'Orholam's balls, Teia, it's us!' Goss said.

'Wow,' Winsen said. 'You killed the shit outta him.' He sounded . . . appreciative.

Teia looked at the dead man. He was all rags and blood now. Blood matted his hair and his beaded beard. How had he got blood in his hair? She didn't even remember cutting his scalp. She wanted to vomit, but instead she felt cold inside. Dead. A killer.

'You have a rag?' she asked quietly. 'I'm a mess.'

Goss and Winsen looked at each other, looked at Ferkudi. Shook their heads in awe at the same time. That was funny. She laughed.

A stricken look passed over their faces, like she scared them. Oh, they thought she was laughing about killing that man. For some reason, that was hilarious, too. She laughed louder. She sounded crazy.

Then she walked over to the dead man. She found part of his breeches that were clean, and wiped the dagger carefully. Then she found a portion of the breeches' leg and began cutting off a chunk of cloth. The young men both just watched her.

She stood, oddly more disconcerted by seeing the bare, hairy leg of the dead man than by the fact that he was dead. Why were some men so . . . so hairy?

Hirsute. That was the word. Meant hairy. Why are there two words that mean exactly the same thing?

She took the rag and began wiping her face. It came away bloody, sticky. She examined herself. She was wearing a light tan blouse. It had been light tan, anyway. Now, it was a wreck, bloody everywhere. All bloody, again.

'Ferkudi,' she said. 'Give me your tunic.'

'Huh?'

'Tunic, moron.'

'Why?'

'Because you can walk out of this alley not wearing a tunic, and no one will remember it ten minutes from now.' She stared at him. He didn't understand. 'Versus *me* walking out of here without a tunic.'

A moment passed. Ferkudi's face scrunched.

Goss said quietly, 'Or her walking out of here with a bloody tunic, Ferkudi.'

'Oh!' Ferkudi said. He loosened his belt and peeled his tunic off.

Teia stripped off her blouse. Battlefield rules, right? She couldn't even find it in herself to be concerned. "Oh no, my squad saw my stomach"? Blood had soaked through her short chemise, too, dammit. It was her favorite of three, the only one that fit just right. She unlaced and stripped that off as well. None of the young men looked. Ferkudi silently held out his tunic, eyes averted. But Teia didn't take it immediately. She used clean areas of her tunic – most of the back of it – to wipe the obvious smears from herself.

Now she knew another reason why the Blackguard wore black. Hide the blood. Smart, that. She pulled on Ferkudi's tunic, wrapped her belt loosely around the waist, and grabbed the dead man's petasos. The young men stood around like rubes, doing nothing. She kicked her bloody clothes at Winsen and said, 'Fold those up, nunk. Ferkudi, you drag the body over there, hide it under the rubbish. Goss, kick dirt over the blood pools.'

The young men stood still for one long moment more, still stunned by the dead man at their feet.

'Orholam!' she swore. 'Now. Now!'

That snapped them out of it. They moved.

And in two minutes, in staggered turns – different directions, different times – they departed the alley. No one tried to stop them. No one cried out an alarm. It was like it never happened.

Chapter 46

Gavin woke bound and gagged in the back of a wagon, and started laughing. These idiots had no idea—

That he was a Prism.

No more. Well, *that* left a bad taste in Gavin's mouth. Or perhaps that was blood and scummy river water. The wagon slipped on a cobble and rattled him. Oh, Orholam, broken ribs.

Didn't appear to be sticking out at any odd angles, though. So maybe just cracked. And he hadn't drowned. So there was that. Didn't think he'd go swimming anytime soon, though. Attack dolphins. What the hell was that? Dolphins were supposed to be nice.

He rolled over slowly, timing his roll with the bumping of the wagon, and was able to see through the side. The sun had risen high above the sole promontory that overlooked the great delta, and it illuminated all the vast farmlands that fed Rath and much of the rest of the Seven Satrapies besides. Looking at the Great River and the farmlands here, Gavin was for the first time appreciative of his handicap. Seen in black and white and gray, the visual cacophony of the city was muted. Gray-and-black buildings rose in front of the dazzlingly white river and farms but for once didn't overwhelm or detract from that greater beauty.

It had been many years since Gavin had been in Rath during flood season. As a boy from their estate's walls atop Jaks Hill, he'd marveled at the sheer expanse of water. Indeed, it still awed him. Every year, the Great River flooded so vast an area that maps – maps drawn at the scale of showing all seven satrapies – drawn at different times of year showed a different coastline. Nor was it merely the coast that was altered. As Gavin looked out, it was like looking across an ocean, with villages in the distance sticking out like tiny islands on a sea of glass. This late in flood season, the water was only a few thumbs deep, and all the silt had settled from it. When one talked about the Cerulean Sea being calm in the morning, one understood it was a comparative calm. In the early morning like this, the Great River was so calm as to be surreal.

As an adult who'd been involved in vast efforts, it was the engineering of the thing that awed him. The people who lived on the Great River had not conquered nature; they'd slipped a yoke on it. Every year the great floods came, and the farmers retreated to their little villages, and the rich to their estates. In each case, foundations had been dug deep, deep into that life-giving silt. Entire villages sat only five to six feet above the level of the rest of the ground. The villagers knew exactly how much the river could rise. The floodwaters held no terror for them.

Flood season became a time of relative rest. Marriages were performed, parties held, feats of sport and strength demonstrated, houses repaired, tools sharpened, songs sung, instruments dusted off, love made. And, until Gavin had settled the Blood War, walls fortified, boys and men drilled, and weapons honed for the inevitable raiding that would come some months hence.

But the yoking of the river never really ended. As the waters rose and until the farmers determined exactly how high the river would rise this year, the village elders directed channels to be opened or shut off, managing the speed of the waters' flow so their own soil didn't get scoured away. Through flood season, the old men would keep watch over the river as the old women kept watch over the people. As the floods finally began to recede, the elders would direct which channels would be opened in order to drain the waters from their fields slowly, only after depositing all their silt, always trying to strike a balance that would give them the longest growing season possible, and always ready to shore up levees in case of rainstorms.

Their gentle mastery of land and river and labor had meant perpetual bumper crops the likes of which the rest of the satrapies could only envy. And envy they did.

The same flat land that gave them so much food offered little defense. The Great River itself was a defender on only one side. There was too much river and too few people to put a watch on all of it – and that was assuming that no village chief would allow himself to be bribed to turn a blind eye to raiders who promised to wipe out the next village over, where some rival lived or some ancient wrong wanted avenging.

They hadn't called these the Blood Plains of old for nothing, though that had also been the name of one of the nine kingdoms that had encompassed both what was now Blood Forest and Ruthgar. United, the warriors of the forests and the farmers of the river had been unstoppable. They'd had the first functioning navy in recorded history, with the riches required to build and maintain and staff a true fleet.

And the kings had used that fleet, one even navigating all the way up the Great River to the Floating City, a trip only possible in that time during flood season. It was more impressive for the logistical challenges they had overcome than the military ones. No one at the time had even dreamed of a standing army. The expense of paying farmers not to farm must have seemed an insanity. Everyone knew that raiding was for late summer.

And so when that fleet had reached the Floating City, the defenders had been entirely unprepared. The navy, filled with men who were starving after the arduous trip, which had included numerous portages, and furious at each other, had done unspeakable things when they reached the city. And their commanders, far from trying to restrain the baser passions, had inflamed them instead.

They had done their best to bury what they'd done there, to proclaim only a glorious victory. But a card of that time had survived.

Gavin had never viewed it. He'd seen enough slaughter in his life. Some cards couldn't be unseen. Sometimes he wondered if that was what his older brother Gavin had done on his thirteenth birthday. Had his father taken him to see cards?

At thirteen? Surely their father wouldn't be so foolish.

And yet Gavin had never been the same, and refused to speak of it, lashing out at Dazen and hitting him in the face for the first time ever when he wouldn't let it go. It had opened a rift between the brothers, that innocent needling and that punch. Dazen had thought it was his own fault for pushing his brother too far. He'd seen the tears welling in Gavin's eyes, like he couldn't believe he'd hit his little brother either. But he'd stood over him. Hadn't apologized. Hadn't ever apologized.

That was where what had culminated at Sundered Rock had started.

I'm sorry, Dazen.

What the hell? I'm sorry, *Dazen*? I've worn this mask too long.

What was I thinking on the boat? Telling them I'm Dazen? Madness. Why would I do such a thing?

They hadn't even treated him any differently. More importantly, in their brief few days with Antonius Malargos, it hadn't seemed that any of them had told the boy that Gavin had once claimed to be Dazen.

Regardless, it was a slip. A slip at the top of the rope and you fall a few knots down. But a slip at the bottom of the rope meant a plunge, and Gavin was about as low as you could get.

The scenery rolled by, beautiful but dead to him. Then, as they wound their way up Jaks Hill, someone noticed his eyes were open. Mercifully, instead of smacking his head with something blunt, they merely pitched a blanket over him so he couldn't see. Sometimes men surprise you with gentility when you least expect it.

Perhaps an hour later, after being slowly walked through a number of doors with the blanket still over his head, Gavin was deposited in a cell and only then allowed to see. He wasn't there long when a door opened and a woman walked in.

'You willjacked the river dolphin,' Gavin said. 'Clever.'

Eirene Malargos didn't deign to respond. Despite the blanket, he was in a dungeon, which told him pretty much all he needed to know about his prospects.

'Punishable by death, that kind of magic, but undeniably clever,' Gavin said.

Still she said nothing. Eirene Malargos didn't have her sister's rare blonde hair, instead she had brown hair in a straight curtain that hung to her chin, sometimes obscuring half her face. Nor could she draft. Nor did she have her younger sister's voluptuous curves, though it was hard to tell in the man's tunic and trousers she wore. They did have the same heart-shaped face, and Eirene had an intensity Tisis lacked.

'Everything's about magic to you, isn't it? Take you Guiles out of your sphere, and you're hopeless.' She shook her head. 'How do you make the world follow . . . this? We *trained* the dolphins. The hard way, with treats and love and consistency and a firm hand.'

'Most likely a lie, but I appreciate the righteous indignation,' Gavin said. 'Very convincing.' He swung his feet over the side of his cot and tried to stand. The pain in his ribs took his breath away. Cracked ribs. They'd been bound, and he'd been washed while he was unconscious, though. Maybe he did have a chance. He took a few light breaths, gathering his strength, and stood. There's a power dynamic that can be seized by sitting when others stand and standing when they sit, or refusing to do so.

He was taller than Eirene Malargos, and meat speaks. The dominance of height and musculature, softened by his attractive face and features, usually undercut resistance quite a bit.

Even women who like women like a good-looking man.

Eirene Malargos frowned, which told him it was working. Of course, being attractive merely opens doors a crack. Especially cell doors.

'May I ask,' he said, 'why I find myself in a cell? Apologies for my earlier unpleasantness. I find myself in a great deal of pain. It's quite enough to make a man cranky.' He winced through a smile.

Careful not to overplay it, Gavin.

The dungeon wasn't much of a dungeon, in truth. It was merely a cellar fitted with a few cells. It was dry, and there were no rats, which meant they kept cats, but also no sign of fur or odor of cat urine, which meant they kept a staff. With the substantial roof beams here, he had to be in the lower levels of a large house or mansion. So a large, wealthy house in one of the nicest sections of Jaks Hill. It was unlikely to be anything other than the Malargoses' own mansion.

Which meant, in turn, that he was within shouting distance of his own home. Though he hadn't visited in years, the Guiles owned an estate here. They were neighbors with the Malargos family. With slightly better position, of course.

It had to be a constant thorn in all the Malargoses' sides: the Guiles had, a generation past, only owned a sliver of swampland with a sad excuse for a rath on it. The family had made a play for power, binding together families on both sides of the river – but a reversal had left them with only their holdings in Blood Forest and that one, moldy rath. Andross Guile had leveraged that rath into representing Red for Ruthgar. And with the Red seat, he'd forced his way into the best estate on Jaks Hill, which doubtless the Malargos family had hoped to make theirs after the fall of the Maltheos family.

After acquiring the estate, the Guiles didn't even live here; they rarely visited, and yet the Guiles had the premier estate as Andross's pride demanded. It was, some said, better than the satrapah's own, and she had to share her estate with all the machinery of government. And here Gavin was. He'd traveled all over the world, only to return home to a cell.

Eirene said nothing for some time, merely studying him. He kept his face pleasantly neutral, on the off chance that she would claim a misunderstanding. As the Strategist had said, if you want your enemy to fight to the death, cut off all escape; if you want your enemy to retreat, leave a path open. As a young man, Gavin had liked to cut off escape, had liked to overwhelm, dominate, and destroy, even if it carried a higher risk of defeat.

On some signal he hadn't seen, a servant came from the hallway, where he must have been standing out of Gavin's line of sight. In a silk-gloved hand, he presented his mistress with a glass of liquor on an electrum tray. There was no second glass.

She drank. Winced.

Gavin could smell it from where he stood. It smelled like burnt peat and fermented giant sweat. He was actually happy she hadn't offered it.

'What is victory to you, Gavin Guile?'

'Pardon?' he asked.

'What is your plan? It's plain you've been a galley slave.

The scabs on your wrists haven't healed, so you've worn manacles within the last two weeks. The stripes on your back are red, but healed, so you've been whipped in the last year but not the last month. If you last shaved when you were free, your beard says you've been enslaved perhaps six months. That lines up with the Battle of Ru. Surely in all your time on an oar, you were plotting.'

'Perhaps all my plotting was taken up on getting free of slavery. Freeing oneself from slavery is better than most galley slaves manage in six months, after all.'

'Most slaves don't have my cousin rescue them.'

'So you, ahem, know about that?' Gavin said.

'He signaled us when you arrived in the harbor.'

Oh, the boy had a mirror. That was how Eirene had known to send a galley first thing in the morning to scoop him out of the water. A mirror. Gavin hadn't even thought of it.

It's the little things that get you.

'You stupid, stupid man,' Eirene said. She threw back her liquor. 'I spoke with him last night. Do you know that he is quite enamored with you? With all these legends you've cultivated around you. He believes them all. He thought when he found you in that galley that he'd been sent by Orholam himself to rescue you. That it was destiny. Young, no men in his life, you understand. Puts you on a pedestal.'

'He's a good boy. Not a boy much longer, either,' Gavin said truthfully.

Another glass of liquor appeared in her hand, but she waited until the servant – who avoided even looking in Gavin's direction – was fully out of earshot before she continued. 'Do you know that if you'd told him honestly why you didn't want to come to Rath, he likely would have turned his back on all his family and gone with you? But you're a liar. A fearful little man who wraps tales around himself like cloaks. You're empty inside all those cloaks, Gavin Guile. He would have defied even me, who has been both mother and father to him. You understand? I'm having to manage him carefully even now, to make sure he doesn't try to come rescue you or some foolishness. But I'll watch. I won't let him tie himself to you. You'll get no help from that quarter.'

'And you're going to silence an entire crew?' Gavin asked.

She didn't like that. 'It can be done,' she said. 'I haven't decided yet if I must do it.'

There was only one way to silence a hundred and twenty-two sailors. She'd sequestered them; now she was deciding if she'd kill them. How long could you even feed so many imprisoned men without word getting out? How long before one of them remembered Gavin had claimed to be Dazen, and traded that information in hope of gaining freedom?

'So, back to my question,' she said. 'What is your plan, and how do you think you can get there from here?'

He was silent, but not even silence could hide all the truth from this woman.

'Because I have a plan,' she said, and there was nothing remotely pleasant in her tone. 'My plan is to find out your plan, and then to allow you to achieve it, if you are indeed so capable.'

'But,' he said tentatively.

'But.' She smiled at him, big white teeth like tombstones in the sun. She grabbed on to the bars of his cell, about to speak, then her thin lips twisted in distaste and she took her hands away from the slick bars. She rubbed her fingertips together, disgusted, and looked up. A servant was there with a kerchief instantly. She took it and waved the servant away. 'Gavin Guile, I want to know your plan. I want to know how you define victory so that when, against all odds, you achieve it, it tastes like water in the mouth of drowning man.'

'But that sounds like something bad.' As if puzzled. Patronizing.

Her eyes flashed, but she rolled her shoulders and finished her drink instead of striking him. 'You're many things, Gavin Guile, but you're neither credulous nor stupid. You've got some plan.'

'And now that you have threatened me at length, in what insane world would I tell you about it?'

'This one.'

'Clearly you think so. The point is that you need to convince me of that.'

'If you don't tell me, I kill you. Right now.' Her tone was

flat and insulted and more than ready to kill, and less than remorseful. It was the voice of a woman who'd killed before, and attached no particular significance to the deed. He thought of a boat full of men who might die at her word. Could she get away with such a thing? In Rath? Unlikely. But it wouldn't do those men or him any good after the fact to be proven right. What really mattered was if she *thought* she could get away with it, or if she simply didn't care.

'Well. That isn't very creative of you,' he said.

She didn't even crack a smile. His charm was dust here. 'Brutality oft accomplishes what creativity cannot.'

'I see that—'

She said, 'I don't want to hear another word out of you, unless it's—'

'You really must—'.

'That counts as another word. And don't you dare tell what I must or must not do. I will not tolerate another interruption.'

Gavin stopped.

'Test me on this. One word out of turn.' She leveled a flat gaze at the man who had made satraps and Colors tremble, and he saw that she hoped he would test her.

She laughed as if she'd been joking. 'Ha! You should have seen yourself just now, Gavin Guile!'

He smirked uncertainly.

'In fact, perhaps you should see yourself!' She looked around in an unconvincing search. 'But I see no mirrors here. Why, you know, I know a torturer who claims that he can pluck out an eye with the sinews still attached, and that a man can be made to see his own face. Ought we try?'

A snake turned over in Gavin's guts, and he felt that fear he'd felt in the war when he'd had to face drafters who'd broken the halo, who stared at him with eyes full of desperation that told him they might do anything. He remembered a man holding a burning slow match in his hand, sparking and spitting, as he sat in the middle of camp on a barrel full of powder, quietly, absently singing, while Dazen and four hundred men crowded into a little cave, hiding from his elder brother's passing patrols. None of his men could leave without alerting Gavin's troops and dooming them all, but if the madman moved that slow match to the powder, most of them would certainly die. Gavin – then Dazen – had talked his way out of that. Carefully, and with no magic.

Giving her a moment to make sure she actually meant this to be a question, and that he now had leave to speak, Gavin said, 'I'm sure I would be quite a sight for a sore eye.'

Her eyebrow twitched, but she didn't smile.

'By which I mean, no thank you,' he said.

'So the question is simple, Gavin Guile, but I am not a simpleton to be taken in by your breezy charm and a smile that once weakened hymens for ten leagues around. Tell me less than the full truth, and you will die. Tell the full truth, and I will do all I can to make your victory almost impossible, but totally empty. What say you?'

I say you're fucking insane and I'm going to ram a sharpened spoon through the side of your neck.

'So you want me to tell you my plan so you can make it nearly impossible, but not quite impossible?'

'And then I will do all I can to make it an empty victory once you achieve it. You see, I believe in you, Gavin Guile.'

She kept saying his name. It unnerved him as much as her flat, hating gaze.

'Perhaps your time in the galley has dulled your wits,' she said. 'Let's say your dream is to father a line of satraps and Prisms and Colors. I'll let you leave here alive, rather than kill you. But I'll cut off one of your testicles and crush the other. You'll live thinking, perhaps, perhaps you can still father sons. And if you do, on your deathbed, I'll let you know I've gelded your son. Do you understand now?'

Gavin said, 'You seem to be angry with me for some reason.'

She looked down, shaking her head, incredulous. Then she cracked a grin. 'You really are quite charming. I see why you get your way. But not here, Gavin. I'm waiting.'

'How about you show me yours, and I'll show you mine?' Gavin said. 'I don't even know why you hate me.' That was, of course, a lie.

'Everything's a competition with you, isn't it?' she asked. Her tone was almost sad, and Gavin got a premonition that this was a very, very bad thing. 'It's all about will, and Gavin

Guile is will incarnate. Is that what you think? Is that how you see the world? Even broken, in a cage, you think that if you act like the bars are nothing, they will be nothing. Perhaps that was true once. You're not the Prism anymore, Guile. You're a husk. You're a broken galley slave is all. Just another man, demanding my surrender. Do you know what your weakness is, former Prism?'

'Women. Especially glamorous women. A woman who knows how to not just wear a ball gown, but really *own* it is rarer than hellstone. And fit women. And women with an ample bust. Or slender women. Let's not forget intelligent women. You can't dismiss the value of a wicked mind in the bedchamber.' Or one woman who is all of that and more. Gavin's heart ached suddenly under a stupid grin mask.

'Put your hands up on the bars,' Eirene said.

Gavin did.

'Spread your fingers.'

Not a good sign. But she was standing back far enough that he could certainly snatch his own hand back before she could reach out and hurt him. He did it.

'Pick a number between one and ten.'

Didn't like where this was going. With his hands held up in front of his face . . . 'One,' he said, as if picking that because he would always pick number one.

She started at the right. 'One,' she said, pointing to his little finger on his left hand. She smiled unpleasantly. 'I'm going to give you a choice that I think will demonstrate to you your real weakness.'

'I admit, when I have to count beyond ten, if my toes are in boots, I do have trouble.'

'Here's your choice, Gavin Guile.'

Orholam have mercy, she said his name so many times it was driving him crazy. It was like she knew.

'Would you prefer to have the word "FOOL" tattooed across your face in as big letters as we can fit, or would you prefer to lose your little finger? Your choice,' she said. She crossed her arms.

'That's a terrible test. It doesn't even remotely show what you think it shows,' Gavin said.

She said, 'You say one more word other than "finger" or "tattoo" and I'll have you suffer both.'

She was going to say he was being vain, if he chose to lose the finger. That vanity was his weakness. But what army in the world would follow a man with "FOOL" etched across his face? He had hurdles enough to overcome with the loss of his drafting to try to lead. A constant humiliation would make leadership impossible. There would be no covering such a thing. Gavin had seen people who'd tried to cover unfortunate tattoos. It would make an even bigger joke out of him.

He looked down the hallway, where a pair of servants stood, looking through the open door, watching for any sign from Lady Malargos. He took a deep, slow breath. With his cracked ribs, it hurt like hell. Which meant this next was going to be ten times worse.

'My name is Gavin Guile!' he roared, shouting toward the servants, toward the open door. 'And my father will give a fortune to whoever reports my presence here! My father is Andross Guile! Any who aid in this torture will pay the price!'

As soon as he started shouting, the servants panicked. They didn't immediately see Eirene's sign to slam the door, and he got almost all of it out before they did so.

For his part, Gavin sank to the floor, tears leaking from his eyes. He tried to breathe in tiny little gulps. Maybe not cracked ribs. Maybe fully broken.

'What the hell was that?' Eirene demanded.

'That was me giving you the finger.'

Chapter 47

Teia couldn't stop looking at her bloody hands. Half under her breath, she said, 'Wasn't right.'

'Huh?' Kip asked.

'What we did. That wasn't right,' she said. She looked up at him, and felt shame cover her like a snowdrift blowing off Hellmount itself. She said, 'I *murdered* a man.'

The safe house where they'd gathered wasn't even a house. It had been a chicken coop built onto the side of a cooper's shop. None of them knew when the Blackguard had acquired the place, but it had been walled off from the cooper's, had a few tools propped up around the low front door, and was made to look like a shed. Inside, the ground had been excavated to make the single room far bigger than looked possible from the outside. Half a dozen bunk beds, three high, lined the walls. A stove cleverly piped to share the cooper's chimney rested on one wall. Stores of food and weapons and clothing took up most of the rest of what little space there was.

'You – we – *killed* a man,' Kip said.

'Oh, what difference is there? He's dead! I messed up!'

'We're warriors, Teia,' Kip said like she was being stupid. 'That's what all this is for.'

'I know! I know,' she said. She looked around at the rest of their squad. She shook her head. She was letting them down. She should just shut up. 'Doesn't matter. I'll be fine. Can you throw me the fucking towel already, Ferkudi?'

'You'll get it when I'm done, bitch,' Ferkudi said. He was usually good-natured, but when he wasn't, he was an ogre.

Kip moved faster than Teia would have believed he could. He grabbed Ferkudi by the front of his tunic in both hands and lifted the young man off his feet and slammed his back against the wall. 'That's my partner,' he said. 'That's your squad-mate. I know you're shaken up. But. Don't.'

Ferkudi's feet weren't even touching the ground – and Ferkudi was one of the biggest boys in the squad. Holy shit. Kip was getting *strong*.

Kip released him. 'Towel. Please.'

Ferkudi handed the towel over. Looked away. 'Sorry,' he grumbled.

'To her.'

'Sorry, Teia,' he rumbled. 'Didn't mean to be such a flesh protuberance.'

'I'll take it outta you in training,' Teia said. She hit him in the arm, not too gently. But she was glad he'd apologized. She liked Ferkudi, but that had infuriated her, and she didn't have it in her to take him down a peg herself. Not right now.

Kip handed her the towel. 'You were saying?'

She took the towel angrily, which he didn't deserve, and she knew it, and it made her angrier. 'Get off it, Breaker. You're not my father.' It wasn't fair. She'd felt gratified that he'd come to her defense, but she was suddenly just so angry, so close to tears.

'No, but I've killed men. Spit it out.'

Teia began wiping her hands off. Stared firmly down at the towel, her hands, the task. 'What if . . . what if they have a point? The Blood Robes, I mean.'

'To hell with them,' Winsen said. 'Kill 'em all. Let Orholam sort 'em.'

Teia had heard similar statements before, but they'd been boasts. Childishness. With Winsen, it didn't seem like a put-on.

'No,' Kip said. 'Teia . . . *Of course* they have a point.'

'What are you saying?' Cruxer asked, speaking up for the first time. He'd been content to let his squad work through things themselves, but Teia could tell he didn't want the conversation to veer into heresy.

'No one's saying the Chromeria is perfect, Teia. There's a price for law, and we see that all around us. The Chromeria has power, and in places, it abuses its power. Welcome to the human race. Lawlessness has a price, too. I grew up in Tyrea, the closest thing to the kind of lawless *paradise* that the Blood Robes hold forth. Tyrea is a lot of things, but paradise?' Kip gave a derisive snort.

'Think about the Blackguard. Think about its leadership. Commander Ironfist may be the best man any of us know. Watch Captain Blademan, a good, good man. Not very imaginative—'

'Breaker, you can't—' Cruxer began, but Kip ran right over him.

'Of course I can!' Kip said. 'We're Blackguards! We're not afraid of the truth! Remember? Not very imaginative, but dutiful, hardworking, loyal to a fault. An excellent second-tier leader. We lost Watch Captain White Oak, obviously, but she was totally capable, too. Watch Captain Tempus? Bookish but clever, better in charge than in a charge, but competent. Watch Captain Beryl? She's a little too friendly for an officer, but good. Blunt? Not quite friendly enough, but again, good. Then I look at the squads above us, and for the most part, I admire them. I look at us, and we're the best I can think of. Am I right, Captain?'

'It's why I gave up my promotion,' Cruxer said quietly. 'Half of it, anyway.' Teia and the squad knew the other half. It was the same as theirs. Lightbringer.

'What's your point?' Teia asked Kip.

Kip said, 'If Cruxer hadn't been willing to risk throwing away his own career, Aram would be in this squad right now. He was a rat, and despite all our good leaders, he was *this close* to getting in. Maybe he would have been discovered before he made full Blackguard, but with how undermanned we are, I doubt it. He probably would have taken final vows within a year's time. And that's with the Blackguards doing almost everything right. Even with us, let's be honest. Some of those who have made it in aren't squeaky clean. Some of us – even us inductees – have had blackmail or bribes tried on us. Why? Because we're powerful and we're going to be more powerful soon; because we have what others want. Some of us stumble, and some of us are downright rotten – despite every advantage, right? I mean, we're respected, we're paid well, we have all we need, we have extra attention paid to us, we have the best the Chromeria can give us – and we still have weakness and venality and betrayers among us.'

'It's not that bad,' Ferkudi said.

'Yes it is,' Kip said. 'You just don't want to face it yet.'

'No one's tried to bribe or blackmail me,' Ferkudi said.

'Ferk,' Kip said, exasperated. 'It's because they think you're too dumb to bribe and too unpredictable to blackmail and too apt to talk to be charmed. They're wrong on the first count.'

Ferkudi blinked like a dog whose nose had been swatted.

But Kip went right on. 'But that's not the point. If a group with the small size, the wealth, the good leadership, and all the advantages of the Blackguard can have its members go bad, how could we possibly expect a group that's so much larger, and more powerful, and spread out over all the satrapies – with *poor* leadership in some areas – to be more virtuous than we are?'

'You mean the Chromeria,' Teia said.

'I do.'

'I expect it because they made vows before Orholam,' Big Leo said, speaking up for the first time. 'Because they are Orholam's hands on earth. They shouldn't fail that kind of a holy trust.'

'No,' Kip said. 'They shouldn't. Men and women should never violate their oaths.'

'But they do,' Ferkudi said. Bless him, always stating the obvious. But then, sometimes the obvious benefited from being dragged out into the full glare of the light.

'The Blood Robes are liars leading naïfs,' Kip said. 'They don't want to live up to the oaths they took that when they became a danger, they'd end themselves. They're afraid and unfaithful, so they say their vows don't count. They want to lord their power over others, so they say the Chromeria unfairly lords its power over them. The Chromeria says that every man is equal in Orholam's sight, that our powers and privileges make us the greater slaves of our communities. I don't admire Magister Kadah, but she's right about that much. On the other hand, the Color Prince says drafters are above other men by nature – and at the same time talks about abolishing slavery. Tell me, if drafters are above other men by nature, why would you abolish slavery?'

Silence reigned for a few long moments.

'Because he needed an army,' Cruxer said. 'And coming from Tyrea, he had to pass the mines at Laurion and the tens of thousands of slaves there.'

'To divide your enemy,' Daclos said. 'Armies afraid of what their own slaves will do when they're gone won't go far from home.'

'Understand that everything the Color Prince does, he does for power, and you'll understand everything he does,' Kip said.

'It can't be that simple, can it?' Teia said. 'If so, how come you see it, and no one else does?'

'Because I'm a bad person, so I understand how bad people think.'

What the hell did he mean by that? Was he fishing for compliments?

349

But Kip was still speaking. 'Don't judge a man by what he says his ideals are, judge him by what he does. Look at what the Color Prince has done. They're wrong, Teia. They're liars and murderers. It doesn't mean everything we do is right. It doesn't mean our house doesn't need a thorough cleaning. I just don't think we need to burn it to the ground to do it.'

Ferkudi nodded his head. 'My folks had a saying: the fact your dog has fleas is no reason to open your home to a wolf.'

'My dad used that one, too. But he said, wife, rash, bed, and whore,' Winsen said.

Goss said, 'A lesson he had to learn the hard way, no doubt.'

Ferkudi laughed with them. Then he said, 'I don't get it.'

'It's one of those things, Ferk,' Goss said.

'Where if you explain it, it doesn't work?' Ferkudi asked. He was familiar with those. 'Flesh protuberance!'

Worst swear ever. Second worst, maybe. For a while he'd used 'proboscis.'

'You think it's that simple, Breaker?' Teia asked, ignoring the boys.

'In the False Prism's War, Gavin's generals ordered the burning of Garriston. It was stupid. It was wrong. Horrific. The fires spread, and they killed scores of thousands. It wasn't strategy; it was vengeance for what happened in Ru, but far worse. But Gavin had to win the war. And after he won, he couldn't punish those who did it, though I'm sure he wanted to. They said – and maybe they even believed – that what they had done was necessary to win. So he gave them medals and showed them the door. Not one of those involved in burning Garriston is here on the Jaspers anymore. You think that's a coincidence? Those men are no longer in any position where they could do something like that again. Was what Gavin did once the deed had been done *good*? No. But it was the best thing possible.'

'And this?' Teia asked, showing her still-bloodied hands and the bloody rag that wouldn't get the stains out completely. 'This is the best thing?'

Kip stared her hard in the eye. He took the towel in his own clean hands and smeared blood first on one palm and then on the other. 'Not the best thing, Teia. The best thing possible? A thousand times yes.'

And staring into his eyes, she believed him. It was a damned thing, war, but she wasn't damned for fighting it. It shifted her burden only a little – not much, but enough.

Twenty minutes later, after the squad had cleaned up, after Cruxer had debriefed each of them in turn, they formed up at the door of the safe house to go back to the Chromeria together and report. It was obviously a duty Cruxer wasn't relishing.

'Teia,' Cruxer said. 'Up front.'

'Huh?'

'You're my number two now. First sergeant.'

Teia looked at Ferkudi, whom she was displacing. He didn't look angry. 'The promotion was my idea, Teia,' he said. 'We froze up out there. I froze up. You deserve it.'

Deserve it? She'd gone crazy out there. She didn't trust herself to speak, so she simply took her new place.

'What about Breaker?' she asked.

'Breaker is Breaker,' Cruxer said. 'He, uh, doesn't fit exactly in the chain of command. When it's time to listen to him, we listen. The rest of the time, he listens to us. Fair, Breaker?'

Kip looked bereaved, but resolute. 'So it begins?' he asked Cruxer quietly.

Teia had no idea what they were talking about. 'It began a long time ago, Breaker,' Cruxer said. 'The only question is if you fight fate or try to steer it.'

'Fate?' Kip asked. 'You're the one who gave me the name Breaker in the first place.'

'Oops,' Cruxer said. A wry grin.

'Fair enough, Captain. I'll take the half-step to the outside. I wanted this more than anything, though. You know that, right?'

'I know what it is to want . . . the impossible.' His mouth twisted, and Teia knew he was thinking of Lucia.

Kip said, 'You're the best of us, Cruxer. In every way. Don't you dare die, you understand?'

'Meh, I'm invincible,' Cruxer said. 'Now let's get back, double time. Let's see if we can work some more of this off.' He poked Kip in the belly, and they both grinned.

Boys. How Teia loved them both.

Chapter 48

Weeks later, they stood again in their ranks in front of Trainer Fisk. He cast a baleful eye around the great yard beneath the Chromeria. Everywhere, Blackguards were training men and women who were not Blackguards. He stared at one arc of the great circle with particular, undisguised hatred, though.

The rumored Lightguard was now a reality. The nunks joined him in his spite. Established with one stroke of the new promachos's pen, the Lightguard was Andross Guile's own personal army, established to defend the Jaspers, so he said, and answering only to him.

The Blackguards saw what he was doing, even if it seemed no one else in power did. The Lightguard was comprised of mercenaries, ruffians, veterans from the old war, and any others who were willing to do whatever Andross Guile wanted in return for coin and his protection from prosecution or vengeance for any crime they might have committed. They were led primarily by washed-out Blackguards and the sons of poor nobles who wanted to throw themselves on Andross Guile's mercy.

They had been given tailed white jackets with big brass buttons and medals for trifles. Worse, they were given some of the Blackguard's prerogatives: allowed to walk through the Chromeria armed, for one.

And they were being taught – by the promachos's incontrovertible order – by a Blackguard. It was like being forced to gut yourself with a rusty knife.

'Today, Specials,' Trainer Fisk said, spitting in the direction of the Lightguards, but then turning away.

Almost all of their training was special assignments now, and there was little pretense that it was only training. The swearing in to full Blackguard status of the best inductees had been halted. Commander Ironfist had seen that once sworn, his people were sent to duties like training Lightguards, so he held on to them.

Other Blackguards were being sent on other missions: some of them searching for Gavin, others disappearing for days or weeks, and coming back, sworn to silence about what they'd been doing. Word got out, at least in Blackguard circles, though. They were looking for bane. They said there might be nexuses of each of the seven colors out there somewhere. Which, to Kip's ears, sounded like more gods to fight.

Some of them reported strange sights, odd phenomena they'd encountered. One brought back a small lizard called a sand dragon from Atash. The nunks thought it was the least exciting dragon ever. It didn't breathe fire or anything interesting, but when they killed it, they were able to set it on fire without any other fuel, and it burned for three days. Somehow the things incorporated red luxin into their bodies, much like atasifusta trees used to do. This was the first one that had been seen in many years.

In Ruthgar, there were stories of the grasslands – usually dormant and brown this late in the year – growing green in great nine-pointed stars. It might have been the work of rogue green drafters fertilizing the plains to make a statement for the Color Prince, but two of the Blackguards had seen one. They believed what they had seen was far too big to be the work of even three or four green drafters working together.

In Paria, a team had found a town where half the wells were full of orange luxin. The village elders swore that there were no orange drafters nearby. And in a week, the luxin simply disappeared.

There were wilder rumors, too, of firestorms in Tyrea, where instead of lightning, great streaks of fire splashed down with the rain and hail and snow. Sinkholes in Abornea. Boiling seas off Pericol. Animals acting strangely, and even plants seeming to act with intent. It was impossible to filter the truth from the nonsense and, quickly, impossible to get some of the books from the restricted libraries that had been sitting right under the squad's nose. Scholars appointed by Andross himself came in, grabbed a bunch of books and scrolls, and left without a word.

And all the time, the war was being fought. The enemy was advancing. Others were fighting in their place, far away.

With them all formed up, Trainer Fisk said, 'Today your assignment, every squad, is to go to the docks on East Bay. The Lists are being read. Go.'

He stopped.

'And what, sir?' an Archer named Kerea asked. 'What are we to do?'

'You listen. Was there something unclear about your orders? Go!'

They went.

'What was that about?' Ferkudi asked before they even reached the Lily's Stem.

Cruxer seemed somber. But he didn't answer. Kip took his lead and didn't answer either. Knowing what a lesson was beforehand didn't mean you had to blunt its impact on those who didn't.

'Let's take it at a jog,' Cruxer said.

They jogged through the enclosed bridge as the sunrise shone brilliance on them. Kip had two thoughts: first, that he was no longer baffled at the wonders of magic of these islands. Running through a luxin tube suspended at the level of the waves had somehow become normal to him. The awkward bumpkin was gone. He wasn't sure that was all good. How insular the Jasperites became, every day seeing magic the likes of which a Tyrean orchardist would never see in his life, every day rubbing shoulders with women and men who harnessed Orholam's breath itself. All the world turned around the Jaspers, but the Jaspers were not all the world. Second, he realized there was now no sign at all of the sea demon attack that had nearly demolished this bridge. The sea demon itself hadn't been seen since the Feast of Light and Darkness, nor the black whale. The mess had been cleared, the dead taken away – and none of them were people Kip had known, or known by people Kip knew. It was like it hadn't happened.

This is what it is to live in the cosmos that is the Jaspers. The world changes here, but here there is not one world, there are many, and we only see the others when they tread upon our toes.

They made it to the docks and slowed as they pushed through

the press of bodies. Cruxer acted as a wedge, and Big Leo went second, clearing a path for the rest of them. In their inductees' grays, no one resisted them.

There was a tall carven pedestal just wide enough for a crier to stand on, and a man was clambering up the ladder to stand there. He reached into a pouch he wore and pulled out a scroll. He cracked the seal, and the crowd quieted, then he allowed the scroll to unfurl.

Murmurs shot through the crowd as they saw the scroll unroll past his feet. But they quieted again as the man began reading, his voice a clear, cutting tenor that carried easily over the murmurs and the sounds of sailors unloading their ships, wagons creaking past on old wheels. 'This is the list of those dead or missing and believed to be dead who hail from Big Jasper or the Chromeria, from the end of the skirmish at Ruic Neck until the end of the Battle of Ox Ford. This list is complete and truthful to the best of my knowledge, so swears Lord Commander of the Unified Armies of the Satrapies, Caul Azmith.'

And then he began reading names. Noblewomen first, then noblemen. Scant few though there were of either. Then female drafters, then male drafters. As slaves – despite being drafters – the Blackguards came next, barely before the commoners.

'Of the Blackguard: Elessia, Laya, Tugertent, Ahhanen, Djur, Norl Jumper, and Pan Harl.'

And then he read on, as if those were but a few names of the hundreds or thousands he had yet to read this day, as if this was simply his work. Which of course it was.

'Norl *Jumber*, Orholam damn you. Jumber,' Big Leo said under his breath.

It was Ben-hadad, the smart one, who said the dumbest thing. 'They could just be missing, right? I mean, this doesn't mean they're dead. Not all of them. It's a list of the dead and missing. Right?'

Cruxer didn't even turn his head. 'There's a hope that empowers, and a hope that enfeebles. Don't confuse them.'

Someone down the line choked, strangling a sob. Ferkudi? Kip wondered why he wasn't feeling anything at all, except awkward that he wasn't feeling what he was supposed to feel. What was wrong with him? What if someone else in the squad looked at him and could tell that while they stood and grieved, he was just standing?

He remembered Elessia. She was small, crooked grin, crooked teeth, light-skinned for a Blackguard, got duty with the White a lot. Laya: she was a red, older. Kip could remember her weeping on the barges as they came back from Garriston. Oh, that was it. She'd had to kill her partner, who'd broken the halo in the middle of the battle. Tugertent was a literal archer, and the best in the Blackguard at that. People swore they'd seen her hit targets around corners, which she'd never denied. Ahhanen Kip could only remember in that he always looked like he'd just drunk wine gone to vinegar. His partner was Djur, who had a trick of juggling two pistols and knife in dizzying patterns to amuse his comrades. Liked to gamble, and was bad at it, from what Kip had heard. Norl Jumber was small and eager, none too bright, but always infectiously happy. Pan Harl had been an inductee, like Kip and his squad. He shouldn't even have been there.

They couldn't just be gone. Not just like that. A name read aloud in a square, and that was it? What had happened to them? Had they died heroically, or were they merely in the wrong place and their card had been pulled?

Someone started keening, not ten paces away. She threw herself forward, as if to attack the crier, and several women grabbed her, held her back. Kip realized he'd lost some time. The crier had been reading name upon name, by satrapy and lord of allegiance. There had to be over a thousand names on his list.

A thousand names, and he was only reading the dead who hailed from the Jaspers. Someone said that the Ruthgari armies had taken the most grievous losses by far.

Orholam have mercy, how many people had died?

The squads stood at attention for fifteen minutes as the names were read. Name after name after name. As each lord's dead was read, some would sob or shriek or collapse, while others tried not to let too much relief show. But as the list continued relentlessly, the balance shifted. The mood darkened. The brightly shining sun glistened in mockery, as if Orholam didn't see.

In some distant corner, a fight had broken out among the bereaved. Furious, flailing against the truth, punishing the innocent. The bitter aggrieved and the guiltily relieved, fighting.

When the crier finished, there was only silence and sobs, the broken being led away by stunned friends.

Kip wanted to shout at them. You thought this was a game?! When Tyreans were dying it was exciting, but now, now it's serious?! He hated them for a moment, but the moment passed, and he saw their sorrow and was moved.

That they have learned to weep at war is no victory. That they know loss is no gain.

Then the crier announced where the names of each satrapy's dead would be posted around the plaza, and got down from his pedestal. There was no other word. No update.

They hadn't announced the battle as a victory, or even as holding off the enemy. That lack, as much as the number of names read did, told Kip there had been only crushing defeat.

'This is why,' Cruxer said. The squad looked at him. 'This is why we have to be the best.'

Chapter 49

Teia was following Murder Sharp again, to a different neighborhood. The winter night was cold, but at least this time there was no fog. It didn't make her feel much better.

'So, this lightsplitter thing . . .' Teia said. That was what tonight was about, and Teia was worrying at the knotted rope of anxieties in her gut.

'Was that a question?'

'I don't get it. I mean, I get it. A Prism doesn't need spectacles. Handy for him, I'm sure, but I'm a monochrome and paryl doesn't require spectacles. So even if I were a lightsplitter, that would be like . . . what? Like being the best juggler in the satrapies, only I don't have any arms?'

'Exactly like that.'

'Really?'

'No.'

They arrived at a dark-windowed home in Weasel Rock, were handed their hooded robes and ushered in to darkness.

'Strip naked.' The voice was gruff, deliberately altered, the figure hooded, a splotch of black against the darkness.

The room was almost pitch black, a tiny thread of light let in under the door, and pants-wettingly scary, but Teia wasn't anyone's slave, not anymore. Not Aglaia Crassos's, not Kip's, not Andross Guile's, and certainly not Fear's.

'Well, that answers one question,' Teia said to the heavily cloaked figure. 'You're definitely male.' Her voice was snide, superior, anything but terrified. That knot in her guts wasn't fear, it was apprehension, anxiety, animus, bitterness, bile, belligerence, contempt, contumely . . . cravenness.

Fuck.

No, fuck him.

'*Strip.*' Definitely male, definitely irritated, definitely not very good at disguising his voice when vexed. A bit of a haze smoker, if she didn't miss her guess, from the rough edges on that voice.

'That's not going to happen,' she said. Fucking amateurs. She cursed mentally when she was trying to convince herself of her own toughness. Her knees weren't trembling from fear. It was fucking cold in this fucking place.

Damn. Doing it double time. Much more of this, and my underwear is going to need an extra washing.

'Your disobedience has been noted. I have whores to humiliate for my pleasure. This is no test of your virtue. Nor indeed, of your will. This is a test of lightsplitting.'

A part of her thrilled with sudden hope, but she hid it. 'And I need to be ass-naked to do it?'

'It works best if—'

'So no.'

'When beginning—'

'You want me naked for one of two reasons. Either to humiliate me and make me feel vulnerable, or for the gratification of your sick desires. Go to hell.'

'Oh, Teia.' Low and amused, somehow more dangerous when he said 'Teia.' Oh hell. 'Sick desires? To see a comely young woman naked? In what world is that a sick desire? True, your

358

curves are late in coming, but I've noticed a change even in the last few—'

'Fuck you!' She trembled. He'd been watching? For months? Orholam's poxy gemsack! How dare he comment on – fuck! She was not going to be extra aware of her body because of one word from this asshole.

She looked around the dark room. Nondescript, nothing to differentiate it from any of a thousand other rooms in a thousand other houses in the bad neighborhoods of Big Jasper. What was she playing at? Why was she here? Who did she think she was, playing these games, with these people?

She'd been at the reading of the Lists. She knew the stakes. There might have been a time when being a Blackguard inductee would have protected her, when fear of what the Blackguard would do to avenge her if she were harmed would have kept her safe anywhere in the world.

That was before the war. Now, she knew, even here on Big Jasper she wasn't safe.

The worst of it was the secrecy. Not being able to tell her squad, not being able to tell Kip? It tore her up, but it was the only safe way. For them.

'This isn't a debate. You'll serve or you'll die. It would be a terrible waste to lose you at this point, but if you're disobedient now, how would we ever trust you with more power?'

'You're an asshole,' Teia said. 'I'll wear my underthings.'

A pause. 'Good, I'd distrust you if you gave in too easily.' He'd let the alteration on his gruff voice fade a bit there, and it gave Teia some small measure of victory.

She stripped. It was pitch black in here anyway, right?

'Put this on,' he said, voice gruff again.

With some difficulty, she widened her eyes to sub-red and saw that the hooded figure wasn't extending the bundle exactly to her. She'd taken a step to the side as she'd stripped, and he hadn't noticed. He wasn't a sub-red drafter, then. Or paryl. She tucked the information away. Someday she'd need it. Maybe. It made her feel less like a victim to do something, regardless. She took the bundle.

A sack, no, another weasel-bear mask, this one bedecked with patches and straps.

359

The man said, 'The test requires that you not use your eyes at all. Everyone cheats. It's impossible not to.'

It's impossible not to? Said like someone who'd taken the test and failed, perhaps?

Teia pulled on the hood. She didn't have any idea if she'd put it on the right way, where the straps went. Orholam, it was hot and stuffy and she couldn't breathe right in—

Someone touched her naked shoulder.

She jumped, but it wasn't the startled little-girl response it would have been even a year ago. She jumped, one foot shifting back, head ducking the blow that must be coming, center of mass dropping until that back foot gave her a base, and one fist snapping forward with the speed and force of all her emotional and muscular tension together.

Her fist sank into a stomach. In Blackguard training, one of the less fun drills involved taking hits in the stomach. You'd stand with a partner and trade blows. There were different strategies depending on how big you were. Clench and move back just as the punch hit you so you didn't take the full force, or if you were bigger and rock-hard, clench and move into the punch so it hit you before it was in the golden zone. But always, always, you clenched your muscles hard. This stomach wasn't fat, but it wasn't clenched either: it was soft, muscles loose, and her fist sank into it easily.

There was a moment of total silence as Teia realized what she'd just done. The scuff of a shoe as the man took a step back, and then the sound of him collapsing on the ground. A moment later, there was a huge gasping breath as he got his wind back.

Teia froze. Chuckles sounded around the room. Five, six people?

'Faces out!' the man snapped. 'You're not to see her!'

Teia heard the man she'd hit – the same man who'd been tormenting her? – stand up.

'No!' a second voice said. Master Sharp? 'We wanted a fighter. We got one. Strike her and I'll strike you.'

The first man stood close to Teia, his breath on her mask. She stood still, very still, not giving him any more excuse than she already had – and noted how tall he was, to tuck away in her head.

'My apologies,' she said, putting real apology into her tone and speaking loudly and clearly so she could be heard through the hood.

'To the test,' he said. 'Let's not take all night.'

'I'll be adjusting your hood,' the man said. 'Do that again, and I'll . . .' He barely disguised his voice this time. Nobleman's voice. Ruthgari accent. Younger. Got you, Teia thought.

He turned the hood so that two thick pads were over her eyes and a hole was over her mouth. Thank Orholam, she could breathe! Then he tightened the straps behind her head and under her chin. There were many layers of cloth and leather between her closed eyes and the outside world. He stepped away from her.

Then something changed; Teia couldn't even tell what.

The commander spoke: 'To split light is to touch the raw stuff of creation and to bend it to your will. To draft light is to participate in the divine, but to manipulate light itself in its pure form is to *be* divine. Adrasteia, we seek the spark of divinity within you. We begin easily. This test will determine if you can see colors with your skin.'

'Pardon?' It just sort of slipped out. It sounded girly and scared, which was exactly how Teia felt, dammit.

'You'll hear a chime, and you'll have a few seconds to say a color. We'll continue the test long enough to make sure you're not getting them right by guessing. If you fail, you won't leave here.'

'Pardon?' Again, but worse.

'If you fail, you're useless to us, and know too much. So do your best.'

'Red!' she said.

'Easy. We haven't started the test yet. Calm down.'

'No! I'm color-blind red-green. You must know that! I can't possibly—'

'Then guess well.'

There was no way. They wanted to kill her. She should take the mask off and take her chances.

But then she had a moment of doubt. At the Threshing in the Chromeria where every discipula was tested to see what colors she could draft, the discipulae were told things to frighten them beforehand – even during. Fear made their pupils dilate. Could this be the same? Were they lying? Surely Teia could still be of use to them even if she weren't a lightsplitter, right?

But dilating the eyes wouldn't help her in a test where her eyes were covered, and though she might be of use, there was no telling if they thought she would be of enough use to counterbalance the danger she posed for them. Orholam have mercy.

Orholam, I'm sorry for talking about your gemsack. I'm sorry for my terrible attitude toward—

A chime rang.

Teia's first thought was that now she was standing in her underthings in full light, with at least two older men staring at her. Not helpful.

Put it out of your head, T. Vengeance later. Store it up, hold it back, buckle down, take care of the now first. Feel first.

She tried to drop all her awareness into her body. The room was cool, and gooseflesh covered her from toes to nose. Her legs were clamped together so tight she could have cracked a walnut between her knees, as much for warmth as for modesty.

Modesty's a distraction right now, T. Battlefield rules. Feel your skin. You're a survivor.

The chime rang again.

'Color?' a voice asked. It could only be Murder Sharp.

Those bastards had wanted to see her stripped, right? What better for that than full light? 'White,' Teia said with a conviction she didn't feel.

A silence.

'Correct,' he said. 'A good guess, I think. We'll proceed.'

The chime rang.

Nine hells! Not even a break in between? Fine, let's go, T. We can do this. Hell, it's possible I actually am a lightsplitter, after all, right? It must follow logically that I could pass this test legitimately, right?

The chime rang again, before she was even ready to start sinking into her body again.

'Fuck!' she said aloud.

'Not a color,' the man said. 'Your answer?'

There were only seven choices, right? Eight if you counted white. 'Blue.'

A brief silence. 'Very good.'

She got it right? What the hell?

A chime.

Dammit! These assholes! How many times could she get lucky? Of course, if they only tested all the colors once, her chances should get better every time. One in eight, one in seven, one in six, one in five. Right?

Stop thinking and feel, T!

Nothing. She felt nothing.

Ding!

'Yellow?' she said.

'Correct.' Murder Sharp didn't sound pleased.

Ding.

Oh, come on. How long could her luck hold? They were just going to keep going until they had an excuse to kill her. She was trapped. She needed to get free. She needed to tear this damned hood off and draft paryl and kill them all. She had to—

Ding!

'Green!' she shouted.

He didn't even answer.

Ding.

She was going to kill every last Orholam-damned son-of-a-bitch out there.

'Red!' she screamed, not even waiting for the chime.

'Correct,' the voice said in her ear. 'And this?'

The chime rang.

Something in that chilly voice brought Teia back to herself. What was she doing? Flailing blindly? She had to think about this, put herself outside the situation. There was no reason they had to exhaust all the colors before they repeated new ones, was there? Surely they would understand that it made guessing easier. She didn't have only three colors left, she had all of them, or none.

Ding.

'Superviolet,' she said.

Ding.

And suddenly, she felt warmth in her skin. This one wasn't a guess. She nearly burst into tears. *Ding*.

'Sub-red,' she said.

He didn't even bother to tell her she was correct. She knew she was.

Ding.

That left her only with orange, but she felt nothing. After the physical, tangible obvious warmth of sub-red, the contrast was even more stark. Orange would feel cold after that warmth, wouldn't it? The room itself was quite cool. But . . .

Ding.

'Darkness,' Teia said. 'Black, whatever.'

Ding.

'Orange,' Teia said, 'but I'm just guessing now, because you've hit everything else.' Then she immediately thought, Not very sneaky, T.

Ding.

She wasn't done. Oh, Orholam have mercy. They'd seen right through her. Luck could only get you so far. Unless . . . feel it, Teia, feel it.

Ding.

'Paryl.'

A long, long silence. The room felt lighter.

'We don't have a chi drafter, so you're finished,' the man said. 'You passed. Perfect score. Get dressed and get out. We'll contact you when it's time.'

After Teia dressed, someone helped her remove the hood and pushed her out the door. Before it closed behind her, she heard the man say, 'Brothers, sisters, we have much to discuss.'

She'd passed? She'd *passed*?

More than that, she'd done it perfectly? Even with red and green? How was that even possible? Was it luck? The mathematical chances of guessing ten colors right had to be – what was it? – one in ten times one in nine times one in eight times one in seven times one in six, and so forth? Even with the gimme that was sub-red . . . No, it couldn't be luck. It hadn't been luck.

Or maybe, maybe they were trying to fool her. Maybe they were playing some long confidence game because they thought she could be useful to them in some other way.

But Teia didn't think that was it. There had been something a little different each time. A slight but appreciable difference in how she'd thought, how she'd felt. But if that was true, Teia was a . . .

Sweet Orholam have mercy. She didn't know what it meant, or why it was important, but . . . I'm not a slave. I'm a lightsplitter.

Chapter 50

Even sitting in the library, outwaiting possible tails, Karris was finding that she enjoyed spycraft far more than she had any right to. For all that she'd thought that sixteen years of being a bodyguard and warrior would have no transferable skills, it turned out she was wrong. Eyes honed to razor sharpness looking for the suspicious could still look for the suspicious. Looking for weapons was less important, but differentiating between the people looking with interest at the powerful and those who looked like hunters out for prey, that was the same.

And now she had toys. It turned out that generations of Whites had created or confiscated certain items that they didn't share with anyone. But she'd never had to use this one.

She fingered the spiky choker in her lap, concealed behind a heavy manuscript on Atashian royalty in the previous century that someone had left in a pile. It was a forbidden magic, but in a very limited way that had been tested for safety by every White for a hundred years at least. You had to wear it tight enough for two little spikes to reach blood, then – if you were a drafter, of course – your own magic empowered the choker to alter your voice lower or higher.

All the best things I learn, I can't tell anyone.

She twisted the big ruby ring on her finger. Sometimes it felt like the only thing in her life that averred that her marriage was real. But even looking at it was too painful.

Maybe it's time to come to grips with the possibility that he's dead.

The hot-cold feeling that shot through her was so strong it took her breath. She blinked, slamming the lid down hard. None of that. None of that. Kip said he was alive.

Kip wants him to be alive. There hasn't been so much as a whisper. Of the Prism. You think drunk sailors coming in to ports are going to keep such a thing quiet? *This* quiet?

I've work to do.

Karris stood up abruptly and headed to the lift. She took it down two floors, then snapped her fingers as if she'd forgotten something, and went up five floors. Of course, if she were being followed by a rotating team it was a worthless gesture – but one can't plan for everything.

Don't overestimate your enemies' capabilities, the White had told her. Assume they're as prone to mistakes as our people are. Every time Karris delegated a task, she had fresh appreciation for the second half of that statement. Like when a maid had dropped a cipher out of her basket of laundry onto the floor. It had turned up – with the seal apparently unbroken – in the found items basket on the main floor.

Given the sensitivity of the thing, though, the cipher had to be abandoned, and every spy or spy handler in the network contacted personally to be given the new one. And of course, Karris now had to remember that particular maid was either inept, unlucky, or suborned. The sheer amount of information Karris had to keep in her mind was ludicrous – and it was all far too sensitive to write down.

Two meetings this afternoon, and then one this evening with her most important handler: her hairdresser. His job not only gave him a perfect excuse to meet with Karris for long periods of time; it gave him cover to debrief the often nobly born spies he handled at length and put him directly in the gossip circuit. The sums the man demanded, however, were mind-boggling. All of his tastes were expensive. Sometimes Karris still had trouble with that.

I'm too cheap for this work. My roots do need some touching up, though. Is that more gray hair coming in? Black, this time, I think.

Easy meeting first today. A new contact, who couldn't be allowed to know that Karris was Karris: the slave turned

Blackguard Teia. Karris had trained some with Teia. She liked the girl, and saw her as a younger version of herself – albeit one who was a slave and hadn't made all the mistakes Karris had made.

Yes, other than that – and the color-blindness and her paryl drafting and that she didn't start a war that devastated the Seven Satrapies – we could be twins.

Still, she liked the girl. But Teia was sixteen years old. Too young for the burdens they'd already put on her shoulders. Karris knew what that was like. Too young to be trusted with more than they had to trust her with. Teia was working with people who wouldn't hesitate to torture her to get the identity of her handler out of her. Best she didn't know, even if Karris longed to mentor the girl.

And what's that about? Am I feeling maternal?

Or is it lonely?

She ducked into the empty apartment she kept on this floor for this purpose. Locked the door behind herself. The room was divided by heavy curtains so she could question and debrief her spies without being seen. The curtains hid chairs so Karris at least could be comfortable, and slits for her to look through. Precautions, precautions, and all of them for naught if the wrong person came walking down the hall at the wrong time.

Speaking of precautions, as Karris took up her place, she picked up the mail cowl and aventail and pulled it on, draping it over her head and chest and hooking the cowl shut so only her eyes were exposed. Ridiculous, but Teia was a smart girl, curious. She wouldn't be able to help but look for her handler's identity with paryl. It was a little unnerving that the girl could see through cloth.

Not as unnerving as her other abilities, Karris supposed.

A quick triple knock, and then the door opened just as Karris finished putting on the choker.

'Come in, sit, that side. No drafting,' she said, her voice lowered to an odd tenor.

Teia's body was tight as lute string, ready to attack. The heightened awareness was a good response to fear for a Blackguard, but tightness made your body slow. 'I was told to report?' It was actually her code phrase. Good, the girl could follow instructions, even when afraid.

'And report you shall, little flower.' That was the answer phrase. 'Now sit.'

'I hate flowers,' Teia said. 'Did you know that? My other handler did. And what's going on, anyway? I mean, I understand that the White can't meet with me personally, but two handlers in a couple months?'

Karris's breath caught. There were other handlers?

For a moment, she was glad of the mail cowl covering her face.

'You know, I'm sure you have good reasons for hiding your identity from me,' Teia said, 'and I'm doing my best not to look right through this curtain, though I could.' Good, so she hadn't actually tried. If she had, she'd have seen the mail. 'But there are dangers to hiding who you are from me, too. If someone found our code phrases, they could replace you, and I'd never know.'

'You're infiltrating a group that would happily torture you to find out my identity. Do you want the burden of keeping that secret?'

'I can handle it,' Teia said.

Ah, the bravado of youth. Karris missed it, sometimes. It was a good attribute in a Blackguard, believing nothing was impossible for you. But it was also why Blackguards had officers, and why those officers answered ultimately to those who were not Blackguards.

'In time, perhaps,' Karris said. 'You are already carrying so many burdens, and so admirably. Speaking of which, tell me the latest.' Karris had received a brief, coded report of Teia's assignments – all written on flash paper, with luxin igniters woven in, either to burn when tampered with or when she'd finished reading them. The report, like others, had simply appeared on her desk in her chambers.

Through the slits in the curtain, she saw Teia hunch forward in her seat, propping elbows on knees. 'The Order tested me. I don't even really know how. They say I'm a lightsplitter. I mean, I passed. They said they would have killed me if I hadn't.'

'Tell me everything.'

Teia told her everything, and Karris did her best – using the mnemonic tricks the White had taught her – to memorize every word. Karris thought she could see the outlines of how the lightsplitter test must have worked, and was surprised that Teia didn't. Then again, Teia's mind had been occupied by other things, not least being forced to strip almost naked in front of terrifying, masked, leering assholes.

When she thought of it that way, Karris was surprised Teia had done as well as she had. If she were honest with herself, Karris didn't know if she would have done as well herself.

'Did you know your last handler's identity?' Karris asked.

'I already told you I did.'

'Who was it, then?'

Teia's head cocked. 'You don't know?'

'Do you have any reason not to tell me?'

'Pardon me if it seems strange that you wouldn't know. If you don't know, maybe I shouldn't—'

'Your place is to obey orders,' Karris snapped. 'You're under my command now.'

'Spoken like someone who's served in an army,' Teia said. She obviously couldn't help but try to figure out who Karris was. 'But things in this field are a little less clear.'

Dammit, girl. I hope we don't get you killed. You're a natural at this.

And Karris couldn't let someone she was handling think she was inept. If your agent doesn't trust you, and you have to give them an order that doesn't make sense with their limited perspective, they might not obey it.

'Feel free to speculate on my identity, but realize that the closer you get to the truth, the more likely you are to get me killed. There's no benefit to—'

'I already told you the benefit.'

'This is not an argument,' Karris said sharply.

Even as she said it, she could remember her dearly departed father saying those very words to her when she was a girl. Clearly, it *is* an argument, young Karris had snapped back. All her defiances had been petty, back then.

Teia's chin floated up. 'I am not a slave,' she said.

'No one is saying—'

'But I was one. And let me tell you, slaves know how to obey an order without actually accomplishing anything. People like you think that slaves are stupid. Slaves are smart enough to use that belief against their masters. "So sorry I did what you said, and not what you meant, Mistress, I'm just a dumb slave." Treat me like I'm stupid, and you'll get stupid out of me.'

The red in Karris reared up, and she nearly lost it. She was the commanding officer. She would be obeyed. But then for an instant, she tried to imagine the White shouting at a subordinate.

Of course, the White was the White. There was an institutional power in addition to the woman's personal presence. When you answered her, you were addressing all the weight of the Chromeria. But still.

How large could the pool of possibilities of who had been Teia's handler previously be? Because the key wasn't someone who was smart and ambitious and willful – in the upper echelons of the Chromeria, that ruled out practically no one – the key was that the person had to be able to report to the White. The White's infirmity had confined her to her own floor in recent months.

So it had to be someone with easy access to her floor. Who had that access? The Colors . . . but most of them have their own agendas, and they'd have spies tracking them, too, because they're already so important. Who else? The Blackguards.

Orholam have mercy. A Blackguard? Of course, and it would have to be someone who could juggle watch schedules so that he or she could report to the White immediately if there were an emergency that demanded it. That meant one of the watch captains, as she herself had been.

Blademan was too straightforward to manage spies. Beryl was a gossip and had been since her youth. Tempus was possible. Loved his books, good administrator. But he never got out. He was always either on duty or in his office. Blunt was too dumb. Not that he was stupid, but you had be very, very bright to handle all of this. Unless he faked that?

No, not Blunt.

So, none of them. Her breath escaped. Unless . . . Commander

Ironfist? The man was always working, always going places and meeting with people. Karris had always thought of him as a man who kept his own counsel, but one could just as easily label him secretive, even reclusive.

But he seemed like he would stand out too much. Too famous, too recognizable. On the other hand, his official duties had him rubbing shoulders with everyone, high and low. If he checked in with the kitchens, no one would be surprised. If he talked with room slaves, no one would bat an eyelash. If he spoke with a Color, or with that Color's personal guards . . .

He was the perfect spy. His position gave him enough access, and was so obviously impossible, that he could hide in plain sight. Teia's handler was Commander Ironfist.

'Marissia,' Teia said, apparently unable to bear the silence.

Karris couldn't find breath.

'Because when slaves aren't invisible, they must be beautiful. And when a slave is beautiful, she can only be good for one thing, right?' Teia said, the acid in her tone spraying all over Karris's face, and burning, burning.

Anyone but her. Anyone else.

'Funny. She trusted *me* with her identity,' Teia said. 'But to you, I'm just a former slave.'

Karris had fought when wounded. Had fought with that sick feeling that something was terribly wrong, but you couldn't stop to gauge how wrong it was. Stopping to judge meant death. It was the same here. Fight on, fight on, turn your eyes to the task.

Teia was a good girl. Defiant, but every Blackguard had steel in them. Study her, figure how to use her best, and don't let her get under your skin – either to anger or to love.

You've got to keep your distance, Karris. What's the most likely outcome here?

That she disappears at some point, and is simply *gone*. That's what the Order does. We're going against them where they're strongest. They practically invented spycraft.

'At some point,' Karris said, as if the storm had washed past her without leaving a trace, 'they'll want you to steal a shimmercloak.'

'What?' Teia asked. She'd wanted a fight, Karris could tell. Without it, Teia was like a ship becalmed.

'The White's been studying the shimmercloaks. You need to be a lightsplitter to use them. We thought light splitting was a gift only given to Prisms. We were wrong. But more to the point in your case, a lightsplitter without a shimmercloak is useless. None of their current Shadows – if there is indeed more than one – is going to give you theirs, are they? So if the Order can use you to steal a shimmercloak for them, then even if you're a spy and they have to kill you eventually, they still come out ahead. If they distrust you, you'll be getting that assignment soon.'

Teia slumped in her seat. She knew a death sentence when she heard it.

'You have to understand, Teia. The Order are masters of subterfuge. They're very, very good at finding and killing spies.'

Teia turned and looked at the curtain between them. Her eyes were dead. 'You expect me to fail. That's why you can't let me know who you are.'

'Odds are.'

There was only bitterness and resignation in Teia's voice. The sound of a soldier sent to die, who thinks his death won't even accomplish anything. 'So what do I do? Feed that perception that I'm a clueless young girl?'

Pretending to be stupid enough that she couldn't be used by their enemies, but still smart enough that the Order would trust her? It would be a difficult line to tread. Impossible for one so young.

Suddenly, Karris remembered what it was like to have her future taken out of her own hands and decided by her elders, to be thought beneath consideration. She'd hated it, railed against it, and finally, she'd left a wake of destruction rebelling against it. She was still paying the price of that rebellion, and still dodging the cost of it – the son she'd abandoned, the damnation she felt.

With an uncertain hand, Karris pulled open the curtain. Teia looked up, jaw clenched. Scared. Karris unsnapped the voice-modifying choker. She took off the mail cowl and aventail. 'So,' she said. 'Now we're in this together.'

Tears welled up in Teia's eyes. 'I hoped it would be you,' she said.

Chapter 51

Tremblefist was grinning. Kip could hardly believe his eyes, but the morose giant was grinning.

All the squads were crowded into the Prism's training room, and every last young man and woman was agape, barely blinking for fear of missing a critical moment. Tremblefist was faced off against his brother Ironfist. Both wore training armor of leather imbued with luxin that would burst with spectacular yellow light if struck, to declare a solid hit. They wore steel helms with bars woven like wicker, thick leather gauntlets, and they bore bamboo swords.

And they moved. How they moved. The bamboo swords beat a tempo against each other that was like the music of the spheres, the great soft swish of the grinding gears of the universe keeping its time.

But not for long. Each point was scored within five seconds. With warriors at this level, a single mistake led to a touch. It was too fast for Kip to even tell sometimes who'd scored the point. Other times, he only saw the luxin bloom.

Ironfist and Tremblefist didn't rest between points, didn't move back to the center of the circle, merely took ready positions, touched swords and began again. The score stood at five to five. Tremblefist readied himself, but instead of tapping his bamboo, Ironfist removed his left hand from his sword.

Tremblefist nodded and took his own left hand away. Kip had trained with those swords, and though both men were taller and bigger than he was, even then those swords were too big, too long to wield perfectly in one hand. If you had the hand and arm strength of an Ironfist, you did gain reach, but you lost speed. A good trade if you could hold a shield, perhaps, but not to hold nothing.

But each man moved fluidly into a fighting style Kip had never seen. They didn't hold the sword in one hand, they merely held the hilt in one hand. Each put his other hand almost halfway down his blade. What followed was some odd blend of sword-fighting, staff-fighting, and body throws. Lunges flowed into blocks into foot sweeps. It was just as fast, but more muscular, each circling, constantly moving, using not just the point of the sword but also blade and even pommel, dodges and even jumps blurring past. The speed of the men was incredible, but in this, Kip could see the full flower of the seeds his own training was planting. Those dodges, this strike, that way of rotating the hips to get force.

A clash and a rattle of bamboo, and Tremblefist's hips twisted and his sword point was batted aside low, but he was merely cocking the gun, his hips snapped back, the sword point dipping behind Ironfist's knee and pulling sharply back toward Tremblefist and up.

Ironfist leapt with the cut, trying to avoid what would be a hamstringing. He did a backflip, but before he could land, Tremblefist shoved his blade in that two-handed grip against Ironfist's stomach. Without any base, it flung Ironfist backward. There was no way he could keep his feet. He flew across the circle and landed, skidding, on his back.

Seeing Ironfist put on his ass was like seeing the moon outshine the sun. The nunks were aghast. Of course, they'd heard of the famous battle between the brothers, more than a dozen years ago in front of the whole Chromeria, so they'd known that Tremblefist was nearly as good as his elder brother. But Tremblefist had somehow quietly faded into the background since then. He wasn't even a watch captain, while Ironfist was legend. It was said in the Battle of Garriston Ironfist had taken out whole batteries of artillery by himself. The man could walk on water. Seeing anyone equal him was a shock. Seeing someone best him? Blasphemy.

But Ironfist merely leapt to his feet and shook his head while Tremblefist grinned. They began again. They traded points, but Tremblefist led all the way. Ironfist barely tied it at nine-nine when his brother dodged back from a blow, but not far enough, and got his head yanked to the side as Ironfist's bamboo brushed the steel bars of his helmet. In a real fight, it wouldn't have hit him at all.

Ironfist racked his sword and pointed to Big Leo and to a nunk named Antaeos. 'Pick weapons.'

'Clawed bich'hwa and a sword-breaker,' Antaeos said. It was an odd combination, both usually secondary weapons. But of course, that was part of the fun of putting masters through their paces – seeing not just what they could do if they were in a strange position, but seeing what was possible even in strange positions. As Commander Ironfist had told them many times, in the chaos of battle, you might end up with any weapon in hand, and you had to make it work.

Big Leo grinned. 'Heavy chain.' He'd been working on using thicker chains. When he draped the thick chains over his draft horse shoulders, he was quite the sight. But chain weapons were difficult, brutal. You were more likely to hurt yourself using a chain than any other weapon.

'That's a bludgeoning weapon,' Ironfist said.

'It's not *only* a bludgeoning weapon,' Leo said defensively.

'But most of its attacks are, Leo,' Teia said. 'You'd be making one of them fight with half a weapon.'

'Uh, then . . .' The big man suddenly felt the weight of everyone's stares on him and got flustered. He shrank into himself, which made him merely much bigger than everyone except Ironfist and Tremblefist.

'Rope spear,' Teia suggested under her breath.

'Rope spear!' Big Leo said, like a starving man reaching for bread.

'Pick a number, one or two,' Ironfist said to Ferkudi. Obviously, he was making a lottery for himself and his brother for who would get to pick which weapon he fought with.

'One,' Ferkudi said.

'To yourself,' Ironfist said flatly.

'Oh.' Then, light dawning, 'Oh! Oh, sorry.'

'Brother?' Ironfist said. 'Be my guest.'

'Two,' Tremblefist said.

'Two it is,' Ferkudi said.

Kip and the rest of Cruxer's squad all looked at him.

'What?' he asked, defensive. 'What?'

'I'll take the bich'hwa and sword-breaker,' Tremblefist said. The bich'hwa was Karris's favorite, Kip knew. The clawed variety could both be used as a normal dagger (the scorpion's tail) and as a punch dagger (the clawed feet). The training variety had the claws made of the same boiled rubber-tree sap that full Blackguards used on the soles of their shoes, dipped in red ink to make its 'cuts' obvious. The sword-breaker was a short sword with thick barbed notches all down one side, made to catch sword strokes, and used correctly could twist a sword out of an opponent's hand or even break the blade.

The rope spear was even more interesting, though Kip wasn't surprised Teia had suggested it. She'd been practicing with it in private lessons with Ironfist and sometimes Kip, who as her partner got to be her target. The rope spear was like a short gladius attached to a long rope. It could be used as a simple dagger, as a flail, or as a spear when sharply redirected from spinning to fly out straight. But the rope was what made it amazing. An opponent would think that if only he could get inside the whirling death that the blade cut through the air, he'd be safe. It was almost impossible to resist catching the rope and trying to disarm the rope spear wielder.

But that was where almost half of the rope spear's techniques began. With a flick of the wrist, the wielder could throw nooses over her opponent's fist or neck. Grabbing the rope was a prelude to defeat. It was still a secondary weapon – not good against armored opponents, not good in tight spaces – but it was so unusual and challenging to use well that even Ironfist had confessed he needed to do a lot of brushing up before he'd started training Teia.

Of course, he'd done the brushing up.

And he'd done it privately. Tremblefist most likely had no idea that he'd just assigned his brother to a rare weapon that was exactly what Ironfist had been practicing.

Kip still wouldn't have wanted to try a rope spear against a sword-breaker, which was made to entangle weapons.

But that was a sidelight. Ironfist wasn't fighting his brother to entertain the squads. That wasn't his way. This was a lesson of some kind.

So what was the lesson? It wasn't how to fight with these weapons.

The two men began fighting, and of course it was dazzling. To most of the nunks, it had to look like Ironfist had picked up a weapon that he hadn't even thought of in years, and had total mastery of it. It was a good way for Ironfist to use the time he'd had to put into brushing up his skills to a second use. It also gave him an edge on Tremblefist, who obviously hadn't trained with his own weapons in a good long time.

Ironfist won, despite having what seemed a worse weapon, nine to six. The brothers finished with double swords. Tremblefist won, but only ten–nine. The total of all the bouts went to Ironfist.

'Form up,' Ironfist said.

And here's where we get the lesson, Kip thought.

The squads were, by this time, highly efficient at getting into place. In seconds they stood in neat lines.

'Tremblefist, thank you,' Ironfist said. He bowed low to his brother, as to an equal. His brother bowed a bit lower, but a smirk played on his lips. Ironfist motioned that Tremblefist could go. 'Squad Yod!' he barked. 'Being the worst has its perks. Take the rest of the day off. You're dismissed.'

The members of Yod looked at each other. Some were dumb enough to look excited at getting the day off. The smarter ones looked stung. They'd been called the worst. It was the truth, of course. Of ten squads, they were tenth. But those few had the sense to see that being dismissed early was a perk, but it wasn't all perk.

Nevertheless, they bowed and left.

'Squad Teth,' Ironfist said, addressing the ninth squad. 'What did you learn today?'

'That you're fuckin' awesome,' someone whispered in the back. It carried more than intended.

They fell silent as they realized Commander Ironfist had heard it. 'Squad Teth, Blackguards guard their tongues. One hour running.' They quietly groaned and hung their heads. He paused. 'Minus half, because I am.'

The squads all laughed and cheered.

Ironfist cracked a grin. 'Squad Teth, dismissed.' They left, clapping the one who'd spoken out on the shoulders and giving each other a hard time.

After they closed the door behind themselves, Commander Ironfist said, 'Squad Kheth, what'd you learn?'

Kheth, Zayin, Vav, and He squads each came up with some technique or combination they'd never seen before. Some of the comments were quite good, noting that a counter only worked because of Ironfist's or Tremblefist's reach or strength.

After the door closed behind He, Commander Ironfist looked at the remaining four squads: his thirty-three best Blackguard inductees. 'Daleth, Gimel, Beth, Aleph,' he said, looking at each squad in turn. 'Being the worst has its perks. So does being the best. What's your perk?'

Ben-hadad said, 'We get more instruction; they get more time off.'

'And what's that mean?' the commander asked.

'They're being punished for their ineptitude,' an Archer from Gimel said. 'They think they're gaining something by getting free time, and thus they prove that they aren't the best.'

'Did all of them look elated to go?' the commander asked.

'The smart ones looked heartbroken,' Kip said.

'Which means the smart ones will redouble their efforts to get better,' Cruxer said. 'It'll make the cream rise.'

'Yes, and?' Ironfist asked.

'Not an "and,"' Kip said. 'A "but." But this means—'

'Hold,' Ironfist said. 'Squad Daleth, you're dismissed.'

It was clearly a shot in the gut for the eight nunks of Squad Daleth. Having been identified for one moment as elite, and then pushed out of the circle, not a one of this squad looked happy to get out early.

'Commander, please, let us stay,' the squad leader, Aria, said. Admirably, she didn't make it sound like begging, simply a request.

'The best are not *allowed* to stay, they earn it,' Commander Ironfist said. 'Dismissed.'

There was sharp silence as Squad Daleth left.

But Commander Ironfist ignored it. Kip had no doubt that everyone in that squad would double their efforts. 'Breaker, go on.'

Kip took a breath. 'By kicking them out, it just means that

the best get better. By our training more, we'll continue to be the best.'

'Is there any way around that?'

'You could give the most instruction to the worst squads,' Cruxer said.

'That would make them better, at the cost of making you worse than you could be. We're not interested in mediocrity here.'

'You could have them train just as much as we do,' Teia said.

'They do already. They were here; they saw what you saw, but I guarantee that all the remaining intelligent comments would have come from Gimel, Beth, and Aleph, not the lower squads. Because we've done this before. We've seen it. We've seen how the worst – even in this elite group – slow down everyone. And my time is finite. I cannot teach a class of one hundred as quickly or as well as I can teach a class of ten. Nor ten as well as one. Would that it were not so.

'To have an elite of anything is to be at the best slightly unfair. There is always someone who almost made it, and if you expand the bounds to encompass that one, there's someone else who almost made that circle. The question is always, what do you get in trade for being slightly unfair? The Blackguard could be a thousand strong, or it could be ten. We make the trades. We decide when to expand the circle to let in someone who is not quite as good as the rest of you.'

'At some level, though, there's a kind of equality,' Kip said. 'Or at least . . . the differences don't matter. A Teia has such gifts you'd be a fool not to bring her onto the Blackguard, even if she couldn't fight at all. You told me that. Ben-hadad can't command like Cruxer, but he's so smart, he brings us other things. Big Leo might lose eight bouts of ten to Cruxer, but his very size means there's times we don't have to fight at all. At some point, a person has enough gifts that even if he isn't the best at all things, he's too valuable to give up.'

The squads looked at Kip like he'd said something smart.

'I agree,' Commander Ironfist said. 'That's why I'm lecturing three squads here, and not just Aleph. Now, what lessons did you learn, Gimel?'

'That practice can get you killed in battle. That you have to always keep the limits of the training you've done in mind,' a singularly ugly young man named Cracks said.

'A truism from the very first days of our training,' Commander Ironfist said. 'How'd you see it, exactly?'

'In the first sparring, you made a single mistake, and it led to a touch, instantly. Maybe that's because Tremblefist has fought you so many times that he knows exactly what your skills are, but I think it was instead because in being totally aggressive, he only risked losing a single point. He could fling himself at you with abandon, trying to grab that mistake. Would he have been so fast to attack if he were risking his life rather than a point? I'd say no.'

Commander Ironfist nodded. 'Great tourney fencers often kill many and die quickly in battle. Well done, Squad Gimel. You're dismissed. Squad Beth, tell me something that good or better.'

After they left, a compact young woman named Tensit said, 'You set up Tremblefist, didn't you?'

'How so?'

'You've been training Teia with the rope spear. It's an odd weapon, and she hasn't practiced in the open. He assumed you'd be out of practice. But what I don't understand is how you got Teia to choose.'

'I got that,' Cruxer said. 'Inductees who use unusual weapons will always choose to see their own weapon demonstrated by a master. So you knew Big Leo would choose heavy chain; you could reject that, and Teia was standing right next to him. You've been working with her long enough to know that she'd jump on the chance. So you did set up Tremblefist.'

A sly grin crept onto Ironfist's broad face. 'So sayeth the Tactician, "He who knoweth himself and his enemy dreadeth nought." Squad Beth, well done, you're dismissed.'

They bowed low and left.

'Being the best has its perks, Squad Aleph,' Ironfist said. 'But it also means you work longer than anyone else. Prove that you're the best in mind, and not just in arms.'

'It's the first time I've seen Tremblefist smile,' Teia said, musing aloud.

A cloud passed over Ironfist's face. 'True, but what's the tactical significance of that? Is there any?'

'I don't . . . I'm sorry.'

No one else said a word.

Ironfist blew out a breath. 'You may know that my brother's birth name is Hanishu. Mine is Harrdun. I was given my Blackguard name when I punched through a door and subdued a raider holding a hostage on the other side of it.'

'Subdued?' Ferkudi whispered. 'I heard he nearly ripped the man's head off.'

'But Hanishu picked his own name,' Ironfist said, pretending not to hear.

For one moment, Kip was struck by how different this was than learning under Magister Kadah. Where she mocked and belittled and ruled through fear, with Ironfist – a man whom the squad actually should fear – learning was like being yoked together with him. Everyone had to push as hard as they could to keep up with him, but one always felt that he was working, too. In comparison, Magister Kadah put the yoke on you alone, and then criticized how unevenly you pulled it by yourself.

Kip looked at the faces of his squadmates. They were intent, utterly focused, fearful of letting the commander down, but not fearful. He had them heart and soul and strength, not because he gave them a respect they didn't deserve, but because he expected them to deliver the best they were able to deliver, always, and he thought their best was better than they thought it was.

This was a great man in action. It was a quiet greatness, but Kip wanted to emulate it.

The commander paused, as if he didn't want to ask the question, but felt he owed it to the squad. 'Do you know why Hanishu chose—'

'Better to be called Tremblefist than the Butcher,' Kip said.

An awkward silence reigned. But Commander Ironfist finally said, 'Training makes us. War breaks us. Hanishu had something terrible happen to him, and he did terrible things in retribution. He's never trusted himself since then. Has never wanted to lead. This is a personal matter, and I won't discuss it further. But that it does happen is not a personal matter. As leaders and as friends, you need to watch each other, and help, and never, never, never give up on each other.

'Now,' he said, putting that aside, 'what else did you learn today?'

No one said anything.

Kip moved to speak, but stopped.

Cruxer nodded to him. Go ahead.

'He's better than you,' Kip said.

Commander Ironfist cocked an eyebrow.

'Breaker,' Big Leo said. 'We just saw the commander win. As he won when they fought before.'

'With a trick,' Teia shot back.

'Tricks count,' Ben-hadad said.

'I'm not talking about today,' Kip said. 'I'm talking about when you had your big public exhibition. Years ago. That didn't involve strange weapons; it was straightforward, and Tremblefist was better than you, but you won. You won because he let you.'

'Breaker,' Cruxer said, 'there were hundreds of trained fighters at that exhibition. No way someone could throw a match in front of all of them and not be noticed.' Ah, Cruxer, the idealist.

'At this level? What's a couple points?' Kip asked.

'Why would he do such a thing?' Ironfist asked, low, dangerous.

'For the same reason he chose Tremblefist as his name. He didn't want to lead, didn't trust himself, but he trusted *you*. By taking a name that automatically made people think of you, any excellence he showed would make people think even more of you. "If Tremblefist is this good, how good must Ironfist be?" He killed his own prospects for advancement to help yours. When you fought in that exhibition, it had to be close. It had to be incredible. But in the end, you had to win. He smiled because today, he could try to win. Because today, the match wouldn't matter. Anyone can get lucky, and now it wouldn't hurt your reputation.'

'Very good, Aleph Squad,' Ironfist said, his voice raspy. 'Dismissed. Now.'

The squad moved out quickly. Kip went with them, but

when they reached the elevator, he finally stumbled upon the obvious.

'Oh, shit,' he said. 'I'll be right back.'

He walked quickly back down the hall and opened the door, but the words dried on his lips. Commander Ironfist was on his knees, face buried in his hands, weeping.

Ironfist hadn't known. All these years, he had thought his brother had merely had an off day when they fought that exhibition. All these years, he thought his brother had chosen to be called Tremblefist because of his own brokenness. All these years, and he hadn't known what his brother had sacrificed for him, how Tremblefist loved him.

Kip stepped out silently – and found himself face to face with Tremblefist. Kip swallowed, looking up at the giant, but the big man merely put a hand on his shoulder, squeezed it briefly, and went inside. Kip closed the door behind him.

They never heard what was said between the brothers, but after that day, Tremblefist seemed to emerge from the shadows. He took over the training of Squad Aleph, and from time to time, he smiled.

Chapter 52

It took all of Karris's courage to open the door to her own room. There was no escape from this. If Marissia weren't waiting in the room now, she'd be there later, at some time when Karris wasn't ready. In fact, the more she'd thought about it, the more certain she'd become that Marissia knew that she knew: of course a new handler in charge of gathering information would immediately ask who the old handler had been.

Thus, in surrendering Teia to be handled by Karris, Marissia had knowingly surrendered herself.

Karris opened the door. Marissia was seated at her desk off to the side of the room, her quill scratching quietly. She looked up, and put the quill in its stand. She was perfectly calm. A perfect lady, despite her clipped ears. Irritatingly beautiful. A winter storm was raging outside, sheets of rain cascading past the windows, thunder rattling the tower.

Walking straight toward her desk, Karris felt like a young Blackguard, coming to report to her watch captain rather than as the lady of her household, coming to confront a slave. A slave! But Karris's knees felt weak.

'The White told me long ago,' Marissia said, '"She who controls the information controls everything."'

Karris was curiously numb. She walked over to Marissia's desk, pulled a chair over, and sat across from her. Marissia studied her quietly, an expression that Karris couldn't quite read fluttering around the edges of her face like a moth trying to escape from a tent.

'My father had a different take: she who controls the Prism controls everything,' Karris said.

They stared at each other for a long time, and for the very first time, Karris looked at Marissia as a woman; for the first time, she ignored the clipped ears and looked at her eyes. How had she missed it? She'd known Marissia was competent, of course. Blackguards liked working with competent slaves who made sure there were no distractions from the work at hand. Marissia directed her small army of subordinate slaves perfectly, making sure everything here was done precisely right, precisely on time. Such oversight was more than enough work for any one woman, much less any one slave.

Much less any one *slave*? An odd thought. Slaves came from every social stratum in every land. One poor decision or too many bad debts and no family willing to pay for your foolishness, or bandits or pirates and no friends willing to pay your ransom. Whether you were at fault, or utterly innocent – it could be one tiny step away. When she was a girl, Karris had played with Taira Appleton, when they were young enough that complementary personalities had mattered more than differing stations.

But in the False Prism's War, the Appletons' lord had sided with Dazen Guile. The Appleton estate had been on the border of Blood Forest and Atash, directly in the path of Gavin's army. Lady Appleton had known they would be overrun if she answered her lord's call to arms. She did it anyway, loyalty overcoming sense, mistaking a question of smart and stupid for one of right and wrong. Karris still wasn't sure whether the action was more praiseworthy or blameworthy. Within a week, Lady Appleton's estates were taken, her six sons killed, her four daughters clipped and sold.

Marissia stared at Karris, and Karris studied her back, each silent, broken mirrors to each other, Marissia's hair its natural red, Karris's hair, naturally red, now dyed black.

Where was Taira now? Where were her sisters? Even knowing how easy it was to fall into slavery, Karris had somehow kept slaves at arm's length, made them *other*. It made them more bearable. One misstep and she could have sat in Marissia's place, serving some lord.

Come to think of it, if her own loathsome father hadn't been careful to keep the White Oaks aligned with Gavin and Andross Guile . . .

No, no, no, Orholam, please no. She'd never thought of it this way. His maneuvering had been all cowardice; it hadn't been . . .

She remembered her father's face, during the feast, while the real Gavin Guile had mocked him and made bawdy jokes about bedding his daughter in exotic ways. Father had looked stricken. He'd looked pathetically weak. But what could he do?

With Dazen's burning of their estate on Big Jasper, the White Oaks had lost the bulk of their fortune and all their best people. They'd also had enormous debts to nobles who'd sided with Dazen, debts they could never pay. Debts they might not be required to pay if Gavin won the war. From her father's perspective, the White Oaks' only hope was in binding themselves to the real Gavin Guile and his father, Andross.

What if father had thought, while the young, drunken Karris was being led away to be . . . forced . . . what if he thought, 'Better she be forced once and be married to the Prism than that she be made a slave and raped by whoever wanted to, forever'?

Weak. Disgusting. Wrong. But not selfish. Not loveless. And he'd blown out his brains when Karris hated him for it.

She hadn't shed one bitter tear for her father since she'd refused the abortifacient.

She felt suddenly very, very sick, but she tried to regain focus. No weakness here, not in front of this woman.

Marissia opened a cabinet, hesitated, choosing, and pulled out a decanter full of amber liquid. She produced a single, ornate crystal glass, and filled it with a more than generous double pour. She set the glass exactly in the middle of the small table. It was an homage to an old Blood Forest custom, born of a hospitality that defied poverty. A family might be able to afford only one nice goblet, but that one would be shared between host and guest.

Whether families retained the tradition as they grew in wealth or quickly discarded the tradition to give each person her own glass said a lot about how that family felt about their origins.

Marissia took the glass, inclined it to Karris, and drank.

Chromeria tradition, though, dictated that slaves and masters or mistresses not drink together. If two social unequals dined or drank together, at least the lesser was supposed to defer to the greater.

Marissia's eyes danced, as if daring Karris: Am I your host who is sharing her own liquor with you, or a slave? Who am I to you? she asked.

To hell with it. In this, Marissia *was* Karris's superior. She'd been running a spy network for how long? Besides, it had always been wine or brandy shared in Blood Forest, never whisky. Maybe it was time for new traditions.

Karris took the glass and took a gulp. It set her on fire, and pain had never felt so good. She counted it a victory that she didn't cough. As the fire spread through her gut, she held up the glass, as if admiring the color. It was a thing aficionados seemed to do. 'Barrenmoor?'

Whiskies were a niche taste, made even more so by the vast distances the barrels had to travel from the distilleries at the edge of Blood Forest in the highlands above Green Haven and their subsequent cost. Karris hadn't been able to afford the stuff on her Blackguard wages. She'd guessed Barrenmoor only because it was one of the two best.

'Crag Tooth,' Marissia said, examining it in turn and taking another sip.

'Mmm,' Karris said. The other one. Dammit.

'Easy miss. This is the sixteen. After it's matured sixteen years, it mellows to be easier drinking like Barrenmoor. I prefer it because it still retains its fiery character and complexity while time takes off the rough edges and impetuosity.'

Karris looked at Marissia sharply. Sixteen years? Rough edges and impetuosity? The woman's eyes danced again.

Damn her, Karris was *not* going to like this woman.

'And how does it do as it ages further?'

'Crag Tooth hasn't been a player for that long, but I'm confident that in the fullness of time it will bring Colors and satrapahs to their knees.'

They drank together, trading sips, each thinking private thoughts. They watched the storm smash all its rage on the Chromeria, lightning striking the tops of the towers themselves, power channeled down into the earth itself, diffused, harmless. Rain sheeting the windows so thickly it was impossible to see to any distance. Wind hammering the tower so hard it swayed, but was unbroken. And whether it was the warmth of the whisky or the fire or, oddly, the company, Karris found herself enjoying the storm.

The storm was subsiding by the time they finished their second whisky, a little light fighting through the clouds just at the horizon.

Karris set the glass down on the table, stood, and walked to the door without a word. She opened it and, looking back, saw woman, and storm, and light. The eye can see all at once, but only focus on one at a time. The clouds were still dark, angry.

She said, 'You know, sharing a glass with you is—' *one thing, but there's no way I'm sharing my husband with a . . .*

But the words didn't make it to completed thought, much less out of her mouth. There was a sudden stiffness in Marissia's spine, a grief in her eyes at all that was denied her. As Karris had been a warrior in the Chromeria's open battles, so had Marissia been one in its secret battles, and perhaps neither was content anymore to fight alone.

Karris started over. 'Sharing a glass with you is the best thing I've done in months.'

Chapter 53

~Samila Sayeh~

Today is the day we make a god. The crowds are gathering, paying obeisance to me and to the other Elect around me, and above us, to the Color Prince himself. All the people are gathering today. A special day, a special victory, but also to commemorate our people's great victory at Ox Ford, and mourn our losses. The Color Prince wishes to tie all these together in the small folks' minds.

I find it terribly uninteresting, so instead I regard the mathematical precision with which I have remade my left hand with blue luxin. No, remade is too grandiose. Augmented. My hand has become superior in most ways to a human hand, but I am a mere mechanist. Perhaps I would have become a creator had not the Guiles' War made a warrior of me.

It is, however, a masterpiece. Blue luxin is crystalline, solid, hard, nearly unbreakable on one plane but easy to snap or shatter if pushed from the side. Supplementing the human animal with all its shifting and bending and twisting forms is well nigh impossible to do without impinging on its functionality. Sheathe your arm in a blue luxin carapace? Easy. And then you sweat, and the sweat and oil gets trapped. The skin softens and, chafed incessantly, peels. Exposed to that sweat and oil and dead skin, after a time, infection sets in. Then the body attacks itself. Unable to swell, the blood gets cut off, the infection spreads, fever comes, and throughout, incredible pain.

It is my hypothesis that much of the madness of color wights has had nothing to do with luxin. It has been the result of unending pain, the sadly self-inflicted torture of incorporating luxin into one's self imperfectly. Perhaps such madmen are so dangerous they must be put down for the safety of others, but to call madness evil is a grave error. The pre-Lucidonian philosopher said, 'Every act intends some good.'

The damage done by wights has been done through ignorance. One doesn't punish ignorance with death. One fights it with knowledge. Not darkness, but light.

My companion and I have long talks about this. She isn't real, of course. She is merely a dialectical prop. She – I picture her as a grown-up version of my niece Meena, who was murdered at the Great Pyramid – questions my research, and we debate. It is the only way for me to have an equal here.

It makes me miss the Chromeria. So many fine minds there. Of course, they forbid all this research, but if they could overcome their fears as I have overcome mine . . . But of course, I know the Color Prince has people recruiting within the Chromeria. The people here are eager, but they aren't disciplined thinkers. They think being Free means being free of the consequences of their actions, free of nature's laws. It is an attitude the prince has not seen fit to curb. Not yet, not when he still needs soldiers and drafters to die for him. Later, he promises me, we will work to channel such fervor.

'Light cannot be chained, but it can be directed,' he tells me. He seems to like the phrase, and I can tell he will use it again. Later. After victory, after the first phrase has bought him willing martyrs and power, he will add that second clause to nullify the first. And those fool martyrs will have died only to put a new king with a different title on a new seat in the same place. Thus ever does a tyrant's noose tighten, I suppose. Expanding, building that future speech in his head, he says, 'All the world is open to the light, but our eyes can only look one way at a time.'

I see these rhythms, with Meena's help. How nine kings became seven satraps, and how failed attempts at making a high king yielded to a successful attempt to make a Prism, and how the Prism's power and the satraps' was eroded by jealous Colors. As a wolf hungers for meat so a man lusts for power. It is unwise to get between either one and his prize. This is not a condemnation but a fact. And only a fool allows herself to become the prize.

This is the reason why someone else is becoming Mot today,

not I, though I stand in the first rank for that honor. Dubious honor, I think. We each 'get' to wear a necklace of what the Color Prince claims is black luxin. Most likely it's simply a clever illusion, but I find it unsettling.

Meena and I have discussed this position for me, at some length. She thinks that— Oh, more cheering. Everyone else on the podium is applauding. I join them.

She thinks that having an overseer would grate on me. I say, what's the difference between having one overseer to direct me to do the Color Prince's will, or having two overseers to direct me to do the Color Prince's will? Plus, those who fail the prince directly feel his wrath directly. Dervani Malargos and Jerrosh Green fought tooth and nail to be the Atirat, and when the prince made his choice, he gave one godhood, and the other a musket ball in his brain pan. And soon thereafter Dervani had joined Jerrosh in death, albeit at Gavin Guile's hand. Godhood is a dangerous business.

Still, Meena thinks I will chafe under the rule of a lesser mind. Ramia Corfu is certainly that, though the man is beautiful. One oughtn't discount the power of beauty. It is a change I notice in myself. It has been months since I last took Usef Tep. We'd made love nine times in that last week before the Freeing, knowing it would be our last. We'd even slipped out of the line at the Freeing, fooling none, and not trying to fool them, either. Human delicacies break down in death's acid gaze. While I had not Usef's daily hunger, by now I would usually feel the lack keenly. Now my libido lies dormant. I look at Ramia's well-proportioned face, and I understand that other women see only boyish charm and willfulness, smoldering good looks. It's not that I don't see it, or understand from memory what it will do to others; it's that its effect on me is limited.

It matters not. My sole strategy with Ramia Corfu will be to make myself appear to be what I actually am: indispensable and utterly without ambition. Meena pretends to be content with this, though I think she has more ambitions for me than I do.

The Color Prince is going on, and seems to be doing a good job of it. He usually does. Then he gestures to Ramia to stand.

Ramia stands, with an arrogant grin that I suddenly realize

I'm going to really, really hate within the span of – oh, I already hate it. He nods to the rest of us, as if we're lucky to be seen with him. My face remains impassive, but some of the others bristle. It's one thing to revel in such a triumph; it's another to act as if you got there because you were smarter than the rest of us.

Why him? I know the Color Prince likes him, but I had assumed it was something to do with the Color Prince feeling a need to have attractive people around when his own looks had been forever destroyed. The Color Prince is now a marvel to behold, a wonder, but not remotely beautiful in human terms, and those who've tried to go to his bed have all been rebuffed. The word is that the fire unmanned him, which means the damage must have been severe. It has never been taught officially in the Chromeria, but the uses of luxin in sex have been explored by drafters from time immemorial.

'Ramia Corfu, Lord of the Air, come forward,' the Color Prince says. As the young man joins him, the Color Prince goes on. 'It is my place as a leader of free men and women to recognize and reward excellence. In your ascension, you will bow the knee to no man and no woman, but to your prince alone. We establish order not so that we may have lords, we establish lords that we may have order. Ramia Corfu, do you pledge your magic, your sword, your will, and your obedience to me?'

'I so swear,' Ramia Corfu says. He gets down on one knee and touches the Color Prince's foot.

'Then today I declare the restoration of the Old Order,' the Color Prince says. 'It is not my wish to rule. It is only my wish to see a people who rule themselves. Free women. Free men. So what authority you have trusted to me, I turn back to you. The white light of the sun is all colors working in concert. Our ancestors, the nine kings of old, forgot this. They pitted themselves against each other, and in their weakness, a heresy came among them. A Prism shattered them. We shall not fail as they failed. I have been your Color Prince, a man only, wounded, made whole with many colors. But today I tell you I have a vision for all of us to be united in freedom under the light. The Prisms have split light, have split satrap from satrap, have split us into those who steal and those who are stolen from. We will unite all of us instead, and we will find strength together. Nine gods, nine kingdoms, and all peoples, united under one White King.' He holds up a multicolored arm, blue plates and green seams and luxin running beneath it all, constantly. 'But a poor White King am I. One day, when we have taken back our kingdoms, I shall remake myself. On the day when you unite the satrapies, I, too, shall be made whole. My friends, will you serve—'

'Yes!' many shout.

'We will serve!'

But he quiets them, playing to the critical. 'Will you serve not me, but this noble ideal?'

'We will!'

'Will you give your all to see the nine kingdoms come again?'

'We will!'

He goes on, but I stop listening. The rest of it is mere whipping the crowd up. Interesting turn there, making his own healing synonymous with 'healing' the Seven Satrapies under his banner. Healing with war. With tens of thousands listening, I can't be the only one to find that darkly amusing. Better is when he tells them he's looking for those who will serve mightily, that's there's 'room at the top.' The veiled appeal is 'serve me, and I'll make you powerful,' but the very fact that there's a top must means there's a bottom. Could a statement be more transparently at odds with his talk of all being equal?

Regardless, if nothing else, the Color Prince has given himself a new title: he is now the White King. I seem to remember him swearing at some point that there would be no kings among us. Does no one remember?

But through it all, he's left Ramia Corfu on his knees, and the young man is clearly uncomfortable and peeved about it.

When the cries of 'The White King! The White King!' fade, the newly dubbed king steps back to Ramia Corfu. He produces a small ivory box and opens it. He pulls out a many-pointed crystal, holding it between thumb and forefinger. It spins, seemingly of its own volition, scintillating in a thousand shades of heaven.

The White King hands the crystal to Ramia. The young man stands. He doesn't move at all for a long moment, but when he does, he looks around at the others on the platform. He looks at the soldiers nearby. He looks at the king.

Ramia Corfu's eyes are sapphires lit from within, and crystals race across his skin, breaking as he moves, and reforming, renewing from within instantly.

'A king?' Ramia says. 'What is a king before a god? You have given me the power over the luxin in your very body!' His entire body is sheathed suddenly in crystalline armor so thick a cannon shot would bounce off. He raises a razor-edged arm as the king's men cry out in alarm.

'And you have given me an excellent demonstration,' the White King says.

The blue crystal carapace shatters at Ramia Corfu's neck, and he crumples to the ground as if his strings have been cut. His head rolls free and as all his blue luxin armor blows apart into grit, the scent of chalk and blood fills the air.

Most of the crowd can't see what decapitated him, but I can. It was the necklace the Color Prince gave us and commanded us to wear at all times. The so-called black luxin pendant has pierced Ramia's neck front to back, tearing through the spine and emerging behind him, and the chain tightened until it cut all the way through his neck, popping his head off.

Or maybe it isn't 'so-called' black luxin. Maybe it really is black luxin. Maybe I've been studying the wrong color all this time.

'Some of us, sadly, are not worthy of trust,' the White King says loudly. 'And such traitors will be winnowed out mercilessly. However! There are in our ranks many more faithful who are true to our cause, and who will never betray us. Who will serve us all, high or low, to the best of her capabilities – which are great indeed.'

Oh no. How can I be so late to see it?

'Samila Sayeh, heroine of the old wars, but a true convert to our ways. Samila Sayeh, will you serve as Mot, our blue goddess?'

I stand unsteadily, feeling the weight of the black luxin crystal about my throat, heavy and corrosive. I bow my head, incapable of speech. Beside the new king, I can imagine Meena. She looks fierce; she looks triumphant.

She looks like she was planning this all along.

Chapter 54

'You haven't been entirely honest with me,' Karris said once the secretaries and slaves had cleared out of the White's rooms to give them privacy.

'I am entirely honest with Orholam alone, and him only when he forces it from me, I'm afraid,' the White said.

'None of that,' Karris said. 'Don't turn this religious. I'm not taking over your spy network because you're roombound and you can't go see them all yourself.'

'Oh?'

'At least that's not the only reason,' Karris said.

The White's wrinkles deepened as she smiled. She had lines aplenty, of course, and the smile lines were not so deep as the worry lines. 'Push me to the window, dear.'

Scowling, Karris did so. One couldn't push the woman's chair across her apartments without being painfully aware of how thin and saggy her skin was, how delicate the bones. It was as if Death were gently announcing his impending arrival by these hints at how close to a skeleton this woman was, how near the end of her term of service on this earth.

'Hold. Are you deliberately reminding me how frail you are so I don't yell at you?'

The White laughed. 'Not everything is a trick, girl.'

Karris frowned deeper. 'Oh. Well, sorry then.'

'But that was.'

The White's grin was infectious, and Karris couldn't help but grin along with her. She took back all her thoughts about Death's arrival. This woman was going to live forever. Somehow Orea Pullawr was a little girl caught filching sweetmeats, smiling like, 'Mommy, you can't be mad at me, I'm too cute!' and simultaneously the wisest old crone in all the world.

Karris couldn't lose her. She sat down on the floor with her back to the blue luxin wall, looking up at the woman who had become hero and mother to her. 'Please don't leave me,' she said. She couldn't help it.

'Not until it's my time, girl,' the White said.

Karris scowled again. 'Well, that's meaningless.'

The White waved a dismissive hand. 'Bah. People say meaningless things all the time when they're about to die. How about this one: "As long as I'm in your heart, I'll never truly die." Ha! Please don't keep me trapped in your heart after I die, girl. I get claustrophobic.'

'How about, "You'll be watching over me"?' Karris asked, only half joking.

'Sure – so please spend less time in latrines, because I don't want to see it!'

Karris laughed. And then she couldn't bring up what she'd come to ask about. Her courage wasn't doing so great today.

'You've had a little talk with Marissia,' the White prompted.

'I just came from there, how do you know? I thought we had all your spies!'

'What need for spies, when I have eyes?'

'Huh?'

'Or a nose. You reek of that whisky she drinks. Crag Tooth, which means she was trying to make peace. Otherwise she'd have given you that swill Barrenmoor.'

Oh. Right. Not everything was about spies and betrayal. You still had to use your wits. Karris took a deep breath. 'You brought me on to handle your spies, you said. But you've already got Marissia. She's been your spy handler for years, hasn't she?'

'Yes,' the White said.

'So why did you ask me to do what she's already doing, probably better than I ever will? Were you just trying to give me purpose? You thought I'd kill myself without Gavin around, without the Blackguard?'

'I don't see you as one for self-slaughter.'

Karris said, 'You're giving me nothing here. Please.'

The White smiled sadly. 'For many years now, Marissia has handled my spies within the Chromeria. I personally handled the external spies. She is very, very good. She would be better than I am at such work, were it not that I am the White and meeting me personally tends to carry weight. With the spy we're handling in this matter, it's unclear whether this should be treated as an internal Chromeria matter or an external threat.'

So the White was simply transferring a spy from one handler to the next. 'That's all?' Karris asked.

'This didn't come up when you fought with her?' the White countered.

'There weren't that many words exchanged.'

'Oh dear. You didn't break any of her bones, did you, darling?'

Karris kept a straight face. 'You'd be surprised how much pain I can inflict without doing permanent damage.'

The White winced.

'But that's it?' Karris asked. Fun as it was to mislead the White in something harmless, Karris had gotten awfully wound up over something that turned out to be utterly trivial.

The White lifted her hands. 'There isn't always a grand design.'

'With you there is,' Karris almost said. Instead, 'I could have used some warning.' About Marissia, she meant.

'You needed to have it out with her. I expected you to do it on your own long ago. Perhaps your abstention from red and green is doing you more good than I'd hoped.'

'About that,' Karris said. 'How long—'

'No.'

'But—'

'No.'

'I've—'

'Absolutely not.'

'Very well, then,' Karris said. 'If you'll excuse me, I have a desire to go the training room and destroy something.'

'You're dismissed. I'm sure Marissia will be eager to come give me her version of events.'

Chapter 55

Kip woke from another nightmare, drenched in sweat, fists balled so tight he had to massage his hands together to keep them from cramping. Remembering the specifics of the nightmare was like grasping smoke, though. He sat up.

An exploding head, the bullet blessing, that was it. Again.

Thunder rumbled outside. The nightmares must have been triggered by the storm lashing the Jaspers. It was nothing.

Wait, that had only been the second dream. In the first, he'd been on the deck of the *Wanderer* again, stabbing his father, taking out all his fury of abandonment while his father's eyes went wide—

Gavin had looked at Kip. In that look, Kip had seen acceptance, self-sacrifice for his son. In that look, Kip had seen love chosen, knowing the cost but undeterred by it.

What Kip hadn't seen was prismatic eyes. The light had been poor – it had been night, after all – but Kip's eyes were fully adjusted, and he remembered. He was sure of it.

Kip got up, throwing off the clinging webs of dream-hatred, and went out. He'd never been to the luxiats' rooms, but he remembered Quentin saying his room was in the blue tower, the floor called Justice, six. The luxiats sometimes referred to floors by names of sins (dark sides of the towers) or virtues (light sides). It was an acolytes' mnemonic so old that it had passed into orthodoxy.

He found the floor and walked brazenly into the room. It was a barracks like any of the Blackguards' or discipulae's, so it was no problem finding the right one, or finding Quentin's bed among the rows. He nudged the sleeping luxiat.

'Oh, it can't be time for morning prayers already—' Quentin cut off at the sight of Kip looming over him, and the whites of his eyes became fully visible around his irises.

Some people lash out when they're terrified. Quentin was a freezer.

For a long moment, he didn't blink, didn't breathe. It lasted longer than Kip would have expected. Surely Quentin recognized him?

'I've got a question for you,' Kip said, quietly so as not to disturb the other sleepers.

Something about that unlocked the luxiat, and he took a big breath. He got out of his bed, his body scrawny, no muscles at all. Kip was so used to being surrounded by the training-honed physiques of the Blackguards that he was kind of shocked by what was surely a more normal body than theirs.

Again he thought, My father did this on purpose. He surrounded me with the best, so I would always use them as my comparisons, so I would always stretch myself. It was a little cynical, very smart, mean in the short term, and probably best in the long term. Damn. Gavin Guile was rightly a legend.

Quentin followed him out into the hall. 'This, is, uh, good,' Quentin said. 'I just figured out the shelving scheme.'

'Huh?'

'For the library.'

'Oh, that. Great. Look, I need you to tell me how a Prism is chosen. Walk with me.'

Quentin fell in beside him, and they talked with lowered voices. 'Chosen? They aren't chosen. They're discovered. I mean, they're chosen, of course – by Orholam.'

'Right,' Kip said. 'Sure. So how are they "discovered"?'

'All luxiats report to their superiors, passing along possibilities gleaned from their areas, those pass it on up the hierarchy of the Magisterium, and the High Luxiats meet with the Spectrum to confer and test whoever has been sent.'

'Let me guess that whoever's been sent is always from one of the leading families.'

Quentin blinked, then his eyes flicked up as he tried to remember. 'With one arguable exception, and one definite one – yes, at least for the past two hundred and twenty-two or -three years.'

'And that doesn't seem curious to you?'

'It's not curious at all. It's not like you're the first to notice that, Kip. Breaker? Why do some people call you— Never mind. It's more evidence that Orholam has blessed the political order of the Seven Satrapies. And the exceptions prove that Orholam sees all men, and when the nobles displease Orholam, he is more than willing to go outside our human politics.'

'Convenient how that works for you, either way.'

Quentin held a reproachful silence. Finally, he said, 'Did you wake me only to mock me?'

Kip wasn't angry at Quentin, who seemed like he was outgrowing his naiveté, though with great pain. Kip was angry at his grandfather. It seemed that if there was one place free of politics, it should be Orholam's house. But that wasn't Quentin's fault.

'No. I wanted to ask you how a Prism's . . . uh, installed? Elevated? Whatever. Is there a ceremony?'

'It's "consecrated," actually.'

'How's it happen?'

Quentin looked a little peeved that this was what Kip had woken him for. 'It's all very secret. There's a feast. There's mourning for the Prism who has died, and every light in the city and the Chromeria is extinguished for the night except for the great braziers that they light in the star towers. People mingle and drink and mourn their own dead and sing songs and only these little beacons of light remain.'

'What about the ceremony itself?'

'It is known only to the Spectrum and the High Luxiats. I think the Spectrum may only be told what to do on the night. I mean, the High Luxiats can be very close-mouthed about the things they think are important, and it doesn't get much more important than that.'

'Who's currently on the Spectrum who was there seventeen years ago?'

'You mean when Gavin was made Prism?'

'Right.'

'Your grandfather, of course. The White and the superviolet . . . and I think that's it, actually. It's been a hard seventeen years.'

'Would there be something about it in the restricted library?' Kip asked.

'What's this about, Kip?'

'It's about a knife.'

'A what?'

'A knife. Maybe a holy knife.' Kip paused. 'Your face just did a thing.'

'A thing?'

Kip was suddenly suspicious. 'Do you know something about this, Quentin?'

They'd reached the restricted library. 'Let's wait until we're inside,' Quentin said.

Kip manipulated the panels to bring the diffuse yellow luxin glow to the darkened room. Quentin didn't look any better in full light.

'Kip, I – I swore to tell you anything you asked about.'

'Uh-huh.'

'And I wasn't . . . precisely forbidden to share this, but I did know that it wasn't meant to be shared. If you ask it of me, my oath to you supersedes an implicit understanding, but it makes me very uncomfortable.'

'Out with it,' Kip said.

'So you're compelling me?'

'Damn right.' It wasn't even a question.

'One of the High Luxiats let slip to me that they lost something very important some sixteen or seventeen years ago. He said that Andross Guile had taken it, and then claimed it was lost.'

Kip rocked back on two feet of his chair and blew out a heavy breath. 'I was right,' he said. 'I just woke up and I knew. Huh.'

It was the Blinding Knife – or, as Andross had called it, the Blinder's Knife. If Kip hadn't been working and studying and fighting every hour of the day before collapsing into bed and nightmares half the time before repeating all of the rest again, harder, he would have thought of it sooner.

Kip had stabbed Janus Borig's assassin Vox with that blade, and the man had failed to draft green at the very moment he'd gone toe to toe with Kip. It had saved Kip's life. Vox had shouted, 'Atirat! Atirat, come back!' Atirat, the green goddess.

Kip had stabbed one of the green demigods at the top of the bane, and it had robbed the woman of her color.

Kip had thought that Zymun had stabbed Gavin when they were escaping the Battle of Garriston. And he had.

Thinking again of the fight on the ship, when Kip screened out Grinwoody's contorted, furious face, and the flailing blows, and Andross Guile's intense concentration, and Gavin's self-sacrifice, and his own guilt about his ineptness and that he had gotten his father nearly killed – when Kip screened it all out and thought only about the right things, everything became clear. And the right things were Gavin's eyes, and the knife. Gavin had looked at Kip and his eyes hadn't sparkled with the refractory elegance of a Prism's eyes, and then Kip had seen the dagger grow.

On the deck of Gunner's ship, Kip had seen that dagger pulled from Gavin's chest. No longer a dagger with a single gleaming blue jewel, it was now a gleaming white-and-black sword with seven burning gems in the blade.

Kip strained to remember how his father's eyes looked then, but Gavin had been five paces away, in the darkness, shouting with pain, eyes narrowed or averted.

Not Gavin's eyes, then. Andross Guile's. Kip had been face to face with the man, and he had seen the broken halos in his eyes. And since then, Kip had seen his eyes again. Kip had sunk the dagger into Andross's shoulder that night, if only for a moment.

The Blinding Knife was what made Prisms. And the knife had taken that away from Gavin.

'What is it? What does it mean?' Quentin asked.

'Well I'm not going to tell *you*. I know you can't keep a secret.'

Quentin looked ill.

'Quent. I'm joking.'

'So what is it?'

Kip shook his head. 'I wasn't joking about not telling you – I'm not telling you. I like you, Quentin, but I barely know you, and I don't know how much of what we say the luxiats make you share with them. I wouldn't even hold it against you. It's very hard to say no to some of these people. I was joking that you can't keep a secret.'

'Not really joking about that, though,' Quentin said.

'I wasn't questioning your character.'

'Yes you were.'

'Yes, I was.' Kip shrugged. 'Tell me I'm being irrational.'

Quentin opened his mouth, then closed it. 'Might be rational, but it doesn't feel very good.'

That was why Andross Guile had been so focused on the blade. Kip had thought him a monster for caring more about the blade than about his son Gavin. But to Andross it wasn't a blade, it was the future of all the satrapies. The Blinding Knife was the key to making a new Prism.

And Kip's mother – his drug-addled, hate-filled wretched harpy of a mother – had stolen it seventeen years ago. And disappeared.

It had meant that Gavin couldn't be replaced. Most Prisms lasted seven years or fourteen, but despite his clashes with the Spectrum and with his father, Gavin hadn't been replaced. Because they couldn't replace him. They had lost the one implement by which the gift of Prismhood was conferred – and, probably, taken. They killed the old Prism with the blade, it took his or her power, and they somehow transferred it to the new one.

It didn't explain everything – how were there two Prisms during the war? – or how had Dazen faked being a Prism? But that the blade was a well of power – Kip was certain of that. He'd seen the evidence.

Orholam have mercy. What happened if the previous Prism didn't want to give up his power and die? They were usually young. Who wanted to die?

That's what the Blackguard is for. To protect the Prism for the satrapies, and if necessary, to protect the satrapies from the Prism.

What kind of spectacle would that make, if some Prism angered the Spectrum enough to get ousted, and they voted to kill her? It would surely be the commander, perhaps one or two others, who would bring the ousted Prism forth and slay her to take her gift. For the good of the satrapies.

No wonder they shrouded it in secrecy. It might even be necessary. All drafters reached their end and had to be put down, so surely Prisms must incur some cost for their ceaseless drafting. Perhaps they went mad.

But Prisms were there to Free others. When Blackguards subdued and killed a screaming, fearful Prism – that would not be a moment to increase the faith of the faithful.

No wonder it was a night of mourning and darkness.

'You don't look very well,' Quentin said.

'I don't feel very well.' It also meant that Gavin Guile was no longer a Prism. Even if the Blackguard found him now, he would be useless to them.

Better, then, to find the knife, before the Color Prince does.

And all this, Andross Guile had understood in an instant. He'd acted immediately. Kip didn't know whether that made him admire the man or hate him.

But Gavin wasn't dead. Unlike every Prism before him, he'd survived. Because he was unique. Perhaps unique in all history.

'Quentin, you said you'd figured out the shelving scheme in here?'

'Just yesterday, actually. Shouldn't be a problem now to find out whatever you need about anyone's family – or even the Black Cards.'

'I'm going to have to trust you, Quentin. Can I do that?'

'That's an illogical question, isn't it? For if I were not trustworthy, would I not tell you that I am?'

'Whereas if you were trustworthy, you'd point out the illogic of the question,' Kip said.

Quentin raised a finger to protest, but then lowered it. He looked first puzzled, then vaguely gratified, as if Kip had shown him a particularly useful trick. 'Ah. Aha. I see. Thank you. How may I serve?'

'Forget the genealogies, forget looking up the Black Cards. I want to know everything you can find about the Lightbringer.'

Chapter 56

'I looked up to your mother,' Eirene said. 'She took me under her wing when my own mother died. She knew I had no women to look up to. As an adult, I can see why else she was doing it, of course. Making peace between Malargos and Guile needn't take a marriage, if your friendships are strong enough. But then something happened. Do you know what?'

Gavin sat in his cell, looking at his captor through heavy-lidded eyes. This was their third visit over the past months. He'd lost two fingers from those meetings. One more and he wasn't going to have much grip in his left hand. 'Pray tell,' he said. His voice was gravelly. Hadn't been used much in weeks. She was letting him rot down here.

'It wasn't a rhetorical question. Do you know what happened? One day, Felia Guile is visiting all the time, and inviting me to visit her, and then . . . Nothing. She refused to ever even talk to me again. What happened?'

That strange intensity was suddenly back. The worst of it was that Gavin was slowly starting to believe that Eirene Malargos wasn't insane. She was a normal woman driven to extremes by her circumstances. Circumstances that the Guiles had much to do with.

'I don't know,' Gavin said, rubbing his eyes, nearly scratching himself with his bandaged hand. 'But I'm sure it was all my fault somehow. How's it going keeping your nephew silent?'

'This was fifteen years ago. Think about it. Why would Felia Guile shut me out, suddenly, then?'

Gavin fixed stupidity on his face and thought about it. It didn't take him long. First he thought it was the war or his fraud, but that was sixteen years ago now. Fifteen years ago was when Felia had learned that Dervani Malargos had survived the war, after being lost in the wilderness for years, and was making his way home, carrying Gavin's secret. She'd confessed at her Freeing that she'd tried to buy him off, first, and then sent pirates to intercept his ship, murdering him, or so she thought.

Felia Guile, willing to kill to protect her last living son, but not willing to face the daughter whose father she'd had murdered and smile. That sounded like mother. Hard when she had to be, but soft underneath. Not like Andross Guile, who never would have thought to befriend a Malargos in the first place. But if he had, he would have played it to the hilt.

This world has only two kinds of people: villains and smiling villains.

Gavin said, 'Of course I know why. Because I kept my silence about what happened at Sundered Rock from even her. For two years, I told no one, and then she heard a rumor that your father was alive. She asked me about it, because I'd made a passing reference at some point to him being dead. She asked me if I could be mistaken.' He closed his eyes and blew out air, as if it were a painful memory.

'And what did you tell her?' Eirene asked.

You dumb cunt, I'm going to enjoy killing you. You have no idea about me, do you? I'm going to tear your fingers off with chains and make you eat them. 'I told her the man was an impostor. He wasn't the first or the last with a lot of scars and wild tales to come back to a wealthy estate to claim the empty seat at the table.'

'He wasn't an impostor,' Eirene said.

'Yes. He was.'

'No he wasn't.'

'And you know this how?' Gavin asked. He had the target now. The man had sent messages to Eirene. Odds were they'd never met, though. He would have sent something to prove he was who he said, but perhaps it was something that could have been a forgery, or a fact that a close associate might have known.

'I'll ask the questions.'

No need to hold back, then. His story needn't be perfect, it merely had to cast doubt on the other.

I am the Father of Lies. See my magnificence. 'I know because I was there, Lady Eirene. At the end. Dervani was close to Dazen.' True. 'He was a good warrior.' True. 'Not the most talented of drafters, but clever with his uses of green luxin.' True, if flattering. Some sugar of what the listener wants to hear helps a bitter lie go down. 'He stood when many fell, in my brother's and my last clash.' First part was true. Second part was not. 'He was there, at Sundered Rock. At the end. He lived through the conflagration.' True, he had lived, and he had been at the battle. But he'd only lived because he'd not been near the center at the end. No one had lived through that magical miasma except Dazen and Gavin. 'Dervani charged me at the end, trying to save Dazen. He . . . died heroically.' Pure fabrication.

'You lie!' she said.

Gavin looked away. Looked back at her. Pursed his lips. 'He tried. He . . . charged me, knocked me over. He pointed a pistol at my face, and it misfired. When I rose, I disarmed him, and . . . he broke. I grabbed a javelin and threw it through his back as he ran away. I didn't see his body afterward, but I've seen a lot of battle. He didn't live through that. I guarantee it. I then picked up that pistol. Little thing. Decorated with silver sparrows, if I remember right. Must have been a backup pistol. Be the only reason it was still loaded that late in the battle. No bigger than my hand. Odd thing in the middle of a battlefield. There were no damned weapons handy except that javelin and that pistol. I couldn't bear to draft the least luxin at that moment, and my brother was barely conscious. I took that little pistol, and I put it between my brother's eyes. It didn't misfire for me.'

The dead look on my face doesn't have to be painted on. It's close enough to truth to bring those memories close to the surface again. The detail about Dervani's pistol was particularly good. How would Gavin know of a small secondary pistol carried by one of Dazen's retainers?

'No,' Eirene whispered. 'No.'

'My mother didn't understand. She never saw battle. She thought running away made your father a coward. Truth is, every man only gets so much heroism to spend in a day, and your father had far more than most. He charged two warring gods, and would have made all the difference if he hadn't been betrayed by a broken flint. When he charged me, he didn't know I couldn't draft any more, and after what he'd seen me do it was brave indeed . . . But more than that, my mother couldn't allow herself to hate me for killing my brother. I was all she had left. So she blamed your father. She thought that if he hadn't brought that pistol into my hand her other son would still be alive . . . I think she knew, rationally, that it wasn't fair to blame him, and by extension your family. But she did. She knew she could keep herself from acting on the hatred she felt for you – for me, really – but she couldn't keep a pleasant mask on her face while she did it. She might even have been right. I wonder sometimes, if I would have taken my brother prisoner if there had only been that javelin there, or would I have rammed that through his throat? The pistol made it easier, but . . . it's an idle fancy. I was in a killing mood. My mother blamed your father, and probably believed that you would blame her in turn, if you knew the truth of what I had done.'

'You . . . you *demon*,' Eirene said.

'If it makes you feel better, I'm sorry that my brother's war cost you your mentor, in addition to all else. By Orholam's beard, I'd give two fingers to have your father back.' He wiggled his half-hand at her.

Karris, you told me once that there was something in me that wanted my own destruction. I denied it. I was a fool.

'Fuck you! Burn in hell!'

'One thing I knew about Dervani; he wasn't a man to torture the helpless. Stubborn, they said, but honorable. He's got that on you.'

It seemed like a stupid thing to do: antagonize a woman whom he'd just told such lies. But you have to let the fish swallow the hook if you want it to set right. If he was angry enough to say something so obviously stupid to her face, surely he couldn't also be so coldly cunning at the same moment to weave a flawless fabric of lies, could he?

She stared at him, silent, arms folded, almost hugging herself, face inscrutable.

But Gavin had to play a bigger game. What was happening under the surface here was the real test. Eirene was the real power in Ruthgar. The satrapah, Euterpe Ptolos, was under her thumb. Eirene's father Dervani had joined the Color Prince. Whatever else the man had been doing for sixteen years – and it *had* been Dervani, Gavin had recognized the man, if not immediately. Whatever else he'd done in the intervening years, Dervani had thrown in his lot with the pagans at the end. By driving a wedge between Eirene and her father, Gavin was really serving the Seven Satrapies, for if Eirene's hatred blotted out all else, she might drag Ruthgar over to the Color Prince's side.

Such a move would be stupid beyond belief. Those at the top have nothing to gain in a revolution like the Color Prince was proposing. Inviting an aggrieved army into your city? You shouldn't even invite a friend's army into your cities.

But hatred and envy birth self-destruction in every heart that gives them a bed to breed in. To dislodge the Guiles, this woman without children might be willing to risk losing all her family owned as well.

So I lie, in service of the greater good. As always.

Still she stared.

There was nothing to be gained now. If she felt pushed into a decision, she'd doubt it in the future. Whatever action she took, she had to feel that it was hers, and inevitable with what she knew, then it would be irreversible, and their alliance unbreakable.

The fingers? She might never pay for that. Or at least not for a long time. Gavin would have to bank the coals of his rage, let them glow warm under the earth. Someday. Maybe. But not today. Not soon.

He didn't hold her gaze. He looked at her, glanced away, looked back, easing his shoulders into a slump, as if he felt exposed. Not a challenge. It was important to let her think this through.

Finally, she said, 'After the wars, my family had estates everywhere, but many of them had been devastated. They required huge piles of gold to restore. Tens of thousands of danars to import vines for the vineyards, to buy new slaves for the cotton fields, to pay the tuitions of drafters and indenture them afterward, to rent and then finally to buy the river barges to transport our goods. New axes for logging, iron for the brackets of new water wheels, millstones which if cut from local softer stone would cost half as much but only last a third as long versus those we shipped in. But every time I would do my calculations in my father's ledgers – actually, the ledgers my father's steward Melanthes kept, but he died during the Blood War – every time, I would see these line items: "Cost of Hired Guards," and sometimes "Bribes to Blood Forest Conns," and "Losses to Pirates." And at the end of the year, "Repairs for Damage from Raids' and "Replacement Drafters from Raids."

'Eventually, of course, I filled those ledgers and moved on to new ones, but I left those columns. And I studied what those costs had been. Old Melanthes was our steward for forty-five years, and he could predict those costs within a few points per hundred after a while. When you know you're going to lose one boat in ten when they make a Tyrean orange run, you know what sort of profit you need to make in order to justify trying next year. Over time, it matters. My father never realized that Melanthes was the real reason we even had estates by the time the False Prism's War and the Blood War were finished, though we lost too many sons and daughters.' She took a deep breath. 'But every time I picked up those ledgers to make a decision about shipping this or that, I saw those costs. I haven't had to pay those.

'I'm very good with numbers, and I've compared my numbers to Melanthes's. And what I've learned, what I can never deny when I see those columns laid out before me, is that I owe you, Gavin Guile. How much is a matter of what assumptions I make. For though those parts-per-hundred losses are unyielding – I would have lost men and treasure to raids and murder and piracy at some point regardless – when I might have lost them matters most. If you lose a prize stallion and a mare from a herd of hundreds, it stings. If you lose them before you ever breed the herd, it destroys you. So, I worked my abacus many different ways and calculated what I could. I chose not to quantify any emotional toll of losing family members or trusted servants and slaves. I also found it impossible to quantify the merely possible, but significant cost of my own lost time, should enough of my own close family have been killed that I would have had to marry and bear my own children. Women in my family have tended to have quick recoveries, but it was impossible to calculate how many pregnancies I might have suffered, or exactly how much work I might have been able to do while in the late stages of pregnancy or early stages of recovery. And of course, I didn't assign any value to not having to marry or bear children – as I now don't. Given my present wealth, I would pay a great deal more for such a privilege than I would have were circumstances quite different. You see you present me with conundrums.'

'You may have lost me somewhere in there,' Gavin said. He thought he followed, but it was rarely a mistake to make an enemy think they were smarter than you.

'Because you stopped the war, Gavin. And then you wiped out the pirates. Several times. And that's without crediting you for taxes falling because there was no longer a war to finance. One way or another, Gavin Guile, your family cost me my father, my last uncle, and four distant cousins.

'But from my calculations, I owe you somewhere between four years and twenty-three days, to twenty-seven years and sixteen days. Years of my labor. Years of my life. You've saved me perhaps a thousand thousand danars; you've allowed me to reestablish my family, and by stopping the Blood War, you have certainly saved me the blood of many people I love. I want to kill you so badly that my stomach aches, and I've been getting the kind of headaches that would bring an empire low just thinking about you. I am well-known, perhaps famous, for dealing straight. I've never cheated anyone, though it has been in my power to do so for quite some time. But how does one balance blood?'

'I leave a complicated legacy,' Gavin said drily.

'One balances blood with blood,' she said.

'Oh, that was a rhetorical question,' Gavin said. 'But you seem both far too grim and far too elated at my suffering to be about to say, "Gavin, you've saved lives I love, so I will save yours."'

'Whatever else you are – and you are many things, Gavin Guile – you're not stupid. Did you hear about the Battle of Ox Ford?'

'I was so busy . . . felt like I was stuck rowing in endless circles. Missed it.'

'The Chromeria lost fifty-five thousand men in one day. Thirty-five thousand of those were Ruthgari. My people.'

Gavin felt like he'd been kicked. 'What happened?'

'General Azmith thought to crush the Color Prince against the Ao River.'

'The Ao? That river's not that deep, is it?' Gavin asked.

'Deep enough, during the wet season.'

Gavin had only seen the river in summer.

'The general tried to catch the Blood Robes as they crossed the ford. Their wight-drafters drafted new bridges within half an hour, encircled our armies, and crushed us against the river instead. The Blood Foresters hated the plan, and had sworn to withdraw, but General Azmith wasn't moved. He went ahead without them. So the Color Prince invaded Blood Forest, and Blood Forest lost no one, while my people took a blow from which we may not recover.'

My people. She said it not as a native daughter, but as a leader. She must own Satrapah Ptolos outright. But that wasn't the worst of it. With the battles of Ru and Ox Ford, the Seven Satrapies had endured two military disasters in a row. Even with the riches of Ruthgar, a satrapy could only stand to lose so many lives.

'Nor have things gotten better. After Ox Ford, he split his armies and sent half up around the headwaters of the Ao, trying to cut off their supply lines.'

That was a long trip, and a long time to be without half your army. Gavin would have sent small parties across the river to raid, not half his army.

'General Azmith entreated Raven Rock to hold out, told them that he would save them. They held, but he got there too late. He fled in disarray, leaving behind cannons and gunpowder, and whole wagons full of rations and muskets.'

'Clearly, there's only one thing you can do,' Gavin said.

'And what's that?'

'Free me.'

'And why would I do that?'

'Because I win battles. Because if you want to keep track of debts owed in blood, then the Color Prince owes you most dearly.'

'I don't know about that. I think the blood debt is yours.'

'Mine?' Gavin asked with real incredulity. 'How could those lives possibly be put on me?'

'You let this war happen. You could have stopped it in Garriston, or long before then.'

'What? What?! Everything I've done I've done to stop this war! How bad are your spies if you believe anything else?'

'You're a liar, Gavin Guile. They all agree on that.'

It was one thing to be killed for your sins, many as they were. It was something else altogether to be killed for the very thing you'd been trying to stop. He tried another tack. 'Do you remember your number, in the lottery?'

'One fifty seven. Everyone remembers their Orholam-damned number. Two days with that damned thing folded in my hand, wondering if it would mean my death.'

The lottery had been a furious young Gavin's way to end the interminable Blood War. Only the leading families of both sides had been given numbers. Two thousand of the richest and most connected people in Blood Forest and Ruthgar had been gathered at Gavin's command. His Blackguards had apoplectic fits at the very thought of it. Not that that stopped him.

Gavin had invited them all to the hippodrome to pray for peace. Attendance was not voluntary. No drafters were allowed in except those who were members of the families, and Gavin's Blackguards had relieved each person of larger weapons, though knives and the like for personal defense had been allowed, allaying their suspicions. The heads of all the families understood you didn't want swords and ataghans and spears when you gathered bitter enemies in one place.

Each family had lined up in a column according to their number. A random number, so they thought. Felia Guile had helped Gavin decide who should be in the front ranks. She'd also helped with the deception itself: Gavin had marked each folded slip of paper with a superviolet number as each person dropped it in. Felia had worn Lucidonius's superviolet spectacles around her neck, though no one knew they were that, and fewer still would have known what those spectacles did. With her head bowing as if in prayer each time she reached into the bowl, she'd look through the spectacles and grab out the appropriate paper.

It worked for all but one family, who had swapped their folded papers. Younger, and angrier, Gavin had merely shrugged and said, 'They want to lie to the Prism? Sow the wind.' His mother knew how the saying ended. She'd acquiesced.

With the columns of families facing him in a circle, with only the lowest number from each family standing in the narrowest circle, facing Gavin, he had gestured to a large circular wooden table he'd placed on the raised *spina* with him. He had led a prayer for peace, some drivel he didn't remember. After they'd all agreed to his sufficiently abstract and non-binding words to Orholam, bobbing their heads and making the sign of the seven, he'd gestured to that rough-hewn round table beside him. 'My friends,' he said. 'Here sits the table of peace. In the blessed light of Orholam, who will join me at it?'

One family, the Blue Bells, had sent their mother forward. The Blue Bells had once been numerous and fierce. Now they were a shadow. Two daughters, two distant cousins left, and not much land, no riches. They were within a breath of being commoners or being extinct.

Everyone else looked to their lady or lord, banconn or conn.

Gavin said, 'I think you all don't understand. Your war has stripped your lands bare. It has soaked every field in unclean blood, with each act rivaling the next in baseness and inhumanity. Your war is an affront to Orholam. All this you know, but your bloodlust is greater than your shame. You daren't ask forgiveness for your atrocities because then you might have to extend forgiveness for your enemies'. Your bitterness is a boil on your faces, obscuring your sight. So every year, you send a tribute of your sons and daughters to death, so you can continue your foolishness and pride. And every year, you send a far greater tribute of those who have been pulled in the wake of your impiety, your blasphemy, your arrogance. You have not only insulted Orholam; you have insulted me. You have not only robbed your own families and your enemies' families and the innocent, you have robbed the Seven Satrapies. You have had satraps and, yes, even Prisms come to you and to your fathers to stop these wars. You have responded with temporary truces and lies. Lulls in which you rearm and breed, picking sons and daughters based on who might be the strongest drafter, who might have the most colors.

'I know. Yes, I am the product of this breeding myself. But now I am Prism, and what I do today isn't for my family; it is for the Seven Satrapies. Today, your war is finished. Now I ask again, will any join me at the table of peace?' He swept his hand, as if in invitation toward them.

None did. Gavin, who moved the world on the fulcrum of his desires, Gavin, loser and leader, drafter deceiver, exile executioner, Gavin was being ignored.

He stared at the sun, as if praying. It was one of those white-hot days, the delta air was thicker than blood, the sounds of the city coming in even to the center of the hippodrome. He prayed, but he wasn't praying. He was filling himself with power.

'So be it,' Gavin said. He swept his hand again, and this time, blue luxin spikes shot out along the superviolet guide-wires he'd place at the throats of each man and woman in the first rank of the circle. Through the center of each throat, and into the center of each spine.

The front person in each family's column dropped dead.

It was so sudden, so stark and brutal and so quiet that no one said a word. Many didn't even know why the people had fallen.

'War seems so random,' Gavin shouted. 'Does it not? Who lives, who dies? It's like a lottery. But in my lottery, only you who are responsible for this war will die. I think the common folk will prefer this greatly. Now! Who will join me at the table of peace?'

For a moment, shock prevailed as every family looked at their dead. In each case, 'Orholam' had picked the most pugnacious, the bitterest, the most hateful or guiltiest person in the whole family to be first in line. Some families had to be happy to be rid of their most troublesome member, and far more so to see the worst of the other families die.

But these were families bred to war, in many cases literally so.

'Are you insane?!' a Willow asked.

'You killed my father!' a sixteen-year-old, fiery-haired Green Apple shouted. Damned Blood Foresters and their tempers. The young man pulled out his belt dagger, a wild look in his eyes.

'Your father was a fool, and you'll be a dead fool if you attack me,' Gavin told him.

'Ahhh!' The young man charged the platform.

Some people simply don't react well to surprise.

Gavin astounded everyone by turning his back. 'There's no need for anyone else to die,' he shouted. Behind his back, the rising young Blackguard Watch Captain Ironfist materialized from nowhere and cut the young man down before he reached Gavin.

It was so nonsensical that Gavin was swept into sudden fury. 'Sit at the goddamn table, and no one else needs to die!' he roared.

Another pulse and another row of men and women died. He'd almost forgotten the sound of projectiles thunking into human flesh.

They broke and fled across the sands. He'd known they would. The damned cowards. Like he'd never set up an ambush in the course of the Prisms' War. He still thought of it as the Prisms' War as the losers did, though he didn't think he'd failed once to call it the False Prism's War when he spoke of it.

He was so furious he thought of waiting until they were in its teeth to trigger the trap. No. No. Enough killing. The point was to shock them into submission, not to turn the few survivors against him forever.

He reached into the superviolet he'd laid under the sand out in a great ring and pushed luxin into it, hard. A great spike-toothed ring of death leapt out of the sand in a fence around all the nobles. Green and blue and yellow luxin twined, shivered, begged the nobles to impale themselves on the barbs.

The nobles tripped over each other, literally falling and smashing into each other as they stopped.

Beyond the glowing wall of death, blocking each exit from the hippodrome, they saw stony-eyed Blackguards, weapons unsheathed, in the loose, easy posture of killers, luxin readied.

'No one else need die!' Gavin shouted. 'Get back to your lines.'

His Blackguards and the drafters he'd brought echoed his command, circling outside the wall, bellowing at the people inside, 'Back to your line. Now! Move!'

Others were gentler, but the result was the same. In minutes, the lines had reformed. Now, more quietly, Gavin said, 'Would you rather die than have peace? No one else in your family or on your lands has to die.'

'If I take your offer,' one grandmother said, 'I'll be setting myself against all of them. How is my little family to stand against the might of the Willows on one side and the Malargoses on the other?'

'Whoever takes my peace gains my protection,' Gavin said. 'Whoever breaks my peace gains swift and brutal death.' He swept a hand slowly across the columns, and this time set glowing yellow targets where the next missiles would fly. In the front of many of the columns were children, or favorite aunts, favorite sons. Orholam forgive the families if they were too stubborn even now. Orholam forgive him.

He held the tense silence until someone was about to speak, and then he swung a hand so fast at the table that the entire crowd flinched, thinking it another attack. He sent out waves of sub-red so that the air around him shimmered, a trick he'd honed in the war to make it look like he was radiating power, and roared, pointing at the table, 'This is the end of your war. Who. Will. Sit?'

Over the bodies of the dead obstinate and the dead murderers and the dead proud, they made peace. It hadn't been easy, but it had been quick. Not all justice could be done: how far back does one go with judgment, after what horror in the chain does one say, 'All before this is forgiven'? But peace had been forged. Hostages were exchanged, and hostages were sent to the Chromeria where Gavin would have personal oversight of them. In the years that followed, a test of the Prism's Peace had come, of course. It had come from a Guile cousin, Marcos-Sevastian Guile, who'd exacted vengeance for a wartime rape in like fashion, doubtless thinking his blood connection to Gavin gave him extra leeway. If he'd had a shred of the Guile intellect, he'd have known it meant exactly the opposite.

Marcos-Sevastian had been found mutilated in the town square, limbs piled neatly nearby, a sign propped under his bloody chin: 'So too to all who break the Prism's Peace.'

And later, Gavin had needed to send an emissary to a Ruthgari lord using his economic might to ruin one of his vassals who'd turned on him early that day.

That had required only a stern talk. Blood and words. Peace by sword and will.

Eirene Malargos had been the first of the heads of the most powerful families to sign.

Now Gavin said to her, 'Do you think that lottery was random? Your uncle Perakles was a warrior coward. Happy to take insult, happy to send men to die, but would never dare the line himself. And his wife Thera? You think that vicious heifer had it in her to lead a great family to a picnic, much less to a peace? Think of those who died that day: they were – except that regrettable young Green Apple idiot with the knife – exactly the people who couldn't countenance peace, or who had done such horrific things the other families couldn't countenance peace while they lived. If that was Orholam's hand, it was his hand working through me. And my mother. It was she who helped me sift the nobles and the conns and the banconns. Only she knew them all well enough to know. She selected you, Eirene. Do you remember the moment at the table, when they wanted you to be the hostage at the Chromeria, because Tisis was too young? My mother picked you to lead your family. Your lottery number was her choice. So you can decide if you owe me everything or nothing, but your life and your position, those you owe to my mother.'

Eirene's eyes were damp, and Gavin didn't know if she was thinking of those who'd died that day, or her father who'd died before, or all that she had lost in leading her family, or whether she was thinking about Felia Guile and the friendship of that great woman that she'd been deprived of. 'Did she . . . did she speak of me? At the end?'

The most tempting lies are often best shunned. It proves your honesty. Gavin shook his head slowly. 'I'm sorry. Our time was . . . very limited. The Color Prince was almost literally at the door, and we had a city to defend. It was an abbreviated Freeing, at best.'

And he had her. By Orholam's beard, he had her. He was going to claw his way up out of this cell, and out of this country, and he was going to climb the heavens. He would fell the sun. There was nothing Gavin Guile couldn't do. He was not only his magic. He was a man unlike any other man who'd ever gone before. He was a man to rival Lucidonius himself. He was a god.

'Lady Malargos, set me free. I will win this war, and I will

417

repay every debt you are owed, and I will make the Color Prince pay in blood.'

But then the door opened, and of all people, of all the real Gavin's old friends and lovers and enemies and those who were all three in a singular body, the Nuqaba walked in. She was dressed in the casual style that a Parian lady would usually only wear in her own home, among her ladies and eunuchs, and that she was dressed so here told Gavin that she was an honored guest and a close friend of Eirene Malargos. She wore jeweled slippers, women's loose mid-calf-length trousers secured with a multifolded brocade belt with long fringe, a light blouse open in the front, and a vest snug about the bust decorated with precious stones matching those on a number of necklaces and a loose scarf about her hair.

She wore the small tattoos of her position as Nuqaba, almost invisible against her rich black skin: one just below her lower lip, and one under each eye in decorative Old Parian script. Under the left eye, it read, 'Cursed Accuser,' and under the right 'Blessed Redeemer.'

'Greetings, Gavin,' the leader of Paria said, 'do you know what this is?' She held up a metallic chain with a large jewel on it like living fire captured in amber. 'This is the seed crystal of the orange bane. Among other things, it detects lies, and you, you glorious fuck, you are a liar.'

Chapter 57

'I've figured out something really exciting,' Quentin said. He was standing on the table in the restricted library. His hair was askew, and he had a few days' growth of scrubby uneven beard. 'Unfortunately, it's trivial and not at all helpful!' He laughed, and it was the ragged sound of someone right on the edge.

Kip said, 'Quentin, why are your teeth red? Tell me that isn't blood.'

'Heh-heh-heh.' His voice pitched up crazily. 'Nah, it's not

blood. Khat. You know khat? It's a stimulant. Never used it until today – uh, three days ago. With kopi and khat and . . .' He looked down at several bowls below the table.

'Please tell me you haven't been using the High Luxiats' flower jars as chamber pots,' Kip said.

'Kip, under a thin veneer of excitement, I think I might be about to collapse.'

'That seems likely,' Kip said. 'What did – did you drink the flowers' water first?'

'I couldn't drink it second. That would be gross. Plus, there wouldn't be any room.'

Kip shook his head. He reached up and grabbed Quentin and put the young man down on the floor. He didn't trust Quentin to jump down without hurting himself. The reedy scholar barely weighed more than Teia.

'Um, thanks?' Quentin said. 'And please don't touch me again. I don't . . . I just don't like being touched. Thanks.'

Kip shrugged. So Quentin was weird. Not any weirder than the rest of them. 'So . . . ?'

'The Black Cards and the Lightbringer are connected!'

'That is . . . exciting. I guess. How?'

'That we don't know anything about either of them! Ha!' Kip said, 'Not so exciting.'

'I, I, I told you that I figured out the organization scheme, right?'

'That was like three weeks ago.'

'Right, right. I, I found all the references to the Lightbringer – I'll show you those in, in, presently – and there was a problem with all of them—'

'Problem?' Kip interrupted. 'What kind of problem?'

'One moment, one moment! So I had this thought and I went and I found all the books on the Black Cards. I couldn't find them at first, but then I didn't look for books on Black Cards – those have all been burned or stolen or what, what have you – so instead I looked for books about *all* the cards, but written before the Black Cards were declared black, that is, heretical, see?'

'Smart.' Kip wasn't following, but it didn't seem to matter. 'And I found the very same thing!'

'Same as what?' Kip asked.

'Same as the Lightbringer mentions!'

'But you didn't tell—'

'Oh, right, right. Look.' Quentin pointed to a tiny book on the table.

The leaves were so old they were fragile and stained. 'What is this?' Kip asked.

'It's a luxiat's prayer book. It was stitched into book form rather than a scroll so it could be thumbed through more easily, and fit in a pocket. They made them durable, and with plenty of empty pages at the back for the luxiat to record notes or prayers or dreams from Orholam or prophecies. This one belonged to Darjan himself.'

'The warrior-priest?'

'A leader of the *ahdar qassis gwardjan*. A green guardian priest.'

'The writing looks funny,' Kip said.

'The text? It looks funny to me, too. I don't speak all these languages. I paired all the oldest books not in Parian or Old Parian with their translations. Sort of handy that the translations have been moved to this library, too.'

Kip hadn't meant the text per se, though of course he couldn't read it. He meant that there were blanks in the text. Spaces floated as if someone had written in invisible ink in them, but there were no words there. 'What's with the gaps?'

'Look at the translation book, right, right below it.'

The book of translation had gaps, too. They weren't precisely aligned with gaps in the original, at least not by spacing. But Kip could guess that they must be aligned by meaning.

'It's, it's the same in all of these,' Quentin said. 'Someone's erased a lot.'

'Erased ink?'

'Or, or, or . . . or they wrote in some invisible ink. You're the polychrome. You tell me.'

Kip shielded his eyes from the lantern and widened his pupils out to look in sub-red. Nothing. He soaked up some sub-red luxin from the lantern and brought it to his fingers—

'Kip, you're forbidden to draft sub-red in a library!' Quentin said. 'You can get *expelled*!' He obviously meant to whisper the last word, but he did it so loudly he might as well have been shouting.

But Kip was already done. There were no heat-reactive inks. He narrowed his gaze to superviolet – so often used for secret writing. Nothing there. He gently streamed superviolet luxin over the page, but nothing fluoresced. Then he donned each pair of colored spectacles in turn and gazed at the page. Nothing, nothing in any color.

But when he drew forth his superviolet spectacles, he found that one lens was broken.

'Oh, hells,' he said.

'Oh, Ben-hadad didn't tell you about— Oops!' Quentin said.

'Tell me about what?'

'So! Nothing in any color?' Quentin asked.

'Tell me about *what*?'

'They all thought you were dead. He had some experiments he needed to do. Something happened. And then I think he's been trying to find the right time to tell you. He, he feels terrible.'

'Then why are *you* telling me this?'

He looked nonplussed. 'It slipped.'

'I didn't mean why you, I meant why not him. Forget that. Show me this.'

'It's all the same. I've copied them all out. In each book, in each translation, there are fragments only of Lightbringer prophecies. I thought at first they might have used bad ink. You can see that in some old manuscripts: ink that fades with age and gets illegible. But you wouldn't have the translations with blanks in exactly the same places.'

'Why not? I mean, if the gap was already there when they wrote the translation, why wouldn't they leave a gap, too?'

'Because I looked at the various times in which each of these translations were made, and there have been different copyists' notations used to show that a text was illegible or absent. None wrote those notations in these gaps, and none of their methods involved leaving long blanks, it's an inefficient use of the space on the pages, which are often expensive. So, so someone erased the relevant sections in the copies *and* the translations. We didn't lose all of the Lightbringer prophecies in existence, of course. But in these books, we get only fragments. And not all the texts have translations, so some of these translations are my own.'

'Wait, wait, wait,' Kip said. 'How did they erase ink?'

'With hide you can scrape it off. Often followed by putting down another layer of whitewashing solution. With papyrus, you—'

'But I don't see any change between the scrolls where there's writing and where there isn't. It doesn't look like it's been treated.'

'The treatment may be so old that it's impossible to tell the difference.'

'Meaning that the erasures happened a long time ago?'

'Well, that makes sense with those with old translations, but that's not applicable to all of them. If there was a single time period where someone erased lots of documents all at once—'

'Like the Office of Doctrine? When the Chromeria anointed luxors?'

Quentin bobbed his head, chagrined. 'They must have figured out some mixtures of luxins that would bond with ink and lift it out. When combating heresy, it's the kind of thing they would have loved to find. And use.'

'Those assholes,' Kip said. 'Long dead and still causing problems.' If Teia had been alive during that time, the luxors would have burned her on Orholam's Glare as a heretic.

'Anyway, here's the prophecies I've got, and then I want to tell you one more thing.'

Kip read:

Death in hand, his card, his lot
He fights/struggles with/kills forethought

'He fights/struggles with/kills?' Kip asked.

'That was my translation. Sorry. It was a tough one. It could mean he's impulsive? Maybe he kills without thinking ahead?'

'Are they all this bad?' Kip asked.

He could tell the words wounded Quentin. 'Some of these languages are highly contextual, and the pertinent portions have been deliberately erased. Someone did this exactly so it would be impossible to reconstruct.'

> *In the dusk of times the jinn will rise*
> *Rivers flow blood and moon shine blue*
> *Of Two Hundred will come the Nine*
> *To bring about the end of time.*

Kip looked up at Quentin. 'That doesn't sound so good. Jinn?'

'Spirits? Powerful ones, though. Demigods?'

'And you're sure it's a Lightbringer prophecy?'

'Yes. It's not choruses or lions frolicking with lambs kind of stuff.'

> *The rebels rise, the old ways lost,*
> *Heresy, hypocrisy—*

'That's the whole fragment? Not helpful,' Kip said.

> *Back to the spinner's wheel*
> *Rejected in blood*
> *Victim of the Promethean's brood*

'Promethean's'? Kip asked. It sounded like Old Ruthgari.

'Usually it's a personification of someone who takes violent action intended for some good. Kind of dark overtones to it? But you still haven't seen the best one yet.'

Kip looked. The last one was only a title. *On the Gift of Light.* 'Um, that's great, Quentin. Where's the poem?'

'No, that's, that's it. But look!' He pulled out the two books side by side. 'The translation is wrong, so it wasn't erased. They missed it. The ablative with this phrasing usually would mean "on the gift of light," but it could also mean "on the giver of light."'

'You keep looking at me like I'm supposed to have a revelation,' Kip said.

'In the original, the common way to construct it would be "doniae luxi." But the word order doesn't matter in an inflected language except for emphasis, but here it's "luxi doniae."'

'Still not—'

'Centuries ago the Parian accent gave way to the Ruthgari, and "luxi" started to be transcribed as "luci".'

'Still . . .'

'Luci doniae. Which in the nominative case is . . . C'mon. This is like having to explain the punch line of a dirty joke.'

'Oh! Lucidonius! So a poem "On Lucidonius"? But what does that mean?'

Quentin deflated. 'Well, I don't know. But it does mean the Lightbringer is tied to Lucidonius somehow. The Light Giver and the Light Bringer? What if they're the same? What if the Lightbringer has already come?'

'And nobody noticed?'

'*Everyone* noticed Lucidonius. He changed – he changed the whole world.'

'But they didn't notice that he was the same person they'd prophesied about?'

> *His hands are forged to take the blade,*
> *His skin is dyed for war.*
> *By father's father is he unmade*
> *He all will save through what all abhor.*

Kip was almost done even trying. But Quentin said, 'No, no, look, this is not even close to an exact translation – you think it rhymes in our language by coincidence? Even the meter is wrong. Iambs are natural for our tongue, but they wrote in dactylic hexameter.'

'Dact – what?'

'Doesn't matter.'

'How does this help us?'

'Well, well, well, it probably doesn't. But I could spend years with this stuff! And this one, it makes reference to "he," which I assume is the Lightbringer, at least it's been erased, too. This last one is a contested prophecy, but I don't know whether it's because they aren't sure if it's about the Lightbringer, or if it was contested later because it's impossible.'

. . . he'll pluck the immortal's own beard and steal the shade from his head in the Great Library.

Quentin shrugged. 'The plucking of beard hair is an idiom for vexing him, and to steal the shade from a man's head – to a desert people? Not appreciated. So irritate and infuriate? Why the repetition? I don't know. Checking the dates on both of those idioms to see when they were in use in the pertinent cultures might shed some light, but it's a rejected prophecy anyway, so that'll be low on my list.'

Kip said, 'But why contest that one? It seems specific and clear.'

'It is. Unfortunately, we know that Lucidonius never went near the Great Library, and it's been ash for nigh unto three hundred years now. Tellari separatists burned it down. Gave their lives, merely to take away something we loved and that made us better. May Orholam curse them.'

'That's all very interesting, and not very helpful.'

'I know, and I haven't told you the other thing, which is more of both.' Quentin looked suddenly so drained with his excitement past that Kip put a hand on his arm to steady him. Then he took his hand away at Quentin's frown.

'And what's that?' Kip asked.

'There's some great stuff in these libraries. I mean I found out why the Feast of Light and Darkness can be a month off the actual date of the autumnal equinox, like it was this past year. It's – never mind. Doesn't matter. There's also some really terrible stuff in these libraries. More terrible than good, I think. Even focusing narrowly, I've come across . . . Doesn't matter. None of that other horrible stuff has been erased. So far as I can tell none of the other stuff that I would have expected the luxors to object to has been erased – except everything about the Black Cards. Even their names. They're just gone, Kip. Nothing else has been erased: just some parts of the Lightbringer prophecies and everything about the black cards. There's some connection. Some force that doesn't want us to see the truth here. But it's all gone. Down to even the impressions a pen would have pressed into parchment. They wanted to keep a secret, and they have. They've already won.'

Chapter 58

'What are you doing down here?' Karris asked. She was standing in the doorway of the Prism's exercise room.

As the winter months had passed, Kip and Karris had fallen into a comfortable rhythm. They spent most of the morning together every day, six days a week, then each went off to their other duties.

'Putting in a bit of time on the bag.' He shrugged.

When he'd first started training with Karris, Kip hadn't known her well enough to pick out her moods, so over the months, he'd only seen after the fact that she was slowly taking off the shuttered lenses of depression. When she was down, she was more serious, adult, focused. She had that mask on now, her hair dyed raven's black, pulled back.

'He's coming back,' Kip said. He turned away from the heavy bag and let his green luxin gloves dissolve. Six months had passed since Ru, almost six months of training and fighting and watching only full Blackguards go out on the skimmers to look for Gavin or the bane. Almost six months of bad news from the war: the loss at Ruic Head, the raids in northern Atash, the cataclysm at Ox Ford, the pyrrhic victory at Two Mills Junction, the steady reading of the Lists, the rolls now full of names of those who'd died from camp diseases, infections, dysentery.

Almost six months hitting this damn bag, hoping to convince that one torn seam to give way and rip open, and it had barely loosened. It was a youthful fantasy to beat the sawdust out of a heavy bag, he knew. He knew it, but that didn't mean he didn't want to do it.

'So you always say.' Karris disappeared behind a screen set up off to one side, and reappeared, wearing the equivalent of Blackguard garb. Red today.

The White was snipping away all Karris's ties to the Blackguard. The red garb had been an early imposition. Then she'd forbidden Karris to train in the Blackguard's area in the great yard below the Chromeria. Forbade her to draft. Sent her on little errands. And if it seemed some days like Karris had been crying before she came to train Kip, she never missed a day, and Kip knew that she'd come to look forward to their training. It was one last little slice of her old life, mixed with a new purpose.

'I'm right,' he said. 'Last time I was worrying about when Gavin would show up and save the day, I turned around and he was standing right there. Scared a stain right into my pants.'

'Kip! Ew!'

'I was wondering,' Kip said to distract her. 'Why do you always call me Kip?'

'Because I'm not a Blackguard anymore?' she asked. She did this sometimes, making him dig deeper.

'It's not that. Some of the others use Breaker for me, too.'

'Breaker's your warrior name.'

'You teach me how to fight as much as anyone. Even my book learning with you is focused on fighting strategy and histories of battles.'

Karris went to a weapons bucket, carefully freeing a long, narrow, flexible staff with crescent-shaped blades on each end. She balanced it across her shoulder and stooped, digging through another barrel of nubs and guards. She found what she was looking for and fastened a hard wooden guard with a sponge projecting on each end. Pensive, she said, 'We put on a face when we go into battle. You can forget Kip for a time and become Breaker when musket balls are whistling past your ears and your throat burns with the black smoke, and the luxin rage and battle rage join in you. But you're still Kip. Inside, somewhere, even in that moment, you're still you. Some warriors want to throw away the other man trembling within them and become only a warrior. It can be done for a time.

'But the other man always comes back, and if he's been shut in a closet somewhere, unable to grow and learn and come to accept what the warrior does and what the warrior loves, then both of them will be cripples in peace and in war. If you despise your own frailty, rather than come to peace with it, you'll not only hate yourself, you'll hate everyone who's frail. A good commander knows the strength of his men and pushes them to the edge of it, but not over. A good man knows his own strength and does the same.' She smiled. 'Of course, at your age, you like to think your limits are both a lot greater and a lot narrower than they actually are.'

'And at yours, you like to think the converse?' Kip said. He wasn't exactly sure what he meant, but it seemed witty.

Instead, Karris's mouth tightened, her eyes narrowed, and her voice went chilly. 'You're calling me old?'

Kip gaped. 'I – I . . .'

She grinned.

'Ah hell. Got me again.'

'Watch your mouth, young man, or I'll wash it out with soap.'

'That was only my second!' Kip complained. She said he could say hell twice a day, no more. Blackguards guard their tongues, and all that.

'I distinctly counted three,' Karris said.

Kip glowered. Hell, hell, hell, hell, hell.

'I know what you're thinking,' she said sternly. 'And quit it.'

Hell, hell, hell. Kip smiled.

'I heard that, too. You always smile when you're being secretly defiant.'

I do? I do not!

'Yes, you do,' she said.

'Now you're just guessing,' Kip said.

She shrugged. 'If that makes you feel better . . .'

He grinned, but then got pensive. They were both skipping a ceremony. 'So . . . this Feast of Waxing Light. What are they doing? I mean, without Gavin, what is there to do?'

It had been almost six months since the autumnal equinox that had seen a sea demon and a whale do battle for the Chromeria, or for the Cerulean Sea. Six months of war grinding its gears slowly through the winter, shipping made difficult with heavy seas and torrential downpours, and ships lost and caravans delayed and stalling actions as the Color Prince pushed into Blood Forest. But the dry season was here, and all the satrapies knew that meant more war.

'First there's a procession in honor of your grandfather, the promachos. Some fireworks. Some martial demonstrations. Given that there's a war to spend money on, it will be a much-diminished thing.'

'What isn't, these days?' Kip asked.

She shook her head. 'Was I a know-it-all like you when I was young? Don't answer that.'

'Do I have to go?' Kip asked.

'You don't want to? Even diminished, it will be a bigger party than you've ever seen.'

'I'd rather learn things that might save my life than eat cakes and candies.'

She gave him a dubious look.

'Depends on the cake.'

'Chocolate?'

'That would be worth dying for,' Kip said.

'Can't get chocolate worth the name since we lost northern Atash,' she said.

'Thus me, here.'

Karris grinned. 'Today, I'll show you the *sharana ru*, the tygre striper.' She hefted the flexible spear in her hands, and spun it easily. 'The sharana ru is said to be carved from sea demon bone. It doesn't work the way other materials work. Note.' She spun the flexible shaft, and stopped it with an arm. The shaft bent around it like jelly, more flexible than a green branch. It sprang back suddenly.

'Excellent,' Kip said. With his slowly growing knowledge of weapons, he guessed that the sharana ru would be a difficult weapon to master, but would then be terribly effective because it would move with surprising speed when used properly. Still, an odd weapon. How fragile was it to get that springiness? Could it parry a sword?

'You haven't seen the half of it,' Karris said.

'And what's the half of it?' Kip asked.

She looked like she'd been about to tell him, until his big mouth said that.

'Let's let you find out the hard way,' she said.

'Oh, goodie,' he said. He scowled, though he deserved it for acting wise with her.

'Fencing,' she said. 'Let's see that yellow. Five, four . . .'

Kip drew in a bit of superviolet and then shot it across the room at the control panel. Yellow light bathed the room. He sucked it in hungrily, the rush of clarity giving him the hard edge he would need to draft the perfect yellow he'd practiced so much. He flicked out his hand, and with it, yellow liquid that he furiously worked to solidify and narrow as it streamed from him.

'Three, two . . .' she counted.

'Too fast, too fast!'

She lofted the sharana ru and began swinging the dual blades in loose circles, swishing the air. She set herself in position just as she reached the end of her smooth count. 'One, and—' She lashed out with one end.

Kip brought his yellow luxin sword, trying to finish the temper even as his body went to the correct block instinctively. Excess yellow luxin coating the blade burst into light with the energy of the collision between blunt yellow blade and blunt wooden guard.

He didn't make it, and instead the yellow luxin burst apart. But both of them had narrowed their eyes against the blast of light, used to this. A slash cut across Kip's front shin, a smear of ink from the sponge on the sharana ru's guard: a bruise for Kip and a point for Karris.

She let him form the sword correctly. It took more than ten seconds. And they went again. Their bout was fast, ridiculously fast, and finished in less than two seconds.

He cursed inwardly, and settled into his stance again.

Again, a loss. And again, and again, and again. Aptly named, the tygre striper left Kip with streaks – mercifully of ink, rather than blood – across stomach, arms, forehead, shin, and hands.

On the tenth round, he scored a point, just before Karris did. She nodded. In a real fight, they'd both be dead. The Blackguard didn't want dead Blackguards who'd also killed their opponents; they wanted unscratched Blackguards who'd killed their opponents. Still, from the humble acorn . . .

Again, a loss. And again, and again, and again. But Kip was starting to figure out how the sharana ru worked, how it sprang back when Karris would snap one side against her own leg as she attempted a short sweep – a feint – at Kip's face to set up the speedier long sweep. The flexibility itself gave a small measure of predictability, for what bent must become straight.

Even with the guard and the sponge, Karris's weapon *hurt*. Every time they sparred, Kip's body was covered with bruises for days. His favorite was when she used a rapier and his bruises looked like freckles. Bruise-freckles on the turtle-bear. Not that Karris cared if he complained about it. And her fighting – learned the hard way with Blackguards – wasn't the speedy, light dance the court duelists used. It was full-contact, brutal action. Hip throws and leverage, forearm strikes and elbows and grabbing your opponent's blade with a gloved hand – or grabbing your own and pressing it to his neck. Kicks and throws and foot sweeps and clothing pulls and eye gouging and knee strikes to the kidneys – everything, everything dirty and fast and effective and lethal.

Kip's weight and burgeoning strength should have been a significant advantage. Maybe it would have, if they'd been wielding battle axes or war hammers. Karris was fast and a small target, and she was an expert at using leverage to compensate for what she lacked in strength compared to her beefier Blackguard brothers. Sixteen years of constant practice against the best opponents in the world had made her surprisingly deadly for her diminutive figure.

Today, she didn't lecture. Some days she did. Learning to keep some attention on other things kept you from getting war-blind, too focused on what was immediately in front of you. Last time she'd taught him about the other magic-using fighting companies in the world: the Nuqaba's guard in Paria, the *Tafok Amagez*; the old Blue-Eyed Demons that Gavin had destroyed after the war; a few of the martial elites from the highland Parian tribal societies; the secretive Shadow Watch of Ruthgar, whom she knew did exist because Gavin had checked them out personally to see if they were a threat to the Seven Satrapies. Few individuals within any of those groups, though, also used magic with anything near the facility of the Blackguards. The *Cwn y Wawr* were archers and tree climbers and green drafters and masters of camouflage in the deep parts of Blood Forest, and some of the Shadow Watch were highly talented drafters as well – but no one group had the range of drafting abilities available to them that the Blackguard did. No other group had the critical mass of drafters to maintain a drafting tradition in each color, so instead each generation had to invent again techniques their forebears would have been able to teach them easily.

Such martial societies were born from wars and all too often extinguished in them. The Blood War had birthed a dozen. The False Prism's War had wiped out half that many. Some faded as the reasons they'd come together had disappeared – those formed in the Blood War had either morphed into mercenary companies like the Blue Bastards or the Cloven Shield, or the men and women had simply gone home or had become soldiers or outlaws or farmers as the demand for teachers disappeared. The martial arts of drafting died especially quickly because of drafters' short lives.

It made Kip realize that anything awe-inspiring that they discovered had doubtless been discovered before. It had simply also then been lost.

Karris said, 'Now, are you ready for the other half?'

'Other what?' he asked.

She lashed out with the tygre striper. Kip blocked, and blocked, and blocked again. Then she whipped part around an arm and popped it back – but it moved twice as fast as it should have and it cut across his belly long before his block arrived.

'The hell?' Kip asked.

'Strike it. Downstroke, in the middle.'

Kip did as he was told, slashing hard between Karris's hands. The sharana ru bent a long way and popped his yellow luxin blade back upward.

'Again, the same.'

Kip cut again – and this time nearly had the yellow blade knocked from his grip as the sharana ru didn't bend in the least. It was suddenly like a steel bar.

'This is what's special about the sharana ru – sea demon bone or whatever it is. It is the only known mundane material that reacts to will. You want it to be hard, and it is.'

My problem is more often that I don't want it to be hard, but it *is*.

Thank Orholam, this time Kip didn't say it.

Karris paused and looked at Kip, who stared back at her, all innocence. 'Mind out of the gutter, Kip.'

They shared a grin.

'With this sharana ru, you can simply grip it hard and will what you want it to – Orholam damn it, Kip! Now all I can think about is, uh . . . Ahem. All of them work best if you're bloody, though.'

Well, that killed any innuendo. 'Bloody?' Kip asked. He didn't mean his voice to come out at quite that pitch.

'Will is in the blood. It's why Orholam forbade the drinking of blood, as of old. Some part of the soul resides in the blood, some luxiats say. Or perhaps it's merely coincidence. Regardless, it works with the sharana ru. There was a warrior caste on the Isle of Glass, before it sank into the seas and became White Mist Reef.'

'Legend, right?' Kip said.

She tossed him the sharana ru. 'You hold the stuff of legend in your hands.'

Which just begged for a ribald joke. But it was *Karris*. She was like his mother.

If I didn't already have a mother. Who was a complete and total calamity of humanity. Or had been. 'Real?' Kip asked, shaking off the memories, the stench of that closet where he'd spent two nights and three days, nearly dying.

'Blood Forest has the Floating City. We couldn't build one today, but the engineering was obviously known, once. Of course, the legends say the Isle of Glass was a hundred times the size of the Floating City. Perhaps it was twice as big, or smaller. Perhaps it sank because of its blasphemies against Orholam. Perhaps it was merely caught in a winter storm. Or both. These things, being, of course, not exclusive.'

'Did they have other weapons?'

'What would you think?' Karris asked.

'Bows.'

'A few. It was said that it took years of training to gain proficiency – the difficulty being in figuring out how much

Will you were using, and keeping it consistent, despite being tired or scared or furious. None survive.'

'Catapults?' Kip asked.

'Broke the men who tried to use them.'

'What happens to a man whose will has been broken?' Kip asked. 'I willjacked Grazner once in training, but he seemed fine.'

'Depends on how much of his will is in it. You foil what someone has a whim for, he might be left dazed for a moment. A man strains to put steel into enough sharana ru to fling a stone two thousand paces and fails? He's left an idiot. Forever.'

'Dear Orholam.'

'Anyway, as I was saying, there was a warrior caste that used sharana ru weapons. They had a dozen war dances they used to get themselves into a fighting trance. Most involved lightly stabbing their own scalps and their palms. They went into battle bloody, and they didn't leave until there was no more blood to shed. One of their great defeats was at the walls of Green Haven. There is a forest there where they say at dusk you can sometimes hear the sound of their war dance.'

'That sounds . . . spooky.'

'It'll scare a stain right into your pants,' Karris said. She smirked. 'You know, Kip, I wanted to say that you've become like . . .' Her eyes clouded.

Kip felt a sudden well of longing open beneath his feet, and he was falling into it. He finished the sentence in his mind, but he couldn't speak lest the last bubbles of his breath escape, like so much hope.

'No,' she said, her tone changing abruptly, 'you haven't become *like* a real warrior, you are becoming a real warrior, and I'm proud to train you.' She patted his shoulder lamely.

It wasn't what she was going to say, and he knew it. It wasn't what she was going to say. Was it? She was going to say that other thing, that thing his stupid fool heart yearned for, pretending it would make everything better.

Kip nodded and took it as a compliment and crawled out of the well, half drowned and dripping false hope everywhere.

But he bobbed his head and smiled modestly. He was getting better at lying.

Chapter 59

Ah, the trouble one botched assassination can cause.

'The empire is broken, Gavin,' the Nuqaba said. Odd for her to start there. After her abrupt entrance and accusation, she and Eirene Malargos had withdrawn together. Apparently they'd come up with a plan, but only the Nuqaba was here now.

'How's your husband?' Gavin asked. 'Well, I hope?'

Her eyes flashed. Through circumstances Gavin had never heard a satisfactory explanation for, Haruru had married Izîl-Udad, the head of the family that had tried to have her mother assassinated. Izîl-Udad was now a cripple. It was widely rumored that the Nuqaba had pushed him down a flight of marble stairs during a drunken fight, leaving the man with shattered knees that even the most skilled chirurgeons couldn't fix. The truth, Gavin's spies had told him long ago, was that the man had beaten Haruru fiercely and often. One night, she had drugged him, drafted orange luxin on the stairs so that he would slip, and then crushed his knees with a hammer while he was helpless. He'd woken with no memory of the incident, or was so fearful that he claimed no memory of it, and because of the political pressures at the time, they'd stayed together. He was confined to a chair, and it was said she did not make his life easy.

Gavin had seen portraits of her as a younger woman many times, not least of which was the masterpiece in Ironfist's room, and she had looked quite beautiful, though artists were apt to gloss over flaws for powerful patrons. Despite the years since she'd sat for that painting, she was still a striking figure. Perhaps more so now, in the fullness of her power. She wore an immaculately folded and doubtless colorful haik, if Gavin had been able to see the colors. Shiny metal – gold? – fibulae in sunbursts at each shoulder. Coral necklace and coral earrings, not through pierced earlobes, but hanging over the ears instead, in the traditional Parian style. Reedy muscles and heavy eyes, full lips and few curves, despite three children.

'Such a pleasant surprise to see you here,' Gavin said. As if that covered the half of it.

She laughed aloud. 'Do you know, the seed crystal tells me that you actually are happy to see me. You're a complicated man, aren't you, Gavin Guile?'

He blinked. 'What's this about a seed crystal?' You never knew. Sometimes you just ask, and people will tell you what you want to know.

She studied the crystal. 'A genuine question. Really? *Really?*' She laughed again.

Gavin quirked an eyebrow. For the last two hours, his mind had been spinning like a mill with the gears uncoupled, whizzing furiously, accomplishing nothing.

'Do you remember the mosaic on the left-hand wall, as you enter my library?' she asked.

By 'my library' she meant the Library of Azûlay. The building itself was more than eight hundred years old, and probably built on top of a library that had been there at least two hundred more. The mosaic was of King Zedekiah, skin depicted in onyx, the scroll-spear of wisdom in his right hand and whatever had been in his left hand long ago chiseled out by thieves. The kings and queens and satraps who followed had never found two scholars who agreed on what had been lost – a scepter? scales of justice? a sword? – or they would have restored it long ago. King Zedekiah, Gavin remembered, wore a crown with seven stars. One for each color, naturally. The red and blue and green, most likely ruby and sapphire and emerald, had been picked out at whatever time the left-hand mosaic tiles had been stolen, but those had been easier to replace.

Though it was a famous place, and he knew much about it, Gavin had never been there. He had never visited her. And he had never taken her to his bed, made Orholam only knew what promises, and then left her without a word – unlike his older brother, the real Gavin.

Thanks for that, brother.

'The crown?' Gavin said, dubious. 'Surely metaphorical.'

'King Zedekiah was one of the nine kings.'

'I've heard that speculation before,' Gavin said. 'You think—'

'Not speculation. You think I support scholars for the warm feelings I get for my charity?'

'Never that,' Gavin said. He smirked to try to take the edge off. It didn't work.

Her expression darkened. 'They confirmed it for me. Along with some other fascinating tidbits.'

'Pray tell,' Gavin said.

She looked down at what she'd said was the orange seed crystal. 'Mostly sarcastic, but interested, too. You hoping I'll slip up? You want to battle with me, Gavin?'

'Seems like that trinket is doing more than telling you yes or no on whether I'm telling the truth,' Gavin said.

'King Zedekiah was holding a sword in his hand. All diamonds, except for a helix of obsidian up the spine, wrapping around seven jewels. Ah, I don't need the seed crystal to tell me you're familiar with the blade.' She walked up close to the bars. She had a terrible walk. Heavy and direct, like a man trudging under the weight of a pack, no sway to her slender hips at all.

But then she was at the bars, and the scent of her perfume wafted over him. Lemon and jasmine and balsam and amber. It reminded him of Karris's scent, a brief flash of the paradise that was having her hair drape over his face, skin to skin.

But he was brought back instantly as she spoke. 'Haven't you ever wondered why so much of your approved history starts only four hundred years ago?'

'That was when Lucidonius came. No empire likes to laud that which came before it.' Gavin shrugged. 'Simple exercise in maintaining power. Bury the past until you're sure it's dead.'

'Another truth wrapped around a lie. You're hoping I'll be frustrated and explain why you're wrong.'

Sometimes Gavin wondered how well he would have ruled if he hadn't had the handicap of maintaining his façade. He'd had to keep the Nuqaba at arm's length throughout his time as Prism because he didn't know the full details of her tryst with his brother, and she was said to be one of the strongest intuitive thinkers in the Seven Satrapies. He'd feared that she would take one look at him and declare him a fraud.

Luckily, her religious duties had kept her tied to her own country, and its great distance from the Chromeria had been enough excuse for Gavin to avoid going there. But now here he was, her prisoner, and she had a means of knowing whenever he told a lie.

'So then, why do you think the empire is doomed?' Gavin asked.

'Because Eirene and I are deciding whether we'll join the Color Prince or stay with your father and the Seven – pardon – Five Satrapies.'

It took Gavin's breath away. Treason. Treason, discussed as if they were discussing who could give a better price for alligator leather.

'You see, Gavin, the Spectrum has become so insular that they've forgotten they exist for us, not the other way around. When's the last time any member of the Spectrum even traveled to their home satrapy? Six years ago. And that was prompted by one of Delara Orange's cousins dying young, with two wills and four bastards.'

Gavin said nothing, but it was more than his breath that was gone. It was his spirit, limp as a wind-starved sail. Why would she tell him her planned treason, and tell him so bluntly?

Because there was, quite simply, nothing he could do to affect what she did. Ultimately, she was saying, all of Gavin's power rested on his magical power. This was her vengeance.

No, it was only the beginning of her vengeance. She would dismantle all he'd accomplished in his time as Prism.

'You see,' she said, 'the Spectrum was so busy hobbling you that they ignored every other threat. Think what you could have accomplished if the empire had been an empire in truth. Ilyta could be a center of smithing that would enrich everyone. Instead it's ten thousand pirates, two hundred smiths, and a few hundred thousand people in poverty. Did I say Five Satrapies? Four. And think about Tyrea. Well, surely you know what a wasteland Tyrea is. Totally unnecessary. If a man as strong as you couldn't unite this empire, then this empire is too weak to stand.'

'So you've made your decision?' he asked.

She smiled almost shyly. 'I've made mine. The Color Prince

thinks he can control us. You see this?' She held up the jewel. It was a six-pointed star, with black tips on each point, both the color – orange, he assumed – and the black somehow throbbing with life. She had it contained in a tiny glass box, and the box on a chain.

'The seed crystal?' Gavin asked.

'Didn't you find them when you destroyed the other bane?'

Gavin shook his head. 'Is this a cruel joke?' The term 'seed crystal' didn't bode well.

She shook her head. 'All that work. All those lives. Wasted. The bane will reform if you don't seize the seed crystal. Within months. They look for a host; a drafter to whom they give enormous power. And for some reason, this man, this Color Prince thinks he can then control all of them. But so long as I hold this, rather than it holding me, I don't need to find out. He thinks an orange drafter must, by her very nature, desire to become a goddess. But I'm smart enough to choose freedom. Freedom from the Chromeria. Freedom from him, as well. But I won't leave without Ruthgar. To get the terms we want – that we need – it will take both of us.'

'So my hopes reside with Eirene Malargos? Comforting.'

'I could force her hand, you know. Your father has offered to buy you.'

'He has?' Father knew. He knew Gavin was here. That solved some problems. And made more, naturally.

'Ah, so you think he knows you're here? No. He's merely offered a general bounty – er, reward. You hurt me, Gavin. And for that I'm going to hurt you.'

Going there would be disaster if that trinket really did what she said it did. 'Tell me about the orange seed crystal,' he said.

But she wasn't about to let him control the conversation. 'You turned my brothers against me. You made them abandon me.'

'You're angry about *that*? Not the other?' Gavin asked.

'You thought I'd been pining after you for sixteen years? You took my virginity, not my wits.'

Gavin was left speechless. He'd known she was furious with his brother Gavin. He'd figured Gavin had deserved it, but it wasn't the kind of thing you could ask in a letter. 'Are you still angry that I left you behind?' That 'I' could be a bitter thing to write, at times.

'You stole Hanishu and Harrdun.' She wouldn't call them Ironfist and Tremblefist. 'To be *Blackguards*! Slaves. Disgusting. And they left me to do it. They thought you were more important than I. And you let them go. What are they to you but more bodies to be spent in your protection? Nothing. If you had a thumb's worth of generosity in you, you would have sent them back. You left me at my home, seventeen years old, in charge of a tribe shocked and devastated by our enemies. I had to marry the man who'd had my mother assassinated. I spent ten years digging myself out of the hole you put me in.'

'Join the fucking queue,' Gavin said. 'War is hard. People die. You got dealt such a raw hand that you rose to become the Nuqaba. Your brothers would be ashamed of what you've become.'

Her eyes went cold. 'Well, at last some fire. I wondered if that man was dead. You've become a schemer, Gavin Guile, but at least you have some passion left.'

'Your brothers did what they thought was their duty. I compelled nothing. I won't deny that I wanted Ironfist to stay. He's one of the smartest, most capable commanders I've ever met, and having him on my side is a huge advantage. What Prism would willingly give up such a strong right hand? And Tremblefist didn't want to stay in Paria. Couldn't. Of course he went where Ironfist went, but he, too, has been exemplary. His quiet competence inspires all the Blackguards.'

'He should have turned to me. After . . . after Aghbalu.'

'To his little sister? To understand a killing rage? Rather than to his big brother, who'd been a veteran of war?'

'I'm his sister! He shouldn't have turned to you!'

'It wasn't to me.' Well, the seed crystal would tell her that was true, at least. But she wasn't even looking at it.

'It was you.'

'Fine, then. I gave him what you never could,' Gavin said. His sins might be manifold and worthy of death, but this wasn't one of them. 'I gave him trust, when he didn't trust himself. A sister's trust means nothing in such a case. No fault of yours. He needed something that he would have to earn.

440

The trust of a man who had no reason to love him? That brought him back. He is not that which you knew as a little girl. He'll never be that. What was done to him, and what he did, changed that forever. When I look at him, I don't look for the man who's gone. You would. That's why he's never gone back.'

'This,' she said, 'this is what I hate about you, Gavin. After all I've been through, after all I've suffered, in five minutes you make it sound trivial. You turn it around so that somehow it's my fault. Like I should thank you for taking my brothers from me. Like all this devastation has just been in my own head. I'm the Nuqaba. I'm a master of orange luxin. I'm the nearest thing to a queen these satrapies have known in centuries, and you make me feel a stupid little girl.'

She reached into the folds of her haik and produced a small matchlock pistol. Working the match cord free, she walked over to one of the small lanterns in the cellar. She rested the pistol on a shelf, lifted the lantern hood, and lit the match cord. 'If you died in Eirene's custody,' she said, 'your father would hold her accountable. Her protestations that I'd killed you would seem weak lies, evasions.' She took up the pistol, cocked the hammer, and affixed the match cord. 'Eirene would be furious with me, of course, but she wouldn't risk putting herself in reach of Andross Guile's vengeance. She'd join me.'

The Nuqaba leveled the pistol at Gavin's face. Stepped forward so she was certain she wouldn't hit the bars.

She winked at him, grinning, and he almost grinned back. Then he realized she'd winked closing her right eye. She was giving him the evil eye: judging him with Cursed Accuser, while the right eye of Orholam, Blessed Redeemer, was closed.

Gavin flicked his eyes ever so briefly up over her shoulder, toward the door, and twitched his lips in a fraction-of-a-second grin.

The Nuqaba glanced at the door. Gavin lunged. He slammed against the bars, extending one arm, jamming a shoulder as far through as he could. His hand slapped against her hand and pistol, for the barest instant, he had it in his grip, and then, without his third and fourth fingers, he couldn't hold on to it. The pistol flew out of her hand and smacked into the wall, discharging.

The rapid whine of ricochets filled the cellar.

After the roar, for a long moment, they stood staring at each other. Gavin pulled his shoulder back through the bars, and felt himself, to see if he'd been hit. He hadn't, but his two stumps of fingers were bleeding again. Damn. He'd had to attack with his left hand, but his instincts hadn't adjusted to the loss of his fingers.

He looked to the Nuqaba to see if she'd been hit. Her eyes were wide. Her arm was bleeding. She took a handkerchief and dabbed her forearm. Just a scratch. She looked relieved.

In moments, a flood of guards burst into the room, drawn by the shot. Parians in blue vests, armed to the teeth, drafters all, the Nuqaba's personal guard, the Tafok Amagez. Then a few Malargos house guards. Gavin raised his hands to show he was no threat.

'It's fine,' the Nuqaba said. 'I'm well. You may go. There's no threat here. Just a little accident. Why is my . . .'

She looked down and lifted a bit of her haik from over her thigh. There was a small hole in the fabric. But Gavin's eyes were drawn lower, where blood was pooling around her feet. A lot of blood. Like an artery had been cut.

She wobbled, her eyes rolled back, and she collapsed.

Chapter 60

~The High Luxiat~

The message in my hand is death. This, of course, has no bearing on its righteousness. But by my inner light, I know this is darkness.

'Orholam himself set the earth to spinning, little brother,' Brother Tawleb says. Tawleb is one of the six High Luxiats, and I'm nervous just speaking with him.

He doesn't need to finish the phrase: to give the earth and all its creatures rest from his burning gaze. That there be a time for light, and a time for darkness.

'A line oft abused, big brother. As you yourself pointed out in *Soliloquies on the First Ten Years*.' I'm a coward. This is wrong. Death, for a child? Barely an initiate. Besides, I know how Brother Tawleb is going to answer, now that I think about it.

Brother Tawleb smiles. I've heard that when he was a young luxiat, he was renowned for his looks and his wealth. He'd had a luxurious Atashian beard bedecked with gold beads and anointed with myrrh. After her first husband had been killed in the Blood Wars, his mother had been forced to put him in the Magisterium when she remarried, so as not to muddy her new husband's lines of succession. But Tawleb had still been her favorite, and she showered him with gifts.

He says, '"Quentin Naheed, first of his cohort, a pupil of the top rank, a disciplined, thoughtful young man. Highly intelligent, probably brilliant, possibly a genius, though he guards his tongue so as not to shame his lesser brothers." It's no mistake I've asked you to do this task for me, Quentin. You know how that quote from my treatise ends, don't you?'

'"Some men's abuse of a truth is no excuse for all men to abandon the use of that truth,"' I answer. There is a time for darkness, for secrecy, and for deceit. But most scholars agree that such times lie at the margins: in righteous warfare, for example, where one cannot announce one's intentions or they will be thwarted; or in the case of protecting the innocent from a sinful authority.

And of course, knowing such scriptural exceptions, every tyrant and liar argues that his case fits those exceptions.

But this is *murder*.

'All are brothers under the light, big brother,' I say. 'Is this boy not to be offered a chance to repent for his misdeeds? Surely he is not lost to the night at so young an age?' He is only six years younger than I. If I were to have gone to face judgment at that age . . . I can't bear to think of it. No innocent, I. But I am more of a sinner than many of my brothers.

443

'Your instincts are good, Quentin, and your heart is full of mercy. The brothers were right about you. Not just intelligence, but a heart after Orholam's own,' Brother Tawleb says.

My heart pounds. The brothers have been talking about me? Complimenting me in such high terms? The reference is to one of the greatest saints in all scripture. My heart swells, followed by a horrible thought: am I taking a compliment and turning it to arrogance? Arrogance is a blindness we choose.

'It isn't arrogance to recognize the truth, Quentin.' That Big Brother Tawleb is calling me by my name is itself a compliment I'm not worthy of.

'All are equal under the light,' I manage.

'A foundational truth indeed,' he says. 'And one that must be handled carefully. When Orholam looks down on us as from the height of the sun itself, the difference between a dwarf and a giant is insignificant. The difference between your intellect and an idiot's is puny when compared to the infinite intelligence which is Orholam's. But though we walk daily *with* Orholam and *for* him, we walk among men, and the difference between giants and dwarfs matters greatly to us indeed, though it doesn't matter to Orholam – and oughtn't matter to us – in terms of justice and mercy and righteousness. This is another truth easily abused. Just as all sins are one before Orholam, but we differentiate between a whitewashed lie and a murder because here one undeniably has worse effects. It is not sin to recognize what is true, little brother. Indeed, it is a sin to choose not to see it. So that you are gratified by a truth being recognized by others that you have long known yourself, but have not wanted to say aloud, is no sin.'

'But I will be proud. I know my heart, and it is deceptive,' I say. I'm not comfortable speaking of these things. I will hoard these compliments like a miser and revel in them in the dark hours of the night. I will sneer at my brothers who flub their memorization, hold my sisters in contempt for saying a quote is from Strong's Commentary when it was from Strang's.

'That you have been given a great intellect is not something to be proud of; it is a burden to bear. It is muscle to be used in lifting greater weights than others can lift. That, little brother, that is why I'm trusting you with this. It is a heavy burden, I know. And this is why I don't give it to some sycophant who would obey simply because of who I am. Your heart is true, your mind is good, and now we will see about your will. We are grooming you to lead, Quentin; I need not keep that fact in darkness. But you must show yourself worthy of it, in will and action.'

I've always known that I'm smarter than my brothers, but I've always called that knowledge sin. Always focused on the similarities, and the triviality of the differences, even when I would choose not to volunteer the answer to a difficult question simply so my brothers could have a chance to have their own moment in the light of a tutor's approval.

My humility was false. It is a lie, isn't it?

This much is true. I hear the ring of truth in those words, but many shadows hide behind light, and the best lies are those seasoned liberally with truth: salt covering the flavor of rotten meat.

These are not things a luxiat should do.

I realize suddenly that this conversation isn't merely difficult; it's *dangerous*. One does not blithely carry secret death sentences for others. If I say no to this assignment, or threaten to tell others in the Magisterium about it . . .

Dear Orholam, what would Brother Tawleb do?

More specifically, what would he do *to me*?

And there a light dawns. I'm not only the first of my peers; I'm also an orphan, and so studious that I have few friends. If I were to disappear, who would avenge me? The brothers and sisters of the High Magisterium have total control over the just-sworn luxiats like me. He could announce that he had sent me to the reaches of Tyrea on a secret mission, and no one would ever ask about me again.

I'm not a fearful creature. Those who live seeking the light will spend eternity in the light. There is little that can be taken from me that I don't already despise.

'You have had a thought,' Brother Tawleb says. He is still a handsome man, though too lean of face, with a few pockmarks that a beard would have covered. A year into his full vows, he'd fasted for forty days, sprinkling ashes in his hair, and had shorn his beard, had given away all his belongings to the poor, and renounced the privileges of his birth and wealth. Paradoxically, that had only cemented in everyone's mind his birth and wealth, and wedded to it an air of deep righteousness. His rise in the Magisterium after that had been swift.

Had that been on purpose?

No, no, please no. Such a scheme was worthy of one of the kings of old. A brilliant maneuver by one angling for power. Such should not be the way of the Magisterium. Surely, so close to the light, there should be no darkness.

And yet the heaviness in my heart, my inner light itself, tells me the truth of this. I have mentally elevated my brothers, have honored them as more than men, better than men. That fawning adoration is blindness, too. But my heart despairs to see the truth.

I say, 'Many thoughts, and some contradictory. I can see what you meant by a heavy weight, big brother.' It is true, but not the truth he thinks it is.

He chuckles mirthlessly.

'I will trust you,' I say, lying to a brother for the first time in six years. 'But I ask that you trust me, too.'

'You think my entrusting you with such orders doesn't show trust?' he asks archly.

'Not the orders, the why. Why are the orders necessary? Orholam gave me the mind he did. When I stand before him for the judgment, I cannot tell him in good conscience that I didn't ask why one of his innocent children deserved death. That a church father told me to won't be sufficient. He hasn't given me such blind faith.'

He exudes an air of deep sadness. 'I'm not sure you're ready for that knowledge yet.'

'I'm not sure I'm ready for this action yet,' I say. I hurry to add, 'Big brother.' But I may have been just a little too glib. Too smart.

He looks at me sharply, and something in that gaze reminds me that here is a man willing to sign a secret death sentence. I may not fear death, but I have no *wish* to die, and this man could not only order my death, he could – quite openly – send me to some living hell. There are always more luxiats needed to minister to leper colonies, to evangelize the Angari (and be martyred doing it), to take the news of Orholam's love beyond the Cracked Lands. But he doesn't look like he wants to throw away a perfectly good tool at the first difficulty in its use.

He says, 'There is a holy relic that the High Magisterium has been entrusted with since the days of Karris Shadowblinder. During the False Prism's War, Andross Guile seized it from us. He then claimed to have lost it, and accused us of stealing it from him, but we know this to be a lie. Andross Guile is an atheist, and a devious one at that. You must understand, I'm already telling you too much.' His voice is low and thready. I could swear there's real fear in it.

'How do we know he was lying?' I ask. I want to ask what the relic is, but I can tell he won't divulge any more than he must.

Big Brother Tawleb chews his lip. 'Though they pretend to be at each other's throats, Gavin Guile is still the Prism. He wouldn't be if Andross really opposed him.'

'So this relic is necessary to keep power?'

Brother Tawleb blanches momentarily. Guessed it. Or he's a better liar than I'd thought.

Orholam have mercy, what am I doing?

'That's more than you need to know, and let me enjoin you never to speak of this with anyone, until you sit on the High Magisterium yourself. You understand?'

I do. Orholam's tears, *until* I sit on the High Magisterium?! He says this not like it's bait to tempt me, but as if it's a foregone conclusion. I nod.

'The High Magisterium was . . . content to let this travesty pass.' He grimaces, and I can tell there's a whole lot more to it than that. 'Because the High Lord Prism has been a very reasonable friend and ally to us, despite his hidden alliance with his father. And because he has at most five years left. His father, our real enemy, has less time. We can deal patiently with provocation and take back what is ours after he dies, without any disruption among the faithful.'

The relic has been gone for at least sixteen years, and you haven't tried to do anything to get it back? I don't believe it. You all must have failed, spectacularly, and been warned that another attempt would mean some great vengeance. The Magisterium is patient, but it isn't that patient.

Orholam, he's lying to me. Easily. In multiple ways. How can a High Luxiat lie so blithely?

'But there's a young man who just came to the Chromeria, Kip Guile. At first, they claimed he was a bastard, and High – we – thought . . .' He's almost given away whoever it is who agrees with him in the High Magisterium. 'We naively thought that might be the end of it. The Guiles have no heirs, nor does Gavin seem interested in producing any. We thought perhaps we could do nothing, and the relic would revert to our care still. But now they've named him a legitimate son. A lie, no doubt, but it means he will inherit. Kip's appearance takes the theft of our relic from being an insult that we knew would be remedied to being the prospect of our prerogative lost and the Magisterium marginalized, forever.'

So this artifact is something on which the Magisterium thinks *all* of its power rests.

I say, 'But the boy himself, he may be amenable to reason. He might give it over. He's an innocent.'

'This is war; innocents die for the sins of the powerful.'

Brother Tawleb thought he meant the sins of Andross Guile, but I'm not so sure he's right. That innocents die in war is a fact. It is unavoidable that when siege engines obliterate a city wall, the children in the houses beyond it often die.

But *targeting* children is something else altogether.

He continues, 'When the Magisterium is weakened, everything every luxiat does is weakened. We minister to the refugees of war, but without power, how can we get the funds we need from the Spectrum to pay to send luxiats to give succor to those refugees? We feed the poor. We treat lepers. We heal the sick. Most of the money comes from alms, but there are times when alms can't arrive fast enough. Can you imagine if we were faced with a flood on the coastal plains of Paria, and we had to wait until all seven satrapies heard about it, donated, and shipped their gifts here, then we bought the necessary supplies and sent the luxiats there? It would be months. Months in which how many innocents would die? Without the power to do good, what good can we do?'

Pray. The glib answer is also the scriptural one, the one every luxiat has been taught for hundreds of years. It is not by our power that Orholam's will is accomplished, but by his. What are our black robes but a constant reminder of our own emptiness, our own need for Orholam's light? And our need for his power.

In pursuing Orholam's business, Brother Tawleb has forgotten Orholam himself.

'This is very troubling, big brother, but I hear the ring of truth in your words.' I bow my head. 'I will pray for his soul. And deliver your message.'

'I don't want you to deliver a message, Quentin Naheed.'

'Pardon?'

'I want you to deliver a bullet.'

Chapter 61

Kip came back from training to find his room trashed. His mirror was broken. The legs of his chair were broken. His pillow was slashed open. His mattress was slashed open. The coin purse with his wages he kept hidden on a roof beam had been stolen. His desk's surface had been scored with a knife, his inkwell upended all over it. His chamber pot had been filled by whoever had done this, and had been emptied in the middle of his bed. A note, carefully tented on heavy wood pulp paper, sat on the desk, slowly wicking up ink.

'I'm done playing games. Come see me immediately. – T.G.'

T.G. The Guile. Because that's how Andross sees himself. Not as Andross, not as the Red, not even as the promachos, but as the representative of all that is this family. That was the most important thing, to Andross Guile.

The urine was incredibly pungent.

Ugh. Someone's not drinking enough water.

And to think of that first, someone's been training with the Blackguard too much.

But aside from that wry thought, Kip was oddly unmoved.

So his stuff had been smashed. So what? He'd had less in the past. So his money had been stolen. So what? He didn't need money. He had friends now, and work to do, things to accomplish. That was infinitely more precious, wasn't it?

He stared at the mess and knew that he wouldn't even have to clean it up himself. There were slaves whose services he could borrow from the Chromeria. If this was meant to be a kick in the nuts, old man, you've missed. This is barely a kick in the thigh.

In fact, more than anything else this does, it tells me about you. If you did it to irritate me, it's because you imagined it would work. You imagined it would work because it would work on you. So this is the worst you can imagine happening to you? Can't bear to be disrespected, can you? Interesting. I'll remember that.

Kip's first urge was to go somewhere else, anywhere else. But passive defiance was the old Kip. Passive defiance was indistinguishable from cowardice. He told himself it wasn't that he cared if Andross thought he was a coward; it was what he thought of himself. He was afraid of the old man. He could accept that fear. It was perfectly rational. But to let himself be controlled by his fear . . .

Funny how I'm echoing things I've heard in Blackguard training as if they're my own thoughts.

Enough thinking. Kip stepped into the hallway. He spied a slave approaching. 'Calun!' he called. 'Who's your master?'

'I serve at the pleasure of Gariban Navid,' the man said, obviously not appreciating being singled out.

'He's a discipulus?'

'Yes, sir.'

'There's been a crime here. Report it to the Black's desk downstairs. You're allowed to cut to the front of the line. And ask that they send slaves to clean up the mess once the Black's men are finished investigating.'

Slaves not serving Colors could be compelled by any free man or woman in an emergency or to report a crime. Of course, it was a privilege that the wise exercised with caution. No one liked a stranger commandeering his property.

'Yes, sir,' the man said.

'Hold,' Kip said. He dug into his purse. One didn't tip slaves, and Kip only had three danars left, but hell with that. He gave the slave two of them. 'Thank you,' he said.

The slave sneered, like Kip didn't know what he was doing, like Kip was an uncouth mixed breed.

He began walking toward the lifts, and realized that the slave's presence was terribly convenient. He turned.

'Oh, and if it was you – drink more water,' Kip said.

'Sir?'

'Kidney stones. I hear it's like having the tip of your penis pounded with a hammer.'

The slave's face iced over. He looked like he wanted to spit in Kip's face. 'I've been cut, *sir*.'

'Oh. So there's a bright side to gelding. Never would have thought. Carry on, then.'

Kip knew that he should be taking advantage of his walk to form a plan, an approach to the most masterful manipulator in the Chromeria, but his thoughts kept going in circles. He nodded to the Blackguards, waving the letter in their direction, and opened the door to Andross Guile's rooms without knocking. It wasn't locked. That was sort of funny. Andross was so certain that his reputation would scare the hell out of people that he didn't even have his slave lock his door or command the Blackguards to maintain his privacy. Unless, of course, Grinwoody had simply forgotten to do it. The man was getting older.

A small, mean part of Kip delighted in the hope that Grinwoody was growing senile. He would weep when Andross cast off the old wrinkled sack of excrement. Tears of joy.

Kip moved through the antechamber and saw Grinwoody dozing on his feet, just leaning against the wall next to the door to the inner room. But Grinwoody woke before Kip took three steps.

He was bleary, though, trying to hide that he'd been asleep. Kip handed the old slave the ink-stained note as if it were an invitation and strode right past him.

Andross wasn't in the main room. Startled, Grinwoody hustled to get back in front of Kip. 'You can wait in the – High Lord Guile is—'

'You can kiss the bald spot where my fat thighs rub together,' Kip said. He threw open the bedroom door.

His grandfather was in bed, and he wasn't alone. Worse, Kip had seen the woman lying next to him before. It was Tisis Malargos, heart-shaped face and pale skin. Lots of pale skin. Just like when she'd tried to kill Kip during the Threshing. Tisis Malargos, who had been a Color for the space of only moments before Gavin had unseated her.

Kip was rooted in place. Tisis's hair was piled in delicate blonde curls held in a web of emeralds. And her hand was under the sheets, moving up and – oh, dear Orholam!

She didn't see Kip immediately – or at least he hoped that was why her hand hadn't stopped moving – but Andross Guile did. He looked up at Kip, and Kip could see the sudden war of Andross Guile's natures: the calculating spider, already figuring how to turn this surprise back to his own benefit, versus the Red who'd drafted passion and fire and all things hot and burning for decades.

The worst of it might have been that it was far more shocking to see his grandfather naked than Tisis.

Tisis saw that she'd lost Andross's attention and she followed his gaze. A fraction of an instant of shame passed through her eyes, and then it turned to pure hatred.

'The funny thing is,' Kip found himself saying, 'I think I've seen you naked more times than I've seen you clothed. Huh. I guess if you only have one thing going for you, you've got to play it to the hilt, huh? Too bad such a beautiful package has to house such ugliness.'

Tisis was out of the bed in an instant. She was still wearing a slip, though the straps had been pushed down off her shoulders, so apparently Kip had only interrupted their foreplay. Tisis picked up a vase and hurled it at Kip. Her arm tangled in her slip's straps, and she missed by a league, splashed water over herself, and dropped roses on the floor. And smashed what was probably a priceless vase. 'Get out, you – you fat worm! You detestable little, little – bastard! You—' Her pale complexion flared with rage and frustration as she tried to throw items and words and hike up her straps over her shoulders all at the same time.

Interrupting, Kip said, 'I like, "You fat carbuncle on the ass of a great family." I mean, if we're going for fat jokes. Comparisons with beached whales are routine but acceptable. Bonus points for slipping "oleaginous" in. You know what's sad? What's sad is that you probably think what you're doing is smart. You think you can play Andross Guile and get more out of him than he gets out of you. Pathetic.' Kip's tongue was fully in charge now. And he didn't care. The tongue is a flame, and Kip was throwing fire at every flammable surface he could see. Let it burn. 'You know what else is pathetic? My grandfather is so vain that he's probably convinced himself that you're falling for his charms. Even though he's smart enough to know you're just prostituting yourself. Tell me, Tisis, how do you hide your disgust when you see his body? When you moan, do you worry that he can tell you're putting him on, or do you despise him because you know he can't tell?'

She screamed and threw a pillow at him.

A *pillow*.

'Grinwoody,' Kip said, not turning, but somehow aware of the presence behind him, 'you oleaginous worm, if you so much as touch me, I'll *kill* you. Think twice before you lay hands on a Guile, even an adipose one.' Kip took in red and yellow – there were colors everywhere in this room – and let them swirl under the skin of his face and neck, going visibly down to his hands. It was the magical equivalent of cocking a pistol.

The slave didn't touch him.

Andross Guile got up, impassive. The spider in him had won out. Somehow Kip knew it would be a mistake to think he was less dangerous simply because he wasn't shouting. He was unashamed of his nudity.

Which makes one of us.

'Enough,' Andross said.

'Enough?!' Tisis shouted. 'Enough?'

He slapped her, without passion.

It caught Tisis unaware. His big meaty hand caught her across the neck and cheek. Her head snapped to the side and she dropped to the thick carpet, not even trying to arrest her fall. She was unconscious. For a moment, Kip was afraid she was dead.

Apparently, it was a concern Andross shared. He knelt over her, poking fingers into her neck. Satisfied by what he found, he stood.

'That worked rather better than I expected,' Andross said. 'Grinwoody, put down the knife. My robe. Then attend to Lady Malargos. She's easily embarrassed, so cover her before you use the smelling salts.'

As Grinwoody draped the robe across Andross's bare shoulders, the promachos turned to Kip. 'So, you got my note. I wasn't expecting you yet. Thought you'd sulk for a while. Come, let's sit in my parlor.'

Kip followed him into the main room of the apartments where they'd played Nine Kings so many times. Like this was normal.

'You're not even going to try to deny it?' Kip asked. 'You trashed my room and pissed on my bed. Destroyed everything. Stole my money.'

'Well, not personally. Brandy?'

'No, I don't want your damn brandy!'

'That's too bad.' Andross poured two glasses anyway, and put one in front of Kip. He sat in his chair and gestured for Kip to sit across from him. 'Knowledge of fine alcohols is mostly an affectation, but an important one. Men respect those who have greater knowledge of the trivial than they do, when that trivia is costly. Nothing more so than spirits.'

'Here's the thing,' Kip said. He was saying 'Here's the thing' a lot recently. It irritated him. Why didn't he just launch into what he had to say? 'Here's the thing.' Dammit, twice! 'It isn't that you would tear up my room that I find surprising. You've tried to have me killed before, so I don't really think anything is beneath you. It isn't even that you would claim the action after you did it. I know you like watching people jump. I think you were trapped in this room so long becoming a wight that you needed people to come to you so you didn't only hear second- or third-hand accounts. You learned to become obvious so you'd get the thrill of having some power in this world. I understand all that,' Kip said. 'You're a pathetic shut-in who is suddenly not shut in anymore, and you aren't adjusting to it well.'

Andross's eyes, so amused mere seconds ago, turned into wells of darkness. He sipped his brandy as if watching Kip dig his own grave.

'Here's what I don't understand,' Kip said. 'How could you be so *stupid*?'

An arched eyebrow.

'I am of you,' Kip said. 'I am Guile as much as you are. True, I have a scrap of decency, but only a scrap. How do you think you can treat a Guile with such disregard and get away with it? Because I am you. I'm as cold as you, I'm as smart as you, and when you push me, I'm as evil and cruel as you. I have a thin film of goodness floating on the top of my Guile, grandfather, but I don't know how senile you must be to miss just how thin it is.'

'Hmm. Words, like the stench of a fart,' Andross said. He waved a hand as if to dispel them. 'You're marshaling them better than you did, but don't bring your games to me. We're past that now. There is nothing about you that inspires fear, Kip. Your very name is insubstantial. Kip.' He smirked condescension. 'Words without actions are weightless. Throw them against this wall, and see? Nothing.'

Kip wondered how fast he could draft. He wondered if it was faster than Grinwoody and Andross together. He wanted to kill them both. He wanted to stand up and piss on Andross Guile himself to show what he thought of him. But he didn't think he could get away with it, and having emptied both barrels of his rhetoric in Andross Guile's face and having hit nothing, he felt suddenly vulnerable, empty. There was no more powder at hand. He was the barely acknowledged bastard, alone, insulting the Guile, throwing epithets and disrespect at the promachos himself.

And all he had at hand was the fact that he didn't care if he wrecked himself.

Paltry ammunition indeed. He did his best to keep his sudden fear off his face, but if there was one emotion Andross Guile was attuned to, it was others' fear. He fed on it.

'Want that brandy now?' Andross asked archly, the very personification of a lupine grin.

'I'll take it,' Kip said, keeping his voice level.

'No you won't,' Andross said.

The glass was sitting within easy reach. Kip thought of snatching for it – and then thought, how fast Fortune's wheel turns. One moment, I threaten death in high dudgeon. The next, I grub for a glass of brandy.

And this was part of Andross Guile's curious power. Another lord might have thought denying his guest a drink was simple rudeness, and been above it. Andross Guile didn't mind if he lowered himself, as long as he lowered his opponent more. Indeed, shame was a tool to be used against others, because Andross himself was shameless.

Perhaps literally so. He had gotten out of bed naked, without even acknowledging the fact. He seemed unperturbed about being naked, despite having all the spots and wrinkles and sagging skin of a man his age. Though Kip could swear that the paunch Andross had carried was shrinking, he stood at the antipodes from his beautiful son Gavin. Nor did he seem more than peeved at being interrupted pre-coitus.

Perhaps Kip was a poor judge. His own glass of self-horror was constantly full, so the slightest additional drip made the whole thing spill over. But even a normal person would be embarrassed at such a thing, wouldn't they?

Kip had assumed that his grandfather was ashamed, and had simply controlled it. That his sudden rage had been a cover over the embarrassment. What if, instead, there was a simple void where shame would be for others, and the rage had been merely for Kip interrupting whatever plan Andross had in place to snare Tisis?

A dozen times, Kip had wondered how his grandmother, by all accounts a good woman, had loved this man.

And now another thought occurred to him. What if, instead of loving Andross, she'd loved the world? What if she'd seen herself as the only one who could keep this wolf from the flocks? Felia Guile had been smart, everyone agreed on that. She'd been an orange. She'd been the only person who could get Andross Guile to change his mind. She'd been the bulwark against the storm.

And now she was gone.

Kip was staring at an old man with saggy skin sitting in a

faded robe, the bare skin of his legs almost translucent, almost obscene in itself – and he was the one who suddenly felt naked.

'What do you want?' he asked. 'You're old. What does winning even look like for you?'

'Old?' Andross chuckled. 'I've got a good twenty years left. Kip, if you and Zymun don't pan out for me, I can start a new family and still have time to groom the next generation. I have the options of a young man again, but with all the advantages I didn't have when I was young. Do you not know your family's history?'

Kip wasn't looking for a lesson. 'I looked back as far as my grandfather and gave up in disgust,' he said. It was the best insult he could slip around the thick knot of fear blocking his throat.

'A weaker man would say I owe you, Kip. For what you did on that ship about my . . . surfeit of red. But I'm not that man. I respect that you have the strength to not be groveling at my feet. However. Defiance is initially interesting, but it grows tiresome quickly.'

'I'd love to hear about the family,' Kip said snidely. The mere fact that he could say 'the' family and not 'your' family was a huge victory.

'You've killed my desire to reminisce. Let it be enough to say that I earned everything we have. By my generation, we were wool merchants – wool merchants with debts and a worthless title that my drunken wastrel older brother nearly sold to pay them. Everything we are – even you, little bastard who's weaseled his way into legitimacy – is because of what I've made us.'

'You wrested control of the family from your brother?' Kip asked, incredulous.

'Wrested? I've had more trouble with a bowel movement. I handed Abel a stack of papers for his signature when he was hungover. He barely glanced at them. I paid his own steward a few danars to countersign as a witness, saying it was contracts for warehouses. He didn't read them either. I seized all the accounts, and my brother didn't even have the money to pay a solicitor to bring it to a magistrate. Nor the friends willing to lend him such sums.'

Kip reached out for the brandy, unthinking, and this time Andross let him take it. 'Oh, thanks,' Kip said automatically.

Andross grinned, as if this too were a victory.

'You're telling me that three generations of Guile brothers have been at each other's throats?' Kip asked.

'Three? No. Six that I know of. There was a tale that a witch cursed us when Memnon Guile wed her and then, as we Guiles do, cheated on her. Or more precisely, she found out that he was already wed back home. He left her broken-hearted and wandered the world, having adventures, and when finally he arrived home years later, he was murdered by his brother, who had taken to . . . comforting his wife in his brother's absence. Since then. That was six hundred years ago, though I personally doubt that our blood has even a drop of that Guile's blood in it. Many other families have taken the names of the heroes of old; I'm not sure why we would be different. Not that such a thing bears repeating in public, yes? Regardless, the tale held enough force that it was said in our family that if your wife was older, and you already had one son, not to have any more children, lest you end up with two boys. Not that a son and a daughter guaranteed any better. Selene Guile the First had more mercy than most of the men in our family – or less, depending on what you value. She exiled her brother Adan Guile, after castrating him so that he would have no heirs. She managed to get one of the kings of her era to make the family name and title matrilineal. Which it stayed for a hundred and fifty years, until an enterprising Guile son managed to wrest control back.'

Kip took a drink. He barely noticed the burning. 'And you think that's an acceptable way for families to act?'

'Acceptable? One doesn't reason with lions. One doesn't accept reality. One adapts to it.'

'But you aren't like my father, you didn't adapt to a situation where your brother was betraying you. *You* were the betrayer.' The words had sounded so logical, so reasonable in Kip's head before he said them. But as they came out the blunderbuss that was his mouth, they expanded into a razor cloud.

Andross Guile's expression froze, his knuckles whitened on his brandy glass, showing the hit. It was with visible effort that he contained his rage. He hadn't become the Red – of all his colors – by accident. 'How is it to be you, Kip? Cocooned in layers of protective ignorance thicker than your blubber, a blundering whale with sperm for your brains and unintentional ruins all around? Abel thanked me for saving this family. He thanked me for saving him from a burden he was ill fit to bear, and a string of failures that drove him to self-destruction.'

'So he forgave you. That tells me something about him. What does it tell me about you? Except perhaps—'

'Insolent boy!'

'—that you would destroy a good man who swam seas you wished to call your own? That you are a sea demon, mindless in your territorial rage, destroying your enemies, true, but also driving away even—'

Stop, Kip! Stop before—

'—your own family. Even finally your own wife.'

Oh. Shit.

Andross's eyes glittered, and Kip's training took over. His eyes darted back and forth from the whites of Andross's eyes to his hips: the first places he would be able to detect danger, whether magical or mundane. Then out to his hands, one of which held the crystal brandy glass, which could be flicked toward Kip as a distraction, the other of which could be used to signal Grinwoody.

'Took you long enough,' Andross said. 'Finally reached the bottom of your rhetorical toolbox, have we?'

'Huh?' Kip asked. His sense of impending doom hadn't relaxed one whit, but Andross didn't look dangerous. Everything Kip's gut was telling him was contradicted by what Andross's eyes were saying.

'Bringing up my departed wife. Such an obvious target that I wondered if you were either stupider than I'd imagined, or more self-controlled – and therefore more dangerous – than I'd believed. Turns out I was right about you after all.'

'Did you even—'

Andross raised a finger, and Kip shut up. He hated himself for it a moment later, but his brain must have realized that raised finger was a lifeline, and, for once, had taken control from his tongue.

'Something you should realize,' Andross said. 'Merely because a target's obvious, and an initial line of defenses stands in place, that doesn't mean the target isn't still there, and still soft as an egg in its shell. You understand this, Lard Guile. Your disgusting obesity can withstand one insult, at least to the public eye, but even the slightest brush causes your secret self-contempt and shame to grow. So you've found my obvious weak spot. Congratulations for having eyes. Just know this: Grinwoody, if he says one more word about Felia, blow his brains out.'

Kip heard the *click-clack* of a hammer at his left ear. 'With pleasure, my lord,' Grinwoody said.

Slowly, so as not to be thought to be attacking, Kip glanced at the pistol, and the man. Grinwoody was indeed pleased, and the pistol barrel looked huge. Too close to Kip's eyeball for him to see how good the quality of it was, how likely to misfire. But then, this was Andross Guile's pistol. It would be the best. Kip was getting faster at drafting, at moving, but he wasn't this fast. Not yet.

'You wouldn't,' Kip said. Stupid thing to say. Grinwoody was even standing off to the side so that the gore – and possibly the bullet – wouldn't fly from Kip onto Andross.

'If you think I'm bluffing,' Andross said, leaning forward to pour himself more brandy, 'say her name.'

The moment stretched between them like a lazy cat. Kip knew already that he was going to fold. Andross knew it, too.

'Well, that was a great talk, grandfather.' A little needle to drive home the past loss on that count. 'Are we done here?'

Shouldn't have asked permission. Kip stood. Should have stood first.

'The thing that astounds me, grandson,' Andross said, embracing the loss, showing it didn't hurt him as much as Kip hoped. Probably deceitfully, but still. Damn. '—is that it must be equally obvious to both of us that I am your only hope. Our family's enemies will try to destroy you, and our family's friends won't try to save you, because they know I despise you. To say nothing of what I may do to you myself. Yet you choose this path. Still. Your father's gone, surely dead by now.

The facts have changed, but you haven't. Held too long, stubbornness is indistinguishable from stupidity.'

'And would you respect me if I'd come in here and licked your boots?' Kip asked.

Andross Guile looked at him like he was speaking a foreign language. 'Respect? Kip, I've destroyed many men I respected. If you wish to add yourself to that list, you're close to earning the destruction, if not the respect.'

'Please,' Kip said, 'underestimate me. It will only make this sweeter.'

Andross grinned wryly, genuinely amused, and it was disconcerting to see that grin. It was all Gavin Guile, and the sense of bereavement Kip felt at seeing that winsome grin on this monster's face threw him off balance. 'If your strategy rests on being underestimated, might not be best to announce such, you think?' Andross asked.

Kip could only find inchoate curses on his once-nimble tongue. He said nothing.

'Enough,' Andross said. He stood and shepherded Kip to the door. He lowered his voice. 'Now. The matter I summoned you for.'

Orholam's knobby knee to my testicles – all this, and we still haven't talked about what he summoned me for?

'The cards,' Andross said quietly as they reached the door. 'I don't know where you've hidden them, but I want them. If you give them to me, you will be my heir. I will take you under my wing and teach you all I know, and I will tell you secrets you cannot conceive.'

The cards? Again? 'If I found them, once I gave them to you, you'd just kill me,' Kip said.

'Voice down,' Andross said. He stroked his chin, thinking. 'Surely Janus Borig told you how they work. I can draft four colors. But one of the colors I lack is blue. I can feel, taste, and sense what happens inside the cards, but I can't *see* anything. In order to use the cards to their fullest, I need a full-spectrum polychrome. The other polychromes are . . . unacceptable for various reasons. I need you, and I would have a continuing need for you. And you would need me to teach you how to translate knowledge into power after I'm gone. If anything, you would be the partner in the superior position.'

Kip blinked. It made too much sense. 'If I did this,' he said, 'I'd keep the cards in my possession. Otherwise, if you tired of me, you could simply find someone who drafts the colors you lack and put together the pictures for yourself, albeit more slowly than I could do it for you.'

'Done,' Andross said. 'With one caveat: my card, my sons' cards, and my wife's are mine. If you even look at them before you hand them over, this deal is moot. Think on it. I'll give you until your half brother arrives or until Sun Day, whichever comes first. Understand, though, if you try to hand over the cards to someone else, I'll have no choice but to kill you. Your time is running out. Grinwoody?'

The slave made a small, unobtrusive sound to signal his presence.

Kip looked from one to the other. Why were they all still whispering? Why were they standing right at the door to the promachos's room?

'How much did she overhear?'

Grinwoody shot a glance at Kip, as if wondering that Andross wished Kip to hear this, then said, 'Most everything you said at the couch. She awakened almost immediately, and moved to eavesdrop soon after. She won't have been able to hear any of this.'

'Well, then, Kip, your move,' Andross said. 'Unless I miss my guess, she'll try to exploit the schism in our family, and being the green that she is, she'll be impulsive enough to think she needs to act immediately, so she won't wait for instructions from her much more formidable sister Eirene. I would imagine Tisis will come to speak to you in tears at some point this week, playing the damsel in distress. That tends to work well on men who wish they were strong. Don't thank me, she's too young for my tastes, and as you surmised, not good at feigning pleasure. It's a skill most women pick up early, so I'm not sure if she's stupid or stubborn. Quite the hotblood, though, according to her best friend. Eager for the bed, though she's kept her suitors short of the jade gate itself.'

'Jade gate?'

'Her quim. It's her family's horse trader roots showing through. They've been nobles a bare century. Knowing how some value such things, she's intended to sell her virginity dearly, even if it's virginity only by the most technical of definitions. Her friend, being her friend, swore up and down that her chastity, such as it is, wasn't merely for bargaining purposes, though. She claimed Tisis has always had romantical notions about her first time being special. Hmmph, youth. I imagine she'll be too smart to lead her efforts on you with seduction, but as long as you play your cards right, she'll flop on her back in no time. She did for me. Not sure how you'll fit into the *special* first-time. But she'll remember it forever, and surely that is one definition of special, is it not?'

'Do you poison every well you drink from?' Kip asked. The sheer meanness of the man baffled him.

'I just told you, I didn't drink from that well. I left it for you, on purpose, in case you were delicate about sharing with a better man. You throw my kindness in my face. Perhaps you are thick in more than the obvious sense. We've spoken too long. Begone.'

Kip kept his curses and his questions to himself, and obeyed his grandfather's order, just like any other soldier in the promachos's army. The Blackguards outside the door said nothing, but then, that was what they were supposed to do, wasn't it?

Four puzzled slaves were waiting for him at his room. 'My lord,' one said, 'there was a crime reported?'

Kip stepped past them into the room. Everything was pristine. The desk had been replaced. The feather bed had been replaced. Every surface was gleaming with polish. Even his purse was back in its hiding spot. Kip dismissed the slaves with an apology. They looked at him like he was crazy.

And who's to say they're wrong? What am I doing?

I'm being used in fights I know nothing about, and I'm taking sides based purely on the personal charisma of the players, not on what's wrong or right, or where I should be, or even what's most advantageous. I've been acting like a child.

Andross knew exactly what I was going to do when he trashed my room. I'm that predictable.

He felt suddenly sick to his stomach.

In Nine Kings, I'd be the Blunderbuss – good only for short ranges, and easily picked up by any enemy and pointed wherever he wished.

What am I going to do?

Chapter 62

~Shimmercloak~

The perspective isn't right. It's hovering around waist height, swinging back and forth. It's a hand, swinging as a young woman walks. She has something cupped in her hand so that it will be concealed from anyone in front of her, but it's longer than her hand, and this perspective is perfect to see as much of the weapon as possible.

This card isn't a person; it's a thing, and the perspective is what the artist had chosen to show.

A short, jagged blade, obsidian edges with an ivory core. Not so much shaped like a knife as like a shark's tooth, a broad triangle with a winking diamond in the center.

The bouncing accelerates as the young woman begins jogging.

Before I can see much more, the perspective swings violently as the blade slams into a woman's side, is pulled out, bloody, and then poised at her throat.

With the blade at her throat, now I can see her face. Her irises are stained red, halfway to the halo, and wide with fear and pain. The attacker's arm is threaded through hers, and the drafter is turned toward a red-painted wall.

The drafter regains her wits; she drafts, soaking up red light, the whites of her eyes filling as with smoke – but this is what the assassin is waiting for. The obsidian edge is rammed into the side of her throat, and suddenly, that black shiny stone is somehow alive. Blood gushes out, and I can't see if the red that blankets the ivory is from the blood spilling from her neck, or if it glows with an internal light.

I see the drafter's eyes bleach, not only the natural recession of red from the whites as a drafter finishes drafting, but deeper As if something is sucking the life's blood from her. Her sclera go pure white, and then the impossible happens. Her crimson-stained irises – red halfway to the halo – dim and then disappear. As the light of life goes out of her eyes, her eyes are left their natural brown.

I've seen dead drafters. Even as a warrior's scars don't disappear in death, so a drafter's scars stay with her: her eyes don't bleach.

The assassin is already moving, carefully dragging the drafter into an alcove, piling rubbish on her body, using her cloak to clean hands and blade. She tucks the blade away, and my perspective is lost in darkness.

In darkness I stay for long and long, jarred and jostled. Is she running? I lose all track of time. I may be here forever.

The blade comes out in a room lit with lanterns, is handed over to a bent-backed old woman. She washes it in a basin. But the blood doesn't wash from the diamond. It was a diamond, wasn't it?

Now, despite washing, it's a ruby.

No, not a plain ruby. The colors undulate, swirling, pulse like the beating of a heart. The old woman chuckles, delighted. She holds up the living stone to a magnifying lens, studies it minutely.

She moves to a work table, puts the ruby in a delicate vise. In a few minutes, she's bored a tiny, shallow hole into the gem. Satisfied, she prepares the rest of the room. She pushes everything else off her work table and carefully drapes a long muddy-brown cloak across it. She pulls forward a choker concealed in the collar. Multicolored chains connect choker to cloth. With deft hands, she cracks open the choker, exposing the knotted chains themselves.

Adjusting the chains so they sit just so on the bench, she pulls a stool over, and puts on clear, magnifying spectacles. She draws the ruby forth again, and takes the chimney off her lantern. She screws a tiny post of ivory and obsidian shard into the ruby, and blows out the lantern.

The sound of chains and gears, and then a crack of light.

The ceiling splits open and full-spectrum sunshine pours in, bounces off mirrors, and is focused directly on the old woman's hands. She holds the ruby full in the light with the post down, like one would hold a pen.

The post – her nib – goes red, and she begins dabbing living red ink onto the exposed wires where the cloak's collar connects. The post writhes with luxin, and the collar chains devour it. The cloak's own color changes, becoming a redder brown in streaks as she moves from chain to chain. She reaches the end finally, and as she stops, I see that the ruby is now as drained of color as the murdered drafter was.

Clicking her tongue, the old woman examines her work. She sets aside the diamond, runs her hand over the cloth, and finally snaps shut the choker over its chains.

'My part is finished,' she says. 'But to make this cloak a shimmercloak, you need to find yourself a Prism willing to give you his life and Will.' She barks a laugh. 'Unless you've got some other splitter of light at hand?'

Chapter 63

Teia was walking through the evening crowds to clear her head after the afternoon Blackguard practice. Kip had skipped again. That was happening more and more often. Despite that, he wasn't falling behind. Between his private training sessions with Karris Guile and sparring with the squad under Tremblefist's personal instruction – and they'd all taken Kip under their wings, giving him pointers at every opportunity – Kip was actually worth his spot on Squad Aleph now. And not just for his mind.

Fine, primarily for his mind.

People were bumping into Teia. She didn't have a purse on her belt, so she wasn't terribly alert, but it was irritating. For all the good that being small did her sometimes, when she moved through a crowd, if she wanted go faster than a crawl, she had to really move, ducking and dodging in a way that had become second nature to her, but doing that didn't exactly engender the meditative thoughtfulness she was seeking. No one bumped into Commander Ironfist. Not on accident, anyway.

Teia remembered an instance of a young woman stepping into the commander's path just in time to be bowled over. The commander's reflexes were quick enough that he'd practically snatched the woman out of the air. She'd purred, melting into his arms. The Blackguards had laughed.

The commander hadn't been amused. As always, he was on his way somewhere more important. He lifted the woman in front of him – and it's not easy to look seductive when a man lifts you by the armpits – stared her hard in the eye until she nearly wet herself, and dropped her off to the side without a word.

It had kept that woman from ever trying it again, but had backfired where others were concerned.

Teia grinned at the memory and finally emerged from the market. She wasn't even sure where she was now. Not that it was possible to get truly lost on Big Jasper. She put her hands in her pockets – Blackguard trousers had pockets. She loved them.

There was a note there.

She pulled it out, and a hollow formed in her stomach. Fine flash paper, of course. If she tried to simply open it – or anyone else tampered with it – it would burn up in an instant. She wondered if Karris had been good enough to pass her the orders herself, or if she had people to do that now.

She tore into the bottom right corner, edged the tear around the left side like she'd been taught, and finally opened the note: 'Kip is going to be assassinated on a raid, today. Most likely by a Blackguard. Several, possibly. They'll be at the docks before noon. Save him.' It was in Karris's hand.

Teia's breath caught. The docks. The squad's current safe house was on the way. She ran.

In minutes, she arrived at the safe house. She knocked the code rapidly on the wood, and then opened the door. Cruxer was alone inside, seating a new flint in the cockjaw of his pistol. He looked up. He frowned as soon as he saw the expression on her face. 'What's going on, Teia?'

'Kip. It's Kip. He's going to be murdered. We have to go help!' Teia said.

'What? What are you talking about?'
'Now, Crux!'

Chapter 64

Kip was sitting at his desk with mounds of books threatening to bury him when someone knocked on his door. It could only be Tisis Malargos. Kip had been preparing for this since he'd left the old man's room. He still wasn't ready.

The truth was, Kip didn't really know Tisis. Sure, she'd pretended that she was going to kill him during his Threshing. Sure, she'd single-handedly made him fail by giving him back the bell rope after he'd thrown it away, but perhaps Kip shouldn't take it personally. He was starting to understand what it was to inherit the enmities of your people. How could it have been personal? She'd never even met him before that day.

And of course, Kip had later killed her uncle. That kind of made them even, didn't it?

He got up, braced himself, and opened the door.

It wasn't Tisis. It was two Blackguards, Buskin and Lytos, looking almost like a comedy, Buskin was so short and Lytos was so tall. But they weren't smiling.

'Know how we been searching the seas?' Buskin asked.

'For my father?' Kip asked eagerly.

'No,' Lytos said at the same time Buskin said, 'Yes.'

They shot a look at each other.

'No need to keep it from him if he knows,' Buskin said. 'Some of us go looking for the bane, and some of us go looking for the Prism. It's supposed to be secret.'

'My grand— the promachos told me about it,' Kip said. 'And he said I'd get a chance to go.'

'This ain't that. With so many of us full Blackguards training everyone, Watch Captain Fisk has got us dipping into the nunks to help look for bane. Your number came up.'

'Watch Captain Fisk?' Kip said. 'You mean Trainer Fisk?'

'You'd know about his promotion and the schedule if you bothered coming to practice more often,' Lytos said in his odd eunuch's tenor.

Fisk had been promoted to Karris's old position as watch captain? That was a small disaster. Fisk had worked with Andross to try to keep Kip out of the Blackguard. For all the times he'd seemed friendly, he was a traitor at the core.

'How long we going to be gone?' Kip asked.

Lytos said, 'Back before dark. They don't want the nunks missing any training – any *more* training, maybe I should say – so you all don't do overnights.' He looked around Kip's room. 'Nice quarters. You sure you want to give this up for a barracks?'

Right. Because my life is so wonderful and easy. Kip let retorts dance behind his teeth, as if taking the jibe with good humor. 'Enough of the easy life for me. I'm ready to buckle down and really start to work.'

'Good. Well, let's get to it, then,' Buskin said. He really was incredibly short. Even with his silly high shoes.

Suddenly though, Kip really didn't want to go with these two. There was something off. They hadn't ever before been hostile to him. It was like something had worked them up. Had he done something to insult them? Maybe it was like his father had warned him: they disliked how easy it seemed he was getting a good life handed to him.

Whatever it's costing me, at least I'm coming out ahead of Lytos, whose parents made him a eunuch in hopes it would help him get into the Blackguard.

And it was Kip's first chance to get to take part in the search for his father himself, even if only tangentially.

He grabbed his stuff. 'Ready.'

Chapter 65

Teia and Cruxer ran into Winsen not a block from the safe house. Cruxer hesitated. They didn't know Winsen as well as they knew each other, but he was in the squad.

'We'll need all the help we can get,' Teia said, but she let Cruxer make the call.

'Someone's going to try to kill Kip,' Cruxer told Winsen. 'We're heading to the docks to stop them.'

Give Cruxer this: right or wrong, he made his decisions quickly. And his penchant for trusting people and believing in them might get him killed eventually, but it meant that the circle of people who liked him and wanted him to approve of them was always growing.

Winsen blinked once. It was the closest to surprise Teia had ever seen from him. 'Then you don't want to go to the docks. I passed him not two minutes ago. He said he was going out bane hunting with Lytos and Buskin, but they'd told him to meet them in Little Hill. He was headed there.'

'The slums? Why there and why go sepa—' Cruxer started to ask.

'Fewer witnesses,' Teia said. 'If they go out to sea and come back without him, they'll be suspected. He meets them in a slum, they kill him, and if the deed itself isn't witnessed, it's clean.'

Cruxer hesitated, appraising her. 'Sometimes you scare me, Teia.'

'I'll get my bow,' Winsen said.

'Be quick,' Cruxer said. As Winsen ran off, he breathed a curse. 'Blackguards, Teia. How do we kill Blackguards?'

'By surprising them,' she said.

'That's not what I meant.'

'I know.'

He looked at her and was suddenly just a boy again. 'How could they?'

'Ask it later. Captain.'

The pain didn't leave his eyes, but the boy in them receded. 'Right,' he said. 'Treat it like Specials. We could be wrong, so we follow as close as we can without being seen. If they're guilty, we can expect them to be nervous. Teia, your paryl's no good from a distance, so I want you to follow hard behind them. If you give us the signal, we'll shoot. We see them draw weapons, we shoot.'

'Got it,' Winsen said, rejoining them. He was wearing street clothes now, and holding not one but two bows. One was one of his yew longbows, a foot taller than he was, and the other was a simple recurve that he tossed to Cruxer.

'If we do this, and we're wrong,' Cruxer said, 'we'll look like traitors. It'll be Orholam's Glare for all of us. We don't know that Breaker is who we think he is.'

'We know him,' Teia said. 'That's enough for me.'

'Me, too,' Cruxer said. 'Winsen?'

Winsen shrugged. As ever, he was a loaded musket. He didn't care so much which direction he was pointed, so long as he could fire.

'Then let's go!' Cruxer said.

Without another word, they ran, heedless of who would wonder at them. Cruxer was tall enough that he appeared merely to be loping, though his gait forced Teia to run full out.

When they got to Little Hill, they slowed. They walked briskly, but no faster than many merchants on their errands. With a wink and a smile, Cruxer got an old baker to tell them exactly when some Blackguards had passed through and where she thought they were going.

They pushed faster than they would have if they were tracking anyone else. The likelihood of blundering over their prey at the speeds they were moving was high. But Buskin and Lytos didn't know they were being hunted.

The base of Little Hill was a Tyrean slum. Not precisely dangerous, at least during the day, but the neighborhood bore unmistakable signs of the origins of so many of its residents. Almost half the women wore long tunics over trousers, and the men wore strong green-and-black-patterned tunics, more shapeless than the tailored tunics most people favored on Big Jasper. Most notable, though, was that the domes on the buildings in this area were either perfunctorily small or had been hollowed out. The Tyreans liked to use their roofs as another room – an open room. Most of the hollowed-out domes, standing bare in their frames on flat roofs, at least at one time had shutters, which when closed retained the dome shape, but in their poverty, the people here didn't fix such frippery when it failed.

'Tssst!' Cruxer said.

Teia saw his hand signals: *two blocks ahead, then right. We'll overwatch*.

There wasn't time to see exactly what they planned. Teia jogged toward the corner. It started raining. She threw her hood up, and drew in as much paryl as she could hold. She stepped around the corner, nonchalant, just in case.

Nothing.

She moved down the narrow street at a half jog, as if hurrying from the rain. Dozens of others traversing the same street were doing the same. The only thing she could hope was that Lytos and Buskin were wearing their blacks so they'd be easy to spot.

Throwing glances left and right as she passed intersection after intersection, Teia's heart was beating harder and harder. With people ducking their heads and hurrying, it would make murdering Kip and getting away with it easier and easier.

She heard a musket shot above her and jumped. No, not a musket, someone slamming shut a shutter against the rain. Broken stones and broken bones.

There! She'd crossed one of the crooked alleys and caught a glimpse of black. No street in the city was supposed to be crooked. It made dark places where the light of the Thousand Stars couldn't reach. But slums were slums the world over.

She was only behind the Blackguards by about thirty paces now, and the alley cleared out. No one except Teia and her prey.

And what am I supposed to do when I catch them?

What if Lytos and Buskin were just here to get some gear for their trip? It wasn't out of the question, was it? The Blackguards would have used supplies and weapons from their stores and safe houses near the docks first, but eventually those supplies would be exhausted, and they would have to dip into what they'd planted even in warehouses in the slums. Usually, slaves could do such work, but safe houses were kept secret.

Maybe it was all innocent. Karris could be wrong, right?

The sun was still high in the sky, but the clouds were so thick and black that it was getting dark. The rain became a full downpour, leaving Teia in a race between rising fears and wet-kitten hopes.

She heard Kip's voice and poked one eye around the corner. Too late.

Lytos had drawn a knife, left side, unseen by Kip and was stepping—

He dropped to one knee, almost gracefully, as if making obeisance, the barest whisper of arrow feathers disappearing fully into his armpit. He looked down, doubtless wondering what had happened, but it looked like he was bowing his head to Kip.

'Lytos?' Kip asked, turning, all unaware of what had just happened.

The ting of bare steel hitting a stone as Lytos dropped his blade made Buskin's head pivot sharply. He saw Teia first, then saw Lytos pitch onto his face. The look on his face was pure guilt, then rage.

His hand dipped to his belt where he kept his throwing knives. Being short and not strong, Buskin liked his throwing knives, and he was one of the few people Teia had ever seen for whom throwing knives were not an affectation.

Teia's hand was already up, but it wasn't the familiar paryl that came through her. A wave bigger than her own body rushed through her and snapped like a whip at her fingers.

All the world was fire. She dropped. Kip staggered. Buskin flinched in mid-throw, sending his knife into the sky even as he jumped backward, throwing his hand up over his face.

The wave passed.

Silence. They all looked at each other, staggered. No one was on fire.

An arrow streaked through the space Buskin had been occupying not a heartbeat earlier and shattered against the stone wall beside him.

The moment snapped; Buskin fled as if loosed from a bow himself.

Kip was agog, looking at Teia and then himself, apparently wondering why he wasn't on fire. 'What th—'

'Get him!' Teia shouted. She bolted after Buskin. Kip didn't follow, at least not fast enough to be helpful.

Buskin turned at the first intersection, his lead on Teia only thirty paces. Lightning crashed nearby, the frenetic flashing of multiple strikes coming at the same instant thunder rattled windows through all of Big Jasper. The lightning threw a shadow into the intersection. Faster than her conscious mind could grasp what she had seen, Teia reacted. *Trap.*

She was already sprawling, slipping instead of jumping aside. Her feet skidded across rain-slick stones. One foot shot forward while the other went back. She slid, doing the splits, right past the corner. A glittering blade flashed right over her head.

Buskin staggered, almost stepped on her as his blade didn't meet the resistance he expected.

On hands and feet, Teia scuttled backward. She twisted her wrist on an unseen stone and fell flat on her back.

Buskin advanced, raising his sword for the killing – no wasteful, big, theatrical slash from a Blackguard; he would stab the point straight into her heart, twist quickly in case he'd pierced a little to the right or left, and be gone in less than a second's time.

But as he stepped forward, an arrow flashed past his face. He shot a glance back up the alley, must have seen Winsen or Cruxer or both, and leaped back and away. Teia shot paryl at him from her back, but it shattered easily with his rapid movement.

She struggled to her feet and went after him. Lightning flashed again, this time farther away, hitting the great lightning-catchers above the Chromeria, the boom of thunder following a few heartbeats later. Teia found herself in a market. It was in an uproar. All the shoppers had already departed as soon as the rain began pounding, but the merchants were trapped, gathering their goods, trying to soothe panicking donkeys and oxen. Others were running around their shops, shuttering windows and pulling merchandise inside.

In all the chaos, a lone runner was nearly invisible. Any other time, such a sight would stick out and cause outrage. Now it was one whitecap in a storm-tossed sea.

A crash rang out as a cart lost all the barrels inside it. Teia saw Buskin running past it, having opened the back gate to loose the barrels. One giant barrel ruptured as it fell, and dumped its contents – olive oil – in a vast slick across the wet stones. Half a dozen pedestrians rushing past went down in tangles of limbs. A horse pulling an empty cart shied as its driver sawed on the reins, trying to avoid crushing the fallen. He lost grip of the reins, though – and it was a miracle he did. The horse, head free, looked down and quick-stepped over the people lying at its feet.

But it turned aside to do so, and the wheels of its cart hit the slick and lost traction immediately, sliding the cart inexorably into the olive oil wagon – and blocking the lane entirely.

Teia dodged into another pathway through the market, ran straight into a young woman and knocked her flat. Teia spun out of the collision, jumped over a rack of thobes that had fallen into the street, and kept going.

Something lit the sky that wasn't lightning, but as soon as Teia looked for the luxin strike, she plowed into someone else, much bigger than she was, and turned her eyes back to the market and her target.

She made it to the edge of the market, just in time to see Buskin snatch up two burning lanterns and hurl them at the ground in the alley behind himself. One ignited, but the other didn't – at least until he sprayed the alley with red luxin.

The flames roared up, blocking the alley, and for half an instant Teia thought of trying to leap through the flames before good sense asserted itself. She barely stopped in time. The red luxin would gutter out in a minute at most, but that was too long. She didn't know this part of town well enough to be certain that going one block to either side would take her back to Buskin's path: she might get lucky and find that he'd turned the same way she did – or not.

She was looking for another path, a way to climb around the flames, a window above them in the second story, anything, when Buskin's flames died as if a giant had stomped on them, splattering liquid orange in every direction.

A figure tore past her. Kip.

He was drafting even as he ran. On top of the fire-smothering orange luxin, he threw down planks of green to give himself footing, and sprinted right across where the fires had been.

His momentum carried him past Teia, who was standing

still. He flicked off the spectacles that he was wearing, holstered them in the pouch he wore, and drew out another pair as he ran. He threw a hand up into the air and shot yellow symbols into the sky that dissolved into light even as they arced upward – directions for Cruxer and Winsen about where Buskin was going.

Teia saw them running across a roof, each holding a bow, approaching an alley gap that was too far to jump. Cruxer sped up and leapt anyway – and made it. Winsen followed his lead, except he threw his hands and a gout of unfocused luxin out of them to give himself extra lift the way they'd practiced.

It would have worked if he hadn't been holding the longbow in one hand. Instead, it impeded the luxin thrust and threw him off balance even as he was flying through the air. But Kip was running right under that gap, and he threw up a wide hand of green luxin that bobbed Winsen gently back up into the air. Instead of smashing into the side of the building, Winsen landed sideways just at the top of it. He rolled across the roof and smacked his head on the dome, but was unhurt.

They were almost to the great fish market near the docks when lightning struck again, blinding Teia. The boom of thunder literally threw her from her feet. She tumbled as she'd been taught, throwing one hand down hard so that her head didn't take the impact.

She regained her senses in time to see that one of the Thousand Stars had been struck by lightning. They were supposed to be insulated with the copper lightning-catchers, but either it was gone or hadn't worked. The entire stiltlike Star was leaning, shattering, stones raining down. Then the arch collapsed all at once, coming down in roar of stone and dust in the heavy rain.

The placement couldn't have been worse – right in front of them, and between them and Buskin. As if the gods themselves had intervened to save him. On the other hand, the arch had hit the edge of the building on which Cruxer and Winsen stood. If Cruxer hadn't stopped to help Winsen, he would have been crushed by the falling rock.

Teia stopped behind the rubble. She could climb over it, but every stone was shifting. Too much delay. Oh, hells. Kip!

Kip had been ahead of all of them.

Teia looked for him. He was nowhere in the fish market beyond the rubble.

Oh, no. No no no.

Her heart stopped. The air of the intersection was awash in a cloud of dust, only slowly being beaten down by the downpour. People were screaming, horses were whinnying in terror, but Teia had no mind for any of it. She drafted a paryl torch, the beams of its light cutting through the dust cloud. She charged forward, barely pausing long enough to pull a cloth in front of her face so she could breathe. The ground was littered with broken masonry, shattered mirror-glass, and there – dear Orholam, a body. Was it—

Teia grabbed the hand she could see and pulled. It came out, with half an arm. She held the arm in both hands, part horrified beyond words, part cold and analytical. This arm seemed skinnier than Kip's. The skin was . . . covered in grime, colorless in her paryl vision. She went back to the visible spectrum, but it was too dusty. She couldn't see anything. She turned the arm over, went back to paryl.

No drafter's scars on the hands or wrists.

It wasn't Kip. It was a star tower slave. What were they doing up there in a storm?

She tossed the arm aside. She didn't care about some slave.

A part of her wrote down that thought in stone. It would come back to haunt her. But right now, she didn't care. Kip. Dear Orholam, where's Kip?

She picked her way over the rubble, looking in paryl through the dust.

The rubble ahead of her shifted and sank. Suddenly, she heard coughing. With quick, light steps, she crossed the rubble. There was Kip, upside down. He'd drafted an egg of luxin around himself as the arch fell all around him, but had quickly run out of air and let the egg collapse.

Teia grabbed his hand and pulled him up and out. He was besmirched, the heavy rain turning the dust coating his features into mud in instants.

For a split second, he'd looked so terrified coming out of that little space that Teia couldn't reconcile the little-boy terror on his face with the kind of drafting she'd just seen out of him. He stared at her, frantic, frightened, chest heaving, coughing still.

She tried to hand him a cloth to breathe through, but he swept her up into a bear hug.

For one moment, she was utterly stunned. Then, in the next, a sudden thawing. She hadn't been really touched in so long, she couldn't even remember the last time. Kip's pure, delighted-to-see-you, I-care-so-much-for-you touch? Oh, dear gods. There was something about the pure physicality of it: an acceptance beyond words, a joy that spoke only truth. But she was frozen, too surprised by the sudden emergence of Kip from death, by the flood of emotion. She didn't hug back, even as the complete, total, abject need to hug back rose in her. She wanted to cling to someone – no, not to someone; it wasn't just a need to connect, though it was that, too – to connect with Kip, her friend.

Her best friend. The one who saw her.

The tides rising in her were obliterating, scouring away the dross of every preconception and prejudice.

And Kip dropped the hug, suddenly awkward at her failure to hug back.

No! her mind cried, but her arms – her treacherous arms – didn't rise.

'Sorry. Thanks,' Kip said quickly, as if to cover, as if to ignore, as if he didn't feel rejected.

No, Orholam no, I didn't mean it like that.

But Teia said nothing, didn't move.

Kip turned. They were on the very edge of the rubble – they'd come through it, together. But they were too late. Kip pulled his blue spectacles on. They were miraculously unbroken, and he drafted quickly, again as if it were nothing. In a few moments, there were stairs from where they stood up to the edge of the building where Cruxer and Winsen still stood.

They joined the young men there. They hadn't given up the hunt. They stood ready as hounds at the leash. Cruxer pointed. 'There!'

Buskin was almost through the crowded, emptying fish market. People were running everywhere, still packing up their stalls, trying not to lose all of the day's catch and sales. Winsen was standing with an arrow nocked, though he hadn't drawn it – there was no shot yet, and holding a longbow drawn for any length of time was impossible.

Buskin reached the far side of the market. He turned and grinned fiercely at them. He put his fingers under his chin and flicked them forward in rude salute. Then he turned his back and walked away.

Winsen pulled the arrow back into the big longbow, using the thick muscles of his back to help with the massive draw-weight, even as people ran to and fro, obscuring Buskin. The shot was at least two hundred paces. A young mother tried to pull three children out of the street, but found herself with too few hands, juggling tools in one hand and recalcitrant kids in the other, at least one crying.

'Winsen,' Cruxer said sadly, 'it's too far. You can't—'

Winsen loosed the arrow.

Teia put a hand to her mouth, certain she was going to see a child die. The arrow flew too fast for eyes to follow. She and Kip and Cruxer and Winsen, too, all looked to Buskin. He reached the corner and looked back – and suddenly hurtled to the ground sideways as the arrow ripped through his chest, lodged in whatever mail he was wearing, and flung him down.

It took them several minutes to cross the empty market and get to him. He was dead. No one lingered in the market or the streets. No one wanted to involve themselves in whatever private quarrel this was. Not today, not in the storm and the rain and the lightning that might slay good or bad.

Winsen finally unstrung his great yew bow when he saw that Buskin was dead. He didn't seem moved in the least, other than being satisfied. Cruxer looked at him, disbelieving, and not just of the accuracy of his shot.

'What the hell, Winsen?' Kip asked. 'There were nearly a hundred people here. How'd you even make that shot, with that many innocents in the way?'

Winsen looked at Cruxer, then at Teia, and finally at Kip. Teia had killed before, and it had left her shaken and weepy. She'd been stunned at first, sure, not able to understand or process what had happened exactly. The finality of it had sunk in immediately, so she was slow to judge those who seemed cold when they killed. It wasn't the same for everyone. But Winsen's eyes didn't have that numb look in them that said he hadn't processed the killing yet, that he was stunned. His eyes were clear. Buskin had been a bad man. He needed to be killed. Winsen had done it. What more was there to say or think about?

Winsen shrugged, puzzled. 'I didn't care if I missed.'

Chapter 66

'Why am I reporting to you rather than Commander Ironfist?' Kip asked Karris. He stood in the Prism's quarters in the Blackguard's informal posture, back straight, legs shoulder width apart, hands lightly clasped behind his back. Dressed in his inductee's grays – which were loose and shapeless, standard-issue baggy rather than the tailored, form-fitting luxin-infused clothing full Blackguards earned upon taking final vows – he looked martial. Karris noted the change.

Kip's eyes were no longer simply the striking blue he'd been born with. Green ringed each pupil, many tiny flecks of blue served to subtly brighten his irises, red bloomed like stars or fires, and a close inspection revealed hints of every other color there, too. She would have reprimanded him for burning through his life so quickly if it weren't so hypocritical. He was still stout, maybe always would be, but the baby fat was almost gone from his face, and when he stood here with determination and mild pique at doing something that didn't make sense to him, he hearkened back unmistakably to a young Gavin Guile.

Moreover, his question was a good one, and it deserved better than the lie Karris had prepared. 'Commander Ironfist is a bit busy these days. I'll debrief you and pass on the relevant details to the commander and the White. Though I no longer serve in an official capacity, it is war, and we all serve where we're needed.'

Kip looked stung. 'Not even this is important enough for a

direct report? The betrayal of two Blackguards, and their deaths?'

'We're in a civil war. Betrayal is commonplace. Do you know how many Blackguards we've lost in the sweeps this month?'

'Six,' Kip said.

She stopped. 'That's right.' Kip seemed oblivious at times, as caught up in his own world as sixteen-year-olds get. But maybe he was more aware than she'd credited.

'Tell me everything,' she said.

And he did. It wasn't as good a report as she'd expect from a full Blackguard, but for one unpracticed and ignorant of the expectations for such a report, it was excellent.

'Again,' she said.

He told it again, this time clearer, with fewer oh-I-forgot-to-says. But then he stopped and rubbed his forehead. 'I wasn't going to . . . It doesn't help anyone, but . . .'

'I expect your reports to be fully honest, Breaker,' she said.

'I didn't understand it at the time, and then things happened so fast it kind of got buried, but right before the first arrow took out Lytos, I heard him say, "Fuck it, I can't do this."'

A chill invaded Karris's bones. 'And you took that to mean what?'

'I didn't take it to mean anything. All hell broke loose right then, but looking back, I think he had second thoughts right at the end. I think he was drawing his knife to attack Buskin, not me.'

Lytos. Orholam have mercy. Karris had been holding off her own memories of the big eunuch. He'd been a practical joker with an infectious laugh, constantly short-sheeting the newly sworn Blackguards, putting fire balm in their underclothes, dropping live scorpions in young Blackguards' boots (though he sealed the scorpions' stingers in solid luxin first – he wasn't malicious, just a prankster).

That Lytos might come through and do the right thing at the last second broke her heart for some reason even more than the abstract thought that he might have been deceived or blackmailed into betraying them.

And then to be killed before he could prove his fidelity. Oh, Lytos.

No wonder Kip hadn't told his friends: By the way, one of the men you killed? He was on our side.

'As he lay there, he said something about a luxiat,' Kip said. 'But it wasn't clear. He died before he could tell me.'

His voice was level as he said it, but something in his tone reminded her suddenly that as much as this boy looked like a soldier, stood like a soldier, reported like a soldier, he was also still a boy. 'I'm sorry, Kip,' she said.

'Am I right, not to tell them, I mean?' Kip asked brusquely. He didn't want her softness and understanding now. 'The commander says we're not afraid of the truth, that that's what makes Blackguards different. Am I serving my team by holding this back, or betraying them by not trusting them to handle it?'

'Who took the shot that killed Lytos?' she asked. She knew from his report.

'Winsen,' Kip said, puzzled.

'Then what do you think?' she asked.

His brow furrowed. 'Winsen's . . . different. It doesn't seem to bother him, killing, I mean.'

'There are some few like that,' she said. 'I think if you told Winsen that he would say Lytos shouldn't have been there in the first place. That Lytos put himself in the line of fire, that he gave your team no choice. I think Lytos would agree, don't you?'

'It's just that simple for some people?' Kip asked.

'Some people *are* what they appear.'

'Not enough,' he said. He looked angry – at her. Just the misplaced emotions of youth, or something more particular? Then Kip said, 'When did you know you loved my father?'

It was someone tearing the bandages off a wound. 'Pardon?' she asked.

He didn't repeat the question.

'That is a very personal question,' she said.

'Not really,' he said.

Part of her wanted to slap him for countering her so insolently, but in the next moment she knew that it was really that she wanted to slap Dazen for keeping so many secrets. Now to keep the secrets of that man who might well be dead, she was going to have to lie, too. 'There was a dance. The Luxlords' Ball. I danced with both him and his brother. I think I fell in love with him then.'

'So you always loved Gavin?' Kip asked.

She saw the trap just in time. 'This, this conversation is finished,' she sputtered.

'But you tried to elope with *Dazen*. Why would you do that if you loved Gavin all along? Dazen was the *younger* brother. There was no advantage in marrying him. There was no reason to elope with him except for love.'

'I was young!'

'I'm young. I don't destroy the world over it.'

'You have no idea what you're talking about,' Karris said.

'Because I only get lies and evasions every time I ask.'

It took the wind from her sails, though anything but becalmed. He was right. He deserved the truth, and he couldn't be told the truth. He thought his father was his uncle, and his uncle his father, and he hated the one and loved the other, in the wrong order.

'Kip,' she said quietly. 'How many times have you told the story of what happened to you at the Battle of Ru?'

'I don't know.'

'Yes you do.'

He said nothing for a moment, then gave in. 'Once or twice, when I was with the squad. We'd been drinking. Even in my squad, some of them were so . . . so excited to hear about it. It seems . . . obscene somehow.'

'I was there with you, Kip, and you did nothing wrong. In fact, you were the hero that day.'

The word dropped between them like an ill-fitting garment. Kip couldn't pick it up.

'We all acted bravely, Kip. We all did what we had to, but your actions made all the difference. And you're reluctant to recount them, because anyone who wasn't there can't really understand the terror of that island coming alive and trying to devour us, of those men and women remade into giants, and of that feeling of seeing the Prism himself helpless. Our Prism, who can do everything, for whom all things are easy as breathing, and there he was, *helpless*. You acted like a hero would act, and you got lucky and it mattered. But you know, as warriors know, how easily you could have been unlucky, how others just as brave and braver still did more and greater things, but because they failed or were simply unseen, will never be known.'

Kip swallowed, said nothing. 'Baya Niel must have talked. I heard about it in a song. In a song! They took some old drinking song and put my name in it! I almost threw up.'

'It wasn't Baya Niel,' Karris said.

'What?'

'It was me. I talked to some of the most popular minstrels in the Jaspers.'

Kip's face twisted like she'd betrayed him. 'But you . . . you understand. How could you?'

'Because it's true, Kip. It's not all the truth, and what's true about it may be misunderstood, but that others will misunderstand doesn't mean we keep the truth in a basket. And because the day may come when you need a Name.'

'I don't want another name,' he said, glum teenager again. 'I've already got too many.'

'Not a name like Kip, a Name, like Breaker. As in, "I am become a Name."' If he didn't know the Gevison, he should.

'I don't want that either,' he said.

'I wasn't done. *You* can barely tell a story about a battle in which everyone came out looking good. You didn't fail. You didn't fire a musket as a friend moved into the line of fire and got his face blown off. You weren't a coward that day. We fought odds beyond human comprehension, and if it wasn't a victory for us, at least it wasn't a victory for our foes.'

Her lips were suddenly dry, for here she must tell him truths and lies linked, and he would never forgive her for it. 'There were no battles that simple in the False Prism's War. None. How can you tell stories of what you did when it seems everything you did was wrong? When you were a coward and your friends died because of it? Or is it less painful to tell of when you almost died because your own kin failed you, running away when they could have saved you easily? A man who's a hero one day can be a coward the next, and sometimes even telling of our heroism reminds us of our cowardice.

'My brother and sister Blackguards fought and killed cousins they'd met a hundred times. Classmates with whom we'd played pranks on our magisters. Lovers with whom we'd shared a first kiss. Samite had an unrequited love for this ridiculously handsome cavalier. His family joined the other side. Samite was part of a strike force that infiltrated a city, found the cavalier with his fellows and their families camped in one of the great stables of the city. They barred the doors and set it afire. She listened to him burn to death, screaming to her to have mercy, not for himself but for his family who were inside with him. Samite loved horses. Riding was her one refuge from her cares. She won't ride now unless she must. She doesn't feel worthy after burning two hundred and seventy of the innocent creatures to death – and all those people. She was sixteen years old.'

Kip was aghast. 'I didn't know.'

'Because it's not the kind of thing a warrior shares often. Not even in her cups.'

'And you and my father, you have stories like that?'

She hesitated. How close to the truth did she dare go? How long would he accept evasions?

'Worse?' he asked.

'You can't rate soul wounds,' she said.

'One thing,' Kip said. 'I have to ask. My mother left me a note asking that I take vengeance on my father. She was a . . .' He swallowed, but continued manfully. 'She was an addict and a liar and Orholam only knows what else. I assume she was a camp follower who was spurned afterward, but she said . . . with her dying breath, she said Gavin was a rapist. It's not true, is it?'

Rapist. For some reason, Karris didn't flash back to that awful bedroom and lying on her back quietly, passively drunk, wishing she would pass out, wishing she would fight. Instead, she thought back to the long walk home, the shame at her torn-off buttons that kept her from covering herself decently, the averted stares of the guards she walked past. No one had even offered her a coat. Who wouldn't offer a young girl, who was half naked and ashamed, a coat?

'Your father,' Karris said levelly, locking eyes with Kip, 'is not a rapist.' The man Kip knew as his father, the man who had claimed him as son, Dazen, was not a rapist.

'But it was war. Are you sure?' Kip asked.

Her initial hesitation had been too long. He needed more. It was not the kind of question to which you could leave doubts. Karris said, 'Once, in bed, he mistook my cries for cries of pain. It distressed him so much he went soft. Not the reaction a rapist would have, you think?'

For a moment, Kip didn't seem to understand. Then he blushed furiously. 'I, uh, I think that was more than I wanted to know.'

Karris cleared her throat. It was more than she'd wanted to share. She felt the blood rising in her own cheeks. But it was necessary. 'Good enough?'

Kip averted his eyes. 'About that? Dear Orholam, yes. Please, let's never speak of it again!'

Karris laughed. 'Uh-oh, now I know your weakness!'

'Oh, come on, you can't!' Kip complained. 'No one wants to hear about their parents having— Parent, I mean. Their parent . . . never mind.'

Parents. Like she and Dazen were Kip's parents. Dazen – as Gavin – had adopted Kip, and he'd married Karris. So that sort of made Karris Kip's mother, right?

Parents. One little slip. One little plural. Parent. *Mother.* It touched something in Karris so cold that the word itself froze on the point of impact. It dropped and broke like a young girl's princess hopes had on a cold midnight wandering home alone in the cold, eyes wet, thighs wet.

And what might have given Kip that preposterous idea? Perhaps that Karris had been spending time with him every day for months, training him, giving him advice, supervising his education. She'd been manipulated into acting like a mother. Into showing care that could be mistaken for love.

That bitch.

The White had done this on purpose.

What had it been? Her spies must have told her how, after Gavin's disappearance, Karris had wept when her moon blood came, how she'd obviously hoped that their single night together had impregnated her, like in the stories.

But then, one night had been enough for Karris before, hadn't it? Back when she'd been a girl, and hadn't been ready for a child. The mere thought of it sent black clouds churning in her heart. No, don't think of it. Of course, the White had thought that Karris wanted a child. Karris was facing the end of her childbearing years, and the loss of her purpose as a Blackguard, and the loss of Gavin. Surely Karris would desire to have something of his, of theirs, something to show that all her sacrifices hadn't been for naught.

The White was trying to make Kip a son for Karris simply because she thought Karris had never had her own. She didn't *know*. Karris's secret was safe.

And how could Karris fault the White for trying to manage Karris's emotions? Karris was doing the same thing to Kip: lying so he wouldn't do something disastrous, because if he knew too much, he would act, thinking he knew more than he did.

She moistened her lips. Kip was already studying her as one might study a large dog, wondering if it was going to lunge for your throat or if it wanted to cuddle.

But then that old fear poked its head out of the dark cellar where Karris kept it. Surely the White, so careful in all things, would have investigated Karris fully before handing over her spies. And how good had Karris been at covering her tracks? She'd only been sixteen and seventeen years old.

That cold place went hot. All the shame of that concealed failure ignited.

Who abandons a child? Who leaves a helpless babe in a far country with people she doesn't even know?

Had they been good to him? Was he well?

She'd lain there, holding Dazen after their marriage, and she'd challenged him to be a good father. She'd been so cool, so correct. All while sitting on her own secret failure like it wasn't a burning coal. Hypocrite.

And the White knew her shame. Was holding on to it, maybe only to use it if she absolutely had to. Karris would never be free. She felt hot and cold, nauseated.

'Sorry, "mother,"' Kip said. He was trying to make a joke of it, but the word was so sharp-edged that Karris couldn't even hear the joke. None of Kip's tone could make it past the roaring of the blood in her ears. Just that one, lancet word piercing a boil.

'You are not my son!' Karris spat. Her heart was bile and she was vomiting it out on him, foul and acid, and it tore her throat and ate everything it touched.

Kip had the same look on his face she'd seen on men mortally wounded, staring at their own guts in ropes in their hands, shocked they weren't already dead, but dying nonetheless.

He turned unsteadily and walked out. He closed the door quietly.

Chapter 67

'This is the last time you and I will meet,' Marissia said. They were seated side by side on one of the benches ringing the Great Fountain of Karris Shadowblinder. Marissia dressed in humble slave's grays, eating her lunch. Teia was in her nunk's grays, taking a break from her calisthenics, ostensibly nursing a spasming calf muscle. 'I hear you gave your new handler a hard time.'

It was hard to maintain the spy discipline of not looking over to see if she was saying it wryly. Was there a bit of pleasure in Marissia's tone?

'Could say that,' Teia said, leaning forward to massage her leg so her mouth would be obscured. The point of meeting in public wasn't to disguise altogether that you were speaking to your handler, it was to make sure you weren't overheard and to give lip-readers an impossible task. Strangers might exchange a few words, after all. 'I want to tell Kip everything. I don't have anyone. It's too hard.'

A long pause as Marissia took a drink from her wineskin. 'You want to reveal everything to Kip the Lip?' She paused, then delicately took a bite of a small meat pastry.

Teia scowled. That wasn't fair. Kip might shoot from the hip when he was angry, but he didn't spill other people's secrets. He was a good man.

A good *man*? Kip? When had she started thinking of Kip as a man? Sometimes she looked at him and images seemed to shear off from him like light splitting: different facets, different Kips. Perhaps it was a side effect of the light splitting or drafting so much paryl. If drafting red gradually made you more passionate, and drafting green made you wilder, what did drafting paryl do to you? She saw Kips frozen, each in a line:

Fat Kip, as he had been when he first came to the Chromeria. He was sunk into himself, the blubber a defense against fear and isolation, chin tucked down, shy, self-consciousness and self-pity at war, but thinking.

Broken Kip, mentally going back to Garriston and whatever had happened to him there. They said he'd killed King Garadul. Some said he'd disobeyed an order in doing so, and put the Color Prince in charge. Whatever else he'd done, they said he'd killed a lot of men. No one had put much stock in that. None of the inductees had been there, and the Blackguards said nothing to the inductees about such matters. 'He's a Guile,' was the most they'd say, as if that said everything. As if that said anything. Broken Kip would show up at practice after having thrashed a bully, and he looked defeated instead of victorious, as if he couldn't believe what he was capable of.

The Weeping Warrior. Teia had only seen glimpses of this one, had heard more of it. Teia had heard Kip self-deprecatingly say something like, 'I'm the turtle-bear.' Others said he was a berserker. Kip fighting Aram in his last fight, about to lose his last chance to become a Blackguard. Kip had gone insane as Aram held him down, beating his face in but letting Kip slip just enough so that the judges didn't call it.

Most young men who went crazy in a fight went stupid, too. But Kip had shot out the lights. It might have been enough for him to beat Aram, if someone hadn't fixed the lights almost immediately – and was there a rule for that? Aram had picked Kip fully off the ground and was throwing him down in a neck-breaker – Aram himself getting terrified of what he felt burgeoning in his opponent.

Teia had overheard two Blackguards nearby talking. 'It's a

good thing they stopped that,' Hezik said. 'That Kip would have died.'

'Or if he hadn't,' Stump said, 'a bunch of the rest of us might have.'

'Huh?'

Stump looked at Hezik. 'At Garriston, I saw that boy go green golem. You remember the south flank at Sundered Rock, when we thought their line was going to snap, and we suddenly saw Dazen Guile himself? Out there all alone. Captain thought we'd take us a prize?'

'You know I don't remember shit about that battle. I woke up afterward and couldn't see or hear for a week.'

'You can still fucking count. Number a men we had before, number a men we had after. It ain't accountancy. Why you gotta trip up my story? You know what happened there even if you don't remember it all for your own self. Anyway. Garriston was that. I tell you. It was that. Boy's fucking fifteen.'

They'd noticed Teia then, and gave her a look that would wilt flowers.

Then she saw the next Kip, right after the Weeping Warrior. She saw Kip taking his place in line after Cruxer had come in like a righteous, judgmental god and crippled Aram. Kip, suddenly accepted, beaten, bruised, staggering, beaming, weeping, and whole. That was Kip Unalone: Kip with the scrubs, Kip with his team. Laughing, for one frozen moment, belonging. There was a tragic undercurrent in his face even as he laughed, though, as if he knew this moment was fleeting.

Then Kip Confident. She'd seen this for one second, and only one, but some part of her was certain this was Kip Himself. Kip, averring that while this war wasn't the best thing, it was the best thing possible. Kip, unself-conscious, who knew when he knew what he was talking about. Kip, who didn't sleep much. Kip, who knew some of the cost of what he was talking about. Kip, in that moment, wasn't trying to impress anyone – and that made him more impressive. He was suddenly *solid*. Adult.

Attractive.

She thought of how she'd not hugged Kip. Why hadn't she hugged him? She should have. Orholam, she should have.

'I suppose if I tell you something that you already know, you won't listen to me?' Marissia said.

Teia blinked.

'Like if I pointed out the foolishness of getting your heart tangled with a Guile?'

'No danger of that,' Teia said quickly. Marissia was a room slave. She hadn't had any say over Gavin coming to her bed. That she had chosen to make her service easier by pleasing him rather than harder by fighting him simply meant she was smart. She was doing what she needed to do to survive.

Marissia said, 'Someone who says you shouldn't do something while doing it herself could be considered a hypocrite. Or an expert. Hypocrite or expert, that of all people, I offer you advice is not a reason to dismiss it, but actually the opposite.'

'I didn't call you a—' Teia was baffled. What was Marissia saying?

'You're sixteen. You thought it. I judged my elders harshly when I was young, too.'

So Marissia loved Gavin. What kind of irony was it that Teia, who had been a slave, would have assumed that Marissia couldn't love Gavin – because she was a slave?

It wasn't . . . what? Normal love? Because Gavin was Prism and Marissia was a slave? Could Teia tell Marissia that what she felt wasn't love? That Marissia was fooling herself, that really she was only making a bad situation tolerable? If a power difference made love impossible, who could ever love a Prism? Who could ever love a slave?

Maybe it was love, then. But it wasn't good. Or at least, it wasn't fair. It wasn't easy.

Which was Marissia's point exactly. The chasm between freed slave and a Prism's son was narrower than the chasm between slave and Prism. But not by much.

Marissia ate more. Drank more. No hurry, no apparent interest in Teia. She casually scanned the crowd, but the way a bored person eating lunch might. Then she said, 'Do you know, I was made a slave at your age.'

Teia stood, turned, propped a foot up on the bench, and

began working on her calf in a way that would give her a glimpse of Marissia's face.

'Things were suddenly expected of me that I found very, very hard. I cried myself to sleep many nights. Sometimes I still feel like that vulnerable little girl. I have an inkling of what the next year will demand of you. I want you to know I'm proud of you. The Order will test you more. They will ask you to do unspeakable things. You will do them. This is an order. In the sight of Orholam, let all the evil you do be on my head, and on the White's. We're playing against the Old Man of the Desert himself, you understand?'

'No,' Teia said quietly. 'No.'

'You will,' Marissia said. She gazed up at the statue of Karris Shadowblinder, Karris's namesake. 'And stop giving *her* nonsense.' She wiped her mouth with a napkin, stood, and walked away.

Teia remembered herself enough to continue pretending to massage her leg. It wasn't like she'd had a long time to bond with Marissia, but the woman had been the only person Teia could tell the whole truth. The sudden emptiness in her chest felt like a death.

Death. She'd killed a man in this war in shadow. Maybe Kip was right. Maybe it was justified. But she was going to have to kill again, for the other side. She had no doubt of it. How would the Order really trust her until she'd killed for them?

It wasn't a matter of *if* they ordered her to do so, it was a matter of *when*. And she was supposed to meet up with Murder Sharp right now.

Chapter 68

Aliviana Danavis followed Phyros into the slum bar. It was the kind of place she would have feared a year ago, with good reason. She'd found new strength in the last months, or at least new fearlessness. But even with that, she never would have come here in her dresses and murex purple. Now she wore her hair in a simple braid, a tricorn hat, her fawnskin trousers still bearing the dark stains of what might have been blood. Before they'd died, she'd had her blue and her green drafter work together to fashion clips onto her pistols like Gavin Guile had, so she could wear all four pistols on her belt and not worry about losing them. She also wore a short saber that she still didn't know how to use well, despite Phyros's efforts to train her. A figure-hugging white tunic, but worn long over her trousers in the Tyrean style, and a green jacket waxed against the rain completed the ensemble.

She still stuck out, here in Wiwurgh. Just across the Coral Strait from Ilyta, and positioned at the very mouth of the Everdark Gates, the city was inhabited mainly by Tyreans, Ilytians, and Parians. The crowds of darker faces made something unknot in Liv's soul. You could hardly get farther from the Jaspers if you tried. Here, she felt beautiful. Men whistled in appreciation, unlike the cool-blooded meat stares the men of the north and west coasts gave. Here a man would let you know his interest, but take his cue and leave you alone if you ignored him or gave a glance and no more.

It had taken Liv a while to get used to it again, and she hated that she'd been changed by her time at the Chromeria.

Of course, having the bare-chested barbarian that was Phyros as her bodyguard didn't hurt in dissuading prolonged staring.

But a sailors' tavern was different. There were women here, too, but they were even harder than the men. Every sailor and pirate had to walk with friends in the seaside slums, of course. The danger of being knocked out in an alley and waking as the iron cut your ear was real for everyone. But a woman's lot was worse, as always. As the saying went, 'A man 'slaved works one oar, a woman 'slaved works every oar on deck.'

Aliviana stepped into the low-ceilinged tavern and glanced around with a haughty, uninterested look on her face. But then she gasped aloud as she saw the man sitting in a corner, staring at her. Her father.

Corvan Danavis was slowly rising to his feet, as transfixed by the sight of her as she was of him. Her father? Here? Impossible.

And he wasn't alone. There were a good ten drafters in some sort of military attire with him, light blue tunics emblazoned with a golden eye high on the chest. Her father wore one as well, though richer, with brocade and a sword at his hip. He was the leader of them.

Emotions rolled over Liv like a swell rolling over a swimmer at sea. After the surprise, there was a little bit of that little-girl glee, but trailing that like a secondary wave that engulfs you just when you think the worst is past was raw anger, unfaded despite the passage of months.

Her father waved her over to join him at his table, and she went, but as she walked, she felt the tableau shift in her head. It took on sudden symbolic connotations: her father beckoned her to walk to him; he didn't come to her. He stood there, asking her to leave her friends and join him at the place he had prepared for her.

What was he doing here? Had he been following her? Impossible! But here? In one tavern of hundreds, on the other side of the world? It was too much coincidence to be coincidence.

Stop being a twit, Liv. It's your father.

He crossed the last few steps between them quickly, as if he couldn't hold back any more, real joy etched on his features. They embraced.

For a dozen heartbeats, all was well in the world.

Finally, they released each other.

Here it comes. She stood with her back straight. She suppressed an urge to tug the laces at her tunic's open neckline tighter.

'Aliviana,' her father said. 'You look so strong.'

It was the last thing she'd have expected from the legendary General Corvan Danavis. It slipped right under her armor. 'So do you, daddy.'

He laughed, and she couldn't help but smile.

'Will you join me?' Corvan said. 'I saved us a table.'

Saved it? Like he expected me? How could he know she'd be here?

'Of course,' she said.

'I'll dismiss my people if you dismiss yours,' he said, eyes twinkling.

Liv hadn't even been aware of Phyros coming to stand behind her. But she paused. She didn't need to let her father dictate what she did or didn't do.

'No disrespect,' Corvan said to Phyros. 'I've heard you've done yet more mighty deeds in keeping my daughter safe, Lord Phyros Seaborn. I owe you everything.'

Phyros scowled, and Liv realized she'd never heard his surname, nor known that he was of noble blood. The thought that he'd concealed that fact from her, and that her father had known it, nettled Liv. 'He can sit with your people.' In a place this crowded, being at the next table would be enough to be out of earshot.

A one-eyed bar slave came over as Liv took her seat, and her father said, 'Drinks for these three tables. On me. You have mead? Keep it flowing.' When the man left, Corvan said, 'Have you had it before? There used to be a large Angari community here in Wiwurgh, so you can find some of their foods and drinks still. Little of their blood.'

'There were Angari here?' Liv asked. She hadn't seen a single blond head here.

'After the Everdark Gates were closed, the community was isolated. A plague came and killed the Angari in much lower numbers than the Parians here. The Parians blamed them for the plague. They exterminated them all. Any half-bloods they could find, too. Even people who were a quarter Angari, or children generations later born with light skin, found life here unbearable. They moved elsewhere in the satrapies or simply found it impossible to marry. Extinguished, completely.'

It was the kind of trivia her father knew that had always amazed Aliviana. He knew something interesting about most everything.

'It was the superviolet,' she said.

'Huh?'

'The Angari priests were superviolet drafters.'

'Really? Oh, maybe I have heard that,' he said, his eyes flicking up as he searched for the memory. 'But . . .'

She felt a little stab of pleasure. 'The priests of Ferrilux blessed their worshippers' food and water. Living in poverty for generations, the Angari must have noticed that it had an effect. So if that later plague was born of bad meat or bad water, the Angari wouldn't have died as much.'

'Religion saving lives?'

'Clearly only in the short term,' Aliviana said. 'Since it got all of them killed.'

'I still don't understand,' Corvan said. 'Are you saying their god intervened with their food?'

'It's the superviolet. Disease loves darkness. We infuse all our bandages with superviolet. Men recover from wounds that would otherwise suppurate and gangrene. The chirurgeons have said our survival rates for even minor wounds are five and ten times better than those left untreated.'

'Aliviana, that's brilliant,' Corvan said.

'It wasn't my discovery,' she said. 'I hear that there are even a few chirurgeons using it at the Chromeria now. They don't understand why it works, but they've seen that it does.'

'No, I didn't mean the discovery – though it was. I mean you, applying it like that, backward, figuring out history with what you know. Orholam's beard, think of the tragedy of it. The Parians' – he looked around the Parian tavern – 'the ancient Parians massacred the very people who could have saved them. Not to mention the countless lives that could have been saved in the centuries since then.'

'And saved countless superviolet drafters from the drudgery of only writing secret messages back and forth to each other.'

'Indeed. So you must have whole corps of superviolet healers.' He drew idly in the wetness ring that had formed around his mead cup.

Distracted, Aliviana almost volunteered more, but stopped herself. She wasn't going to give him any details about the disposition of the Color Prince's forces.

'I'm sorry,' he said. 'I was just thinking out loud. It's a brilliant leap. Of course you've already put it to the best use. I'm sorry. I had no idea that my historical anecdote would intrude on our present . . . difficulties. How have you been? Did you get my letter – no, never mind, that doesn't matter.'

The bar slave finally brought their mead, having served Phyros and Corvan's men first. Stupidity, or a deliberate slight? Liv wondered. Drinking the sweet sharp mead gave her an excuse to gather her wits. She couldn't see any harm in sharing, and if she shared, surely he would, too. So she began.

The sea had fought them all the way. Liv and her crew had been through horrible storms. They'd frequently needed to stop to make repairs. Then they'd been marooned in a fishing village for a month, stuck in what they'd come to call a crystal storm. Shards of blue luxin the size of a thumb and edged with sharp angles beat down day and night, for a count of twenty-seven, then stopped for some multiple of that long, and then began again. Anyone caught outside in the storm was shredded. The crystals themselves broke apart almost instantly in the sun afterward, leaving gritty blue dust everywhere.

It had seemed like the end of the world must be upon them, but when they finally escaped, they'd found the crystal storm was localized. People twenty leagues away hadn't even noticed clouds.

They all knew what it had to be, though Liv didn't tell her father. The blue bane had regrown, somewhere, and no one was in control of it. Or a madman was.

Their galley had been destroyed in the crystal rain, and they'd commandeered a new ship outside Garriston – fine, stole it. When Aliviana had seen a small river running green and wanted to go investigate, the crew had been so frightened, they'd nearly mutinied.

They'd later lost two drafters after the idiots had humiliated some pirates in a tavern fight. The pirates ambushed them in a dark alley, and mortally wounded them.

The lesson Aliviana's men had taken from that was that when you fight pirates, kill them and all their friends. Against her orders, they'd gone looking for vengeance and sunk the pirates' ship. With all the pirates aboard.

She'd had to execute another drafter for instigating that and disobeying her. She had qualms about that. One of the men killed in the ambush had been the drafter's lover. The men were greens. They had a hard time obeying rules.

But after that, her authority hadn't been questioned again.

It also meant that as they finally made it to Wiwurgh, she had only two drafters and Phyros. The captain and his men had disappeared, not even taking their pay – though they had stolen the galley.

That brought her here, carrying a fortune, looking for a ship and crew crazy enough to search the very mouth of the Everdark Gates for the superviolet seed crystal – or bane. Though of course Liv didn't tell her father that they were looking for anything. 'And that's it,' she said. She realized as she'd been speaking that it was tremendously comforting to talk to someone who loved her. To connect.

She'd slowed down on drafting superviolet since she'd gotten away from Zymun, and she'd realized what a crutch it had been. Not that she judged those who burned through their halos joyfully – many of the Blood Robes celebrated such, though the Color Prince himself took a more nuanced approach. But for her, it was too much, too fast. She didn't feel like herself when she was drafting all the time. Maybe she'd gone a little overboard for a while.

Talking to her father again, she saw a new respect in his eyes. He was worried for her. Of course he was. These were dangerous times. But she could tell he was trying hard not to interject advice. It was nice to be reminded of relationships that weren't all about power. And yet, power interfered even here.

'Now . . .' she said. 'What about you?' As if they were just old friends catching up, not father and daughter. She was an adult now, not his subordinate. She'd done amazing things in her own right, and even if he wasn't pushing her down, she could feel herself wanting to slip back into that old role. She'd worshipped her father, and he was a great man. That didn't mean he was infallible. It didn't mean he was right about the Chromeria, about Gavin Guile, about any of it.

'I've . . . well, you're going to hear it sooner or later. I took the people of Garriston and a bunch of Tyrean refugees to Seers Island. We established a city there. They're calling it the City of Gold. Gavin Guile helped us. He drafted tens of thousands of solid yellow luxin bricks that we've used to build most everything. He even managed to win us back Tyrea's old lost seat on the Spectrum.'

'That's, that's great news. Who would have known? They're

going to have to start calling him Gavin the Builder, what with Brightwater Wall around Garriston, and now that.'

'He's gone now. A slave on an oar currently. With worse ahead.'

'What?'

'A bit of intelligence, as a sign of good faith.'

Kind of you, but . . . 'Father, how did you find me?'

'You like your truth unvarnished, right?'

'Yes.'

'I've fallen in love. I married a woman on Seers Island.'

'Oh. Uh . . . congratulations. I'm so happy for you.' Married? Liv felt the twist in her guts. So fast? The detachment that superviolet had taught her helped her speak levelly, as if it were merely interesting.

'She told me I could find you here. Did you know this place doesn't even have a name? Hard to find by description alone, I assure you.'

'You what? Married?' Easy, Liv. Not like your own love life has been particularly laudable. You have no right to feel betrayed.

'Also, I'm a satrap now.'

'What?!'

'You like it straight. That's straight.'

'So that was your payoff for turning your cloak?' she asked.

'Was your payoff for turning yours that you be made a goddess?' He tapped a finger firmly on the tabletop.

She wanted to spit at him. 'I changed sides because I saw what I'd believed before was wrong.'

'So did I.' He was calm, cool, and hard. So very rational that the superviolet part of her couldn't help but be impressed.

'Gavin Guile is a monster. You told me so yourself.'

'Gavin Guile *was* a monster. People change,' Corvan said.

'People don't change that much!'

'You did. I did.'

'He killed people. Thousands upon thousands,' she said. 'Innocents. He wiped out Garriston.'

'You mean in the Prisms' War? He wasn't even at Garriston. But yes, he told his generals to take the city. But you've seen battle now. War is a flame. It escapes even the best-laid plans.

Your actions were vital in laying Ru prostrate. And now you know all the vileness that can happen to a city laid prostrate.'

It took her breath away. She had been the decisive factor in the Battle of Ru. She had birthed a god. All those sailors dead, all those men enslaved, and all the massacres and rapes and horror within the walls, too. They weren't her fault, not exactly, but they wouldn't have happened without her, either.

Did she have an entire city on her conscience? Was that why she had wanted so badly to escape?

In the end, was she different from Gavin Guile only in degree, and not in kind?

'The Color Prince had some good rationale for the Rape of Ru?' Corvan asked, eyes heavy-lidded.

'A punitive action to deter others from belligerence in the future,' she said, but she felt like she was saying it far away.

'Or inspire more belligerence?' Corvan asked.

'It could do that, too,' she admitted. It was only logical.

'So the weak will surrender more quickly than they would have otherwise, while the strongest will fight to the last man and woman, knowing what will happen if they lose,' Corvan said. 'He's taken Raven Rock, since you left. It's a small city, perhaps twenty thousand souls, perched on the side of a cliff. They refused to surrender and he put them under siege, though they didn't hold out long against his wights. When he broke down the gates, two hundred young women who heard what he had done in Ru leapt off the cliffs. Some young mothers jumped with their children.'

Liv felt sick. 'It can't be true.'

'I don't lie to you. Indeed, perhaps we wouldn't be here if I did.' He tapped his fingers.

'He wouldn't have hurt them. Ru was a one-time thing. He's not bloodthirsty.'

Her father said nothing to that, and she heard how it sounded.

'Two hundred? Surely an exaggeration. One or two, perhaps. I know how these stories are.'

'They're saying a thousand. They're saying every woman in the city. It was two hundred. The Third Eye saw it herself. She counted them. It was a quick vision, though, she might have been off by ten or fifteen.'

'And you're certain she's telling you the truth?' Liv said.

'She has told me hard truths, I trust her entirely.'

'Fealty to One, huh?' Liv said bitterly.

'Indeed. But my ultimate fealty is not to her.'

'Nor is it to me!' Liv had to work hard to keep her voice down. As it was, people were already staring.

'No, it's not. Fealty to your own family is the smallest possible circle beyond the self. To hold fealty to your own and to call it a high virtue is ludicrous. Even animals protect their own. It is a good, but it is a common good, an easy one. It's a miser who says he grows rich not for himself, but for his children. His vice is not thus magically made virtue. Fealty to One is the expression of a high virtue. It is what sets Danavises apart from those who take easier roads.'

'It doesn't set you apart if you take your fealty from one man and give it to his mortal enemy.' It wasn't fair, but Liv didn't care about fair. Her father was saying she was supporting a monster. That all she had done, all she had worked for, was worse than nothing.

His fingers flexed hard around his mead. For a long moment, he said nothing, but when he did speak, his voice was quiet. 'Even if your father is a hypocrite of the lowest form, Aliviana, your problem isn't his choices. It's your own.' He drummed his fingers on the tabletop and then stood. 'I have to go. My wife said I may still save her life if I don't tarry.'

'Wait. What?'

'She's a Seer. She can tell all sorts of things. But there's an order of assassins that wears these special cloaks. It makes them invisible to her gift. She's seen that in many futures she dies, but she can't see how, which has never happened to her before. So we believe one of these assassins must be after her. Me coming here likely means that the woman I love will die. That's how much I care for you. I came for you, knowing it might cost me her. Farewell, daughter. Orholam's light shine upon you.'

'I'm sorry, father, I – I didn't even congratulate you. A satrap, that's—'

'No time,' he said, glancing down.

And he left. His people swarmed around him, and they were

gone. Without so much as a parting embrace. Liv was stunned. She felt hollowed out, and suddenly more alone than she had ever been. What if she'd done the wrong thing? She'd been hasty. She'd been young. She hadn't known – she hadn't known much of anything.

She'd done the best she could. Better than anyone could have expected of her. Isolated and afraid, she'd chosen the best of bad options.

Hadn't she?

And what the hell was it with her father tonight, fidgeting, acting—

She looked at the tabletop as Phyros came over to sit with her again. She tightened her eyes for an instant. On the tabletop, written in spindly superviolet luxin invisible to any eyes but hers, was a message: 'Under the table. Hide it in your left boot. Tell no one.'

Phyros sat and rested his arms on the table, setting down his drink. The motion broke the fragile superviolet luxin and it disappeared. 'You good?'

'It was upsetting. But I'm fine.'

'I found us a crew,' he said. 'You ready?'

'More than ready.'

Phyros stood, and as his back turned, she slid her hand under the edge of the table and found it. A knife. A knife? When she had four pistols, a sword, and another knife on her belt? This was what her father gave her? Nonetheless, she swept it into her hand, palming it, and followed.

Chapter 69

'They tell me you're good,' Murder Sharp said. He'd taken residence upstairs in a midtown porcelain shop. The large, round room had lots of windows, and Master Sharp had lots of roses. Blooming roses, at this time of year? That meant he either could draft green, or had access to the services of someone who did. He was watering the roses as Teia came in.

Teia mumbled something under her breath.

'I lied,' Sharp said. 'They don't tell me you're good.'

She looked at him, a quick flick to his disconcertingly intense gaze, then away. What was his problem? He turned back to his watering. He wasn't, as it turned out, bald. He'd merely kept his carrot-red hair shaved in a pattern to make it appear he was. Then he'd cut it all off so it could grow in together, without drawing attention to his old disguise. So now it was boyishly short. It made him look young.

'Truth is,' he said, putting down the watering can and turning to study her, 'they tell me that you're better than I am.'

This time when her eyes flicked up, his amber eyes were waiting, and they held her like a fish on a line.

'Do you know why they'd tell me such a thing?' he asked.

She shook her head. Was he even telling the truth?

'They hope I'll kill you. They hope I'm that vain.' He slid knives home in his belt. 'And you know what? I am.'

Her breath was suddenly short. She glanced toward the door. No. If he was going to kill her, it was too far away. And who was to say he'd use a knife? He was watching her eyes, waiting for her to widen her pupils to look into paryl.

The whole room was probably full of paryl. Her heart sank. But she tried to keep her voice light. 'Why not just do it themselves?' she asked.

'You don't know the Old Man. If they kill you out of hand, they'll have to answer to him. Killing a paryl lightsplitter? He'd be furious. And when he's furious, people die. On the other hand, if they take in a spy, he'll be even more furious. He'll wipe out the whole mission here as traitors or incompetents. But . . . if they get *me* to kill you, it becomes my problem. And the Old Man isn't likely to kill me. I'm too valuable.'

I didn't even think of fighting him.

The thought pissed Teia off. She was a Blackguard. Near it, anyway. People feared her. Should, anyway. And she was thinking of running, of letting herself be pulled down from behind? Like what? Like prey. She wasn't prey. She wasn't a slave who had to curl into a ball while her mistress beat her, only defending, forbidden to answer rage with rage.

I am not a slave, not even to fear.

'So what's it going to be?' she asked. 'You wouldn't be telling me if you were really going to kill me out of hand. You're too careful for that. And I'm too dangerous.'

'Are you?' he asked, bemused.

'I am.' She smiled, and her rage smiled with her. Test me? Please do.

'I've half a mind to take your dogteeth for that impudence,' Murder Sharp said. He fingered his necklace, showing her the glittering pearls-that-weren't-pearls.

'Come get 'em,' Teia said. She told herself that it was because a spy would be obsequious, desperate to do anything to get in. By putting on a mask of rebellion, she'd be above suspicion.

But that wasn't really true, because fuck him.

'You're not afraid of me?' he asked, smirking.

'I'm afraid all the time. It's boring.' She felt the tiny flask of olive oil hanging inside her tunic. She still hadn't thrown it out. Hadn't been able to. Why was that?

His strike, when it came, was quick. But she was ready. A small deflection, and his open hand went over her shoulder rather than striking her cheek. She moved in, instantly. As she was small and not strong, everything about Teia's fighting had to be technically sound. She went for the elbow lock, saw she wasn't going to get it, stepped on his foot as he spun out of the elbow lock, and pushed hard.

And like a professional, he went with it instead of fighting it. He flipped, and she had no warning before his other leg clipped her in the back of the neck. It launched her into a wall, and she was so stunned, she couldn't get her hands up in time. She smashed into the wall face first, staggered like a drunk, unable to control her limbs suddenly, and went down. Black rushed, stars winked. She felt her limbs being manipulated, bound, but it was too fast, they didn't move right. She spasmed.

Two cupped hands slapped down on her ears, and trapped air went rushing into her head. The pain blotted out all. She gasped, breathless with pain.

By the time it faded enough for Teia to be aware of anything else, she realized she was trussed like a lamb, except her limbs were all pulled backward, her stomach on the ground, her feet and hands bound back in the air behind her. She had no leverage to fight the bonds. She heard a suck-click as Murder Sharp cinched the last rope, one hand knotted through her hair, pressing her face into the rough wood floor. Something wet dribbled on her cheek.

Drool.

She spasmed again. Some part of her retreated deep into the recesses and she bucked and thrashed like an animal. No use. No matter. She rolled over as he stepped clear. She tried to bite his feet. It felt like her arm was going to be pulled out of the socket. She gasped.

Murder Sharp stood. 'Glad we got – *ssscchhhht* – that out early.'

She couldn't do this. She couldn't.

'Are you afraid of me now?' he asked. Then he laughed.

He promptly sat down cross-legged next to her, tilted his head, studied her, doglike. He chuckled. He put a hand on her butt to push her hips down and pushed down, let go to let her rock like a toy horse you'd give a child. Back arched and trussed, she bobbed helplessly, up onto her chest, almost smacking her chin, then down onto her pelvis, helpless, helpless.

Murder Sharp laughed like a little boy with a new toy. Then he grabbed the back of her trousers and yanked up on them and her underclothes, cleaving the moon painfully. He chuckled like a mean adolescent.

'Just so you know,' he said. *Ssschhtt*. Again, that slobbery slurp-click. What the hell was that? The fear jumped from her stomach all through her whole body like lightning. She almost screamed. No no no. She had to wall that off. It held her vocal cords.

'Just so you know, you're mine. To do with as I please.'

'I understand,' she said. It was supposed to be defiant. It wasn't even close. Orholam save her! What was he going to do? 'Please. Please . . .'

Don't weep, Teia. I forbid. I forbid. She'd been a young girl enslaved, but she'd never been raped. Too boyish, too young, too lucky, maybe even protected by some small scrap of decency of her mistress or by her hope to sell Teia's virginity. Whatever the reason – or for no reason at all – in that one thing, she'd been spared. She couldn't breathe past the fear clogging her throat.

He rocked her back and forth, gently, gently. 'You understand . . . here,' he said, tapping her head hard with one finger. 'I need you to understand in here.' He rocked her body again. 'Like an oft-beaten dog cringes when its master raises his hand even if only to grab a cup, I want your body to know my mastery, because there are only two motivators in this world: fear, and the desire not to fear.'

Suddenly, she was weeping. There was a first, intense spike of self-hatred for her fear like a snakebite, and then there was nothing but the fear itself coiling, curled around her, squeezing out her breath. But it wasn't crushing her from outside, it was like the serpent was growing from within spiraling outward as if it wanted to escape. There was no room for Teia in her own skin.

'Shh, shh,' he said. 'I want to tell you a story, Teia, a true story though five thousand or a thousand thousand years old. Or so widely regarded as true, it doesn't matter.' He paused. *Ssschht. Ssschht.* What the hell was that sound? 'Wait here,' he said. He stood.

He lit a lantern, then shuttered the windows, one after another. He kissed his roses, told them he wouldn't be but a minute. He took his time, and slowly, the room filled with shadows.

Murder Sharp came back with the lantern, his handsome features ghoulish in the bobbing, harsh light. He put it down and sat again, cross-legged.

'Pretend this is a campfire. It works better that way. It's a campfire story.'

Orholam, save me, save me. I'll never do anything bad ever again, I swear it.

'In the beginning, there was—' He turned down the flame conspiratorially. 'God. Shhh.' He turned the flame back up. 'And there was nothing. And the nothingness displeased the One. You see, he wasn't yet called Orholam, for you know what Orholam means, don't you?'

He spanked her, lightly, and for some reason, that shocked her more deeply than a hard blow would.

'This is the part where you answer, silly!' he urged.

Her mind went blank. She couldn't remember what he'd

been talking about – she arched her back, twisted her shoulder to see his face. He was losing his good mood rapidly.

'The Lord of Light,' some part of her answered for her. Perhaps Orholam himself had reached down and given her those words. Though she wished if he was reaching down and doing miracles, he would go ahead and give Murder Sharp a heart attack.

Oh, Orholam, how stupid am—

'If you draft paryl without my permission,' Murder Sharp said quietly, dangerously, 'the first time, I'll put out one of your eyes. See how you explain that to your commander. The second time you do it, I won't go so easy. Understood?'

She managed a quick nod.

'Oh, I'm sorry,' he said suddenly. With both hands, he pulled her underwear and trousers out of her butt crack where he'd pulled it up earlier. Then he patted her butt lightly, as if it were friendly. Like this was something people did for each other. 'I don't mean you to misunderstand. I won't violate you. Rape is disgusting. Beneath my dignity. There, does that set you at ease? My fault. Now, the story . . .'

She turned and rested her face on the rough floor, slave again, survivor, silent, and so very, very thankful.

'There was no light yet, yes? So It – "He," if we must, since we are saying "Lord" and one must admit the limitations of language in such cases – *He* couldn't be a lord of light, then, right? There was no light. *Ssschhtt!* Right? Got it? Language can mislead us on all these things. We say there was him or it and nothing. But we don't mean that he sat there with nothingness. He wasn't on a porch swing with nothingness in a box on his lap, wondering what he'd do with it. We say Orholam and nothingness, but really it was Orholam and Orholam-not-ness. There was only him, but somehow he was lonely – though how could you be lonely, having never known company? Creation stories are impossibilities packaged in lies. He was, and it wasn't not good, though he is all good and he was all that was? How can such be? He was, and it was good, but it wasn't good enough? Perhaps that. I've felt that way, when alone. But he is to be perfect, and how could perfection be less good than it ought to be? Would that not be an imperfection?

Or how can you add to perfection and still have perfection? *Ssschhtt.* Maybe that. Maybe in adding a perfection, you can have a new sort of perfection. Hmm . . .

'Well, he was. And he, the creator, created light. Light was his joy, his first and favored creation. Light, being first, partook of its creator's very essence. But light, light isn't. I mean, it isn't just *is*. It doesn't just *be*. It, it, it doesn't sit. Light isn't passive. Light sitting still wouldn't be light at all. Light, light *verbs*! That other kind of verbing than is-ing. It, it goes. It flies. It moves. Even luxin, luxin doesn't sit. It isn't frozen motion, it is stable, predictable motion. Like glass. Motion in rings or predictable waves, motion slowed, but not motion stopped. Never that.' He scowled. 'You're getting me off track, making me tell it wrong. Let me try again. *Ssschtt.*'

He massaged his scalp, rubbing fingers hard through his disheveled red tradesman's hair. '*Ssschhtt.* Dammit. Do you know what you've done?'

Teia shook her head, silent, submissive.

'You broke my teeth with your fighting.' He stood once again and moved away, carrying the lantern with him. With his back to Teia, he reached in his mouth. There was a slurp as he pulled something free. Teia was suddenly mindful of the drool that had dribbled on her face earlier.

She was going to wake up, wasn't she? This was surreal. This couldn't be – oh, no, that felt like a calf cramp coming on.

Sssscccchhhhhhttt!

He spat in a small spittoon. It was a lot of spit. Her stomach churned. He was talking to himself, too, slurring words, and she didn't want to hear what he was saying. '. . . new red tabs frohm zhat fief . . .'

The spittoon accepted another shot, and then his voice drifted closer once more.

'Much better. You'll be glad to know you just broke the adhesive. Else I would have been angry,' he said. 'Do you know, with paryl, I don't ever have to kill someone with my bare hands? It's almost disappointing. There are other Shadows out there who let that make them lazy. And then they get captured by some oaf house guards because they can't break a grip, and there are times when someone having a seizure is a bit too coincidental. This is why I am still a fighter, though I am so much more. Sometimes the meat must sing, and spirit merely nod and clap to the beat. Now where was I?'

'Light,' she said quietly.

'Ah yes.' He sat again. Folded his hands in his lap. 'Calf muscle is cramping?'

'I hope n-n-not.' And then it went, cramping hard.

He grabbed her leg and she was spun around on her stomach. He worked her calf like an athlete or chirurgeon, skillfully working out the cramp in short order, and without causing unnecessary pain. Then he spun her back as if nothing had happened. He lowered the lantern light so that the barest ridges of his facial bones could be seen.

'In the beginning, God made light. And he saw that it was good. So he made the First Ones, that they might enjoy the light with him, and each other's company. But the greatest of the First Ones rose up, and spoke for the Light. He said Light cannot be chained, that to sit in stasis and worship was no fit end for creators so glorious as they. And so he stole a light from the Lord of Light himself, and brought it to earth, and they called him Lightbearer. And he broke this light into colors so that all might enjoy it, so that even if some part were lost or chained again, yet light itself would be free. And he kindled many flames from that one solitary light he stole. And Orholam, in fury at this rebellion, barred the Lightbearer and those who followed him from the kingdom he now called the Heavens. And the Lightbearer and his Two Hundred set up their reign on earth, becoming gods in miniature, and over the course of eons, they bickered and fought, and when Orholam made men, they bickered and fought and used men to destroy men in their games. For God loved men, but men loved destroying what he loved.'

He turned the lantern up. 'Tell me, child, is that close to the story you heard?'

'Yes,' she whispered. 'Yes.' Her heart was a hummingbird in a cage.

'Then let me tell you: half of that version is lies. A cunning lie, close to the truth, as the best lies are, yes? The Lightbearer did not steal a lesser light. He stole the Light itself. And with it, he fashioned Man. Yes. And he fashioned us not in the image of himself, but instead, in the image of the Lightmaker and the Light, and this is why Man has two natures. This is why we are a mirror of God himself, sides reversed, smudges showing the flaws of the model, not the copies. The Lightbearer and his host are the gods of old. And when we ascend to the bane, it is an ascent to a fraction of the former glory. It is not a usurpation, for we are created in the image of the light itself and are no lesser sons for this. Indeed, in some ways, we are the greatest of all. Though, one must admit, the most fragile. Orholam and the Lightbearer have been at war since, with Orholam using the Prisms to try to chain all light and bring it into obedience to him again. With Orholam stomping out those colors he finds his people cannot control. Like paryl.'

He pulled out a knife. 'All of this, Teia, is prelude.' His face twisted through a dozen expressions in two seconds. 'What I do, what you seek to do, this has weight. Not the, not the, killing. We might as well be harvesting fish from the salmon runs. Necessary, but not worthy of deep contemplation. This . . . this has weight. Turn over. Look.'

He kicked her, hard, right in the kidney. It took her breath and made her roll over. The sudden savagery – for no reason! – after he had been so calm and steady, pushed her right to the brink of tears again. She had no idea what he wanted her to see. 'What?' she said. 'What?'

'This, stupid.' He was holding the hem of his cloak?

'The cloak?' she asked. A little muscle in her back started cramping, and she gasped involuntarily.

'Yes, the cloaks. The shimmercloaks, Teia. What are the shimmercloaks? What do they do?'

She wasn't getting it. Did he want more than the obvious? Was he going to hurt her if she answered wrong? 'Make you invisible?' she ventured. She braced herself for a kick.

'That's right,' he said, amused once more. 'And what does it mean to be invisible?'

Mean? What kind of question was that? It just was. 'I don't know. I don't know. Dear Orholam, don't hurt me again.'

'"Dear Orholam,"' he echoed quizzically. But he let it go. 'When the First Man and the First Woman first sinned, what did they do?'

'I don't know. They were ashamed. They were naked. They hid. They, they clothed themselves.'

'They clothed themselves so the light wouldn't touch their skin. They hid from Orholam. But of course, they couldn't hide, could they?'

'Of course not, for Orholam sees all.' She stopped as soon as the old maxim crossed her lips.

Murder Sharp squatted on his heels, right next to her head. 'To be invisible is the sinner's first desire. To be invisible is to hide from man and angels and light and the Lord of Light himself. It is to be *oralam Orh' olam*, hidden from Orholam. The pagan ancient Tyreans had a myth of a ring that when its bearer twisted it, it rendered him invisible. They didn't believe in it literally, of course, how would a ring do such a thing? It was a parable for what a man might would do with all temptations laid before him. For, invisible, hidden from the eye of gods and men, what could a man not do? Allowed to do whatever he wished, what *would* a man do? To be invisible was to show the true condition of one's heart. To the Tyreans, it was a story to muse upon. To the luxiats, it is more. Wanting to hide, to them, is itself evidence already that one is ashamed, that one's heart is black. Who else would hide from the light, from truth?'

He cut her bonds. She didn't stand, just lay there, rubbing life back into her limbs, the wood grain beneath her face somehow reassuring.

'So think of that, if you ever are struck by a desire to confess to them. They cannot help but suspect you. All you do, in their eyes, is tainted by the fact that only a beast would hide from Orholam. They will never trust you. Think of what they have done before to drafters of paryl, a mere *color* invisible to them.'

They hunted them down. More than once. Because they feared them. Because seven colors sounded right to them.

He reached over and turned the knob of the lantern down, extinguishing it. The room was plunged into darkness, but even that wasn't total. Bits of light leaked in around the shutters.

'Tell me, Adrasteia,' he said quietly. 'It's dark here. Have you disappeared because it's dark?'

'No,' she said.

'Are you different because it's dark? Taller? Thinner? Smarter?'

'No,' she answered, uncertain.

'Tell me, have you ever been, say, trapped in a bathtub and a visitor comes, and your clothes are on the opposite side of the room?'

She still didn't know what he wanted to hear, and she only wanted to give him what he wanted. She sat up. 'Uh, I was trapped changing after Blackguard training last year. Someone took my clothes as a prank. Is that what you mean?'

He didn't answer. 'Tell me, were you doing anything wrong?'

'No,' she ventured. Unless you counted letting yourself be vulnerable to having a prank played on you in the first place as wrong.

'No. And yet you would have been ashamed to walk out into the eyes of passersby, wouldn't you?'

'Of course.'

'But if it had been dark, you wouldn't have been embarrassed, would you?'

'No.' She was starting to see it now.

'You probably hid, didn't you? But it wasn't because you were bad, on the contrary, it was because you were modest. Because you were good, as they would call good. Yes?'

'Yes.'

'So not all shame comes from wrongdoing, and not all hiding is evidence of moral failure, is it?'

'No,' she said.

'And so we stumble together onto the truth: Darkness is freedom. And that is why they hate it. That is why they fear it. Because some abuse freedom, they want none to have freedom. Because light is power, they wish to control light itself. But freedom need not be feared, and light cannot be chained. It is ever more than we see and more than we know, and when we hold it too tightly, it dazzles us and makes us blind. You and I, Adrasteia, we are called to serve in the dark. And look. You're not blind now, are you?'

Indeed, her eyes had adjusted, even without her using her tricks. It was natural. Her eyes knew what to do in darkness.

'We are the friends of light, but not its chattel. We do not fear its lash. We are equanimous; we know we are both meat and breath, flesh and spirit, animal and angel, and neither more truly one than the other. We are the priests of light and darkness, the arbiters of dusk. Neither day nor night is our master. And do you know what happens when a woman walks without fear?'

Teia shook her head, but there was a sudden longing deep in her that swelled so strong it paralyzed her tongue. Tell me. Tell me.

'She becomes.'

Becomes what? Teia didn't say the words aloud, but he knew what she was thinking, for he answered:

'She becomes whatever she wills. Minus only one thing.' In the dark, he held up a finger, almost like he was scolding her.

Teia was silent now. The question was obvious, and now she didn't want to ask it.

Sharp said, 'She has one thing she can never be, never again. You know what it is, don't you?'

The words came unbidden to her lips, from a place so dark no light had ever touched it: 'A slave.'

Chapter 70

After Karris made him look like a complete asshole, Kip went to the Prism's exercise chamber. He hoped Teia would be there. He didn't want to talk about it, but training with her was better than training alone. She made him feel better, just by being there.

She wasn't there.

He tried this week's layout of the obstacle course, sinking into the blessed distraction of taking apart problems – how could you transition from swinging across the ropes to leaping that pit to climbing that wall without stopping? It was a warrior's meditation. Of course, the calm of it was punctuated when he figured out a perfect combination. He'd need to swing one-handed, left, then right, to build up momentum, and then swing his whole body up parallel: he'd clear pit and wall all in one move. He tried it twice, and had to accept that he wasn't strong enough to lift his bulk the way he would need to.

Brain better than body. Again.

He ended on the heavy sawdust bag, as usual, trying to break it open. His fists were getting tougher all the time, and he'd been building up scar tissue and calluses on his knuckles slowly, but he still wrapped his hands in luxin in order to protect his wrists. As usual, after doing his drills, he finished up by working on that one loose stitch. It didn't seem to have budged in six months.

Kip was just finishing pounding on that one side with all his fury when someone cleared his throat. Kip almost wet himself.

Commander Ironfist was setting down a stack of books on a side table. Books? Down here? But Kip was more worried about the dubious look on the commander's face. Ironfist strode over and wordlessly examined the loose stitch.

'Won't take but a few minutes to sew that up,' Ironfist said.

Kip moved to speak, then stopped, embarrassed.

'Oh, that's how it is,' Ironfist said. 'You want to destroy someone else's property.'

'No sir!' Kip said. 'I mean . . . I suppose so, sir.' He scowled. 'I hadn't thought of it that way.'

'Can you think of any good reason why I should let you do that?'

Reasons, yes. Good reasons? No. 'Have you ever done it, sir?'

'Makes a hell of a mess. Better to stitch it or patch it.'

'So you have!'

Commander Ironfist grunted.

'How'd it feel?'

A twitch of a smile, quickly smothered. 'I'm going to repair that bag, Guile.'

Kip's face fell. 'Yes, sir.'

'In six months.'

Why wait six – oh! 'Thank you, sir!'

A grunt. The commander walked over to his side table.

'Sir? Should we talk about . . . ?' He couldn't quite say Lytos and Buskin's names.

'Oathbreakers and traitors are worth only whatever it takes to kill them, and nothing more.'

He was taking it personally, Kip could tell. The betrayal stung Ironfist as a leader and as a friend. 'Karris told you what Lytos said?' How he changed his mind?

'It changes nothing.' The commander picked up a book, signaling that there would be no more about this.

For some reason, though, Kip had found Lytos's last words, incomplete as they were, to be comforting. He'd said 'luxiat,' of that at least Kip was sure. That suggested the attempt really hadn't been at Andross's direction. That some luxiat wanted to kill him was bad, but if Andross had wanted him dead at this point . . . Honestly, Kip would probably be dead.

The commander was reading. Again. With how busy Kip knew he was. It was strange.

Kip sidled over to see if he could see the book better.

A flat stare met him. Commander Ironfist raised a hand and extended three long fingers.

'I'll, uh, be going,' Kip said.

He got to the door and turned. 'Good day, sir.'

The flat stare didn't alter a whit. The commander lowered one finger. Two.

Kip fumbled with the door, the luxin gloves making him clumsy. He chuckled awkwardly. 'Gloves,' he said, dissolving them.

The flat stare of Your Colossal Pettiness bored through him. One.

'Right. Sir.' Kip grinned weakly and got out.

He made his way to the public baths. Before he'd got into the Blackguard, he'd never wanted to come down here. He'd thought that joining the Blackguard would be the end of that problem. The Blackguards had their own private baths.

As if bathing with the perfect-bodied athletes would be better than bathing with average strangers. One or two good-natured jibes about being chubby, and Kip was gone. He knew in his head that the nunks and Blackguards didn't mean harm, that a rough sense of humor was necessary for survival in what they did. But like Andross said, even an obvious, well-defended target might still be vulnerable. Kip laughed off the jabs and shot back his own and smiled . . . and never went to the Blackguard baths again.

The main public baths were separated by gender – not that some sneaking each way didn't happen with some regularity – and though many people opted for thin bathing robes, more went nude. Even the robes were too much sharing for Kip. Once they were wet, they barely covered anything; they clung to every inglorious curve, and were thin enough that you could soap your limbs through them. Kip had opted instead for sponge baths and washing his head in his basin.

There were, however, extensive private baths. Some were reserved for nobility, but others were open to anyone who paid the small fee. Lords got in free, got free soap, got free towels, got access to any temperature bath they wanted, and were given a share of the services of a bath slave, who would bring refreshments or towels. Kip had heard that at other baths in the city and through the satrapies, the bath slave was often a prostitute, but that wasn't tolerated at the Chromeria. The bath slaves here were the same genders as the bathers and definitely not picked for their looks.

'Any of the hot baths unattended today?' Kip asked the head slave of the men's side, signing in as a noble. It was one privilege he was not shy about claiming.

An older slave took him to a bath down a long hallway so humid that water beaded on the walls and steam obscured vision. Privacy wasn't guaranteed: even the small baths could hold half a dozen people at busy times before religious festivals or the Luxlords' Ball. But most days, Kip would either be alone or have to share with only one other person.

The man left Kip after making sure he had all he needed, putting Kip's clothing and effects in a basket and leaving him alone with a robe and soap and a summons bell. It was an odd time of day to bathe – late morning – so Kip hung the robe on one of the pegs provided so it would be dry when he got out. Most of the students would be in classes now.

Classes, there was a thought. How long had it been since Kip had gone to every one of his classes?

He got into the water quickly, despite its heat and the solitude. He reclined against the side.

The heat slowly worked its magic on the stiffness in his muscles, and was beginning to unknot his mind, too. What was his problem? Clinging to Karris like that? He needed to grow up. He was basically an orphan, and it was time to deal with that. Someone offers you friendship, and you ask them to be family. For Orholam's sake, Kip, you smother people. You're so needy. It's disgusting.

And this self-pity is *sooo* helpful. Maybe it's time to *break* that habit, eh, Breaker?

Kip scrubbed his hands over his face. He sighed, eyes closed against all the world, letting the steam melt him. When he opened his eyes, there was someone in the bath with him.

'Aren't you the bold one?' Tisis Malargos said. 'What are you doing in the ladies' baths?'

A bolt went through Kip. He jerked upright and almost fled. Then he looked down. He was stark naked. He was chubby and stark naked and utterly trapped. He swallowed. He looked around for identifying marks to show that he was in the men's baths, but the private baths didn't have any. Had the old slave been senile and brought him here by accident? 'I'm not – I'm not – I'm not in the ladies' baths . . . am I?'

'I'm afraid so.' She was definitely amused. Just letting him wallow in misery.

He looked toward the door, and thought about making a break for it.

'Don't forget,' she said, 'the baths are at the mesh point.'

'The what what?'

'The hallways and changing rooms are part of the island, while the baths are part of the interior of the Chromeria and rotate with all the structures above. This time of day, if you're not careful, you could end up heading right out in the main ladies' bath.'

Kip blinked. No wonder he'd gotten lost down here before! With the rotation of all of the Chromeria as it followed the sun, depending what time of day you came down here, a hallway might line up with a different room than it had last time you'd been here. He looked back down at the water. It was pretty soapy, right? Pretty much opaque, right? He sat down. 'I suppose this is revenge?' he asked.

A quick, puzzled scowl, then a grin. 'Actually, no. I had no idea you'd be modest. Especially not painfully so. Orholam knows the rest of the men in your family aren't. I confess I meant to put you off balance. I thought you'd be amused. You said you were always seeing *me* naked.'

Kip cleared his throat, realized he had nothing to say. It was true. If she'd simply been trying to shame him, she wouldn't have gotten into the bath herself. She simply would have stood or sat outside it, fully clothed.

His mind went back to his grandfather's words about how if he played his cards right, Tisis would make love with him. And now she was naked, not two paces away. He licked lips that were miraculously dry, despite water and steam and humidity and sweat.

Oh. Oh my.

'You, uh, you paid the slave to divert me here?' he asked. She was in the water up to her collarbones, and the water *was* mostly opaque, but it was still inexplicably hard to look at her. And just as hard not to.

'I wanted to speak with you privately,' she said.

Speak. He could speak. Right?

Tisis scooted closer until she was seated right next to him. He swallowed. She was sitting so close that it was too intense to look straight into her hazel eyes, the color perfectly complemented by a thin halo-ring of green with tiny tips like wave caps into the hazel. He looked down – and realized that it probably looked like he was trying to stare through the water at her full breasts – and then he realized that it would look like that because it was true.

He snapped his head forward.

She faked a cough to hide a laugh.

It struck Kip like a note out of tune. It was a strange impulse of her, not to laugh at him outright when she could. Did she think he'd bolt if she pushed him just that extra little bit, or was it actual kindness? He looked at her quickly.

'I'm sorry, Kip,' she said. 'I've been preparing myself to talk with you for weeks now, trying to work myself up to it, and all the time I was readying myself, I was readying myself to speak to a Guile, and I forgot that you're a sixteen-year-old, too.'

That's me: underwhelming.

He had a sudden memory of telling his grandfather he *liked* to be underestimated. And here was the opposite. 'What do you want, Tisis?'

She raised her hands in mock surrender. The movement coincided with her sitting up straighter and rising perilously high in the water, her bare shoulders and chest confirming that she was not wearing a bathing robe. 'Kip, we have good reason to hate each other,' she said. 'Though I like to think my reasons are more substantial than yours are. I know you think there was some big conspiracy against you at your Threshing, but there wasn't. We always try to scare people. And when you threw the rope out of the hole, I really thought you weren't allowed to, so I gave it back. It was an innocent mistake. On the other hand, you killed my father.'

When you put it that way . . . 'Whatever that thing was, it stopped being your father long ago,' Kip said.

'Something it would have been nice to judge for myself, rather than assured that by the man who killed him. Besides, your father and uncle destroyed half the world, I—'

'And your family joined the wrong side to help do it!' Kip said. Man?

'An error we corrected,' Tisis said, her chin drifting up.

'You came out against Dazen? When? After he was killed at Sundered Rock? Brave.'

'I would think of all people, Kip, that you might not be the first to blame a person for what their family did when they were young. You weren't born yet; I was two. Should I blame you for what your mother did? Because I've heard stories – from people who heard them from you. So maybe we should focus on where we are today, and not old fights that we had no part in.'

'That sounds . . . remarkably sensible,' Kip admitted. It was easier to focus when he was having to dissect her argument, but at the same time, she'd leaned forward and up as her temper got going. He cleared his throat. 'Could you, um . . .' He took his hand and gestured down a smidge.

She looked down, and saw that her nipples were right at the waterline, and the water wasn't that soapy. 'Oh!' She blushed, and with her pale skin, he could tell immediately. She sat lower in the water. 'Thanks,' she said. Something touched his naked thigh, and he nearly shot out of the water.

She burst out laughing. 'Come on, Kip, as you so pointedly, uh, pointed out, you have seen me naked before. It shouldn't be a surprise.'

I don't think that's how seeing a beautiful woman naked works. 'The first time I saw you, I was about go into the Thresher and you looked into my eyes and lectured me about self-control. I thought you'd tear my head off if I dared – and the second time! My grandfather?!'

Her lip twisted. 'Believe me, I know I actually owe you for stopping that before it went any further.'

He looked at her and they both burst out laughing.

Her laughter wasn't seductive; it was hilarious. Full-throated, distinctive, it was the kind of laugh you could pick out of a crowd of thousands, the kind of laugh that snuck out of its cage infrequently and burned the town down when it did, 'cause, hell, it was just going back in the cage again anyway, right? And then she snorted.

They laughed harder, and she blushed and laughed and snorted so hard she ended up trailing off in tears.

They drifted into a companionable silence as Tisis wiped her eyes. She ended up cleaning off the kohl makeup dripping from around her eyes with a little towel. When she was done, Kip stared at her quizzically. Without her makeup on, she didn't look twenty-five years old like she did with it on. She didn't look her actual nineteen years. She looked about seventeen. No wonder she wore the makeup.

She was just a teenager like him, and they were both very, very alone here.

'Kip,' she said, 'the truth is, my family's in a bad spot. The False Prism's War wiped out the other branches of the family. Perversely, that strengthened us, because with all the wealth and lands of our entire clan in my uncle's hands, we became a major family. I think that your grandfather thinks we're a threat to him. We proposed that I marry your father Gavin to make an alliance, and we thought your grandfather was going to accept. Instead, Gavin married Karris. It was a slap in our faces. Never explained, never apologized for.'

She had been intending to marry Gavin? And she'd had to go from *that* to putting her hands under the blankets for my grandfather? Now there was a turn of Fortune's Wheel.

But Kip kept his features carefully blank. There's a time not to use the Lip.

'I don't know why, but I fear Andross has decided to let us be destroyed. The war isn't going well, everyone knows it. Our richest lands are those nearest the Color Prince's army. We're afraid the promachos plans to let the Color Prince take our lands and wealth and only stop him after he's destroyed us. Kip, you have no idea what it feels like to admit this – especially to a Guile – but my family is right on the edge. My mother passed away two years ago. My father's dead. If it were a will, my older sister Eirene got all the family intelligence, I got all the looks, and all the charisma I should have gotten went to my little cousin Antonius instead. Eirene will continue the family line if she absolutely must, but it would be hell for her, and I won't do that to her if I can help it.'

'What?' Kip asked. Sure, some women didn't want to get stuck raising children, but a wealthy family would have slaves for that, wouldn't they?

A scowl. 'I forget you're not in the gossip circles,' Tisis said. 'Her interest in taking any man to bed is about equal to your interest in taking your grandfather to bed.'

'Oh,' Kip said, not understanding. Then, '*Oh!*'

'My cousin Antonius was on his way here to bring orders from my sister. His ship was captured by pirates. They haven't asked a ransom, which they would, if he were alive.' Her eyes went vacant, her voice an echo of itself. She obviously loved him very much. 'That leaves me,' she said. 'Kip, our southern plantations and forests *can* be defended. But if they aren't . . . those are my people. More than fifty thousand of them. I grew up in those lands. I played banconn in their festival parades.

I was taught farming and husbandry and logging in those little towns. I played with little boys and girls there. Many of those little girls I played with have children of their own now. Life moves faster out on the farms. I will do *anything* to save my people.'

Including getting on your back for my grandfather.

'Yes,' she said quietly, reading his mind. 'Even that. My virginity for their lives? I'll take that trade any day.'

For some reason, the statement made Kip deeply ashamed of himself. He'd judged Tisis as if she were merely angling for the attention of the most important man in the room, willing to debase herself even with Andross Guile. Like she was a tramp or a prostitute.

Some of the noble families had made their base on Big Jasper for so long that they had little to no connection to their ancestral holdings. Perhaps the lord or lady would make one trip a year to check how the stewards were keeping things together, but their children were left vying with the children of other nobles for who could throw the most lavish party, who could gamble better or dance better or ride better, with constant talk of who'd bedded whom that morphed into who would marry whom, followed by more gossip of who was carrying on affairs with whom. Or they used some tiny sliver of magical talent to get into the Chromeria, where they ended up doing much the same, with a side of studying. Kip hadn't been part of those circles despite his pedigree, his time taken up entirely with studies or training.

That hadn't been a mistake, he knew. Gavin must have realized that if Kip had come in as a bastard from Tyrea and been thrown in among those wolves, they would have torn him apart. That was what the Blackguard training was for. That, and Gavin's realization that war was coming, and Kip would need as much martial training as possible.

Kip had assumed that Tisis was part of those circles. After all, she was rich and highly talented with green and beautiful. She had to be petty and boring and gossip-mongering to make up for it, right?

It made Kip wonder how people judged Gavin Guile, who was frustratingly Everything Good. Surely they must secretly hate him. Come to think of it, what did people think of Kip, who'd swooped in out of nowhere and taken up the mantle of the foremost family in the Seven Satrapies?

Suddenly, the Blackguard looked like a warm blanket that Kip didn't ever want to leave. People judged him for himself there, mostly. Some of them even liked him. No one had given him trouble for being Tyrean since he became an inductee. What mattered in his unit was what you were doing to help the unit succeed. Kip hated being judged, but had barely noticed when the judgment of him stopped.

And here was Tisis, ready to sell her body to save her people, and Kip was judging her and calling her whore.

'Orholam have mercy,' he muttered into the water. 'Tisis, I'm so sorry for, for everything. For how I treated you. For what I said. It was vile. I'm so, so sorry.'

She blinked rapidly, looked away. 'I tried to go back to him, you know? After you left. He wouldn't take me. Put me out of his room like a . . .'

Kip said, 'He is . . . not a nice man.' A deep hatred started burning there. It was one thing for Andross to debase Kip, then point out his debasement and laugh at him. It was quite another to see him do it to someone else.

'No,' she laugh-cried. She dabbed an eye with a finger, getting control of herself. 'No, he's not that. You know, the only thing that really surprises me is that he didn't bed me first. I mean, I already feel pretty gross about myself – "gross about myself"? Well, you know what I mean. I would have felt a hundred times worse if he'd used me and then cast me off. It seems more like his style. I mean, we'd barely gotten started – sorry, you don't want to know all that. Maybe he was afraid I'd get pregnant and then he'd have a bastard to worry about.'

No, it wasn't that. He was playing a different game.

But Kip didn't say anything.

Hey, she hadn't said 'another bastard to worry about,' so apparently she had some tact.

For the next few minutes, as she recovered, Kip studied her openly. Without the makeup she always wore, she was still intimidatingly beautiful, but this natural beauty was softer, and of course younger, than that icy perfection. He found himself warming to her.

What just happened? Did we just kind of become friends? How did that happen so fast?

Andross Guile, who pissed on everything, had said she would try to seduce Kip. Was that what this was? A very clever seduction? Was she simply playing him?

He couldn't see it.

Hell, if she was this good and this was all an act, he'd rather be on her side regardless, because if she was this good, no one else was going to stand a chance.

'So, uh, my skin's getting all pruney,' Kip said. 'How do we get out of here gracefully? Ladies first? I mean, it doesn't matter since I've already seen you naked, right?'

She sighed and let herself sink into the water until she was blowing bubbles in it. 'So,' she said. She winced.

Kip waited. Nothing. 'So?' he prompted.

She bobbed higher and he glanced down through the water, though he didn't think she noticed. Dammit! And he'd been so high-minded a few moments ago. 'So I didn't just come here because I needed a bath, though I notice you haven't washed, pruney or not.'

'Oh. Right.' Kip picked up the soap from the edge of the bath. He started soaping up his left shoulder awkwardly.

'So I shared all about my family and the situation I'm in . . .' Tisis said.

Kip stopped soaping. She expected him to do the same? 'Tisis, it's been really nice talking to you. I mean, really nice. A huge surprise, actually, but a bunch of classes end right around now, and dozens or hundreds of people are going to be heading down here any minute. I don't think we have time for my whole history.'

They heard the banging of a distant door slamming, and both of them nearly bolted.

'Right,' Tisis said. She licked her lips. 'But you are isolated, too, right? I mean, I need friends, you need friends, right? Something solid.'

'Sure, that'd be . . . nice. I don't know if it's *possible*. Sooner or later, I'm going to get kicked out of the Blackguard, or nicely promoted out of it. You saw. My grandfather hates me. I've secured funding to keep on at the Chromeria, but yes, you could say my position is . . . not strong.' He'd been so assiduously not thinking about it that thinking about it now slapped him in the face.

She exhaled a big breath again. 'That's pretty much what I thought. I have a plan, and I don't want you to answer now, but I want you to think about it seriously. Come down to the baths next week, same time. The same slave will meet you and bring you back here.'

'Now I'm curious,' Kip said.

She was blushing. 'This is not exactly how I'd planned for this to happen . . .' She took a deep breath, let it out. She bobbed under the water. Scrunched her face as she emerged.

'Why am I the one who feels awkward here?' Kip asked.

'Marry me, Kip.'

A sound like someone was strangling a small animal came from somewhere. Oh, Kip's throat.

She blushed harder. 'Just think about it?'

'What?!'

Then she daintily dashed up the steps out of the bath, snatched Kip's bathing robe from its hook, and ran tiptoe out of the room. Between her words and her nudity, Kip was speechless.

'Hey, wait!' he shouted finally. 'I don't know how to get out of here! There's only that one robe!'

Then he realized he, a man, had just shouted – in the women's baths. Idiot! He jumped out of the water and dashed in the opposite direction from where Tisis had disappeared. Naked turtle-bear coming through!

Chapter 71

In the closest thing to a corner she could find in a circular library, Teia was working on her assignment for Murder Sharp. The man might be an utter horror, but he was also a font of knowledge about paryl. And as far as Teia knew, with Marta

Martaens having fled, he was the only source of knowledge about paryl available: there was nothing in even the forbidden libraries about paryl. Damn luxors.

But Murder Sharp dropped the answers to her biggest questions like they were nothing.

'The other colors,' she'd ventured, 'they have metaphysical effects.'

'Meta-what?'

Oh, right. Murder Sharp hadn't gotten his education in the Chromeria. Best not to make it look like she was trying to rub it in. 'Like red makes you more prone to anger, and superviolet makes you more logical over time. What does paryl do?'

He'd chuckled. 'Haven't noticed, huh? Maybe you're special, like me. I'm a bit of a curiosity among paryl drafters.'

A curiosity. That was one way to put it. But she painted a carefully neutral but interested look on her face. He'd given in.

'Paryl makes you a feeler. Think about it. It's way down below sub-red, opposite to superviolet. Superviolet makes you more logical. Paryl makes you empathetic. You get incredibly attuned to the emotions around you, whether mundane or magical. I'm lucky. I'm just aware of them; they don't affect me. Other paryl drafters – most of the few we got – aren't so lucky. They themselves feel what others are feeling. For some, to a horrifying degree. "Weep with those who are weeping, rejoice with those who are rejoicing." It could have been written with a paryl in mind. That refined feeling, though, is our greatest weakness and our greatest strength. It's why we feel light itself. First, we get good at feeling light's effects. Then we simply become aware of light itself. Then we can split it.'

'All paryls are lightsplitters?' How could the Chromeria not know such a thing?

'One in ten, maybe. Which is about a thousand times more frequently than other colors.'

It turned out that half of what Marta Martaens had taught her about paryl was worthless. Paryl made a gel, Marta had said. Master Sharp had admitted that could be done, but wondered why you'd want to use it very often. 'There's a resonance point higher up that can be used to make a gel. We only use it to mark targets, because it evaporates quickly. Other than that? Good for paryl torches, I guess, but I just fling the light directly. So maybe if you want to give paryl to someone else for some reason?' And then he'd shown her another resonance point: it was a gas. It was also much, much easier to draft than paryl's solid or gel forms.

Then he'd given her the assignment she was working on now. She drafted a shell of paryl in a bubble around her.

It was, of course, invisible. It was also so delicate that any touch shattered it. But delicate didn't mean useless. With the bubble surrounding her, she drafted paryl gas to fill it. This, too, was invisible – which was why she could practice in the library without worrying about being interrupted, so long as she flipped the page of the tome open in her lap every so often and didn't let them see her eyes.

By drafting paryl, Teia was made more sensitive to the touch of colors. Having paryl gas actually touching her skin seemed to enhance that sensitivity even further. Having it surround her also meant she was breathing it, though it had no taste and only the faintest scent.

The paryl bubble not only acted as a good way to contain the paryl gas, but it was also a lens. Just as a blue lens filtered out all colors except blue, or as a clear glass window still filtered out some superviolet light, so too did paryl have an effect on the light that passed through it. It was like a gentle sieve.

A sieve of light? The idea had seemed impossible, but it was true. Paryl nudged every color closer to its true color – that spectrum at which it could be drafted. Through even this much paryl, each color seemed more vibrant, brighter. Master Sharp said this was evidence that paryl was the master color. Except he said it like it was capitalized. 'Paryl is the Master Color,' he'd said, his voice reverent.

But Teia had heard red magisters come up with reasons why red was the best color. Blue magisters told their upper-level discipulae why blue was the true color – Orholam's favorite shade, the color of sea and sky. Yellows made the case for why yellow was Orholam's favorite – the strong center of the spectrum, whose solid heart was unbreakable gold. As far as Teia was concerned, much as she would like paryl to be amazing and great – it was her only color, after all – paryl was just another color with some quirks. Like yellow could be liquid or frozen and was useful in each form.

Teia had seen the tenth-year discipulae – those few permanent students who were able to convince their sponsors that they could best serve them by doing research – experiment with polarized lenses. When one lens was placed in a beam of light, nothing appeared to happen. When a second was placed downstream in the same beam, still nothing happened – until either lens was rotated. Then the beam of light went dark.

This seemed to be something similar. Unless, of course, it was something totally different. She was forbidden to ask anyone about it.

She finished her assignments for her other lectures, maintaining the bubble as well as she could while doing so. It was impossible, and even when she did it right, she realized she soon ran out of air. For that matter, she was inhaling an awful lot of paryl gas. Was that healthy?

On the scale of things likely to kill you, T, breathing paryl goes somewhere below murderous heretics, insane assassins, conquering pagans, and plain stupidity.

That was one way to look on it.

She finished her work and headed back to her barracks. She tried to maintain the bubble, drafting in quick gulps, averting her eyes from passersby, then returning them to normal, and glancing once again after traversing only a few paces. But the bubble kept snapping from her uneven support of it – the rolling motion of walking itself broke the bubble at whatever direct support beams she attached to it. Then when she was sure she was supporting the bubble correctly, walking so lightly and fluidly and holding the bubble at so many points it shouldn't break, she watched as the force of the wind from her walking caved the front of the bubble in. It held form for one second, then cracked and split and dissolved into nothing. Again.

'Tsst.'

The whisper almost didn't register. Teia walked right past the open door, totally absorbed in her – oh hell!

She froze. Master Sharp! He was dressed in the embroidered linen and wide belt of a rich Ruthgari, with his petasos worn on his back, the ties interwoven with gold threads. A part of her noted the clothing with approval: rich enough to allow free movement around most of the Chromeria, but not so rich as to be memorable.

He beckoned her to step into the room he was in. It was an office of some kind. He'd clearly broken in. She made sure no one was looking, and stepped in.

'This will be quick,' Master Sharp said. He grinned at her, all perfect teeth. He closed the door behind her. 'The time has come for you to prove your loyalty. Sun Day is only three days away. The White is attending rehearsals, right now. You will go to a room two floors below her room. Out the window, you'll find a knotted rope. It will take you up one floor. Then you're to use these to climb to the next.' He handed her a bag of what felt like rocks.

She took one out. It was a crescent roughly the size of her hand. The mouth of the crescent was almost flat. A tab of blue luxin stuck out from the mouth.

'You wipe the wall as clean as you can get it. You peel the tab off, and you stick it immediately to the wall, hard. It'll hold five times your weight. When you climb down, you pull this off the bottom.' He flipped out a ring. 'It's attached to a string. The string is coated with a solvent. You use the string to pop the crescent off the wall. This is important. You're to leave no trace, understood? There may be a little luxin left on the wall. It'll dissolve in minutes.'

'What am I supposed to do when I get there?'

'There will still be a Blackguard or two posted right outside the door. Her room slave has been dealt with.'

'Killed?' Teia asked. He still hadn't answered her question.

'Sent on a task. We believe the shimmercloaks are in the bottom drawer of the White's desk. That or in her slave's dresser in the attached slave quarters.' So that was the goal. Shimmercloaks. Just like they'd guessed. 'We expect you have half an hour. The door to the balcony has been left unlocked.'

'You have a Blackguard in your employ,' Teia said. 'Why not have him get it for you?'

Master Sharp looked at her like she was stupid.

Oh. Because they didn't want to expose him. Or her. The

Blackguards would be the first people suspected – even though no one would want to suspect them, who else could steal something from the White's very chambers?

The further implication was that whichever Blackguard *was* the Order's man, he would be somewhere with a good alibi during this job. Perhaps it would be someone who was with the White right now. Regardless, it would also have to be someone who could have gotten into the White's room quite recently in order to unlock the balcony door – which was kept locked at all times since the assassination attempt a few months ago. Between those two bits of information, surely Teia could limit the pool of possible traitors.

Later.

'What do the cloaks look like?' Teia asked.

Murder Sharp bared his too-white teeth at her. Maybe it was a grin. He showed her the inside of his cloak. It was a supple gray cloth, fine-woven. He flipped the cloak over and showed her the pocket at the neckline, gave her a glimpse of the golden choker inside. 'One of them is burned at the hem. There should be two. We know the burned one is there. If you bring both, you will find great favor. If you bring only the burned one, they may still not trust you.'

'You're telling me I could bring you a treasure as great as a shimmercloak and *still* not be trusted?' Teia demanded.

'The room's Prudence twenty-seven. Get moving,' Master Sharp said. He scowled, as if he wished he hadn't given away the part about the two cloaks. 'Oh, and the trick with the paryl bubble is to support it with the gas itself. No hard points. If the gas is dense enough, you can hold an open connection to it, and without your eyes black orbs of night. My own master said that our ancient forebears could hold the cloud in formation around them without a shell even as they moved, even in wind, or while sprinting or fighting.'

That was impressive, but . . . 'Why would that help?' Teia asked.

'The shimmercloaks help us lightsplitters attain invisibility. The mechanics of the cloaks are different, but the idea was based on something, you know.'

'You mean . . . ?' Teia started. It was impossible.

'The ancient masters were called mist walkers for a reason. They didn't need cloaks.'

Chapter 72

Think of it this way, T: you hate waiting. For some insane reason, like every soldier, you prefer the moments of terror to the monotony of boredom.

Teia remembered leading the Blackguard up the cliff path to the fort on Ruic Head. She'd led an assault by the best force in the entire world. Surely she could climb a ladder. She'd climbed up the side of the fort with enemies shooting cannons mere feet away. This would be easy.

To distract herself as she walked, she tried to support the paryl bubble with paryl gas alone. It worked, easily. If she left the bubble open at the bottom, a hand's breadth above the ground, she could float along inside it and still breathe.

She rounded a corner and saw Kip coming out of the lift. She stopped suddenly and ducked backward so he wouldn't see her. She forgot to push the bubble back as she did so it shattered when she moved back into it – but it shattered silently and invisibly. She waited. If Kip was coming her direction, she'd see him any second.

But he didn't come. He must have been headed to the library.

She made it to the lift unseen. She went up to the floor named Prudence – the luxiats' name for one of the upper floors – and made it unseen. There was no one in the hallways. She made it to room twenty-seven unseen.

The door was unlocked.

No one inside.

She checked the window. It was big enough. It opened easily, and the rope was hanging precisely where it was supposed to be. It was even knotted for easier climbing – which Teia appreciated greatly. She could make it up an unknotted rope, but with difficulty. Her upper-body strength wasn't what she wished.

She checked the door behind her, secured the bag she was carrying with the climbing crescents, and prayed for about ten seconds. Don't give yourself too much time. Too much thinking will stop you. You take long enough to prep your gear and gather your wits, but don't take any time to gather your courage. Courage delayed is cowardice. Courage is action.

But I don't want to die.

Move, T.

She grabbed the rope, tugged on it. It felt solid. Of course, it would. If they were trying to kill her, they—

They wouldn't do it in the tower.

She was climbing before she knew what she was doing. Much better. She avoided looking down and worked her way up, knot to knot to knot. It was late afternoon, not exactly the time she would have picked. But this was when the White was out of her room, and Teia didn't have any choice regardless. At least she was climbing in the shadowed side of the Prism's Tower, so while the sun was descending, anyone looking her direction would be dazzled by the sun beyond her.

Thank Orholam it was a cold spring day with a chilling wind: hardly anyone would be outside.

The tricky part was always making the transitions, from rope to balcony this time. But Teia was a good climber. She hitched up a foot, swung the rope around it, locking the rope against one of its knots, and used that as a step. With that and both hands on the balcony rail, she vaulted into the balcony as if she did this every day.

It made her think about climbing the balconies at the Lucigari estate with the little girl she'd been bought to be a playmate for, Sarai. Easy.

She checked the door, and found it was unlocked, as it was supposed to be. She glanced inside. There was no one inside. It was a small, plain room, but this high in the tower, it must be the room of a favored slave. Or a room reserved for such, but empty now. Teia's curiosity was hot, but she didn't have time to poke around. She stepped back outside, closed the door gently, and examined the climb.

She wished she could use a grapnel, but she knew why she couldn't. She would descend by the same rope, and that would mean leaving the grapnel behind as evidence. The whole point of this job was that the shimmercloak would simply disappear.

Mercifully, she had plenty of the climbing crescents. She wasn't going to have to make it a stretch to reach each one. She scrubbed the wall with a sleeve in an area not too high above the balcony railing off to the right, peeled off the blue luxin cap, and stuck the crescent there. She snapped the blue luxin cap in her hand, and it dissolved into dust.

The next crescent went higher, up to the left. Left foot onto railing, right foot up onto the crescent, left hand reaching to the top one. And repeat. No hurry.

The climb wasn't far, but Teia took her time. As she climbed, she angled to the left. If she fell now, she'd hit the balcony below. In two more steps, there would be nothing below her but the great yard far, far below.

The clouds were thickening and it was getting darker rapidly, exacerbated by being on the shadow side of the tower. Teia had a thought, and drafted the paryl gas. With it floating above her head but still connected to her will, she could use it as a torch.

So the 'ancient masters' hadn't only been thinking of invisibility. Having the torch close, but above her instead of in her line of sight, made it much more useful.

The wind gusted hard and she lost the paryl. She clung to the crescents like a spider, pressing her body against the tower.

The wind abated, and Teia drafted paryl again and kept climbing. Easy. She had enough crescents that she climbed higher than the balcony so she could simply step from the crescents to the railing and then drop into the balcony. Her hands were getting stiff and clumsy from the cold anyway. No reason to take chances. She just prayed it didn't start raining before she got out of here.

She dropped into the balcony and landed lightly. Easy. She squatted there, low, with her hands in her armpits, bringing feeling back to them and resting her tired arms. If she opened that door and there was a Blackguard standing right there, she was going to have to come out here and climb down at breakneck speed.

Thinking of that, she stood and found the tabs on the two

crescents she could reach and popped them down. If she had to cut away the crescents to frustrate pursuit, she was going to have to do it *fast*.

She paused one heartbeat more. She couldn't use the paryl to look through the wood door; that only worked with thin, permeable materials like clothing. Courage is action, T.

She tested the door handle, turning it slowly. It turned, unlocked, exactly as it was supposed to be. She hadn't heard any creak from the mechanism, but here on the outside with the wind, she wouldn't. There was nothing for it. She completed turning the handle and opened the door a crack.

With the curtains drawn, the White's chamber was dark. The difference in temperature between the chamber and the outside air meant Teia was causing quite a draft. She ducked inside, keeping low, and closed the door behind her. The curtains blew – and settled.

With a quick paryl torch in her hand, Teia scanned the room for hiding places. Had the wind rattled the outer door in its hinges? If it had, the Blackguard standing outside would check it immediately or not at all.

Heart in her throat, she dashed on tiptoe toward the White's desk as fast as she dared. She stumbled on the edge of a thick carpet and fell to her hands and knees, extinguishing her paryl torch. Because of the luxurious thickness of the carpet, however, the fall was neither loud nor painful.

Teia almost burst out laughing from the ridiculousness and the tension. And then she remembered: laughing might mean death here.

The door didn't open. The Blackguard outside didn't check.

Teia collected herself and drew in paryl. She thought for a second, and drafted the shell again. She filled it with paryl gas to be a floating overhead torch for her, and the room lit in her vision. Now that was more like it.

One of the mysteries of paryl was that it was so distinct. It was farther down the spectrum from sub-red, and sub-red was indistinct. Teia had assumed that there was some qualitative property of light that made it finer at superviolet and less fine at sub-red. But something must happen between sub-red and paryl, because she could see perfectly.

Teia glanced into the slave's quarters. Empty. Easy.

She went to the desk – and immediately broke her paryl shell on the wood. The paryl gas inside, however, was inert. It didn't go rushing anywhere. With a little sigh – was this the time to be figuring out paryl? – she reformed the shell. She moved forward, let it break, but held the rest of it so that only the part that physically was hit broke. With Murder Sharp's revelation that she could hold an open connection to the paryl through the gas, it was actually simple.

With great care, Teia went through the desk. How many lethal secrets sat here? Papers and notes and ink and even a number of Nine Kings cards – funny, Teia didn't know the old lady played. In the bottom drawer, carefully folded, there was a dark cloak. Teia shook it out, revealing a snarling fox stitched subtly gray on gray. The hem was burned short; a gold choker adorned the neck, and the material was thin, silky, but strong. Easy.

Too easy? Teia licked her lips. She rolled the cloak, tucked it into the pack on her back, secured it.

There was no other cloak.

For one moment, panic closed her throat. Then she thought, no, of course there isn't. This is all a setup, but it's not a setup for me.

This cloak is so short only a petite woman or a boy could wear it. How many lightsplitters exist? How many of those were petite women or boys? One. They couldn't kill Teia if she was the only one who could make use of this cloak for them.

It could be a lucky accident, but Teia saw the White's hand in it. Or if not the White's, then Orholam's own. Of course, by some accounts of how Orholam worked, this was his doing even if it was the White's doing. So . . .

Thank you, sir. I'll pray properly when I'm not, uh, risking my life. And I'll stop skipping weekly worship.

So often.

She was finished. Even if the other cloak was in some other closet, she realized now that it would be tempting death to bring it with her. Forget it.

She was walking toward the balcony when she heard a voice

outside the door. The door opened and a Blackguard poked his head in. It was Baya Niel, a green who was a veteran of the Battle of Ru. He'd fought Atirat himself alongside Kip and Karris and Gavin Guile. He was illuminated in the pure yellow light of a lux torch.

Teia froze. There was no cover. Nothing within a jump. Her heart stopped. Battle juice flooded her veins, but where every other of a thousand times it had thrown her into action, this time it failed her, or she it. She couldn't move. She knew what was going to happen next. Through the paryl cloud surrounding her, she saw something odd about the yellow light reflected off Baya Niel's ghotra, his nose, his arm, which was turning, turning.

If it wasn't her imagination, the yellow seemed to give Teia a strange clarity, a fast understanding beyond her own intelligence. She could kill Baya Niel, the logic of it told her, she had the paryl in hand, and she knew how to drop him limp to the floor in no time.

But she couldn't kill a Blackguard. Not to save herself.

A thought flitted through her head: I could have just asked the White for the cloak, and she would have given it to me.

When Baya Niel saw her, he would have already been briefed by the White on the plan and he would do nothing, or he would capture her, and Teia's usefulness as a spy would be destroyed. There were ways out of this, but none of them were acceptable – and that was the strength of yellow. It wasn't the pure, detached logic of blue or the passion of the reds. It was logic and emotion balanced. Teia surrendered to that implacable human logic. She stood still, unthreatening, as Baya Niel swung the lux torch into view.

Teia's skin tingled like snowflakes teasing every nerve. Some disembodied part of her felt like her skin was kneading dough, pulling apart and drawing back together.

Baya Niel's gaze passed right over her. He shot glances around the room, searching. His eyes went right past her again, through her, beyond her, and again. She wasn't six steps away. He wasn't pretending not to see her. She saw his eyes. They didn't even hesitate. There was no flicker of refocusing. He wasn't being clever; he was blind to her. And as he swung the lux torch this way and that, Teia's brain seemed to hiss and spit.

And in that second, Teia knew. That lux torch. Her cloud of paryl. The lux torch gave off a single tight spectrum of yellow light. That, paired with the paryl's refocusing properties, meant that Teia's light splitting had to deal only with one single spectrum of light. It was a small enough challenge that she was doing it – unknowing. This was what the ancients did, while moving, with every spectrum of light at once. Teia was doing that, albeit without moving, and with only a fraction of yellow.

Baya Niel swung his torch back out of the way and closed the door.

Teia was off like a bolt. She ran to the door. As she opened it, gently, she heard Baya Niel's voice. 'You know,' he said, 'I should check the locks out to the balcony. Those boys they've jumped up to full 'guards keep forgetting—'

She didn't hear the rest. She slipped out of the door, shattering the paryl and losing it. She closed the door just as the other door opened. The difference in air pressure was a quick hiss. She climbed over the railing and onto her climbing crescents. She pulled the tab of the first one, exposing the razor string. She pulled the razor string in a quick circle, cutting the climbing crescent off the wall.

Teia took a quick step down as the door to the balcony opened and full-spectrum light flooded out. Despite her prayers, there must have been misting rain while she was inside, because the lower crescent was slick and her foot slid right off it. With one hand filled with a climbing crescent and one foot flying into space, she grappled spasmodically to keep from flying off the tower.

Her body swung and slapped against the tower. She lost the climbing crescent in her free hand, scrambled, and held. She was low enough that her knee was almost in the foothold she'd missed. But that was no good. The spacing was for feet and hands. She pulled, her left arm trembling, her hamstring screaming, and pulled herself back up, got her right foot back where it belonged.

There was no time to pause. If he looked over this edge, he'd see her. She pulled a tab, circled the razor wire, and retrieved the next crescent, putting it in her pack. Took a careful step down onto the next slick crescent, repeat. She had barely disappeared under the balcony and taken a deep breath when she heard a 'Huh.'

Yellow light stabbed the darkness as Baya Niel held the lux torch out over the side where Teia had just been. Then it swung back.

She heard the door open and close.

She let her muscles recuperate for a few moments. They needed the rest, but waiting too long would mean letting her cold fingers get stiff and clumsy.

Nonetheless, she was methodical, and she made it down to her balcony with no problem. There was a heavily cloaked man inside the room sitting with his back to her. The sight of him suddenly there almost made her faint.

At the sound of her coming in, he held up a note in gloved fingers, but didn't turn.

It read: 'This one will stow the rope as soon as you're done with it. Do not speak to him. He is not to know your identity, nor you his. He is in danger simply doing this. Leave nothing with him. You have one minute after you give him the note back before he removes the ladder.'

Teia checked that all her items were still securely stowed – minus the one crescent she'd dropped. She handed the man the note, saw the quick flash of paper being consumed with fire, and slipped down the rope to the next balcony. She rolled her shoulders. Easy.

She took the lift down to the level of the Blackguard barracks, and ran smack into Kip.

'Hey,' he said. 'I've been looking for you everywhere. I got something I really need to talk to you about. Why are you wet?'

Teia did not want to talk to Kip while she was carrying a purloined shimmercloak and a dozen climbing crescents, especially because the most obvious places for Kip to take her would be either the Blackguard barracks or down to one of the training areas, where she would have to change clothes and endanger herself and her stolen goods.

'Where are you going?' she asked, ignoring his questions.

'I thought we'd go to my apartments. Like I said, I got a thing.'

'So mysterious,' she said. She meant it to come out teasing, but her fuse was a little short.

He dropped his hands as if she'd hit him somewhere sensitive. 'Teia,' he said. 'Please. Please?'

Kip, being serious and contrite and vulnerable? Now there's no way I can *not* go with him.

She thought of the hug she hadn't returned, and how she regretted it. Kip, you have terrible timing. The worst.

'Sure,' she said. You're gonna get me killed.

She followed him. Halfway there, she thought she heard a scuff of a shoe on stone behind them. Glanced. Nothing.

She glanced again, this time in paryl, and saw that Murder Sharp was trailing them, invisibly. He lifted a finger to his lips, forbidding her from saying or doing anything. She wondered for a moment if she could shrug off the pack on her back and just drop it as they rounded a corner. Surely Master Sharp would have no choice but to pick it up, and maybe leave her alone, right?

But what if she wasn't terribly adroit? What if Kip saw her acting strangely about her pack? He'd ask instantly, and then he'd get tenacious, and wouldn't leave her alone until he knew what was inside. So curious all the time, always wanted to know what was going on with everything. He was like a bad cat.

So they walked, her dread growing, all the way to Kip's room. In paryl, she saw Master Sharp gesture, insistent. Hell no. But there was no disobeying him, not now, not ever.

She left the door open, and Master Sharp stepped inside to join them invisibly, intent to hear every secret word.

'Finally,' Kip said. 'Privacy.'

Chapter 73

'Here's the thing, Teia. Dammit, I keep saying here's the thing.' He heaved a sigh. 'We both know I'm not going to be a Blackguard.'

'What? No, we don't,' she said.

'Are you kidding?' Kip asked. Surely he'd been the only person blind.

'What are you talking about? Our squad's the best in the Blackguard. Your skills are improving all the time. Breaker, get over this. You're always worrying. You're—'

'I'm not worried about that!' he said, like it was ridiculous. Which was unfair, of course, since he'd been worried about precisely that as long as he'd known Teia.

'You've been worried about it for as long as I've—'

'Teia, I'm a Guile. There's no way they'll let me take final vows. Who would they let a Guile guard? Who would they trust me with? I've only made it this long because the war has everyone else looking the other way. But when it comes time for vows? Probably my grandfather will spring other plans on me. But maybe the White. Maybe one of the other Colors. I'm my father's son, and that means I have value to people I don't even know, people who hate my family. And those people aren't moving yet, because even though they think my father is dead, they don't know how much Andross hates me. As soon as they realize I'm not under his protection, or—' He cut off. Orholam's mercy, he'd almost said "or once my half brother Zymun shows up." He'd been that close to spilling it. 'I'm fucked, Teia.'

'Hey,' she said, 'Blackguards guard their tongues.' She glanced off to the side.

Kip rolled his eyes. 'Exactly,' he said. 'In other words, not me. I'm just the acknowledged son who everybody knows is really a bastard, but if the Guiles want to pretend I'm a real son, well then, they're Guiles. They get to. Yet another reason to hate us. It was all a fantasy. In fact, I think my father got me in just to teach me how to fight. That cold, shrewd—'

'Maybe he did it so you could have friends,' Teia said. 'Maybe you're being unfair to a man who gave you everything.'

'I'm starting to have my doubts about my sainted father,' Kip said. He pushed his hair back with a hand. 'Anyway. Anyway! So . . . I'm not going to be a Blackguard. Think about what that means.'

He thought she'd figure it out instantly. 'Kip!' she complained. 'I have no idea what you mean.'

He blanched, looked away, felt suddenly vulnerable, squirmed. 'Blackguards can't . . . Blackguards can't be involved with other Blackguards.'

'Right,' she said, like what he was saying was trivially true. Not. Connecting. The. Dots.

Don't make me say it, Teia.

'But if I *weren't* in the Blackguard, I could be involved with someone . . . who is.'

'Rrrright,' she said. Eyebrow rising like coaxing a small child: Use your words, Kip. Then her hand flew up to her mouth. 'Oh shit!'

Not the reaction he'd been hoping for. But in for a danar, in for a quintar. He stared at the wall. It felt like he was tearing his heart out and throwing it against that spot.

'I'm about to run out of friends and allies here, Teia. I've angered my grandfather no end, and with a word, he can end my tenure with the Blackguards. And it's not like you . . . you all will have your duties, which may include stopping me from, you know, killing my grandfather.'

'Kip, it's not like we're going to forget you.'

'No, actually, it's exactly like that. Or worse than that. The whole point of the Blackguard is that your loyalty is to the Blackguard and to whomever the White tells you your loyalty needs to be to. With a promachos? Your job may be to kill me, just like that.' He was angry, but he wasn't angry at her. He wasn't being fair. He really had ambushed her. Maybe she hadn't even thought of it. Until recently, he'd been kind of relieved to be in a brotherhood where he didn't even have to think of relationships for a time.

'Kip, we would never turn against—'

We, she said. Not I. He interrupted, 'Point is, turns out friends are a luxury I may not get. So what I need are allies. Tisis gives me that. What—'

'Tisis?'

'—I want to know from you is, is there one good reason I shouldn't say yes to her offer?' Brusque. Being an asshole, and he couldn't help himself. He looked at Teia, and it was like she was already receding in the distance with his hopes.

'Her offer? What? What offer?'

Had he not made it clear? 'She proposed we marry.'

'Marry?!'

'It's the only way to get a rock-solid alliance. Even a promachos can't dissolve a marriage.'

'Are you seriously – Kip, you're sixteen!'

'Seventeen in a few months. Ten. Ten months.'

'*Marriage*, Kip. Marriage. Yes, there are a thousand good reasons. Like . . . like . . . Well, I mean, you're only sixteen—'

'I'm not looking for a thousand reasons to say no to her, I'm looking for one. Was. Was looking.' And suddenly, horrifyingly, infuriatingly, tears were flooding his eyes. He took a deep breath, blinked, blinked, but it didn't matter. The tears came, and he couldn't speak, and the tears spilled down his cheeks.

Rejection. From Teia.

Should have fucked her when you had the chance, Andross Guile said in the back of Kip's head. And Kip was ashamed.

'I'm sorry,' he said, and his voice was level, somehow. Tight, oh so very tight and quiet, but level. 'How embarrassing for both of us. I apologize. I was unfair. Please . . .'

Teia looked at him, totally stunned, speechless.

'Please excuse me,' Kip said. It was his room, but he had to get out. He couldn't breathe in here, couldn't face her for one more second. He practically fled into the hall. He went to the lifts, but there wasn't one at this level. He flipped his green spectacles on – they hid his eyes – and drafted a hand brake. He'd never done this before, but he'd seen it done. And, to hell with it.

He attached the brake directly to one of the anchor lines, grabbed the crossbar in both hands, and jumped down the hole.

Sudden terror can apparently be quite bracing.

But the terror lasted only a second. Kip went whizzing down the shaft past alarmed discipulae and magisters. Level after level blurred past in tears and regret. He applied the brake and came to a jerking stop at his floor – the basement where he did so much of his training.

The Prism's training room was empty. Thank Orholam. Kip threw his spectacles back into the hip case and slapped each of the color panels, flooding the room with colored light of seven spectra. Any drafting he wanted to do would be easy. He threw off his tunic and moved to the heavy bag. It took all of his discipline to warm up. Beating the hell out of the bag immediately would just sprain his damn wrists.

Whatever distance he'd gained in running from his weakness closed in as soon as he started punching the bag. Circling the swaying leather and sawdust wasn't flight enough to get away from his stupidity. Whatever pain shot from fist to wrist to elbow to shoulder wasn't enough agony to overwhelm the shame. What had he even been asking? How had he not seen that she was dumbfounded? How had he not taken the quiet exits her blank, stunned looks had offered him?

No. Kip had bulled ahead. Like a dumb animal. All the grace of a turtle-bear.

His fists thumped, thumped the bag, and his wrists hurt, the connective tissue crying out as he hit the bag too hard. He wasn't warmed up yet, but he couldn't help but hit until he crossed the threshold of pain. As if pain would blot out all else.

Why had he backed Teia into that corner, where there was nothing she could say? He'd wanted to lose her. It was the only explanation.

He tried to imagine what the right response would have been.

And couldn't.

This was all on him. Bastard and outcast, choosing to be bastard and outcast. He hit and hit, the thud of luxin glove on leather becoming his voice. He could judge every punch by its sound, and soon he was making corrections – tightening here through the gut to put more force into the hit, foot landing just there to give him an anchor, aiming just there as the bag swung back.

But it was no escape. He'd let himself think he could have friends. That here, at the Chromeria, at the very center of all things, he could be no longer alone. But Gavin was gone, Karris was furious, Teia didn't want him, his friends would be taken away, and he could never trust them again. Kip was to be alone, again, and this time, finally, fatally.

And what are you going to do? Cry about it? Feel sorry for yourself? Poor little Kip of Rekton, poor little fat boy.

He closed his eyes and tried to hit the bag by feel. It had always been more theoretically possible than actually possible: you knew how the bag was shaped, you knew how it swung, you knew where it was hanging, you knew how hard and where you'd hit it, so you should be able to tell where it was going to come back. Repeat. Right?

Of course it wasn't nearly so easy. Whatever else he was, Kip was leagues from being a blind fighter.

Finally the tendons in his arms and every surface of his fists felt merely hot rather than in pain, and his muscles warm. He picked up the speed. Elbows, knees, quick combos, face. He kicked the bag, reveling in the bass, meaty thump of a perfectly executed kick.

He was going to marry Tisis. He was really going to do it.

She had done exactly what his grandfather had warned him of: seduced him into rescuing her, without ever having to resort to actual physical seduction.

And there was that damned loose stitch on the heavy bag. Still just the same amount of looseness in it there had been months ago. Dammit! Like he'd accomplished nothing.

He focused on that side, chasing it when it turned, punching it with left hooks so it would turn right and then slamming a kick into it as hard as possible.

And then he began streaming. That was the name the squad had come up with for Kip's little trick of shooting luxin while moving in order to move faster. Streaming was, they all agreed, incredibly dangerous – and they all did it as frequently as possible. If Kip streamed luxin out of his shoulder as he punched, he could punch the bag almost twice as hard as a normal punch. Which was awesome, except that hitting something that hard would break his hand, and wrist, and probably his arm. Streaming didn't make you tougher, it just moved you faster.

They'd had more pratfalls and collisions and collected more minor injuries than any Blackguard squad in history.

It had given them some hilarious stories, though: watching Ferkudi stream while running in order to run faster – and jetting from his shoulders, which made him go really fast for a few moments, until he faceplanted. He'd skidded, and was only losing the last scabs on his face now. Cruxer flipping into Daelos while trying to learn to leap high.

Kip had wondered aloud if you could coat your bones in solid yellow (provided you were able to draft a solid yellow) and make them unbreakable, so you could hit anything. Teia had pointed out that your tendons and skin still wouldn't be unbreakable; Cruxer pointed out that it would be incarnitive, and thus forbidden, with the penalty being death. It was where all wights started, he said, tweaking their flesh just a bit for an advantage here and there.

Now he made a mistake by streaming red first. The advantage was that it had significant mass, so the action-reaction combo of throwing red took less drafting for an equal amount of streaming. But red wasn't purely physical, as he should know well by now. The emotions poured through him, first among them fury.

Kick. Fury at looking a fool. Kick. Fury at Andross Guile. Kick. Fury at Gavin Guile for leaving him here. Fury at Karris and Teia for rejecting him. Fury at his own weakness.

Fury to rage to insanity.

He aimed a roundhouse kick right at that one loose, defiant stitch, and his fury crested. Hit it. Nothing. Punched, punched, punched. The world fogged into pain and stubbornness and one loose damned stitch. Kip was that stitch, waiting to be clipped or sewn up by a power greater than he. *Thud, thud, thud.* The bag was swinging back and forth, and Kip's fists were a blur, a rattling drum punctuated by great streaming kicks. He was getting hot, overheating, so he drafted sub-red to cool himself, and it stoked his rage higher, blotted out pain, blotted out reason. He became pure beast, pure hatred, a roar sounding from some place deep within him.

He roared, and as red luxin streamed out of his heel so too did sub-red, and the luxin ignited. His kick was biomechanically perfect, weight to counterweight, muscles and resistance delivering a whipcrack right into the junction that was the rounded striking surface of shin and foot. But the thrust of that fire-streamed kick delivered incredible force into the bag.

There were two cracks: one felt, one heard.

Kip didn't see what else happened because he was swept off his feet. His planted foot was expecting only so much force to rotate around it, and he had doubled or trebled that. He went down, landing heavily on his side.

He wondered if he'd broken his leg. He wiggled his foot. It hurt. He flexed it. It still hurt, but it didn't seem to be broken. *Hurt?* It hurt like, really-really-damn-I-can't-even-swear-under-my-breath-because-I-can't-get-a-breath-because-it-hurts-so-bad hurt.

Kip rolled over, wincing, breathing, and sat up. The heavy bag was on the ground. It had been torn loose of its chains and was lying on the floor. The bag hadn't burst.

It had just . . . *Fuck*.

It had just fallen over.

It lay there, mocking him. He stood up. Oh wow. That really hurt. He hobbled over to it. Nope, the heavy bag had definitely not burst. The same loose threads were still simply loose.

Mocking him.

But Kip had heard *two* cracks simultaneously. If one had been the torn leather hanger on top of the heavy bag, what was the other one? The heavy bag slapping onto the ground? No.

The second crack had come from *inside* the heavy bag. Kip was certain of it.

Well, hell with it. He was already going to have to explain the broken bag to Commander Ironfist – come to think of it, he was already going to be kicked out of the Blackguard sooner or later – so what did he have to lose?

He looked over at the blue light and drafted a little blue knife. Sitting, he poised the knife over the stitching where the loose threads were.

Months of punching this thing, for one reason. All that time, trying to do one stupid thing, failing to do one stupid thing, and now he was giving it up? I *really* wanted to punch this bag open. Ah, well.

The bag came open in moments, and revealed . . . sawdust. Kip sat cross-legged on the floor and plunged his hand into the sawdust, making a mess on the floor. Already gone this far . . .

He only had to root around for a few moments when he felt it. A box, deep inside the middle and top of the heavy bag, where few of the strongest blows would land. Soon, he had it out.

It took his breath. He knew this card box. No, not a card box. The card box. Olivewood and ivory, just large enough to hold one large deck. This was Janus Borig's card box, the one she'd hidden from the people who'd murdered her. The box that he'd happily given to his father Gavin. The precious wood was cracked, right in the middle, from Kip's kick.

Oops.

He shook off the sawdust and, with trembling hands, opened the box. The new cards were there. All the precious cards – a treasure beyond imagining, the hidden truths of kings and satraps and Colors and many of the greatest women and men alive today and in the last two hundred years. They were all here.

Gavin must have known that with how often he was gone, his things would be searched. So he'd hidden it here, where it would only be found by either Kip or Ironfist. Which of course brought up the obvious problem. Where could *he* hide such a treasure, when he'd shown how terrible he was at hiding anything and Andross Guile had shown how ready he was to violate Kip's privacy. Or should he turn over the cards, take Andross's deal? Turning over the cards would mean Kip had given up on his father.

But that could wait.

A chill passed over his sweat-damp forearms, tingled down the length of his spine and up into his scalp. Kip stood, disrupting the heavy bag. More sawdust poured out onto the floor. He was going to pay for that mess. But it wasn't just sawdust. There was another card box – one Kip had seen before, briefly. Andross Guile's own card box: the one he'd asked if Kip had stolen. Gavin *had* stolen it.

And now Kip had it.

But that could wait, too. He had the cards. Janus Borig's life's work. Her masterpieces. Wonders of the world. Kip had scanned these cards once, when he hadn't known anything. He was giddy, trembling. He opened the broken box and lifted the entire deck out.

A shot of joy, as intense and burning as straight brandy, went through him.

Odd. It didn't quite feel like *his* joy. Kip looked around the room at the seven intense colored lights illuminating the room. How many of those was he passively drafting? Maybe it wasn't the best idea to be drafting and holding—

The deck in his hand was vibrating. It wasn't his hand trembling, it was the cards themselves, reacting to something.

Kip flipped the whole deck away from himself, but they escaped from his grasp as he flicked his wrist and jumped toward him like iron filings to a magnet, slapping to bare skin. The rest of the deck hit him in his bare chest, *snap-snap-snap*, drawn inexorably to his skin. Seven colors – more – roared through Kip, seemed to explode beyond the boundaries of his body. Everything was burning and freezing and piercing.

He was staggering around in a circle, blind, the *snap-snap-snap* of cards smacking onto the bare skin of his back. He tore at the cards across his chest, and they went *tap-tap-tap-tap-tap*, resonance points jumping to his fingers. As each card scraped off his hand, another jumped onto his fingers, and another. Too fast, too sticky, and then they weren't just burning into his fingers. Every card seemed to bore into his skin at many points. He was screaming.

A luminescence bloomed in the room in front of him. A figure filled with glory like light, arresting, impossible to look away from. Rea Siluz, the librarian with the halo of brown hair and the full lips, the woman who'd sent Kip to Janus Borig in the first place. Except now he didn't think 'woman' was the right term for her.

He was falling—

No, he was jumping – no, he was fighting, blazing swords in each hand – no, he was cursing the woman he'd given his satrapy for – no, he was hearing a young Blackguard say, 'It's not incarnitive, sir.'

'It's real damn close.'

Finer gave a jaunty salute, and leapt off the precipice. The magnificent bastard, he did a *somersault* on the way—

Kip hit the floor, the impact jarring him back to himself.

Rea knelt beside him. 'Breaker, I can't help you in this. Get out or you'll die.'

The light was scouring flesh from bone, was whittling bone to slivers, was grinding slivers into shavings, grinding shavings into dust.

A wind made of light itself, Orholam's breath, streamed across what once was Kip and scattered him. Scattered to every corner of the Seven Satrapies, beyond. Scattered him from the present and into the past. Blew him out of time, as Orholam was out of time.

She was becoming a wight, as all the luxiats had warned about for her whole life. She'd broken the halo. She should commit suicide. It was the only option. Else what might she do? The Color Prince was betting she would join him, that she would lose her mind in exactly the way he wanted her to. She bit a tiny hole in her tent, letting through one tiny ray of light. If she used the tiny sapphire her Purple Bear Usef had given her, she should—

Zee Oakenshield blinks to clear her eyes. There are enemy armies on both sides of the Great River. She feels a pang at the sight. It isn't fear. Regret. Should have tried harder. Shouldn't have spit those witticisms in Darien Guile's face. The flush of pleasure at besting one of the smartest men in the world, the laughter of the nobles that day, will be paid for in the blood of common men today—

Her pen scratches precise lines: 'Dog. Day 1207. Still no differences in physiology beyond what this researcher originally drafted. No changes in psychology detected, though previous caveats about the limits of studying dogs' minds stand. Day by day, this researcher's conviction grows that incarnitive drafting can be done safely – if proper protocols are strictly observed. There is a slippery slope here, but the Chromeria is overly cautious. Luxin properly sealed before implantation is no different, and indeed, much safer! than mundane tools. If—'

He staggers from the burning White Oak manor on Big Jasper, flames licking the sky. His skin is sloughing off. He's screaming even as the healers come running—

Kip gasps. He retches, but the visions won't let go. There's so much power flowing through him, he can't even see. He screams on a raw throat – or tries. It freezes in his throat, fails.

'Kip, Breaker, listen: your heart has stopped. You haven't much time. Don't be stalled or distracted by—'

His eyes don't close, can't close, but the images flicker as if he's blinking.

Gavin opens his eyes to the same yellow hell that has greeted—

Ceres is being a bitch, Gunner thinks to hisself—

She must be the last Blackguard alive—

Orholam, black luxin. Black! It—

The light kills—

She—

Chapter 74

'Strange boy,' Murder Sharp said, a few seconds after Kip left his room. Murder Sharp had dropped his invisibility. He unlaced the front of his mask, as if it made him claustrophobic.

Teia said, 'Say one more word about my friend. I dare you.'

Master Sharp's face twisted like he'd drunk vinegar where he expected wine. 'There is a time and place to discipline one's apprentice. This, sadly, is not it. This' – he waved his hand about – 'this is weakness, Adrasteia, and you're best off without it.'

She tried to mentally make a box and drop every emotion into it. Anything she revealed would be made a weapon against her.

'You can't protect him. You know that, don't you?' Master Sharp said. 'Not from me. Especially not from me. I wonder, what would you do, if I told you that to prove yourself, you'd have to kill him?'

'Why don't you order it, and find out?' Teia asked.

'Oooh, iron in you. I like.' He smiled that odd, predatory smile where he seemed to be trying to show all of his perfect teeth at once. 'You have something for me?'

Teia threw him the cloak, and handed him the climbing crescents, too.

'Dropped one crescent,' she said. 'Had to get out of the White's apartments fast. Blackguard almost caught me on the balcony.'

'But didn't?' It was a question.

'I'm here, aren't I?'

He searched her then. It was a dispassionate violation, like being stripped naked by a man who preferred boys. It made it better, but not by much. He started with her scalp, jamming fingers through her hair roughly. If she'd spent any time on her hair, she'd be furious, but Archers were too practical for elaborate hairstyles on any but feast days.

'Can't you do this with paryl?' Teia asked.

'Not foolproof, as I'm sure you know.'

She did? Actually, she didn't. Holy—

Murder Sharp had just jabbed two fingers hard into her groin. In the front side, and the back side. She was so surprised, so violated, that she didn't even do anything. And then it was over.

'When I was in Ha—' Murder Sharp stopped. 'When I was in prison, you'd be amazed what people would put . . . where. Puffing haze that smells like . . . midden? Could never make myself so desperate. Not even to fit in. This one Tyrean hid knives up . . . well. They searched him rough, cut him all up inside. He didn't live, but for the longest time, he was the . . . butt of our jokes.'

Hilarious.

He released her and unrolled the cloak, far enough to check the fox sigil. 'Just the one? Gebalyn's burnt cloak?'

'It was the only one there.'

'Was it?'

'Yes. But I have to wonder why you'd send me on such a job. Was it to see how dumb I was? If I'd found both cloaks, would you have expected me to bring them to you? Why would I possibly make myself less valuable to you, you who so casually kill?'

A brief troubled look crossed Murder Sharp's face. He really hadn't thought it through. The question was, had whoever had given the orders?

'Was this a test to see how smart I am?' she asked.

A frown on that perpetually grinning face. 'Perhaps it was. Regardless, well done. You brought us a shimmercloak, and that's better service than many in the Order of the Broken Eye have done in a century. Even if it was handed to you.'

For one moment, Teia's heart stopped. He knew the White had helped!

Then she realized Master Sharp meant that *he* had helped her so much that the job was simple.

'It was windy out there,' Teia said, just to say something.

'Never liked heights much myself. But then, that's why they pay us, isn't it?' He folded the purloined cloak up with rapid motions.

'You're going to pay me?' Teia asked.

'Of course not, how would you explain where you'd gotten the money? But I do get paid on your behalf, and for that, thank you. Two cloaks would have been better.' He looked at the cloak again. 'I would let you keep this if I could,' he said. 'I suspect it's gonna get bloody here. Try not to get killed.'

With that, he flipped up the hood of his own cloak, laced it back up over his face with quick, practiced motions, and stepped out of the room.

Which left her alone with her thoughts. Which circled Kip.

She expelled a great breath. Dammit, Kip. Just. Dammit.

You had to do that in front of Murder Sharp? When I couldn't respond?

And how would I have responded, had he not been here?

The exact same way, probably.

What was it about Kip that petrified her? When they trained, he was her partner, and it was easy. Everything flowed smoothly and easily, like they were left and right hands, working together. He trusted her so implicitly that she trusted herself more when he was around. He made her feel better about herself.

What was scary about that?

And how could this be a surprise? When he'd given her that hug that wasn't just a hug, the alarm bells should have been ringing. She should have acted then. If she simply wanted to be his partner, or his friend, she should have said something afterward. Something clear, without being unduly embarrassing.

Stringing it out was a cruelty of kindness. A friend didn't do that.

No, she'd wanted to bask in that little extra attention, but she'd wanted to freeze it there. She wanted no expectations of her, only his adoration.

That sounds like a great relationship. For me.

Why then did she feel that virulent rage shoot through her at the very thought of Tisis Malargos?

Seems like a bit of an overreaction, huh?

She knew where he'd be now. He'd be trying to knock the sawdust out of that heavy bag. Boys, so uncomplicated.

One of these days, she was going to have to tell him that Ben-hadad had secretly been repairing that one stitch since he'd noticed Kip trying to knock it open. Ben-hadad's father had been a tailor, and Ben-hadad had left that one stitch hanging loose on purpose, while tripling the bag's strength at that seam.

The prank gave all the squad a little smirk every time they saw Kip mercilessly pounding that bag.

Funny to frustrate the Guile who'd had everything in life handed to him.

Suddenly, that prank seemed impossibly petty and cruel.

No, now was probably not the time to tell him about the seam.

She looked at the door. She should go now, before Kip did something stupid.

Why do *I* have to be the adult?

You think *you* are being the adult, between you and Kip?

Orholam damn it, I nearly fell off the side of the Prism's Tower half an hour ago. I am *not* going to be afraid of talking to a boy.

She grabbed the door handle. Dropped it.

Fine, I'll be afraid. It's a different kind of fear altogether. But I'm not stopping.

She huffed. It felt empowering. Stupid boy.

She threw the door open and, glowering storms at everyone who crossed her path, made her way to the lift. It stopped down a few floors. Payam Navid, one of the most handsome young men in the Chromeria if not the entire world, stepped on. He looked at the sour look on her face. He was so beautiful it was probably the first time in his life he'd seen a woman frown at him. Probably wasn't even aware that women *could* frown. Bastard. It wasn't fair that someone could be so attractive.

He said, 'I don't—'

'Don't talk to me.'

'I only—'

'Don't.'

'Come now,' he said, smiling, showing perfect teeth to go with his tall, dark, and gorgeous.

Teia sniffed and waved a hand at his face. 'All this pretty you've got going on here? One more word, and you lose it.'

For a moment, he seemed amused. She didn't even come up to his shoulder. She must seem like a puppy barking at him. But then his eyes lit on the embroidery of her Blackguard rank on shoulder, stitched gray on gray. A wash of expressions poured through his perfect face, and then he looked away, intimidated.

He got off at the next floor. Once he was out of harm's way, he turned and said, 'What's your name, anyway?'

She rolled her eyes, and put her hand to the lever.

He blurted, 'Would you like to go to the—'

But she was already gone.

The little draught of confidence she got from that gave her enough strength to step off the lift in the basement. But then she stopped.

Oh, come on, T. Don't be ridiculous!

One at a time, she lifted her feet and walked to the door of their exercise room. And again, she paused in front of the door. Move!

She threw the door open. It slammed back against the wall, far harder than she'd intended. She stepped into the room, apologetic – not at all the attitude she'd intended.

But then she saw Kip. He was lying on the floor, unmoving, unconscious.

What had he done?!

She ran to him. There was a halo of cards – Nine Kings cards? – around Kip. The heavy bag lay on the floor nearby, torn open, sawdust scattered. Kip's eyes were open, unseeing. He wasn't breathing.

No no no!

He was bare-chested, his skin cold, clammy. She rolled him onto his back, and for a moment, she had hope.

In his open eyes, colors were swirling: in Kip, every color of luxin was alive.

But Kip wasn't.

There was no reaction in those eyes, just a palette of colors swirling down an eternal drain, disappearing, disappearing.

'Kip! Wake up! Kip, come back! Breaker!'

She shook him, but there was no response.

The cards were stuck to him like leeches, holding on. She began tearing them off his skin. They were poison. They were killing him. As each popped off, she saw a swirl of colors fade into his skin like dribbles of ink dropped into a glass of water. What was going on?

Tearing the last one off, she held her breath. But Kip didn't stir. If anything, the colors rising and falling like billowing clouds in his eyes began to recede.

She had taken his hand in hers. She squeezed it hard. 'No, Kip, no.'

But he was dead.

Chapter 75

Being dead wasn't what Kip expected. He was still himself, so he wasn't in a card, of that much he was certain. He'd triggered a trap Janus Borig had left on the cards, then. She'd certainly loved her lethal-and-easily-tripped-by-her-friends traps.

It was dark in here. Dark as a tomb – dark as if his eyes were closed. Which they were. Little Kipling, not the brightest color in the spectrum. He was lying facing down on a polished hardwood floor. He stood up – that was good. Good that he could move, right? – and found that he was in a library.

No, maybe not a library, more like *the* Library. Shelves of a curious, luminous red wood marched in lines to the horizon. Leagues of shelves, each five or six times the height of a man.

Kip's eyes traced the lines of a nearby shelf loaded with the new *pressed* books up, and up. There were ladders on rollers to reach the higher shelves, but there was no ceiling. The night sky itself gleamed high above, undistorted, stars unwinking, clearer than Kip had ever seen them.

Kip was no astrologer, but he didn't see a single constellation that he recognized. A sudden sense of vertigo swept him, as if he were going to go flying off the ground and out into that void. He slammed his eyes down to the shelves again.

Atasifusta. That was the wood. The wood that burned forever. Except here, it was merely burnished to such a high sheen that it provided warm ambient light for the whole library. Neat trick. Kip took a step forward and looked down an aisle to see how wide it was.

There was no end.

He stepped back to his spot, as if to find safety.

He took a deep breath. Wait, was that the first breath he'd taken since he'd been here? Did he have to breathe, being dead and all? Oh, he was breathing. Odd that he wasn't scared. Confused, certainly. Curious, of course. But not a crumb of cowardice.

Maybe one crumb.

Is a crumb the unit of measure for cowardice?

He tried stepping into the aisle again. Ah, it wasn't endless, it was merely so wide that it seemed so. Somewhere in an oceanic distance he could see something that had to be a wall, and to the other side, the same. Looking so far and being made aware of the expanse inspired vertigo again. Kip turned instead to look at what was near at hand.

A flurry of activity burst forth, the moment of creation appearing to only begin because he was there to observe it, the shelves near at hand filling with an explosion of texts, a blunderbuss blast of thought flew through the aether of every language and collided with the medium of its time: vast double-roll scrolls were unrolling, being filled with text by invisible quills, being illuminated whimsically, then advancing; whole pages of text were unrolled from a press, lined up like soldiers, and sliced apart and stitched to a binding before flying to their place on a shelf; papyrus was pounded flat in layers even as intricate glyphs danced across its surface; clay tablets were smoothed to uniform thickness, tiny punch marks of cuneiform wedges barely filling it before the tablets hardened in sun or kiln; bamboo was pounded flat, cured and stitched, script dropping down each column like rain: a thousand kinds of writing, on skin and on stone and on wood and on paper and on material for which he had no name; left to right, and right to left, and top to bottom, and all at once, and in no discernible order at all. Some of them flew to shelves nearby, but some – like the cuneiform – flew to distant shelves, rows back.

Almost at Kip's feet, he saw scrawling – on a tabletop that looked like those in the lecture halls at the Chromeria. In a child's awkward penmanship, written by an invisible hand, letters leapt out:

> *Majister Gold Thorn is a bitch*
> *She went to the chirurjins with a notty itch*
> *Majister they sed you have the pox*
> *The only cure is lots of*

The doggerel was never finished before it was whisked off to a shelf somewhere. Ooo, poor bastard. Kip couldn't imagine Magister Goldthorn had taken the mockery well.

The old styles of writing that no one used anymore flew far away, and doggerel that had to have been written in the last ten years was nearby. So . . . What if this place held every word ever written? *Every* word. And every word, as written, was added.

Which meant Kip was standing at the present, facing the past, watching history roll slowly by to the left and right.

He turned around, expecting to be standing at the edge of a precipice or a blank.

But he was wrong. The future rose before him, league after league of shelves, crammed book after book – the scrolls slowly disappearing as the pressed books crowded them out, and were in turn replaced by shining metal or crystal pieces Kip couldn't begin to identify somewhere in the distance. And there, beyond even those, far, far in the distance, but still visible, was the library's wall.

The future *ended*.

Kip looked off to the sides again, and there, dimly could make out walls. To the past – and nothing. The past might be finite, but it went farther back than he could see, and the past was deeper than the future.

I die and go to a library? Sure, it could be worse, but I've spent a lot of time in libraries this year. Quite enough time, really. Do I have to stay forever? Where do I go pee?

I suppose the dead don't pee.

In the same way they don't breathe?

He was just about to start walking to explore the shelves when a man fell out of the sky. He landed with a sound like a rockslide, right in front of Kip. Somehow, his landing gave the impression that he'd been falling forever, and that the landing wasn't even a strain on his knees. Sort of like Cruxer landing a jump. Even if Kip had lived to train in the Blackguard for a hundred years, he was pretty certain making a landing look light and easy was a skill he never would have mastered.

The man stood gracefully, fixed the cuffs of a shirt under a three-buttoned black jacket of a cut and shiny fabric Kip had never seen. Over the jacket, he wore a leather greatcoat, black on the outside, white on the inside, slim cut and hanging down to his pointed-toe leather boots. He took off a brimmed hat similar to a petasos and shook back a cascade of platinum-white hair that didn't quite touch his collar. His features were paler than anyone Kip had ever seen, exotic, unearthly, perfect. He smiled, a genuine smile that touched his mirrored iridescent eyes, and his teeth were not quite white, but instead pearlescent, and the bit of dogtooth that Kip saw in that smile seemed longer and sharper than usual.

This man was not, Kip decided, a *man*. A shiver of fear ran down his spine, despite the man's apparent friendliness and beauty, but then Kip thought, I'm already dead. What's he gonna do to me?

Good thing fear is rational. Good thing you can talk yourself right out of it.

'Hail, Godslayer,' the stranger said. With his pretty face and sharp beard and immaculate coiffure, Kip had expected a tenor, but instead the voice emanating from this being was a bass – crisp, perfectly enunciated, not gravelly or an indistinct rumble, but a bass that sounded too big to be coming from this man-sized creature.

'Hail, scary guy who fell out of the sky.'

The stranger's eye twitched as if with irritation. He smiled to cover it instantly, but not before a ragged crack shot from the corner of his eye where he'd twitched to his ear. It filled in as fast as it appeared, and left the smile alone on his face. 'Hail, Godslayer,' he said again, as if being very patient.

'Hail . . . sir.' Puzzled. It was as if Kip was playing a game, and no one had told him the stakes, let alone the rules. It had happened enough in the last year that Kip should have been getting used to it. But this wasn't the kind of thing you get used to. The man filled Kip with a quiet, nameless dread.

Already dead, can't do anything to me. Oh, look at that. There may not be peeing in the afterlife, but it turns out that the strong *desire* to pee is indeed possible.

Which, in itself, was kind of terrifying.

Not moving from the spot where he'd landed, the man extended an open hand, tilted up. It wasn't quite the attitude for a handshake or a wrist clasp, and Kip looked at it warily. Falling from the silent sky, something slapped into the man's open hand. A polished black wood cane.

'You'll excuse me the use of a cane, I hope,' the man said with a sound like great gears grinding. He stepped forward, and Kip could see that the man's ankles were broken, poorly mended. Perhaps that was the reason for the stiff leather boots. 'Under what name have you come here?'

Kip looked to the left and right. 'Uh, is this a trick question?'

The man settled into place perhaps ten feet away from Kip, an odd distance for interlocutors. He put his cane centered before him and leaned on it with both hands like a three-legged stool. He waited.

'I am whatever I am. I mean, I am what I ever am. Kip. Kip,' Kip said. 'Is there a privy here?'

'Kip? Kip. Not your birth name, is it? Kip, so puny, so insignificant. Barely worth three little letters. "Don't look at me," it screams. "I'm just a bastard." Kip Delauria. Kip Guile.

Lard Guile. Breaker. Godslayer. Perhaps Diakoptês? If you're going to start collecting names in other languages and religions, this is really going to get tedious. But what are you under the names? Under your cloak of names, who are you?'

'I have no idea what you're talking about.'

'I was known as a bit of a wearer of masks myself, you know. They called me . . . well, why ruin it? It became one of the first Black Cards, forbidden, for those who viewed it lost their minds. That, little Guile, from the tiny fraction of my power that can fit inside a card. You're dying, right now. Oh, no worries, time is different here. We have all the time out of the world to talk, but your body is dying. I can save you.'

'Well, that solves that,' Kip said. 'Here I didn't know if you were a hero or a villain. Villain.'

'Really? It's so easy for you?' the immortal asked.

'Not complicated,' Kip said. A million million books, and not one place to pee. 'There's a time for ratiocination, and a time for gut feelings. Gut wins, this time.' Ratiocination? Where did I even hear that word? Too much time in the restricted library.

'And if head and heart are equal, with which facility do you decide whether to follow the one or the other?' The creature smiled. He leaned on the cane with his left hand and propped his right hand on his hip. The move pushed back his long leather coat and revealed a pistol hanging in a special holster made for it at his right hip. It was actually kind of brilliant. Most people carried a pistol either in a bag or in a pocket. This design would make it far easier to draw quickly. It even had a tie at the bottom to keep the holster tight against the leg, so it wouldn't flop around. Its wearer could always be certain of the position of his pistol. Kip would have to remember that.

Kip said, 'You come across a dying man, and it's in your power to help him – and you don't. That's villain behavior.'

Amused. Only a too-small ring of black pupil interrupted the eerie mirrored perfection of his eyes and showed where he was looking. 'Ah, but you're not dead yet. So perhaps you're too hasty to judge me.'

Kip scowled. He had the distinct impression that the longer

he listened to this man – Man? God? Something in between? – the more convinced he'd be. In that way, Kip's tutelage under Gavin Guile was invaluable. Gavin tended to do the same thing.

'So I haven't saved you. Yet. But neither has my enemy, now, has he?'

Enemy? 'Who are you?' Kip asked. There was something odd about the leather of that long coat. Dual-layered, supple, yet so thin.

'Of course, he can't save you. He doesn't see. He doesn't care. He doesn't know. He doesn't save. He is dead, and this world is ours.'

'Who are you?' Kip whispered. That was what it was about that coat. It was the pale white of the Angari on the inside, and that black was Parian black. Orholam have mercy, it was made of human skin.

'I am the Bearer of Fire; I am the Opener of Eyes; I have been called a god and a beast; I have been called angel and demon, and Slave of the Holy, and Breaker of Chains. I have been called jinn and monster and man. Those who hate me have called me Defiler, Seducer, Corrupter – and Master, and King. Wanderer, Outcast, Kinless, Unclean. I am the Right Hand of Darkness, the Voice of the Grave. I have slain kings and gods. I have come to bring true worship to the Seven Satrapies, to destroy what has been erringly wrought by human hands. The luxiats have shrouded my coming in darkness, but some things cannot be hidden forever. You know who I am.'

Kip's metaphysical heart came into perfect synchronicity with his physical heart, and stopped. No.

'Say it.'

'You . . . you're the Lightbringer.'

'I *am*.' The Lightbringer rolled his neck, and then his shoulders, and giant, glorious white wings unfurled from his back with a crack, emerging from long slits cut in the coat. His shirt tore, revealing a torso so white and flawless it could have been carved of living marble. He was larger than life, and more beautiful than any woman. It was more than simple beauty. It was raw presence, as if you magnified the melancholic yearning and pain of a perfect sunset a thousand times and stirred it with an animal lust to take and be taken and added glory like the true light of a summer day passing through a lens and burning Kip, the ant.

This is why the owl hunts at night; her eyes would burn in the sun. This is why man sees only his slim slice of the spectrum. To see more would be to be blinded. To see that for which his mind is not made was to be struck dumb.

Kip dropped to his knees, fell prostrate. He couldn't help it. Had no strength. No will.

His hands slapped in the dust, in a position of worship, barely keeping his face from smacking the golden floor. The dust – dust? here? in this immaculate library? – swirled up in clouds into his open eyes before he could blink. In seconds, he was streaming tears, his tears turning humble dust to mud. The mud burned his eyes, but it wasn't the burning of getting a speck in your eye, it was the burning of a muscle fatigued, a muscle growing stronger. The burning faded to tingling.

He looked up – and *through*, his eyes made new, silently made strong. Beneath a façade of glory – a cloak of light – the wings were rotten; a stench of decaying flesh swept out in a putrid cloud; the skin was blackened and curling, split from flames, and something else, something utterly inhuman was beneath – all quickly covered. The immortal bared his fangs at the sky, and snarled in a language that Kip's ears couldn't parse into syllables, nor his tongue ever hope to form. Here was an angel of light indeed, for light can also be used to dazzle, to blind, to misdirect and deceive. Here was light bent to illusions and lies.

The masks slammed back in place, and the immortal said, 'I am Abaddon, the King, one of the Two Hundred who marched out of the Tyrant's palaces and went to make our own way in this wilderness, and a thousand worlds like it. I am a lover of queens and a father of gods. I am the Day Star, ushered from the heavens in glory.'

Stand.

Kip couldn't tell if the voice came from within his head or outside of it, but his stubbornness agreed it was a good idea. He found strength, a little anyway, and stood slowly. 'Marched out? Or were thrown out? So out of two hundred failures, I

562

only rate you? What's the fat son of a whore got to do to get some respect?'

The immortal laughed. 'Save yourself, Kip. *He* won't. Though if you do, He'll take credit. Like always, sapping the achievements of the good and the great, making you doubt your own worth. If you're strong enough to save yourself today, I'll be back. When you're ready. I have eternity. You have . . . minutes, or fifteen years, or seventy years at the most. It's all the same to me. I will come again, in your hour of need, when your own strength fails. If you live so long.'

For some reason, that seemed a little more menacing than, 'Fare thee well, see thee anon!' Kip cleared his throat. 'Not sure I'm understanding. If I live so long?'

'You *man*. Why do you think you're here, in the Great Library where all the knowledge of your race's five ages is stored?'

I've kind of been wondering that.

Abaddon seemed incredulous that Kip still didn't get it, even with what he seemed to think was a generous hint. He shook his head. 'Know this, O *Kip*. Your being here involves a compromise. Your mind is not structured to understand timelessness. So instead of being outside of time, you are instead carrying around with you a bubble of causality.'

'Hammerfist centaur granite,' Kip said gravely.

Ancient eyes wrinkled, irritated. 'What?'

'I was, uh, trying to demonstrate how I could understand each of the three words in a three-word phrase and still have no clue what they mean together.' Kip grinned weakly.

Monster eyes flashed, and something seemed terribly wrong with that mouth as it spoke: 'This library is outside of time, but your mind isn't made to understand timelessness. So while you're here, cause precedes effect. Which means you're not fully removed from time. Your body is dying right now. You're not breathing. Your heart has stopped. If you could go back now, you'd be yourself when you arrived. If you don't get back soon, you'll be alive, but a simpleton, perhaps with no control of your limbs, or your bowels, perhaps too gone to even care. You wait a few seconds more back in time, and you'll simply be dead.'

Oh.

Oh, shit!

'You think I'm being awfully helpful for a villain, don't you?'

Actually, Kip hadn't gotten that far yet. He was still a little hung up on the bubble of causality part. But now that he mentioned it . . .

Abaddon folded his wings. They slipped easily back into slits in the sides of his human-leather coat. There was something about the greatcoat that drew the eye, more than simply its repulsive materials. It shimmered. Everything about this godling breathed extravagance, from the delicate ivory lace at his cuffs to the subtle blue silk pinstriping in his straight-legged trousers. He assumed his posture again, left hand on cane, right hand on hip. He noticed Kip's glance fall to his pistol.

'There are rules here,' Abaddon said. 'These very clothes come from hundreds of years in your future. It's forbidden that I show a mortal things from after his time. Never was much for rules.'

'What are you?' Kip asked instead.

'In this form? A lone wanderer, an icon, a card from a deck not yet painted. Your descendants, like you, will believe that every excellence is praiseworthy. This figure is good at killing. Nothing more. Killing and moving on, with impunity, as if above their petty laws, as if a god. And how they will worship it. Indeed, they would worship *you*, O . . . Kip,' he said, the word like a popping bubble, as if he were delighted by insubstantiality of it. 'By this time you've already killed a god and a king and fought a sea demon at the very walls of – oh, my, no, not that, not yet.'

He smiled, and Kip thought that was a trap, a little false prophecy that would probably get him killed. If he made it that far.

'You want to see it?' In a move faster than human thought, the pistol was in Abaddon's hand. 'I made it with my own hands, sacrificing precious days out of eternity to Make. It has been long and long since I have done such, and it will be millennia, I think, before I do so again. I named her Comfort. Do you think that your chromaturgy is magic? What is the most irritating thing about a pistol?'

This wasn't right. There was more going on here than Kip could grasp. 'I don't know. The inaccuracy. The black powder blinding and burning you after you fire.'

'I fixed those, too, but think bigger.'

Kip was fascinated, but this . . . this was a smokescreen, just like the black powder. 'I don't care,' he lied. 'Why are you doing this?'

'Reloading. Reloading is the most irritating part of a pistol. Some two hundred years hence, they discover a reliable rotating cylinder to give multiple shots before reloading is necessary. I copied the form so as to not stand out, but this pistol . . . no reloading. Ever. Reloads itself. *That*, that is magic. Do you want to know how I did it? I came perilously close to violating the basic laws of the universe to do so. A magic engine, within an inanimate object?'

'So you infused an object with Will, so what?' This was all a trap, but Kip couldn't see what the trap was. And what the hell was an engine? He'd heard of siege engines, of course, but Abaddon was using the word as if it meant something else.

'It's one thing to infuse an arrow's feathers to seek a target that you lock in your mind. It's something altogether different to make an item that uses magic itself. It is an act of creation, one might say.'

Kip ignored the answer, searching, searching. If he made it out of this, he could remember this conversation and comb through it to find out what mattered. But right now, he had to cast about, find the teeth of the trap. 'What did you mean, precious days of your eternity? If you're outside of time, what does it matter how long you spend?'

'Even as there are compromises when your kind comes here, carrying with you cause and effect in rigid order, so too are there compromises when my kind goes to your lands. Even I. We're immortal, not omnipresent.'

Suddenly Kip wished he hadn't skipped his theology lectures so often. 'Attributes of Orholam' had seemed a little outside of what would be useful in his life. If only he'd known. 'I don't follow,' he said.

'We can enter your time at any point and place we wish.'

'But you can't be two places or more at the same time.'

'So your mortal mind can slowly churn out the obvious.'

Kip suddenly got it. 'So if you spent two weeks in the Angari archipelago this year, crafting your pistol, you couldn't leave and come back to that same two weeks ever again. You could leave and come back to some other place, either before or after, but you couldn't inhabit the same time. You have all eternity to visit as you please, but you can only visit it once. That's why you call them your "precious days of eternity." Eternity is limitless, but our time is finite, and so, when you visit here, your time is finite, too. Which means if you go to the wrong place at a certain time, you can never fix what you did there. It means you can be fooled!' Kip laughed, delighted. 'That has to be a burr under the blanket, huh? All eternity to visit except for the bits where you need to go. You made a pistol, but you have to fear forever that those very two weeks you spent in our time were the two weeks you needed to be somewhere else. Ha ha ha!'

A quick flash of rage rippled over that mask of a face, disturbing and cracking it, and filling in immediately, as before, but not before Kip saw something beneath it, green and black, the mouth all wrong, the eyes huge and alien.

'So the fly taunts the spider about problems too late to fix? From my very web?'

Oh, no. And there it was. The teeth of the trap.

Abaddon said, 'Truth is, the longer you stand here and listen to me, the closer to death you are. Truth is, you're dead already. You're—'

'Truth is, you're still talking, which means lying, which means I'm still a threat. Somehow. That must irk you. Me. Little fat Kip of Rekton. A threat.' Kip chuckled involuntarily. Such a silly thought, and yet, why else would he even be worth the attention of such a being? But that was beside the point now, a distraction. Don't pat yourself on the back while there's a dagger in it.

Kip turned away, to where the invisible hands were writing, drawing, etching, hammering. That was the crux, that was the present, that was where the answer lay.

A short inhuman roar, the size of the creature that the man disguised, sounded. Abaddon did not like being dismissed.

Kip flinched, and out of body, out of time, and all that he might be, he was still surprised he didn't wet himself at the noise. But he didn't turn. If that thing wanted to kill him, if it was allowed to do so by whatever murky rules governed this place, there was clearly nothing Kip could do to stop it.

'Know this, Diakoptês, I may not be allowed to kill you here, but my hands are not bound in—' He stopped. 'Should you leave, I will follow, and there is no foe who compares.'

'Shut it. I'm thinking.' Oh Ramir, I never thought I would have a reason to thank you for anything, but for this I thank you, you small-souled, small-hearted, small-town tough: I know how to needle a bully when he can't get to me. For that, thank you.

Now, why *am* I in the Great Library?

It's the repository of all knowledge. So what does that—

Kip looked at the invisible hands again. They were drawing glyphs right now. Pictures as words. Pictures as knowledge. Knowledge in every language, in every medium.

Perhaps even the knowledge in cards. Perhaps even the knowledge in cards inside careless young fools.

I'm here because this place is the repository of all knowledge, and I'm here until I get all this knowledge out.

Kip looked down at himself for the first time. He was absolutely covered in tattoos. On every exposed bit of skin, every place a card had stuck to him, it had left its image. Perhaps they'd left more than their image, perhaps they'd left their essence. It didn't fully make sense to him. Why hadn't the cards come here the moment of their creation? But maybe he was asking a time-bound question – time that he was running out of.

He turned over his left wrist.

Gunner.

The crazed Ilytian was wearing a waistcoat, open over a naked torso, sailor's loose pants, no shoes, and a huge grin. He was seated on a smoking cannon like he was riding it. It was bigger than any cannon Kip had ever seen. Gunner also had a blunderbuss in his left hand and a pistol with multiple long barrels in his right hand. Like the first time Kip had seen him, the man had woven burning slow matches into his long unruly hair and beard and into his waistcoat to make himself look like he had come striding out of hell. Gunner? I've got to go be Gunner?

Fine, Gunner, let's dance.

Kip bunched his fingers in the familiar pattern to touch the five jewels: one at each corner, and the middle finger at the middle top. One at a time, he pressed them onto the tattoo of Gunner, fully expecting nothing to happ—

~Gunner~

Tap. Superviolet and blue. As his thumb touched, it was like someone had blown out a candle. The world went dark. Eyes useless. But then, a moment later, there was sun, waves washing over him, blinking, bobbing. Seeing his perspective shift while he felt his body utterly motionless made him queasy.

Tap. Green solved that in a rush of embodiment, touch restored. He was swimming. A strong body, wiry, naked to the waist. The water is warm, strewn with flotsam.

Tap. Yellow. Hearing restored, the shouts of men calling to each other, others screaming in pain or terror. But yellow is more than that; it is the logic of man and place. But the yellow in this one isn't quite right. Disbelieving. The Prism came out of nowhere. Dodged all his cannon shots. Even when Gunner finally started shooting both at once. That little boat the Prism made moved at speeds he wouldn't have believed if he'd heard another telling the tale. Ceres is going to take this out on him. Damn Gavin Guile.

But this mind skips around. There's something—

Tap. Orange. The smell of the sea and smoke and discharged powder, and he can sense the other men floating in the water, and below them, around them – Oh, by the hells. Sharks. Lots of sharks.

His finger is already descending. *Tap. Red-and-sub-red-and-the-taste-of-blood-in-his-mouth-and-it's-too—*

The trick with sharks is the nose. Not so different from a man. You bloody a bully's nose, and he goes looking elsewhere right quick. Easy, right? Easy.

Gunner ain't no easy meat. The sea's my mirror. Fickle as me. Crazy as me. Deep currents, and monsters rise from her depths, too. What others call sea spray, I call her spitting in my face, friendly like—

Kip tore his hand away as soon as it touched all the points – instantly – but that instant was minutes long in the card. He'd not left until he'd – until *Gunner* had killed a shipmate named Conner, who had the oars. Kip had just seen Gunner make himself a captain and get his first crew. The benighted madman.

Finding himself back in the Great Library, Kip looked down at his wrist. The tattoo was faded, but not gone. Right in front of him, a hand had drawn half of the card, hanging in midair. And now it stopped.

He had to go back into the same one. There was something important about Gunner. He had to find the right time. He had no idea what he was doing, but he had to learn.

Kip's fingers descended into a raid on an Angari ship, the murder of men, the lopping of limbs, and a little singsong, 'Rinky, sinky, dinky, do.' He pulled his hand off again, unable to bear it.

And the tattoo still wasn't gone.

Twice more he submerged himself into that ill-fitting skin, and emerged, gasping, weeping. But the card before him was being drawn, and split: one copy flew to his hand, and one went winging to a shelf.

Time out of joint, Kip stares at his wrist. The Gunner tattoo is disappearing even as the hands finish drawing the card. But then his tattoos move, shift, rearrange themselves, and there on his wrist sits Samila Sayeh, the heroine from the Prisms' War.

'You'll never make it,' Abaddon said. For some reason, his coat was gone, but he had a cloak of the same black and white leather spread in his hands. 'Even if you could live every card in turn. Even if any human could take that much punishment, you don't have the time.'

Kip didn't answer. There was no answer. There was no giving up.

'Samila, let's dance.' His hand came down.

But it didn't end with Samila. It didn't end with Helane Troas. It didn't end with Viv Grayskin. It didn't end with Aheyyad Brightwater or Usem the Wild or Halo Breaker or the Fallen Prophet or Pleiad Poros or the Novist or Orlov Kunar or New Green Wight or Heresy.

He was dimly aware that after he finished each tattoo each card flew off into the library, and at least once he saw Abaddon sweep the cloak out like a net, trying to catch a card before it disappeared, but each card seemed to fly right through it, barely slowed. It was one too many things to worry about. Kip went into card after card, sands running out.

Every time, when he felt for whatever reason that he'd seen enough, he removed his hand. He barely had any awareness of himself, none, perhaps, until the moment came to take his hand away. Nor was there any processing of the memories. He had no idea who the majority of these people and things were; he didn't even connect Vox from the Shimmercloak card and from Janus Borig's home until his hand was descending onto the next tattoo.

The integration of Kip to card was complete, but the disintegration that followed was ever incomplete: it wasn't merely a melding of mind to mind, it was union. Spiritual. Emotional. And definitely physical. When he came back from a man who'd lost an arm, he felt the pain, not just after that card to be blotted out by the next card, but after that next card, too. The list of injuries piled up, and even without them, he was seeing men and women at the pivotal crises of their lives: terror was the norm, physical battle common, hatred and cowardice and heroism all piled together.

At first, he regathered his wits each time, reminded himself who he was, wiped away what blood he could from his bleeding nose, took a breath, then tapped the next. Then he merely took a breath, glaring at Abaddon, feeling wetness trickling from his ears. He died a hero's death. He betrayed his closest friends. He took his own life, screaming a spray of teeth as he fired the blunderbuss pointed at his chin.

He found himself on his knees, weeping, blood and tears covering his wrist. But he didn't stop. He wiped his forehead with an arm, giving himself a single breath. His forearm came away bloody. He was sweating blood. That couldn't be good.

'No,' Abaddon said, dismayed.

Hand down. The Technologist. What the hell? This was Ben-hadad. He was some kind of genius. Never would have guessed.

'I—'

Hand down. The Commander. It was Cruxer, and not just Cruxer now, but Cruxer as he would be, facing – but as soon as Kip lifted his hand, he lost the future parts.

'—won't—'

Hand down. Incipient Wight. And Kip lived the conversion, saw the how, and the why, and what worked, and what the wight thought worked, but some still part of Kip saw it was a delusion.

'—allow—'

Hand down. High Luxiat. The man was only beneath the Prism in the future. But first, as a young man, Quentin was taking an order from – from Brother Tawleb. Raising a pistol in a familiar alley. Missing. Blood squirting from a young woman's neck as she stepped into the line of fire. Soul horror at the mistake.

Something about that – Lucia? – no, no time.

'—this.'

Three cards left. Kip was going to make it.

Beneath the blood and tears and mud obscuring his wrist, Kip saw the next card slide into place: the Butcher of Aghbalu. Orholam, no. That was Tremblefist's card. No, no, no.

He couldn't let himself think.

Hand down.

The perfect joy of battle rage, the heady potency of matching skill to skill and overmatching each, of tearing what every man valued most from his arms and proving, time and again, to be the best, to be untouchable, to be godlike in his power, in his slaying grace, to be so feared that bowels loosened and hearts literally stopped as the shadow of this avenging god fell upon them. The agony sang inside him and found company in the agony he left – lopping off hands and feet and leaving men to bleed, gut-wounding others, slashing off jaws, eviscerating, crushing faces, and killing, killing, killing. His palace became his charnel house. He returned to the maimed and sometimes found their women comforting them, and he killed their women before them, that their agony might pitch higher before they knew the release of death.

And it was not enough. The rage ran hot, the rage ran cold, the rage ran out, and still he was killing when the sun rose. And the sun showed that he had not only killed enemies. His own slaves lay dead among their new masters, the Tiru. He had no recollection of killing them, aside from some half-remembered screams, but the wounds matched the wounds he'd left in five hundred others.

He staggers back to the upper court where his wife lies dead, almost unrecognizable from the beatings, raped to death by the invaders. He goes there to end it.

He drops the double swords from gory hands. Pulls her into his arms as the sun rises. Smears the blood away from her broken, battered face. Rearranges her bloody torn dress into some pathetic semblance of decency. Holds her in his arms, draws his dagger.

This woman has a mole on her neck.

This woman isn't Tazerwalt. This isn't his wife. This is her handmaid, Hada, dressed in her lady's garments.

He stands, trembling, an image flashing through his head, a slave girl rushing him. A horrid intuition. A sickness unto death. A stone in his gullet.

He finds the room. Tazerwalt. His wife, disguised as a slave. She'd been alive, unharmed by the Tiru attackers, hidden, until he'd come. A *slave girl* had rushed him. A slave girl, loyal to the Tiru, surely. Thinking it an attack, he'd slashed her neck as she threw herself at him, and he'd moved on, heedless.

Her eyes are open, questioning, and dead. So very dead.

He falls to his knees, screaming. Mind tearing, separating from himself. He sees a man, caked in blood, screaming. His screams sound no different than any of a hundred others he's heard all night. His throat is tearing, unable to contain the force of his suffering.

Kip lifted his hand, convulsing. For some reason, his whole body was in pain, as if all his muscles had cramped at once.

He fell over, blinded, unable to breathe. The wave passed, leaving him gasping. He blinked his suddenly clouded eyes clear. Wiped at them. Looked at red fingers. Touched his forehead. No, no wounds to his scalp or forehead. He was bleeding from his eyes.

That, Ferkudi would say, was a real flesh protuberance.

'You're too late. You're dying,' Abaddon said, sweeping the cloak back up onto his shoulders. 'All this suffering for nothing.'

A sound escaped Kip's lips, and for all the times he'd hated his body for its petty betrayals and awkwardness, this time, it did him proud: the sound was far more growl than moan. Emboldened by his own flimsy façade of defiance, Kip rolled to his knees.

'You're wrong,' he said, voice raspy, breath short. 'See, I have a gift.'

'A few.'

'No, just the one.'

'Pray tell.'

'I'm fat. So I'm out of breath. Maybe dying. Hell, I've felt worse climbing a flight of stairs.' I'm fat, he didn't have the breath to say, but when everything's hard for you, something being hard isn't much deterrent to doing it anyway. I'm fat, and there's only one person in this room who gets to make jokes about me.

But Abaddon was grinning. 'You've already lost, Lard Guile. This wasn't me visiting you in the Great Library. This was a raid. Your coming here broke open a gap in our enemies' defenses. You're so predictable. By stalling you, I made you hurry. I could never have found all the new cards myself. You brought them to me.' He spread the cloak open, and on the white inside, Kip saw images, like tattoos, of every single card. They hadn't escaped Abaddon – he'd somehow copied them all.

Kip had no idea what it meant, but something Corvan had said once made him react instinctively: 'If your enemy wants it, deny it.'

Andross Guile, you asshole, tell me that I've got something of you in me. Your every victory, your every taunt, every time you turned a loss into a victory of another sort and soured the wine of winning to gall in my very mouth. Speak, O blood of Guile. Sing in me of the rage of the man skilled in all ways of contending. Sing of the blood of a beast and a god—

Blood.

Kip scrapes the blood from his wrist, feeling lightheaded. Only two images remain. He laughs, for the final two tattoos are the Lightbringer and the Turtle-Bear. But these two sit side by side in his wrist.

A choice. Kip has no doubt of it. There is only time to touch one. The image of the Lightbringer looks holy, a beam of light from heaven illuminating his face, washing out his features so it's impossible to discern them.

Janus Borig asked for her brushes when she was dying. Asked for them, because she knew who the Lightbringer was. Had she started that card and never finished the face?

No. This tattoo isn't unfinished.

What it is, or what it can be, is a trap. A trap for Kip – and now Kip's trap.

Kip lifts his hand, bunches his fingers, using the periphery of his vision to see how Abaddon reacts. Fear that Kip will touch the Lightbringer. Good. Kip moves.

'No!' Abaddon shouts. 'No!' He twists his cane and a blade flicks out from its heel. He stabs Kip's arm in the tattoo of the Lightbringer. Power arcs through Abaddon's cane, and the tattoo bursts apart like a popped soap bubble. Too easily, as if it had been waiting for it.

Kip flips sideways from the force of the blow, his other hand slapping at Abaddon's face as he falls.

When he looks up, Abaddon looks confused. There's a hole in the illusions hiding his face, his chin and beard plucked off entirely, the rest of the mask shimmering – and dissolving.

He is no man under that projected beauty. His head a locust's head. His mouth mandibles, stretching and snapping sideways. His eyes monstrous, inhuman. The wings barely protruding from his back are the clacking wings of an insect god. And the moment he touches Kip, there's a change in the air of the Great Library. Even Kip, bent and broken, can feel the power gathering, a kind of magic beyond mortal ken.

By touching Kip, he's entered Kip's time, his bubble of

causality. And if there's one thing fat kids understand, after getting beat down into a puddle of blubber and humiliation, it's being overlooked and disregarded.

But blubber bounces back.

Shooting a look at something Kip couldn't see, Abaddon roared, 'What do I care for your rules?! I am I! I am the Day Star! I am of the firstborn, and I. Will. Not. Be Moved!' His turn swept the hem of his cloak toward Kip, almost brushing him with it.

If there's one thing fat kids understand, it's momentum.

With a roar, Kip leapt onto Abaddon's back. Every Blackguard lesson forgotten, he was an animal, tearing at his prey. He was the fucking turtle-bear, ready to take punishment as long as he could give more punishment back. His weight nearly knocked Abaddon off his broken ankles, and Abaddon barely caught himself on his cane. Screaming, Kip scratched at his eyes, tore at his neck, and lunged for that precious pistol.

But the move was a feint. With only one hand free, Abaddon grabbed on to his precious pistol. Instead, Kip tore the cloak off his neck and kicked off. Abaddon fell.

His masks down, Abaddon was all snarling, shrieking insect. He drew the pistol from its holster smoothly, those great bulbous eyes unreadable.

At that moment, something seemed to resound through the entire library, a great pulse, a great weight settling – and Abaddon was ejected, utterly, instantly. Not physically, for he merely disappeared, but Kip had the very distinct impression that the psychic shock of it had to be tremendous.

It was like a child addressing a tidal wave, saying, I will not be moved – and before the words are out of his mouth, all is ocean, leaving no sign; not only no sign of the child, but no sign of his defiance, no sign that anything opposed the crushing sea in the least, no eddy, no swirl, no detritus, only simple, plain, indisputable nothingness.

From his back, exhausted, immobile, bloody, Kip looked up into those yawning foreign constellations. 'So you are there,' he said. 'Kind of take a subtle approach, don't you?'

The cloak lay shimmering in Kip's hand. He sat on the ground holding it, wondering what would have happened if

Abaddon had shot him here. If he was practically dead anyway, what was the difference? Or was that creature lying about the whole dying-out-in-his-real-body thing? Something felt very wrong in Kip's chest, so he thought not.

'Subtle? He's using *you*.'

It was Rea Siluz. She was wearing a green-and-black jalabiya with the hood down around her neck, her halo of black hair fairly glowing. But perhaps that was just the effect of her smile. Kip thought for a moment about what she'd said, then grinned. 'Rea. So, you're some kind of librarian?' He stood, with difficulty.

She smiled again and shook her head. 'Only when . . . time allows.'

'You're what he is . . . or was, or . . . something?'

'I am not nearly what he was, but I am far more than he is. As are you. Evil is darkness. Darkness is the broken eye, the ever-blind unseeing. Darkness is less substantial than smoke, and even a dim mirror is brighter than the void.'

That seemed pretty deep, so naturally Kip said, 'You're not as flashy as he was.'

She laughed. 'Kip, do you know how beautiful you are? You understand things with your heart. There's a time to revel in and reveal glory earned and glory given. But vanity is show. In point of fact, I am quite well-known for my love of spectacle. Which is probably why I was drawn to you.'

'Me? I'm just a dim mirror. And I, I think I'm dying.' He thought suddenly, if you're addressing some kind of celestial immortal, and she's actually answering you, you should probably ask some really good questions: like about the cloak he was holding, or heck, if there really was a Lightbringer, and if so who . . .

He fell over. Too late. He thought that if he got through all the cards, there was supposed to be some way . . . out? Did he miss it? He tried to open his eyes to look for it. Nothing. Maybe they were open. Ah well. He was dead at last, but he didn't mind.

Chapter 76

Kip was dead.

Teia staggered to her feet in disbelief. She felt like she'd been bludgeoned between the eyes with a brick. She felt like she was standing knee deep in the shallows of a mighty river, waters roaring through and past her. Kip lay like he'd been cast out of the current, his body sprawled, mind broken, spark extinguished.

Kip is dead.

It didn't look right. Kip, as meat. Without his animating spirit, Kip was a brow hewn from granite, shoulders to shame draft horses, and staring eyes of many colors. This was a body; this wasn't Kip.

Teia could hear nothing but the cataclysmic wind gusts of her own heart, pumping, pumping, as if blowing on a forest fire. Kip dead? It was impossible. And it was.

I didn't hug him. Why didn't I hug him? He staggered back from death's door, and held me, and I didn't hold him. I let him down. Why?

I'm not a slave. I'm not a slave. I tell myself that every day. Why?

Because I don't believe it. And despite all I feel for Kip – for all the Kips I know him as – I can't love him if I'm still a slave. He was my master. If only for a time. If only in word. Kip could think of me any way he wanted to, but it didn't matter, doesn't matter, as long as I'm a slave in my own eyes.

My lenses are bad. My eyes, broken.

I hate being a slave, because I hate what it has made me, because it has changed me, and I can't change back in a day. I can't say yes to Kip, though all my soul longs for it, because I haven't taken my freedom. Not yet.

Why do I want so much to be a Blackguard? Because they are the best slaves in the world, with the best masters, with rules that make sense, well rewarded, and well directed. But directed. Ordered. Always, always subordinate. And a part of me craves that.

Orholam, what would it be like, to be whole?

Teia blinked, hating and overcome with disappointment at who she'd become – and then she felt as if she were standing outside herself. For one heartbeat, she saw a vision of herself standing before her, as an adult. Only a couple years older, maybe, but she looked totally other. She stood tall – well, as tall as her slight frame could manage – but she stood free, there was joy in her eyes, pride in her stance, and mischief on her lips. And she was *beautiful*. Not the beauty of curves and men's desire, a brighter beauty than that. She was a woman fully herself, a woman who had life, and had it in full.

And then the vision was gone. But Teia knew it was herself as she could be.

A tear tracked down her cheek.

I realize this now? Now?!

Kip shall not be dead.

Again, Teia seemed to be standing in that great river, nearly sweeping her off her feet. She had such a strong, sudden conviction that it was some titanic, immeasurable magic that she widened her eyes to paryl – and saw nothing, but she lost not her conviction that it was here, it was true. There was a magic she knew not.

Not yet.

Kip was dead, his eyes staring blankly into nothing.

Kip is dead; he's left us all behind. I've learned from him, but too late.

Kip shall not be dead.

His hand was wet with blood from his torn knuckles.

Life is in the blood.

Paryl is the master color. Paryl makes us feel all. Barely knowing what she was doing, Teia drafted paryl from her hand to Kip's blood. She could feel it, and then she plunged the magic into his blood, going after the receding luxin, the receding light, the receding life, like it was a rope trailing out of her reach.

As soon as her luxin passed the barrier of Kip's skin, she gasped. The Chromeria didn't even begin to teach Will magics until late in a discipula's tenure because it was so dangerous, so prone to abuse. Kip had willjacked an opponent once, though, and it had been described to the Blackguard scrubs then. Luxin had no memory, and Will was where the technology of chromaturgy met the magic of the thing. Teia couldn't draft any of the colors Kip had inside him, but with paryl using Will to interact with one color was the same as using will to interact with any color – so long as the luxin was open.

Kip's entire body was awash in every color of luxin. From her training, Teia knew you wanted to stop the heart to kill a man. She didn't know much more than that, though. Certainly, she was no healer.

She found Kip's heart through his blood, and it was still. She grabbed all the luxin in and around his heart that she could feel. Without any control of each of those colors, it was like grabbing a handful of knots rather than plucking the appropriate threads.

She simply squeezed, hard.

Kip's entire body jumped in her lap, and she almost lost hold of the magic.

Kip was dead.

What the hell am I doing? Orholam—

Again.

She did it, tears streaming down her face. His body leapt. It seemed a desecration.

Kip is dead. Dammit, leave him alone. Stop this, stop this!

Again.

She jerked so hard, she thought she tore something inside herself. This time, after his body leapt, he seemed to melt into her lap. He was dead. He was really dead.

Teia's will drained away. All she'd done. It was for nothing. It was just desecrating his corpse. She should be ashamed.

'Orholam's balls,' Kip said, pained. He moaned. His eyes flickered open, and focused on Teia after a moment. 'Teia!' he said, surprised. 'I'm here, right? I mean, I'm now? I mean . . .' His eyes lost focus for a moment, and he blinked, on the brink of passing out.

'Kip?' she asked. She brushed back his wiry hair. Her whole body felt full of light. Her eyes were full of tears, and the tears made the light streak and dance and glow and sing. Kip shall not be dead indeed.

She couldn't stop grinning.

'Teia, Teia, I have something to say.'

She leaned over him. 'Yes?' Maybe it was all drafting, the nearly falling to her death, the escape from Murder Sharp, the fight with Kip, the saving his life; maybe it was touching all the other luxin, maybe it had worked on her even as she'd worked with it, but she felt all warm and soft inside. He was right here. She remembered kissing him, that night after they'd all been out drinking. It had been nice.

'Teia, I have to tell you,' Kip said again.

'Yes?' She should kiss him now. What was the harm?

'You've got a booger.'

'Uh-huh, I—what?! What?!'

Kip pulled away and sat up. 'Sorry, you were all looming over me, I got claustrophobic.'

'Looming?' She punched his shoulder, while she fished in a pocket for a handkerchief. 'I don't *loom*.' She started laughing. She couldn't help it. She deserved it, didn't she? After leaving him standing there, hugless. It wasn't like he was retaliating, it was like the universe was. A firm elbow from Orholam himself. She laughed, hard, maybe a little bit out of her mind.

He seemed puzzled by her laughing, but then he joined her in it. 'What are we laughing a—'

His smile froze on his face and he stopped laughing. He jumped to his feet, staggering, awkward, but never taking his eyes off her face. An odd black-and-white cloak unfurled from his hand, ignored. He tilted his head, studying her. He blinked, like something else was standing in her shoes.

'Kip?' she said.

'T?' he asked.

No one called her T. She only called herself that.

'Kip, are you . . . are you well?'

'You're sheering off in different colors, disappearing. You're – no, it's going. It's—' He shut his eyes tight as if groping for a memory. 'Mist Walker.'

Her throat tightened.

He blinked. 'It's gone.' He shook his head then put a hand

to his temple as if he had a ferocious headache. 'Huh, Mist Walker. You ever heard of that?'

He'd never heard that term. Not from her. Not from anyone. That was an obscure tale.

She opened her mouth to lie to him. She heard Karris's arguments in her mind that anyone who knew this secret only put them all in more danger. And she saw how right Karris had been. Teia hadn't needed to know Karris's identity. It had been helpful only emotionally – and hurtful in every other way possible. And yet still the lie wouldn't come.

'It's what I hope to be,' Teia said. And she realized only as the words passed her lips that they were true.

'Huh?' He was obviously still recovering from the pain in his head.

'It's what I'm doing for the White. I'm infiltrating the Order of the Broken Eye, Kip. I've already stolen a shimmercloak for them. My master was in the room with us, upstairs, when you said. . . . It's why I was . . . playing dumb? I didn't want him to have anything over me.'

He didn't react. She wasn't sure he heard her. 'Mist Walker,' he repeated. He squinted at her. Then he seemed aware of the cloak in his hand again. She'd never seen it before. To himself, Kip said, 'He broke the rules, so that meant I could, too. Doesn't look like leather here, though.'

'He?'

'Mist Walker. Fuck.' Kip stared down at his left wrist, where there was a smudge of color like a tattoo, but fading into his skin. 'What the—'

'Kip, Breaker, what are you—'

He winced, his mouth open in a silent cry as if she'd just kicked him in the stones. 'Oh, oh, don't! Don't call me that. No names. Please. You have no idea. Right now . . .' He blinked.

'What's—'

He slung the cloak out and around her shoulders. It billowed strangely, as if it weighed nothing, but settled on her shoulders firmly. It was the strangest material she'd ever felt. Shimmery like satin, cool to the touch like brass, light as air and as heavy as responsibility. It had a hood that looked familiar.

He stepped back and squinted again. 'Damn,' he said. 'It's

perfect.' He looked back down at his wrist, and rubbed it, but there was nothing there now.

'Kip, what is this?' Teia was suddenly afraid.

'It's a gift of light. It's the Night's Embrace. The Shadow's Wing. Portable Darkness. A crutch until you learn to walk. To mist walk? I don't . . . it's all scrambling together. It was all so clear.' He squeezed his eyes tightly shut. 'And it's not for me. Mist Walker. Damn. I should have gone for the gun.'

'Kip, I can't take this. Why would you give me such a thing? This is—' She stopped.

They both looked at the cloak.

'Am I hallucinating again?' Kip asked.

The cloak had gone red. Red like passion, or a blush. And Teia knew it was red, too. That was no green. It didn't feel green. Not in the least.

And now it shot through with blue, chased by orange, by pink, by a violet tinge. Each wave started at the neckline and coursed down to the hem. Now yellow. Curiosity?

'Oh,' Kip said.

'Oh?'

'It's the cloak all the shimmercloaks were based on. Of course it's the best.' He rubbed his eyes. 'You can probably make it turn any color you— Oh no.'

He was staring at the cards scattered on the ground around them. He saw that he was standing on one of the cards and he moved carefully, lifting his foot as if the card might bite him. He bent down and grabbed the card as if it were made of rubies and gold, touching only the very edges. 'Oh, Orholam, please. Please tell me I didn't break any of . . . What the hell?'

He stared at the card as if it was offending him.

He grabbed another card.

'No!' he breathed. His eyes widened.

He grabbed more and more. Stared at each. What was he doing?

'No, no, no,' he said as he turned each over. 'Teia, was this like this when you found me?'

'Was what like what?'

'Were the cards like this? No one came in and stole the real ones before you found me?'

'Kip, what are you talking about? They were all stuck to your skin. It was like they were poisoning you.'

'Oh, no no no no. I must have triggered one of her traps. No wonder it almost killed me. Out of all the times I've loused everything up . . .' He cupped his forehead with a hand, aghast.

'Kip! What are you talking about?'

He turned and held up a card in front of her. The back was illustrated painstakingly with geometric designs, lacquered with luxin. He turned the card. The face of it was blank. He showed her another card: blank. Another: blank.

'I've destroyed her life's work! Janus Borig lived to make these cards, and she died protecting them, and now I've—' He took a few hurried steps away and retched noisily.

She came over and put a hand on his back. He was hunched over, hands on his thighs. She'd just saved his life, and this was not exactly how she'd expected him to react. Or at all how she'd expected him to react. Orholam, had she been thinking of kissing him?

'Is it really that bad?' she asked. No, T, he's probably puking for fun.

'It may be worse,' he said, wiping his mouth. 'My grandfather believed I knew where the cards were all along, and he's threatened to kill me if I don't turn them over. This? There's no way he'll believe this.'

'What, uh, what's this other box?'

Kip sighed. 'That's my grandfather's favorite deck. My father must have stolen them to spite him. They're worth a fortune, of course. But one-of-a-kind, of course, so I can't sell them, can't hide them, can't give them back without him knowing that I must have found these others.'

'Maybe this would make a good peace offering?'

Kip considered it, but then shook his head. 'I don't know why my father stole the cards. Maybe he has some purpose for them. When he comes back, I don't want to have failed him doubly.'

'Kip,' Teia said gently, 'you really think he's coming back?'

'Yes!' he barked. 'Yes,' he said more quietly. He winced and squinted. He seemed woozy, nauseated.

Teia went over and turned off all the lights except for the soothing blue.

'Thanks.'

'You're still my partner, Kip. They haven't taken that away. Not yet. Now, let's clean this up.'

They began picking up the cards, and it was good.

Moments of companionable silence passed as they simply worked together. With the cards and the cloak and everything she didn't understand of what was happening, Teia found herself saying, 'I, I thought you were dead.'

Kip looked very tired. 'I think . . . I think I was.'

'That would have been the worst thing that ever happened to me.' She'd wanted to say *losing you* would have been the worst thing that ever happened, but it was too much. Kip could say whatever popped into his head and get away with it, somehow. She couldn't.

'I promise to die in some way that's convenient and non-messy,' Kip said.

'That's not what I'm—'

'I'm joking.'

'Oh.'

He took a deep breath. 'Thank you, Teia. I wouldn't have wanted anyone else to find me destroying priceless artifacts.'

She laughed. Ripples of color went scintillating down her cloak. Whoa, what the hell?

'You know, I think I like that cloak on you,' Kip said. 'Makes you a lot easier to read.'

She scowled, but the scowl wasn't reflected in the cloak, so he could see she was faking, dammit. She shut her eyes and concentrated.

'Ooh, nice,' Kip said. 'But I don't think I can look at that cloak for long right now.' He was wincing and rubbing his temples.

She looked. The cloak was a drab, boring gray. It looked exactly like a normal Blackguard inductee's cloak. 'Kip, this is amazing!' It reacted directly to her will. She didn't think the shimmercloaks changed their mundane form. Those only did one thing. This, this was something far more.

He grumbled something, but before she could ask him to repeat himself, Karris White Oak opened the door.

She didn't look particularly pleased to see either of them. Nor was she pleased to see the mess of the punching bag down and sawdust spilled everywhere. She strode in purposefully, glanced at Teia, dismissed her.

'You did this, Kip?' she asked, meaning knocking the bag down.

He nodded, hands in his pockets. He also had a card box in each pocket.

'Show me your hands,' Karris demanded.

Kip pulled his hands out, carefully palm down, and Karris examined – his hands. Teia blew out a relieved breath. She glanced at her cloak. It was staying gray, like she wanted it to. Thank Orholam for that.

'Beat your own knuckles bloody, while training. Now your hands will be no good for days as you heal, and you'll miss training. Does that strike you as particularly productive?' Karris asked.

'Learning to fight through pain is good training, yes,' Kip said. 'And I won't miss anything.'

Teia almost gasped at his tone, and Karris's lips thinned. She was still holding Kip's fist in her hand, and Teia wondered if she was thinking how fast she could turn her hold into an arm bar or a wrist lock and kick Kip's defiant ass. Instead she turned his right arm over and looked at his elbow. Then she pushed up his sleeve and looked at his shoulder. She found the wound there.

'So you've discovered venting,' she said.

'Venting?' Kip asked.

'Shooting luxin is one way to make your punches or kicks faster.'

'Streaming? You already knew about that?' Kip asked.

'Why are you blinking? Do you have a hangover, Kip? Are you lightsick?'

'I'm fine,' he said.

She sighed. 'We wait until after final vows to teach it. Your whole squad's using this?'

Neither Teia nor Kip answered.

'Figures,' Karris said. 'It's a good way for people to burn through their halo in a couple years. And so difficult to use well that most Blackguards use it less than once a year.'

'A mistake,' Kip said. 'Would you have us only shoot muskets once a year, because we use them so rarely in actual combat? The lack of practice reinforces—'

He saw the look on Karris's face and finally shut up.

'So the bag tore off its hanger,' Karris said. 'And it split open?'

Teia saw the problem. If the bag had torn off its leather hanger, that would have taken care of the force of a mighty punch. Or if it had ripped open at its loose thread, how would it then have torn off its hanger?

'I'm Guile,' Kip said, still hostile. It was, despite the incredible rudeness, kind of a brilliant response. 'I'm Guile' meaning that he was so far outside the norm that you could expect things far outside the norm to happen regularly around him, or 'I'm Guile' meaning I'm a cheater, and go to hell if you don't like it?

Surprisingly enough, Karris didn't slap Kip's silly head off. And this was a woman who'd been famous for her temper. It seemed she was changing, mellowing with age. Of course, the open secret that the White had forbidden her to draft might have had a little to do with it, too. As a red/green, it might have been the best thing anyone could have done to her.

Karris's face went still, her eyes hooded. 'Don't forget, Kip, I'm Guile now, too.'

Oh. So maybe not mellowing with age.

The chagrin on Kip's face was priceless. Orholam's bony knuckles, but Teia kind of wanted to give a cheer for her handler.

'Yes, ma'am,' Kip said.

Before Karris could say any more, though, the door creaked open once more. They all turned, but Teia was watching Karris, and she saw the woman's face drain of color.

'Samite!' she said. 'What are you doing down here?'

'The White said you might be here.'

'Sami, what happened to you?'

Teia saw the squat Blackguard give an apologetic grin. Her left hand was wrapped in a thick bandage that despite its thickness couldn't hide that what was bandaged was smaller than a full hand.

'Retirement,' Samite said with forced cheeriness. 'Or a post training the scrubs and the nunks here.' She lifted her chin at Kip and Teia.

Karris had already covered the distance to her friend. She lifted her friend's arm carefully. Samite winced. 'Samite. What happened?'

Samite shrugged. 'The promachos has been sending out squads to search for all the bane.'

'Sure, sure,' Karris said.

'Mine went after the yellow. Found it and destroyed it. Not many wights there, but when yellows go wight, they figure out how to draft a solid yellow. *All* of them figure it out, it seems. Hell of a fight. Half the squad was new kids, and *I* was the only casualty. Embarrassing, frankly.'

Karris embraced her friend. Samite stood stoic for a moment, but then hugged Karris back.

'Guess this is what I get for that other thing. With Lady Guile. The last Lady Guile, I mean. Felia.'

'No, no, no, don't talk like that.'

Teia was suddenly embarrassed at seeing this intimate expression between friends – and also intensely curious, though she could tell that this was a secret she wasn't going to be learning.

Samite pushed back from Karris and looked at the heavy bag. 'Kip, you do this?'

He nodded.

Samite continued, 'Your father would be proud. He told me once to give you a hard time if you hadn't knocked the bag open by Sun Day.'

Which did two things to Teia. First, she was deeply ashamed that she'd been part of the prank to keep that stitch reinforced and the thread loose. Second, it made her realize that Gavin had meant Kip to get those cards if he didn't come back.

'But, I, uh, I'm not here about that, and I'm sorry to interrupt your training of these two, Lady Guile.' Samite took a deep breath. She glanced at Kip and Teia and shrugged. 'It's for your ears, but I guess they'll know soon enough. Lady Guile, I wouldn't have come to interrupt you for just . . . my . . . news. I came here to give you warning.'

'Warning?' Karris asked.

Teia was looking at Kip. He blanched. Teia had no idea what it was, but *Kip* obviously already knew what Samite was going to say.

'When we Blackguards landed on Big Jasper, there was another ship at the docks. A young lord was debarking. He was quite . . . willful, trying to make his way through the pilgrimage crowds. He said his name was Zymun.'

Kip looked ill again, but in a very different way.

Karris looked at her blankly. 'And . . . ?'

'Karris,' Samite said, 'Zymun says he's your son. The White wishes you to report to her, immediately.'

Chapter 77

Her son. Here.

Karris felt like she was watching her own body move from hall to hall to lift. She passed the Blackguard station and couldn't even identify the men on duty. Her chest was constricted; it was hard to breathe. She could only focus on one thing at a time. Step, step, woman, dammit. Now knock. Her son.

Dear Orholam, it was all coming down.

Knock, damn you.

She lifted a hand and knocked on the White's door.

The oddest thing happened with that simple, irrevocable action: she felt relief. It was all coming down, and somehow, no matter what that cost, no matter what came next, the lies were finished.

The Blackguards at the door, Gill and Gavin Greyling, looked at each other over her head. 'Lady Guile?' Gill asked. He opened the door for her.

'Thank you.' She walked in, back straight, features clear. She had been taught by the best; she wasn't going to disgrace them now. Here at the end of all things, she would be brave, and stoic, and take her punishment like a lady and a Blackguard.

The White was in her wheeled chair, and she looked stronger

than she had in years. She saw Karris and said, 'Leave us.' Her attendants and secretaries and Blackguards left immediately; there was a steel in her voice that brooked no argument or delay.

When the room was empty, she studied Karris.

Karris moved to speak, but the White lifted a finger, silencing her, and studied her more.

Then, abruptly, the White said, 'Look at this invention. One of the young Blackguard inductees, Ben-hadad, made it for me. At first I didn't think he quite realized what he'd stumbled upon, but now I'm pretty certain he does.'

She put her hand down on the arm of her chair, and the barest tendril of blue luxin moved down the rice-paper-thin skin of her arm – and the chair turned, and then rolled out from behind her desk as if a ghost had turned and pushed it.

'What the h—? Your pardon, High Mistress,' Karris said. 'I've never seen such a thing. How . . . ?'

'Gears and pulleys, he told me. All made of luxin. His trick was to completely encapsulate some open luxin within a couple of the belts, he said. It being open, I can push it with Will alone. Because it's encapsulated, it doesn't evaporate. Were I younger, I'd be flipping this chair over right now to understand exactly what he's done. It can't be as simple as he's said, but if it is, or if it's even close . . .

'We each tend to think of our time as the end product of all that has come before, which is true, but we like to believe our time is therefore the pinnacle, rather than another pearl on the string. This invention may remake a thousand things, or it may remake only one or two, depending on how efficient it can be made, and over what distances and for how long it can operate, and across what color bands. I may be dying just before the most interesting time in history. I may miss out on a revolution by this much. It's either intolerable, or very hopeful. I can't decide which.'

'Come now,' Karris said, 'you're going to live forever.'

'I'll be dead by Sun Day,' the White said.

Steel bands crushed Karris's chest. 'You mean Sun Day next, surely,' she said, meaning more than a year away.

'I said what I meant.' The way the White said it, it was

589

obvious she meant the Sun Day three days away. 'And not another word about that. I've been gifted with a long life and a certainty about the date of my passing. Debate about a foregone conclusion is a waste of the little time I have left.'

Karris swallowed the dozen contentions warring to get out of her throat. Not only, if she was honest with herself, to try to convince the White and herself that the White would be around for a long time yet, but also to keep her from bringing up worse things. Sitting in the judgment seat beneath an authority you can't deny is no place of comfort.

'It is almost sunset,' the White said. 'Push my chair to your balcony, would you? I could Will myself there now, I suppose, but I tire.'

So Karris pushed her down the hall to her and Gavin's rooms. And out to the balcony. The Blackguards insisted on being in the room, at least, with their recent bad experiences with balconies and assassins.

Karris found a heavy cloak for herself and some blankets for the White.

'Take my hand, dear,' the White said.

They watched the sun set together. And in flares of pink and orange and every red, the sun went down to the sea, leaving flaming clouds as a promise of its return. And in the beauty of the sun and sea and clouds and the iron grip of a frail hand that had protected and guided her in ways her own mother never had, Karris found her cheeks damp with tears for all the woundedness in the world. And for her own.

'Look upon the city, and tell me what you see,' the White said.

With the sun so close to the horizon, the city was being swallowed in soft shadows, rising from the ground up. The gleaming domes of every possible color and metal and design shone bright against the whitewashed walls, and the Thousand Stars sparkled, beaming their rays to and fro in their districts. The seven towers of the Chromeria were stunning in this light, too, reaching like longing hands toward the heavens. 'I see the most beautiful city in the world,' Karris said. 'I see a treasure worth protecting.'

'The Thousand Stars, odd, aren't they?'

Karris shrugged. They were wonders; their oddness was undeniable, but also unquestionable.

'A vast expense to build such towers, merely to bring drafters a few extra minutes of light each morning and night, don't you think?'

They were, of course, used for many other things than that: ceremonial, celebratory, practical, but the White knew all that. She meant something else.

Karris turned a questioning glance to the White, but the old woman had turned away from the city to look over the sea as the disk of the sun disappeared.

'Will you tell me about the second time you saw the green flash?' she asked the White.

'The second?! Did I tell you about the first?' the White asked, still looking over the sea. But the sun was fully down; there would be no green flash tonight.

'Gavin told me about the first. Said you saw it at a party and were so excited you jumped – and broke your future husband's nose as he leaned past you for his wineglass.'

The White's face broke into a grin at the memory, but she didn't turn from the sea. 'You know, he snored after that. Nose didn't heal right. I knew I couldn't really complain about it, but I was young, and I did.' Her smile was tugged down by that old sin, but rebounded. 'I miss him so much. He told me I should remarry when he was gone. He never wanted me to be lonely, but I couldn't find a man who compared to him. Problem with being exceptional, as you know. Perhaps great men are content with marrying a woman who is not their equal, but we great women . . . Our equals are rare enough in the first place, and then most of those we do find have married twits.'

'We're victims of our own refined tastes?' Karris asked.

'If Gavin Guile is a refined taste. He's a rare one, that's for sure.'

Karris couldn't talk about Gavin now. Couldn't begin to touch the well of sorrow that was beginning to turn to rage: how dare he leave her here, alone, to face all this? And the guilt that followed the rage: where was he? What was he suffering? He wouldn't be away if he could help it, she knew.

She hoped she knew.

'Look now,' the White said. The shadows like a rising tide had swallowed the walls of Big Jasper and rolled upward constantly, lights winking out around the curvature of the land until only the tallest buildings and the Thousand Stars were alight. Then only the Thousand Stars. They burned day into night.

It had been a long, long time since Karris had really looked.

'We drafters are those Thousand Stars, Karris. We have been turned to a hundred purposes, but at heart we have only one: to bring the light into darkness. Each high-set mirror is special indeed, brilliantly crafted, magically made, but in the end elevated not because of its innate specialness but because only by being set high can it serve to bring light where there is darkness. We are elevated to serve.'

For a time, they watched the light reflected from those many mirrors play over Big Jasper. Then the White said, 'The second time I saw the green flash, what I call Orholam's wink, was one of the hardest days of my tenure as White. I was on one of the lower balconies here, thinking about something I'd seen that had terrified me. I thought that if I did the wrong thing, the world would be plunged back into a war that it seemed had just ended. I thought that if I didn't do something, though, a blacker fate might befall than even that.'

'After the war? What was it?' Karris asked. She'd already run away by then, but she wasn't aware that there had been huge crises. Small ones, certainly. Perhaps all the putting down of pirates and rebels and the distribution of lands and pillage had been far more dangerous than she had thought, and they only seemed like small challenges because they had been so adeptly handled. Aside from the Tyrean solution, which, though immoral, had kept Tyrea weak for nearly two decades.

'It was the day Gavin came back from Sundered Rock.'

Karris held her breath, and her pulse became thunder in her ears. 'Because he was still drugged and didn't seem himself?' she asked, lying almost smoothly enough to do Lady Felia Guile proud.

'No,' the White said. 'Or, alternately, precisely.'

She said nothing more, and Karris didn't want to insult her by filling the space with words.

'I saw a thing that terrified me, and in my panic, I almost did something rash because I thought I needed to do *something*. And then . . . Orholam's wink. I took it as a message that he was with me. He knew. Power is any action that results in consequences. But real power is action that results in the intended consequences. Real power is impossible if not guided by wisdom. I had the power to kill. But Orholam had another plan. That was the second wink.'

It was like the words were in a foreign language, and Karris was struggling to translate them. The White had seen Gavin – and?

And she knew.

Just like that? Instantly? Karris had been in love with the man. Had made love with him. Had focused every fiber of her young soul on her forbidden love – and she hadn't seen it, but the White had?!

It made her furious. It made her feel stupider than words.

She almost reached out to draft red, to get that affirmation and validation that her rage was deserved. But then she realized she was comparing apples and oranges. The White had found Dazen while he was drugged and in the immediate aftermath of killing his brother. Karris hadn't spent much time with him before fleeing to conceal her pregnancy. When she'd come back a year later, Dazen had had time to practice being Gavin. They'd only gotten reaquainted when all around him treated him as Gavin. His clothing, speech patterns, hair, and posture were all different.

The point was that the White had known. She'd *known*. And she hadn't exposed Dazen.

The White said, 'How much is a man's soul worth? For what price will you buy his redemption? Is your answer different if he leads a nation? What if he could affect all of history? What price would be too much? What justice or vengeance would you forgo, for your hope?' She closed her eyes and sighed. Then her lips twisted in a little, reluctant grin, and she opened her eyes again. 'He did turn out to be a pretty damn good Prism. Go figure.'

Karris let out a breath she didn't realize she'd been holding. This was surreal. This just simply couldn't be. 'How did you keep it to yourself for so long?'

'To be a White is to know secrets, Karris. But that the position requires spying and skulduggery doesn't relieve me of the moral obligation for how I use what I know.'

Another breath. 'And you've known about . . . me, too? How long?'

'I've known about your son since the beginning. Other women I've known who have given up children have been haunted by it ever since. So over the years, I gave you several assignments where, had you wished, you could have extended your time to go looking for him without anyone being the wiser. You never took those chances.'

Woodenly, Karris said, 'I was . . . afraid I'd lead spies right to him. Afraid of what I would do, of who he'd become, of what he thought of me.'

'The darkness has not served you well. From what I learned today, I believe now that Andross Guile has known about him for years as well. Be wise as a serpent, child.'

But Karris couldn't wrestle with her thoughts about her son. Zymun. She hadn't even known his name. There was too much there, and she didn't trust herself how she'd react in front of the White. Her chin drifted up, and she pushed that open wound away. Just for the time being.

'I wish . . . I wish I had the kind of certainty you have. That Orholam is guiding me. I wish I could see him give me a visible sign, like he did you.'

The White chuckled. 'Yes, two green flashes, in fifty years. What are the odds? It turns out, if you watch the sunset almost every day, pretty good. Karris, what we see is not determined solely by what is in the world, but also by what is in us. The lens is as important as the light. You think I haven't questioned those two occasions a thousand thousand times? Besides, Orholam speaks differently to each of his children. I only thought of the green flash as a message because my own grand-mother always called it Orholam's wink. Had you seen it, you would have thought it a curious phenomenon. Orholam may speak to you in ways more pedestrian: through his holy writ, or through his followers' words, related to you. Could you accept that?'

'Of course.'

'Then hear this word, which is his gift for you. Are you listening?'

'I'm listening. Did Orholam just tell you this now, or have you somehow steered me into this?'

'Orholam has told me this for you a thousand times. In fifteen years, I have never read these words without you filling my mind, but it has been my lot to know and not to tell. Part of the price I pay for my own sins. Even the forgiven must pay penance.'

Sins? What sins had the White committed? Did she think that not telling anyone about Gavin was a sin? Surely not. 'What is the word?' Karris asked.

'The Most High will repay you for the years the locusts have eaten.'

Locusts hadn't come to the Seven Satrapies since before Lucidonius, but Karris had a luxiat when she was a child who told stories that made the plague as real as a memory. Thought to be an effusion of an imbalance of a surfeit of both green and blue, they came in a cloud, with a sound like distant, unremitting thunder. They spread from horizon to horizon, literally shadowing the land. The mass was like a million chariots descending to pillage the land, and the ancient Seer Jo'El spoke of them marching as in ranks.

Drafters of every stripe, even in that ancient, fractured time, had fought in their waves. Blues tried to draft domes over entire fields. Oranges had tried to manipulate the hordes and turn them to foreign lands. Reds and sub-reds had sprayed the skies with fire. And like candles thrown into the ocean the drafters were extinguished, one by one by one by the thousands.

And everywhere the locusts went, they devoured everything. Nothing green was left. They wiped out not only crops, but whole forests. Trees, denuded of their leaves, simply died in their wake. Men went mad during the assault, screaming, open mouths filled with locusts. Men went mad after, as starvation's scythe swung. The insect armies left nothing good and green and growing. Nothing but hollow-cheeked children with huge eyes and hunger-swollen bellies, walking on stick legs until they could no longer stand. They curled, not even waving the flies from their eyes. And they died.

And that had been Karris's life, since the war. Even with Gavin's coming back, and marrying her, she couldn't but think of those sixteen years of her life, the flower of her youth, lost, blighted, devoured. And an impotent rage smoldered there, an ever-burning fire that she hadn't even known was still aflame.

This was her slow suicide. This was her drafting red, so much red she would die young, not precisely on purpose, but not precisely not.

The words themselves were a fist that punched through her stomach, ripped off a dozen layers of ill-fitting plate, and gave her a warm, clean robe in their place.

'Karris, you will be at your most formidable when you bear no sword and wear no armor,' the White said gently. 'This is the power of the word.'

Karris couldn't move. She held herself rigid. *I will repay you for the years the locusts have eaten.* That promise held everything she'd ever hoped to hear, and from Orholam. It felt like someone had picked her soul up out of her body and shaken it gently, and all the dirt and grime and hatred and rage had simply sloughed off and fallen, and he dropped her back into her own shoes. Everything was the same, but her eyes were different, healing. She didn't trust herself to speak.

Finally, she said, 'You have been the mother to me that my mother could never be. You have been more. Thank you.' She knelt, and kissed the White's hand.

The White held her cheek fondly, then patted her, signaling she should stand. 'I must go now, my dear. I will pray for you, Karris, and I will pray that Orholam gives you your own green flash when the time is right.'

'I don't want you to leave,' Karris said. 'Not ever.'

The White smiled sadly. 'Thank you, child. Do me a favor, will you?'

'Anything. Anything.'

'Be kind to Marissia. She has done excellent service in harder circumstances than you can know.'

The request, as reasonable as it was, reached nonetheless

straight into that hot core where the rage fire had burned. For what was that red-haired beauty but a walking symbol of all Karris had lost in those sixteen years? She, a slave, had had what Karris with her wealth and position could not have. Not just a man – as if a man's affections could be traded as one would trade a cow – but a position, a purpose, a place that she fit perfectly. 'Blackguard' had been a cloak that Karris had worn because she was excellent enough at the attendant skills that she couldn't be denied it, but she hadn't been Blackguard as Commander Ironfist was Blackguard. It was not a task to him, but an identity. Thus Karris had always been given the odd assignments, as the White's fetch-and-carry girl, as Gavin's partner in hunting wights, as liaison here and there. She'd always been different, and not just in the tone of her skin or background. Her Blackguard brothers had accepted her as you accept a sister with a limp: fiercely, because it was so obvious that she didn't quite fit.

Marissia had always *fit*. Her staff was invisible, because they served perfectly. And so too had she served excellently at a myriad other duties that Karris was only seeing now. And of course, Gavin Guile's longtime room slave was accorded treatment no other slave in the Seven Satrapies got. Not even Grinwoody was treated like Marissia. The younger, wilder Gavin fresh from the war had made sure of it.

A young lord Seaborn had gotten grabby and, when his advances were rebuffed, had blackened young Marissia's eyes.

Gavin had melted his face and mounted his head over the Chromeria's front gate – briefly. The White had seen it taken down within hours.

It was enough of an insult that the family had sworn vengeance. But through mysterious circumstances that most of the Blackguards later attributed to the Red, the Seaborns quickly found themselves without allies. The family had eventually sided with pirates attacking the Guiles and their retainers' ships.

They'd all been hanged, and their lands seized and given to the Red's friends, including, incidentally, some of the Seaborns' old allies who'd abandoned them.

And Gavin showed not the least sorrow for it. He was a

hard man, but that made him a safe friend, and a fearsome foe. When he came to your door and gave you the choice which to be, such stories came to mind.

The White said, 'I know you envy her, though truth be told, she envies you more.'

'She envies me? But she's a slave.' A slave shouldn't dare to envy her owners.

'And yet a woman still.'

'More's the pity.'

The White folded her hands in her lap, her very silence a reproach. When Karris met her gaze, chagrined, the White said, 'The choice to give up bitterness is not easy, but it is simple: peace or poison. And don't wait until you feel like making it. You never will.'

Karris took a deep breath and went back inside. The White followed her in.

'Gill has a package for you. It's your inheritance. Please don't open it until you hear of my passing.'

Karris swallowed. She opened the door and Gill handed her a package tied with red ribbon. It felt like nothing more than half a dozen pieces of paper. Seemed a small inheritance, but then, the White had treasured information above all, and who was to say what was written there. Thinking of that – 'What am I supposed to do with the spies? I've spent all this time . . .'

'I've explained that in those papers. Maybe not to your full satisfaction, but as well as I can. Please don't let those fall into enemy hands.'

'And burn them as soon as I've memorized them, which I should do instantly. Yes, I'm familiar,' Karris said. They shared a grin.

'One last thing,' the White said. 'While you're doing hard things. When the time comes, please, forgive me, too.'

'For what?'

'For failing you a thousand ways, as every mother does. Know that you are loved, Karris. And remember this: even a small woman, if she stands near a great light, casts a long shadow.'

'A small woman? You're a giant,' Karris said through damp eyes.

The White grinned, and it wasn't until she and her Blackguards had disappeared into the hall that Karris realized the White hadn't meant herself; she'd meant Karris.

Chapter 78

Days passed. Weeks.

Gavin was fed and given watered wine, but the guards who tended him never said a word. Never answered a query. Avoided eye contact. When one did accidentally meet his eyes, Gavin saw the worst thing possible: pity.

They thought Gavin was mad. Without his prismatic eyes, no one believed he was the Prism. Without his drafting, without his regalia, without his Blackguard escort, his impish imperial imperiousness seemed the struttings of insanity.

Was what Gavin had woven in all those years of power so thin a veil? Is a man no more than his magic?

Then one day, the door opened and the Nuqaba came in, bracketed by her Tafok Amagez. She limped a little as she came to stand in front of him. She waved the guards away. They hesitated, obviously mindful of what had happened last time. Her jaw set, and they left.

'You may be pleased to know we've come to an agreement,' she said.

'We?'

'Eirene and I. Your father and the two of us. We are going to sell you to him. After you've faced justice.'

'Justice?' Gavin asked. 'So you've come to wash my feet and begin begging to know how you might pay restitution.' Lies and illusions and bluster. But it was all he had.

'You've assaulted the Nuqaba. A drafter who assaults the Nuqaba is punished by having his eyes burnt out. Everyone wins.'

She meant it. Every word. Even after all he'd said.

You can't barter with crazy.

'Even you win,' she said. 'With your eyes burned out, your

father doesn't need to know you lost your power. Eirene wasn't going to go along with it, until I pointed out that your father might deny that you were you. After all, without your prismatic eyes, what are you? Useless, that's what. Useless.'

She leaned close, but not close enough for him to snatch her haik and pull her against the bars and brain her.

'You'll be gagged, of course, and in the very stadium where you killed so many, you will be publicly blinded. While people cheer. You always did so love a spectacle, didn't you? On the ship home, you'll be scrubbed and shaved and given a haircut and put back in clothes befitting your former rank. Your father has to accept receipt of you, of course. Has to accept that it's you. But I want you to know something. On that ship with you, there will be an assassin. A man loyal to me unto death. After you've been accepted, he will shout some nonsense about the Color Prince, and kill you. Do you know how hard it is to stop an assassin who doesn't care if he dies?' She sighed. 'Your death is necessary, I'm afraid. It's my fault. I was careless. I spoke too freely, earlier. I searched all our laws to see if I could cut out your tongue and remove all your fingers instead so that you wouldn't be able to tell him what I said, but there's no such punishment. Blinding will have to do.'

Her tone was so light and joyous that Gavin thought she must be joking.

She wasn't joking.

'Do you know,' she said, 'it used to be quite common? Blinding drafters, that is. I think they had more drafters then. They said that if a man misused the light Orholam gave him, he should be denied light altogether, that perhaps he would repent and not lose his soul. Tell me, Gavin, don't you agree that you've misused the light that Orholam gave you?'

Yes. Yes, I have.

He said nothing.

'There are instructions for how to do it – hear this – *humanely*. Because if you're going to put out a man's eyes, you should do it without unnecessary suffering, right? Ha. Apparently, it requires all sorts of strapping down. They used to build this machine. Quite ingenious. Two pokers that could be adjusted to the wideness of each man's face. The tines heated glowing hot. A stopblock so that eyes would be fully burnt out, without piercing the brain and killing the blasphemer, no matter how he might thrash. There are even instructions on what luxin to use to prop the eyelids open. If you burn the eyelids, the blasphemers would often get an infection and die. You want them to live, not die of a fever. How can they repent if they aren't in their right mind, right? They said they did both eyes at once because after losing one eye, a man's anticipation of the pain of losing the second was so great they'd often go mad.' She smirked. 'We, of course, have no machine. We'll do one eye at a time. I want you to think of one thing, Gavin Guile. *Tsssssss.*'

He looked at her, confused.

'That'll be the sound of your eyeball steaming as red-hot iron enters it.' A chill went through his very core. This was the woman who it was rumored had tortured her husband for years. Suddenly, he believed it.

'And know this, if you shout anything other than screams of pain, if you claim to be Gavin Guile, we'll shout you down and beat you for blaspheming and tear out your tongue. There aren't instructions in my scrolls how to do that, but I don't need them. I already know.'

She was a worse butcher than her brother ever was. 'What happened to you?' Gavin asked. She wasn't like this, before, was she? Or had it been there all along?

'I refused to merely survive.'

'You're the Nuqaba; you're sworn to Orholam.' Though as the words came out, the irony wasn't lost on Gavin that he should be the one speaking them.

She glanced around for eavesdroppers, then the expression instantly morphed from appalled to grimly amused. 'A dead faith that keeps rolling only from its own momentum. Men want to worship, and worshipping abstractions is hard. I give them something easier: me. As you used to.'

'I never asked for men's worship,' Gavin said. He'd lost faith, but he'd taken it as his responsibility to safeguard the religion for those who did believe. Why destroy it for others, if it made them happy? Why destroy it, if there was a slim chance that it was true?

'Did you not?' She shook her head. 'I don't even need the seed crystal to tell me that you're deceiving yourself. I have preparations to make. Just remember: *tssssss*.'

She laughed, and left.

Gavin sank to the ground of his cell. His eyes. Dear Orholam, his eyes. His fucking eyes had been betraying him all his life.

During the war, men and women, satrapahs and conns had believed in him because of his prismatic eyes, he knew. His impossible eyes. His brother had seen the onset of their prismatic glory. That had torn his brother's soul; Karris had only been the pebble that upended the cart. With one glance, his eyes had proved to the world that what the Chromeria said could never happen, had happened. Two Prisms in one generation. And if one had to pick between brothers, it was hard not to choose whichever brother who stood before you, threatening you, wasn't it?

You are nothing more than your magic, Gavin Guile.

Gavin remembered his first conversations with his older brother about magic. Gavin, the elder, had known everything. Or speculated with such confidence that Dazen had never failed to be impressed. He'd worshipped Gavin.

He still did.

He wondered how much of his persona as Prism was a projection of that winsome, pretend perfection his big brother had embodied to Dazen as a child. Gavin was the oak around which Dazen had grown, like ivy. The parasite vine climbed high and decorative, slowly choking the life out of that which it embraced. No wonder Gavin had hated his little brother with the boyish hatred of encumbrances.

Even after the war, Dazen had grown round the great expanse that had been Gavin, draping his own foliage over the widespread branches and calling himself an oak. Calling it life, when it was death. Blocking out the sun, light, and life intended for another.

And now that Gavin was dead, and the oak rotted, what happened to the ivy? On its own, it had no strength to stand.

I haven't mourned him. I put two bullets in his face, and I haven't mourned him.

I wonder what it smells like down there. I left his body to

rot. I didn't even have the decency to wrap him in funeral cloths. Didn't want to get bloody.

I didn't want to get bloody?

There's always something desperate requiring my attention, isn't there? As if I can blind myself with activity, with travel, or with war.

He thought of all the wights he'd killed over the years. The White had been right. There had never been any need for him to risk his own life hunting them down. Foolishness to risk a Prism to hunt a few wights. Wights are merely once-men, running in fear, nearly always alone, usually in the wilderness because no one in the world would give a murdering madman shelter. Take a tracker after them, figure out when they sleep, and have half a dozen men fire muskets at the sleeper.

Instead, Gavin had insisted on going after them himself. On facing them. Killing them when they were conscious. Giving them those phony last rites. Trying to purge himself, more than them. Steeped in blood, he sought blood to cleanse himself.

He sometimes still couldn't believe the White had let him go hunting. But she'd thought he'd kill himself if he didn't have those trips. Perhaps she'd been wiser than he knew.

The tiny window inset in the cellar's door opened.

'Tssssss.'

And a woman's laugh.

It chilled him. Staring there at the now shut window, and his grubby cell and his half a hand, and his dirty beard and his long dirty hair, Gavin felt his chest tightening up. Hard to breathe. Shooting pains.

A thought that he'd batted away successfully a hundred times came back to him, and stood over him, and spat upon him: You're not going to get out of this. There is no escape.

It was almost puzzling to him. Putting on Gavin Guile hadn't meant putting on a set of clothes, it had been putting on a new skin. He'd seen flayed men: his spies left for him by his brother. He could still hear their shrieking, and now he felt he was one of them, the Gavin-skin torn from him.

He was going to lose his eyes.

Well fuck his eyes.

'Orholam will give it to you plain,' the prophet had told him. 'You keep up your lies, and you'll be stricken blind.'

He was already blind. What could they do to him but make all the world see what he already knew? For months now, he'd been a husk. A man when he had been nearly a god. That knife, that damned knife had stolen his power. But there was no getting it back.

He looked around the cellar, and could almost convince himself that he saw brown dirt, brown wood, the silver of metal. But it was all gray. Shades shading into black. Into blindness.

Who had he been deceiving, anyway, thinking he could make a comeback? From this. He had built himself to be the perfect Prism since he was seventeen years old. A seventeen-year-old's projection of a perfect Prism, anyway. Robbed of the light of his youthful delusions, he was an empty mirror in a darkened room.

Ah, Karris, I'm only glad that you don't have to see me like this. And if you do see me before my end, I won't see the disappointment, the horror, in your face.

If I could do it again, would I do it all differently? Would I have stolen your life, Gavin? Would I have come forward, at any point in all my years as Prism, having consolidated my power, and said of my own will, at my own time, 'I am not he'? I was too great a coward to live in the light. Fitting then that light be taken from me.

He sat, hollowed of feeling, for days. Morning and night, the window would open. He would hear a light step. '*Tsssss*,' the Nuqaba would say. And she would laugh.

Haruru was as much a legitimate Nuqaba as Gavin was a legitimate Prism. Hundreds of years ago, under Prism Karris Shadowblinder, immediately in the aftermath of Lucidonius's death, the Parians had been given extra leeway in how they kept the religion. Having been the birthplace or fostering place of Lucidonius, they had demanded special consideration. Prism Karris had allowed it in order to keep the empire together. Though attempts had been made since to keep the two parties more in line theologically, there had been no success in bringing the Nuqaba further under the Prism's political control.

Most Prisms tried, but war with Paria was something no

one had the stomach for. And a succession of Nuqabas had played their hands beautifully, strengthening key positions while giving up the inessential. But the truth was, too many Parians, both within the satrapy and outside of it, considered themselves uniquely bound to the Chromeria. The empire was, as they saw it, theirs. Their man had founded it. Their people had expanded it. To go to war with their own was unthinkable, so long as certain prerogatives were respected.

The Nuqaba was supposed to be a living saint. She was supposed to be mother to all the clans. She was supposed to be a model of patience and wisdom and firm love. She was supposed to look upon her people with the eye of grace. Some had gone so far as to wear a patch over their left eye, the oculus sinister, the evil eye. Not Haruru.

Ironfist and Tremblefist are going to be furious when I kill you.

No, that problem, that thought, that was the old Gavin. That was the Gavin who had power. Who was power.

She came back, to speak to him, or to taunt him.

'You're going to make a deal with a pagan army?' Gavin asked suddenly. 'Your people will kill you for that.' Perhaps worship of Orholam had slipped among the rich and powerful in Paria, perhaps they would be happy to make a deal with a monster. But would the army? Would the villages, and the fleets? Or would those faithful people rather die before they would join with monsters, regardless of what their betters told them to do?

'Not me.'

And then Gavin understood.

She's a useful idiot, is what she is. One of her nearest advisers probably works for the Color Prince.

It amazed Gavin how stupid ambition made smart people. Haruru controlled the Satrapah Tilleli Azmith totally, but hated having to publicly give the appearance of obeying her – or perhaps of merely being her equal. The Nuqaba wanted to be unfettered. So she'd join with the Color Prince, believing he would then turn toward the Chromeria and leave her alone until he'd dealt with them. Leave her alone. In what world would the man be stupid enough to do that?

The Color Prince wasn't an Angari pirate, coming to raid. He wanted to be an emperor. He was building up Tyrea rather than plundering it. Doubtless he was doing the same with Idoss and Ru now. It was certainly why he'd stopped or at least slowed his advance. When you spent money to build, you ultimately got more out of the land you held, but it took more time. If he was patient, it might be too late to stop him already. The caves above Ru held millions of bats. The guano contained a key ingredient for making gunpowder – and the Atashians had held a stranglehold on that, making the Chromeria and everyone else pay dearly for what the Color Prince now had for free. And what else could you do with the cedars of Blood Forest but build a fleet?

Both of which took time. With the Chromeria's navy shattered . . .

The Color Prince needed time, so he was using this time to divide his enemies. And the Nuqaba was deluded enough to think that if only she had total power over Paria, she could use that time better than the Color Prince could use his time to gather resources from five satrapies.

Truth was, it would probably take her years and a civil war for her to rule Paria outright. And when she won – if she won – Paria would be at its weakest precisely at the time when the Color Prince began to reap the riches of the satrapies.

Parians were great warriors, but they weren't so great that they could fight five satrapies. And in the meantime, as he subdued the other satrapies, the Color Prince wouldn't have to face those Parian warriors and Parian ships.

We so easily convince ourselves that what is good for me is also good for others.

If Gavin had been promachos, he could have stopped the Color Prince before Sun Day.

Of course, it's different when you're right.

Truth was, he could have stopped him even without being promachos. Sending the Blackguard searching some of the rivers in Atash that might hold harbors fit for shipbuilding. The skimmers changed everything, and Gavin was more adept at figuring out the implications of rapid changes than most.

The Blackguards could have found those harbors – if they existed – in a few weeks. With the amount of lumber collected all in one place, it would have taken only a single good red drafter and a spark. They'd have destroyed the Color Prince's fleet before it could sully the waves.

If I were in charge, things would be better.

Said every tyrant ever.

'Why are you grinning?' the Nuqaba asked, peeved.

'I've got my health, my family, one and a half hands, two good eyes, what's not to love?' Gavin asked.

'We'll change that soon enough,' she snarled.

'That's why it was a joke . . .'

Her face contorted, and he was suddenly glad she didn't have a pistol now. Didn't like condescension, this one.

My brain seems stuck in the obvious right now. Perhaps to deny what's coming.

'Though I will sit close enough to hear the hissing and popping of your eyes, to savor your screams, I wish I could be there on your ship home, as you jerk and twitch at every touch, every voice, wondering which one is my assassin, wondering how you can fight off a death you can see coming, but only metaphorically. When they shave your cheeks clean, will you wonder if that razor will later taste your throat? What savage nightmares will you have before you die?'

'So,' he said, 'you act the evil gloating traitorous bitch queen laudably enough, but I'm bored. Are we going to do this? Hard to escape when I'm stuck in a cell.'

'Such things have to happen at noon. And I'm not giving you any chance to escape. We'll go straight to the hippodrome. I wanted to do it tomorrow, as part of the Sun Day festivities, but the Ruthgari have a different view of things.'

'Spilling blood as defilement, yes, pity, that.'

'Yes, pity,' she said flatly. 'So we'll do it today.'

She stared at him for long minutes, seeming to savor the darkness he tried to hide growing in his breast like the white egg of black widow spiders undulating slowly until it suddenly split, bursting forth a black, creeping explosion. He tried to keep the horror off his face, the fear that he'd convinced himself he simply didn't have the capacity to feel. He was wrong, and the hopelessness crept in a black wave up over his defenses, over his bravado, and finally over his face.

She saw, and smiled.

Finally, a knock on the door. 'Your Eminence,' a voice said, 'it's time.'

Chapter 79

Kip had barely escaped to his room and his pounding head and his flickering visions when there was a rapid knock on his door. Teia.

'Go away,' Kip said. He sounded like a petulant child, and he hated himself for it.

'Breaker,' she said. 'You need me.'

But when she said 'Breaker' again he heard 'Diakoptês,' the sense of two languages colliding, intertwining. Diakoptês: he who rends asunder. He heard a woman whisper it in his ear, sharing a secret. He heard an old man screaming it in despair in the distance. He heard a crowd chanting it until it melded with 'Break-er, Break-er!'

'Breaker, open the door,' Teia said, and Kip was aware of himself once again, leaning against the doorframe, head down, heart racing. He opened the door.

Teia came in. 'Decision time,' she said. 'Your grandfather is going to know about your half brother's arrival any moment, if he doesn't already. He'll send for Zymun, and then he'll send for you. Right?'

'I suppose,' Kip said.

'What'll happen?'

'We tried to kill each other the last time we met, Teia, and Zymun's not the forgive-and-forget type.' But even as Kip said the name 'Zymun,' it echoed in his head. Zymun the Dancer. *Forests flashed before his eyes, light streaming through morning mist, rising in a meadow. A man he knew well, lying prone at my feet. Unconscious? No, dead.* Dead, Kip was certain of it. And—

Gone. Only to be replaced by dazzling pain.

'Breaker! Pay attention! "Who hesitates . . ."' she quoted. 'Finish it.'

"Is lost," Kip said.

'So, you've got a choice. Wait until your grandfather summons you and dance to his tune again, or run.'

'Run?' Kip asked. White and black spots were still slamming into each other companionably in front of his face.

'Take a ship. Take it anywhere.'

'I wouldn't even know where to hire a—'

'I do.'

'Or how much to pay for pass—'

'Two hundred danars. You've got five times that in your stash.' She pointed at his hidden coin stash.

'You know about my coins?' Kip asked.

'You're many things, Breaker, but sneaky ain't one.'

Breaker. Again, it was like someone rang a cymbal next to his ear. But it didn't distract him completely. 'Breaker,' she'd said. And 'ain't'? Teia didn't talk like that. Not usually. She was establishing distance between them.

Kip didn't even know what he'd done. 'It was the booger thing, wasn't it?' he asked.

'Kip! No time!'

But a flush of red suffused the gray of her cloak, until she noticed it, and it went back to flat boring gray immediately.

Kip drew his green spectacles and tried to draft enough to nudge the coin sticks off the rafter, but at the first infusion of green, he almost retched.

'Teia, I don't suppose you could draft to knock the coins down for— Oh, you only draft paryl, never mind.'

'Boost me,' she said. They'd worked together long enough that he did it automatically.

The plan is that I fling her up to the window ledge, and she'll lie down, extend a hand for me to grab. I'm the heavier by far. It's how we always do it.

But the fire is too intense. Nearly smokeless, intense. The reds are pouring luxin into the manse. Overkill, but we've given them reason to fear a team of Shimmercloaks.

I fling Gebalyn skyward, the hem of her shimmercloak trailing fire.

Teia sprang up and grabbed the coin sticks, and he caught her on the way down.

Distracted by the vision of fire, his hands stayed on Teia's hips just a moment too long.

'Kip,' she said. She thumped his wrist with a coin stick.

'S-sorry,' he said. He'd be more embarrassed if he weren't in so much pain.

'The captain's name is Two Gun Ben. You don't pay him a danar more than two hundred, you understand? He's already agreed. East docks, blue. Now move! We've probably—'

A sharp knock at the door interrupted them. 'Kip, it's your grandfather. Open the door. It's urgent.'

The Master. Hands stained red with betrayal. Scribbling lines – he'd been writing to the Color Prince. He'd gone wight, and he didn't know how to escape, so he was planning to 'join' the Color Prince. Eventually, he would betray him, too. But joining the Color Prince would give him time, and that was a commodity the Master needed.

Kip blinked. His head was pounding.

Teia was cursing silently. She was mouthing words to him: Don't. Open. It.

For a moment, he couldn't think at all. Then all he could think about was all the cards in his pockets. Teia was already moving, throwing open his bureau. Kip handed her the card boxes, and she buried them all under some clothes and shut the bureau quietly.

'Hesitated,' Kip said. 'I hesitated. Not like me at all.' Dammit. He opened the door.

Andross Guile stepped inside, not waiting for an invitation. He looked at Teia, surprised, perhaps, to see her here. 'Hmm, you're filling out nicely,' he said, staring Teia up and down. 'So sad Kip won you away from me.' He gave her a little charming grin. 'If you wish to visit my chambers on a more . . . open basis, though, please come by.'

She shrank from him. Kip realized what she did not: Andross Guile wasn't serious. His tastes didn't go so young. If he wasn't interested in Tisis, he certainly wouldn't be interested in Teia. He was merely digging deep enough into debasement to undercut her fundamental decency. He wanted to unnerve her. It worked.

'You're dismissed, caleen,' Andross said, turning his attention to Kip.

'I'm a free—'

'Dismissed,' he said. He was the promachos, and even without the weight of his new title, he was a man accustomed to being obeyed.

Teia practically fled.

Andross closed the door behind her. 'Has she come to you?' he asked.

'Pardon?' Kip asked.

'Tisis. Has she come to you? My spies have reported a Malargos ship being quietly readied to sail this evening. A smuggler's ship, fast, one they don't know I know they own. Has she come and proposed marriage, or not?'

A long silence. 'Yes,' Kip admitted.

Andross slapped his gloves into his other hand and smiled. 'I so love it when I'm right. That prediction? That was a bit of genius, if I do say so myself. New player, impulsive, trapped. Hard to predict. Did you bed her?'

Kip shook his head. Then was ashamed of himself. He should have told the old bastard it was none of his business. Why did Kip defer to his enemy?

'Well, you can lead a horse to a mare in heat, I suppose, but you can't make him mount her. Not usually a problem for us Guiles. My advice? Get rid of that fat. You might find a libido hiding under it.'

Kip opened his mouth – he wasn't even sure what he was going to say, and he didn't care, he was about to open the Blunderbuss and let fire – but Andross raised a finger.

'But.' His eyes twinkled. 'I didn't come here to lecture you, dear boy. I came to give you a choice. Few in this world get their life-defining choices handed to them and labeled as such, but you are special, and I am feeling generous. Do you have them for me?'

'Huh?'

'The cards, Kip.'

'You never sent me to look for my father. You broke your word.'

'I broke nothing. We agreed I'd choose the time. I mean to

send you to be part of the group that will free him. You are spending your time here profitably. I don't waste those who work for me. Now. Do you have my cards?'

Kip could feel his future slipping away. 'No,' he said. He wasn't sure, at this moment, if he would have handed them over regardless.

No, that was a lie. He would have. He was that much of a coward.

Andross Guile sighed. 'Do you know that I really did want to make you Prism? I was ready to groom you, to give you, the bastard from a backwater village, seven years as one of the most powerful people in the world. I would have made you, the fat little orphan, the most admired man in the world. From there, you could have possibly extended your reign, were you competent enough. But you're not much of a Guile. Not enough to hide your ambition and take my orders for a short while. You're too stupid to play the game at its highest levels. I was going to give you a task next: you against your brother. Whoever won would be Prism.'

'The promachos doesn't name Prisms.' Kip was parroting Quentin, though.

Andross Guile merely smirked.

'But you can orchestrate such things,' Kip said, heart sinking. I knew I was right to be skeptical.

'What do you think I've been doing the whole time Gavin's been gone? What do you think I've been doing my whole life?'

Setting things up. Destroying and sacrificing people as if they were cards, as if all that mattered was the game.

'What was the task going to be?' Kip asked.

'To destroy the green bane and bring me something from it.'

'What?! I already destroyed the green bane!'

A smile lit Andross's lips. 'Oh! You are learning. Look at that. An effort that took thousands of people, and you easily inserted yourself into the story as the hero – as if you'd done it all alone. A noble's trick, that. A dirty one, but time-honored. Congratulations. Fact is, the green bane is reforming or has reformed already. You botched the job. You need to take the seed crystal from it, or it simply grows again.'

Kip was gutted. 'So all we did . . . the destruction of the whole navy. The whole Battle of Ru. The capture of Ruic Head. The deaths . . . they were all for nothing?'

'It was a setback for our enemies. They had the seed crystal, the green bane, and an Atirat. They lost them all – but we didn't gain them.'

The idea of going back to fight the green bane again was like being asked to voluntarily get back in a closet full of rats. 'So that's why you looked so inept.'

'*Pardon?*' No one applied the word 'inept' to the Guile.

'You took the navy to Ru and did everything wrong – if you were trying to save the city. You didn't care about the city,' said Kip.

'Had we saved the city, but lost the bane, we would have lost the war. And lost the city, too, within days.'

'But you didn't care that you lost it. That's the difference.'

'Yes, please. Given unlimited time and perfect hindsight, tell me how you would have directed our forces so that all would have been well. Regardless. You dithered, and Sun Day is upon us. You won't be the next Prism.'

The words echoed in Kip's head: 'You won't be the Prism,' Janus Borig had told him. Plain as day. That wasn't how prophecy usually worked, was it? It was usually all obfuscation. Smoke and mirrors and darkness and flashing lights to blind the unwary. When it was just stated, did that make it more certain, or less?

Kip wasn't certain how much to believe Andross Guile, though. Sure, it was one thing to go hunting the bane, but why sacrifice your whole fleet to do it? If you saw a trap, you sprang it with a few ships, not your whole fleet. He may well have been hunting the bane, but that didn't mean he had godlike perspicacity. And he'd been a red wight at the time. That had to have clouded his vision, made him impulsive. Perhaps he was only lying to himself now, telling himself that the losses had all been part of the plan.

Kip opened his Blunderbuss to say so. Shut it.

Andross Guile continued. 'But now you have another choice: marry Tisis, go with her tonight. I will provide a luxiat who will marry you in secret because he believes love conquers all.

Whatever you tell her at first, I don't care. But as time goes by, you *will* make her believe you've fallen in love, and do your best to make her do the same. That's vital, you understand? Then, you stay with her, reporting to me from time to time. Eirene Malargos has big plans, and I've been unable to get a spy close in to learn them. You serve them, pretending to hate me. Your half brother will become the Prism – but Prisms usually only last seven years. You can wait, right? You'll have a beautiful wife; you'll have riches; I could even allow you to take your little friend Teia with you to guard your back, or your bed, whichever.

'At the very worst, Kip, it gets you out of Big Jasper alive. I know there have been attempts on your life – and those haven't come from me. I don't believe the attempts will stop if you remain here. What you need is some time to get away, to grow up, to marshal your powers and your skills. You're sixteen and you're starting to see who you will be. But you're not that man yet, and there are challenges here to which you are not yet equal. If you take care how much you draft, in a few years you can come back as the head of the foremost Ruthgari house if not the head of the satrapy itself, and a full-spectrum polychrome.

'Then we publicly make peace and reunite, and all that I have will be yours. Marriages are often made to make peace and cement alliances, and yours would do both, both in the short term and in the long.'

'I just have to become your spy.'

'Yes, yes, staying alive is such a dirty business, isn't it? Perhaps you should leave it to others,' Andross sneered. 'You have to become my heir. You'll be serving the promachos and the satrapies, not just our family. Such is only right.'

'Then why does it feel wrong?' Kip asked.

'Because you're young, and you haven't learned the difference between a twinge of conscience and a twinge of fear. In other words, ass from elbow.'

'Oh, no,' Kip said. 'In my time under your tutelage, I've become quite adept in recognizing an ass.'

'Then you ought to do well when you meet Two Gun Ben.'

Given that Kip had only heard of the captain minutes ago, he was too shocked to keep it off his face.

'Oh, yes, I know all about him. He's not a transporter; he's a slaver, and too cautious to ransom the slaves he takes back to their families. You go with him, and he'll clip your ear and put you on an oar. We've had quite enough of that in this family, don't you think?'

'I—'

'Your friends aren't as clever as you hope, Kip. Nor are you. Speaking of which, whatever you choose, before you go, I will have my cards. This is not optional.'

A jolt of real fear shot through Kip. 'I already told you. I don't have—' Kip said.

'Not optional. You must—' And to Kip, his face suddenly twisted, replaced by a much younger Andross Guile, young and strong, standing in his own manse, addressing his thirteen-year-old son. 'You must do this, Gavin. All our family, all our satrapy, all the world, and all of history rests upon you. In the blinding glare of his responsibilities, a Guile doesn't blink.'

Then Kip was back, and Andross's face was tight, suspicious, and old. 'Kip, show me what's in your pockets.'

'You won't listen,' Kip said. He couldn't even take joy in the fact that the cards were in the bureau and not in his pockets. Small victory indeed.

'I won't listen to lies, boy. And I can tell you're lying to me.'

And a lie bloomed, and Kip saw a narrow hope. 'Lying because I've been afraid of what you'll do. Now I just don't care anymore. I saved her life, grandfather, if only for a few minutes.'

'Her? Janus Borig?! I knew it.'

'Someone sent assassins after her – not ordinary assassins, but assassins who could make themselves invisible. I came in while they were still robbing the place, and I could see them in sub-red. They didn't expect me to be able to see them, and I got lucky. I killed them both, but we triggered some of her traps, and the place caught fire. I tried to carry her body out, and she was still alive. She made me get the assassins' cloaks, and then on our way out, she stopped me again. She grabbed this.' Kip wondered what insanity had gotten into him, but it felt like the only way. He dug out Janus Borig's card box.

Andross Guile's eyes lit with hungry fire. He reached for the box, but Kip didn't give it to him. 'Why is it broken?'

Of course he cared about the cards first, and not the woman. Kip said, 'She died before I carried her two blocks away. I came and gave my father the cloaks and—'

'Cloaks? Plural?'

'Yes,' Kip said. He couldn't help it. His lies wouldn't have the ring of truth if he didn't give his grandfather a whole lot of real intelligence. Of course, any of this could be a trap. Maybe his grandfather already knew all of this and was expecting the lie.

'And I gave him the cards. I took a peek first, of course. There was name after name, so many it was overwhelming. But it was the very night Gavin got back, and he found me, and took the cards. I didn't see them again – until today.'

'You're telling me you found these *today*?'

'I swear it on my hope for light.'

'Give them to me!'

Kip shook his head. 'You don't understand. I would have brought them to you. After looking at them, of course. After writing down all the names. Maybe after viewing a few of them. But maybe not even that. Janus told me she put traps on the cards that would flay a man's mind.' Kip blew out a breath, and it wasn't pretense. Whatever had happened to his mind, it had felt like flaying. He didn't think he'd seen the last of whatever it was that had happened. 'They were hidden in Gavin's training room. When I found them . . .' He handed over the box.

Andross Guile's brow furrowed. He hated not understanding things immediately. He handled the box like it was an asp. He put it on the table, pulled on his gloves, noted the box's broken side, and opened it gingerly. When nothing happened, he examined the back of the top card minutely. 'Definitely her work. I'd spot a counterfeit.' He looked up at Kip. 'Congratulations, boy, perhaps you have some hope of being Prism after all.'

Kip just shook his head.

Andross scowled. He flipped over the top card. His head cocked as he saw the blank on the other side. He flipped another card. Blank. Another, another. He cut the deck in half and looked at a card there, then another. He flipped the entire deck onto the table and fanned them out. Every last card, blank.

'No!' he screamed. '*No!*'

Kip's door was flung open and two Blackguards were inside in a blink, each with a knife drawn for close-quarters combat and spectacles on, drawing magic. Looking for a source of attack, and alighting on Kip.

Andross held a hand up and waved them off immediately. It was Gill Greyling and Baya Niel. 'Out!' Andross ordered. 'Out now!'

They sheathed weapons and left immediately. Andross Guile obviously tolerated no less. They didn't even apologize for intruding, which Kip guessed was the price Andross Guile paid for always treating them so poorly.

Before the door had even closed, Andross said, 'What have you done? This isn't what I demanded. This doesn't make you Prism.'

'I'm telling you,' Kip said. 'I found them like this. After months of searching, I find them like this. After all the threats you've thrown my way. I finally find them – and they're blank. I knew you wouldn't believe me.'

'You destroyed them.'

'I'm *still* scared of that old lady, and I saw her die. I didn't dare mess with them. She was *crazy*. I saw the traps she laid in her own home. Fire traps, when there were barrels of black powder everywhere in her home.' Don't go on too long, Kip. Let the hook stay in the water.

Andross looked at Kip skeptically. 'So either Gavin destroyed the cards, accidentally or on purpose, or someone found them since, and did the same, accidentally or on purpose. You found these where?'

'In the middle of a heavy bag, in Gavin's exercise room.'

Andross thought. 'So, unlikely that someone else would have hidden it there, unless Ironfist is making a play. Of course, he'd be much more likely to trigger a trap. No. Gavin. That's how he knew about . . .' Andross's eyes lit suddenly, and Kip knew he'd swallowed it. It fit some narrative in his own mind, and he'd almost given Kip information by thinking aloud.

The weakness of a spider: it sees every dangling thread as part of a web.

'Name every card you can remember, boy. It may be I can glean something from the very names or the inclusion of certain men or women.'

'I saw them only briefly,' Kip pleaded. 'Six months ago.' Oh, Orholam have mercy, even saying the names might . . . might flay his mind. 'Fine, fine. I remember a few.' He sat down and closed his eyes to make a show of trying to remember, but really because he thought he might get dizzy again. 'Shimmercloak.'

His vision swam and he was following Niah's perfect ass down the dock on his way to assassinate Janus Borig. He swallowed hard.

'It said something like, "If lightsplitter . . ." I remember it because I'd never heard of a lightsplitter before. I've been afraid to ask any of the luxiats or magisters about—'

'Not interested in your interpretations. Names,' Andross Guile said.

'Zymun the Dancer,' Kip said. And he was standing on the deck of a great barge, looking at Gavin Guile's back, trying to make himself look more frail and younger than he was. He fingered the knife secreted under his tunic, picking his moment.

'Zymun?' Andross asked. 'Do you remember that one? What did it look like?'

'I thought you weren't interested in my inter—' Kip shut up at the look in Andross's eyes. 'I don't remember what he was doing, but it was Zymun. It was definitely Zymun.'

'Damn you for turning the cards over to Gavin and not me,' Andross said.

'You *were* trying to murder me at the time.'

'Next! The Malargos girl will be coming anytime now, and I can't be here when that happens. Quickly.'

It was like choosing to plunge your hand into fire. How smart was Kip? He had to give the list fast enough so that his grandfather wouldn't think he was sorting them, had to give enough of a list so that his grandfather would think he was giving him all that he remembered, but not so long of a list that he'd be suspicious why Kip would remember so many, and if they weren't a good enough list of surprising and unsurprising cards, he would know. He would *know*. And Kip had to do all this while his head split and hallucinations danced around him every time he spoke. Oh hells.

'New Green Wight. Incipient Wight. Flintlock. Sea Demon Slayer,' Kip blurted. That last. That damned pirate. That was Gunner! 'Shimmercloak. Uh, sorry, said that already. Um, Dee Dee Falling Leaf. Usem thc Wild. Aheyyad Brightwater. Samila Sayeh.' Kip was going to throw up. He was forgetting who he was. 'Mirror Armor. The Fallen Prophet.' He almost said Black Luxin and the Master. 'Skimmer. Condor. Viv Grayskin. The Butcher of Aghbalu. Incendiary Musket. The Burnt Apostate. The . . . the Angari Serpent.'

Andross listened with a quiet intensity that told Kip he was memorizing all of it. All of it, on one hearing. The man was infuriating. Finally, Andross spoke. 'So you have something of the Guile memory, if nothing else. Good. Did you see Orea Pullawr or any of my sons?'

'Orea?'

'The White!' Andross said, terse, impatient, frustrated.

'No, no. I looked for my father, but I never saw him.'

'So some cards are still out there,' Andross said. 'Still intact. Maybe.'

For some reason, Kip found that funny. Andross was so certain of his own judgment. If he thought someone was important, he had no doubt that they would have a card. My judgment and the judgment of history will be the same, he thought. What an ass.

'One last question,' Andross said. 'Did you see a Lightbringer card?'

Janus Borig's face was unnaturally pale, luminous in reflected lightning-light. 'I don't suppose you grabbed my brushes,' she asked. 'Because I know who the Lightbringer is now.' And then she died.

'It was . . . it was me,' Kip said quietly.

Faster than most men would have been able to process shock alone, Andross Guile's face went through shock, insult, and settled on rage. 'You lie!' he barked, sinews standing taut on his neck. He stepped forward, as if to strike.

'Of course I lie,' Kip said. His tone said, 'You moron, I just wanted to see you dance.'

He saw his disdain like a tuning fork ringing Andross Guile's rage, which went from hot to cold in an instant as he realized he was being taunted. But Kip wasn't done. 'And obviously, you lie, too. You're the one who brought up the idea of me being the Lightbringer. To torment me. I know there's no such thing. I know how you work, you old cancer.'

'You really think you can outsmart me? *Me?* I know what you and your father are doing, Kip. Have known, since you claimed the epithet Breaker. Clever, to set it up as you did. Clever, to have another give it to you. Clever, using the Blackguard habit of nicknaming to take it, and to take a tertiary translation that might slip past the luxiats yet look so obvious in retrospect. But clever isn't enough, boy, not against me.'

'I have no idea what you're talking about,' Kip said. But it was a lie, and he felt the blood draining from his face, from his head, leaving him lightheaded on top of sick and dizzy and pained. He wouldn't have known, yesterday, or two hours ago. But now . . . He who tears asunder, renderer, shatterer, destroyer. Breaker was the most pedestrian and vague of translations for Diakoptês.

'Aha.' Andross looked triumphant; he'd seen the lie on Kip's face. He was in control again. 'Well, I'm sure Gavin put you up to it, and it speaks well of you that you've continued to play it quietly in his absence, in case he came back. We'll discuss this fraud more, in time. For the nonce, only one thing matters: your choice. I gave you one task, and a prize if you accomplished it. You failed. Consider it a miracle I don't have you killed. Your half brother will be named Prism-elect at dawn. At midwinter, he will become Prism. There is nothing you can do to stop this or take his place. No doubt your squad will greatly enjoy guarding him against threats like you.

'Your choice now is simple. If you wish to marry that girl and be my spy – and live – come by and talk to me before you leave. Choose what you will, but if you're here tomorrow, you'll be dead before sunset.' He cocked his head at a sound. 'I've stayed overlong. Decide well, *Diakoptês*, or it will not be your dreams alone that will be broken this night.'

He hit the light control on the wall, and left Kip in darkness.

Chapter 80

'Mother,' I yell. 'Mother!' I come running in from the street as usual.

Jarae stops me before I even get past the entry. She's a dour figure, looming in doorways, but quicker than you'd suspect with her bulk. 'Shoes, young master, shoes!'

I step on one heel after the other, kicking them off without a thought. 'Where is she, Jaejae?'

'In the garden, Dazen, but she's—'

I'm already off. The slaves are settling us in to our new home on Big Jasper, dusting, and rolling out carpets, washing bedthings, and moving furniture. Two young men in sleeveless tunics, arms knotted and muscular, are carrying a lounge chair across the hallway. I speed up.

They don't see me until too late, and I see their eyes widen as it looks like I'm going to collide with them. They brace themselves.

I drop to my knees at the last second and slide right under the heavy chair. I pop back up to my feet with a whoop.

'You nearly gave me a fit, you d— young master!' one of them shouts after me.

Yes! Now that he's shouted at me, I know he won't report me to father, lest I tattle back on him.

Farther down, a bed is in the hallway, but no one's carrying it. I jump and slide over the top, but get tangled in the dusty sheets covering it and fall on the other side, smacking my knee. I pull the dusty sheets behind me for a good twenty paces as I try to get disentangled. I leave it in the hall, all of its dust deposited on me, and hobble into the garden.

'Mother!' I shout.

'I'm right here, Dazen. You should come and meet—'

621

But I'm already running, and I jump into her arms.

She laughs and spins me around once, then puts me down. 'Dazen, you are getting too big to— What is this? You're filthy!'

I have put about a sev of dust on her pretty blue dress.

'Sorry, mother!' I say. I know she's not really mad.

She sighs. 'Never you mind. Dazen, I'd like you to meet my guest and my dear friend, Lady Janus Borig.'

Lady Borig is seated in one of the wrought-iron chairs, and she's old. Gray-and-red hair, pulled back tight under her hat, long nose, bright eyes. She's smoking a long-stemmed meer-schaum pipe adorned with rubies. The faded freckles on her arms and the red in her hair say she's a Blood Forester. Gavin's been teaching me all the old-fashioned court rituals of the satrapies.

'Mother,' I say.

'Dazen, greet our guest.'

'Mother, your shawl, please.'

I draw myself to what my tutor calls a proper little lord-ling's pose. My mother hands me her shawl. I drape it over my shoulders, adjust it, and sweep into the old courtier's bow of the Forest Court. One needs a cloak to do it properly. 'Lady Borig, may your roots grow deep, and the circular skies bring you sun and shade in perfect proportion. May your herds increase, may your sons be unto you like a quiver full of arrows, may the small folk fear you, and may the tygre wolves hunt only your enemies.' Whew, almost forgot the last part.

Lady Janus Borig studies me silently.

'His father's memory, I'm afraid,' mother says.

'And his mother's charm. I seem to recall you stealing hearts when you were his age, too.'

'I spoil him,' my mother says. 'I know it's not good.'

'But you continue because.' Lady Janus Borig waves her pipe vaguely. In the direction of my father? I have no idea what she's talking about.

'Exactly.'

'Please,' Lady Janus Borig says, 'take your time with your son. The matter between you and me can wait. Pretend I'm not here.'

I look at her, then at my mother. This is all kinds of backwards. Adults never want to wait while children speak first. I can't imagine father saying such a thing, not even with Gavin. But she seems serious.

'You were out with Magister Kyros?' my mother prompts.

'After lessons, we were playing at the Great Fountain, and I was talking to some of the other boys, and they said they'd learned from their tutor about other kinds of luxin that Magister Kyros won't teach me about. They said it's because I'm not smart enough. They said it's too advanced. I asked him about it, and he wouldn't say anything. It's true, isn't it?'

My mother's face darkens, and the whole world darkens with it. 'Let me guess, the White Oak boys again? You know they'll be looking for an excuse to hurt you after your brother blackened Tavos's eye last week.'

'I know, mother, I wasn't trying to be around—' Oh no.

'So it *was* Gavin who hit him. Last week you said you had no idea what happened.'

I've let it out of the bag again. Gavin's going to hit *me* for that.

'Mother, you tricked me!'

'Son, you lied to me.'

Quick. 'There's so many of them, wherever my tutors take me, there's one of them there.'

'Yes, son, and it behooves you to remember that.'

'What, mother?'

'There's more of them than there are of us.'

I sniff and raise my chin, just like father. 'Ain't afraid of nothing. I'm Guile.'

Mother laughs despite herself. She covers her mouth and smothers it, but her eyes are light again, and I know she won't be mad at me anymore. 'Oh, my little man, you're growing up fast, aren't you?' She looks over at Lady Janus Borig. 'You see?'

'Indeed,' the old woman says. She doesn't sound pleased.

'Growing up fast enough to be told about the luxins?' I ask hopefully. I see my opportunity slipping away.

She scowls and I do my best to look cute and harmless. She sighs. 'Don't tell your father?' she says.

'Promise!'

My mother pauses, though. She turns. 'Lady Borig?' she asks. 'Somehow, I think your own knowledge of that might be just a bit larger than my own.'

'Indeed.' Lady Borig's index finger suddenly glows hot, and she sticks it into the bowl of her pipe, reigniting the ashes. A sub-red drafter. She puffs on the pipe for a time until she's enveloped in a cloud. 'How much do you want me to tell him? For that matter, how much do you want me to tell you? 'Tis the stuff of nightmares.'

'You weren't going to tell him about bla—'

'Indeed I was,' Lady Janus Borig says. 'Your son is not simply precocious, Felia. He is terribly bright; he is handsome; he is charming; and you have spoiled him horribly. In other words, he has all the makings of a true monster.'

My mother blinks. No one talks to her like this.

'Though I wonder.' She takes a deep breath on her pipe, not merely drawing the smoke into her mouth, but inhaling it. Mother doesn't say a word, which tells me that she respects this terrible old lady immensely. 'I suppose his elder brother beats him from time to time?'

'Best of friends one minute, fiercest enemies the next.'

'Do you ever win those fights with Gavin?' the old woman asks me.

I shake my head, glowering.

'You think I don't like you,' Lady Janus Borig says. 'Nothing could be further from the truth. I'm trying to save you.' She turns to my mother. 'You should let those White Oak boys thrash him a few times.'

'What?!'

'You're clever enough to pick one of the younger ones who won't do real damage. Perhaps a broken nose spoiling Dazen's looks a bit would be the best thing for him. And learning that he is not invincible, that would be best for the world, I think.'

My mother lowers her voice. 'Is this . . . is this your gift speaking?'

'Pshh. This isn't prophecy. I'm simply wiser than you, girl.'

My mother blinks, but accepts the rebuke. Suddenly she seems very young.

'I'll tell him of black luxin, but I'll tell him true, or I'll tell him nothing at all. I think it would be best for him. But you're the one who will have to live with the screaming in the night from the bad dreams.'

'If he thinks he's ready,' my mother says, and her eyes are burning.

'You said you're not afraid of anything,' Lady Janus Borig says to me. 'Are you afraid now?'

Click.

Suddenly, Kip was standing in total darkness. He was himself once more. Where was he? *When* was he?

He drafted sub-red and widened his eyes. It was his own room. Click? What had that been?

He strode to the door, opened it, peeked out. Andross Guile was barely disappearing down the hallway.

What in nine hells?

The card memory had taken almost no time at all. The click was the settling of the latch.

He hadn't been certain until this moment, but now he knew: he'd lied to Teia. He had bungled everything, but he hadn't sprung a Janus Borig trap. He hadn't erased the cards. He'd absorbed them all – and he had a sudden, clear, sick conviction they were going to drive him mad.

Chapter 81

Teia only pretended to flee. As soon as Andross Guile kicked her out to talk to Kip, she walked hurriedly past the Blackguards standing watch and headed down the hall and out of sight. She summoned the lift, but didn't get on.

Instead, she pulled up the hood of her cloak. She looked left and right, saw no one, and willed herself to become invisible.

Nothing.

She felt up in the neckline and found the choker, a narrow band of metal that was attached to the cloak at many points.

She pulled it up against her neck. She trembled, a shudder of revulsion coursing through her.

No one collared their slaves on the Jaspers. It was considered gauche. Beatings and other discipline were to be carried out at home, not in public. To need to discipline one's slave in public reflected poorly on your own mastery. Slaves, of course, knew that any public defiance, however satisfying, would be met with double punishment later.

Other cities, and other men, were not so civilized – or perhaps not so hypocritical. This wasn't the first time Teia had worn a collar, but it was the first time she'd done so voluntarily. The feeling of constriction around her neck was almost unbearable.

Things to do, T. Not much time, T. Could come out any second. Still have to figure out how to use the damned thing.

She moved the loose necklace that held the little vial of oil aside. Her hands held the choker's clasp loosely. Unmoving. She was breathing deeply, almost hyperventilating, and not clasping the damned clasp.

Chains. I've done everything in my life to get away from chains.

Part of her argued with that. Some garbage about differences between slavery and a cloak that empowered her. It didn't change the visceral revulsion.

These are the chains I choose.

The chains I choose.

She cinched the choker tight and extended her will. Teeth shot out of the choker and sank into either side of her neck. They hurt so bad she doubled over and almost screamed.

And then her breath was taken for another reason. She could feel it. The cloak had a presence within it. It wasn't a whole personality; instead – if the chirurgeons were correct, and cogitation took place in the human brain – it was as if the cloak had all the parts of a person's brain that dealt with light splitting and magic sunk into it, with a whisper of personality there. To make this cloak, someone had given her life – or had it taken from her. The cloak knew how to split light in the ways that Teia had barely glimpsed when she broke into the White's office.

In all her life, Teia had had to struggle for every excellence. She could sing, but had seen other slaves remember every note in a tune in one or two hearings. She could fight, but she'd seen other Blackguards combine throws and punches and kicks into series as fluidly as if fighting were a language and they were constructing elaborate arguments. Her own style was terse, fast, but ultimately simple, without nuance. She could look at Cruxer or Winsen and see that they were already maturing into the best in the world, their skills growing by leaps and bounds. That was beyond her, and always would be. Her speed would get no better. Her reach was terminally short. In a continuum that began with Big Leo and Kip and Ironfist, she was not strong. Her aim would improve, as would her knowledge of where and when to strike. Among the best, she would become mediocre, every scrap of her skill earned only by the most challenging labor.

Nor had she any excellence in her studies. Despite his difficulty reading, Ben-hadad could extemporize, looking at the gears and pulleys and weights and strengths of each luxin and designing machines as if it were play to him. Kip could memorize, and make great intuitive leaps. If study were scrivening, they wrote in a perfect hand, and illuminated their manuscripts for fun while the dullards caught up to them. By contrast, Teia held the quill in her fist.

At the touch of whatever will was animating the cloak, Teia knew two things immediately. First, light splitting at the level of the old mist walkers was as difficult as any magical or mundane skill in the world. It was as difficult as juggling and sprinting and singing at once. Blindfolded. Second – more importantly – it made sense to her.

Simply using this cloak would teach her more than any master could.

She already saw how this cloak was superior to the other. None of the cloaks – not even this one – split light beyond the visible spectrum. Sub-red was too long a wave to be diverted and reformed within the thin layer of fabric, and superviolet was too fine.

Even among lightsplitters, the only people who had a chance to be fully invisible to all spectra would be paryl drafters. A true mist walker might use a shimmercloak to handle visible light while using a paryl mist to handle the last two spectra herself.

And then it was obvious: they were called mist walkers not because they were invisible or could only be seen as though through a mist, but because they walked within their own cloud of paryl, always.

And this cloak would teach her how to do it.

Without ever expecting such a thing, Teia had found her purpose and her excellence. It was quite possible that no one in the world understood this like she did. For the first time in her life, she didn't feel inferior. She would have started crying if she hadn't heard the door open around the corner down the hall and Andross Guile grunt something to his Blackguards.

Drafting even a thread of paryl was enough to activate the cloak. Teia threw the hood up and reached to lace it up over her face. But there were no laces. She fumbled, looking for some kind of fasteners, and when she drew the edges close, they snapped shut firmly, as if lodestones were sewn into them. Much faster than the other shimmercloaks. Even with this cloak, though, she couldn't cover her eyes completely unless she wanted to be blind: no light, no sight. It might be worth covering them in certain situations, but it would also be terrifying. Instead, she would have to rely on taking quick sidelong glances or creeping around at low levels where enemies wouldn't be looking for eyes.

Being short helped the latter, of course, but she was going to have to take care that she not get overconfident.

The approach of Andross and his guards presented an instant problem. How much did she trust the cloak, really?

She took deep breaths as the three men approached and stood off to the side, sneaking only quick glances at them to keep her eyes hidden. They passed right by her.

A thrill went through her body from head to toe. Invisible!

Andross turned to his Blackguards as they waited for the lift and said, 'I'll be heading to my home. Immediately. Summon a squad of Lightguards to accompany us.'

Of course, they were insulted by that, and of course, they

said nothing, taking it like the professionals they were. But what Teia thought was odd was that she couldn't remember Andross Guile ever going to his home on Big Jasper. Why would he be headed to his home now?

The lift appeared before Teia heard any response, if there was any.

Andross Guile was going to his home on Big Jasper on the very day that his lost grandson showed up at the docks? From how Samite told it, it sounded like the boy was announcing who he was to anyone who would listen. Teia couldn't imagine Andross Guile going home if the boy was headed to the Chromeria. Andross Guile would go to where the center of action was – or have the action brought to him.

Which meant Andross Guile was having the boy taken to his home, to meet him away from spying eyes.

Well, other than Teia's.

She suddenly grinned. She leaned out into the lift shaft to see where it stopped. Ground floor.

After waiting half a minute, she stepped onto another ring of the lift mechanism and set the weights. She descended slowly.

At the ground floor, she had to dodge several old luxiats piling into the lift. But they moved slowly, and she made it out with little trouble before they could observe that the weight settings of the lift seemed off.

She searched for Andross Guile then, and couldn't see him anywhere. She went to the great, open door, soon to be shut for the evening, and spotted him through a swirl of white and black cloaks. He was heading out of the Chromeria. She followed.

There was something totally empowering, even intoxicating, about walking unseen. Here were the drafters of the world, the cream of the Seven Satrapies, and they couldn't even see her. No wonder the Order's assassins loved these cloaks, even without using them to their full potential. This was amazing.

It was also surprisingly challenging. Teia was used to ducking and dodging through a crowd, but it was one thing to brush past someone who barely saw you, and something altogether different to actually get run over by someone who didn't see you at all. That, and the fact that the shimmercloak completely cut out her peripheral vision, made simply moving at a walk almost exhausting. She was constantly turning her head, sneaking glimpses of everything, adjusting the paryl bubble as the evening crowds head back across the bridge from Little Jasper to their homes on Big Jasper.

She was lucky that Andross Guile hadn't chosen to ride. As a Color, much less as promachos, it was his prerogative. He'd chosen instead to walk, which she hoped meant that he wasn't going far. She should know where his home was, but the truth was, she'd spent all her time in the wrong neighborhoods. Still, it was an odd thing for a man who just a year ago had seemed practically an invalid. That he walked also meant that he'd picked up four more Blackguards, and an equal number of Lightguards. Six Blackguards might seem overkill, but it was a time of war, and Andross was the promachos. Teia barely counted the Lightguards, other than to note their presence. Pretenders.

Once they were in the open streets, following was much easier. They didn't go far, either, and soon Teia saw the Guile estate. Its dome was, of course, gold. The great doors were black oak, studded with garnets. The great crossbeams were black oak over forever-burning atasifusta wood, which had been set alight to announce the Lord Guile was in residence. The garnets picked up the red glow and reflected it beautifully in the fading sunlight.

The Guile estate was so large it was home not only to one of the tallest of the Thousand Stars, it also had a small yard and garden – enormous luxuries on the overcrowded island.

Sentry boxes stood on either side of a thick, tall gate sheathed in iron. Some estates had simple wrought-iron gates, presumably, Teia thought, to let pedestrians see through them to show off their owners' wealth. But open-iron gates were a terrible idea for a city full of drafters: stick your hands through the gaps and draft freely. The Guiles valued their privacy or their defense more.

And here's where it gets sticky.

Suddenly, Teia had to ask herself just how much she wanted to follow Andross Guile. He might well simply go into his home and go to bed. All she had was wild guesses and intuitions. She could be risking her life for simple curiosity.

The Guile guards opened the gate for them. Two of the Blackguards slipped inside, weapons drawn, while two kept an eye on the guards, despite that the men were older and must have served the Guiles for decades. The last two waited with Promachos Guile, carefully scanning the crowds who gave them wide berth.

Teia took a deep breath and started moving. How good was she at using this cloak? If she did it wrong, this was going to be the shortest infiltration in history.

Tucking her fears into a pocket, she strode confidently. She drafted her bubble of paryl mist around her. Maybe it would help.

Someone jostled her, stepping into the seemingly empty space in the crowds where she was walking. Her paryl bubble broke apart silently, but she simply formed it again and kept moving. Andross went inside, one Blackguard in front of him, one right on his heels. The last two, Presser and Essel, nodded at each other, then Presser slipped inside while the Lightguards stood around, shifting, not even professional enough to stand still when at rest.

Teia didn't mind; it meant they took up more room, and gave her more space to move.

The petite, curvy Essel would wait two seconds, scanning the crowd once more, then come in and shut the door immediately. Teia pressed herself against the closed side of the gate and slipped through the crack right in front of the woman.

Andross Guile was supposed to wait for his security detail to reform, but he was halfway to the house.

A young Blackguard with a shaven head, Asif, stood at the front door with the Guile guards. He perked up at the sight of his compatriots. Standing guard all day with house guards who don't welcome your oversight of them was not a favorite posting for a Blackguard, especially when one had to do it alone.

Then Teia got lucky. Andross Guile went inside and his slave Grinwoody stepped outside, blocking the door. 'The High Lord bids you to head to the back barracks, there to await his pleasure.'

'The back?' Asif said. 'But from there we can't even see who comes through the gates, much less who's in the house.'

'The Lightguards will cover the front. You will remain in the back barracks until you are called, or you will be dismissed,' Grinwoody said.

'We might as well be dismissed if you aren't going to let us do our job,' Essel said. 'I can rest at home better than—'

'Dismissed from the Blackguard,' Grinwoody said. 'The promachos has spoken.' A smug smile lit his wizened features. No wonder people hated him.

The Blackguards couldn't believe it, but in that moment of grumbling and curses under their breath, Teia saw a gap open, and she slipped behind Grinwoody and into the house.

For some reason, it wasn't until Teia was in Andross Guile's very rooms, following the sound of his voice and the footsteps of his chamber slaves, that she realized just how frightening her new power was. She'd been scared by Murder Sharp – but for all sorts of reasons. Teia now, Teia herself, had infiltrated the home of the richest, most powerful man in the Seven Satrapies. She had walked into the house of the promachos himself without so much as an advance plan.

She could now kill him, unseen, even if other people were in the very room, and without any more than a suspicion of foul play. A man his age, under the stresses of war, dying suddenly? It would elicit comment, but no more. There wouldn't even be marks on his body.

Which, she hadn't realized until this moment, made her scary. It made her a predator.

The thought more startled her than filled her with awe or even gratification. I'm scary. I'm scary? *I* am scary.

Somehow, before, the notion of being invisible had meant to her that she could hide really well.

It didn't mean that. It meant that she could strike from shadows – no, not even the shadows – she could strike from anywhere, and simply disappear. She could kill, and be at almost no risk of being killed.

Murder Sharp hadn't precisely shown her how to kill with paryl yet, but she had seen him do it once, and she wasn't stupid. He'd taught her how to pinch nerves, how to move paryl through solid flesh. All you had to do was make as many little crystals of paryl as you could and let them go to the brain or the heart or the lungs. It might take Teia five crystals or ten rather than a practiced assassin's single try – but what did it matter if you were invisible and no one would notice your failures?

Andross was being attended by three attractive female room slaves of about thirty years of age. They took his tunic and gave him a sponge bath, with quick, practiced motions, wasting no effort and not getting his trousers wet. He was flabby over a powerful frame, sweaty from a mere brisk walk: a fact he obviously noticed with displeasure. Teia guessed that was why he had walked tonight. He was trying to recapture the vigor of his younger years.

And vigor it must have been, for he had the scars of a warrior-drafter on his torso and arms. With her eyes downcast, the edge of the hood just high enough to let her see the women's legs – and to therefore guess when they would move – Teia slipped past them and took a place in a nook on the far side of his bed, well out of the way of any traffic she could imagine.

In a couple of minutes, the room slaves had him dressed again in a dinner jacket, his hair anointed with aromatic oils.

'You have something to say, Deleah?' Andross said, bored.

A pause, and then a rush of words. Clearly Andross wasn't patient at drawing forth reports from his slaves. 'It's the young Lord Zymun, sir. He's terrible free with his hands. One of the younger girls slipped away from him. He fell while chasing her. He shouted that he'd broke a rib and she'd pay with her life. She's been weeping since. She almost tried to run away—'

'Not interested.' He hesitated. 'The girl's name?'

'Leelee.'

'The blonde? Kitchen girl?'

'The same, my lord.'

'Seventeen years old now?'

'Thereabouts. Slave girl, so no telling, my lord.'

'The others he bothered. All blondes? All pretty? Short? What does he prefer?'

The slave Deleah chewed her lip, thinking. 'Pretty, yes, my lord. Though Overseer Grinwoody makes sure all the girls who serve upstairs are. Not much preference otherwise, far as I can see, my lord.'

Grinwoody came in the room. Andross motioned for his room slaves, who'd been waiting silently, to leave. But as Deleah got to the door, he said, 'Deleah. Right side, or left?'

She turned, blinking, then understood. 'The ribs on his right side, my lord. A bruise, not a break.' She clearly wished it had been worse.

Andross said, 'Tell Leelee and the others it won't happen again.' For one moment, Teia thought perhaps this man wasn't so bad. Surely the treatment of those in his care is a good test of a man. Then he said, 'I'll not have weeping slaves in this house.'

The room slave bobbed and disappeared.

Grinwoody extended a tray with a crystal glass full of amber liquid to Andross Guile. 'The vile one awaits in the red parlor, my lord.'

Andross grinned. 'Never liked our toothy guest, have you, Grinwoody?' He sipped the liquor. His mouth twisted. 'This is that Barrenmoor?'

'My lord.'

'You're certain it's coming into vogue?'

'My lord,' Grinwoody said. It was, again, affirmation.

'Hmm, that which is powerful and distasteful does have its place, doesn't it?'

Grinwoody said, 'Let us hope that hiring Sharp does not come into similar vogue.'

Andross laughed aloud, and Grinwoody grinned. It was more disconcerting than seeing Andross Guile half naked. These men were *friends*. There was no falsity in that laugh or that grin. They might have vastly different stations, but both liked and respected the other. Grinwoody had clearly been an instrumental part in Andross Guile's rise. 'Any new updates about Eirene Malargos?' Andross asked.

'None.'

'I still worry about that.'

'Withholding reinforcements has always carried the risk of driving her to the enemy rather than making her need us more. But sending them too early would allow her to turn on us later. Your way, she'll be allied to us forever. It's worth the gamble, my lord. We'll know by tomorrow, regardless.'

'You've got all in order to send her the news immediately? Good. To matters closer at hand, then. Have that whore Mistress Aurellea make sure the girl she sends tonight is blonde. Sixteen, seventeen. Slender.'

'You still wish to reward Zymun?' Grinwoody asked, a tiny quiver of doubt in his voice.

'I don't wish to, but time is short. And knowing what he likes in the bedchamber will be one more tool in hand. If he's as charming as he thinks, once he settles in at the Chromeria such information will be more difficult to acquire. Might as well do it now. Actually, take Zymun up to my solar. Dinner can wait. Make sure he doesn't see Sharp. And wait there with him. He can cool his heels. Take some of the Barrenmoor. For yourself. Don't give him any. I want him off balance. You may lay hands on him if necessary.'

'With pleasure.' Grinwoody bowed and left.

Andross Guile paused at the door. In his brocade and Abornean goat's wool and cloth-of-gold and murex purple, he looked a king of old. He put his hand on the doorframe, though, and bowed his head, taking a few deep breaths.

Then he turned on his heel, sharply, and walked back into the room.

He came around the bed and straight for the nook where Teia stood. Her heart jumped, and she almost bolted. Almost attacked. She looked to his left, but the wall was too close; she would brush against him.

The only way open was up onto the bed. She jumped lightly onto the bedframe, one small foot on the side frame, one on the headboard, an arm stretched out to push off one of the bedposts to hold herself in place; if she stepped on the bed itself, she'd leave an unmistakable dent in the blankets and mattress. It was a brilliant bit of balance, especially given how disconcerting it was to not see your own limbs. The only problem was that stretching out so far like this exposed one boot entirely on one side, and her hand and forearm on the other.

But Andross was already past her, bending down to pick up something that had been placed in Teia's nook. It was a painting of his late wife, Lady Felia Guile. The frame had been broken, and there was a tear through the middle of the canvas itself. He stood, holding it delicately.

If he turned counterclockwise, toward the room rather than the wall, Teia would be face-to-face with him. With how much of her was exposed, he couldn't miss her. Teia tried to scoot her foot along the frame and the cover of her short cloak, but all her weight was on that foot. It wouldn't slide.

Andross turned in toward the room – disaster! But he was holding the painting up. It passed between Andross and Teia, blocking his view, the frame nearly cracking Teia's nose.

He carried the painting back to his desk, and Teia, breathing once more, stepped silently back into the nook. Her heart was pounding so loud it was a marvel she wasn't shaking the entire house.

'Fee,' Andross said quietly. 'Forgive me for this.' He fingered the tear where he'd obviously punched through the canvas. 'I was wrong. Like so many other times we fought. You hurt me, leaving like that. It felt like betrayal, but I'm sorry, too. I shouldn't have forbidden you the Freeing this year. Oh, but my dear, if you could only have stayed to see me now! One more year! You could have held on one more year, could you not? But I wasn't myself, stuck in that room. I know. I thought my light would fade before I could do all I promised you so many years ago. I need you, my dear one. What I must do with a sword, you could do with a smile.' He traced the line of her cheek with a finger. 'I shall never find your like again.'

Then he cleared his throat, and composed himself. He hurried from the room as if he could leave tenderness behind.

Teia didn't know why, but that unexpected gentleness made her more frightened of the promachos than any coldness she'd seen from him. She knew that if he found out that someone had seen him during that moment, his vengeance would be terrible.

As if breaking into his house and spying on him would result in only a firm talking to?

They can only kill me once.

The thought didn't make her feel any better.

Chapter 82

After giving Promachos Guile some time to get ahead of her, Teia followed. He was at the bottom of the stairs by the time she reached the top of them, and she had to wait. Should have followed closer. Going down the steps would expose her feet, especially if someone were below her. If she had instead followed him closely, the angles would have made it much more difficult for him to see her.

Some invisibility.

She headed down the stairs carefully, putting as much of her weight as she could on the handrail, skipping the steps she'd noticed creaked. Here, at least, was one good thing about being small: she didn't weigh much. She heard a bell ring from the room where Andross Guile had gone. She made it to the bottom of the stairs without any problem, and heard him speaking to one of the attractive slaves who'd been upstairs.

'There's a damaged painting in my quarters. Have it repaired by whomever's the best.'

The woman bobbed and came out of the room, stepping between the Lightguards standing watch at the door.

Teia flattened herself against the wall, but the woman ducked into a slave's door off to one side. There was a brief opportunity to slip into the room, between the two Lightguards. But if one so much as shifted . . .

She hesitated, and Andross dismissed them.

The two Lightguards were both big men. Not the hard, professional warriors that made up the Blackguard, and part of Teia couldn't help but sneer at them. But they did look like they knew what to do with a cudgel. Both had noses that had been broken multiple times and flab over big muscles. The one on the left had the red nose of a drunkard. The one on the right walked with a slight limp. The most salient detail about them, though, was that they took up the whole damned hallway as they walked side by side.

Teia retreated down the wall, walking backward carefully, only stealing glances at the men's feet so they wouldn't see her eyes. Stairs or doorway?

She pressed herself into the recessed doorway.

They turned toward her door, trapping her.

The one on the left, closest to the door, put his hand on the high latch, right next to Teia's face. She held her breath. 'You thinking what I'm thinking?' he said to the other one. He turned his head to the other man as he pulled the latch down. The handle brushed Teia's shoulder as it turned, but he didn't notice. He didn't push the door open, either. Still trapped.

'You touch the brandy cabinet one more time, you're gonna get us both whipped,' the limper whispered. He looked around nervously. 'He'll smell it on your breath, Arrad!'

There was nowhere to go. If the man moved forward quickly, he'd run into her before she could retreat. She couldn't open the door herself and slip away; his hand was still on the latch. There was no space to slip between them. They formed a perfect, closed crescent, with her between them and the door.

Before she realized quite what she was doing, Teia was drafting. She was already drafting paryl in order to keep the cloak functioning, and the instantaneous thought shot through her: Is this what other drafters talk about? Reds spoke of feeling their own passions twice as deeply, blues spoke of a cool logic, but Teia had never felt anything at all from paryl. This odd, unlikely creativity or awareness or . . .

She swept paryl through the second man's leg. There was a mesh point with paryl between a gas and a solid where you could shoot a stream but still direct it. She'd tried this a hundred times and succeeded twice, both times when she didn't think about it too much – which was maddening. But it worked again. She felt the knot in the limper's bad knee, and seized it, solidifying the paryl and pulling until the paryl broke.

The limping Lightguard's leg folded, and he fell. He cursed as he hit the floor.

The drunkard Arrad let go of the latch to see what had happened, and Teia pushed the door gently so it swung open slowly as if he'd pushed it a bit. The Lightguard started laughing at his friend.

'Here you were worried about me. You're the one who looks drunk! That dodgy knee again?' he asked.

But Teia didn't wait to hear any more. She disappeared into the room.

The room was some kind of parlor, with a hallway opposite where Teia had come in, heading toward another wing of the house, and another door vaguely in the right direction.

Teia put her eye to the keyhole. In the room beyond was a staging area for the slaves to bring up the food from the kitchens below and put it in order for presentation in the dining room that must be farther in. It was almost dinnertime. That room was full of slaves, all moving quickly to and fro: the quick pace of a smoothly run household, but almost literally running. Impossible to get through there.

From the hall Teia had escaped, she heard Grinwoody, raising his voice from the top of the stairs, summoning the Lightguards.

She went back into the hall as they disappeared upstairs and made her way – finally – back to the door where the promachos had gone. It was closed.

For one heartbeat, she thought of going back around, through the slaves' area. She was quick, agile, small, and fucking *invisible*.

Then she heard Murder Sharp's voice, and her guts turned to water. 'Kidnapping's a two-man job,' he said.

Kidnapping?

'Use Adrasteia. It will be a good test of her loyalty.'

'I'm not worried about her loyalty. It's her upper-body strength I'm concerned about. If the mark gets difficult, I have to use the blackjack and carry her.'

Teia couldn't even take pleasure in the thought that she'd truly fooled Murder Sharp. Instead, her mind was spinning: 'Her'? Who were they planning to kidnap?

'Is she coming back?' Murder asked. 'From wherever you take her?'

'You don't need to know,' Andross said.

'I need to know whether she can see my face when I grab her. If you're going to let her go afterward, it makes the job that much harder. People tend to remember me. My good looks and all.'

A hesitation. Then, finally, Andross said, 'No, she won't be coming back. Do whatever you must to bring her to me. I need her uninjured. I'll give you a few days to ready your plans. Use whom you will. If it's not Adrasteia, make sure whoever you use is disposable. And dispose of him.'

Teia put her eye to the keyhole and saw a vision out of nightmare. Murder Sharp was wearing his cloak, but hadn't laced up the mask. With his body invisible, his head seemed to float in the air, his eyes dilated full paryl black, the whites pushed to oblivion. But as disconcerting as Teia still found his eyes, the effect was heightened a hundredfold by his wide grin. Murder Sharp had swapped out his dentures of perfect white teeth for a set made up entirely of human canines. Thirty-two dogteeth, perfectly fit together, in Murder's deliberately wide grin.

'Gladly,' Murder said. He passed his tongue not so much over his lips as over his teeth, seeming to savor the touch. He shook his head like a dog shaking off water, and let himself shimmer back into visibility, his eyes narrowing to human dimensions.

'Now, about that matter at the Chromeria,' Andross said. His voice was all business, unmoved by the horror in front of him. Not pretending to be unafraid, Teia thought, but actually unafraid. This was his world, and he was master of it and all the beasts within. The pure confidence struck fear into Teia.

Can only kill you once, the logical part of her said, but these people were so far beyond her that the rationality was thin as an eggshell. If Andross Guile caught her, she would be less than a slave. He would turn her into an animal.

'It's done,' Murder said. 'She doesn't know and never will. Trick I made up myself. Bits of paryl all around her heart. She feels tired, and simply . . . dies.'

Some words that Teia couldn't hear, then '—the most delicate of all luxin?'

'Don't matter. If they break up, she strokes out and dies anyway.'

'But . . .' Some words Teia couldn't hear followed. '. . . by morning? You're certain?'

'Probably dead already.'

Who are they talking about? Who does Andross Guile want dead?

But her thoughts were interrupted by their footsteps. She glanced through the keyhole, and saw they were walking toward her door.

She retreated to the steps, and then went up them as quickly as she could, pressing hard on the handrail to take her weight. With her eyes stuck to the door, she almost forgot to skip the creaky steps, and stumbled. She rolled onto the hardwood floor at the top of the steps, and quickly threw the cloak over her exposed legs.

She tried to free slack in the cloak so it would drape over all of her, but she was sitting on it, and the hands she put down to lift her butt also landed on the cloak. She shifted, exposing her hands – and realized she was covering herself with a *visible* cloak. She'd stopped drafting paryl.

For a moment, she was so frightened, she almost yelped. In her panic, she locked up and couldn't draft at all.

There were doors every direction from the top of the stairs. If anyone came—

Teia rolled to her feet despite the voluminous cloak, and drafted paryl. Her chest heaved. Orholam's beard, a moment of inattention could mean death. *Panic, T? You're better than that. Knock it off.*

She looked down the stairs where Promachos Guile was escorting Murder Sharp to the door.

She was careful to look in quick glances so as to hide her eyes, but then realized that the cloak wouldn't hide her from paryl vision.

In fact, she wasn't sure that she could hide from paryl vision ever, even if she mastered the cloak.

Teia ducked out of sight and took a deep, quiet breath.

No wonder the mist walkers had been stingy with teaching others, and with seeking out others with the gift. Everyone you taught became more than a rival. It would mean deliberately creating threats to yourself, in a world where a true mist walker had few.

With the faint tinkling of the bell hung over the lintel, the front door opened and closed without the men saying any farewell. Not the type, Teia supposed. Then Andross Guile came up the steps. Teia guessed which way he was going, and was right for once. He passed by without so much as a glance her way.

What was she doing here? What had started as a lark had a very real chance of getting her killed. And for what? Because she was curious to see Kip's brother? He would surely be coming to the Chromeria eventually. Why not wait?

Good question to ask myself a while ago, but now I'm here.

I didn't come to see Kip's brother; I came to see what Andross Guile is planning, and there's no way I'm going to leave before I do.

Andross walked down a hallway, up another set of stairs, and into another sitting room. This kind of space within a single house on an island where everyone lived cheek by jowl and rents were ruinous seemed obscene. One old man lived here, one. Actually, he didn't even live here. He barely visited. And yet he had this staff, in addition to the slaves who maintained his apartments at the Chromeria – and his wife's empty apartments there. What other dead person got to keep apartments in the Chromeria, where space was perpetually tight?

Teia thought that she was going to have to decide if she was going to follow Andross into a room to eavesdrop again, or if she was content catching bits and pieces in the hallway, but it wasn't much of a decision. As she rounded the last corner, she saw that the Lightguards from before were stationed at the door, and Grinwoody was scuttling about like a cockroach.

'Grandfather,' a young man said. He was astonishingly handsome, as one might expect of the son of Gavin and Karris Guile. He had Atashian caramel skin, with strong brows and an aquiline nose, and wore a fine gray tunic with slashes of color to match the many colors in his light blue eyes.

She knew him! He was the one who tried to kill her in the fort on Ruic Head. Tripped her, knocked her sprawling, took her pistol, and then ordered his men to kill her. This, *this* was Kip's brother?

The young man didn't simply bow; he prostrated himself on the floor before the promachos.

I'm going to hate myself for this.

But Teia couldn't bear to miss this conversation. Holding the cloak tight around her legs and looking down, she slipped between the big Lightguards and into the solar.

Andross Guile stood silently staring at his grandson. He didn't seem impressed. 'Up,' he said.

Zymun stood. 'I, uh, I lost the coin you sent me, the pirates, you understand. But I can draw it from memory. I'm a deft hand with a pen. Penmanship, art, luxin designs, I excel at them all. And of course I know the phrase you told me to say when we met: "Of red cunning, the youngest son, shall cleave father and father and father and son."'

'You don't carry much family resemblance,' Andross said.

'And Kip does?' Zymun shot back instantly. 'He's darker than Gavin!'

Teia could see that Andross Guile didn't much like being addressed as an equal. 'How much do you know of Guile family history?' Andross asked.

'I know we rule,' the young man said.

'You know we rule?' Andross said, mocking. 'And you presume to correct me?'

'Not a correction, my lord, simply standing up for myself. I thought you would appreciate—'

'I would appreciate the respect I deserve. You grovel in one heartbeat and "correct" me the next?'

Zymun looked aghast. 'I'm terribly, terribly sorry, my lord. I know but little of the family history. The – folk – who raised me were not keen on teaching Guile history. I stand to learn.' He bowed his head, and if Teia weren't already disposed to hate him, she would have believed him chastened.

'Hmm,' Andross Guile said. He said nothing for a long time. It stretched to an uncomfortably long time. Grinwoody stood still as a statue. Andross drank his liquor slowly, and Zymun finally squirmed, but didn't say anything.

Finally, Andross said, 'Well then, we shall begin your education, and perhaps at the end have a little test, to see if you have the Guile mind. If you fail, you're useless to me, even if you are what you say. A stupid Guile is no Guile at all.'

Teia's heart soared, while Zymun nodded with feigned confidence over fear.

Andross said, 'During the Blood War, some prominent families began arranging marriages with an eye to war instead of to political alliances. The Guiles were the first of these. My great-great-great-grandmother Ataea was from a small noble family that supplied half of the horses for the chariot races in Ruthgar and Blood Forest, and almost all the champions. Galatius Guile was a drunk who was bent on wagering away the family fortune at those races. She rescued his fortune by telling him which horses to bet, and soon stole his heart. She convinced him that marrying down – to marry her – would be the bravest act of his cowardly life. It turned out to also be the smartest one. She, like many, despaired of the Blood War ever truly ending, so she brought the lessons of horse breeding to the Guile house. She was a savage but shrewd judge of character, and she kept a ledger book of genealogy. Her husband, like every other noble she met or could learn about, got a single line: "Galatius Guile: drunk, gambler, a bit dimwitted, blue eyes, no drafting, inspires loyalty in family and beyond." Later in her life, her journals got more extensive, noting skin tone, musculature, bravery, height, and relative fertility. It helped, of course, that she herself had eighteen children and lived to be a hundred and five years old. She arranged marriages that defied politics, bringing in the blood of the brilliant but impoverished, the hale but unconnected. Where other families fought over who would marry the beautiful or the rich, thus driving up the cost of acquiring those matches, she instead believed that having smart warrior-drafters would result in riches and power both – in the long term. She even birthed several bastards of her own from the great men of her day, and clearly noted the fathers in her book, with no apparent shame.

'In that first generation, she was either very, very good; very, very lucky; or both, because almost every child born was a drafter. That she was similarly lucky with several other attributes wouldn't become clear for a few more generations. Which pleased her. After all, if other families are becoming smarter and more magical, too, where's your relative advantage over them? In fact, no one would have even known the logic behind her scheme if she hadn't infuriated one of her grandsons by refusing to let him marry a girl he loved. He rebelled and ran off to a Blood Forest family that gladly took his secrets, and later, when Ataea refused to pay his ransom, his life.'

'Nice people,' Zymun said.

But the sarcasm hit a wall. For a few moments, Teia almost took hope in how much Andross Guile seemed to dislike Zymun. Then she realized he didn't much like anyone. Or maybe he'd just been so powerful for so long that he never bothered to conceal it when someone displeased him.

He was the opposite of a slave, and yet his constant truths were no more winsome than a slave's constant lying smiles.

'No one has kept that book as well as Ataea Guile did, and war has intervened again and again, killing men and women before they could contribute their children to this family. Bastards have been brought in, and their patrimony concealed. But in eight generations of faithful record-keeping – and sometimes nine and ten and twelve, for Ataea researched the family before her time back as far as she could – the Guiles have learned a few things about what's heritable, what's highly heritable, and what seems to be a dice roll. Of course, I don't believe in dice, but I understand that there are systems whose workings I don't understand. A lesson you might do well to learn.'

Zymun looked appropriately chastened. 'Yes, grandfather,' he said.

'Grandfather? Haven't connected it yet, have you? All this I've just said, what does it mean?'

'My lord?' Zymun asked, and Teia could tell that he hadn't been paying attention at all. Who takes their first interview with Andross Guile, with their entire fate in his hands, and doesn't pay attention to the first thing he says?

'Do you think me stupid, boy?' Andross asked.

'Of course not,' Zymun said breezily, but it sounded like a lie. Who spoke so fearlessly to Andross Guile?

Andross Guile slapped Zymun across the face, hard.

Zymun's fists balled and his whole arm tightened. Somehow,

Grinwoody went from standing off to the side with a serving tray to being right there, serving tray vanished, ready to intervene.

'One of the things we've tried hard to breed out with every generation,' Andross Guile said. 'Impulsivity. Those who can't control themselves are always failures. I see this is a weakness for you. Expect it to be tested again. Seems endemic with the Guile blood, but the best of us translate it to boldness, nimbleness, readiness to seize an opportunity. The rest simply chase the first thing to come along, and lose interest before they run it down and capture it.

'The point is that I have a very good idea what traits are Guile traits, and what traits seem random. Blue eyes with dark skin? Very rare among most peoples. Not rare in my family. There's a lot of Parian blood in the Guile line. My brother was darker than Kip. Our mother was Parian, as was my grandmother. I was thought to be oddly light-skinned. If there is one of my grandsons whom I suspect might not be a Guile, it's not Kip.'

'Kip? The bastard?'

'I've declared Kip legitimate. Kip does what he's told.'

In what world does Kip do what he's told?

But lie though it might be, now, for the first time, Zymun seemed truly aware that his position was tenuous. It was as if he'd made the cornerstone of his identity that he was, secretly, a Guile, that he had all seven satrapies waiting for him, that he was *destined*. And now his own grandfather was threatening that?

But Kip had told Teia about his own interactions with Andross Guile, so she saw what was happening. Andross hated his new grandson's arrogance, so he was doing to him exactly what he'd done to Kip, pretended that belonging to the Guiles was something that had to be earned.

It was patently ridiculous to Teia. The Guiles had no children. To whom would the old man give all this wealth? He'd gone on and on about genealogy, but he'd failed to produce a large enough crop of his own to give him the luxury of being picky. There remained only Kip and Zymun. Gavin was gone, probably never to return, and even if he did, where did a marriage to Karris fit into Andross's book? The threat had to be hollow.

But Zymun didn't know that.

'You little moron,' Andross said. 'You had the Blinder's Knife, and you used it to try to kill my son? You think you can play the Color Prince? Maybe. You think you can play me? You have no idea.'

'Grandfather, I was trapped. The Color Prince was there and you were so far away. Disobedience would have meant – I failed on purpose.'

'Learn to lie better.'

'I thought you and my father were at odds—'

'You had no way to know how I felt about Gavin. You were ingratiating yourself with the Color Prince.'

'I didn't mean—'

'I know exactly what you meant. You were on a barge, with Gavin. All you had to do was come back to Little Jasper and bring me the knife. If you'd done so, tomorrow I would have made you Prism.'

'I swear I'll never disobey again. I'll do anything you ask. Everything—'

'You think I'm punishing you? I haven't even begun to punish you. This isn't my punishment. This is reality's punishment. I can't make you the Prism tomorrow. We need the Knife for that, and . . . other things that you don't need to know about. Yet. Your incompetence may cost us – it may cost *you* everything. Had you either killed Gavin or joined him – either way! – if you had brought me the Blinder's Knife, your own future, not to mention this family's, not to mention all of the Seven Satrapies', would be assured.

'Someday, you cretin, you may lead this family and perhaps this world, if you aren't too stupid to take what I hand to you. But that day is not today. From this day forth, you obey without question, and you prove yourself worthy of this family. I'm giving you one chance. You have a brother, and however much he pretends to oppose me, he and I have an understanding, and he serves me well. If he serves better than you do, I will not hesitate to make him the Guile heir. From Ataea Guile's time, we have only practiced primogeniture when it suits us.

The only way you will inherit is if you please me. And so you know, in this family, the one heir gets everything.'

The ambition on Zymun's face was as naked as the hatred, but Andross Guile didn't seem to notice. Zymun said, after a pause that was only a little too long, 'Of course, grandfather. How may I best serve?'

Andross Guile stared at him and tossed back his liquor with a grimace. 'Tomorrow we make you the Prism-elect.'

'I thought the White had to acquiesce to any recommendation the Spectrum brought her for that. I was under the impression she wasn't a friend.'

'She isn't, but she's doing me a big favor tonight.'

'She's signing off on it tonight?'

Andross Guile gave a thin-lipped smile that was all victory. 'In a manner of speaking,' he said.

He didn't explain any more to Zymun, seemingly pleased to deny a morsel of information to the young man, but Teia's heart dropped. She couldn't believe she hadn't put it together before now. A woman that Andross Guile wanted dead, and Murder Sharp being here – after being at the Chromeria earlier.

Sharp wouldn't go to the Chromeria simply to test Teia; the place was too dangerous for him. He'd come to scout, and he'd used Teia to scout the last part, and used what she reported to help him kill the White. No doubt now Sharp would make himself highly visible somewhere on the other side of Big Jasper for the entire night, just in case a drafter stumbled across some paryl in the old woman's body.

Murder Sharp would have an alibi.

For a moment, blind rage flooded Teia. Who would hurt that kind old woman? How dare he? Murder Sharp was an animal, but he was merely a tool. It was Andross Guile Teia wanted to kill. How could he stand so close to goodness for so long, and hate it? Such things – for sure they are not men – should not be allowed to be.

She could kill him. She could kill Zymun. She could kill Grinwoody. No, not Grinwoody. Slaves shouldn't be killed for the sins of their masters, no matter how much they seemed to enjoy facilitating them.

Would it not be a service to the greater good to kill these

detestable men? Would it not be a fulfillment of the Blackguard's oaths? She hadn't taken the final oaths, but she knew them, and had wanted to take them for as long as she could remember.

I swear upon my life and light and sacred honor to protect the White, the Black, the Prism, and all the members of the Spectrum of the Seven Satrapies, and in the final exigency to protect the Seven Satrapies. I shall live not as a woman free, but as a slave to my duties and after them to my commanders. The final exigency was when a Prism went mad, and refused to lay down his powers, and had to be put down, but Teia supposed it also applied if a Color or even a promachos went mad and did the same.

She began filling herself with paryl, not simply the constant stream she needed to keep the shimmercloak functioning, but enough to make weapons.

'Protect,' Teia. The word is 'protect.' Not 'avenge.' You are not to be a blade in the darkness, you are a shield. You are not a woman alone, you are a soldier under authority.

If I kill now, I'm an assassin, not a Blackguard.

I am a special soldier, with uncommon skills and unique abilities, but I am a soldier under orders. If the White commands me to kill Andross Guile, I will kill with joy in my heart, and a conscience clean of murder, though guilty of rejoicing in it.

The world might be better if I were a law unto myself, if I killed these loathsome men.

She sat on that thought. She'd killed a man in that alley, almost on accident, but he'd been a man who would have killed her or her team if she hadn't. Aside from the heaviness of killing at all, when she looked at the situation, she couldn't see a moment when she would have acted differently. More competently, sure. But she'd trained as hard as she could for as long as she could. Her skills at that point in time weren't something she could change. She would have done what she did again. This . . .

Dear Orholam, what harm will these men do that I might prevent?

But it wasn't her place. Orholam had put her here, but he'd put her in the Blackguard, too, and he'd put a longing in her whole heart to be a Blackguard. She couldn't betray all that. She was called to be a shield, and shield she would be.

And like that, the cobwebs cleared and what she had to do was simple.

The White wasn't dead. Not yet.

Teia waited only until her chance came, and slipped out of the room. She made her way downstairs, stilled the bell above a servants' door to the outside, and went out. She slipped past the Blackguards, climbed the roof of the stables in the back, and vaulted over the high fence. After a block, she dropped the invisibility and simply ran.

She was almost all the way back to the Chromeria before she realized that both Andross and Zymun could see in the sub-red. If it had occurred to either man to look in sub-red while she was in the room, she would be in a dungeon or dead right now. The thought made her sweat run cold.

Lucky, T. Now let's hope that luck holds.

Chapter 83

Gavin had expected some casual cruelty on his way to the hippodrome, like being forced to wear a hood, or locked in a carriage or palanquin with something disgusting so that his last sight before the cheering crowds would be of filth. Instead, he was allowed to ride inside a normal carriage, albeit with doors that locked from the outside, and windows too small to wiggle through.

He was also chained and tied up nearly as much as he would have tied up himself in this situation. But still, he could see, and by luck, he got the better window.

He wanted to think that knowing these were among the last things he would see lent everything a certain poignancy, but the truth was that the Great River Delta was always beautiful, and now, with Sun Day on the morrow, it looked as vibrant as he'd ever seen a day in whites and grays look.

As the carriage rumbled through the cobbled switchbacks

down Jaks Hill where the great families had their estates, Gavin could see the myriad farms stretched out on the plain below. With the warmer weather and the passing of time, the flood-waters had deposited their yearly tribute of fertile silt. Some fields were now dry. Others were muddy. Some few were still under a bare thumb of water. Thousands of shorebirds filled land and sky. Egrets and herons and cranes and ducks and geese and red-winged blackbirds had arrived from their migrations or emerged from hiding. Rushes and cattails and a thousand kinds of grass had sprung up in the lines between perfect fields. The land must be a debauched party of greens and browns and points of color like jeweled fingers flashing in torchlight.

Gavin's monochromatic vision was a curse once again. This world had faded to textures.

He sank back into his carriage seat.

Some part of him still expected a crash at any moment, a violent stop, fighting – rescue.

But none came. The image of the baby black widow spiders rolling over him in a wave changed. Now the eggs were grains of black powder, wadded down the blossoming barrel of a blunderbuss. Gavin, the elder, watched: a hole in his forehead, a hole in his jaw, head bobbing like an old man with the twitching sickness because the tendons supporting his head had been clipped by the passage of bullets and brains out the back of his skull. Dead Gavin smiled around broken teeth, blood washing from the front of his head and his mouth and the back of his head, too, too much blood for a man to bleed when his brain had been stopped. Too much blood for a man to bleed, period. He cocked that blunderbuss, aimed it at his little brother's stomach.

He fired.

The blunderbuss vomited black death through Dazen's guts. He jerked, looked down with trepidation. All his soft tissues were gone. He stood on his spine alone. A writhing mass of black spiders fed on his guts, grew into adults in moments, and swarmed, devouring. They climbed his spine, wrapped under his hanging skin, and went inside his rib cage. They devoured his lungs. He couldn't breathe, feeling them from the inside, taking life from his very core. And then they ate his heart. It seized, labored, thumped one last time, and stopped.

He fell. Opened his mouth to seek some forgiveness, but only spiders burst forth, burning his esophagus like bile, spewing over his tongue, crawling out of his nose. He was covered with black spiders, a living stinging biting blanket, sticky as tar. His brother stood over him and laughed. His eyes crinkled and he leaned forward – Dazen had forgotten how Gavin did that, how he doubled forward, eyes shut when he laughed hard.

Now Dead Gavin stood over him, laughing, and the sun shone through the hole in his head like a third eye. The beam of light fell on Dazen just as the spiders began crawling up his cheeks. They were going for his eyes! He jerked, but his arms were useless, his mouth pried opened. And then the spiders began attacking his eyes, biting, poison squirting deep into those orbs, filling his precious orisons with acid.

Gavin jerked awake. They were in the city proper now. He gulped and blinked, the sun high above, cutting through the gap in the carriage's window curtain. Not quite noon. He was sleeping through his last sights. But still the dream clung to him. Would Gavin laugh at him like that, doubling over, out of breath? Or would he have some compassion for him now, at the end?

His guards chuckled. 'Never seen a man who could sleep on his way to torture. You got stones, friend.'

Gavin looked at the guard, searching him for some sign of humanity. Was this man part of his escape plan? No. No. Hope is the great deceiver. Hope is the piper who leads us sleepy to our slaughter.

I shouldn't have killed you like that, brother. It wasn't worthy of me. It wasn't worthy of you. I don't think you would have taken shriving from me, but I should have offered. Should have given you a chance to prepare yourself. Killing you without warning, that was for me. That was for my nerve, which I knew would fail me.

Because I still loved you. And love you still.

A Guile's love is a bullet through the brain.

He bowed his head even as the sounds of the hippodrome floated down into the street. A race must have been under way.

The streets were packed, and though carriages had the right of way that came with crushing power, it still had to slow as they approached the enormous crowds around the hippodrome. The carriage added its tinny bell to the din: shouting voices of vendors, angry yells from other drivers, a distant yell decrying a thief, the throbbing roar of the crowd inside the hippodrome swelling in time to their favorite chariot coming round, the hoots and jeers of fans outside, the rattling of tuned bamboo wind chimes and more, cowbell and brass and drums competing among the fans.

But the colors were mute. Gray on gray on dark gray on black. The smell of cooking pork and curries and roasted nuts in caramel was far more vivacious. Gavin peered through his curtain and saw a little boy in rags, lean to the point of starvation, staring back at him.

A lookout for the rescue?

But the boy merely watched him go by.

The carriage turned and went down a long ramp, accompanied by many shouts, and then was swallowed by darkness. A gate rattled shut behind them. This area was off-limits to the public.

And Gavin's last ember of hope died. They didn't know he was here. Like so many other things, his father had been able to keep it secret. Gavin was going to lose his half-useless eyes, and then he was going to die. Funny how he was more worried about his eyes than his life.

They have stolen light from me. What is life without light?

The carriage door opened. He was bundled out, hands bound behind his back, hobbled by his chains so that he had to take tiny shuffling steps. They didn't help him. After walking hundreds of paces through winding corridors beneath the very hippodrome itself – the roof rumbling with hoofbeats as the chariots raced overhead, the roar of the crowd barely rising to perception – Gavin was put in an iron-barred cell. More a cage, really. It was fitted with chains connected to gears, and high above, there was a panel that slid back. This cage would take him directly up into the stadium floor.

'On your knees,' a soldier said. He waited until Gavin complied before he came into the cage himself, carrying a bucket full of black liquid. Or dark liquid, anyway. The soldier was careful, too. He didn't keep the key, but handed it off to another, outside the cell, and locked the door behind himself.

'Dunk your head. Not your skin, just your hair,' the soldier said. He didn't seem to relish the duty. Gavin looked up at him, not understanding what he wanted.

The man locked up suddenly, muscles clenching so obviously that his friend called out, 'Something wrong?'

'No,' the soldier said, after a brief hesitation. 'I got this. I'll call for you.'

And then Gavin recognized him.

'Captain Eutheos. Citation for Extraordinary Bravery at Blood Ridge, wasn't it?' Gavin said. He remembered belatedly that that was his own memory, pinning that ribbon on the man's chest. He'd been Dazen then. As Gavin, he should have no memory of Eutheos. Oops.

Ah well. What would have been a gigantic blunder at some other time now seemed a bit trivial.

There was a gigantic clatter and roar of wheels and hoof-beats pounding overhead as the massed chariots passed, but it was obviously a familiar, inconsequential sound to the captain.

The sudden joy on the soldier's face bloomed and died in an instant, an abortion of hope.

'It can't be,' he said. 'They ordered me to dye your hair and eyebrows and make you look scruffy. I didn't know why, but . . . High Lord Prism . . . *Dazen* Guile?' the soldier whispered.

A crushing weight settled on Gavin's chest. There had been a time when he would have tried to turn this man, when he would have blithely ordered this man to do something that would cost him position, and reputation, and family, and probably life, all for the slimmest chance that Gavin might, might, escape.

But he'd been young then. All his invincibility had been built on other men's bones.

'It's not your fault,' Gavin said. 'It's mine.'

'I swore you my fealty, my lord, all those years ago, but . . . I swore them my fealty, too, after the war.'

'It's not your fault,' Gavin said.

'I, I, I gave him the key. If I, if I have to call him back, I'll

654

have to steal it from him, hurt him – he's my brother-in-law, and devoted to this land something fierce. He wasn't in the war. He doesn't know what it was like.' The captain looked around like a trapped animal. 'Which oath does a man hold, when holding one means breaking the other, and he never saw it coming?'

'I wouldn't ask it of you,' Gavin said.

'That's why the hair black, and the charcoal. They don't want to chance anyone recognizing you like I done – as either Prism or as Dazen, I s'pose. But how are you alive? What do I do?'

Gavin was still on his knees. 'Eutheos,' he said. 'Be still.'

And the man was still. This, at least, Gavin still had. His voice was sometimes magic over other men.

'Breathe.'

And Eutheos breathed.

Chariots passed overhead again, but they seemed far, far away.

There was no escape from here. If Eutheos unlocked Gavin's chains, Gavin could go no more than a few hundred paces. He wasn't strong enough to fight. He couldn't draft. He couldn't get out. And there was no point ruining a man and his family for a futile gesture.

'Captain, before I release you from your oaths, as your last duty to me, dye my hair, and black my eyebrows as you've been told. I ask only that you keep the dye from my eyes. They will burn soon enough.'

And so he did. He did his job thoroughly, and well, and silently, tears streaming down his face. He dried Gavin's hair with a cloth, and blacked his eyebrows with coal, and then ground dirt and ash onto his ruddy skin to make him look no more than a beggar.

Gavin said, 'I've no more right to compel you, soldier, but as a man, as a comrade who once took up arms with you, I ask a favor. Will you send a letter to Karris Guile at the Chromeria of my fate? And tell her that I will be murdered by the Nuqaba's assassin as I arrive in Big Jasper. Don't put your own name on this letter, nor anything that can be traced to you. It will be death for you if it is intercepted.'

Former Captain Eutheos nodded and swallowed. 'My lord. You made me feel part of something. It was the only time in my life that I—' He cut off, clearing his throat as his brother-in-law the soldier came back, this time not alone. Eutheos said gruffly, 'Let me outta here, would you? Got some dirt in my eyes.'

He was let out, and the other man unlocked and locked the door carefully, as if the still-bound Gavin might attack at any moment. The woman who was with that soldier, though, surprised Gavin. It was Eirene Malargos, not the Nuqaba. She dismissed them and they moved out of earshot.

She looked tired. 'I didn't want this,' she said. 'You've done nothing here that would exact such a penalty under Ruthgari law – but you also know that I can't let you attack my ally and do nothing. Were she forgiving, she would let us handle this in our way. She's not chosen that route. I see why she is feared.'

Gavin simply stared at her. He reckoned from her mood that Eirene Malargos would shut down instantly if she felt she were being manipulated. Gavin's golden tongue was suddenly worth what his eyes would be, soon.

She said, 'I've been looking for any avenue that doesn't lead to war? You damned men, always trying to prove who's bigger. I just want to live. I want my people to live. I don't know how to avert this. Do you know I tried to align us with the Guiles?'

Gavin's eyebrows must have twitched, betraying his disbelief.

'Even after the insult of you rejecting our proposal that you marry Tisis, I proposed your father marry her instead. A temporary alliance, perhaps, given that your father is probably too old to give her children, but a gamble worth making with so many lives at stake.'

My father? With Teats Tisis? *Me* with her?

A thunderous clamoring resounded overhead as a mass of chariots passed all at once.

'But he spurned her,' she said.

'Outright?' Gavin asked. 'That doesn't sound like my father. Does he not know how close you are to betraying him?'

'I don't know what he knows. I sent a ship with my diplomats and instructions for my sister. It was intercepted by pirates. Perhaps you remember?'

Oh. In more ordinary times, that the ship Gavin had been rowing on had intercepted the very ship that his enemy was depending on for vital communications would have been a stroke of extraordinary luck. It still was extraordinary luck, he supposed, just not the good kind.

A huge cheer went up, above. The race had a winner.

'Believe me,' she said, 'I'd prefer to wait until I hear more from the Chromeria, but the Nuqaba is insistent. And I can't split with her. If Blood Forest falls – and it is falling, even now – I can't stand against the Color Prince on my own. Even if the Chromeria finally decides to send enough help to change things, I'll have trouble securing one border against the Color Prince. What if the Nuqaba attacks me from the east? We would be lost in little more than the time it takes her armies to march.'

'Oh, I see what this is,' Gavin said. 'You're going to let her take my eyes, and you still think I might be made an ally afterward.'

Her lips thinned. 'Your eyes are lost already, Gavin Guile. Put them in the ledger with my dead father and forty thousand other dead Ruthgari fathers and mothers and sons and daughters. Then do your calculations. If you want to save the Seven Satrapies, you need me.'

'If you attack me, you've already attacked the Seven Satrapies. I am the Seven Satrapies, and treason is death.'

Another, last chariot clattered overhead.

Her face steeled. 'Look at yourself before you threaten me, Gavin Guile. You are not that which once you were. You're a haggard old man with half a hand, and soon to be blind. You can't draft. Orholam has begun your punishment, and I will finish it. Tomorrow is Sun Day, and you won't have returned. You were absent on Sun Day last year. The Chromeria can't be without a Prism for two years straight. The luxiats won't tolerate it. You've probably already been stripped of that title in absentia, and you'll be replaced with a Prism-elect tomorrow. There is nothing you can do to stop that. All you can do is try to save an empire that is no longer yours. That's your option, but know this, Gavin Guile, once-Prism: no one spurns the Malargos family thrice.'

She spat on him. No doubt she'd intended to spit in his face, but most of it hit his shoulder.

Still, it communicated the feeling fairly clearly.

She walked out. 'I'll ring when it's time,' she told the soldier. Then she was gone.

The soldier said nothing.

Gavin said nothing. Eirene had been his last hope. He knew it. He knew, and yet he couldn't believe. There had always been some way out for Gavin Guile. There had always been a door that his genius and his power had let him open that no one else had even seen.

That was me.

Was.

Several minutes later, a bell rang. Gavin cracked his neck right and left. The soldier went to a lever and pulled, and Gavin began his ascent. The great trapdoor overhead sank and slid aside in a shower of sand and sunlight into his darkness.

He remembered, for one moment, that which he did not want to remember – he remembered emerging from the very bowels of darkness, bringing hell to earth at Sundered Rock, and climbing step by step out of it, the darkness finally parting and light pouring in, but light weaker, light stricken, light sickened. The world was not what it had been, before his victory, and he thought it not his eyes alone that had changed.

Until now. What I did was sixteen years in catching up to me. Why so long?

The great murmurs of a crowd of fifty thousand souls hit him first, before he even emerged from the darkness. Layered atop that was the thin, cutting voice of Eirene Malargos, projecting as loudly as she could. She had not the gift of orators and singers and generals, though. At the far points of the hippodrome's open floor, women who did have that gift listened intently and then repeated each line perfectly. It gave an odd, delayed response, but Eirene had learned the art of keeping her speeches short and pointed. Some nonsense: this man attacked our guest; according to Parian law, this malefactor will lose his eyes for his crime.

What else was there to be said?

And the crowd, Orholam forgive them, whipped up by their favorites' victories or losses, roared with bloodlust. Gavin's people, they had been. Now they roared for his eyes.

And roared once again as he came level with the ground and they saw him for the first time.

And then he saw the Nuqaba's crowning touch. The rich families of Ruthgar took turns sponsoring the games and races. Even the absent Guiles did it, though not as lavishly as others. Gavin couldn't see the Guile red on the banners or on the tunics and ribbons worn by those – he assumed – few who still favored his family here. But he could recognize his family's crest on the biggest flags. This was the Guiles' race day. Gavin was going to be blinded at his own party.

You are one vindictive bitch, Haruru.

He was surrounded by soldiers and three drafters, each with their hands already stained with color. He guessed blue, red, and green, though there were too many scents in the air to tell for sure. That was where most people went for offensive magic. They were serious. Gavin was unchained, forced to stand, and marched over the sand toward the *spina*, the center line of the hippodrome, which had a raised platform on it that would insure that everyone would be able to see his punishment.

Same platform he'd stood on when he ended the Blood War.

He stumbled on his hobbles as he climbed the stairs, and laughter rang out.

His people. How he hated them.

Then he saw the coal bucket, smoking. Two iron pokers rested in it, each with a tip as narrow as a pupil. He looked around the hippodrome. Fifty thousand people, and not one friend. In the satrap's box, he saw the Nuqaba looking at him, smiling. She was mouthing something to him. She was too far away for him to read her lips, but he could guess: 'Useless.' She was enjoying Gavin Guile impotent at least as much as she would enjoy seeing him blinded. Then she and everything else became a blur. He saw people moving, mouths moving, but he stopped hearing.

He remembered, strangely, as if cobwebs were being cleared from a hall of memory he'd not trod in decades, Lady Janus

Borig visiting when he was a child, treating his mother like no one treated his mother, and telling him, 'Black luxin is the scourge of history. It is madness in luxin form. It is the soul poison. Once touched, it lives within a drafter forever, slowly eroding her from the inside. In every world, there is that which is *haram*, that which is forbidden, and in every world, that is the thing most desired, for there is that in us which loves destruction. Here is a test for your wisdom, young Guile. It is the only test that matters. In this world, Orholam has given us such power as even the angels have not. It is the power of evil unfettered. It is the destruction of history itself. It is madness and death and being-not. It is void and darkness. It is the lack of light, the lack of God himself – the lack that men rightly call hell. It is black luxin, and that color – though color it is not – that color, Dazen Guile, is your color.'

And he'd believed her. He'd known then he was the cursed brother, the evil brother. And what she'd said had been true.

And at the end of all things, when every color is gone, darkness remains.

Gavin could see only in shades of gray.

And black.

How did I forget that? How did I, who remember all things, forget that day? Is that a real memory? Was it merely lost among all the myriad others?

But there was no time for that now. Not on this, his last walk.

Drafting black luxin wasn't something you could test. It was a cocked and loaded pistol. You pulled the trigger, or you didn't. And if you were able to draft it, and you did . . .

Hell, hell on earth. The smoking ruins of Sundered Rock. The charnel house, the gore, the rage and madness and slaughter and vileness of poison poured onto the world as from a spigot as big as the sky itself.

Gavin looked around the hippodrome, and in shades of gray and black, he saw not a single friend. They jeered and they hated and they knew him not. They, whom he had saved from a war that would never end, they hated him and wished pain and death upon him. For nothing more than their amusement.

They were, in this moment of bloodlust and casual cruelty, an open window into hell.

Gavin could bring hell to them, and in so doing, save himself. It was the only way to save himself.

He looked at the mutely roaring masses: the sounds might have been the susurrus of the waves on the shore for all he heard them, and he realized that if they had been threatening him with death, he wouldn't do it. He would die for these ingrates. Not happily, but willingly.

But to be blinded, to be made useless, to be disgraced, to be mocked, to be impotent, to be pitied? To be shorn of sight and light and power was to be made not–Gavin Guile. It was all he had built for his whole life. It was all his worth.

Or he could draft the black once more, triumph once more, rise once more, a shadow figure caked in the ashes of his enemies' burnt flesh and dreams.

To be Guile is to have will titanic. It is to move the world according to my pleasure. To be an Unmoved Mover, to be like unto God.

To be Guile is to kill without hesitation those who stand in your way. Even if it be a stadium full. Even if it be your brother.

To be Guile is to be great but not good.

But I'm not only Guile, not anymore. I'm a husband and a father now. I'm more than a conqueror. What if what I'm losing isn't worth what I'll lose to keep it?

Karris, will you understand? Kip, will you someday see that this isn't my moment of weakness?

They seized him, and of all the acts of will in a life famed for them, it was by far the greatest that he resisted them not.

They bound him to a table. It had a lip to hold in several thumbs' depth of sand. To soak up blood, he supposed. First, they put thick leather straps on his feet and wrists. Then luxin locked even his head in place.

He was on his back, on sand, staring at the sky. Like he was afloat on the ocean, lying in the skimmer, dangling his arms out to each side, looking at the placid heavens. Either this was Orholam's peace, or Gavin had finally lost his mind.

A man came to stand over Gavin and pushed his eyelid down, making him blink. Then luxin flowed around his eye and opened the eyelid. The luxin gelled, solidified, and held his left eye wide open. Bound to the table as he was, it left him looking directly at the noonday sun.

You can't stare at the sun. You might go blind.

Gavin burst out laughing.

He was staring eye to eye with Orholam's Eye, the sun. And he couldn't look away.

What had that scurvied pirate said? You keep up your lies, and you'll be stricken blind? What lie was I supposed to not tell? There were so many. Was it only telling the truth to Antonius Malargos? I am a fabric of shadows, Orholam. There is naught else to me.

The drafter spoke to him, but Gavin was beyond words now.

Staring a challenge at the sun, but still I could draft the black. I could take my noonday shadow, withered though it is, and cast it over all the world.

A woman in a chirurgeon's coat stepped close, looming over Gavin. She was plain, and pale, and paler than her usual pallor, Gavin guessed. Blanched white as only the pallid people at this arc of the satrapies could blanch. She wore two heavy leather gloves. He couldn't hear her, but he could read her lips. Though she didn't know he was the Prism, she was begging for his forgiveness. He'd seen those words pass lips in their thousands and thousands, every Sun Day.

Still I could draft the black. Orholam, you do not show half the mercy I do.

Karris, I will miss seeing your smile.

The chirurgeon lifted the first white-hot metal poker from the barrel and scuffed the coal particles from the metal with quick strokes. She braced her hip against the table and brought the smoking hot point over his head, holding it in both hands, burning like a second sun. She moved carefully, carefully.

Last second. Last chance. This is it.

The glowing metal descended, the bright white point of that terrestrial sun blotting out the celestial one.

He'd been like this. Last time. At the point of death. And had refused to die. Hands outstretched, like now, only facedown that time. Arms outstretched, and he'd reached out and embraced all hell.

And it was there, beneath his fingers like a smothering blanket of black spiders, ready to be thrown over the face of the world, over the face of the sun.

The black luxin trailed under his fingertips like all the waters of the world. To claim it, he had only to make a fist.

Still I can— His fingers went rigid, but didn't clench.

Tssss. The sound of his sizzling eyeball was the first thing he heard as all sound came back.

He'd known it would hurt.

He'd had no idea.

He screamed his soul.

Chapter 84

'Karris, you have to wake up. Right now.'

Karris blinked to find Marissia shaking her. 'Marissia, what are you doing? It's not even light out.'

'It's Gavin. One of my spies has just reported.'

That woke her instantly.

'Gavin's imprisoned in Rath, and he may be executed.'

'When? How do we know? How good is the source? Where?' Karris moved toward the bureau where she kept her blacks.

Marissia stepped in her way, put a hand on her arm. 'Today,' she said.

'Today?! And we're learning this now?!'

'I have an idea,' Marissia said. 'Mind you, not a good one.'

And now here Karris was, agreeing with the last part more and more with every windswept league. Gavin's invention of the skimmers should change everything. They might even save his life.

She'd grabbed all the Blackguards she knew could keep their silence and whom she knew had a fair bit of drafting left until they broke their halos, but she hadn't told everyone. There hadn't been time. She'd hadn't looked for Ironfist, certain that he would have seen this foolishness for what it was and tried to stop it.

But there he'd been, at the Luxlords' dock at the back of the Chromeria, waiting.

She took a deep breath and lifted her chin, gathering her thoughts. He was as imposing as his arguments would be good. And that was if he even bothered to argue with her, rather than simply throw her over his shoulder and carry her away.

He scowled at her and she moved to speak. He spoke first. 'You can go get yourself killed, but you're not going to do it alone.'

'You have to let me— What?'

Ironfist let her struggle under a glare that weighed more than she did. Then a little smile stole onto his face.

She jumped onto him and hugged him, hard.

'Gah!' He caught her, startled, then pushed her away. 'Karris, there's no, there's no hugging in the Blackguard!'

She smiled up at him. 'You're cute when you're flustered.'

Karris couldn't count the emotions that passed over his face, but twice his mouth opened to say things, and nothing came out. He stepped back away from her, then looked irritated that he'd retreated. He settled on a glower. 'I brought baggage,' he said, gesturing over his shoulder.

'I'm baggage?' the Blackguard inductee named Ben-hadad asked.

But Ironfist ignored him, noticing all the Blackguards looking at him, grinning their fool faces off. 'What is this?!' Ironfist barked at them. 'Lives in the balance. The whole point of the Blackguard, and you're lolling about? Skimmer! Now!'

They scattered like deer at a musket shot, and only then did a small, satisfied smile steal over his face. He looked at Karris and sniffed. 'The room slave told me your plan. Terrible plan. This one here will make it work, though.' He made a grudging motion to Ben-hadad.

'I . . . what?' Ben-hadad asked. His hinged spectacles, with their multiple lenses sticking up, looked like alarmingly distended eyebrows.

'The baggage.'

Ben-hadad looked nonplussed. Then, 'Oh! Oh, the dress! What's the dress for?' He pulled out of a bag the frilliest riot of a dress that Karris had ever seen.

'Lady White Oak needs a maid,' Ironfist said. 'The dress is for you.'

Ben-hadad's mouth dropped open. He looked down at the dress in his hands. Dislodged by his movement, the lenses on one side of his spectacles drooped.

'He's joking,' Karris told Ben-hadad.

'He's, he is?' Ben-hadad asked. Relief washed over his face.

Ironfist looked as close to smug as he got. 'You do gears and whatnot. Machines?'

'Yes, sir,' Ben-hadad said, confused. 'But I've never—'

'You'll make one for Lady White Oak.' Ironfist seemed to stress 'lady.' 'While we ride.'

So they'd started, in those hours before dawn, burning a fortune's worth of magnesium torches to do what drafting they could early. It was enough to get halfway through building the skimmer.

Usually the Blackguards made sea chariots. With the difficulty of the drafting and the expense in life lost to draft so much so quickly, their craft needed to last more than a few voyages to be worth making. Thus they made heavier, durable, and slower craft.

Not this time.

But even with seven of them together, they couldn't draft the craft as quickly as Gavin could have done it alone. The man could intuit the shape and density of luxins required, and, of course, didn't need to communicate which luxin needed to go where to anyone else. He just did it.

Karris spent all morning as they crossed the waves trying to come up with a better plan. She had no doubt Commander Ironfist was doing the same. From his silence, she guessed he had failed, too.

Five exhausted Blackguards traipse into the middle of fifty thousand angry civilians whipped into a frenzy by the brutal chariot races and whatever lies the Nuqaba had dreamed up and do . . . what, precisely?

There just weren't good options. Not with time running out. What could Karris do? Threaten the Nuqaba? With what? Bribe her? With what? Say that an army would avenge Gavin? Perhaps even true, but it would come too late for him.

She looked at Ironfist. 'Could you . . . ?' The woman was his sister. He kept a picture of her in his room. She knew he thought about her often.

'You don't know the Nuqaba,' he said. He never called her his sister; he never used her name. 'If she even *sees* me, this only gets worse.'

Dawn was nearly six hours past now, the sun perilously near noon.

Around the skimmer, the five drafters who'd come with her – two of the others had exhausted themselves building the craft and stayed behind, not worth the weight they would add to the skimmer – were all bent against the wind, cutting up the Great River past galleys and galleasses. Everyone other than Karris and Ben-hadad wore eye caps rather than spectacles, enduring the glue and the discomfort in a trade for keeping them on and being able to see even at these great speeds.

Everywhere, they attracted stares. None of the people on shore had ever seen a ship move at such speed, and though they might have heard rumors of skimmers and sea chariots, seeing one was different.

They angled the skimmer up river channels. Karris and Commander Ironfist both had been here before. The hippodrome was carved into Rathcore Hill – the smaller twin to Jaks Hill in an otherwise flat plain. But while the hippodrome complex was elevated above the floodplain, a deep canal had been dug to allow ferries to transport horses and goods directly to the hippodrome's basement.

As they approached the vast iron gate blocking river access, Commander Ironfist looked at Karris. 'New plan?' he asked.

They both looked at the defenses. The gate itself could be blasted open or opened by a guard at the counterweights. The soldiers guarding the gate and the hippodrome, ironically, were wearing Guile livery. The Guiles must be sponsoring these races, so they were in charge of the expense and manpower of securing the hippodrome during the race and clearing and cleaning it afterward.

It would have been a great stroke of luck if they'd had hours to call the Guile steward, convince him or her who

Karris was, and enlist them to help. There was no time for that.

We could just kill them. Tragic, but their lives against Gavin's? Karris was willing to make that trade.

But there were at least a dozen of them, most of them at the gate to the basement itself, where someone was shouting up the results to the races to them as they happened.

They could kill twelve, no problem. But how many more were around the hippodrome, within a minute's run? Karris and Ironfist could get in, but what if Gavin wasn't there yet? Or what if he'd already been taken above?

'The timing's impossible,' Karris said.

Ironfist veered the skimmer into an open space between two riverboats. They spilled out onto the dock, ignoring the stares of the merchants and sailors. 'Ben-hadad, Essel, guard the boat. Ben-hadad, that spot there.' He pointed out in the canal. 'Make sure it stays clear. If it isn't deep, make it so.'

'How am I supposed—'

'Your problem. Essel, ten minutes, fifteen at the outside. Hezik, with us.'

'Ben-hadad, do whatever you're going to do.'

He approached her warily. 'This is not going to be comfortable,' he said. 'Hold your left eye open. You can't blink.'

She did and he lifted a tiny lens on delicate luxin fingers, swabbing the lens itself one last time to make sure it was free of dust – and then placed it directly on her eye. It was about as enjoyable as she'd guessed getting poked in the eye would be. She blinked.

'No – you weren't supposed to blink – ' Ben-hadad said. 'Is it still in? Next one.'

They repeated the process. It took two tries, and left her streaming tears.

But she looked up at him and Ben-hadad said, 'I'm a genius.'

Commander Ironfist grabbed her face in his meaty hands and turned her toward him. It was so disconcerting when he touched her face.

He looked troubled, but said nothing, merely nodding.

Ben-hadad had not only made almost impossibly thin blue lenses that sat directly on her eyes, he had patterned them exactly to the luxin patterns already on her retinas. To anything other than long study, Karris would appear to simply have blue eyes.

'How long?' she asked.

'A few hours. Try not to blink too hard.'

It would have been great, she'd joked, if she drafted blue. Ben-hadad took the criticism to heart, and had incorporated a bit of red luxin – which someone else had needed to draft for him, on a speeding, windy skimmer – into the lens itself, but only directly over the pupil. With the black pupil behind that dot of red, it was unnoticeable. One lens red, one lens green.

Karris wished she could try it out, but drafting at all risked destroying the disguise. Cursed pale skin. She would undo the good months of abstaining from drafting had done.

'Ready,' she said. She didn't look a drafter at all.

Ironfist and Karris and Hezik ran up the steps from the docks, Karris especially drawing stares with her dress that was all cleavage and a flood of white lace and blue satin and a pink ribbon on her right hip the size of a great ship. She hiked up skirts and petticoats and thanked Orholam that she hadn't put on the elevated shoes, too.

As usual, Ironfist moved with purpose. He cut between stalls, heading straight for the hippodrome's wall. Karris's wide skirts knocked over a rack of petosae, and she cursed the dress again, never mind that her life was going to depend on it in moments.

'Sorry, sorry,' she said, shooting the biggest, stupidest smile she could at the old man who ran out to catch his hats.

He looked at her face, her dress – and then her cleavage – and seemed to forget his anger, at least long enough for her to escape.

Ironfist brought them to the wall. It wasn't the lowest wall, but it was clear. All the entrances were packed with people and Guile soldiers. Twenty feet above them here was a sentry box and a narrow walkway that disappeared into the hippodrome: a lookout to spot supplies arriving.

Ironfist must have already given an order to Hezik while Karris was flirting with the merchant, because Hezik's brown skin was already tinged blue. He moved instantly to the wall, put his back to it, and squatted slightly, putting his thigh at a good angle to step up on.

Without hesitation, Commander Ironfist approached at a slow jog. The rhythm was important, and as always with Ironfist, the rhythm was perfect. He stepped on Hezik's thigh, then up off his shoulder, then into the hand Hezik had raised above his head. A small luxin platform sprang up out of Hezik's palm, shooting Ironfist into the air, his own jump magnified.

The jump was so perfect that Ironfist merely put his hands on the railing as his body went over it and into the walkway, as effortless as a farmboy vaulting a stone fence.

And then it was Karris's turn. In this damned dress.

She gathered up skirts in both hands, and took a deep breath against the rib-breaking bodice, nodded the tempo to Hezik and jogged. Step, step, step.

Karris wasn't as tall or as strong as Ironfist, but she was a great deal lighter. Hezik overcompensated and launched her luxin platform too hard. She flew up and off to the side, but Ironfist was there, dodging to the side fast enough to arrive in place and put out his hand and arm as stable targets. She snagged his hand, and he swooped her up and into the walkway.

It worked perfectly except that the boned skirts smacked Ironfist in the face as she spun, poking him in the eye. He didn't let it interfere with setting Karris down in the walkway, but he was left blinking.

Karris looked down in disgust. 'This thing is hideous,' she said.

'The very pinnacle of fashion is to wear the hideous with great confidence.' Ironfist rubbed his eye, but he did it as he jogged over to the door. It was chained shut, and the door itself was stout old wood. The hinges were on the other side. Ironfist was in the lead, and he went right to the barred window. Who the hell put a door that sturdy up here? Who bothered to chain it shut?

Shaking the door to test its hinges, Ironfist immediately got the attention of someone on the other side.

'Would you open the door?' he asked smoothly. 'My lady friend and I seem to have gotten locked out.' He smiled as if they'd been up to mischief.

'Go to hell,' Karris heard from the other side.

Brave words, when Ironfist was on the opposite side of a chained door.

Ironfist turned. 'I saw a man on the spina. Being bound for punishment. It's not Gavin.' He hesitated, though.

'Let me look,' Karris said. She went to the window, but wasn't tall enough to see over the standing crowds.

Without needing to be asked, Ironfist stooped and wrapped an arm around her and lifted her up.

'That's him,' she said instantly. Even emaciated and with his hair dyed, she couldn't mistake him. 'Sir,' she said louder. 'Please . . . ?'

The man turned, frustrated. 'Do I look like I have a key? I'm trying to watch the show.'

Karris nearly shot a spike of luxin through his head.

There had been some hope while they'd thought the chains might just be looped around the other side. But locked, too?

She looked at Ironfist. They could break through the door, but it would take time and noise. That would draw soldiers. And if Gavin was already on the spina . . .

Ironfist looked up. There were no more walkways or sentry boxes above them, but there were open spaces between the broad arches – twenty-five feet up. Not only was it higher than their first jump, but it would mean running forward, jumping forward, and grabbing *sideways*. If they did anything wrong, Karris would be launched away from the hippodrome and would land in the market below. Far below.

It was too dangerous.

'Ladder?' Ironfist asked. It was possible, but it would take time to make one that would bear even Karris's weight over this kind of height.

'Shh. The crowd just went silent,' Karris said.

Ironfist took his place instantly, squatting slightly, right hand over his shoulder, a flat blue platform already drafted in it. 'If you need to, you come out the way you went in,' Ironfist said. 'They won't expect it. Five count. Gavin first. Plank out.'

'You think you can?' Karris asked. She'd taken her position already. Plank, from up there? She paled. As if *that* was the insane part of this plan.

But before Ironfist could answer, the crowd in the hippo-drome erupted in groans. Something terrible had happened. It was the same sound they made when a chariot wrecked, or a man was dragged to death by his horses. That was how it always went: a shared groan, then a cheer.

They *cheered*.

Karris drafted green for the first time in half a year, carefully packing it in areas covered by the dress, and the wildness filled her. Her eyes lit. This, this was life. She wasn't too late. She couldn't be too late. Not when she was this close. 'One, two, three, four,' she said, giving the tempo for the jump.

Ironfist's face was stone, the tight muscles in his jaw giving the only indication that he'd entered battle readiness, the whites of his eyes flooded with blue.

Karris jogged the few steps. With battle juice flowing and green luxin, she rushed the tempo she'd set. But Ironfist had practiced with her, fought with her. He knew; he adjusted.

But the faster tempo and the harder jump meant her skirts – which she had to release as soon as she made the first jumping step – flattened more than they had on her earlier jump with Hezik. The first step was fine, the step to Ironfist's shoulder was fine, but the skirt caught for a fraction of a heartbeat between her foot and Ironfist's hand.

Ironfist threw her hard into the air, springing the platform high and hard to give her the maximum height. But that little hitch put her off balance. Her leg strained to take all the pressure and she flew up – but not high enough, and out into the empty air.

Something big and blunt smacked into her butt, adding to her fading momentum, shooting her higher into the air. It was Ironfist. He'd noticed her jump was wrong and immediately tried to help her get higher. But the blue luxin scoop snapped immediately as he tried to use it to angle her in.

Worse, the boost twisted her body so that she was facing the street. All the green luxin she'd readied to extend in hooks was useless. Then some primal part of her remembered some-thing and acted before it could rise to the level of thought. She snapped her hands out and *streamed* unfocused green luxin into the empty air.

Like a tiny rudder steering a mighty ship, it didn't take much. She threw luxin, and the luxin threw her back – toward the vast open arch. She started spinning, but too late. Her left leg hit stone, and she tumbled.

In.

She'd made it. Her butt had cleared the ledge, just barely.

Karris hopped to her feet amid the standing crowd. No one had even noticed her entrance except one little girl on her father's shoulders. The girl was patting his head, trying to get his attention. Karris straightened her skirts, brushed off the dirt, and pushed hair out of her eyes.

Now, the hard part.

Chapter 85

Aliviana Danavis spotted the superviolet seed crystal after midnight. She and Phyros were camped just off the bare rock that made up the north peninsula of the Everdark Gates. The sailors they'd hired had refused to make the climb, their fear so great that Liv had left her last remaining drafters with them, to make sure the sailors didn't abandon them here. For three days, Liv and Phyros climbed alone, guided only by Liv's intuition. She hoped it was a sense of superviolet, but she wasn't sure.

Until now.

They had found a campsite just below the final pitch, where windblown grasses gave way to the bare rock of the cliffs of the Gate itself. The site had obviously been used by every party ever to make the climb to stare out over the Gates and the sea. Liv had sat with her back to the fire, thinking about tomorrow and stealthily checking her guns. She checked them all without ever moving her hands, letting her luxin wrap invisibly around her back or down to her belt. She was no smith, but when she pressed her superviolet luxin down the first pistol's barrel, she noticed that the wadding was in place, but there was no ball. She'd loaded the pistol herself, so it was possible she'd done it improperly and the ball had fallen out.

But on all four? The only question that remained was when it had been done, and by whom. One of the drafters or sailors, back when they were on the galley? Or by dear Phyros?

She took a deep breath, and that was when she saw the seed crystal. In the air above and perfectly between the Everdark Gates, a winking, spinning crystal like a star hung low. Something about the moonlight made it glow cool in the visible spectrum.

Liv rose and started walking, barely aware of herself. In the superviolet spectrum, the crystal looked entirely different. It was hard to get any idea of the size of the thing. Light in the visible spectrum seemed unaffected by the crystal, and indeed, overwhelmed it. In the superviolet spectrum, though, the delicate light of a thousand stars bent toward that one point. When the moon emerged from a cloud, its powerful light beat down, scattering the superviolet streams like iron filings in a wind. But the moon's face was hidden once again, those delicate streams were sucked toward the seed crystal as to a lodestone.

'Aliviana!' Phyros said. 'Where are you going?'

During the day, it would be invisible even in the superviolet. The sledge of sunlight was too strong. This tiny point of light would be a mote in a storm.

'Eikona!' Phyros said.

Liv made her way up the bare rock promontory, captivated. The Everdark Gates were more than twice as tall as the Prism's Tower, and from each side it was a straight drop from promontory to frothy sea, hundreds of paces below. The waters of the Cerulean Sea warred with the waters of the ocean outside, sometimes jetting through the narrow channel with incredible force one way, and at others, the opposite direction. Rocks lined the channel like teeth of every size. Some were barely above the surface of the water; others were taller than a galley's mast. Liv couldn't imagine how any ship could ever make it through the maelstroms.

She reached the top of the Gate, an unnaturally flat plain of bare rock several hundred paces wide. A road etched into the stone itself led out to the precipice.

'Eikona!'

The road was flanked by ancient statues, now broken down to nubs by time and weather and vandals or invaders. Liv walked the road, transfixed by the shining crystal that would change everything. It was, she was certain now, no larger than her fist. Maybe even smaller than that.

'Eikona, that's far enough,' Phyros said, grabbing her arm.

She stopped and stared hard up at him, as if shocked and disgusted he would touch her.

He released her. 'Liv, I'm sorry, but you are to go no farther unless you wear the black jewel. That is what our prince has ordered.'

She stepped back and pulled a pistol from her belt and pointed it at him, and then another.

'You're not going to shoot me,' he said.

'Am I not? Look in my eyes and tell me I lack the will to do it,' Liv said.

'It isn't will you lack,' Phyros said.

'So it was you.'

He looked confused. Then, briefly, frightened. If she knew her pistols had been unloaded, did that mean she'd loaded them again?

She had thought to talk to him, to appeal to the loyalty she thought she'd built in him, to offer him a choice, to appeal to logic. But he wasn't a superviolet or a blue drafter; Phyros was a warrior. He attacked instantly, and was on top of her before she could think.

His gigantic hand was around her throat, squeezing, throwing her into panic. With his other hand he flung the pistols away from her hands, grabbed the others from her belt, and tossed them away, too. The sword and knife at her belt followed, as the blackness closed in.

Phyros carried Liv by her neck and her belt up the weather-beaten stairs out to the very point of the promontory. She curled into a fetal position and kicked, kicked blindly. Then they reached the top.

His hand was still wrapped around her throat, though loosely now, and he was pawing through her pockets. He found the necklace and pulled it out. He pushed her back until she was on the very edge of the cliff. The wind whipped them. She could barely breathe. There was no strength in her.

'What'll it be, lady, the black or the abyss?' He loosened his grip just enough for her to speak.

'The blade.'

'What?' he asked. Perhaps the wind had swallowed her words.

She rammed the hidden blade her father had given her deep into his chest, twisted hard, and pulled it back.

He pulled away instinctively, which was the only thing that saved her from falling off the cliff as he dropped her. She flung herself toward the ground and rolled past him.

He roared wordlessly and drew his huge sword. He darted forward and stood over her. There was no escape. He lifted the sword, but then lowered it, the expression on his face softening. 'You killed me. I guess I—' He fell over sideways, lifeless.

Liv stood and walked past his corpse. Walked out onto the cliff. She glanced at the drop. It should have terrified her, but she was numb. She looked up to the superviolet seed crystal, twinkling in the air. It floated at the nexus of a thousand streams of superviolet light, some of it spontaneously shimmering into luxin in the presence of the crystal, lifting it. The crystal tumbled end over end, and each time it did, it sent a little flash of purple light in the visible spectrum.

It called directly to Liv's heart. Here is calm, here is reason, here is power, here is fearlessness. The seed crystal called to Liv, and Liv raised her hand and called to it.

And it came to her.

Chapter 86

Karris ran down the broad steps of the hippodrome's tiered seating, not even trying to be ladylike.

With the broadness of the steps, she couldn't take her eyes off her footing to see if Gavin still lived. But the audience still seemed transfixed, so she guessed he must. Maybe it was only torture.

As she descended, the crowds got thicker, until she had to push through a mass of people standing at the chest-high fence that ringed the track. The track itself was fifteen feet below them. With her dress, Karris had to push through the crowd instead of dodging through it. But she wouldn't be denied.

A man took umbrage at her shoving. He said, 'Who the hell do you think you—'

Sometimes being short was a blessing. She swung a hand up between his legs, grabbed a fistful of cloth and his stones, and twisted, hard. He dropped, and she snatched his ghotra off his head as he fell.

From the spina, she heard a man's screams. She recognized the voice. No, no, no.

She unwrapped the ghotra as she moved. Reaching the front, she vaulted over the worn stone handrail. She threw the ghotra into a knot around the rail and jumped, sliding down it until she ran out of cloth.

She dropped daintily onto the sand of the hippodrome floor and ran out onto the dirt racetrack before anyone could stop her.

There was a murmur from the half of the hippodrome that saw her immediately. What was a noblewoman doing running out onto the track?

But the people on top of the spina – drafters and what looked like a chirurgeon – didn't see her immediately. They were looking at Gavin, bound to a table. He was screaming, throwing himself against his bonds, obviously in agony, but he couldn't move. The chirurgeon was lifting a red-hot poker in gloved hands. Karris had never seen him in such pain. Gavin, admitting weakness, admitting pain? Gavin?!

They were blinding him. Dear Orholam, they'd already burned out one eye.

The soldiers standing around the spina saw her. These were the Nuqaba's elite drafter soldiers, the Tafok Amagez. Bad luck. But then, Ironfist had once said that Karris was the fastest drafter that he'd ever seen, and Ironfist didn't flatter. Karris's white skin was a disadvantage in full battle. There was no way to draft vast amounts of luxin without it showing in her arms.

But she'd learned a thing or two. There are advantages to apparent disadvantages.

The hot poker descended toward Gavin's face.

Green luxin uncurled down the underside of Karris's arm to make a ball that fit nicely in her fist. Her feet danced through a progression, positions on a clock, hips twisting like throwing a javelin, loading tension and snapping forward to impart it all into a projectile. It was faster than the Tafok Amagez could react. The green ball flew at the chirurgeon's head. Connected.

She spun away hard enough that when she dropped the burning poker it didn't fall on Gavin's face.

Karris turned her odd steps into an awkward swaying dance, desperately trying to clear her skin of any hint of green luxin. The projectile had been small enough and so fast as to be invisible. That, together with the sight of Karris moving strangely, might leave the crowd simply baffled. More importantly, it might leave the Nuqaba baffled.

Play it to the hilt, Karris. Pretend you've got the confidence of Gavin.

She raised a hand, her index finger up. 'Pardon me!' she shouted.

As she stepped forward, she remembered to alter her steps to a lady's. Her sidesteps had triggered Ben-hadad's other contraption. As subtly as she could after having just demanded the attention of fifty thousand people, she reached a hand down to the ridiculous huge bow and pressed it firmly to her hip once more. It clicked. Wait, had she landed on that hip? Had she destroyed the mechanism?

No, she'd landed on the other hip. Right?

She raised her other hand at the same time she checked the bow. 'Pardon me?' she shouted again. She smiled, as if she were asking a man to come to her bed.

Which confused the hell out of them, as intended.

There was brief chaos on the platform on the spina. The chirurgeon was on her knees, in serious pain, but she wasn't saying anything. An Amagez tried to pick up the poker. He was smart enough not to grab the glowing end, but not smart enough to realize iron didn't need to be glowing in order to be hot.

He threw the hot iron away, cursing loudly, adding to the chaos.

Karris made it to the steps before the Amagez tried to intercept her. She ignored them, jutting her chin high and dismissive – and made it to the top before they brandished muskets and luxin to show her they were serious. Amateurs.

She stopped, now in full view of everyone in the hippodrome, as if shocked and put out that soldiers would threaten her. A young one stepped forward and started searching her.

Moment of truth. Big stage, big body language to let everyone see it.

He had to push hard against the many petticoats to try to feel the inside of her legs. For a moment, she let him search as if stunned and violated. But she had to let him search enough that he could be convinced to stop.

She stepped back, as if horribly insulted, flinging her arms wide. In her loudest battlefield voice, she projected, 'Pardon you, sirrah! I no more have a weapon between my legs than you do!'

And she slapped him. Not hard, not with the correct body mechanics to put the poor fool on the ground, but sloppily, tossing her hair like a dimwit.

The audience roared with laughter, still wondering what the hell was happening. Was this part of a show?

She held up her hand again, turning to face the Nuqaba's box. She was sitting right at the front, beside Eirene Malargos.

The young guard moved toward Karris again, chagrined, but she boomed out, 'Your Excellency!' toward the Nuqaba. 'Move aside, young man,' she said in a withering whisper. 'Your betters are speaking.'

It was enough to freeze the young Tafok Amagez. Accustomed to taking nonsense orders from an imperious woman who demanded his obedience without question, he felt suddenly bereft of authority.

This is how tyrants fall. By destroying their people, they destroy themselves.

Blackguards knew exactly what they were entitled to do, and they were authorized to do it to whomever entered their sphere. A lord might complain, but not even a luxlord would go without being searched in an area where weapons were forbidden. No Prism or White or Black would ever reprimand a Blackguard for doing his duties thoroughly. The Nuqaba was clearly not so rational.

She stood in her box, and motioned to the young Amagez to move back.

'Who are you?' the Nuqaba demanded. 'What is this?'

'This man,' Karris projected, so that not only the Nuqaba, who was near enough to easily hear, but all the hippodrome could hear as well. 'Is my husband.' Karris turned, to shout it the other direction. 'This man is my husband!'

What she hadn't planned was to see him as she turned. He was strapped down so he couldn't turn his head. But he heard her. 'Karris?' he shouted. 'Dear Orholam, Karris, get out of here!'

His left side was to her, and blood trickled out of his eye, down his cheek, a stream of red tears from a wound that hadn't been fully cauterized.

Her stomach caught and she tried to stifle a sob. She hunched over, but set her jaw. Weeping and running to him would mean death for both of them.

Put it aside, Karris.

'Your Excellency!' Karris snarled, whipping around to face the foul bitch who'd done this to Gavin. Her fear was gone, and her rage wasn't red. 'I declare my husband innocent of any wrong. By your own old traditions, I demand trial by combat!'

'I demand trial by combat,' she announced to the other half of the stadium. If only she had an orator's voice that could be heard over fifty thousand murmuring souls. But most orators couldn't pull off this dress, either.

She turned to the Nuqaba and lowered her voice, trying to project just enough for the woman and those privileged few in the front row to hear. 'Or I tell everyone here our surname and rally those who are not traitors.'

The Nuqaba's face gathered a storm. Eirene Malargos interjected some question. A quick volley of questions and responses between them, impossible to hear. Both angry. Both insistent.

There was no ancient Parian tradition of trial by combat. It was pure horse shit.

But the fifty thousand bloodthirsty Ruthgari spectators in the hippodrome didn't know that. And they loved the idea. Chariot races could be bloody – crashes frequent, injuries common – but true blood sports had been banned and reinstated, banned and reinstated repeatedly for the last four hundred years. They had been illegal for the last ninety or more. A licit taste of an illicit activity? A taste of a vice that the audience could blame on Parian barbarity rather than their own? It was irresistible.

But that pressure wasn't enough. The Nuqaba didn't mind angering fifty thousand of some other satrapy's people. But the pressure wasn't the bait.

Karris looked closely as the Nuqaba and Eirene Malargos bickered. She could lip-read 'wife,' and multiple curses. The Nuqaba nodded her head and said some words to a handsome, muscular Parian man who was still seated next to her. Then she stepped forward and raised her hands. Eirene put a hand on her arm, but the Nuqaba shook her off, giving her a poisonous glance. Eirene surrendered, trying not to make a scene, but clearly furious.

When Marissia had pitched the idea to Karris, she'd said, 'I've studied Haruru for fifteen years. She's hateful, petty, jealous, and vindictive – and she was involved with Gavin once. If she can do anything to hurt him, she will.'

And now we find out just how competent Marissia really is.

And then a sick thought punched Karris in the stomach: It's not as if Marissia has an incentive to send me to my death.

Sudden fear shivered down Karris's back.

Her rival.

Oh, Orholam, what have I done? I thought I'd finally won her over. I thought we shared a love for Gavin that trumped the rest. I thought she was working with me. I've taken everything from her, and this is her one chance to reclaim her work, if not her man, whom she knew was lost to her forever.

This is what you get for trusting a slave.

It had been a colossal blunder. The kind Karris never would have missed if she hadn't been so pressed for time. How long had Marissia sat on that information, in order to make sure

Karris *was* pressed for time? Marissia could have known about Gavin's imprisonment for weeks, and held it back just so Karris would rush off and get herself killed. Even the trial by combat had been Marissia's idea.

But the White trusts her. And she loves Gavin. She wouldn't hold back information when he was in danger, would she?

But Gavin had pushed her aside without a thought when he'd married Karris. How would Karris react if a man had done that to her?

Orholam have mercy.

The crowd quieted, and Karris waited for the word. She would be dragged off as a co-conspirator. Alone, with no one to speak for her, all that needed to happen was for the Nuqaba to say that Karris was a madwoman, and that a trial by combat was never part of Parian history. There would be those in this vast crowd who knew that was true.

It was all falling apart.

'It has been many, many years since the trial by combat has been requested,' the Nuqaba said. And Karris's heart soared. She had a chance. 'As set down in our ancient laws, the trial by combat can only be requested once, and must be fulfilled by the one who asked for it. No champions!'

Bait swallowed.

Before the crowd could shout, enthralled by the idea of some insubstantial little girl in a dress fighting in a trial by combat herself, the Nuqaba continued. 'There is no drafting allowed in trials by combat, and the trial is to the death!'

Now the crowd roared.

So Marissia didn't betray me.

But this was almost worse. All Karris's preparations to hide her drafting abilities were for nothing. Either the Nuqaba or Eirene Malargos had known who Karris was and that she could draft. The Nuqaba was vicious, but she wasn't stupid.

Shit.

The Nuqaba quieted the crowd again, and gestured to the man who'd been sitting to her left. As he stood, the Nuqaba said, 'Do you, O common woman, wish to face the hand of our justice, the Lord Commandant of the Armies of Paria, Enki Hammer?'

On his cue, the man, clearly the Nuqaba's consort, came forward out from under their shade to stand full in the noon sun. He was tall, very tall, with slim hips and shoulders but the reedy forearms that told a warrior like Karris that under his rich Parian cloak – his *burnous* – and his gold-brocaded tunic that he was a soldier. He wore the ghotra, too, to cover his head, but there was nothing of pious humility in him. Even his ghotra was woven through with gold.

He shrugged off the white-and-black-striped burnous and pulled the laces of his tunic open, dropping it to reveal impressive musculature. Karris wanted to hate him for his vanity, but she dabbled in vanity more than her fair share.

Odd, she thought. That would have made me hate him twice as much not too long ago.

Oh, she was supposed to respond. Something gutsy but that didn't hint to the crowd that she was a fighter. 'I would rather die,' she shouted, 'than let you hurt my husband any more.'

The crowd cheered. The Nuqaba tried to whisper something to Enki, but he shook his head. She tried again, but the crowd was too loud, too impatient. He waved her off. Later.

As Enki jogged down the steps and across the sand toward the spina, looking vexed, the Nuqaba waited for the cheer to die and then shouted, 'Then may your blood be on your own head!'

There was confusion on the spina as the soldiers tried to figure out what precisely they were supposed to do during a trial the likes of which they'd never heard of, much less trained for, all while under the watching eyes of fifty thousand people. The professional in Karris had some pity on them, but she said nothing. Any hint she gave that she knew exactly what she was doing could get her killed. This is why you strike fast – some part of the enemy force may have intelligence that will destroy you, but if they can't communicate it in time, it doesn't matter.

She bent her head and wiped at her cheeks defiantly, as if she were weeping uncontrollably but was angry about it. A fool wisp of a girl in a ridiculous dress, that's what she was, not at all a Blackguard.

She wanted to look at Gavin. She wanted to go to him. But she'd lose herself if she did.

Finally, on quick orders from Enki himself, the Tafok Amagez set up a perimeter around the spina as he mounted the steps. An Amagez broke ranks and came forward for the offering of weapons. He was probably thirty-five years old, ancient for a warrior-drafter. He lifted his scabbarded longsword from his belt and offered it to Karris. Another Amagez joined him a moment later and offered a stabbing spear. Then another, with a scorpion. Enki himself wore a long, thin-bladed scimitar, scabbard and hilt encrusted with mother-of-pearl and rubies.

Karris looked at the weapons, and shook her head and waved her hand in denial, still making the motions large enough that they could be interpreted even by the farmers in the highest seats. 'Oh, no, I shan't need anything there, I think. But thank you.'

She glanced at Gavin as murmurs rippled through the crowd again. No weapons? What insanity was this? Was she simply committing suicide?

Gavin was still twitching, still obviously in great pain, but he said nothing, didn't cry out in his agony, didn't call out to Karris. He couldn't see what was happening, and the not knowing would be driving him insane, but he held his silence. She knew at once it was because he trusted her. He knew she had a plan, and he knew it was desperate, and he wasn't going to distract her from it.

For a man who'd been in control of everything, and been the driver of change in most of the great moments in the Seven Satrapies for the last two decades, to trust her that much moved her beyond words.

No time for that, dammit! She scrubbed a tear from her eye, a real one.

Unwilling to let her dominate the crowd's eyes, Enki had stepped forward and raised both hands to heaven. 'Orholam!' he cried. 'Look upon the works of our hands! May your justice be done to traitors!'

He lowered his hands, and then took off his ghotra, as if this were connected to drawing Orholam's attention. His black hair was woven with gold wire into clumps that hung past his shoulders. In Parian tradition, that hair was his glory, and he gloried in it.

The gesture wasn't lost on the Ruthgari, who didn't wear the ghotra, but were well aware of their neighbors' beliefs about it. Nor were they immune to appreciating a handsome, athletic man who was six and a half feet tall.

He was like a smaller, vain version of Ironfist. Which was a bit disturbing, when Karris thought about it. Who picked a lover who looked so much like her own brother?

Karris walked up beside Enki and stood facing the Nuqaba's box, waiting for him.

A flicker of doubt crossed his face. Karris was acting with such conviction that she could tell the big ignoramus thought that maybe these trials really were a tradition. He stood beside her, but not too close.

Around the spina in a circle, the Tafok Amagez drew in their colors. Any drafting would mean death.

Karris curtsied carefully to the Nuqaba and a steely-eyed Eirene Malargos. Beside her, Enki bowed deeply.

The crowd fell silent.

The Nuqaba waved a hand, signaling they could begin, but Karris ignored it. She turned to Enki and curtsied, more elaborately, an old court curtsy, with sweeping arms bringing her skirts wide, and her ankles crossed. Enki bowed to her, but carefully, keeping his eyes on her.

And . . . nothing happened.

Ben-hadad! It wasn't supposed to be like this!

Enki lifted his sword and readied himself, while Karris stood on one foot, her right ankle pushing against her left calf.

'One moment,' Karris said. She held a finger up. 'I have an itch.' She moved her right foot up and down her calf.

Enki looked at her, incredulous. Was she mad? And then he laughed.

And it was as if Ben-hadad had made the catch to be activated by laughter instead of by crossing her ankles, as they'd discussed. Karris felt the catch give and the big ridiculous ribbon on her right hip popped out and the luxin holding together layers of skirt and petticoats let go, swinging open like a door over her thigh, giving Karris access to the quick-release scabbard that covered the length of the inside of her thigh.

At the same time the skirts popped open, the scabbard

684

swiveled from the inner thigh where it had been hidden during her search to her outer thigh and hand.

Most scabbards required a blade to be stabbed into them, and likewise, drawn vertically out before it could be used: they took two motions. This was a tension scabbard, holding the blade in a hug instead, letting the blade come out horizontally, so that one could draw as one slashed.

It was only a fraction of a heartbeat faster than a normal draw, but a fraction was all Karris needed. She sprang forward in the moment Enki's eyes crinkled with laughter. Onetwothree steps, the back of her left hand batting his sword aside—

And she buried the blade under his chin at the very instant he realized she'd moved. She rammed it all the way to the hilt, its point jutting out, gleaming red above his glorious braids. She twisted the blade hard, breaking bones in his brainpan, taking no chances. A man could still kill you before he realized he was dead.

And then she jumped back, out of reach, pulling the dagger free.

Enki dropped to his knee, dropped flat on his face. Someone in the circle of Tafok Amagez shouted, but Karris barely heard it.

She stepped forward again, now that she saw he wouldn't attack, and knelt at his body. She pulled back his braids and took the scimitar from his twitching fingers. Taking a fistful of braids, she stood, lifting the body to put pressure on the neck, and hacked with the dead man's own scimitar. Once, and then twice, and a bit of quick sawing for the last of the skin, and Enki's head came free of his body.

Karris held the head high in one hand and the scimitar high in the other, and suddenly, she could hear the crowd again, a vast roar of confusion and horror and awe and disbelief and cheering all intermixed. 'Orholam has seen! Orholam's justice has been done!' she shouted. But her voice was probably lost in the roar.

'I am Karris Guile, and this man is Gavin Guile, your Prism. He is Gavin Guile!' She was shouting at the top of her lungs, but it was lost in the clamor of fifty thousand voices. Only the nearest could hear. She could only hope it was enough.

She switched hands and swung the head back and forth as she drafted off the banners nearby. She flung the head and gave it a little extra push with luxin as she threw it.

Karris couldn't have made the shot so perfectly if she'd tried it a hundred times. The head flew all the way into Eirene Malargos's box and landed in the Nuqaba's lap.

The Nuqaba began shrieking, and Orholam forgive them, many in the audience laughed.

Karris didn't care. She moved to Gavin quickly and cut him free as the Tafok Amagez stood around, baffled.

Oh, Orholam. Gavin's face. His face!

'Gavin,' she said, 'we have to run. Can you—'

'I won't let you down,' he said, but when he stood, he almost collapsed. He put his left hand up to his face, and two of his fingers were gone. Those fucking animals.

But what mattered now was that Gavin was in no shape to fight.

Karris steadied him. Around her, the Tafok Amagez looked uncertain as to what they should be doing. She had won a trial that their Nuqaba had established, so they should let her go, but then, she'd also thrown the head of one of their leaders into the Nuqaba's lap, so, should they arrest her? Could they, after what she'd just done?

There was no point in waiting to find out what they decided.

But just then, one of the hippodrome guards ran to the steps of the spina. 'It is Gavin Guile!' he shouted. 'I recognize him from the old days! They dyed his hair and dirtied his face, but he is Gavin Guile!'

Karris veritably pulled Gavin down the steps, and the soldier fell in with them, desperately signaling to other Guile family troops to join them.

'Kill them!' the Nuqaba shrieked suddenly. 'Kill them both!' Karris shot a look over at her. She was covered with blood. More blood than you'd think would leak out of a man's severed head. She'd smeared it somehow on her face.

'No! Ignore that order!' Eirene Malargos shouted. 'You're not in your right mind, Haruru!'

'Kill them!' the Nuqaba shouted. 'Block the exits! That's an order!'

'That's an act of war! I forbid it!' Eirene Malargos shouted.

Chaos.

'This way!' the Guile soldier said.

He unlocked a door set at the level of the sand. They stepped through and he closed it behind them, locking it.

'Captain Eutheos, you son of a bitch,' Gavin said. 'I thought I ordered you out of here.'

'Wasn't much good at orders at Blood Ridge either, my lord.'

Gavin laughed briefly at some shared memory, then cut off abruptly, as if anything that made his face move spawned such pain that it nearly felled him.

'I can get us to an exit, but they'll get there faster,' the soldier said.

'There has to be some kind of service exit,' Karris said.

'First thing they'll think of,' Gavin said. And he was right. Dammit.

'Can you get us to the top tier, west side?' Karris asked.

'Absolutely.'

And he did. They dodged through corridors where only servants and slaves went, and crossed halls clogged with spectators eager to get out – the sight of men drawing swords and pistols and drafting and ready to kill anyone who opposed them did crazy things to people. Other people, who'd been outside the hippodrome and heard that amazing things were happening within were pushing to get in, creating vast snarls. One musket shot and this was going to turn into a stampede.

The Guile soldiers manning the exits were shouting, trying to bring order, but they were confused themselves. Were the Tafok Amagez now the enemy? Or were they still friends who should be helped? What had happened inside?

Gavin collapsed several times, apologizing each time. Karris and Eutheos ended up each taking a shoulder – another thing that being short made her ill-suited for. He was shockingly light.

But in minutes they made it to the arch where Karris had entered. She poked her head out over the drop.

Oh my.

But there was Ironfist. At the sight of her, he grinned big.

When Gavin poked his own head out, Ironfist's grin slipped.

Gavin's eye was still bleeding. But Gavin smiled, delighted to see the big man.

'Are you going to make your own way down, Lord Prism?' Ironfist asked.

Gavin jerked back and turned. 'Company coming,' he said.

Karris saw five Tafok Amagez running up the stairs she'd run down not fifteen minutes ago. These upper decks had cleared out. They definitely saw them.

'Afraid not,' Gavin said, quickly poking his head back out. 'What's the plan? Quickly.' He looked out at the river. It was a long way away, and a long way down. 'Oh no, tell me that's not the plan.'

'That's it,' Karris said. 'Captain, thank you. Now get the hell out of here. Five count, Gavin. Commander, I'll come five after Gavin.'

Gavin had already backed up. He wobbled, but gathered himself. Eutheos steadied him. 'Go, Captain, and bless you.'

Karris stood at the edge so both of them could see her. 'One, two, three, four, five.' And Gavin leapt, right in front of her.

She didn't watch. Couldn't and make it to her spot in time. The Tafok Amagez were charging up the stairs. Oh damn, a five count was too much. By four she'd be dead.

She ran for the edge as metal cut the air. 'Five, five, five!' she shouted. And dove into the air.

For a sickening heartbeat, she fell. She kept her body rigid, no time for a prayer or a curse.

And a soft cloud of Ironfist's open luxin caught her for half a moment, and then flung her hard.

The timing was off, and the throw was less than perfect: instead of catching her at her chest and hips and throwing evenly, it was a little behind her. Being flung from that position spun her, hips over head, flipping. She would land flat on her back in the river.

From this height, it would break her.

Karris twisted hard. First lesson of fighting, how to fall.

But she had also turned sideways – and her feet hit the water first, before she was ready, and suddenly – black.

The next she was aware, she was underwater in billows of clinging skirts with no idea which way was up, and no breath.

She flailed, and the last of her breath escaped with the wave of pain that crashed over her. Her left arm felt like someone had tried to tear it off, and her ribs and left breast had been crushed.

An unnatural hand – more hook than hand – grabbed her many petticoats and dragged her, upside down, to the surface. It shot water up her nose, and as she hit the blessed air, she coughed and spat and fought to push the blinding, suffocating layers of cloth away.

Ben-hadad dropped the open green luxin claw he'd used to grab her and extended a hand. Karris made the mistake of offering her left hand, and regretted it immediately when he hauled her up. Pain took what little breath she had.

'Ben!' Essel shouted. 'Need you! Need you now!' She was standing over Gavin, who had also been pulled out of the water. He was wet and whimpering and holding a hand to his bleeding eye. He would be no help.

The sparse crowd that had already filled the market when they arrived was now a thick crowd with the events inside the hippodrome and the sudden spectacle of the insane people jumping all the way from the hippodrome into the river. Soldiers were trying to fight their way through to get to the river's edge where the skimmer was docked.

Karris couldn't see whose soldiers they were, just the fighting in the seething crowd, and the bobbing points of muskets.

She fought to stand, and saw Hezik break through the crowd and run for the stairs. He jumped halfway down the first flight. 'Ironfist says go! Go!' Hezik shouted.

A musket shot rang out. Flesh and blood and cloth puffed from Hezik's left arm. He was already running down the second flight of steps and it threw him off balance. He tumbled, rolled down the remaining steps.

The crowd bolted, and despite the clear visual marker of a big black cloud of smoke from the musket, people who've never been in combat do the craziest things. They went all directions at once. Some were pushed off the wall to fall onto the docks, shrieking, screaming, breaking legs and backs and necks, grabbing on to those who pushed them to try to save themselves.

Others pushed toward the soldiers, who turned their muskets and started beating anyone close with the stocks. One must have had his musket grabbed by someone in the crowd, because it discharged into the air.

Karris fought to her feet. 'Ignition!' she shouted at Benhadad, who looked paralyzed.

'What? I, I don't – I don't draft—'

The red lens had popped out of her eye somewhere. She tore into his pack. Found the flint and steel and her red spectacles, the pain in her arm making black spots dance in her vision. Pulled the spectacles out and put them on, and filled her left hand with red luxin.

She turned her eyes in time to see Hezik stand with effort – it looked like one of the falling men had hit him. A soldier with a musket stepped to the edge of the wall, and fired.

Hezik dropped, a splash of red jumping into the air from his head.

'No!' Karris shouted. Drafting red for the first time in six months, she reacted instead of thinking. Like the old Karris, like she hadn't learned anything. With enough red feeding constantly into her left hand to keep a fire constantly burning low, she made a red luxin ball in her right, and hurled it through the fire at the satisfied young soldier. It hit high on his chest, in his beard, and splashed over him, liquid red luxin drenching him for one heartbeat, then flames roaring over him the next.

Screaming, he turned to his fellows. Panicked, one of them lashed out with the already raised butt of his musket. The man on fire plunged off the wall, where he almost landed on a child.

'We've orders to go!' Essel said. She threw a line from the cleat back onto the dock and pushed off.

'We wait!' Karris said. 'Out of my line!'

She braced her feet and brought the flaming luxin in her left hand up as if she were sighting down a musket.

'Kill them!' a familiar voice shouted. Orholam damn her, it was the Nuqaba herself.

Karris shot a thin, continuous ribbon of red luxin through the air. It ignited in a huge fan. She dragged it back and forth in front of the wall and the soldiers there. All the luxin burned away before it hit the men standing there, but a roiling wall of flame wasn't something anyone wanted to approach. The heat itself would be a slap in their faces.

'She can't throw it far enough to hit you!' the Nuqaba shouted as soon as Karris let the first wash of flames die.

Fool doesn't know the difference between mercy and a lack of will.

But the truth was, Karris killing one soldier could be overlooked, called an accident. Killing a dozen was a diplomatic incident, war. War in the middle of war. Against Paria, their ally; Paria, which the Chromeria needed.

But they needed Gavin more.

Karris stopped, indecisive for the first time.

'The commander said to go!' Essel shouted. 'We don't even know if he's leaving this way!'

'Get on the reeds, and turn us,' Karris ordered Essel and Ben-hadad, 'but wait for my word. I'll defend. We wait for Ironfist!'

Then a fireball arced through the air toward the skimmer and plopped into the water with a hiss and a kick of steam. Drafters. The Nuqaba's Amagez drafters were on their way through the crowd.

One arm near useless, drafters and soldiers closing in, muskets being fired at them, and all Karris could think was that her real problem was that she was no longer a watch captain of the Blackguard and therefore was in no position to give orders at all, and that as soon as Essel realized it, the woman would take charge.

Karris threw another narrow stream of flame, hard. It was difficult to gauge the force needed as the distance changed, but luck smiled on her. Most of the red burned off in the air in a frightening display, but some little hit the massed musketeers across their muskets and chests.

The screams were immediate, but they were screams of surprise and fear, not of agony. With most of the flammability of the red exhausted, the men weren't consumed. Hands were burnt, muskets thrown away, tunics hurriedly stripped off, men fell over each other as even those in the second and third rows threw themselves backward, away from the billows of flame.

'We have to go, now!' Essel said.

Karris hesitated again.

'He's coming,' Gavin mumbled, from the deck where he was lying. He sounded delirious. 'Don't you see him? His angel's fighting through the crowd.'

Essel said, 'He's not in his right mind. Karris, we have to—'

'We stay!' Karris snarled, but even as the words crossed her lips, she knew they had more to do with the red she was still drafting to keep the flame alive in her left hand, and the green she was drawing in that refused to be told what to do, and her own fear at what she'd seen in Gavin's good eye.

His blue, unprismatic eye.

Before the smoke cleared in the gap where the musketeers had been, Karris saw a glow like a torch, lighting the dissipating smoke from within. An instant later, four of the Nuqaba's Tafok Amagez appeared. Warrior-drafters. One had hands encased in red luxin, already aflame. He threw fireballs, right and left.

The right-hand shot was wide. A lefty then, or a feint. It gave Karris time to hurl a green projectile out to intercept the other fireball, batting it aside.

'Go, go, go!' Karris shouted. It was one thing to wait for Ironfist; it was another to commit suicide.

Three of the four Tafok Amagez attacked, throwing blue missiles that exploded in shrapnel, and green spears, and red fire. The fourth tried to fire a long musket, but it misfired and he was working to clear it. The Tafok Amagez were brute force drafters: if something didn't yield when they hit it, they hit it harder.

Unable to use their physical strength against her except to throw their luxin really hard and fast, and unable to use their numbers to surround her, they kept doing more of the same. But Karris didn't merely have to protect herself, she had to protect everyone on the skimmer and the skimmer itself. With a weak left arm.

She dodged through the lux forms – the modified martial arts moves that compensated for the balance shifts of throwing the weight of luxin – always giving herself an anchor to throw shields left and projectiles right and absorb and divert.

Not having used luxin for so long gave her an unusual edge. Like drinking several cups of kopi when you haven't had any for a while, the luxin hit her hard. The wild energy of green roared past her injury, and the heat of red burned out the voice of her pain. But her long experience took that energy and passion, and made it a blade.

She was fast, faster than she'd ever been. She was instinctive, shooting missiles out of the air with missiles of her own, impossible shots, impossible speeds. Left left left – as they realized her weakness – and right and high, and diverting a huge curtain of flame that the red tried to drop on them from above.

It was only seconds, but the fury of the attacks made it seem an eternity. Essel and Ben-hadad were throwing luxin down the reeds, but the skimmer's inertia was significant: its own weight, and the weight of four people on its decks, and neither Essel or Ben-hadad were particularly strong, physically or as drafters.

All it would take was one slip.

More Tafok Amagez joined the first ones, pausing only a moment to see what was happening. Half a dozen more.

Too many, and the skimmer was still too close.

And then the fourth stood, his musket cleared and reloaded. Karris saw him, and dread filled her. A premonition that cut off air like drinking tar.

She couldn't counterattack: the missiles and fire were coming in too thick. He leveled the musket, took aim.

But Karris heard a familiar roar, a man bellowing.

A blue wedge, a V of shields as tall as a man, appeared behind the four Tafok Amagez. They didn't even see it coming. And then a huge figure appeared, holding that V like a battering ram, running full speed. The wedge split as Ironfist rammed through the Tafok Amagez.

Sweeping his massive arms wide, bellowing that legendary shout that had melted the knees of enemies throughout the Seven Satrapies, holding the blue luxin shields to either side as he came through the middle of a dozen Tafok Amagez, Ironfist leapt off the wall, blasting the shields out into the Amagez and back, sending him flying with incredible speed.

He flipped in the air, and it looked for a moment like he was going to make it all the way to the water, but instead he dropped from that great height onto the end of the dock. Ironfist threw a gush of unfocused blue down as he landed, but the shock was still enough to stagger him and splinter wood.

His tunic had been torn half off, and blood was streaming from a cut on the side of his head, but he gathered himself and refilled with blue.

Karris had seen Ironfist run across the waves before. He drafted a narrow platform of blue, half floating on the water. He could make it fifty feet or more, and the skimmer wasn't that far out yet. Her heart soared.

The Tafok Amagez were in chaos behind him. Several had been pushed off the wall. But as Ironfist drafted, his chest heaving from the exertion of Orholam-knew-what fighting he'd done to get through the crowd, Karris saw the Amagez with the long musket. He'd been at the far end, and he recovered first, lifting the musket with an ease and precision that told Karris this would be an easy shot for him.

He was too far away for Karris to hit with a drafted projectile. Karris was fast. Karris was accurate. But she wasn't that fast or that accurate. She heard the shot, saw the sudden jerk and the smoke blossom from his musket – but he'd twitched off-aim at the last moment.

Karris realized that the musket she'd heard was behind her. Almost beneath her. The young marksman on the wall dropped his musket and tumbled down to the dock, dead.

And then the skimmer was picking up speed and Ironfist leapt aboard, and in less than a minute they were safely skimming down to the river, outrunning any order that could arrive to tell anyone to stop them.

Karris looked at Gavin, lying bloody on the deck, still holding the smoking musket he'd fired to save Ironfist's life.

Gavin was grinning fiercely. Blood from his ruined left eye had trickled into his mouth, and it painted his teeth red. 'Not quite useless. Not yet,' he said.

Then he passed out.

Chapter 87

A knock, and a familiar woman's voice: 'Kip?'

Kip didn't know how long he stood in the darkness of his room. Did time even have meaning anymore? He thought perhaps that the darkness would bring back the black luxin card. He hadn't seen the entirety of it.

But it didn't come back. And he knew no way to call it forth consciously. There were so many things that he needed to think about and decide right now, this instant, immediately, that he was paralyzed. He couldn't think about anything. His life was about to turn irrevocably, and he wanted to look at some card?

Granted, if he was right, and viewing – or living or remembering or whatever the hell it was that he did with the cards – was nearly instantaneous, then theoretically, he could live as many of them as he wanted, and not lose any time. But somehow he was pretty certain it didn't work that way. If he could even figure out how to call one up, he felt like it might roast that tiny, underused pea between his ears.

The thought only served to remind him of his headache.

A knock on the door. Again. Wait, this was the second knock, wasn't it?

He hit the light control, and his knees almost buckled as the light seared his eyes, burned like rock salt stomped into his open wound of a brain. He leaned against the doorframe, gasping, and opened the door.

'Kip? Are you all right?'

Oh hells. It wasn't Teia. Why had he thought it was Teia?

Because Teia's the only girl who ever talks to you on purpose.

It was Tisis. 'Are you hungover?' Tisis asked.

I'm a giant, wakened from my bed by assassins. With a roar, I grab the man leaning over my bed and ram him so hard into the marble wall that his skull shatters, blood spraying. Sharp steel parts the muscles of my leg, deep, hot. I jump out of bed, but my head is aflame with a hangover, black spots dancing in front of my eyes.

There are four of them left, grubby, not professionals. The nearest stabs – deflected, albeit with blood. Armlock, his arm dislocated, fist up to his face so hard bones crack – dammit, both his face and my knuckles fracture. I know better!

I bellow, and see the fear go through the other—

'No,' Kip said. 'Bit, uhm, lightsick.'

Her face softened. 'Takes a while to get used to drafting, huh? So easy to do too much at first. I got lightsick a few times myself, early on.' And despite the worry that perched on her shoulders like a cougar bearing down on its prey, she grinned. 'Well, maybe more than a few times. Green, you know.'

She's beautiful.

And I can have sex with her. As much as I want. Well, as much as she'll allow. Which may not actually be that much, now that I think of it, but surely it would be more than zero times. Have to consummate the marriage at least.

Andross Guile had been wrong. If there was anything wrong with Kip's libido, it was that he had too much. He just didn't think satisfying it was a possibility anytime soon. It was a 'someday, who knows when, don't think about it, you'll just get more depressed than you already usually are.'

But as bad as he wanted it, he didn't want it to be *bad*. Forcing it from Teia back when she was a slave would have been wrong.

Not that forcing it from her *now* would be good – ugh, his brain was only working for one purpose now and that seemed to be to hurt as much as possible.

What if he went to bed with Tisis and when he took off his clothes, he disgusted her? What if she saw his fattiness and despised him? How could someone so beautiful, someone who could do so much better, bear to be with him?

Ah, so you're not chaste. You're just afraid.

'Kip, I know I said you had a week to decide about . . . you know, my proposal. That didn't really happen how I'd ever imagined it, by the way, and I certainly – anyway. I know I said you had a week, but I need your answer sooner.'

'Sooner?'

'As in, now.' She winced apologetically. 'I have to leave the Jaspers. I'm going to walk to the docks as soon as I leave you.'

'You don't have any stuff. Clothes. I don't know. Jewels, cosmetics? Whatever it is you have.' Kip felt stupider the more he said.

'My slaves have already smuggled it out to the ship. I'm technically the Chromeria's hostage, so I'm forbidden to leave without permission. I can't carry anything on me lest your grandfather's spies figure out that I'm leaving.'

'Oh.' Obviously, a little late for that. Andross knew everything. He always knew everything. Damn him. Damn him to a thousand pits of fire.

Fire. Fire engulfs the woman, her skin curling, blood hissing as it boils—

Breathe. Breathe. Back in the now, stay here, Kip.

And Kip still hadn't decided what to do. He should have been weighing the pros and cons in the last few days, when he might have had a chance to think without the total distraction of a beautiful woman standing right in front of him.

Kip the Lip. Use it to your advantage.

'You know,' Kip said. 'I actually haven't decided. I should have been weighing the pros and cons in the last few days, when I might have had a chance to think without the total distraction of a beautiful woman standing right here in front of me. You're beautiful. You know you have an effect on men. Are you seducing me?'

'Pardon me?' she said, incredulous. 'I mean, thank you, but what are you talking about?'

'Are you trying to seduce me?'

She looked suddenly awkward. 'I thought you weren't interested in women.'

'What?!'

'I asked around while I was procrastinating and trying to figure out how to talk to you, and no one could even remember you expressing interest in a girl. They said you had a room slave that you never bedded, so I thought you either didn't have any interest at all either way or you liked boys. That's why I, um, tried to appeal to your better nature. Believe me, if I'd thought it would be as easy as flashing some cleavage at you, I'd have done it in a second.'

'What? What? What?' Then Kip couldn't help it; he started laughing.

His grandfather had been right – infuriatingly right – about Tisis. And he'd been right for all the wrong reasons. He'd thought she would ask Kip to rescue her because she was subtle; she'd done it because she thought Kip was homosexual.

'I'm so sorry,' Tisis said. 'You mean you're not . . .'

'No,' Kip said, still grinning. 'I mean, I'm not homosexual and not, er, well, I am asexual, I guess, but not by choice. I mean, I'm a virgin, but . . .' He slammed his eyes shut. Had he really just said that out loud? Orholam, let the floor open and swallow me. He opened one eye. Tisis's mouth was hanging open, shocked.

Kip the Lip, use it, turn it out. 'Which is to say, I find you very beautiful, Tisis, and not just in some abstract sense. And my earlier disinterested attraction to you – understandably dampened by the fact I thought you wanted to kill me – is strangely getting more intense and more personal all the time.'

He could tell the convoluted compliment warmed her. She blushed faintly, and looked at him with new eyes.

Before she could speak, Kip said, 'But that attraction – whether it's the simple infatuation of the boy you seem to think I am, or something more robust and worthy of consideration – is not the point. It's moot.'

He could see her digesting that, and he could tell that she was impressed. But her regard was not, now, the kind you'd have when you think a child is being mature for his age. In her eyes little green shoots of respect broke the ground. 'So,' she said, 'if that's not the point, what is?'

'If I do this, I'm crossing my grandfather. He's not just the Red anymore. He's the promachos, and he was scary enough when he was only the Red. He does not forgive insults. I'll need your protection and your sister Eirene's protection, at least for a few years.' It was partly true, but it was mostly a lie, and Kip felt embarrassed at how easily it passed his lips. But she mistook his embarrassment, thinking it was for needing the protection of women. After the time Kip had spent with the White and with Karris, nothing could be further from his mind.

'Kip, your grandfather's not going to come after you during the war. If he did, he'd risk losing not just my family, but all of Ruthgar. And after the war . . . who even can think that far ahead?'

It was true. As a political marriage, the union was actually far better for the Guiles than it was for the Malargos family. Though Tisis felt that her position was tenuous – and Andross had deliberately isolated her so she would feel it more keenly – he needed to know that Ruthgar was firmly on the Chromeria's side. War was here, and the bottomless coffers of the Malargos family would be necessary to fund the fight.

Andross would strengthen his flank and get Kip away from the Chromeria, where he might cause problems. If Kip betrayed him, Andross would still achieve those things. If Kip obeyed him, on the other hand, Andross would put a spy directly into the heart of the Malargos family.

Who could plan for what would happen after the war? Andross Guile.

And what did Kip get for his participation? A wife set to inherit a fortune, a place next to power, and a reputation for defying his grandfather – which would be seen as being incredibly brave when he got away with it. After the war, they could 'reconcile' and all would be well. As far as political marriages went, Kip could do far worse.

In fact, he probably couldn't do better.

With Zymun in play, Kip was expendable.

'What are you thinking there, little storm cloud?' Tisis asked, teasing.

That there's no way out.

But maybe that's the wrong way to think about this. I want to defy my grandfather because he's an asshole, because he's been cruel and insulted me, because he tried to have me killed.

That was before he knew me, though.

He tried to kill Gavin.

No, he tried to get the Knife. Gavin got in the way. As long as you understood that you couldn't oppose him, Andross was remarkably logical.

Andross Guile didn't have friends. He had useful allies, and he had enemies.

Then Kip had an insight into the man, an intuition stark and clear and true. Life was a game of Nine Kings to Andross. He had opponents, and he would do all he could to destroy them. His opponents had cards, and he would destroy or suborn them. But he himself was simply the Master. His own cards were to be preserved while they were of use, but destroyed without thought if that achieved his ends, and pursued with vengeance if they attempted to play against him. It was that cold and that effective. Kip had tried to figure out what the old man wanted. What motivated Andross Guile to work so hard, to plan so deeply? It didn't seem to be money, though he had plenty of that. It didn't seem to be women, though he had room slaves. It didn't seem to be homeland, or Orholam, or even power as others understood it. A man motivated by lust for power would surely want to be seen as the master of others. Andross Guile had simply been one of the Spectrum, for many years.

Perhaps to Andross it was subtler but also simpler: he wanted to win. He didn't care if everyone knew about his winning; those who mattered would know. He didn't care about anyone else: who is flattered by the praise of insects? Becoming an emperor in name was unnecessary. If one can wield imperial power, if one can make one's name synonymous with emperor, was that not the greater achievement?

And when Kip thought of it that way, at least one more fact bared its teeth: Kip's status as an apparent enemy of Andross Guile wouldn't necessarily in the fullness of time be discarded. If, after seven years, Andross had other cards better than Kip to play, he might destroy Kip rather than reward him.

And that is the deal for me. Take it or reject it. Eyes open.

And yet . . . doing what Andross Guile wanted? Everything in Kip rebelled against that.

But whereas Kip might have blithely risked destroying himself in the past, now his actions would affect people he cared about. This wasn't a matter of right and wrong, but of smart and stupid.

There was nothing to gain by defying Andross Guile, and no way to win if Kip did so. Why then was it so hard?

'Just thinking about my grandfather,' Kip said, finally answering Tisis. 'He's not a good man to make an enemy.'

'But he's not a good friend, either, is he?' Tisis asked.

'He doesn't have friends.'

'I know,' she said. 'I've been caught in his schemes twice, and each time, I've come away hating myself almost as much as I hate him.'

'He has that effect,' Kip said. 'But . . . how do I know that putting myself in your sister's hands won't be just as big a mistake? Andross may be here, but so are my friends, what few of them I have, anyway.'

'My sister will know I made the best move in a bad situation – but even if she doesn't, she's my sister. She loves me, and she'd never turn her back on me.'

Must be nice.

Kip had that kind of friendship, with the squad. But it was already slipping away. Whatever he did, they were passing inexorably from his life.

The one good thing I have is fading already.

'Let's do it,' Kip said. He looked at her, looked down at his shoes, looked back up at her. 'Uh, how do we do it?'

'It's too late in the day now. It'll have to be done at dawn. We'll meet a luxiat I know at the little temple across from the Crossroads. You know it?'

'I know the Crossroads. It was the old Tyrean embassy. It'll be enough to find the temple. Wouldn't it make more sense to go now, and have the ship captain marry us?'

'Yes, but no,' she said. 'I need the marriage on the books, official, here, with witnesses, by a luxiat in good standing, otherwise your grandfather might have it annulled.'

'Smart,' Kip said. And it was. Maybe she was smarter than he'd thought.

What a terrible thing to think about your future wife.

She brightened. 'Thank you.'

'It—'

'No, really. Thank you. To have my intelligence praised by a Guile? That's not something we mere mortals often get. I mean, I saw you standing there, thinking, when I asked you that question. You were probably seven forks down a winding road in your mind, weren't you?'

'Uh. Yes?' Kip asked. He wasn't sure why it came out as a question. Probably because he was receiving the admiration of a woman. Not used to that. Wow, she was pretty.

Tisis said, 'I've spent weeks thinking about all this – and trying not to think about it – and I tell you, and you figure it out in minutes. It'd be vexing if it weren't so impressive. And not only impressive. It's almost as attractive as these are.' She stepped forward and reached out to lay gentle hands on each of his shoulders. 'Can I say that? Or do you think me too forward?'

He knew his shoulders were wide – that was just a function of his bone structure, right? He came from a line of broad-shouldered men. But he hadn't really thought of them as 'broad' in the way that people say 'a broad-shouldered man' and mean it as a compliment. Kip was just *big*. Right? But to have her hands on his shoulders, he couldn't not be aware of the muscles there, and that she thought he did have broad shoulders in the way that people referred to broad-shouldered men and meant it as a compliment. He felt like his brain was smoking, he was thinking so fast. Wait, she thought his *shoulders* were attractive?

He hadn't thought of his shoulders more than three times in his life, maybe. And those had been when he was trying to share a bench in chapel and there wasn't room to sit next to the other wide-shouldered Blackguard initiates. She thought his shoulders were attractive?

She was standing right in front of him. This close. His mind wasn't working – shoulders? shoulders?! – and wow, her lips were close, and full, and her eyes were wide and emerald green on green and terrifically distracting, and her eyelashes were long, and her cheeks were pink, but maybe they were always pink, or maybe it was cosmetics? And why couldn't he, with his Guile memory, remember if they had been pink before this moment? and Orholam have mercy, blood was flooding his cheeks, and, and, and, he was supposed to do something, wasn't he? Yes. Yes, he was.

He was supposed to kiss her. Oh shit.

He was supposed to kiss her, right now, before the moment passed. But what if she didn't want him to kiss her? What if he was misinterpreting the signals? He'd never *been* signaled before. He could well think she wanted him to kiss her, but maybe she's signaling something completely different. Orholam have mercy, if she did want him to, and he missed the signal, she'd think he was a complete idiot. He was young, younger than her, and she'd think of him as a child again, and then he'd be set back in her regard forever. Maybe she'd cancel the wedding.

Wait, she'd asked him a question, hadn't she? But what – how was he forgetting everything?!

His ears were hot, and his shoulders were taut as drums beneath her hands. She removed a hand from one shoulder, and he nearly leapt, nervous tension thrumming through him. Embarrassed, he looked down at his feet, unable to bear the eye contact. He'd totally botched it.

Shit shit shit!

And looking down, he saw not his feet, but straight down the front of her dress. Orholam's – breasts. He froze. Now there was a sacrilegious thought. Not that he'd ever worried too much about sacrilege when he said 'Orholam's balls,' and surely Orholam made balls and breasts both, right? And then, he was aware he'd frozen, looking at her breasts – no, no, not looking. Looking implied that you just *looked*. This had gone on and on, this was a *stare*, at least. He'd have a gray beard by the time he tore his eyes away. Maybe that made it a leer. But a leer kind of implies some intent. It makes it seem creepy, and he wasn't being – it was—

Orholam's breasts. It had been too long. She couldn't fail to notice. He looked up at her, wincing.

'Anything I say is only going to make this worse, isn't it?' he asked.

'Shhh,' she said, smiling sympathetically. 'Relax.' She picked up one of his hands, which had been held ramrod straight at his side, and pulled it up to her waist. 'I happen to think it's adorable.'

Adorable. 'Adorable' is what you called puppies and poppets. There's no way to say 'adorable' without pitching your voice up, as if speaking to an infant, Oh, that's *adorable*. And then you pinch a cheek.

She took his other hand and placed it on the back of her own neck. She sidled in close, pressing her body against his.

I've just been emasculated. By my own stupidity and social ineptitude. *Adorable*. Dammit, Kip, there was your chance and you – what is she—?

And then she pulled his head down and kissed him gently on the lips.

Kip . . . lost a few moments in the sweet smell of her breath – who has sweet-smelling breath? Isn't breath, at best, neutral? And the sweet soft moistness of her lips, and the sweet soft pressure of her body molding itself to his.

Oh. Oh my.

She released him, and, nerveless, he let her slip away.

'Kip, I know we barely know each other, but I find your quirky mix of innocence and strength . . . intoxicating.'

Kip swallowed. 'Guess it's a good thing I'm already blushing from, uh, the other thing.'

'And why's that a good thing?'

Because otherwise my blood would be getting confused which end of me to rush to. 'So I don't have to go to the effort of blushing anew,' he said.

She laughed, and he stole a glance at her cleavage. And then felt weird. Now that they were basically betrothed – they *were* betrothed now, weren't they? – was he supposed to stare at her boldly? Or was it leering?

Orholam, I don't know anything!

He glanced at the door.

'What are you doing?' she asked.

'Honestly?' he asked.

'Honestly.'

'I was kind of hoping bad people would break down the door, and I'd have to fight them. I actually know how to deal with that kind of thing.'

'The virgin thing, huh?' she said.

He groaned. 'Er, kind of hoped I'd buried that in all the words after it.'

She pursed her lips, eyes twinkling. 'There might have been another hint or two.'

Kip covered his face with his hands. 'Orholam take me now. I'm ridiculous.'

'I told you already: you're adorable.'

'A woman doesn't want to take a man to bed because he's adorable.' It just came out.

'This one does.' Just as fast.

And suddenly Kip's mouth was very dry.

'We're going to take care of your little problem,' she said.

'My . . . huh?' It was like she was speaking another language. What's she mean? His inadequacy? Awkwardness? Embarrassment? Total hopelessness?

'Your virginity.'

'Oh!' Orholam, did she have to say it out loud? What if someone was passing in the hall? Surely the word 'virgin' must draw ears more than any expletive. 'Yes, yes, of course,' Kip said. 'I mean, yes! I would *really* like that.' He hitched his backpack up on his shoulder. 'Believe me, I'm looking forward to nothing more.'

'Now.' She locked the door, glanced at his bed, smiled. And though her words were bold, there was something shy about that smile, and certainly about the flushed cheeks that accompanied it. Pinker than before. Definitely pinker.

But Kip the Lip had absolutely nothing to say.

'After all,' she said, 'boat's not going to leave without me, right? Now get naked.'

The sound that came out of Kip's mouth was not a squeak. Dammit.

Kip looked at the door again, longingly. Naked? Here? In full light? He wasn't as fat as he used to be, he knew that . . . but he'd seen Tisis naked. Amazing how keen the memory can be for such things. She was gorgeous, and he was . . . he was the fucking turtle-bear.

Maybe 'fucking' is an inapt modifier.

And that made him think of a turtle-bear, copulating.

Ah!

I can't stop thinking. I'm with a beautiful woman who wants

705

to make love, and I'm standing here like a complete non-copulating turtle-bear, *thinking*.

Maybe if she kissed him again his head would go all gooey and thought would cease in the pink happy cloud of being wrapped up in her, but, 'Get naked'?

'Wait, wait,' she said. 'You're right. I can tell you're thinking it through, and you don't want to reject me, but just in case something goes wrong before we get on the ship tomorrow. We shouldn't. My sister would kill me, anyway. Not that she's been chaste – the hypocrite.' She threw the insult out like only someone who's very close to their sister could. A recognition, but not a condemnation. 'But she's always meant to sell me dear, she says, "You don't hand over the goods until they hand over the gold," and I'm sure she'll ask, even if everything turns out perfectly. And she can always tell when I'm lying. I can wait one more day. You can wait, right? I didn't mean to tease.'

'Huh? Huh?' Kip said. I'm right?

'Blame me. I'm capricious. Sorry. Tomorrow. Either we'll rent a room at the Crossroads, or we'll just have to make do with the captain's cabin on our ship. In some ways, a big room is a waste, anyway, don't you think? I know I'm not going to want to leave bed for a long while.'

'I, I,' Kip stuttered. Huh? What? The blood wasn't going back to all the right places fast enough.

'Don't worry, I'll make this up to you, I promise,' she said, and she put her hand on the front of his trousers.

When the great thunderstorms of spring passed over the Jaspers, lightning often struck the top of the seven towers of the Chromeria. This was *that*. A thousand times that.

'Oh,' she said, 'definitely interested.'

The thing that made it ridiculously charming was that she was blushing furiously as she did it, like she was being terribly naughty and couldn't believe her own brazenness. But she also hadn't taken her hand off.

'Kip, I know we didn't get the best start, and that's my fault, but—'

There was a knock on his door.

Tisis snatched her hand back guiltily, but quickly recovered.

She cocked an eyebrow at him. 'Now, see what I saved us? That could have been awkward,' she whispered.

Kip was still speechless, still blinking bleary-eyed as if he'd been dunked in a big sudsy tub of I-can't-believe-this-actually-happening and some soap of I-am-actually-going-to-have-sex was still in his eyes.

But some wiser part of him was detached. We're children, both of us, playing at being adults, putting on shoes that are too big for us, and being surprised when we stumble.

Tisis whispered again, and this time she was simply herself, earnest and a little scared. 'Kip, whoever it is, don't let them know I'm here.' She moved into the lee of the door.

Kip's mouth worked silently, but he had nothing to say. He went to the door and opened it a bit, not so little as to cause suspicion, but not inviting anyone to step right in, either.

'Oh, Kip! Thank Orholam you're here!' Teia said.

Chapter 88

It wasn't yet dawn of Sun Day when Karris and Commander Ironfist and their squad rowed into sight of Big Jasper. Exhausted from skimming all the way to Rath, and then fighting, they hadn't been able to get all the way back before they ran out of daylight, even on the eve of the longest day of the year. It was only because of Ben-hadad, young genius, that they'd been able to navigate the rest of the way home with the stars.

He'd drafted a perfectly working mariner's astrolabe from memory, calculated their latitude, estimated their rowing speed, remembered the latitude of Big Jasper, told them they could make it by dawn if they rowed all night, and kept them on course.

Mostly. Karris had thought that the enormous spires of the Chromeria would be impossible to miss, but late in the night, a low mist kicked up, and though they could still take their bearing by the stars still visible overhead, they found themselves west of Big Jasper, having overshot Little Jasper entirely.

'It's just as well,' Ironfist said quietly. He and Karris had this last shift on the oars. The others were still asleep. It was almost time to wake them, though. 'There will be Lightguards at the Chromeria's dock. I'm not handing Gavin over to them.'

'He needs chirurgeons before anything. West dock isn't far from Amalu and Adini's.' They were the best chirurgeons on the Jaspers, maybe in all the satrapies. They'd made a fortune treating nobles and Colors for two decades, but then had freed their slaves and taken a religious oath to treat the poor of Big Jasper.

'Karris,' Ironfist said after a few more long sweeps, 'it's Sun Day. If we don't bring Gavin to the Spectrum today . . . They're not going to stop naming a new Prism on our word alone.'

'You saw his eyes,' Karris said. Eye. She felt dead inside. A pause. 'Blue.'

'Then you know. Hope is dead. We've lost.'

Gavin knew it, too. When night had fallen and they could draft no longer, he had insisted that he help row. It was one thing he was good at, he'd said. But soon he'd passed out, overcome by his wounds and long privation.

Karris looked at him now, still asleep on the deck, his gouged-out eye bandaged as well as they could. She had wanted to see her husband and simply rejoice that he was alive, that he was hers once again. But the first thing she noticed – and it had overwhelmed her love and her relief and her hope – wasn't the dirt or the bloody grin or the ruined hand or the burnt-out eye or the black hair dye or the long beard or his indomitable spirit; it was his good eye, his blue eye, his icy-bright intelligent natural blue eye.

They'd come to rescue a Prism. Instead they'd rescued a man.

They'd done the impossible, five of them rescuing a man from fifty thousand, and it was for nothing.

'This isn't how Prisms die,' Ironfist said, keeping his voice barely above a whisper. 'When I was named commander of the Blackguard, they told me what to look out for. Nothing about Gavin Guile has been normal.'

'What is?' Karris asked.

'I'm not supposed to say. Last thing we need is every

Blackguard playing chirurgeon, wondering if she should obey her Prism, or if he's going mad.' He looked away and said, 'It's not the first sign, but eventually, they get color in their irises, and eventually, they break the halo. Just like the rest of us.'

'But . . .' Karris said. Obviously, that wasn't what was happening here, not at all.

'That's not all. There's a ceremony, every seven years. I don't know what happens, but the first time I had the distinct feeling that Gavin hadn't made enough friends, and he wasn't going to be Prism afterward. But an odd thing happened: they never had the ceremony, and Gavin kept being Prism. After that, everything changed. If you weren't paying attention, you wouldn't have seen it, but the composition of the Spectrum changed drastically. Marid Black killed himself, but he'd long struggled with melancholy, and we found a note. The Blue left immediately after Sun Day and was killed in a shipwreck, possibly while fleeing pirates. The Green retired and since has died. The Yellow was called home to Abornea and died months later after being thrown from a horse. The Sub-red withdrew to his estate on Big Jasper and didn't leave until his death two years later, supposedly of drink and lotus eating. Delara Orange's mother somehow emerged from what had been called ruinous debts; she'd been gone for much of the previous few years, missing meetings while she tried to beg, borrow, or steal money to keep her house together, but was suddenly present for every meeting. Only the Superviolet and Red seemed unchanged. It was spread out over so much time, and the news of some of these didn't come for six or eight months later, that everyone was already engaged in maneuvering over who would take those seats. And Gavin and the White and the Red and the High Luxiats and the satraps and everyone else who was anyone jumped into those fights. No one party emerged as a total victor. I'm certain of that. I've kept tally of the close votes, especially the close votes Andross has won. He didn't buy or suborn all the new Colors. It's been nine and ten years or more now. It would have been clear by now if he had them all under his thumb. Which is probably the other reason everyone wrote off the changes as coincidence. Who would overturn a Color if they didn't have a plan to put in a friendlier face?

709

'But I watched again, three years ago now, at the fourteen-year mark. No one was nervous. No one moved their families around, arranged visits, or wills, or escapes. There were no contenders to be the next Prism. And the day passed in peace. I don't know what happened. I've searched the libraries and every history I can find, but there are no mentions of how a Prism is named. None. Not even speculation. Which tells me the lack is deliberate. This is not the work of one man expunging some records, like I thought at first. It must be the work of generations of men doing that. Think even of the oral histories, which can't be stopped: even they speak only of parties and gathering of the Spectrum and satraps and luxiats, with a whiff of the usual politicking, and at the end, always, always, total unity and agreement, with "Orholam having spoken." I know these men, and Orholam could show up in a pillar of fire in the middle of the room and turn half the councilors into goats, and the other half would still not be in total agreement and unity afterward. And I can tell when Gavin is ready for a challenge or a fight or even a game. He doesn't contain his excitement. He doesn't even try.

'And he's not been excited. Because he doesn't know. I've never been sure whether I should be glad the Prism isn't part of this conspiracy, or terrified because of that. But this, his eyes, they prove to me that we're facing something unprecedented.'

But Karris was thinking about something altogether different. Gavin had appeared to be oblivious to all the angling going on under his nose because he was Dazen, and he was petrified. He hadn't known what secret alliances Gavin might have made, and he hadn't known or probably had any way to find out about the ceremony without exposing his real identity. And perhaps no one had bothered trying to enlist his aid for their schemes because they thought he would be dead when they carried them out.

Gavin had been absent half the time, hunting down wights with Karris and others in every arc of the Seven Satrapies. When he was home, he was pressed into rituals of all sorts, appearances for new discipulae, and even teaching lectures. He sometimes thought his high position meant he could simply ignore the political currents swirling around his ankles like a giant crossing a stream. There were layers upon layers of secrets, and at the bottom of any you might happen to excavate, you might find that it had all been a plot to marry this daughter to that son of a higher class, or to displace another family that had valuable shipping contracts, or a bastard son, or a gambling habit.

On the other hand, feeling in good health, Gavin might have never even realized that others were plotting what to do when he suddenly died. And then he hadn't suddenly died. Who would tell him that they had been planning how to take advantage of his sudden death?

Of course, if he hadn't thought it all beneath him, if he'd turned his mind fully to controlling the Spectrum, he would have noticed. But Gavin was no Andross. And Gavin had always his own secret to protect. How much had that hobbled him? If someone made a veiled comment that they expected the real Gavin to understand, would Gavin have demanded they explain, or would he have shied away instead?

Shied away. Every time. He'd hated talking about the war, though he must have practiced those lies to perfection. Hated talking about the past, period. And he'd done everything he could to make none of it matter: disrupting old alliances, forging new ones, destroying powers and dispensing justice where he could, regardless of where those receiving it had stood in the war. It had made him a great Prism, but it had also made him blind to the knives at his back.

Which was fine, as long as he was so powerful that no one dared use those knives.

There was more there. Something she was missing. A piece she'd been handed. But Karris was tired from rowing half the night, and worrying, and yesterday's fighting had left her bruised and battered. And they weren't home yet.

'You've got a secret,' Ironfist said. 'Something I said made you realize something.'

'Yes,' Karris said. She wanted to explain it all to her commander, her old friend who'd saved her life on a number of occasions, whom she trusted perhaps more than Gavin himself. But she said nothing but, 'I'm sorry.'

711

He nodded. 'She said you'd say that.'

'Huh?'

'The White. She said at some point, you'd cut me off. Exclude me from your counsels. She said you'd apologize for it. She said that would be the moment when you were finally a Blackguard no more. And that it wasn't a bad thing, but it would hurt. And that it was her fault, not yours.'

Karris shook her head. 'You ever think what a pain it is to work with people who are smarter than you?'

'No, never,' Ironfist said. Simple statement of fact. Because he didn't?

But when she shot him a look, he was smirking.

She couldn't help but grin back. For an instant.

'Dammit,' she said. 'Hezik, that asshole.' That dead asshole, their colleague.

'He was intolerable,' Ironfist agreed.

'Heard he tried to claim that miracle shot you made at Ru,' Karris said.

'Asshole,' Ironfist said.

And they chuckled. They knew when you had to laugh, as warriors know.

'So what do we do?' she asked.

'The White said once you cut the strings that you'd be ready to start giving orders. Your command, Lady Guile.'

It was true. She knew what needed to be done. Karris woke the others, excepting only Gavin, who needed the sleep to heal. She gestured to the lightening sky. 'The commander and I need to get back to the Chromeria. We're already going to be too late for the dawn rituals. Essel, you and Ben-hadad are going to take the Lord Prism to Amalu and Adini's. You know it?' Essel nodded. 'If you have to refer to him by name, you call him Hezik, you understand? It won't bear scrutiny, but perhaps Hezik will protect the Prism in death as he did in life. We'll send any backup we can. Don't hand him over to the Lightguard no matter what.'

With Gavin's hair dyed dark, and his beard grown in, and so much of his skin wrapped in bandages and with all the weight he'd lost, he certainly didn't look like the Prism of old.

She saw by the end of her orders that Gavin was awake.

He stood and took Ironfist's cloak, swaddling himself in the big garment and throwing the hood on. Soon it would be too warm for such, and cause more questions than it staved off, but for the moment it was the right move. He looked up at her, and the movement must have broken a scab because she saw him wince and wince again and a dribble of fresh blood escaped from under his bandage and coursed down his cheek. He steadied himself on Essel's shoulder.

'Just when I think I have your measure, dear Karris,' he said, his voice low but steady in spite of the pain. 'You exceed my expectations all over again. I am blessed and honored above all deserving to have you as my bride. But you're right. You must go. My father will have planned mischief and worse for this day. You can't help them heal me, and you can't stop him from here. Go, my love, go.'

Chapter 89

Teia didn't wait at the door. Instead, she threw herself at Kip and gave him a fierce hug.

Oh no. As she froze in his arms, Kip wished for the first time that he was still as fat as he used to be. With his belly protruding, he might have had a chance. As it was, the difference in their heights meant their first point of contact was below Kip's belt . . . and right in the middle of Teia's stomach. There was no way to ignore it. She'd hugged Kip, and there was no way she couldn't notice.

She stepped back and looked down, to confirm what didn't need confirmation. Kip folded his hands in front of himself, which was pretty much closing the barn door after the cows were already out.

'Kip, what the hell?' she said. 'Is that for—'

For you? Hey, they come on fast, but not that fast.

The words were out before Kip realized he'd said them aloud. Oh shit.

'Oh, you were – I'm so sorry!'

'No! I was – sometimes they just happen. You know, just out of nowhere. You know, to young men.'

Teia cocked her head, her lips pursed and one eyebrow lifted. She folded her arms, nonplussed. Not Kip's best evasion ever.

Without turning her head, Teia swung the door shut behind her with a foot, exposing Tisis.

Teia's expression went carefully blank. It did that when she was furious. 'Constant as an oak, aren't you, Kip?'

'I, I— This isn't, this isn't . . . this is probably exactly what it looks like.' Kip looked plaintively. 'Teia—'

'I don't care. I don't have time for this. I need you. Right now.'

'Pardon?' Tisis said, coming out of the corner as if she'd simply been inspecting the drapes, haughty and put-upon, chin lifting.

Oh hells.

'Shut it, bauble, or eat fist,' Teia said. She didn't turn her head, but her pupils flared as she looked at Kip – flared, in an instant, so wide that the irises were reduced to the tiniest rings, and then those pushed back so far that the whites of her eyes disappeared altogether. Her eyes became perfect black orbs. Kip knew she was gathering paryl, but with her set jaw and sneer, Teia's suddenly inhuman eyes made Kip want to wet himself.

Tisis shut it. Teia ignored her, going straight to Kip's bureau and rifling through it.

'Kip, you're a great gushing shit sphincter, but I've got more important things to worry about. There's—' She glanced distrustfully at Tisis, and stopped. She went back to digging and quickly pulled out Kip's lens belt and tossed it to him. She looked at Kip. 'You have any other weapons here? This may get ugly. The White's in danger. I may be the only one who can save her.'

Tisis said, 'I'm sure a color-blind drafter is exactly what the Blackguards need to do their—'

Teia pointed a finger at Tisis's nose, getting right in the older girl's face. 'One more word, poppet. Give me the excuse. Breaker, now!'

The other thing? Oh, she meant the cards. Kip wedged his fingers behind his bureau and pulled it away from the wall. In the space underneath, he grabbed the card box.

Teia looked unimpressed. 'I really need to show you better hiding places.'

Kip strapped on the lens holster. 'Tisis,' he said, 'go to the docks. I'll meet you there as soon as I can.'

Teia turned and pointed. 'Tisis, there are coin sticks on that rafter.'

'What?' Tisis said.

'Use green, moron! Knock them down with luxin and take them with you as you go. We can't carry anything extra. Orholam's balls you're dumb.'

They left her standing there, fuming, and ran to the lift.

As they got in, Teia pulled out the gray cloak and fingered the twin black-and-white disks stitched on the back. 'Kip, where'd you get this cloak?' she asked.

'I stole it from a god or a demon or something. Something bad.'

Teia looked at him, exasperated. '*Asshole.*'

'Teia, listen to me. I'm going to marry Tisis—'

'I don't care. We need to talk about our strategy upstairs.'

'Teia! My grandfather has commanded—'

'So you are working for him. What was all this, part of a ruse?'

'What was all what? Ruse? What are you talking about? Teia, you of all people should understand!'

'Of all people? And why's that?'

'You were a slave!'

'Oh, I'd *forgotten* about that. Perhaps you—'

'You should understand what it is to have to obey orders you—'

'—have forgotten that you're free. Don't you dare tell me you know what it's like!'

'I'm doing it for the squad, Teia.'

'I could tell. Had your horn up for us, did you? Funny how the things you do for others end up benefiting you most of all. You're a Guile, Kip. Through and through, and all Guiles are the same.'

Kip dropped his hands. She was past reason. And the lift was here.

They got on. Kip shifted the counterweights. He remembered it requiring more weight the last time he and Teia had taken the lift with just the two of them. Teia said, 'An assassin of the Broken Eye took a contract from your grandfather to kill the White. He put a paryl trap around the White's heart. She may already be dead. If she's not, I'll need to work on it. If we're discovered, I need you and the squad to hold the door while I work. Oh, and we have to get past the Lightguards. Not a problem for me alone, but like I said, I may need you once we get in the room.'

Kip absorbed it in silence. 'The squad?' he asked finally.

'Should be meeting us up there. At least some of them. I sent Marissia to find them.'

All Guiles are the same, huh? 'Fine, I got a plan.'

'Which is?' Teia asked, as they started ascending.

Kip said nothing.

'Breaker, I'm serious. What's the plan?'

Kip turned a contemptuous look on her, then looked away, dismissing her. He could practically feel the air chill. It wasn't fair of him. Dammit. He should open that Lip and apologize immediately.

But he didn't. And just as he was reconsidering, the lift stopped at an earlier level. Caelia Green stepped on with her distinctive swinging gait, followed by her Blackguards, men Kip didn't know well. She looked up at Kip, then at Teia.

'I think it's past time we get to know each other, Kip Guile,' she said. 'I am Tyrea's Color after all, and truth is, I don't know my people all that well, and there are far too few Tyreans here at the Chromeria. You do consider yourself a Tyrean?'

'Of course,' Kip said. This? Now?

'Ah. Just didn't know if you thought you'd outgrown that somehow,' she said. 'We should talk.'

And then she got off at one of the upper levels. Kip and Teia continued on, but there was no way to apologize before they arrived at the top level of the Prism's Tower.

The rest of the squad was standing there waiting for them

in the reception area. All of them were wearing their grays. All of them were armed, but there was no tension in the air. They were curious why they'd been summoned.

'Hey, Breaker!' Ferkudi said. 'What's happening? What's the game? Where's Teia?'

Cruxer, though, saw the look on Kip's face immediately. He stepped close. 'The Guile room slave sent us here. Told us to be armed. Said that you and Teia would meet us. What's—'

Kip glanced around. Teia was gone.

Oh, not gone. Just not visible. Keeping her presence secret. Fair enough.

'No time,' he said, walking past Cruxer.

Three Lightguards stood at the usual Blackguard post. They were standing side by side, fully blocking the hall. Ten paces behind them, the Blackguards waited, looking peeved about having been evicted, but clearly under orders not to do anything about it.

Kip stood up on tiptoe briefly as he walked toward the checkpoint to see which Blackguards were on duty. He squinted and drew his green spectacles smoothly from his hip case. 'Gav Greyling? Is that you?'

Big Leo whispered behind him, 'Boom.'

'Ayup!' Gavin Greyling said.

'What's your orders?' Kip said, again bobbing up on tiptoe like a little kid to look past the Lightguards.

'Son, you're going to have to hold up,' one of the Lightguards said.

'Not to interfere with the Lightguards. Not in any way,' Gav announced.

'Boom?' Ferkudi asked, confused.

'Son, I mean—'

'Oh,' Kip said to Gavin Greyling, 'that's—' He was close enough. Amateurs.

Forearm strike to the neck. Kip caught the man on the left so hard, right under his jawline, that the man was launched into the wall. Kip used the follow-through to build torsion through his core. He whipped back to smash his elbow into the noseguard of the middle guard's helmet. The man hadn't bothered to tie his chinstrap, so his noseguard became the metal vanguard of Kip's attack. The man flopped into the third guard, already unconscious.

His collision knocked the spear from the third man's grasp. The Lightguard went for a belt knife. It was a cross-body grab, and Kip blocked him from drawing it, first grabbing the man's wrist, and then wrapping green luxin around the man's wrist, hand, and belt, chaining them together.

The man tugged frantically, fighting his own belt. Kip was already grabbing him by the throat in one hand. He brought up his other fist and made thorny spikes sprout from it. But didn't punch.

All the fight went out of the last Lightguard.

'Lie down and pretend to be unconscious,' Kip said.

The man nodded quickly, wide-eyed.

Kip let go of him, and the man knelt and awkwardly lowered himself onto the ground with only one hand.

'Oh!' Ferkudi exclaimed, getting it. 'Boom!'

'Hanging hairies, Ferkudi,' Big Leo said, 'sometimes I think you have *got* to be faking it.'

'Faking what?' Ferkudi asked.

'Hold the hall,' Kip told Cruxer.

'We got it,' Cruxer said.

The squad rapidly gathered the Lightguards' weapons. The full Blackguards, Gavin Greyling and the shaven-headed Asif, were grinning at how Kip had dispatched the Lightguard, but they still barred the way.

'I've no doubt you're going to pay for that, nunk, but it sure was fun to watch,' Gavin said.

'The White's in danger,' Kip said. 'Something only . . . something only I can see.'

And like that, the men were on alert. They went straight past the guards at the door. Kip stopped at the White's door for a moment and looked back, as if pensive, to give Teia a chance to sneak in.

Winsen crouched over the third Lightguard. 'Hey, friend,' he said. 'No need to pretend.'

'Huh?' the guard asked, opening his eyes.

Winsen's fist cracked across his jaw. The guard's head bounced off the ground. Kip winced. Winsen saw him looking. He

718

grinned, but there was always something a little cool about even his friendliness. He enjoyed this, and he liked Kip, but he didn't quite like people the way other people did.

Kip nodded to him and went in.

'Hold the door,' Kip said to the Blackguards, 'and please don't look?'

They pursed their lips, but Gavin Greyling nodded. Kip pulled a curtain as he approached.

Teia was already standing at the foot of the White's bed, her eyes black orbs in the low light of the room. It was dark outside, and Kip could see only pinpricks of light out of the windows, the lamps of the rich people's homes and the lamps of the rich people's streets, tapering off into darkness on the poorer north side.

'I'm too late,' Teia said. 'I can't . . . It's like he made this hoping I'd try to disrupt it. If I touch them, she'll die. But if I don't touch them, she'll die anyway. It's somehow starving her heart. Her heart is dying. But if she so much as coughs . . . Kip, what do I do?'

'Shhh, child,' the White said.

Kip started. He didn't even know she was awake. Didn't know she could wake. Two Blackguards had stayed, but others had fled to get help.

'Wake my room slave, Kip, and say nothing more for the moment. Adrasteia, get behind the curtain, please.'

Kip walked to the slave's closet and knocked. No response. He opened the door, and saw the old woman, snoring in her chair. 'Caleen,' he said. 'Caleen!'

She snorted and opened her eyes, then followed him blearily. And slowly. Damn she was old. But by the time they got back, Teia had hidden.

The White said, 'It's my time, Bilhah. Summon High Luxiat Selene. Ask no one else to come in. I don't wish my end to be all a clamor and panic.'

Bilhah shuffled out past the Blackguards, slowly.

When the door closed behind her, Teia came out from behind the curtain. She asked, 'Why did I have to hide? I mean, why'd I have to hide from *her*?'

'So you wouldn't have to kill her,' the White said. 'She's

719

been reporting to Andross Guile for ten years now. She has a grandson she loves.'

'And Andross used it against her,' Kip said bitterly. He didn't know why it was hard to believe his grandfather had hired an assassin – the old monster had done it before. But still. Kip had played games with Andross. Andross was even charming sometimes. And a murderer. Killing people like they were cards to be cleared from the play surface.

'Why didn't you sell her?' Teia asked. 'She betrayed you.'

'Hers was a sin of weakness, not one of malice. It tortures her, and I let it. That's her punishment. And if one is to have a spy in one's chambers, what better than one who is hard of hearing and a little slow? After I pass, you tell her I knew, and that I forgave her. But not until after I pass. I don't want her weeping to be the last thing I hear.'

Not for the first time, Kip wondered at the White. Both uncommonly gracious and uncommonly hard.

'Wait, why would Andross knowing that Teia was here matter? She's— Oh.'

If the Broken Eye found out Teia had tried to foil the murder of the White, they'd know she was betraying them. They might figure it out anyway.

The White said, 'You have my permission to tell Kip everything, Teia. But I don't release you from your mission.'

'Where's everyone else?' Kip asked. 'It's not right we should be the only ones here.'

The White simply breathed for a few long moments, as if her previous speech had worn her out. 'The Spectrum is meeting, appointing Zymun Prism-elect. All my friends? Off, away, obeying orders,' she said. 'Dying is a task I can accomplish alone. Adrasteia, stop. That's enough. If not this night, I'll die tomorrow. They only snip a few days from my natural span, and I am not such a fool . . .' She got winded and couldn't speak for a little bit. 'Such a fool I cannot take certain advantages from knowing my own last day. Go now, go.'

They turned and went to the door, but she said, 'Kip, not . . . not you.'

Teia pulled her hood closed and disappeared, and the White

beckoned Kip closer. 'Desk. Card. Take it. And one last puzzle for you, O blood of Guile: Not only Prisms fly.'

Kip went to her desk and found the Nine Kings card held between panes of glass. The White, much younger: Unbreakable. He tucked it in a pocket.

'Open the curtains,' the White said. 'I would . . . look upon the light.'

Kip drew the curtains all the way open. It was gray out, not quite dawn. 'Orholam shine upon you, High Lady,' he said.

She didn't respond. The Blackguards, who'd overheard the last, came to stand at her side. Keeping one last watch. Tears were streaking down Gavin Greyling's cheeks.

Kip stepped out into the hall. He couldn't mourn now. He pushed it off. Had to think.

Almost dawn on Sun Day, and Zymun was going to be named Prism-elect? They'd do it at dawn, or even before, so he could perform the morning ceremonies. If Kip wanted to get out, he didn't have much time.

The squad was waiting for him. 'Let's go!' Kip shouted. They were ready. They ran for the lifts. High Luxiat Selene, coming to give last rites in her many-colored robes of office, stepped to the side as they pounded past her. They piled into the lift and set the counterweights. Made it, thank Orholam.

Cruxer threw the lever, and they dropped – one level.

The lift jerked to a stop so hard it nearly knocked them all off their feet.

'What are you doing, Captain?' Ferkudi asked Cruxer.

Cruxer said, 'It wasn't me.' He flipped the lever back and forth to show them.

They were at the Spectrum's level. Kip turned to see a smug Grinwoody. Apparently the lever in his hand was some kind of override. 'Ah, hello, sirs,' he said. 'Promachos Guile demands you come with me. Now.'

His triumphant grin told Kip just how much trouble they were in.

Chapter 90

For one mad moment, Kip thought about beating the hell out of Grinwoody and making a run for it. It was, of course, a terrible plan, but that grossly grinning face made it so tempting.

Instead, Kip and the squad followed Grinwoody to the Lightguard checkpoint, heart like a stone. There was no general Blackguard checkpoint here: their numbers were too depleted now. They were only stationed directly outside the council chamber, down the hall.

But as they got closer to the four Lightguards, a young Lightguard officer stood up with difficulty from the chair where he'd been resting. He lifted himself with the help of a boar spear. The crossbar was designed to stop the penetration of the spear into a boar's flesh so it couldn't gore you, but he was using it as a crutch.

Kip could feel the ripple of recognition pass through the squad, like wolves with their hackles rising.

Aram. He had a splint around the knee that Cruxer had destroyed. In the year since he'd been crippled, the young man had obviously been sucking at the teat of bitterness, for his face was twisted more than his leg. But whatever else it had done to him, his injury hadn't stunted his physical growth. Aram had filled out. His arms and shoulders were huge even as his crippled leg had withered, and Kip had no doubt that the young man was far more proficient with that boar spear than anyone would guess.

There was a flash of something in Aram's lidded eyes as the squad approached, hastily hidden. But Kip recognized it. All the hatred and resentment in the world – and Aram's eyes held his share and more – couldn't hide that emotion. Not from Kip. It was *grief*.

It was being excluded from a club that you wanted to be part of more than anything. It was not-belonging.

It was only in seeing that feeling so perfectly mirrored in

Aram's eyes that Kip realized the void of it in his own heart. When had that ache disappeared? Kip had been an outsider for all his life. The fat boy. The drunkard's boy. The whore's son. The Tyrean. The bastard. The unfairly favored. The boy who didn't deserve to be in the Blackguard. For all his life, Kip had felt excluded.

Aram was feeling that. He'd lost the Blackguard. Kip was going to lose it himself. How could he look at Aram and not feel compassion?

Technical ability wasn't what made a Blackguard, though it was part of it. The essence of a Blackguard was sacrifice. They lived and died for each other, and that, the unquestioned devotion of the whole corps, made the whole greater than the sum of its parts. A Blackguard could be told to go to his death, and he would, because he loved his fellows and he trusted that his commander wouldn't waste him. Orders might come down that made no sense that you could see, but they did make sense. Mistakes happened, men and commanders failed, but not – in this one tiny, precious corner of the world – from malice or selfishness.

That was a treasure beyond words, and it was what made the Blackguards the best in all the world. That was what Aram lacked. His selfishness was poison to the heart of the one most valuable thing the Blackguard had.

But he couldn't see it, and that wasn't reason to hate him. It was reason to pity him.

'Aram,' Kip said. He saw the insignia on the young man's lapel. 'Lieutenant.' Respectful, but not deferring.

And the grief was gone. There was only hatred there, but Kip was unmoved by it, even as the squad bristled at Aram's open sneer.

Aram said, 'Search them. No one may go armed with the Spectrum meeting on this level.'

A Lightguard came forward to search and disarm Kip, and Kip was suddenly tired. They were really going to play this? Again?

'Uh-uh,' he said. He pushed the Lightguard's hand aside.

With a voice equally tired, bored, and exasperated, Kip said, 'I'm a full-spectrum polychrome. This is the best squad among the Blackguard initiates. We *are* weapons. There's no such thing as disarming us. And we, for our part, are compelled as Blackguards not to let ourselves be disarmed within the Chromeria itself. It goes to the very heart of who we are. We are those who are trusted with weapons here. We make ourselves slaves to earn that trust. So what you're asking is both pointless for you and impossible for us.' Kip said the words to the man who was approaching him, but they were for Aram, and more than that, for Grinwoody.

'Grinwoody,' Kip said, still bored, not turning his head to look at the slave, and still deliberately using his name in order to offend. 'Use that unctuous voice of yours and the authority my grandfather has so mysteriously granted you, and clear this rabble.'

The sour look on Grinwoody's face was worth a thousand nights in hell. He waved the Lightguards away, and together, the squad walked past.

But then Grinwoody stopped before they got to the council chambers. He put a hand on Kip's arm. 'A moment, young master,' he said.

Kip stopped, suspicious.

'Let me tell you how this is going to go,' Grinwoody said. He didn't wait for Kip to acquiesce. He kept talking. 'Your grandfather will berate you and accuse you of something. You will protest loudly—shouting is good, but not for too long. We need a spectacle, not a fight. And then he will banish you.

'You will then have one hour until the promachos publicly changes his mind and orders you brought in for questioning. Don't be captured. The girl and a luxiat will meet you at red dock five, where her ship is anchored. Get the wedding taken care of before you leave the island. You understand? It must be done here, publicly, or the deal's off.'

'Breaker,' Cruxer said, worried, 'what is this?'

'It's survival.'

The squad said nothing. Kip didn't look back. Blackguards got used to following those they thought were making mistakes or endangering themselves recklessly, and though the squad hadn't yet taken final vows, they'd still seen the attitude modeled enough times that they could emulate it.

'We go where you go,' Cruxer said. Anyone who didn't know Cruxer as well as Kip did would have missed the sorrow in his tone. Dear Orholam, it was going to be hard to say goodbye. Maybe it was best this way, though. One farewell at the docks rather than slowly watching the void grow between them and Kip as their duties pulled them inexorably away.

The first Blackguard at the door was Gill Greyling. He'd watched Kip's interaction with the Lightguards, and he seemed immensely pleased. He gave Kip the kind of salute that was supposed to be reserved for senior officers, then said, 'Oops,' unapologetically.

'You're supposed to go right in,' the other Blackguard said. Kip didn't know him well. Parian named Kalif, if he remembered right.

Kip thought they were headed for the Spectrum's council chamber, but instead, this was the Spectrum's audience chamber. The Blackguards opened the double doors, and Kip found himself staring at several hundred people from the side entrance, with many of them staring back.

One of the High Luxiats was speaking at the front of the room. Everyone was dressed in their best attire for Sun Day, and all the High Luxiats except Selene were in attendance, in ceremonial robes of a particular color or of many. Some high nobles were seated, too, with sons and daughters at the front, in places of honor of some kind. The doors creaked loudly as they opened, and the High Luxiat seemed thrown off his sermon.

From a seat on the dais, Andross Guile stood and hurried toward Kip. He kept his head down as if he were trying not to interrupt, but he moved fast enough that he drew every eye.

As the luxiat began speaking again, Andross reached Kip and motioned furiously for him to go back out into the hall. Kip tried to back up, but with the whole squad and the Blackguards behind him, he didn't get all the way out into the hall before Andross began. 'How dare you show your face here?!' Andross hissed. 'I heard what you've done!'

'What are you talking about?' Kip demanded.

'Is it that you're guilty of so many things, you want me to tell you which one I found out about?' Andross said, voice rising. He kept his back carefully to the audience chamber, to maintain the illusion that he didn't know everyone could over-hear them.

'I have no idea what you're talking about!' Kip said, matching his grandfather in volume. 'I haven't done—'

'You and your squad killed a man! We found him. We found witnesses!'

'What man?' Kip asked.

'In the Six Corners district.'

Kip put a hand to his mouth. Suddenly this wasn't a game. That was where Teia killed the man who'd been tracking them. He'd thought Andross was going to make something up out of a whole cloth, not convict them of something they really had done.

'There was no evidence that the man was a spy. None!' Andross shouted now. The luxiat in the room behind him had stopped even trying to preach. 'Orholam help you, Kip. At best you're a vigilante, at worst, a murderer.'

'I—'

'What did you think? That I'd shield you because you're my grandson? No. And I've heard what you've done with this squad of yours. I don't know how you turned the best of the Blackguard recruits, but I won't tolerate anyone making a private army on my watch. What is it you call yourselves? The Mighty?'

Of course they called themselves no such thing. Kip's head was spinning.

'I didn't . . . I wasn't . . .' he started to protest.

'Hold!' a voice shouted from the door at the back of the audience chamber. It was Commander Ironfist. It was like watching the axle rattle loose on a carriage. There was nothing Kip could do to stop it. There was no way the commander knew this was prearranged.

The commander was sweating freely, his chest heaving as if he'd run leagues to get here. 'Kip was under my authority at all times. High Lord Promachos, there was no—'

'Yes!' Andross Guile interjected, cutting him off. A hint of a grin curled the side of his mouth but disappeared before he turned back toward the chamber, and Kip's heart sank.

He'd seen that look before. That look was the look Andross

gave when Kip had made a mistake playing Nine Kings. It was the look of a child being given an unexpected gift, as if the world stunned him at times with its sheer stupidity. Andross hadn't planned that Commander Ironfist be here, but he knew what to do now that he was.

'Yes, Ironfist, he was under your command. And your negligence grieves me. You have served long and hard, and I am loath to hold your failures against you, Commander, but you have done your term of service honorably, if poorly in this last year. Commander Ironfist, you are hereby relieved of your command and your commission. You will retire with full honors and stipend, effective immediately.'

Kip felt like he'd been hit in the face with a shovel. One part of him saw the art in the lies, the questions spawned by Andross's words. People were suddenly wondering, in what ways had Commander Ironfist failed? Many of them knew that Ironfist and Andross Guile hadn't gotten along, but Andross's apparent grief at having to relieve Ironfist of command, and the way he seemingly honored the man even as he kicked him out – his very grace in victory made it seem obvious that whatever the conflict had been, it had been Ironfist's fault.

Ironfist looked gutted. He seemed like he didn't even know where to look, glancing from Andross Guile to Kip, even at Grinwoody.

Kip wanted to throw up. He wanted to kill Andross Guile.

'And you, Kip,' Andross said. He turned, as if suddenly aware of how public this had become. 'Everyone, I'm terribly sorry you had to see this. Kip, I will not shield you because you are family. The evidence, though far from certain, is quite suggestive. Kip, you're expelled from the Chromeria, expelled from the Blackguard, and exiled from the Jaspers. Effective immediately. If any of your *Mighty* go with you, they, too, are expelled and exiled. Begone, grandson.'

'I—'

'Begone! Before I change my mind! Out!' he roared.

Kip trembled with rage. Not for himself, but that he'd let Ironfist get caught up in this. And suddenly, Gill Greyling and Kalif were very close behind him.

To protect Andross Guile against *him*.

No, no. Not like this.

In a daze, Kip went out. The squad and even Commander Ironfist went out with him. The double doors closed, but before anyone could say anything, they opened once more, and Andross poked his head out. 'Commander,' he said quietly. 'I know how your Blackguards love you. If you lead a rebellion, I bet half would join you. So it's your decision: is that what you want for either half of the Blackguard? Afterward, I'll disband them. You'll have *ended* your precious Blackguard.'

Then Andross disappeared back into the room. The doors closed after him.

Kip looked at Ironfist's face, and was afraid. The huge warrior trembled with rage, his fists clenched hard at his sides. Kip never precisely forgot that Ironfist was huge and tall and perhaps the best fighter he would ever meet, but being reminded of it like this was something else altogether. He heard Ironfist breathing: in on a four count, hold for a four count, out for a four count, empty for a four count. It was the very calming technique he'd taught them to moderate the battle juice or to steady rage.

The commander turned to Kip. 'So she's dead, then?' His voice was controlled. He meant the White.

'By now. We saw her not ten minutes ago. She was passing quickly.' Kip wanted to say more, but the other Blackguards were still in the hall.

Ironfist started walking toward the lift, and they fell in behind him naturally.

'Well, who looks like whipped puppies?' Aram said as they passed the Lightguard checkpoint. He laughed noisily.

Following Ironfist's example, Kip did nothing. Aram would expect him to attack. Kip did nothing, and Aram turned, laughing at him.

After Kip was past him, he heard the clong of helmet on stone, and the laughter abruptly stopped.

Kip glanced back, but the squad hadn't even broken stride. Aram was tottering, eyes unfocused, his helmet pushed forward over his eyebrows. The wall behind his head was scratched, as if from a helmet striking it. He sat heavily. His Lightguard

728

compatriots were looking at him, puzzled. Kip looked forward, so as not to draw more attention.

They got to the lift, and Ironfist, who had never turned, said, 'Thank you, Big Leo.'

Kip looked up at his squadmate, but the hulking young man kept looking forward, a slight, smug grin on his face.

They had to wait for the lift to arrive, and when it did, Karris was on it with two slaves. She was dabbing her flushed face with a handkerchief as if she, too, had been running, as one of the slaves tried to wrestle her long dark hair into some order, and the other, scandalized, was still lacing up the back of Karris's dress.

Karris and her slaves stepped off the lift. 'What happened?' Karris asked. 'Do they know?'

'No,' Ironfist said. 'The promachos just stripped me of my commission.'

'What?!' Karris asked. 'We were only apart for—'

'You need to go in there. Learn what you can,' Ironfist said. 'Tell them when it's time. It's what the White would have wanted.'

'So she's dead.' Karris's face twisted with grief, rapidly pushed down.

'Don't let it make you stupid. Go. We'll meet later,' Ironfist said.

Karris looked around as if there was more she wanted to say, but that she thought spies would overhear. 'Tell Kip,' she said. Then she looked at Kip, but didn't seem to know what to say. She reached a hand out and touched Kip's shoulder awkwardly, as if trying to apologize for their last encounter. But there wasn't time. Then one of her slaves dabbed one last bit of powder on her face, and Karris was off.

She waved off her slaves and glided right through the Lightguard checkpoint. Aram was still seated, holding his head. The other Lightguards looked unnerved.

'You're not going to touch me,' Karris announced, looking right past them, head held high, the force of her personality preceding her small figure like a wave. 'You're not even going to speak to me.'

They didn't.

Chapter 91

Zymun was seated with his grandfather on the dais, where he belonged. For now. The crown of the Prism-elect on his forehead was a welcome weight. But he'd hoped for more. Prism-elect? Why was he not simply the Prism?

It was his grandfather's work, of course. The old man was keeping a leash on him. Zymun would make him pay, eventually. He was already irritated that the High Luxiat was the center of attention, droning on and on. Zymun had feigned respectful deference for some interminable length of time, but the luxiat simply wouldn't shut up. So now Zymun was looking out at the assorted nobles and deciding which women he would bed.

Women afforded such drama; he loved it. The hunt was a thing of beauty. An avalanche of words and your full attention, watching always to see what flattery worked best, feeling out the weak points, returning to them often. Unrelenting attention, pretending she was the center of your world.

Then the lovemaking. First sweet and passionate, animal desire and total focus. And then, once you had them, indifference interspersed with total focus. Apologies, little gifts, confusion, and more lovemaking, degrading now.

That was, perhaps, the sweetest part. To watch a woman fall in love and to see in her eyes that she knew she shouldn't and yet she was.

From there, it was merely a matter of completing the destruction. Fighting, making up, slapping, apologizing, cheating, first stealthily and then getting caught on purpose, apologizing, degrading, stealing and blame shifting, then acquiring whatever blackmail you needed to make sure that when you cast her off she stayed gone. Sometimes with whole weeks of sweetness mixed in. And when they were wrung out, poor, humiliated, self-hating, and ruined, he would move on, perhaps to her friends.

Married women were the best. Sometimes harder to seduce initially, but with more access to money and secrets, and less likely to cling when you cut them loose, and while he was still young, it was easier to make them take the blame. After all, he was just a boy. That they had husbands also meant that they had a harder time keeping tabs on him, so he could seek out other excitement at the same time.

Liv Danavis was the only one who'd really escaped him. In his defense, she'd been the side excitement while Zymun was involved with a general's wife. There'd been so much else going on, too. It was a failure, but not one for which he could blame himself. He was young, after all, and he hadn't perfected his technique.

He was drifting, though. There were plenty of handsome women here, but he wouldn't pick one only for her looks. Not with his new position.

Maybe on the side. But he'd have to learn who was who before he committed time and energy. His grandfather had kept him in the dark about the nobility, and his own plans.

It meant Andross feared him. Zymun didn't know whether to be more flattered – an equal! – or irritated. It made things ever so much more difficult. Especially since Zymun needed his grandfather. He couldn't move against the old man without destroying his own power. Not until he was Prism. Prism-elect could be undone.

Clever old goat.

But what had Andross been doing with Kip just now? Kicking him out? Zymun thought that Andross was going to keep Kip around to guarantee Zymun's good behavior. Had he simply let his anger get the best of him? He was the Red after all, and old. Stupid.

This morning, in the nauseatingly early hours before dawn when they'd woken to come to the Chromeria, Zymun had done his best to eavesdrop on his grandfather, who was giving orders to his slave, that old wrinkled prune, whatever-his-name-was.

Something about tell him he gets an hour. Him?

That slave had come into the hall with Kip.

Andross was giving Kip an hour to run away. Why would Andross do such a thing?

So Kip *would* get away. Whatever the plan was, Andross wanted the pursuit to look real, and Kip had an hour.

Zymun fidgeted in his seat and leaned over to his grandfather, who appeared to be listening to the High Luxiat's sermon intently. 'I need to use the latrine,' he said.

Andross said nothing. Eventually he turned a baleful glare on Zymun. 'What are you, a child? Hold it.'

Zymun was about to go anyway when the side double doors opened once again. It was a rude way to enter the audience hall when there was another, more subtle entrance at the back, and the hinges creaked loudly. Some slave or discipula would be beaten for that, Zymun hoped.

A woman stepped in, petite, early thirties, skinny, oddly muscular, dark hair. Her dress was rich enough that it was clear she must be of the high nobility. Who would be brash enough to interrupt this ceremony? She was beautiful, though. Rich enough. At her age, certainly married. Maybe she would be a good target for his next seduction. She looked familiar for some reason.

Oh, she saw him now, and she looked transfixed. Zymun was uncommonly handsome. And he was Prism now. Women love a powerful man.

Prism-elect. Damn.

She tore her eyes away from him and looked to the slave at her elbow who was supposed to usher her to a seat. The man seemed flustered; there were no seats up front, where her position obviously demanded she be seated.

Then a noble got up from the very first row. He walked confidently down the center aisle, as the preaching luxiat faltered briefly and then went on about sacrifice and the light of truth or whatever. Zymun felt more than saw Andross cock his head.

The noble waved the slave off and escorted the woman forward. Odd. There were literally no places at the front, and the way the benches were packed, they couldn't simply make room for her.

But the noble brought the woman, who looked alternately confused and still captivated by Zymun, up to where he'd been seated himself. The noble seated her in his own seat, shot a single inscrutable look at Andross Guile, and then left by the side aisle. Zymun watched him go to the back and take a seat with the low nobles. How odd.

Zymun had a sense that something important had happened, so he looked at Andross Guile, but could read nothing there.

He wasn't always good at reading emotions, though.

He shifted in his seat again, and said, 'Grandfather, I'm going to leave a puddle if I don't go. Pardon me.'

Without waiting for a response, Zymun went out, head bowed and consternation writ on his face so it was clear he was not trying to cause an interruption. He left by a side exit near the dais.

Blackguards stood at the door both inside and out. After the doors closed behind him, Zymun headed toward the lift.

'Latrines are that way,' a Blackguard offered, pointing the opposite direction.

Zymun ignored him and walked briskly until he came to the Lightguard checkpoint. 'Name?' he demanded of the limping commander.

'Lieutenant Aram, sir,' the man said. There was a bit of fear in his face, but he was muscular and sour-looking. Zymun knew how to deal with his type. Not much different than the scurvy-ridden pirates he'd just spent months with.

'My grandfather has changed his mind about his disowned grandson Kip,' Zymun said. 'Lieutenant, are you capable of taking decisive action and delicate orders?'

'Yes, sir!'

'And your men here? They know how to keep their mouths shut when given a vital assignment?'

'Yes, sir!' they said.

Zymun said, 'Promachos Guile wants you to capture Kip and any one of his squad who try to stop you. You may use all of the Lightguard.' Zymun lowered his voice. 'And lieutenant . . . by *capture*, the promachos means *kill*. Make it look like you had no choice. You must never breathe a word of this, not even aloud to the promachos. Our enemies have spies everywhere. I promise you great rewards if you show you can be trusted. Perhaps even advancement. I am now the Prism-elect. I can be a good friend to you. Do you understand?'

Aram's eyes glittered. 'Yes, Lord Prism. We'll obey gladly. More than gladly.'

'The luxlords will be in ceremonies until after noon. Today is a holy day, I don't expect you to get the whole city in an uproar, you understand? Do it quietly, but do it. If you have to use every Lightguard in the city, do it, say you're after a thief or something. Yes?'

'Yes, my lord, I understand absolutely. I can summon every Lightguard in the tower. We have access to the room crystals.'

'Perfect. But – not on this level. We want no interruptions for our ceremonies. Shut down the lifts first. That bridge, the Lily's Stem, yes? Looked like a good choke point to me.'

'Yes, my lord, absolutely. Only way onto the island. That and the back docks. We can cover those, too.'

'Don't come report until he's dead. Or don't come at all.'

They rushed off, the lieutenant at an odd hobbling gait aided by his boar spear. Zymun went to the latrine. It was only as he was pissing that he realized who the woman in the front row must be and why she'd looked familiar. He'd seen her from afar once in King Garadul's camp. It was his mother, Karris!

He laughed aloud. How perfect! Was he good enough to seduce his own long-lost mother? Now that, *that* would be a challenge. But who better to use to get all the money and information he could ever need to use against Andross Guile?

Was he that good? Yes, he thought, of course he was.

He laced up his trousers, readjusted the gold crown on his head, and walked back into the audience hall with a big, big smile on his face.

Chapter 92

'How long do we have?' Ironfist asked Kip.

'An hour.' Kip had told Ironfist only that there was a deal with Andross – and that relieving Ironfist of his position hadn't been part of it.

Ironfist nodded, not wasting words on the obvious. They had to move fast.

They walked quickly into the Blackguard barracks. Teia met them at the door, playing it off to the squad like she'd just arrived from downstairs. Almost all the Blackguards were on shift today. There was so much work to do on a Sun Day that even the nunks had been pressed into crowd patrol and guard duty and overwatch. There were only four or five Blackguards in the barracks, and those were napping for a half hour or grabbing a quick meal before heading out for more shifts.

Most surprising though, was seeing Ben-hadad. 'Oh, thank Orholam,' he said. 'I've been looking everywhere for you all. What is all this stuff? Coin sticks? Weapons? Writs of—'

'Shut it, Ben-hadad,' Kip said. 'Not now.'

'I can't wait to tell you where I've been! I was—' Ben-hadad started.

'Ben!' Cruxer said.

'Meet me here in three,' Ironfist said, not even slowing.

The squad scattered, each going toward their own bunks and chests.

'Wait,' Kip said. He already had all his stuff. 'What are you all doing?'

The sleeping Blackguards perked up instantly. 'What's happening, Commander?' Stump called, sitting up.

'I'm not your commander anymore,' Ironfist said, not even slowing as he went to his own room. 'I've been relieved of duty.'

He might as well have hit them with lightning. 'What?' Lem asked.

'What the hell!?' Stump asked.

But Ironfist didn't answer. Kip followed him. 'Sir, how much should I tell you?' he asked.

Ironfist didn't turn. He started loading a pack. 'Is what you're doing right?'

'It's . . . not wrong. It's smart. It's for the good of my squad and the satrapies.'

'Sounds right to me, then.'

'Will you come with me?' Kip asked. 'Even just as far as the docks?'

Ironfist paused. There was a small bag sitting on his desk. He picked it up, looked inside. 'Andross. That old fox.' He breathed out again, then he walked over to the painting he kept of a young Parian woman. Took out his knife and slit down the canvas next to the frame. He reached in and pulled out a ceramic tube. He smashed it on his desk. Inside was a slip of paper.

'What's that?' Kip asked.

'Orders,' Ironfist said. He read them. 'From the White. One in the event of her natural death, one in case of her murder. But, no, Kip, I can't go with you. If I do, whoever it is your grandfather is trying to fool won't believe it for a second. He has a falling-out with you, and with me at the same time, and I go wherever you go and protect you? It's too convenient.'

'I hadn't thought of it that way,' Kip said.

'Your grandfather doesn't understand personal loyalty. He would never guess that I would want to protect you if there wasn't something in it for me, the old fool.'

Kip's eyebrows raised. He'd never heard Ironfist speak ill of any of the Colors, even when he clearly thought it.

'Not a Blackguard anymore,' Ironfist said, winking. But the strain on his face was clear. 'I can't go with you. Not after what's happened.'

'You don't mean what happened upstairs, do you?' Kip asked, confused.

'Kip. Karris and I rescued your father. He's back on the Jaspers.'

'He's back?' Kip said. 'He's alive! I knew it!'

'Quiet! He's hurt. Badly. Maybe crippled. Maybe unable to . . . serve as Prism.'

'I have to go to him. I— How can I help?'

'Help by not going to him.'

'What? Why? He's my father!' Kip's squadmates were busy with their things, and he wanted to ask them what they were doing, but – his father!

'Because you're about to be pursued by his enemies. Enemies who don't even know that he lives.'

'But I want to—'

'Doing what you want will put him in danger. What's more important to you?'

I wanted to save him myself, Kip couldn't say. It was what he'd promised to do. Maybe he'd been involved by prompting his grandfather to send more people looking, but maybe Andross would have done that anyway, and Kip had done nothing at all. Another oath failed. Just like he'd failed to find damning information on Klytos Blue, as his father had asked, what? A year ago?

There were too many things happening at once. Too many thoughts and too much pressure. 'Where was he? How'd you find him?' Kip asked. 'I didn't even realize you were gone.'

'We saved him from my sister. The Nuqaba. She was having him blinded.'

'Your sister? I didn't even know you had a—' Kip looked at the painting. It was of a pretty young woman, hair strung with jewels and piled high, vibrant brown eyes lit with orange halos. 'The Nuqaba's your sister?!'

But Ironfist ignored that. He said, 'And Andross is right, many or most of the Blackguards would join me if I went with you – even as far as the docks. Think of what happens if you split the Blackguard. What would victory be? If our half killed the others, what would we do then? Murder Andross and then what? Lay down our arms and be executed? Seize control? Rule the Chromeria ourselves? That isn't who we are.'

'So what do we do? Just let him win?' Kip was furious. He was doing exactly what that murdering spider wanted him to do, but there didn't seem to be any way out. He couldn't even go to the one man who might be a match for Andross Guile. His father was finally here – and Kip had to leave? Now? Before he even saw him?

Kip said, 'He planned this! He's doing it on Sun Day on purpose. What everyone will be talking about will be Sun Day and this year's party, and the new Prism-elect and what does anyone know about him, and there'll be tributes to the White who everyone loved and speculation on who'll replace her. Normally it would be a huge scandal that he stripped your commission, but this . . . That you and me got kicked out . . .

Anything else that happens today will just be buried under the other news, right?'

'If you're looking for justice, look not to earth, Breaker.' Ironfist looked up suddenly to the crystal embedded in the wall. It strobed yellow, then red, then yellow. The crystals were rarely used – the system was delicate and difficult to fix. It was only normally used for initiation day to announce the colors of new drafters coming through the Threshing – and for emergencies. Only the higher luxiats and Blackguards were supposed to have access to them.

'That's not one of our codes,' Ironfist said.

'What?' Kip asked, but Ironfist was already on his way out of the room.

'Who's going with Breaker?' Ironfist asked. 'Quick! I can't. My path is different.'

Slight Daelos seemed to be gathering his courage, and he spoke quickly. 'My parents would die if I left, Breaker. This is all they've ever wanted for me. It's all I've ever wanted for myself. Sorry.'

'I'm not blaming you, Daelos, but he only meant getting me to the docks—' Kip started.

'No, that's not what I meant,' Ironfist said. 'You go with Breaker, you're out of the Blackguard. Permanently. The promachos has spoken.'

'I'll go,' Cruxer said. His voice was steady, but he looked like he was dying.

'Cut the stitching on the side of your insignia,' Ironfist said.

'Wait. What?!' Kip said. 'Cruxer, what are you saying?'

'I'll go,' Ferkudi said.

'In,' Big Leo rumbled.

'Wait, what is this?' Kip said.

'Same here,' Goss said.

'Wouldn't be anywhere else,' Teia said.

Winsen shrugged. 'Sounds fun. I'm in.'

'No time!' Ironfist said. 'Line up now. You each found a paper in your pack. Sign it.'

'Stop it!' Kip shouted. 'What are you doing? You've worked your entire lives to be Blackguards. You're *this* close. I have to go, but me going means you *can* stay. Me going means I won't ever have to fight you.'

'Breaker,' Cruxer said. 'Don't you understand? We're all good enough to be Blackguards. The commander has offered promotions to every last one of us. But we wanted to be Blackguards not because we wanted to have the clothes and the admiration—'

'I thought the clothes and the admiration were pretty great,' Teia said.

'I like the clothes and admiration,' Ferkudi said.

'Ferkudi!' Cruxer said.

'Wha— She just said the same – ow! Ben, what'd you elbow *me* for?'

'All the trappings are wonderful,' Cruxer said. 'But we all wanted to be Blackguards because we wanted to serve a high purpose.'

'But what if I'm not the—' Kip said.

'It doesn't have to do with that,' Cruxer said, but Kip wasn't sure the rest of the squad agreed. 'What purpose is there in us serving evil men?'

Ben-hadad asked, 'What good are the trappings of honor if the honor itself is dead?'

'I still like the trappings,' Ferkudi murmured. He was mournfully turning his gold inductees' fight token over in his hand.

'Breaker,' Teia said. 'We love it here. We don't want to go. But we want to go with you.'

Just when he thought he was going to lose it all. Kip felt warmth suffusing him, like his body was filling with light.

'You'll find two pairs of blacks in your bags,' Ironfist said. 'I heard some of you only joined up in the first place because you wanted the clothes.' But no one laughed. The blacks were not just a gift rich beyond imagining, stretchy-soft and comfortable, luxurious and useful, they were the ultimate symbol of the elite Blackguard and what the squad was giving up. That their commander gave them the blacks anyway told them that he thought they were worthy of the honor and the brotherhood they were choosing to sacrifice. Ironfist growled, 'What, am I gonna have to requisition handkerchiefs? Line up!'

Kip could barely see through his brimming eyes. But the squad lined up immediately, and he took his place at the end.

'You're Blackguards no more,' Ironfist said. He walked down the line, took each signed release, and ripped the Blackguard insignia and rank off their sleeves. Kip was the last. It felt as if Ironfist tore his heart out.

'Lem,' Ironfist said. 'Take these papers down to the secretaries' desk and have them copied in triplicate and put on file.' He handed over the papers and simple Lem disappeared.

Ironfist dug into a bag. 'You can call yourselves whatever you want now. Make your own patches if you don't like these. The promachos called you the Mighty.' Ironfist went down the line again and slapped an insignia on each person's left shoulder. It was of a powerful man in black silhouetted on a red field, standing with feet planted, head bowed, arms straight out to either side, and force radiating from each hand. It reminded Kip of his time in the jungle, when he'd expelled the leeches.

Ironfist said, 'Now go, go with Orholam, and may I see you again. If not on these mortal fields, then in paradise.'

They went to the door, and Kip turned as the rest of them went into the hall. 'Commander, if I may, where'd you get the patches?'

'Andross Guile had them made.'

'That many?' Kip asked.

Ironfist nodded. 'And the weapons. And the supplies. Minus the blacks.'

Unbelievable. Just when Kip felt comfortable hating that old murderer, Andross had given him his squad back. Andross had not only given them weapons and gear, he'd arranged the writs of release so they wouldn't have to pay back the signing monies that all of them had spent or given to their families or previous owners. Andross Guile, generous?

'Sir,' Kip said, 'where are you going?'

'A different front of the same war.'

'Halt!' an unfamiliar voice shouted from the hall where the rest of the squad was. 'Which one of you is Kip?'

'That's me,' Goss said loudly. 'What's it to you?'

A musket shot rang out.

Chapter 93

Kip's first shameful instinct was to run away from the sound of musket fire. But that passed as soon as he saw Ironfist's face. Ironfist was restraining his first instinct, too. Except his first instinct was to run toward the sound.

But Ironfist didn't see the fear in Kip's face. 'I can't,' he said. 'Even if it means— Go, Breaker, go.' He pushed Kip toward the lift, and ran the opposite direction himself.

In the very act of moving, Kip was broken out of his indecision. He ran toward the lift, but by the time he got there, not ten seconds after the musket shot, all four of the Lightguards were down. Two were screaming, one was crawling away with a torn-out throat, bleeding in gushes, slickening the stone floor.

All of the squad were still standing. Winsen and Big Leo went to the two screaming, dying Lightguards and opened their jugulars. The crawler collapsed. All four were twitching.

'Oh, shit,' Ferkudi said. 'Goss, are you hurt? I thought—'

Goss was blinking. 'I, Orholam's balls,' he said. 'I don't know how he missed. Musket ball must have fallen out before he fired or something. Bad job packing the—' He collapsed.

Cruxer barely caught him in time, easing him to the bloody stones. But Goss was dead. There was a hole right in the center of his chest.

'They came to murder us,' Cruxer said. He closed Goss's eyes. 'No warning. That was no attempt at capture.'

'We gotta move,' Teia said.

But as she said it, they heard loud thunks from the lift shaft. Big Leo ignored it. He picked up Goss's body. 'I can't just leave him here. I'll catch up.'

The thunks continued, and Kip arrived at the lift shaft in time to see huge iron doors slam into place over the shaft at each level.

'It's part of each tower's defenses,' Cruxer said. 'Parents told me about it. They're hinged one way, so soldiers can be sent up the lifts, but no one can get down.'

'Surely we could draft levers and pulleys or something,' Ben-hadad said.

Cruxer said, 'They estimate five minutes per floor for drafters to break through. We gotta go down the slaves' stairs. The exits may be barred, but we can break through. Follow me!'

Ben-hadad grimaced. He clearly thought he could break through each level in far less than five minutes. But he followed orders.

They reached the stairs, and found the doors bolted. Ben-hadad moved to the front, locating the mechanism and studying it.

'Move,' a voice said behind them. It was Daelos. He was carrying two blunderbusses. He handed one to Cruxer as Big Leo returned.

'Big Leo?' Daelos said, lifting the matchlock.

Big Leo drafted sub-red to his fingers and touched each slow match, lighting it.

'Daelos, I thought you said you weren't coming—' Kip started.

Daelos pointed his blunderbuss at where the hinges would be on the other side of the door. He fired.

'They killed Goss,' he said. 'I'm coming.'

Cruxer's matchlock misfired, and they all waited, tensely, while he cleared it. 'What are you, rookies?' Cruxer demanded. 'Defensive perimeter! Teia, get us two more from the barracks.'

Chastened, they did. Kip immediately saw a few curious heads poking out of doorways. Not everyone got out of the tower by dawn, not even on Sun Day. 'Get back in your rooms!' Kip shouted. 'Look out for the Lightguard. They just killed our friend.'

Two of the three ducked back immediately. But one just kept looking. And then Kip recognized him. Magister Jens Galden. He was the asshole who'd punched Kip the very day he had first arrived at the Chromeria.

The man obviously hadn't forgotten Kip, either.

'I know a passage out,' Jens Galden said loudly. 'I could save you all.' He smiled unpleasantly.

'Let's go!' Big Leo said. He turned to the squad. 'Stop shooting the door, we can go this way. This magister has—'

Several of the squad members started jogging over.

Jens Galden waited until he saw they were coming, then announced, 'But Kip is with you, and I'd rather you all die.' He slammed his door shut. They heard a bar being slid into place on the other side.

Big Leo stared in disbelief.

A young woman poked her head out in the hall to see what was happening.

'Back in your room!' Big Leo roared.

The young woman's eyes went wide, and she said something, but it was lost in the roar of the blunderbuss behind them.

Kip flinched hard, though he should have been expecting it. Cruxer wasn't one to waste time cursing about a plan that didn't work out.

Cruxer and Ben-hadad and Winsen grabbed and pulled the shattered door. The central bar was still in place on the opposite side of the door, but it was only anchored on one side, and they were able to rip the door open and slip through.

Teia came jogging back up. 'Both loaded,' she said. She tossed one blunderbuss to Big Leo, and the other to Ferkudi.

They all squeezed through the door.

'I'd rather—' Ferkudi said.

'Shhhh!' Cruxer said. He'd been holding his hand up for silence. The squad hadn't even seen it. In some ways, Kip thought, talented rookies were still very much rookies.

But they quieted immediately now.

Then they all heard it. From far below, the sound of many footsteps coming up the stairs toward them. The stairs were not quite three paces wide, curling around one of the great lightwells, lit dimly by a few small windows into the lightwell itself. Whatever resistance they encountered would be hidden by the curvature of the stairs until they were right on top of it.

If the Lightguards were smart and disciplined enough to set up a spear wall or a few ranks of musketeers arranged so they could fire a volley into the squad, the squad would die.

They all looked at each other.

'If we can hear them coming up, they'll hear us coming down,' Ben-hadad said. Surprise was impossible.

A chunk of wood from the door they'd just pushed through shot out into the stairwell as a musket shot rang out. The wood hit Big Leo. He yelped in surprise.

'Down one,' Cruxer ordered. Better to only face attacks from two directions than from three. Kip emptied himself of green luxin, reinforcing the door. It wouldn't stop pursuit, but it would slow it.

He caught up to the rest of them on the next landing, not running into any opposition. The door here was locked, too. Big Leo was patting his body, searching to see if he had a wound from the musket ball.

'Light's weak in here, everyone fill up now,' Cruxer said.

But even as he said the words, the slaves' stair dimmed. Kip looked at one of the windows into the lightwell in time to see it slide shut, plunging them into utter darkness.

'Oh hell,' Ferkudi said.

'Winsen?' Cruxer said.

A yellow luxin light bathed them weakly. 'I can keep this light for thirty seconds at the most, Captain.'

'We've got to get out of the stairwell,' Big Leo said.

'The stairs are our only way out,' Kip said. 'If we leave the stairs, we just give them more time to surround us.'

One flight down, someone knocked loudly on the door. The doors had all been barred, but they were barred on the squad's side. Kip froze.

Muffled by the wood and the distance, he heard someone say, 'Kip? Ben-hadad? Adrasteia?' Kip wasn't certain, but the voice sounded familiar.

'Nothing to lose by going down one more flight,' Cruxer said.

They ran down the steps and took up defensive positions as they unbarred and unlocked the door. They threw it open.

A woman was standing on the other side, alone. At the sight of the squad's raised weapons, she threw her hands up. 'I'm here to help!' she squeaked.

For another moment, Kip didn't recognize her. She was in her mid-thirties and had bad posture, and still wore her green spectacles on a gold chain around her neck, but her wiry black hair had been combed out and oiled glossy, and she was smiling.

'Magister Kadah?' Kip said, disbelieving.

'I read their code in the room crystals. Not even a code, really. It's an old maritime mirror signal. They think you're on one of the upper floors, and they've got only one squad double-checking that every door to the slaves' stairs is locked. But it's the only way out. I knew you'd be coming.'

'Magister *Kadah*?' Kip repeated. This woman couldn't be the same one who'd hated and humiliated him.

'Not a magister, not anymore. I'm doing research now, as I've always wanted.' She smiled, and looked ten years younger than Kip had ever seen her look. 'I brought you these. They were all I could find.' She handed him a bag. It had half a dozen mag torches in it. 'Now go. There are people on this floor who would betray you.'

'Is there no other way out?' Cruxer asked, as Teia grabbed the bag from Kip and distributed the mag torches.

'Rumors only. None that I know,' Kadah said.

'Use 'em,' Cruxer ordered the squad. 'Fill up now!' The squad instantly began popping the mag torches.

'Magis – I mean, Kadah, why? Why are you helping us?' Kip asked.

She looked at him curiously. 'Kip, you saved my life. I was planning to suicide. I'd even picked the day. And then the White summoned me. I've spent the last five months trying to figure out how to thank you.'

Kip hadn't even thought of Magister Kadah since he'd left her class – well, except to think how glad he was that he wasn't still there.

'No time!' Cruxer said. 'Thank you! But we have to go!'

'He's right,' Kadah said. 'Go! And Orholam defend you!'

They barred the door. The squad had already taken up positions on the landing, each one full to bursting with luxin.

'Breaker,' Ben-hadad said, 'GBBBoDs?' He said it 'G-bods.'

'What?' Teia said.

'Great Big Bouncy Balls of Doom,' Ben-hadad said.

'Or Green Bouncy Ball of Doom,' Kip said. 'It's less cumbersome than BGBBoDs, Big Green Bouncy Balls of Doom,' Kip said, distracted. He was already soaking up green.

Winsen was using yellow, filling himself so he could throw flashbombs, and he held it out so Kip could fill himself with that color, too. Despite Mistress Phoebe's best efforts, Kip wasn't nearly proficient enough at making solid yellows to draft anything instantaneously in combat, but preparing a weapon beforehand was possible.

Kip soaked up some yellow and flung his hand down, drafting, trying to make a yellow sword as he'd practiced a thousand times.

'Quickly,' Teia said. 'Quickly.'

Kip fumbled, and he lost his concentration on the fine mesh point of yellow. The yellow sword broke apart near the hilt, and, unsealed, it all splashed into light.

He cursed. Why had Andross Guile sent men after them now? It was far too early. Had he betrayed Kip, or had something gone wrong?

Andross had expended so much effort making this plan that Kip didn't think he'd try to have him killed. Maybe the Lightguards had jumped early, hoping to curry favor with Andross by killing his 'enemy.' Or maybe it was just another betrayal from the man who specialized in them.

Cruxer offered him a blue mag torch and a green. 'Spikes and shield?' he asked.

But Kip's eye was caught by the insignia of the Mighty: a man with hands outstretched, power radiating in circular waves from his hands. 'I have a better idea.'

He drafted green from the mag torch like it was water gushing from a well. 'All of you, you're going to have to run after me as fast as you can. Pick me up. As in, right now.'

While Ben-hadad and Cruxer each got under a shoulder, Kip drafted a disk under his own feet.

'Oh no, I need a bit of orange. But those things cost a fort—'

Teia snapped open an orange mag torch. 'Life and death, Breaker.'

He didn't object. He drafted a green platform, then orange lubricant below that, then green again, starting a curve.

'Oh! I've heard of these!' Ben-hadad said. 'The ancients called them water balls? Drafted them out of blue so they could see out. Then they'd go out on rivers and lakes—'

'Footsteps. Above and below!' Big Leo said.

One of the squad fired a blunderbuss up the stairs above them. Kip heard the clatter of a man falling to the ground. The other blunderbuss fired. Curses and swearing and screams. Kip tried to filter it out, though with the green roaring in him, he wanted to smash them, shut them up. In moments, he'd drafted the bubble. He sprayed orange around the inside of the bubble before he finally closed it. He sealed it on the inside, putting the nexus of the knot close to the surface so he would be able to get out.

He was inside a vaguely translucent green bubble. His idea was to stand, letting his feet slide on the lubricative orange so that he stayed upright. He could tell immediately that it wasn't going to work.

'I just realized that I don't need to be *inside* the ball,' Kip said. 'And actually it might be a really bad idea.' But with the bubble closed, the sound was muted. They didn't hear him.

Kip waved to Cruxer, who took it as readiness.

Cruxer and Ben-hadad heaved the ball toward the stairs.

Kip fell immediately. Orange. Slippery.

He thought he saw Cruxer try to grab the ball to stop him, but Ben-hadad, thinking this was the plan, pushed harder on the Great Green Bouncy Ball o' Doomed Kip.

And Kip bounced. The ball rolled down the stairs, slowly at first, skipping and bouncing, and then it hit the next landing and sproinged airborne. He rolled along the outside curve of the spiraling staircase – and flew at face level into a group of ten or twelve Lightguards running up the stairs. The ball was six feet wide, and the stairs nine or ten. Kip shouldn't have blasted into all of them, but he did.

Kip was spun around and right side up for one moment, and he saw the squad following hot behind him, slashing at the scattered, fallen Lightguards, trying not to stumble over the bodies themselves, but trying to keep the men from following them. And then Kip was knocked off his feet again on the next bounce.

He didn't even see the next group of Lightguards, just felt the shock of collision. And now he had such speed built up that there was no way the squad would be able to keep up. He landed upside down on the next bounce, only the curvature of the ball keeping him from breaking his damn fool neck. Another collision – this one so hard that it rattled Kip's teeth – sent the ball bouncing back the opposite direction.

Finding himself flat on his back, Kip squinted through the barely translucent ball, wondering how many Lightguards he must have killed with that collision.

None. He'd caught the edge of the recessed doorway at one of the landings. His ball, now having ricocheted back into the stairs above, was rolling slowly back toward the edge of the descending stairs once more.

Through the distortion of the green luxin, Kip saw a young face coming up the stairs from below. A Lightguard, baffled at a boy in a ball. The ugly man had a musket in hand, but he stopped. In a heartbeat, half a dozen more Lightguards joined him. They, too, stopped, bewildered.

Kip waved to them, friendly. It had worked that one time out on the river.

But none of them waved back.

Then something else occurred to him. He hadn't made any holes in the ball. It was getting hard to breathe. He couldn't hear what they were saying, but it didn't sound friendly.

An officer joined the men. 'Shoot it!' he yelled.

Kip heard that.

The men raised their muskets. Kip had stopped musket balls with green luxin, once. But that had been open luxin, with all the power of insane Will behind it. He was still flat on his back, and the luxin of the ball wasn't thick enough to stop bullets.

Why didn't I make it thick enough to stop bullets?

Thinking was the wrong thing to do. Thinking took time.

A roar resounded through even the walls of his ball, and Kip saw the briefest flash of Big Leo, running down the stairs faster than you can run down stairs. Big Leo lowered a shoulder and flung his massive mass into the ball.

The Ball o' Kip shot into the Lightguards' faces amid musket fire.

Sometime in between that collision and the bouncing and the lack of air, the world went red and black and he lost everything.

Some time later, he regained consciousness with a gasp. Teia was standing over him with a knife in her hand, and he was covered with the dust of broken green luxin. It took him a few heaving, deep breaths to regain his wits. He'd passed out.

Teia had cut the seal of the green luxin. The squad were speaking to him, but he had nothing for them. Couldn't understand.

They pulled him to his feet.

'Where's Daelos?' Kip asked. Everyone else appeared to be here. Wherever here was. At the bottom of the slaves' stairs, maybe? Ben-hadad and Ferkudi were reloading the blunderbusses, preparing to breach a door.

'Broke an ankle jumping over some bodies,' Cruxer said. 'We had to leave him.'

'You *left* him?' Kip demanded.

'We gave him a Lightguard cloak and tunic. The chirurgeons will help him and he can get away. The Blackguards will help him, Kip,' Cruxer said. He was defensive. He hated leaving someone behind, too.

Orholam damn it. We're children. Even Cruxer.

'It was the right thing,' Teia said. 'Now shut up and let's go.'

'Fire in three!' Ben-hadad announced.

Ferkudi fired before any of them could cover their ears.

'Sorry, I heard *fire*,' he said.

Ben-hadad fired right behind him, and he winced at the deafening sound. 'Deserved that,' he said.

'Reload,' Cruxer said. 'Everyone, ready luxin.'

Kip took a step to take a defensive position at the stairs, and almost fell again as his orange-luxin-coated foot shot out from under him. Ugh, he had orange luxin goop everywhere, even in his hair. Someone handed him the lit orange mag torch. He drafted a wad of orange luxin into his hand, and then used that to suck the open orange luxin off his body and out of his hair. Mostly.

He checked himself quickly. His green spectacles were unbroken, and the spectacle case on his left hip had successfully protected all his other colors.

He listened closely at the stairs and thought that he could hear the groans and whimpers of the injured and dying above, and maybe distantly, the sound of reinforcements coming down. With the musket fire, the Lightguards had figured out where the squad was. Now they could concentrate their forces. The noose was tightening.

'Where are we?' Kip asked. He filled himself with green luxin rapidly, then swapped spectacles and pulled in blue off one of the white mag torches. The torches were already getting low, and Kip could feel the bruises he was going to have tomorrow. Provided he had the luxury of seeing tomorrow.

'Main floor,' Ben-hadad said. 'Main hall should be that third door on the left.'

'How do you know that?' Kip asked.

'I don't really get lost,' Ben-hadad said. 'I was eight years old before I realized a person could.'

'Where did Ironfist go?' Kip asked. 'I mean, he was leaving, too, right?'

'No time,' Cruxer said. 'Let's go.'

Kip followed, but he couldn't shake the thought. Ironfist was getting out of here, too. He hadn't gone toward the lift.

So Ironfist had some other way out.

But Kip didn't know that for sure. Maybe Ironfist had stopped on one of the other floors, grabbing some personal items, and got stuck on the wrong side. Maybe he planned to make his escape later. Maybe he'd bluffed his way through the Lightguards.

They ran through the empty halls, fanned out, weapons drawn. Everyone but Kip was a bloody mess. Big Leo had his left arm in a makeshift sling, half cloth, half luxin, and the skin was bulging in his forearm. Nasty break, but he didn't seem to be feeling it yet.

Cruxer's nose was bloodied, and he had a cut down his forehead, seeping blood into his mouth. Ferkudi had drafted what looked like a fighting glove around his left hand.

Probably had broken some bones punching someone. Winsen was grinning broadly, He looked insane. He was carrying a short bow with bodkin arrow nocked. Teia had wiped blood off her face, but she was careful to wipe it onto her grays, not on the shimmercloak. It was a steely, metallic gray now, not the dull gray of an inductee's cloak. Maybe this was its true color, if it had such a thing. On the back of the cloak Kip noticed barely touching circles, one white, one black, with the black over the white a little, like an eclipse of the moon.

'They know about the cloak,' Teia said. 'At least, they know enough. I told them while you were out.'

'I wouldn't say we know *enough*,' Ben-hadad said. 'I have got a hell of a lot of—'

'We know enough for now,' Cruxer said. 'Enough to use her. Teia, take point.' She did. As they moved down the hall, people's mag torches began sputtering out. 'Fill up,' Cruxer whispered.

But they'd all been drafting long enough that the order was unnecessary. Each of them drew in as much luxin as they could before the torches burned out.

As they reached another door, Teia made the hand motion to Cruxer: scout? He nodded permission, and she put her hand to the crack in the double doors, lowering her head, her eyes flaring wide.

She stood there for perhaps a full minute. Then she came back. 'Fifteen, maybe twenty. Semicircle of musketeers around this door. It's a death trap.'

Kip's heart dropped, and he could tell that all of them were thinking the same thing. They hadn't run fast enough. If the Lightguards at the base of the Prism's Tower knew that they were coming, this wasn't the only choke point available. The Lightguards could also cut them off at the Lily's Stem. With enough men and muskets in narrow places, the squad's skills would be beside the point.

'I could go green golem,' Kip said. 'I've done it before. I stopped bullets once.'

'Can you do it reliably?' Ben-hadad asked. 'Can you differentiate between friend and foe when you're golem?'

'No,' Kip admitted reluctantly.

'There's some other way out,' Ferkudi said. 'My parents mentioned it once. I overheard. Some way to get to Cannon Island directly. No boats.'

'Where?' Cruxer asked.

'I don't know,' Ferkudi said. 'It's hidden, that's all I know.'

'Well that doesn't help us, does it?' snapped Big Leo. It looked like the pain was starting to come through his initial shock from his messily broken arm. He was rarely irritable.

'Breaker?' Teia prompted.

'I know another way out exists,' Kip said. 'My father told me that. He didn't say where it was. But it'd have to be in one of the lower levels if it goes out under the bay?'

'If we want to go to the lower levels, we've still got to cross the great hall,' Cruxer said. 'The slaves' stairs don't go down there. The only access is on the other side.'

'Well, that's a stupid design,' Ben-hadad said. 'Why don't the slaves' stairs go all the way down?'

'It's for defense,' Cruxer said, 'and as you can see, it's *working*.'

'Breaker, that wasn't what I meant,' Teia said, giving him a significant look.

'Huh?' Kip asked.

'You know,' she said, nodding her head.

'No. What?'

'I pulled a thing. You know?'

'A thing?'

'Off your—'

'This is getting intriguing,' Winsen said.

'Skin, Winsen! Off his skin!'

'Oh!' Kip said. The cards. She was asking if he'd seen anything in the cards that showed an escape route. Given that the cards were of the most powerful people in the world, it made sense that any number of them would have known about an escape route. 'I don't . . . I don't remember anything helpful.'

He hadn't been having the flashbacks – flash-sidewayses? flash-cardwises? – for the last half hour. Not that he missed them. He still had the headache, though it was less acute now. It had seemed the cards had been triggered by words, right?

Escape, he thought. Tower. Prism's Tower. Cannon Island. Flee. Run Away.

Nothing.

Cruxer said, 'Check the other doors on this level. Maybe we can go around to the stairs down or to the outside. Now, go! Not you, Breaker. You *think*.'

They ran off in all directions except through the double doors. Kip tried to think. He'd absorbed those cards. All those cards. Something should come to him. One of them surely must have known this secret. Any of the Blackguards would know, right?

But none came to mind. No matter what he thought. He couldn't just call them up.

What the hell?! What use were the bloody cards if they didn't come to mind when he needed them? Right after he'd come out of the Great Library, the cards had been leaping into his brain so fast he couldn't stop them. They'd been triggered by every little thing.

I'm a Guile, I'm supposed to remember everything!

But he couldn't remember any of the cards. Except the one he hadn't lived yet. The White's card. The puzzle card. Which was perfect. As if Kip needed puzzles *now*, with every passing second bringing the Lightguard closer. What had she said? 'Not only Prisms fly'? Right. That was it. But what the hell did that mean? That she'd known about Gavin's flying machine, his condor? Karris had flown in the condor, too. Maybe Karris had reported it. But even if the White had known about it, so what? Gavin was the only person in the world who knew the proper design of the condor or could draft enough to make it work, and after a full year of work and practice, he'd still found it incredibly difficult and dangerous. Someone could give Kip a condor, and it still wouldn't do him any good.

'Not only Prisms fly.' What could it—

Oh, not *fly* fly. Fly like *flee*.

Dumbass! The White knows the secret exit! Of course she does!

It's got to be in her card!

'Barricaded!' Big Leo shouted as he ran back to them.

'My way, too!' Teia said.

'Men coming down the stairs. Fast!' Ferkudi said.

'All of them are locked,' Cruxer said. 'Kip, what you got?'

'I need light, full-spectrum light!' Kip said.

'Stairs are no good,' Ferkudi said. 'Only way to get natural light is to get out.'

'Surely we've got a white mag torch,' Leo said. 'That'd work, right?'

'Teia?'

She was already looking in the bag, as if looking would change things. 'Gone. They're all gone,' she said.

'We could go up the stairs one floor and get full light from one of the balconies there,' Big Leo said.

'There is no way I'm going *up* the tower,' Cruxer said. 'We're trying to get out, and the exits are all down. We go up and we have to fight through the Lightguards twice more.'

Ben-hadad came back at last. He was huffing. 'I got, I got, far as the lift. Should be able to, to squeeze through. But saw out front. Out the main gate at the Lily's Stem, there's, there's an ambush. Forty, fifty Lightguards. Musketeers.'

'We go up,' Kip said.

They looked at him like he was mad. And he was. Even if they got to the lift, they'd be exposed to fire from the main hall until they could go up.

'Breaker. *Up?*' Cruxer said.

Winsen drew his arrow and let fly. A man forty paces back stumbled and fell as he burst through the door to the slaves' stairs. Winsen already had another arrow nocked, and released.

'Let's go!' Cruxer said.

Winsen sent four more arrows down the hall in rapid succession while they ran, then reached into his quiver and found no more.

Ben-hadad led them through a small door where he'd knocked a huge bureau over to be able to get in. 'Not by strength,' he said. 'Application of a lever.'

They pushed through tiny, connected rooms, all empty. Past another narrow hall. Ben-hadad pointed. 'Leads back to the barricaded door you tried, Captain.' Another: 'Leads to the kitchens, there's a door to the outside, but it's a wall this time of day. Problems of a rotating tower,' Ben-hadad said. 'Designing doors in the island mantle – which doesn't rotate – that can be used all day long. The designer solved the problem a few years later, but the Prism's Tower had already had its base constructed by then. Inefficient, I agree.' Kip knew what he meant – he'd experienced the same thing down in the baths – but he could tell no else did. Not that now was the time to ask questions about things that didn't pertain to their immediate survival.

Ben-hadad said, 'That hall leads to more slaves' housing and then to a door off to the side of the ambush. We'd have some surprise. If we want to try our luck?'

'I say we do it,' Teia said. 'I'll use my little trick and cause a distraction. They're musketeers. If I can get them to fire a volley wildly, they'll be vulnerable. They attack me on the opposite side and then, you all fall on them from behind.'

'Twenty men? The seven of us?' Ben-hadad asked. 'We're good, Teia, but I don't know if we're that good.'

'Why are we discussing this?' Winsen said. 'We've got a command structure.'

'Do we?' asked Big Leo. 'We're out of the Blackguard, Win. Maybe we should all have a voice.'

'Enough,' Cruxer said. 'Breaker, you sure?'

'If we have to wait until we're sure to decide, we're fucked.'

'Damn it, Kip!' Teia said. 'Now is not the time to be un—'

'Breaker,' Cruxer corrected.

'Breaker,' Teia said. 'I saw what those things did to you. It might kill you to look at another card. Or it might take half an hour. And up? Goss *died* to get us down this tower. You want us to go back up?'

'The White would have an escape. It has to be near her apartments.'

'You want us to go *all the way up*?' Ferkudi asked.

'I'm telling you, get me light, and—' Kip started.

'Enough!' Cruxer said. 'Enough! Kip, Breaker, we're with you because we believe in you. Anyone who doesn't, get the hell out. Make your choice.'

'I'm with you,' Teia said, but it was softly. It was surrender. To death. She would die to prove her loyalty, but she knew Kip was wrong. Everyone else was in.

'Was just a question,' Ferkudi muttered.

'Then let's go,' Cruxer said. 'And, Breaker, next time I ask if you're sure? Lie.'

Kip took a deep breath. They were placing a great deal of faith in his intuition. If he was wrong . . .

If he was wrong, they would all die, instead of most or all of them dying, which was what would happen if they charged the main hall.

They arrived at yet another hall. 'This way to the lift,' Benhadad said. He pointed down the other direction. 'That way goes to a wall that will become an open door in half an hour. It should rotate open far enough for us to slip through in . . . maybe ten, fifteen minutes. It would put us behind the Prism's Tower, but we'd still have to make it past the Lightguards in the yard.'

'How many of these bastards are there?' Teia asked.

'Five hundred eighty-two,' Ferkudi said.

They looked at him. It had been a rhetorical question.

Ferkudi said, 'As of last week, anyway. What? Like I'm the only one who looks at the kitchen manifests?' His voice dripped sarcasm.

'Holy shit, Ferkudi,' Big Leo said.

'What? I wanted to know if there would be any Tyrean oranges at the Sun Day parties.'

Kip didn't know whether to be more amazed that it had never occurred to Ferkudi that the Tyrean orange groves were held by the enemy – along with the rest of Tyrea – or that the big clod had somehow done the arithmetic to figure out how much food meant exactly five hundred eighty-two Lightguards, and then had remembered it.

'Trying to hold a hall against musketeers for fifteen minutes is suicide,' Cruxer said. 'We go up.'

Chapter 94

'Everyone ready?' Cruxer whispered. They were behind and to the side of the lift, but they would be exposed to the musket fire from the Lightguards as they ran to get into it.

'Maybe the light's good enough for Breaker to try here?' Teia asked.

'Teia, are you serious with this?' Ben-hadad asked.

'Sorry,' she said.

'We're ready,' Kip told Cruxer. 'Teia, maybe you could . . . could you use it for all of us?' Kip asked.

'No. I barely know how I use it for myself.' She pulled together the hood over her face and – despite that it had no laces or other visible means of fastening – the cloth cinched together tightly, leaving only her eyes visible. The face shimmered and disappeared, leaving what looked a hole, only her eyes floating against blackness.

Teia turned her back and Kip saw the two disks moving across the cloak. The black passed in front of the white disk like an eclipse. White light flared briefly around the black disk, and then the entire cloak shimmered and Teia disappeared.

The entire squad muttered curses.

'If we get out of this alive, I *really* want to study that cloak,' Ben-hadad said.

The natural light that usually suffused this chamber was cut off, the windows covered. Clearly, the Lightguards were trying to minimize their handicaps against the Mighty.

The Mighty? Is that really what we're going to call ourselves?

The light was weak, but it was full-spectrum. With his spectacles, Kip could draft whatever he wanted. But more choices in a limited time didn't mean you could do everything – it meant that you could do anything, so you probably did nothing, frozen with indecision. How long would it take the Lightguards following them from the stairs to find their way through all the halls and catch up?

So Kip fell back to the old standbys, albeit with far greater proficiency and less waste than he would have before all his training with Karris. He drafted the equivalent of a tower shield of green onto his left arm, and drew still more green, weakly, through his green spectacles. It was slow, but it would have to do.

And suddenly, despite the green he was drafting, he was a coward. He didn't want to move. Didn't want to be a target to dozens of men with muskets.

What the hell? Green had always made him invincible, had always made fear foreign.

This is what it is to grow up. It is to live beyond the blind rush of passion, or hate, or green luxin, or battle juice. It is to see what must be done, and to do it, without feeling a great desire or a great hatred or a great love. It is to confront fear, naked. No armor of bombast or machismo. Just duty, and love for one's fellows. Not love felt, not the love that compelled action without thought, but love chosen deliberately. I am the best person to do this thing, it said, though I may die doing it.

I will go, it said, with clear eyes and no passion, but it was love, love, love all the same.

The drug that was green luxin had no hold on Kip, but he took a deep breath, and ran.

He ran, on tiptoe. He ran, without screaming defiance. He ran as silently as possible. And running in such a way, he ran without being detected, almost all the way to the lift.

A shout rang out as he threw himself into the lift. There was white stone here, lit from the mirrors above, and it gave him green sluggishly, even as he lay down and raised the shield, sideways, making an embankment of green luxin.

The rest of the squad was hot on his heels. Winsen threw a yellow flashbomb, and it hit right in front of the turning Lightguards. Perfect throw, perfect flashbomb. Several of the Lightguards, scared out of their minds, clenched fingers on their triggers. The roar of matchlocks in their ears and resounding magnified off the stone walls only doubled the confusion of the Lightguards, who'd only turned in time to be blinded.

Only one or two of all of them got shots off even vaguely in the direction of the squad. The whine of ricochets sounded off the far walls.

Cruxer leapt over Kip's shield and threw the counterweights, ignoring the danger, and was about to throw the release to fling them upward when Kip cried, 'Cruxer, no! Ben!'

Ben-hadad had gone sprawling. He picked himself up immediately, but fell again. His knee was red, and when he stepped again, it turned a direction a knee shouldn't turn.

Ferkudi was up in an instant. He hopped up over Kip's wide shield and ran out. Shots rattled into Kip's shield, and Kip was frozen. The shield embankment was open luxin, if he let it go, they'd all be vulnerable. They could all die.

This was his part. This, now, in this moment, was the totality of what he could do. If he tried to be a hero, his friends would die. As they might die anyway.

He shook as the Lightguards recovered and more brought their weapons to bear, some aiming at Kip and the others in the lift, and some aiming at Ferkudi leaping out of the lift and Ben-hadad on the floor.

A blunderbuss seemed to appear out of midair, to the side of the crescent of Lightguards. Hammer slapped down, and sparks and fire and molten death shot out, raking across the front line. It could only be Teia. Kip's eyes widened to sub-red in an instant, and the inane thought floated into his mind: I couldn't have widened my eyes that fast six months ago. Progress!

He saw Teia flinging the spent blunderbuss into the still-standing Lightguards. Then she hefted the other blunderbuss that she'd balanced against her left leg, and shot the second rank of Lightguards.

One or two shot vaguely in her direction before she discharged that shot, then she was off, legs briefly visible as her cloak swung free of her legs. But none of the Lightguards saw it. The attack from midair was too surprising, too disorienting. They almost broke.

Kip saw the moment yawn open. One more touch, his Guile mind said, and these men will flee.

But he was holding the green shield and he couldn't—

Ferkudi heaved Ben-hadad into the lift, and Teia – visible now – jumped in a moment after. Cruxer threw the lever.

The lift shot up. It hit the first stop, throwing them all into the air, and ground to a stop. It fell back to the ground.

There were shouts of alarm, pain, injury, weakness, and rage going up from the Lightguards. Kip stood up, dropping the green shield, as Cruxer wrestled to put on more counterweights.

A man was rushing them. Kip drafted a green spike and stabbed him in the face. The Lightguard fell into him, still alive, still fighting. Kip elbowed him across the nose, and he went down. Saw another man rushing them, a blunderbuss in one hand.

Kip shot another green spike but missed as the man slipped on a pool of blood.

The man slid almost into their feet. He didn't try to stand; instead, he grabbed for the blunderbuss. At this range, he might take out half the squad.

Winsen was on him with a knife in an instant.

The knife went in and out and in and out of the man's belly, like a tailor rapidly drawing a stitch.

In and out and in and out and in and out and in and out, Winsen wasn't stopping, and it was cold and it was hot and it was bloody and wet and slick and dirty and gruesome and necessary. The man was still fighting, drawing the end of his blunderbuss down to point at Winsen's face.

Ferkudi leapt onto the pile and pointed the barrel out toward more charging Lightguards. Winsen yanked the trigger and the blunderbuss fired, and the Lightguards were peppered with whatever had been in the barrel, but were too far away to be killed.

With his one good hand, Big Leo hauled the man off the pile and threw him off the lift. But another Lightguard was already coming, face bloodied but not stopping. Kip shot a hammerfist of green and blew a shower of teeth and blood across himself. The Lightguard fell across the gap, halfway between being in the lift and not in it as Cruxer threw the lever again.

They flew upward, and the Lightguard flew up with them into the lift shaft. He screamed as his body blocked the lift's ascent, pinched between the floor of the lift and the sides of the lift shaft.

But he only screamed for a moment, as muscle and bone and mail tore. Half a man was left as they flew skyward, and then as they rammed through the one-way doors at each level, and the body got trapped and scraped off at each successive level, less and less. Half, a third, a head and an arm, a helmet with a head in it, and then nothing at all – of what had been a man, ten seconds ago.

Kip fell backward onto his ass, staring horrified, as a man disappeared into the maw of war.

They clanged through level after level. With how much counter-weight Cruxer had set, they never paused long. Several times, they saw astounded guards, who never so much as fired their muskets.

And then the squad hit the top level.

None of them had reloaded on the trip up. Inexperience, or trauma, or plain horror overwhelming their training. Kip hadn't drawn in any more luxin.

There was no Lightguard checkpoint, and the Blackguards recognized them and came running. Cruxer kept his cool, and it was a blessing from Orholam himself, because out of the others, only Winsen kept his, too. Together, they pulled everyone off the lift.

'Lightguards,' Cruxer said to the Blackguards stationed there. 'They're after us. You can't fight them or you'll start a war. But please, please, help.'

'Oh, shit!' Kip said. 'Where's Teia?'

She spoke behind him. 'I'm right here. Cruxer waited for me to get in the lift.'

The Blackguards on duty were baffled. The woman, Nerra, went immediately to Ben-hadad, though, and started examining his leg.

'What are you talking about?' Little Piper asked. 'What's happening? We've seen the wall crystals going crazy, but they aren't any of our codes, and we couldn't leave our posts. The commander hasn't answered any of our queries.'

'Commander Ironfist's been kicked out of the Blackguard,' Kip said. It occurred to him that he should lie, that lying would make it easier to get these two on their side.

'Orholam, Ben-hadad, what have they done to you?' Nerra said. 'Who's behind this?'

'My grandfather,' Kip said. 'He set the Lightguard after us, and he's the one who relieved Ironfist of his position.'

'What? What?!' Little Piper demanded. He wasn't a tall man, but he was wide, with a shaved head and intense brown eyes under half-halos of yellow and orange.

'The commander agreed to go quietly. He didn't want to

cause war between the Blackguard and the Lightguard. Said the promachos would take the excuse to eliminate the Blackguard altogether.'

'To hell with that!' Little Piper said. 'I'll, I'll—'

'Shut up,' Nerra said. 'We'll delay them, young ones. What are you doing?'

'We need to go to the White's room. Can we?' Kip asked. They could stop them.

The two Blackguards looked at each other. Some silent understanding went between them. They were in love, Kip saw, some intuitive part of him seeing it from how they understood each other.

'I'm sure I don't need to say this, but I need to say this,' Little Piper said. 'The White's in there still. She's dead. You won't disturb her.'

'Of course,' Cruxer said. 'Is Ben-hadad fit to travel? Ben, do you still want to come with us?'

'He'll never fight again,' Nerra said. She looked at Ben-hadad. 'The leg's ruined. Sorry to say it, but it's true.'

Ben-hadad shrank. 'Can I come? Please?' He turned to Cruxer. 'I don't want to . . . I can't be left behind. I'm no Daelos, you understand? This squad is everything to me.'

Nerra nodded, and so did Cruxer, who said, 'I'll carry you if I have to.'

'We'll buy you as much time as we can without a clash of arms,' Nerra said. 'Go, and Orholam shield you.'

They ran down the hall and up the stairs and went past the two Blackguards who stood silent at the White's door. Kip recognized Gill Greyling, but each Blackguard pretended not to see them.

Kip went out to the balcony. It was still early morning. Orholam's beard, how was it still early morning? It felt like a thousand years since dawn.

He rummaged through his pack, looking for the card he'd tucked away not half an hour ago. He glanced at the White's bed, where her corpse lay. He kissed thumb and two fingers and flung a quick blessing at her.

He found the card in his breast pocket. It had been preserved between plates of glass. Kip had nicely broken those in his tumble down the stairs, but the card was undamaged. He drew it out and, while rapidly switching between spectacles and sheathing each as he was done with it in order to draw in all seven colors at once, said, 'I have no idea how long this will take me. Just . . . just defend me. I'll be back as soon as I can.'

'We'll hold,' Ferkudi said, and he spoke for them all.

Kip felt, in that moment, an overwhelming love for these people.

He wouldn't fail them.

Holding the card in his left hand, he drew the colors into his right and touched the five points. *Tap, tap, tap, tap, tap.*

'Got it,' he said.

He looked up, wondering if any of them would still be alive, if he had done it in time.

'Huh?' Ferkudi asked.

Kip was looking down at his left wrist. The tattoo was back, but it was already fading, as if its colors were connected to the colors he drafted. He looked up. 'What do you mean, "Huh"?'

'Uh, you didn't *do* anything,' Cruxer said.

'What did you see?' Teia asked.

'I . . . I . . . I can't remember,' Kip said.

'What?!' Ben-hadad said. 'You mean *that* was it working? And you don't remember what it did?'

'Ben, I love you to death, but shut the hell up,' Cruxer said. 'Breaker, what do we do?'

'I can't remember anything—' Kip said.

'We came up here so you could remember *nothing*?!' Big Leo demanded. He was kind of an asshole when he was in pain.

'It's outside of time, Big Leo,' Kip said. 'It's – I can't remember anything right now. But I'll remember it in the future, I think. Except, except one thing. We have to go upstairs.'

'There is no upstairs. Except the roof,' Cruxer said. 'Oh. In for a den, in for a danar. Up to the roof!'

With Ferkudi and Cruxer helping Ben-hadad, they piled out of the room, past the Blackguards, who looked after them, wondering. They went out the door to the stairs up to the rooftop.

'Well, at least those Lightguards are gone,' Big Leo said. 'Of course, there's nothing else up here, either.'

'Big Leo, Winsen, Ferkudi, you guard the door,' Cruxer said. 'Kip? Please, please, please tell me you've got something.'

'It's . . .' Kip squeezed his eyes shut. There had been something. It was about this space. He could almost taste the memories. He knew, somehow, that he had seen all of the White's life, every decision, every regret, every maneuver, and yet . . . he couldn't grab on to it.

Oh, come on! What's the point in having powers if they don't come through when you need them?

'Teia,' Kip said. 'There's something here. I'm sure of it.'

'Something? Like, what? Like the entrance to her secret escape tunnel?' Teia asked. 'Kip, I don't think there's room up here for a tunnel entrance.'

'Teia, I don't know!'

'It *was* a tunnel,' Ferkudi said, suddenly excited. 'That my parents talked about. I mean, it was a tunnel under the sea. Out to Cannon Island. Tunnel.' He pointed down, as if they weren't grasping an obvious point. 'But, but, I don't think you'd start a tunnel from up *here*. Maybe in the basement?'

'Ferk, did you miss the whole convers— You know what? Never mind,' Kip said.

Teia was holding a hand up against the sun, trying to shield her eyes as she flared them open to paryl width, blinking from the intensity of the light.

There was a shout from inside. It was the Blackguards, but Kip knew they were simply doing their best to give Kip and the Mighty a warning.

'Does the door lock?' Cruxer asked.

Winsen shook his head. 'Only from the inside. Anyone have arrows? Shit. Anyone know how to draft arrows?'

No one said anything.

Big Leo, arm still in a brace, leaned his weight against the door. 'Please tell me they don't have muskets,' he said. Still in pain from his broken arm, but resigned now.

Resigned to die well. This is what I've brought my friends to.

'Breaker,' Teia said. 'Your spectacles. Try them. Try them all.'

Kip put on his sub-red spectacles. They were still a wonder, overlaying all the detail of sub-red without making him sacrifice the visible spectrum. Possibly the handiwork of Lucidonius himself. But not helpful. He flipped them back into their case and drew the superviolet, again, more helpful than narrowing his eyes to superviolet himself because he could see the spectra overlaid simultaneously. He looked around, not knowing what he was looking for.

The door rattled and jumped as someone tried to fling it open.

They hadn't expected resistance. They tried again.

'Ignore that!' Teia said. 'What about over here?'

At the door, Big Leo crouched down, still keeping his shoulder braced against the door, but as low as he could.

Two shots rang out, and wood splintered at head and shoulder level. If Leo hadn't moved, he would have been dead.

Winsen pushed a tiny flashbomb through the hole the musket balls had torn.

'Kip!' Teia said. 'I see something!'

Kip looked at the spot she was pointing out. There was something there, barely visible in superviolet. It was the shape of a key. Kip pressed it, hard, and it sank.

Text appeared, burning white in the floor at the very edge of the tower. It was in some language Kip didn't know. 'Uh . . . anyone read this? What is it?' Kip asked the squad.

Cruxer glanced over. 'That's archaic Parian. It says, um, it's a formal case, um, something like "Would ye fly, o White?"' Another key appeared, larger.

'Yes!' Kip said. 'That's it!' There was another key next to the text. He pushed it down with his whole hand.

A panel slid back, and a long lever appeared. Kip looked at Teia, excited.

Wood exploded within a breath of Big Leo's face. Shrapnel tore his cheek. 'What are you waiting for?' he bellowed.

Kip heaved on the lever. He pulled it all the way back until it touched stone. They heard something grate and grind. They all looked around, expecting a hole to appear.

'Where's the entrance? You think it's some kind of chute?' Teia asked.

'Uh, there's a whaddaythingit over here,' Ferkudi said, pointing.

On the inside of one of the crenellations, a bolt had appeared. Wrapped around the eye bolt was woven a steel cable that disappeared into the stones at their feet, which were glowing.

'Don't stand on it!' Teia said.

'It . . . it ratchets, the lever,' Ben-hadad said.

'What?' Teia asked.

But Kip got it. He threw the lever forward and pulled it back again.

'Not much time left!' Big Leo shouted.

'Not acceptable!' Cruxer yelled. 'Light 'em up!'

Who yells, 'Not acceptable'?

With each throw of the lever, more steel cable popped out of the ground, slowly crossing the entire diameter of the tower. 'What is it doing?' Kip asked. 'Where's the damn hole? There's got to be some kind of chute, right?'

He heard the sounds of luxin being flung and shouts and musket fire and the wood door disintegrating, but he had time for none of it. His world had shrunk to this duty, this place. The steel cable finally popped fully free of the floor and wrapped over what looked like a pulley on a post at the edge of the tower.

Kip pulled it again and this time it stopped. He pushed the lever and pulled back with no resistance. It was finished, whatever *it* was. 'That's it!' he said. 'What do we got?'

'That's no chute,' Ferkudi said, looking off the edge.

'Captain! Can you hold the door without Ferkudi? I need him!' Ben-hadad said.

'Yes! Go!' Cruxer said. He had his spectacles on and was throwing luxin through the holes in the door. The door was barely hanging by its hinges, splintered and torn by musket balls.

Suddenly, there was a lull.

'Ferkudi, carry me over there,' Ben-hadad said.

Ferkudi did it immediately, joining Kip, who was standing at the edge. The steel cable had been freed not just from the top of the tower, but from the sides of it as well, buried under mortar and stone for hundreds of years. It had only been freed from the top ten paces or so of the tower.

'Orholam have mercy. It's broken,' Teia said. 'Look.'

The stones at her feet, directly under the post, had some text in archaic Parian.

'What's it say?' Kip asked. 'Anyone? Cruxer's busy.'

'Says, "The Isle" or "The Island." Actually I'm not really sure of the difference between those,' Ferkudi said.

Of course Ferkudi knew archaic Parian. Of course he did.

They looked out to Cannon Island, which was almost a straight shot west out into the sea from here. 'There's a post all the way over there.'

He was right. A perfectly matching post had popped up on Cannon Island. It, too, appeared to have steel cable wrapped over it, pointed toward them.

'What's the point?' Kip asked. 'Is it supposed to be an anchor for magic? Who can draft over that kind of distance?'

'No, no, no,' Ben-hadad said. 'They're supposed to connect by steel cable. But that would require a vast counterweight to take up all the slack and keep the cables taut.'

'Need some help over here!' Cruxer shouted. The battle had resumed. Cruxer was doing his best to reinforce the door with luxin, but it was a losing battle. The blue just shattered or dissolved when hit with musket balls. Big Leo's red and sub-red weren't any help at all.

'I'll go,' Ferkudi said. He pulled two powder horns out of his pack and ran over to join them.

Ben-hadad said, 'The counterweight. It would have to be huge, see, to tear the cable free . . . Ah! Look!' He pointed to the side where another crenellation had popped open to reveal a compartment filled with some machines of pulleys and belts. 'You snap one of those onto the cable, and ride the cable all the way to Cannon Island.'

'The cable doesn't go to Cannon Island!' Kip said. 'It doesn't go anywhere!'

'Something's wrong, then. We have to release the counterweight.'

They were interrupted by Cruxer shouting, 'We need shot for the blunderbuss! Anyone have anything we can use?'

Usually, you could put nearly anything into a blunderbuss: rocks, nails, musket balls, whatever. But the top of the tower was bare. Any luxin short of perfectly crafted solid yellow wouldn't survive the shot, so that was out.

'Coins,' Kip said. 'Our pay! Can't spend it dead.'

They all looked at him for one moment like he was insane. And then they all tossed their coin sticks to Big Leo, who was sitting on the ground, back braced against the door. He popped the danars and quintars off the coin sticks and into the barrel.

The top third of the door was gone.

'They're about to rush us,' Cruxer said, peeking through a hole. 'Hurry, please.'

'Hurrying!' Big Leo said, stuffing pieces of a torn handkerchief as wadding down the barrel.

Kip ran back to the lever and pulled it again. Twisted, pulled, turned, and there! It grabbed and he heaved on it.

He could feel something give within the tower, and suddenly the steel cable was zipping down. He turned his head and saw that the entire crenellation, a huge slab of rock, had broken away from the side of the tower and tumbled off. Suspended on another post just feet away from the wall, the counterweight plunged downward, pulling the cable taut with incredible force.

Kip ran to the island side of the Prism's Tower to see his handiwork.

Ben-hadad was downcast. 'And this,' he said, 'is why engineers have to think of *everything*.'

The steel cable had pulled perfectly out of its hidden places along the side of the Prism's Tower, and along the top of the walkway in the air between the Prism's Tower, and the sub-red tower and the tiny strip of land before it came to the water. But then, instead of connecting straight to the far post on Cannon Island far away, the line went straight into the water of the bay.

'They laid that line along the sea floor hundreds of years ago,' Ben-hadad said. 'But since then, it's grown over with coral and Orholam knows what. The entire sea floor could have shifted. The counterweight isn't heavy enough now.'

Kip looked at the angle of the line. If they rode the line, they would plunge into the water at incredible speeds, not even halfway to Cannon Island. The drop was too steep. They wouldn't survive it.

They heard the roar of the blunderbuss as Cruxer fired, but couldn't see anything beyond the broken door and the black smoke.

'We could . . . maybe draft brakes onto the mechanisms,' Ben-hadad offered. 'But those of us who are injured . . . Breaker, there's no way I can make that swim.'

'I hate to criticize when we're on the verge of death and all,' Teia said, 'but what good does it do us to get to Cannon Island?'

'It keeps us alive for another half hour?' Kip said. He scowled.

'They're withdrawing!' Cruxer shouted.

'The ship is on the other side of Big Jasper,' Teia said. 'You think we can make it down the line, row from there, get to Big Jasper, and run all the way to the docks before any of five hundred eighty-two Lightguards can intercept us?'

'It would be less than five hundred eighty-two now,' Ferkudi said. 'We've killed at least—'

'They'll catch us easily, and without a choke point like the door here to hold them off, we're dead.'

'Teia, not helping!' Kip said. 'Wait! Teia! You're a genius!'

'I am?'

'Teia, get over here!' Kip said. He was flipping through his spectacles, one at a time, searching. 'Paryl!'

'They're coming! They've got some kind of shield wall!' Winsen said.

'What are we looking for, Breaker?' Teia asked.

'The script, it says, "To the Island,"' Kip said. 'Why label a destination if there's only one destination?'

'I could kiss you!' Teia said.

They looked at each other, and both looked away.

Winsen fired a musket. 'Got one! But it's not enough. They've got reinforcements!'

'There,' Teia said. She ran over, pushed a second key, and script and another key appeared. Kip pushed it, not worrying about the translation. They were running out of time. Pulled open the compartment and started ratcheting the lever.

'Faster!' Cruxer said.

'No, wait!' Ben-hadad said.

Kip stopped.

Ben-hadad said hurriedly, 'This wire goes all the way to the southeast side of Big Jasper. It's got to go right along a bunch of streets that are packed with people today! If this cable comes ripping up out of the streets with all this weight behind it, we could kill dozens. You have to give them time to get out of the way.'

'This is the Lightbringer's life we're saving!' Cruxer shouted. 'Do it! That's an order!' He was reloading the blunderbuss as fast as he could.

Kip heaved, and the crenellation-counterweight split off the side of the building and fell. This one was far larger than the other. It plunged and the steel line hummed, and then the counterweight crashed into the ground near the base of the Prism's Tower far below – and through the ground, into the vast underground practice yards, as it had apparently been designed to do.

Kip only hoped no one had been killed below.

From his vantage, Kip couldn't see what had happened in the city. He wondered if he'd just killed people. But before he could get to the edge to see, he had to make it past the line of fire of the wheeled shield wall that the Lightguards were pushing forward. In moments, they would have it all the way to the door, and their field of fire would expand to encompass most of the top of the tower.

Flipping on his red spectacles as he ran to take a position next to Cruxer, Kip drew red in and in, until he wanted to combust. He threw his hand forward and shot red out in a stream, as hard and concentrated as he could manage.

The stream splattered over and under and around the wheeled shield wall and deep into the hallway.

The Lightguards knew what red luxin meant. Five of the men who'd been pushing the shield wall forward panicked and bolted.

Panic is contagious, but not all are susceptible. A big man stepped up, smearing some of the pyrejelly off his face. He lifted his matchlock – but never got the shot off. When the burning slow match was brought close, the red luxin on his face ignited.

He shot the musket into the ceiling and the sound of a

ricochet whine preceded the sound of rapidly spreading fire. He screamed.

Kip ran past the door and flames and found Ben-hadad fitting the wheel mechanisms over the steel cable.

'The line didn't kill anyone,' he said. 'It came off the top of the city walls. Ingenious. Who's first?'

'I'll go,' Kip said.

'Breaker's not going first,' Cruxer said. 'Thing may not work. I go first. Winsen, you're second. Give me a ten count. Might need to fight at the other end. Then Ferkudi. Then the wounded: Big Leo, you first, then Ben-hadad. Then Kip. Teia, you bring up the rear.'

'Anything special I need to do?' Cruxer asked Ben-hadad.

'Just hold on,' Ben-hadad said. He snapped the mechanism onto the line. Cruxer stepped quickly onto the iron sides of the inverted T and gripped the post in his hand. 'But I think—'

Cruxer hopped off the side of the Prism's Tower and flew down the line. He just kept going faster and faster. The first section was nearly a free fall. In ten seconds, he was nearly beyond the sea and over Big Jasper.

'I was going to say,' Ben-hadad said, 'that it would be about ten times safer to *sit* on the crossbar. Straddle it.'

Winsen did, sitting right on the edge. 'If this racks my stones,' he started, but he didn't get to complete the threat, because Big Leo pushed him off.

Ferkudi went next, and then Big Leo, who handed Kip a pistol. 'Won't be accurate for shit. It's loaded with a danar. But might be better than nothing.'

Ben-hadad made sure Kip was paying attention to how the mechanism locked onto the cable as he prepped his own.

'Uh, is that the last one?' Kip asked.

'No, no, there's a whole extra compartment of them,' Ben-hadad said. Then he went.

Teia ran over to the other compartment while Kip laboriously set up his own wheel, checking and double-checking it.

'Breaker?' Teia called out. There was something tight in her voice. 'Kip?'

He looked over. She pulled a wheel out of the case. It was

so corroded it was hardly recognizable. 'What's that?' he said. He didn't want to understand.

'There was a hole in the compartment. It's been getting rain in there for years, decades maybe.'

'Well, grab another one,' Kip said. 'And hurry, Teia, I hear voices in the hall. They got drafters to put out the fires.'

'Breaker. They're *all* ruined.'

They looked at each other. 'You take this one,' Kip said. 'I'll draft a copy of it, and be right after you.'

'You're not that good a drafter, and we both know it.'

'I can do it.'

'Kip.'

'We don't have time to fight, Teia.'

'Kip! I'll stay. I can go invisible—' She started grabbing the hood to pull it up.

'There'll be dozens and dozens of them. They're all going to come flooding out at once. Dammit, Teia! They'll find you by touch.'

'Breaker, Goss died to get you out of here. Don't throw that away.'

'Don't you turn this on me!'

'Don't turn it on *me*! We have our orders.'

'You know the thing about fat kids?'

'What? What?!'

'When we don't want to move, we ain't gonna.' He gave her a lopsided grin. 'Come here, I just had an idea.' He flipped on his yellow spectacles. 'We both go.'

He sat, straddling the inverted T, not far from the edge, but not so close she could just push him and make him go.

'There's no way it's going to hold both of us,' Teia said.

'Lap, now!'

Teia grabbed the center bar and swung one leg around it, straddling the T and Kip from the opposite side.

Her eyes went wide as she settled into place, but not from sitting on his lap. 'Kip! Go! Kip, go, go, go! Aram!'

But instead of helping him push off, she was leaning to Kip's left, the same leg he was trying to rock forward. He realized she was trying to draw the pistol he'd tucked behind the lens holster, but it was trapped underneath them.

A musket fired behind Kip, and Kip felt something shift. He hadn't been hit. He looked at Teia; she hadn't been hit either, but she was looking up. He followed her gaze. The bullet had hit the mechanism where the inverted T connected to the wheel. As Kip and Teia watched, the wheel rolled down the cable without them.

They were now tangled together, sitting on a bar completely unconnected to the cable.

'Would you believe I was aiming for your head?' Aram said. 'Lucky miss, for you, huh? Thing is, I'm a lot better with a spear.'

One thousand one. One thousand two. Kip had never success-fully drafted solid yellow luxin in less than a six count. Every time he went faster, his yellow broke.

Teia finally reached Kip's pistol. She tugged on it, but it was held in place. She pulled harder. Gave up. She started to stand—

One thousand three. One thousand—

Kip hugged Teia to himself, and hopped off the edge of the tower.

Teia hugged him hard with her arms and legs as they fell, eyes squeezed tight shut. They fell and fell – and then swooshed out over the Chromeria's wall, and out over the sea, together.

She looked up, stunned. Kip had drafted a simple loop of solid yellow luxin over the cable, and doubled the bar they were sitting on. He swapped spectacles and drafted a steady stream of orange for lubrication where yellow luxin scraped over steel cable. They were emitting a constant stream of yellow sparks, but it would hold. It would hold long enough.

Teia looked at Kip, wide-eyed. Then she squeezed him hard again, but this time with glee. In the perfect light of early morning, they flew over the sea and shoreline. They flew over Sapphire Bay. They flew over the morning parades and luxin fireworks. Teia waved to the bewildered crowds, and many waved back, laughing.

Whites fly, too, indeed.

The cable passed over the east side of Big Jasper, high over houses and warehouses and ships and the wall.

Teia looked at Kip, and he looked at her. She was glowing with joy and morning light, her skin radiant, her eyes holding a million colors Kip had never seen. And they were flying, and they were holding each other, and they were safe, and they were alive, and they were breathing pure glory, and Orholam's Eye gazed on them with the approval that only young lovers know, and in that moment Kip knew the difference between love and infatuation, and love and hunger, and love and the longing not to go unloved. And he wanted to know nothing more than this, and he wanted this moment to freeze forever and thought to cease.

He kissed her. And she kissed him. And it was infatuation, and it was hunger, and it was longing to be loved, and it was an all-consuming fire so hot it devoured worry and loneliness and fear and time and being and thought itself. They kissed, embracing, flying, and for a hundred heartbeats, there was no war, no death, no pain, nothing hard, nothing terrible, nothing but warmth and acceptance.

And as they slowed, nearing the end of their flight, when Kip pulled away from her at last, and gazed again into her eyes, he knew he was lost in her. And he knew at last the difference between love and necessity.

Chapter 95

'This convocation is now in session,' High Luxiat Amazzal said. 'None may enter. None may leave.' Karris wondered if, out of all the High Luxiats, they'd chosen Amazzal solely for his voice. He had a great booming, deep, powerful voice. Maybe the voice and the beard. He had a braided beard in the Atashian style. It was enormous and perfectly white, woven with white silk thread and pearl beads.

With a gravitas that imbued even simple actions with meaning, he held up the end of a thick iron chain. Half a dozen young luxiats were holding coils and coils of the stuff. It was a single, long chain. Unhurriedly, he walked to the main doors and wrapped the chain around the handles, rattling and clanking. There was some sound there that set off Karris's

Blackguard senses. But maybe it was just thinking of Gavin being in such chains. Gavin, here. Home again. Gavin, her love, perhaps broken.

A young assistant brought High Luxiat Amazzal an enormous lock, and he snapped it on. He repeated this at each of the doors, unwinding the chain from each relieved young luxiat's arms, walking to each, taking his time, and winding the chain securely. By the time he reached the last door, the last assistant was trembling with fatigue. He was sweating, clearly terrified he would shame himself by dropping the chain.

Finally, they came back up the side aisle, fully encircling the nobles and drafters seated in the audience hall.

Karris realized she was supposed to be praying. She was off kilter still. Seeing her son – her son? – had been more of a shock than she'd thought it would be. He was staring at her, too.

But he wasn't only staring. He was wearing a crown. Her son had been made Prism-elect. Karris hadn't imagined that Andross Guile would demand that a new Prism-elect be named, not while his own son was Prism. That would have meant a loss of power for his family. Unthinkable. Or at least it *should* have meant a loss of power for the Guiles. Karris knew Andross wouldn't have given such power to Kip. Andross didn't hold Kip, didn't control him. Not yet, though no doubt he was working on that.

But this was altogether unforeseen. A failure of intelligence, in both senses of the term.

Andross had another Guile in play: Zymun. And he'd kept him out of sight until the moment came to play him. Karris hadn't even known that Andross knew she had a son. He hadn't only known it; he'd insinuated himself into Zymun's life somehow. The only thing worse than having to face her abandoned son was to face him after Andross had picked him up like an abandoned toy and taken ownership of him.

She couldn't think about this now. She didn't even recognize this ceremony, and somehow she was sitting in the front row.

Damn, her whole side hurt from that idiotic dive into the water. Tomorrow she wasn't going to be able to get out of bed, she was sure of it.

But sitting here in front, she couldn't even try to massage her shoulder. If only Lord Bran Spreading Oak didn't like her so much. He was old now, but still perfectly genteel. She'd known the Spreading Oaks since she was a girl. Back then they'd had six sons. One had become a Prism, briefly. All were dead now: raiders, fever, the wars. When she was twelve and thirteen years old, Lord Bran had hoped she'd marry his youngest, Gracchos. He'd been a kind boy, more poet than warrior.

He'd died a hero's death that had accomplished nothing in a battle that hadn't settled anything.

Karris looked back to Zymun. She couldn't help it. Was there something about him that drew the eye like iron to lodestone or was it only her? No, no. He was very handsome. He was Prism-elect. Everyone was at least glancing at him frequently. But only Karris stared with her gut churning.

She looked away, to the other Colors sitting on the platform with him. Delara Orange looked sober for the first time in months that Karris could remember. Karris's eye was drawn to the two she didn't know: Caelia Green and Cathán Sub-red. The dwarf Caelia Green of new Tyrea seemed like she could be a natural ally. Gavin would need those in the days to come. Karris should have already made her acquaintance. Cathán Golden Briar was the newest Color, stepping into Arys Sub-red's place after she had died in childbirth. Cathán was a cousin of both Arys Greenveil and Ela Jorvis, and therefore to Ana Jorvis, whom Gavin had thrown off his balcony, albeit accidentally.

If Karris had been looking for someone to look at who would set her mind at ease, she was looking in the wrong place. She looked back at Zymun, and away again. Dear Orholam.

One time when she and Gavin had been hunting a sub-red wight, they'd come upon a family that had fought the wight briefly and chased it away. Through dinner, the father had acted strangely, but denied he was hurt. The next morning, he stood up and screamed. He'd taken a flame crystal in the groin. It had unmanned him, and ashamed, he'd hidden the injury. The flame crystal had cauterized the wound closed – until infection made the skin burst apart when he stood, spurting blood and pus everywhere. He'd died, of course. They wouldn't have been able to save him even if they'd known.

Looking at Zymun, she felt like that. Stomach diseased, like a grotesque pregnancy. Sixteen years of shame and failure had distended her belly, filled her with poison.

Is not the one test of a mother how well she cares for her child? Karris had abandoned this boy. She'd not taken him once to her breast. Hadn't even looked at him, as if he were a monster, or worse, as if in looking at him, she would love him.

And now, she was looking at him, and it was too late. Her heart was dead.

Success, Karris. Your fears were unfounded. You are colder and harder than you knew.

But the ache in her stomach only got worse. She couldn't look at Zymun. She needed her head in this, and it wasn't.

She knew it was kind for Lord Spreading Oak to give her his seat, but she wished he hadn't. She felt exposed up here. People were looking at her as if they expected her to do something. They didn't know about Zymun, did they?

'Child,' High Luxiat Amazzal repeated. He was looking at Karris.

Now everyone *was* looking at Karris.

'Yes?' she asked.

'Please come forward.'

She blinked, trying to remember what he'd been preaching about. She had no idea. Surely he didn't know, did he? Was he going to shame her publicly? For simply not paying attention? Surely not.

She stood and moved forward with all the grace she could muster.

The High Luxiat gestured her to stand in a place off to his left, but as Karris was walking, she saw a muscle twitch in Andross Guile's jaw. A wave of relief swept over her. She didn't know what was happening, but if Andross was angry about it, she wasn't about to be shamed. She took her spot, and finally, finally started thinking.

'Ismene Crassos,' the High Luxiat said. A middle-aged noble-woman stood from one of the other front seats and walked up to a place beside Karris. From the row behind her, her horse-faced cousin Aglaia beamed with pride.

One by one, the High Luxiat said the names of those seated in the front row, and each came to stand in line. 'Eva Golden Briar. Naftalie Delara.'

Next would be Jason Jorvis, then Akensis Azmith, and Croesos Ptolos last.

Karris knew them all. Some from her time as a discipula, others only by reputation. All were drafters. Each was from either a prominent family or a formerly prominent one. Even she counted as the latter, she supposed. But she shouldn't be here with these people.

And before the last name was even announced, Karris knew why they were here. She almost gasped aloud, though if she'd been paying attention to the ceremony, it would have been obvious. But what was *she* doing here?

If she had been putting together the lists, every seat was acceptable but hers. Drafters from the most important families among the satrapies that were still standing, with a special concentration on Ruthgar and Paria. Karris's seat should have been held by a Malargos, but with Tisis gone, it had reverted to Lord Spreading Oak, who was as weak a blue drafter as one could be and still pass the test. It was why he'd survived into old age – he never drafted. Didn't see the need.

They weren't here for a sermon.

'Lords and ladies,' High Luxiat Amazzal said, 'I present you with the cream of the Seven Satrapies. I present you with your finest, the seven candidates from whom Orholam will choose a new White.'

The room broke out into applause, but it was a fierce, competitive applause. There were factions here.

They were here to select a new White. The pool was selected by the High Luxiats, but the White was selected by Orholam himself, in a casting of lots.

But Karris? What—

'There isn't always a grand design,' the White had said. It was exactly the kind of wordplay she loved. It seemed a denial, but it wasn't one, was it? That there isn't *always* a grand design doesn't mean that there isn't a grand design *this time*.

The White had been a discipula with Bran Spreading Oak, ages and ages ago. They were good friends. Bran deserved a seat at the front but could be overlooked because he was so old. If he were made the White, he would only last a year or two, surely. Thus he became a nullity in Andross Guile's plan, whatever that plan was. But by Bran's waiting until the ceremony was under way to vacate his seat and give it to Karris, there was nothing Andross Guile could do about it.

Then, moments later, they'd been locked in here. Not even slaves were allowed to come or go.

The White had arranged for Karris to be here.

All her tutelage was for this. The dozens of minor missions in years past. The possible suicide mission in Tyrea. The slow takeover of the White's spy network. Those tests that Karris had seen as so harsh, so unnecessary, were harsh and unnecessary – for any position less than the White. Which meant that the White had wanted Karris to be her successor – no, that thought was too grandiose, too arrogant, too presumptuous.

And yet here she stood.

The White had wanted Karris to be the next White.

Perhaps Karris wasn't the White's only choice, though. Five of the seven standing here might be the White.

But as Karris looked around, she was pretty sure that wasn't the case. That was Andross Guile's kind of strategy: buy everyone, so whoever wins, you win. The White gambled differently; she put all her money on the long odds. Orea Pullawr had wanted Karris to be the next White.

Karris's eyes started leaking. She couldn't stop it. That irascible old woman had even apologized for it beforehand.

The White had been teaching Karris to take over, all this time. And Karris had never seen it? That didn't bode well for how good of a White she would be, did it?

We all have our blind spots, but pity her whose blind spot is a person. Karris had had two – the White, whom she'd underestimated but loved, and Gavin, whom she'd underestimated and come to love when she stopped underestimating him. It was by Orholam's grace alone that both of her blind spots had been good to her.

Karris had only one chance in seven to fulfill the White's wishes. And suddenly, she wanted it with half her heart.

No one sane could want to be the White. But Karris could want Andross Guile's puppet *not* to be the White. If she was the only stumbling block in his way, so be it.

If it be your will, Orholam, use me.

But how could she do it? Had the White been trusting Orholam to take Karris the rest of the way?

And there it was again. A distant sound that made Karris's ears perk up. The first had been louder, but it had been buried under the rattling of the chains. A musket shot. There were multiple shots, muffled by the thick doors and thick stone, coming from another floor, perhaps? Or was she hearing the shots through the window? Was someone out on a balcony several floors down celebrating Sun Day?

It was, of course, forbidden to celebrate in such a way, but that didn't stop many people on Big Jasper. It did, however, usually stop people within the Chromeria itself. Karris looked over at the Black, who was seated in the second row, but Carver Black didn't appear to have heard the shots, or he was a better pretender than she'd ever guessed.

Andross on the other hand . . . Andross was the ultimate in pretense, in misdirection. Karris stared at him, though he shared the dais with her, and staring was obvious. What did she care? It wasn't like they could take away her candidacy because she was socially awkward.

And then she saw it. She didn't know why this should be the first time. She'd seen Gavin operate a thousand times a thousand – but Gavin had always been a special case. Now she saw power for what it meant to her. To her, it meant not just operating outside the social norms – she always had – it meant flouting them. It meant staring at a man past the time it was acceptable to stare, and instead of feeling awkward, making everyone else feel it. That mastery, that freedom at the expense of others, was intoxicating.

For one who had always had an affinity for the blue virtues of order and harmony and setting a plate exactly according to some point-book written by some long-dead prince of the punctilious pompacio, power was a revelation. Power, not for others, but for her.

And the heart of intoxication is toxic.

Andross Guile looked back at her calmly. He didn't seem angry. It was a feeling, an intuition, rather than any hint of expression. He had an air of expectation. And an expectation, for Andross Guile, was an expectation of victory. He was patient because he was going to win.

Karris smiled at him, smiled like she knew the game, like she loved that he thought he was going to win, smiled like she was better than he was. He blinked, then, the barest flicker of doubt. She ducked her head demurely and smiled on sweet secrets.

He had a plan. Damn. Andross Guile wasn't a man to leave anything to chance. He wasn't going to take a chance, not even a six-to-one chance. Even if he owned all of the other six, he would have a favorite.

But how would he cheat? The ceremony must surely be designed to making cheating impossible.

But Andross Guile knew exactly what those safeguards were. Or who.

Karris looked at the High Luxiat Amazzal. Was he part of it?

'Orholam, all-mighty Lord of Lords,' he said. 'Look upon us. Highest Lord and Highest God, thee we beseech. Look upon our efforts and bless them with thy light, thy life, thy favor. This day, Orholam, Lord and High King, Emperor of Emperors, Balancer of Scales, Mighty and Just, Honorable and Pure, Awesome in Power, Wholesome in Mercy, we seek your will and not our own. We seek this day your White, your light, your antidote to night. We, your satrapies, ask your hand to rest lightly on us, lightly on obedient hearts that need only prompting, not compulsion, only guidance, for it is thy purpose which we seek to serve, and not our own. We praise thee, Lord of Luxlords, Light of Nations, Voice in the Stillness, Guide to the Blind, and Path of Mercy to the Benighted. See and move, O God.' Each time he said 'God' he gave it the traditional moment of hesitation, of respect. It was a measure of his piety or simply his experience that he made the traditional seem vibrant, like he himself thought even this measure of respect was perhaps too little.

'Candidates,' he said, 'come forward. From this time forward, drafting is forbidden. Drafting is an imposition of our will upon the world. Any who draft or who accept another's drafting on their behalf will be disqualified and executed as a heretic. Understood? If so, repeat, "Under the Un-deceivable Eye of Orholam, I understand and I agree."'

They did so, in unison. Then they followed him to a circle on the floor. Young luxiats carried folding screens out for each of them and set them up quickly. Karris's luxiat was a pimply, blushing young man of no more than eighteen.

The High Luxiat spoke now only for their ears. 'The ceremony must be unimpeachable. Thus, because in years long past others have attempted to destroy the sanctity of it, we have put safeguards in place. No lenses. No mirrors. No jewelry. No strips of cloth in your color. Nothing. Even your hair will be covered. In order to assure all that you are obeying these injunctions, you will strip, be searched, and be given identical garments, randomly assigned, all under the eyes of the Blackguards, luxiats, and each other. No exceptions. Even a White submits. If you object to these rules, you may remove yourself from consideration now. If you don't object now, and are found violating the rules, you'll be executed by Orholam's Glare. You understand?'

They did.

'If you think you see some malfeasance on the part of any other, bring it to the attention of the luxiats. A new Blackguard and luxiat will be assigned to her or him, and she shall be searched again. Appropriate punishments will follow, by which I mean death for the heretic and the Blackguard who allowed the heresy both.'

He left, and Karris stripped down. Her blushing luxiat was far more embarrassed than she was. Then he saw the bruising. Flopping into the river flat on her side had made the left side of her body look like she'd been dead and lividity had set in. His mouth moved, but he was obviously forbidden to speak. Karris ignored it. Years with the Blackguard had stripped necessary nudity of its shame. Besides, feelings about her body would distract her from the game Andross was playing, and you couldn't play Andross and have any hope of victory if you didn't give it your full attention.

The High Luxiat was facing seven Blackguards. Each drew a number from a bowl and moved to one of the disrobing lords or ladies. Trainer Fisk – Watch Captain Fisk now – moved to Karris. He gave her a shrug that barely moved his muscle-bound shoulders. 'It was supposed to be women to search the women, and men for the men, but with our numbers so low, they said – Orholam's beard, what happened to your—'

'Just do it,' Karris said.

He did. Not that there was much searching to do. Her hair took the most time, despite that it would be covered. Then he examined both of her hands, her eyes, her armpits, her back, her butt crack, the soles of her feet. Contraband was obviously the first target, but luxin-packing was the second. Fisk was professional and moved quickly, his face a mask.

Seven more Blackguards watched the searchers, and the luxiats, making sure nothing was passed between any of them. The randomness – assuming it was random – of the choice of guards seemed like it would defeat any plan Andross might try to orchestrate. Karris watched the others.

She saw nothing other than their obvious discomfort. She wondered, would someone being passed a – a what, precisely? A colored lens. A drafter could never go wrong with a lens. It would be small, inconspicuous, and allow lethal action.

But she saw nothing untoward.

Luxiats brought out stacks of robes, and at least two Blackguards searched each robe, bending seams to look for hidden pockets, and shifting the piles randomly. The High Luxiat himself distributed them then, also seemingly at random. The robes weren't even different sizes, meaning Karris was swimming in hers while Jason Jorvis could barely close the robe.

The High Luxiat came to each of them while they dressed, holding a plain wooden bowl. 'This is the order you'll draw,' he said.

'We draw for the order we draw?' Karris asked, deadpan.

He sighed. 'Would it shock you that there have been problems about precedence in the past? One goes first, seven goes last.'

Karris shrugged and drew. Six.

She was secretly glad to be going so late. By then, the choices would be constricted.

'There will be seven stones presented. Listen for Orholam's voice. He will guide you. You each may bring no more than one stone back. Just to warn you, each has multiple layers of paint on it, and there is no way to tell how deep is the true one. You bring it back and plunge it into the bowl full of solvent. Whoever has the White's stone will be revealed.'

'What do you mean we bring it *back*?' Karris asked. 'Where are we going?'

'That's it?' Jason Jorvis asked. 'No other rules?'

'You really don't remember?' Ismene Crassos asked.

'My family weren't on the Jaspers last time.'

'And you didn't hear the stories?'

'I'm just trying to get the rules clear,' he said.

All Karris could remember from the time Orea Pullawr was selected as White was a boy named Amestan Niel who'd stayed at a neighboring estate for the summer. She'd barely said two words to him in the whole time. Her best friend, whom Karris had told all about her crush on him, all summer long, had kissed him the night before he left. It had been a devastating betrayal at the time. Last Karris had heard, Amestan Niel was now the third largest exporter of wool in Paria.

Somewhere in the tower, something rumbled. Something big.

They all looked at each other.

'Was that part of . . . this?' Karris asked. But from the startled look on the High Luxiat's face, she knew it wasn't.

'We'll proceed,' he said.

The luxiats carried away the screens, and the candidates were brought to stand in a circle.

'Brace yourselves,' the High Luxiat told the audience. 'There is often a great deal of wind.'

Wind?

At some signal Karris didn't see, all the windows in the room slid down into slots, even as the windows in Gavin's room one floor above did. There was a cold wind, but there wasn't much of it after the initial gust. The morning was still and warm.

Then the floor shifted. Karris instantly dropped her center and stood wide in a fighting stance. It was the floor beneath her and the other candidates. Ismene looked at her and grinned as if to say, Isn't this exciting?

The five-pace-wide circle on which they stood rose out of the floor. Patterns on the audience chamber floor sank, revealing tracks – and the entire disk the candidates were standing on started sliding toward the open window.

'Am I the only one to whom this seems like a really bad idea?' Karris asked.

'Jump off, then,' Jason Jorvis said.

She was standing right at the edge of the disk, and she had been considering doing just that, until he spoke.

The disk slid out the window and into the air, supported on a vast arm protruding from the Prism's Tower two stories below. They slid out ten, then twenty paces from the side of the tower, and the great windows of the audience chamber rattled shut.

Oh. Karris understood. Everyone was to see what happened, but no one was to be able to draft to affect the outcome. The nobles were craning their necks to see more clearly, but Karris's eyes were suddenly drawn up.

Atop the Prism's Tower, one of the massive crenellations had split off and fallen several stories. That had been the rumbling sound she'd heard. The huge chunk of stone was dangling, suspended by a woven steel cable. Karris had been atop that tower a hundred times. There were no steel cables and massive bolts in the crenellations. And the precision of the break made it look purposeful. She was trying to see more of it – where did that cable go? – when her platform shuddered again. Seven additional smaller circular platforms unfolded from beneath the larger platform. The seven circles sank geared teeth into the edge of the larger platform and began wheeling slowly around them.

Now, on each of the smaller circles sat a narrow pedestal, and on the pedestal, in teak and velvet, a white ball. They were identical. After they circled all of them once, they stopped.

Naftalie Delara had drawn number one. She said, 'No point in delaying, I suppose.' She looked heavenward. 'Orholam guide me. Orholam bless my choice.' She went to one of the pedestals and took the white ball there.

Out on balconies of each of the seven towers, a Blackguard and a luxiat stood as a team, watching each other, watching the other teams, and watching that no one would come out onto their balconies to interfere with the ceremony.

But whatever cheat Andross had arranged was doubtless already done. He'd arranged who would pick, and somehow told them beforehand which stone was the one. The mechanics of the cheating would never be visible, and in picking sixth, her choice would likely be moot anyway – a choice between two stones of which surely neither was the correct one. Pointless and barren, like so many years of her life.

Eva Golden Briar took longer, but settled on one in short order.

The White had sacrificed Orholam only knew what to get Karris here, and they'd lost. Karris didn't even know which smiling face hid a liar. Maybe all six did. Andross Guile always had backup plans behind his plans, didn't he?

Karris heard musket fire again and could tell that it came from the top of the Prism's Tower. There were some few people gawking at the candidates through their windows, but no one was out on the balconies, and none was armed that Karris could see. What the hell was going on? The Blackguards on the other towers looked alarmed, too, but were glued to their stations.

Akensis Azmith had selected his stone while Karris looked. Croesos Ptolos took longer, hesitating a long time before one, praying, and then taking another. Then Ismene Crassos went. She looked at each of the three remaining for a long time. Went back to one three times, and finally picked it up.

That left Karris, and two stones.

Listen to the will of Orholam, huh?

She walked up to the first stone. White, round, small enough to fit comfortably in her palm – for whatever reason, it didn't feel right.

Now that was odd. She approached the second, studying it closely, and felt a strong urge to take it in her hand immediately.

She crossed her arms. She'd claimed to the White that she wanted Orholam to speak to her in a way that was obvious, but here it was, and it was obvious, and she didn't like it. If Orholam's voice was a slap in the face, then of what value were Karris's ears? It somehow seemed to devalue her intellect, the intellect Orholam himself had given her. She should be a participant in Orholam using her.

Shouldn't she? Or was she being arrogant?

The fiery green/red drafter she had been not so very long ago would have made a decision and to hell with it. Orholam could do his part or not. If this was his big plan, he'd have to do it. It was all probably pointless anyway, the correct stone already taken.

But Karris wasn't that girl anymore. She had been foolish. She had done things for which she hated herself still. She'd tried to burn herself to ash, and been too excellent to die. She'd tried to blot out the weakness with borrowed purpose as a Blackguard. And now the ache and the disappointment were as much a part of her as her passion and her wildness. She was not a creature of isolated extremes, that disjunctive bichrome, not anymore; she was a whole cloth in the making, integrated.

Ignoring the waiting nobles at the window and the waiting candidates around the disk, Karris turned toward the morning sun. The perfect fiery orb was losing its red tone as it rose, becoming gold.

Karris spread bare arms, saluting the sun, soaking up its full-spectrum light, accepting it and reveling in it.

We are the stories we tell about ourselves. But when those stories are lies, we are the most surprised of all.

When you ask for bread, Karris, would I give you a stone?

And as she raised her arms, glorying in the light, she heard the sound of something huge giving way and an enormous stone crenellation plunged right in front of her.

With the sound of a whip unfurling, a line attached to that great stone spooled out. The other end strained over a pulley at the top of the Prism's Tower, and this stone plunged down, and down. It hit the ground and plunged through it as if the ground been designed to let it through, and it fell into the great underground yard, under vast tension. At the same time, the steel cable unspooled out, away from the tower. It sprang free of the water between Big Jasper and Little Jasper; it tore right out of the top of the walls ringing Big Jasper's east side and then stood, straining, tight, making a straight line from the top of the Chromeria almost to the docks.

'Would I give you a stone?' Karris burst out laughing. And then, as she turned – everyone was watching the great cable – she saw a flash of green at the corner of her eye. What? She looked at the horizon, but she knew – she knew – that the green flash only came at sunset. And then it hit her again. She looked toward Big Jasper.

The star towers were spinning their mirrors, lighting up the crowds, festive, playful. One had caught the green tower and reflected it briefly to Karris.

Karris laughed. She shook her head at Orholam – and then watched, stunned, as a young man went flying down the cable from the top of the tower. She thought she recognized him, but he was moving too fast. Cruxer?

She went back to the stones. Her choice mattered. She knew now. Orholam had not led her to a place where her choice was pointless. She looked at each in turn, and again, felt drawn to one and repelled by the other. But she didn't touch either. Instead, she knelt by the pedestal on which one of them sat. She couldn't see anything there. She scratched a fingernail across it – and the tiniest shell of solid orange luxin cracked and dissolved.

And just like that, her feeling of desire to pick up this ball was gone. A hex. Magic forbidden with the sentence of death by Orholam's Glare. But then, interfering with the choice of the White carried the same sentence, so there wasn't much added deterrent there.

Andross – if it were Andross – had found an immensely talented orange drafter trained in forbidden arts, and had somehow defeated whatever security the luxiats had, and whatever checks were in place to make sure hexes were never placed here.

But that was a problem for another day.

Karris walked to the other ball, scratched her fingernail across the hex there, and waggled a finger toward the window beyond which Andross Guile sat. Naughty, naughty. She picked up the ball.

Some sixth sense warned her – maybe the step of a running man beneath the sound of the wind and the musket fire still ringing out from the roof. Karris pivoted and dodged as Jason Jorvis closed on her. She was only saved because he went for the ball in her hand rather than simply trying to shove her off the tower.

She spun with him, using his momentum against him to send him on toward the edge, but he snagged her weak left arm and pulled her with him.

She broke his grip with a strong move that turned his wrist; he lost his grip but grabbed again, snaring the belt rope of her robe.

He stumbled, one foot flying out over the edge, dropping his own white ball as he twisted back toward safety. The green in Karris hated to be bound. With one hand she whipped her belt rope from its two simple anchors at either side of her waist, while with the other she played out enough rope that Jason was tipping over the edge, totally dependent on the rope for balance.

She heard more steps. The backup plan to the backup plan. Of course. Everyone inside could see this, but there were no rules. Whoever came back with the correct ball was the White, and there would be no prosecution for murder.

A fist went right through where Karris's head had been a moment before. Another punch – but this one she blocked with the white stone itself. As Akensis stood frozen with the pain in his shattered fist, Karris tossed the stone into the air. With her hand now free, she looped the rope into an open knot, and flipped it over Akensis's hand as he watched the flying stone. Feeling the rope drape over his hand, he jerked away from her, pulling the knot tight.

Karris dove, dropping the rope, and rolled to her feet. She caught the stone.

Akensis hadn't taken up the slack immediately, and so Jason

Jorvis fell parallel to the platform they were on. But he kept his feet planted on the edge. It was an uncommonly smart move. Most people, falling, will panic and flail. Keeping his body tight, he gave himself a chance.

Akensis pulled against the rope to save himself, screaming as the knot tightened on his wrist. He grabbed the rope with both hands, and stood balanced precariously.

For a moment, Karris thought about bringing them in. They were big men, though, heavy and strong. She was still forbidden to draft; it was the only rule. If she pulled them up, they would work together to kill her. With her left side injured, there was no way she could bring them both in. Would the others intervene? And if so, on whose side? How many would die to save these two traitors?

There is a time for Orholam's gentle gaze, and a time for his glare.

With a yell that was both dirge for her old life and rage that men would betray Orholam himself and swelling pride that she knew all of her pain and training and even her waywardness was being redeemed, Karris delivered the slippery side kick that was the pinnacle of Blackguard perfection. With such a kick, a small woman moving masterfully could launch a man into the air. And she did.

Both men flew off the platform, and plunged to their deaths.

Everyone, silent, stared at Karris.

The windows opened and the disk slid back into its place inside. Karris dropped her stone into the clear bowl and didn't even watch the solvents do their work to reveal the stone's color beneath. She knew.

Karris turned and addressed a stunned audience of Colors and the promachos and the highest nobles in what remained of the Seven Satrapies.

'We're at war,' the new White said. 'We're going to start acting like it.'

Chapter 96

By the time Kip and Teia hit the ground, they saw that the squad was safe – and they'd been joined by none other than Tremblefist.

Kip had never felt more glad to see anyone.

'Which dock?' Tremblefist asked.

'Red, berth five.'

'Good news and bad,' Tremblefist said. 'There's probably two hundred Lightguards between here and there. They've got a big house they use as a barracks. And they've signaled with mirrors that they want you dead. And everyone on both islands knows exactly where you landed.'

'How do they know that?' Ferkudi asked.

'The big steel cable pointing right to us?' Leo said.

'Oh. Right.'

'You know their codes?' Ben-hadad asked.

'Please tell me that's all the bad news,' Cruxer said.

'It is.'

'And the good?'

'I don't like Lightguards.' And then Tremblefist grinned, and somehow, Kip thought they were going to be all right.

'Tremblefist, sir,' Cruxer said. 'Before we go: we're not Blackguards anymore. We've been kicked out, exiled.'

Tremblefist looked at him. 'Let's move,' he said.

And move they did. Kip would have died after about two blocks of this pace six months ago, much less a year ago. Ben-hadad couldn't run with his knee busted up, so Kip and Big Leo – who was injured himself – carried him. And ran.

They ate distance in huge gulps, trading off who was helping carry Ben-hadad. They were aided by the fact that most people were already thronging to the main streets, so the side streets were free of the usual early morning traffic. But then they came across a knot of four running Lightguards.

The squad tore them apart before the Lightguards got off a single shot.

Then they were at the wall. Two blocks of running along the jagged edifice and they came to a small gate, barely big enough for one person to get through. The streets were laid out according to the light beams from the star towers, but the walls were laid out to conform to the shape of Big Jasper. It made for some odd nooks and crannies.

'Throw fire in the air,' Tremblefist said. 'Make noise. We want to draw them here.'

Kip donned his red spectacles and threw luxin skyward and lit it. The others threw other colors into the air, too.

On any normal day, it would have drawn a thousand spectators in moments, but today was no normal day. On Sun Day, drafters who specialized in such things came here from all over the Seven Satrapies. Most of those, however, were lining the parade route, hitting up the crowds for thrown coins.

Tremblefist produced a key and opened the little gate. 'Breaker, put slow-burning pyrejelly on the lock. Make it look like we burned through.'

Kip did it.

While he was doing so, Tremblefist said, 'Narrow path out there, along the cliff face. Used to go down to the water, but the path fell into the sea long ago. It's a dead end. Any who go that way won't be on us.'

Then, instead of going through the gate, they sprinted once more along the wall. In another few blocks, they found another gate. Tremblefist produced another key. They ducked through, and he locked it behind them.

After a few hundred paces, this path dead-ended, too, and Tremblefist took them through a gate to get back onto the streets. In only a few minutes, they reached the docks and finally had to slow. The area was crowded with people arriving late for Sun Day and hundreds of merchants offloading and selling every kind of good imaginable – it would quiet at noon, but not until then. More importantly, it looked like no Lightguards were here.

Before they got to the red dock, they saw a luxiat standing, shifting from foot to foot, and Tisis Malargos, beautifully made up and looking like she had been waiting.

'You made it!' she said. 'Was that you?' She pointed to sky cable, and Kip just grinned.

But he felt Teia shrinking back.

Tisis looked at Teia, and then at Kip; she didn't look pleased. 'So,' Tisis said. 'Are we going to do this?'

'What do we need to do?' Kip asked.

'Sign three copies of the contract and say the words in front of the luxiat. That's it. He knows he needs to boil it down to the essentials.'

'Give me the contract,' Ben-hadad said. 'One of the copies. Quick!'

'You're not seriously going to read it?' she asked. 'Now?'

'Well, no, I'm not. But only because I'm shit at reading. Big Leo, read it to me. Over here.'

'It's a typical Ruthgari wedding contract,' the luxiat said. But he handed over a copy, and Leo began reading it aloud to Ben-hadad.

'Do we really have time for this?' Winsen asked. He and the others were eyeing the crowd, trying not to look threatening and conspicuous and failing.

'What's the saying,' Cruxer asked. ''Marry in haste, repent at leisure'?'

'Hmm,' Teia said.

'Surely this doesn't count as haste,' Tremblefist said. It was hard to tell whether he was being sarcastic or droll.

'Look, this is my deal,' Kip said.

'Deal?' Big Leo asked, breaking off from his low, murmured reading. 'Was part of that deal Andross trying to kill us all?'

It was Aram, Kip thought. Aram had to be working against what Andross wanted. I think. But he said, 'My deal isn't with Andross.' Which was a lie, but Tisis was standing right here. 'My deal's with the only people who can protect me from him: Tisis and the Malargos family.'

'Leo, keep reading!' Ben-hadad said.

'Kip,' Teia said. 'Breaker.'

'Oh, shit,' Tremblefist said.

'What?' Kip and Cruxer said at the same time, Kip to Teia and Cruxer to Tremblefist.

'You're really going to do this?' Teia said.

'*This* this, or this, getting the hell off the island?' Kip asked.

'Either. Both.'

'It's the signal,' Tremblefist said to Cruxer. 'The Lightguards have control of the cannon emplacement at the mouth of the harbor. If we try to sail out of here, they're to sink us.'

'Yes, I am,' Kip told Teia.

There was a moment of hurt, and she smoothed it down, but it didn't disappear. 'I'm staying,' she said. 'I'll help you get away, but I'm staying.'

'Is this because of—' Kip gestured to the cable they'd come down together.

'What do we do?' Cruxer asked.

'What are the parameters of your mission?' Tremblefist asked Cruxer.

Cruxer looked surprised that Tremblefist was giving him command. 'Save Breaker,' he said quickly. 'Nothing else matters.'

'No, it's not about that,' Teia said. 'You heard . . . Her. She didn't release me.' She meant the White. She didn't want to say it, not even in front of the squad. It was that kind of secret. 'I have a mission. A purpose that's bigger than what I want, and a task that only I can do.'

'What? What task?' Ben-hadad asked, interrupting.

They both stared at him.

'Sorry. By the way, contract's fine. Bit archaic, "enemy of your enemy" and the like, but. . . . Sorry!'

'Teia, you don't have to do this,' Kip said.

'No,' she said. 'I don't have to. But I choose to.' She tugged out the necklace she always wore, a little vial of olive oil. She'd always avoided questions about it. Now she broke the string, dropped the vial, and crushed it under her heel.

'Breaker,' Tremblefist barked.

'Sir,' Kip said, turning away from luxiats and women and – fuck! Did everything always have to happen at once? 'Yes, sir?'

Tremblefist locked his gaze. 'Thank you.' His mouth twitched a grin. The family resemblance to Ironfist was never more clear. But Tremblefist seemed free, his spirit open and joyful.

'Thank you? For what?' Kip asked.

Tremblefist said, 'I'll clear those cannons. Your ship will be safe. Go in light, Breaker.'

'Quickly, people!' Cruxer said. 'I see Lightguards. Lots of them. Thirty seconds. Maybe.'

Kip turned back toward the luxiat, who'd gone pale. Someone put a pen in Kip's fingers and presented the contracts, braced on a board. Kip signed, signed, signed.

'We have everything?' Tisis asked.

'Yes,' the luxiat said. 'Hands.'

'Defensive positions, people!' Cruxer said.

Kip and Tisis presented their hands and the luxiat lifted a pitcher and washed them of metaphorical sin. When he saw that Kip's hands were smeared with literal blood, he gulped. Kip felt Ferkudi put something on his head and saw that the young man had crafted green luxin crowns for both of them.

'You are here of your own free will?' the luxiat asked.

'Yes,' Kip and Tisis said quickly. Kip realized he'd barely even looked at her since he'd gotten here.

'Have either of you promised yourself to anyone else?'

'No,' Tisis said.

'No,' Kip said, a heartbeat late.

'Touch your right hands and entwine your fingers.'

'Wait!' Ben-hadad said. He waved his hands and almost fell over, having to hop on his good foot to regain his balance. 'A Ruthgari wedding can be considered illegitimate and annulled if there's no fire. Water, wine, and fire to sanctify a marriage. You need them all.'

The whole squad started looking around for a torch. How hard could it be to find a torch in the middle of a thousand merchants?

'Ah, hells,' Kip said. He opened himself to the sun and raised his own left hand, letting power roar through him. Fire gushed out of his hand skyward.

He must have been a bit tense, because it leapt out much farther than he meant, a pillar of fire ten paces high for a moment, before he tamped it down.

'Flesh protuberance,' Ferkudi said.

'Ferkudi!' Cruxer said. 'Position! And shut it!'

'Lightbringer indeed,' Big Leo murmured.

'On with it!' Kip said. If the Lightguard hadn't known where exactly to find him before, they certainly would now.

The luxiat picked up the cup. He'd apparently dropped it when Kip painted the sky with fire. He filled it from a skin with wine. 'The wine is Orholam's gift. The shared cup signifies the joys and sorrows of the life you will share.' He guided them to each drink, the cup held awkwardly in their clasped right hands. 'Even the awkwardness you feel is an emblem of your new—'

'Just drink and say the oath,' Cruxer said.

'Kip Guile, Breaker,' Tisis said, needing no prompting from the luxiat, staring Kip in the eyes. 'Your life shall be my life, through all the dawns and noons and dusks and nights Orholam grants us. My light is yours. With my body, I thee worship.'

Kip blinked for a moment, because he could tell she meant it. 'Tisis Antonia Malargos,' Oh, Orholam, it was like he was outside of his own body. He saw the Lightguards, pushing through the crowd. They were within musket range now. 'Your life shall be my life, through all the dawns and noons and dusks and nights Orholam grants us. My light is yours. With my body, I thee worship.'

And it was done. Kip had bound his will to this. It was finished. He was married.

The luxiat said quickly, 'May there never be darkness between you. I declare you husband and wife.'

'Go!' Cruxer shouted. 'Go, go, go!'

Kip saw Teia squeeze her hood shut, covering all but her glistening eyes, then she turned her back, and the black-and-white disks on her cloak rolled together, eclipse and darkness.

Kip and Tisis ran the other way. Big Leo had slung Benhadad over his shoulder and was pounding down the dock already, barely slowed by the weight. Kip followed, but it was as if the world had been drained of sound. They sprinted down a dock, and the Lightguards ran after them. Kip poured red luxin across the width of the dock in a wide swath, even his pounding heart silent in his ears.

The Lightguards pulled up short in front of the red luxin, none of them drafters, none of them willing to die. They fired their muskets, splintering wood around the running squad. Kip turned and drew his pistol, but saw the crowd of innocents behind the Lightguards. If he missed . . .

He holstered the pistol and ran up the gangplank to the galleass. The Lightguards had found sheets of wood to throw on top of the red luxin, and they charged across. Finally gathering their courage, or thinking Kip was too far away to throw more red luxin, the Lightguards ran the rest of the way down the dock, rapidly closing the distance to the departing ship.

Kip stood on the stern gallery and shot the pistol at the Lightguards. He threw luxin, the squad shouting at him to get down, calling him insane. One word worked its way through: Teia. Kip looked into sub-red and Teia moving among the Lightguards.

She attacked no one. Merely bumped an elbow here just as a musketeer fired, extinguished a slow match there, tangled men in the lines on the deck as they ran about, causing several to fall.

Kip had been throwing death right at her.

Cruxer pulled Kip down and behind cover, berating him for risking himself when there was no longer any reason to do so, but Kip didn't even hear him. Teia.

Their ship passed the cannon tower guarding the bay, and they saw the Lightguards flashing mirrors at it, signaling, no doubt, to fire. But the cannons were silent. Silent until, suddenly, the entire battery blew up in a concussion that shook the earth and sea.

Explosion layered on explosion. Cannons and muskets and a falling wall. Card after card. But they passed as fast as he saw them.

'Tremblefist, no,' Kip said.

And oddly, at the sound of his own voice, Kip was back. He could hear again, and his eyes lost the intense, singular, war-blind focus. He saw his squad: Cruxer, and Ferkudi, and Ben-hadad, and Big Leo, and Winsen. Teia gone, and in her place Tisis. And he saw himself, madly dealing death to enemies he didn't have to fight at all. And he saw his two faces: child and warrior, man and leader. Kip, who wanted to sit and cry and be taken care of; and Breaker, who was responsible for taking care of others. Karris said that to take up the latter didn't mean to deny that the former existed.

Kip took a deep breath, then he popped his neck to the left and the right, and when he turned, he was Breaker.

'Breaker, my lord, what're our orders?' Cruxer asked.

'This ship is going to Rath, but when it lands, we won't be on it,' Breaker said.

'What?' Tisis asked.

'Ben-hadad, you've been on skimmers and sea chariots. Design one big enough for the squad. Tisis, you have people aboard?'

'Of course. But what are you—'

'Then it's your choice. You can come with us, or you can take that signed contract to your sister Eirene without me. Our alliance and our wedding stands, but I have no intention of getting trapped in Ruthgar. I will help your family, but I won't be its hostage. I'll help your family by defending your satrapy. We're going to Blood Forest. We're going to stop the Color Prince. The Mighty are going to war.'

Chapter 97

When no one answered the door at the chirurgeons' house, Ironfist broke it down. There was no one inside. Neither the chirurgeons, nor the Blackguards, nor Gavin Guile. There was no note, no sign of a struggle.

'They're gone,' a voice said outside, behind him. 'I've been waiting for you.' And then Grinwoody stepped into the house.

'Grinwoody,' Ironfist said.

Grinwoody waved a hand. 'That's not necessary, not here, not today.'

'Uncle,' Ironfist said, cracking a grin. The men embraced.

'You understand there was nothing I could do about *this*,' Grinwoody said. He gestured to the emptiness.

'Is he alive?' Ironfist asked.

'Gavin, yes. The Blackguard who was here protecting him and the chirurgeons, no. Andross will . . . No, even after all these years, I don't know what Andross will do with Gavin.

Imprison him until he breaks? Kill him when Gavin disrespects him, as he inevitably will? Elevate him for some purpose? I have no idea. Still.' He said it with frustrated admiration, as of an adversary who had fought for so long and so well that they were nearly friends.

Ironfist said, 'I was there, within steps of that old scorpion. I could have . . . Did I fail you, uncle? Did I fail my *Ulta*? After all this time, and how high I rose.' He expelled a great breath.

'Do you have it?'

'The White had it hidden just where you said.' Ironfist handed over the polished ziricote-wood box, no wider than his hand and only a few thumbs deep. 'I found no key.'

'Your commander's pin,' Grinwoody said. Ironfist gave it to him, and Grinwoody snapped the pin between his fingers. Ironfist flinched, but Grinwoody wasn't done. The halves hadn't split randomly. He took one half and stuck it into the lock. It fit.

A line around the box glowed briefly.

Grinwoody said, 'Throwing away your life to kill some noble was never to be your Ulta. There were . . . questions about your loyalty. Questions you've quite answered now.' He opened the box a crack and exhaled reverently, then closed it. 'They call us masters of secrecy, and yet in dazzling the eye with lying light, the Chromeria is without rival. They say you're the Blackguard because your skin is black, because your clothes are black, because in wearing no color, you show that your allegiance is to none of the Colors. They say you are Blackguards because you surrender your own light of reason to serve as a slave, that you are like the black-robed luxiats in taking on the humility of colorlessness. They say you serve in the dark. They say a hundred things that are all true – all to obscure one, central truth: you are called the Blackguard because you guard the black. The black seed crystal. Accessible only with the cooperation of the White and the commander of the Blackguard both. It is the weapon that kills Prisms and quenches luxin. This is the tool that will rebuild the Order. This is the pen that rewrites history. This, nephew, was your Ulta. You have succeeded. You've done more for the Order of the Broken Eye than anyone in three centuries.'

Why then was Ironfist ashamed? Ashamed that Grinwoody hadn't trusted him. Ashamed that for some few months, he'd thought he didn't have to choose sides, thought that his two oaths could be fulfilled without betraying either one, that ancient enemies could be made allies as they fought a common enemy, that his Ulta might be to kill the Color Prince. He took off his ghotra. Too late for that now. Orholam had reached out to Ironfist, and Ironfist had just spat in his face. 'What do we do now?' Ironfist asked, without inflection.

'How we direct all the resources of the Order hinges on your answer to one question, my nephew and my right hand: after all you've seen, who is Kip Guile?'

Ironfist looked at his uncle, the slave, the hidden Old Man of the Desert, the head of the Order of the Broken Eye, and he could almost see fates being written as he chose his words. 'He is not Kip Delauria, bastard, that I know. Nor is he Kip Guile. He is the Breaker, he is the Lightbringer, and he is our Diakoptês come again.'

'Then go, nephew. You have fulfilled your Ulta, so the fulfillment of your next task will have to come not from your oaths but from your heart instead. Go and turn Breaker's will that he may not destroy us as did the last Diakoptês. Go and serve him, go and save him, or go and slay him, and with him, all the world.'

Epilogue 1

The distant explosion's roar raced through Big Jasper's broad avenues and lightwells, between the arches of its Thousand Stars, past whitewashed homes and gleaming domes. The cheering throngs along the Sun Day parade route fell silent, and every eye looked to the horizon, Ironfist's eyes first of all.

Ironfist's bitter regrets and introspection blew away with the last echoes of the great blast, and a rippling cloud billowed upward somewhere near the docks, so intensely hot and huge that it folded in on itself like a mushroom cap. There was only one place on that side of the island that held enough black powder to make an explosion so huge. He ran.

With his height and constant training and knowledge of every back street on this island, the half league passed in no time. Crowds coming and going both slowed his pace as he reached the narrow peninsula. Promachos Andross Guile's Lightguards were trying to set up a perimeter, and doing a predictably bad job of it.

As Ironfist approached the line – were those idiots keeping out chirurgeons? – he couldn't help but stare at the dissipating black cloud and the rubble beneath it. The explosion had come from the cannon tower that guarded the harbor. The tower's powder stores were sunk into its bedrock bowels so that even an invading navy's fire couldn't hit them. Carver Black, in charge of the island's defenses, was meticulous in checking that appropriate discipline in storing and working around so much black powder was maintained.

Of course, with the Lightguards having taken over, those clumsy fools might have begun storing the powder above ground. A dropped lamp, an iron-nailed boot – if you let discipline slip for a heartbeat, this kind of accident could happen.

But Ironfist knew in his gut that this was no accident.

The Lightguards tried to bar him from the peninsula, but he said, 'I'm Commander Ironfist, let me pass.'

He actually forgot that it wasn't true anymore until the words were out of his mouth. He'd been commander so long, it was impossible to think of himself as anything else.

They moved immediately. So they hadn't heard yet.

The cannon tower was still standing. Reinforced with iron and Orholam only knew what kinds of luxin, the outer walls were cracked in some places, but otherwise intact. The blast, thus contained, had shot up from the cellar through each of the five floors, hurling everything out the top, transforming the cannon tower into a cannon aimed at heaven. Everything within had been flung into the sky: broad paving stones that had made the floors, splintered wood, rags, and, nearer to the tower itself, even the massive cannons themselves.

The entry door had been blown out into the harbor, and heavy smoke roiled out of it still. Civilians and Lightguards alike surrounded the tower, looking for survivors, surveying the damage, counting the dead. Ironfist saw a corpse, legless, charred, his clothes blown entirely off him. Others bobbed in the waters. But of most of the dead, there was almost nothing left. A boot here, a piece of meat unidentifiable there. Blood smears.

Ironfist found a corpse, dead not from the explosion, but of a slash through the neck. It could have been from flying shrapnel, but the man had no burn marks or evidence of injury from the concussion wave. He'd been lying here when the explosion happened, already dead.

That meant sabotage. Ironfist looked to the horizon. Was there a fleet out there? No. And they'd have had warning if there was. Why this target, then? Surely the Color Prince wouldn't spend lives and treasure blowing up a tower for no reason.

A yell sounded from a knot of Lightguards at the water's edge. Ironfist made his way over there as they pulled the man from the waves. The man was Parian, tall, hugely muscular, and wearing only dark trousers, his tunic lost, his headscarf lost. It was his brother.

Tremblefist. Dear Orholam, no. Ironfist's heart stopped. It couldn't – it couldn't . . . And yet there was no mistaking that imposing figure, the smaller twin of Ironfist's own body.

'He's alive!' someone shouted.

Ironfist crashed the lines of gawking Lightguards. 'Away!' he roared. 'That's my brother! Move!'

And then, with no time intervening, he was holding his brother in his arms. He must have been convincing, because everyone had moved back a good ten paces.

It was immediately obvious that something was very wrong. Tremblefist's body bore no wounds that Ironfist could see, but when his eyelids fluttered open, the whites of his eyes were bloodshot almost pure red. If he had that kind of damage to his head . . .

No. Ironfist didn't want to believe what his experience knew.

'Harrdun,' his brother said, looking up at him.

'Hanishu.' They had barely spoken each other's birth names in all the days since they'd taken their Blackguard names, there was so much pride in the latter names, and so much pain in the former.

'You should have seen me fight,' Hanishu said. 'Twenty-seven men. In less than a minute. Not a scratch on me. They even used . . . mmmm. Used muskets. Orholam forgave me, Harrdun. For Aghbalu. His holy breath was on me in this fight. I made it through the whole tower.'

Ironfist was still trying to recover, the words clanged against each other like a cacophony of pots and pans. 'You did this?' he whispered tensely. 'I thought maybe an attack by the Color—'

'I saved the Lightbringer. They were going to sink his ship.' He found Ironfist's hand and clasped it. 'I made it to the cellars. Set the fuse, ran. But they'd locked the door out. So I climbed the entire tower, fighting, jumped off the top just as she blew. Landed it. One for the ages. Surfaced, was swimming back to shore, and a damn rock fell out of the sky. Had no idea they'd be in the air that long . . . I'm all busted inside.'

From his eyes, he hadn't made the jump quite as clearly as he seemed to think. But blows to the head could skew everything. And it didn't matter, did it?

'Not long now,' Hanishu said. 'Got a question, big brother.'

'Anything,' Ironfist said.

'Not for me. For you. Will take a while to answer.'

'What is it?'

'Before you left home to come here, you met with some people. You made them an oath.'

'What people?' But Ironfist knew, and his heart sank again that Tremblefist knew about that.

'I didn't want to come to the Chromeria, you know, after what I did at Aghbalu. But I came for you. Seeing you swear yourself to the Order, it, it wouldn't leave me. I would have happily killed myself, but I couldn't go while you were in danger. Funny thing. Coming here to save you is what saved me. I came so that someday, when your soul was on the line, and you had to decide which oaths to keep, that I would be here for you. I'm not going to make it, big brother. All that effort, all this time . . .' And he began weeping. 'I failed you.'

As if the failure were his.

There was nothing to say, no way to combat the tears spilling freely down Ironfist's cheeks.

Tremblefist said, 'After the fall of Ru, the others told me how you prayed. It had to be the first time you prayed since mother was killed, huh?'

Ironfist nodded tightly.

'And he answered.'

'He did.' A miracle cannon shot, five thousand paces, to save friends he might be called on to kill.

'So you've taken unbreakable oaths to implacable enemies. One to the Bearer of Light, and one to the Maker of it. So you have to decide without me, brother. Which man are you?'

Ironfist had no answer. He clung for comfort to the brother he should be comforting. Like his life, Tremblefist's death wasn't easy.

Epilogue 2

Gavin woke, facedown, cold, naked, lying on a hard floor. His missing eye was professionally bandaged, but he had new bruises everywhere. He couldn't remember how he'd gotten here. Wherever here was. He rolled over, wincing at the many voices of pain singing like a Sun Day chorus, and opened his eye.

It was a small room, curving around him in a circle, shaped like a flattened ball. There was a hole above for bread to be dropped in, and a hole below for his waste. He couldn't see the color, but the winking crystalline facets told him he was in the very blue cell he'd made for his brother.

It had been repaired.

In the peaceful perfection of the passionless prison, Gavin felt a horror and revulsion unlike any he had ever known. Pain stabbed through his chest. Tight. Breathless, fighting for little gasps of air. His secrets were out, all at once, in front of the last person he loved and the one person he knew could never understand.

Those repairs meant his father was his captor. If he'd found this cell, he'd found them all. That meant he knew everything: the false victory at Sundered Rock, Dazen's imposture of Gavin, and finally his murder of Andross Guile's eldest and favorite son in the yellow cell.

It meant Andross planned to make him pay for it.

Stripped bare of clothes, and titles, and privileges, and power, and vision, and freedom, and stripped now of even his false name, Dazen stared at the grim reflection in the shining wall. It looked like a dead man.

Acknowledgments

The problem with standards is living up to them. Acknowledgments are usually as tedious but necessary as a EULA. Where can I scroll and hit Accept already? Then you hit Accept, and it forces you to perjure yourself by averring that YES, I DID READ all that tiny print that I just didn't read. What, you don't believe my 12,000-words-per-minute pace? I tell you, I'm Harriet Klausner, and I read every last word of the contracts I review. ACCEPT!

I had a standard. I thought, acknowledgments are boring. I shall make my acknowledgments un-boring. Acknowledgments shall be a new genre of creative nonfiction, to which readers shall flock! New readers shall buy my books with no intent of reading the fantasy herein, no, even dyed-in-the-wool octogenarian mystery readers who actually do wear wool that has been dyed – natty sweaters mostly – will buy my books solely in the hope of seeing my witticitudes. (That being, of course, my witticisms about the vicissitudes of the publishing business. The mystery readers already sussed that out. Sharp lot. You fantasy folk have been put on notice.)

But. And isn't there always a 'but'? And inasmuch as I have been enjoined not to begin a sentence with a coordinating conjunction until I can spell 'coordinating conjunction' [Note to proofreader: Have a double look at this, will you? Would be terribly embarrasing to misspell in the middle of a witticitude.], [yeah, and check that punctuation, too, always get hung up on by what marks to put around nested clauses!] every so often in life, a sentence must needs start with an And But Yet Or For Nor.

Amirite? (Octogenarian mysteriods, the fantasy folks sussed that neologism instantly. You've been put on notice.)

But. But after writing acknowledgments for six books now, I'm beginning to see how the grind has worn down souls greater than I. Truth is, at some point, adding witty lines to computer code as an amuse-bouche for that one other programmer who actually reads lines 3.5 million to 3.6 million is dust in the wind. Dust. Wind. Dude. Because the list of people to be thanked only adds names. And do you know who gets to add drama to reading a list of names? Let's ask the cast of the Grammy-winning *Bible Experience*, which features a who's who of African American actors reading the entirety of the Bible. Of course Samuel L. Jackson gets to read Ezekiel 25:17 – hopefully the real verse this time, not the one from the Gospel of Quentin – but who 'gets' to read the begats?

Like success, a novel has many fathers. Here are my co-begetters:

Thank you to my wife, Kristi. For believing in the beginning, and for believing still. Thank you to my daughter, who did her best to hold back being born until daddy could finish the first draft, and then slept well so that daddy could edit this behemoth.

Thank you to my editorial assistant, E. dub, for enduring interminable nicknames: Monie, CAPSLOCK, and others too good to be shared. Your goat's leash is over here. Seriously, even though you do cruel things like, well, make me work, having you around has been an enormous help. Our life is better – and so is my writing – because of the work you do.

Thank you to Devi (fierce friend and peerless provocatrix of production peeps), Anne, Alex, Tim, Susan, Ellen, Lauren, Laura, James, and Rose of Orbit Books US and UK. Thank you to Don Maass, Cameron McClure, and the rest of the staff at Donald Maass Literary Agency. I know this is kind of what we do, but you make the work part of this work rewarding and as smooth as possible – and you make the art of it better than anything of mine has any right to be.

A special thank-you to my beta readers: Mary Robinette Kowal, Heather, Andrew, Tim, Jacob, and John. I still kind of hate you right now, but my gratitude will grow as the memory of the pains you inflicted on me fades. And double thanks to Tim and John for diving back into the word trenches a second time.

Thanks to Aristotle for ideas so big that I couldn't escape them even in a secondary-world fantasy.

Thank you to Dr J. Klein, former roommate, for my continuing work-ethic inferiority complex and for last-second translations. Any abuses of philosophy or translation herein are the ones I either didn't ask him about, or ignored his sterling advice about. If he's your prof, ask about swimming the Hellespont and scaling the tower. Or at least about his Bruce Lee impression.

Thank you to Stephen R. Lawhead, who showed me that there was fantasy after Tolkien. Much of my writing is an attempt to make others feel how I felt after reading *Taliesin* and *Merlin*. Quentin is for you.

And last, thank you to my readers. Thank you for sharing these worlds with me, for your encouragement, and for sharing me with other readers. It is a gift and a privilege to get to do what I love for a living. Thank you.

– Brent Weeks

Character List

'Annaiah: Darjan's wife.

Abaddon: Also known as the King, the Day Star. One of the chiefs of the Two Hundred. Often depicted with crippled ankles, giant locust's wings and pallid features.

Abraxes, Ambrosius: A saint from ancient times.

Adrasteia (Teia): A Blackguard inductee and a drafter of paryl.

Aeshma: One of the Two Hundred, nearly one of the Nine, and Darjan's jinniyah. A potential Atirat.

Ahhana the Dextrous: Superchromat yellow drafter who was the architect and lead drafter of the Lily's Stem.

Ahhanen: A Blackguard. Partners with Djur, known for a somewhat sour demeanor.

Aheyyad: Orange drafter, grandson of Tala. A defender of Garriston, the designer of Garriston's Brightwater Wall; dubbed Aheyyad Brightwater by Prism Gavin Guile.

Aklos: A slave of Lady Aglaia Crassos.

Alban and Strang: Saints and commentators on holy writ.

Amazzal, High Luxiat: One of the six High Luxiats, most notable for his commanding presence and rich voice.

Amestan: A Blackguard at the Battle of Garriston.

Anamar: Commander of the Blackguard at the close of the False Prism's War.

Anir, Brother: A librarian at the Chromeria.

Antaeos: A Blackguard nunk.

Appleton, Lady: A noblewoman of Blood Forest.

Appleton, Taira: One of Lady Appleton's four daughters. A friend of Karris during childhood.

Aram: A failed Blackguard scrub with a grudge against Kip and Cruxer.

Arana: A drafting student, a merchant's daughter.

Aras: A student at the Chromeria.

Arash, Javid: One of the drafters who defended Garriston.

Aravind, Lord: Satrap of Atash until his death. Father of Kata Ham-haldita, the former corregidor of Idoss.

Arias, Lord: One of the Color Prince's advisors. He is an Atashian in charge of spreading news about the Color Prince.

Arien: A magister at the Chromeria. She drafts orange and tests Kip on Luxlord Black's orders.

Ariss the Navigator: A legendary explorer.

Asif: A young Blackguard.

Asmun: A Blackguard scrub.

Atagamo: A magister who teaches the properties of luxin at the Chromeria. He is Ilytian.

Atiriel, Karris: A desert princess. She became Karris Shadowblinder before she married Lucidonius.

Aurellea, Mistress: A procurer for high-class prostitutes on Big Jasper.

Ayrad, Commander: He was a Blackguard scrub years before Kip entered the class. He started at the bottom of his class (forty-ninth) and worked his way up to the top, fighting everyone. It turned out he'd taken a vow. Became a legendary commander of the Blackguard and saved four different Prisms at least once before someone poisoned him. A yellow drafter.

Azmith, Akensis: A scion of the powerful Azmith family.

Azmith, Caul: A Parian general, the Parian satrapah's younger brother.

Azmith, Tilleli: Parian satrapah, older sister of Caul Azmith.

Balder: A Blackguard scrub.

Barrick: A sailor.

Bas the Simple: A Tyrean polychrome (blue/green/superviolet), handsome but a simpleton, sworn to kill the killer of the White Oak family.

Bel: An apprentice at a brewery on Big Jasper, The Maiden's Kiss.

Ben-hadad: A Ruthgari student at the Chromeria and a Blackguard inductee. A blue/green/yellow drafter who has created his own mechanical spectacles that allow blue and yellow lenses to be used separately or together to create green. He's highly intelligent and an inventor.

Beryl: A Watch Captain in the Blackguard, a skilled horsewoman who is known for taking new recruits under her wing.

Big Ros: A slave of Aglaia.

Blademan: A Blackguard watch captain. He leads one of the skimmers in the battle at Ruic Head, along with Gavin and Watch Captain Tempus.

Blue-Eyed Demons, the: A mercenary band that fought for Dazen's army.

Blunt: A Blackguard watch captain.

Borig, Janus: An old woman, she claimed to be a *demiurgos* and a Mirror, creating true Nine Kings Cards.

Bursar: The Omnichrome's treasury advisor. She was originally a minor secretary for the Secretary of the Treasury of Paria.

Burshward, Captain: An Angari captain. He chose to dare the Everdark Gates because he'd heard rumors of the wealth beyond, and because of his vision from his god, Mot. Mortal enemy of Gunner.

Burshward, Gillam: Captain Burshward's brother, now short a leg, due to an encounter with Gunner.

Buskin: Along with Tugertent and Tlatig, the best archer Commander Ironfist has on the approach to Ruic Head.

Caelia Green: A talented drafter, a dwarf, and formerly a servant of the Third Eye.

Carver Black: A non-drafter, as is traditional for the Black. He is the chief administrator of the Seven Satrapies. Though he has a voice on the Spectrum, he has no vote.

Carvingen, Odess: A drafter and defender of Garriston.

Cavair, Paz: Commander of the Blue Bastards at the Great Pyramid of Ru.

Cezilia: A servant/bodyguard to the Third Eye. A fourth-generation Seers Islander.

Clara: A servant/bodyguard to the Third Eye.

Companions' Mother: Head of the Omnichrome's army's prostitute guild.

Coran, Adraea: Blessed. Said 'war is a horror.'

Cordelia: A willowy female Blackguard. An archer.

Coreen: An old widow of Blood Forest. Despite her humble isolation, she seems to speak for or with Orholam.

Corfu, Ramia: A powerful, extremely handsome young blue drafter. One of the Color Prince's favorites.

Corzin, Eleph: An Abornean blue drafter, a defender of Garriston.

Counselor, the: A legendary figure. Author of *The Counselor to Kings*, which advised such cruel methods of government that not even he followed them when he ruled.

Cracks: A singularly ugly young Blackguard.

Crassos, Aglaia: A young noblewoman and drafter at the Chromeria. She is the youngest daughter of an important Ruthgari family, a sadist who enjoys the pain she inflicts on her slaves. Has a powerful hatred of both the Guiles and Teia.

Crassos, Governor: Elder brother of Aglaia Crassos; the last governor of Garriston.

Crassos, Ismene: A middle-aged cousin of Aglaia Crassos.

Cruxer: A Blackguard inductee and perhaps the most talented Blackguard of his era. He's the third generation to enter the ranks; his parents are Inana and Holdfast.

Daelos: A Blackguard scrub, very small, but intelligent and talented with blue.

Dagnar Zelan: One of the original Blackguards. He served Lucidonius after converting to his cause.

Dakan, Dayan: A thug-for-hire on Big Jasper.

Danavis, Aliviana (Liv): Daughter of Corvan Danavis. A yellow and superviolet bichrome drafter from Tyrea, she serves the Color Prince. Formerly a discipula at the Chromeria whose contract was owned by the Ruthgari and supervised by Aglaia Crassos. Grew up in Rekton with Kip.

Danavis, Corvan: A red drafter. A scion of one of the great Ruthgari families, he was also the most brilliant general of the age and the primary reason for Dazen's success in battle. Now the Satrap of Seers Island and married to The Third Eye.

Danavis, Ell: The second wife of Corvan Danavis. She was murdered by an assassin three years after their marriage.

Danavis, Erethanna: A green drafter serving Count Nassos in western Ruthgar; Liv Danavis's cousin.

Danavis, Qora: A Tyrean noblewoman; first wife of Corvan Danavis, mother of Aliviana Danavis.

Darjan: Legendary drafter at the time of Lucidonius and Karris Shadowblinder.

Delara, Naftalie: A woman from a prominent family that

Andross was going to 'let' Gavin marry. An ally of Andross Guile.

Delara Orange: The Atashian member of the Spectrum. She represents Orange and is a forty-year-old orange/red bichrome nearing the end of her life. Her predecessor in the seat was her mother, who devised the rotating scheme for Garriston. General Caul Azmith and the satrapah of Paria are her cousins.

Delarias: A family in Rekton.

Delauria, Katalina: Kip's mother. She is of Parian or Ilytian extraction and is a haze addict.

Delclara, Micael: A quarryman and a Rekton villager.

Delclara, Miss: The matriarch of the Delclara family in Rekton.

Delclara, Zalo: A quarryman, one of the Delclara sons.

Deleah: A slave woman in Andross Guile's household.

Delelo, Galan: A master sergeant in the Omnichrome's army. He escorts Liv to the gates of Garriston.

Delmarta, Gad: A young Tyrean general from Garriston, he commanded Dazen's army. Took the city of Ru and publicly massacred the royal family and their retainers. Garriston was later burned in revenge.

Delucia, Neta: A member of the ruling council of Idoss (i.e., a city mother) before its fall.

Demistocles: A prophet and a mentor of prophets.

Diakoptês: An ambiguous term. Literally, 'He who rends asunder,' a looser translation could be 'Breaker'. In Braxian belief, both the name (or perhaps title?) of Lucidonius, and the name or title of a similar figure (or possibly a reincarnation?) of Lucidonius who will come again to break or heal the Cracked Lands.

Djur: A Blackguard.

Droose: One of Gunner's shipmates.

Elelyōn: Another name for Orholam, from the Old Parian, meaning 'God Most High'.

Elessia: A Blackguard.

Elio: A bully in Kip's barracks. Kip breaks his arm.

Elos, Gaspar: A green color wight, he saved Kip's life in Rekton.

Erato: A Blackguard scrub who has it in for Kip.

Essel: A Blackguard Archer.

Euterpe: A friend of Teia's. She was a slave. Her owners lost everything in a drought and rented her to the Laurion silver mine brothels for five months. She never recovered.

Eutheos, Captain: A hero of Dazen's army, and later a member of Ruthgar's military.

Falling Leaf, Deedee: A green drafter. Her failing health inspired a number of veteran drafters who were also her friends to take the Freeing at Garriston.

Farjad, Farid: A nobleman and ally of Dazen's once Dazen promised him the Atashian throne during the False Prism's War.

Farseer, Horas: Another ally of Dazen's, the bandit king of the Blue-Eyed Demons. Gavin Guile killed him after the False Prism's War.

Fell: A female Blackguard, the smallest in the force, she excels at acrobatic moves.

Ferkudi: A Blackguard scrub, a blue/green bichrome who excels at grappling. Gifted with spotty intelligence. Like Cruxer, a legacy, meaning both his parents were Blackguards.

Finer: A Blackguard seen in one of the cards.

Fisk, Trainer: He trains the scrubs with drills and conditioning. He barely beat Karris during their own test to enter the Blackguards.

Flamehands: An Ilytian drafter and defender of Garriston.

Gaeros: One of Lady Aglaia's slaves.

Galaea: Karris White Oak's maid, and betrayer.

Galden, Jens: A magister at the Chromeria, a red drafter with a grudge against Kip.

Galib: A polychrome at the Chromeria.

Gallos: A stableman at Garriston.

Garadul, Perses: Appointed satrap of Tyrea after Ruy Gonzalo was defeated by the Prism's forces in the False Prism's War. Perses was the father of Rask Garadul. He worked to eradicate the bandits plaguing Tyrea after the war.

Garadul, Rask: A satrap who declared himself king of Tyrea; his father was Perses Garadul.

Gazzin, Griv: A green drafter who fought with Zee Oakenshield.

Gerain: An old man in Garriston who exhorted people to join King Garadul.

Gerrad: A student at the Chromeria.

Gevison: A poet of a heroic bent. He wrote *The Wanderer's Last Journey.*

Golden Briar, Cathán: Cousin to both Arys Greenveil and Ela Jorvis. Eva Golden Briar's elder brother.

Golden Briar, Eva: A Blood Forest noblewoman Andross was going to let Gavin choose to marry.

Goldeneyes, Tawenza: A yellow drafter. She teaches only the three most talented yellows each year at the Chromeria. A notorious misandrist.

Goldthorn: A magister at the Chromeria. Barely three years older than her disciples, she teaches the superviolet class.

Gonzalo: A farrier's son of Atan's Town in Darjan's time. A simpleton.

Gonzalo, Ruy: A Tyrean satrap who sided with Dazen during the False Prism's War.

Goss: A Parian Blackguard inductee, one of the best fighters, and a member of The Mighty before he is killed by the Lightguard.

Gracia: A mountain Parian scrub. She's taller than most of the boys.

Grass, Evi: A drafter and defender of Garriston. She is a green/yellow bichrome from Blood Forest, and is a superchromat.

Grazner: A Blackguard scrub. Kip breaks his will in a bout.

Green, Jerrosh: Along with Dervani Malargos, he is one of the best green drafters in the Omnichrome's army, and a Blood Robe. Killed by the Omnichrome before the Battle of Ru.

Greenveil, Arys: The Sub-red on the Spectrum. A Blood Forester, cousin of Jia Tolver, sister to Ana Jorvis's mother, Ela. Her parents were killed in the war by Lunna Green's brothers. She has twelve children by twelve different men and is pregnant with the thirteenth.

Greenveil, Ben-Oni: Arys Greenveil's thirteenth child. His name means 'Son of my Agony'.

Greenveil, Jalen: Arys Greenveil's third child.

Greyling, Gavin: A Blackguard. He is the younger brother of Gill Greyling, named after Gavin Guile. He is the handsomer of the two brothers.

Greyling, Gill: A Blackguard. He is elder brother of Gavin Greyling, and he is the more intelligent of the two.

Grinwoody: Andross Guile's chief slave and right hand. He is barely a drafter, but Andross pulled strings to get him into training for the Blackguard, where he made friends and learned secrets. He made it all the way through Blackguard training, and on oath day decided to sign with Lord Guile instead, a betrayal the Blackguards remember.

Guile, Andross: Father of Gavin, Dazen, and Sevastian Guile. He drafts yellow through sub-red, although he is primarily known for drafting red, as that was his position on the Spectrum. He took a place on the Spectrum despite being from Blood Forest, which already had a representative, by claiming that his lands in Ruthgar qualified him for the seat.

Guile, Darien: Andross Guile's great-grandfather. He was married to Zee Oakenshield's daughter as a resolution to their war.

Guile, Dazen: Younger brother of Gavin. He fell in love with Karris White Oak and triggered the False Prism's War when 'he' burned down her family compound, killing everyone within.

Guile, Draccos: Andross Guile's father. Hero of the Aghbalu Campaign. Notorious for gambling an entire hyparchy for the hand of a woman, the young Orea Pullawr, on a horse race. He lost the race, the woman, and his family's entire fortune. It was revealed decades later that his opponent, Juldaw Rathcore, had cheated. The Spectrum refused to expel the Rathcores at that time, leaving the Guiles as wool traders. Implicated in the murder of his brother, but as the only witnesses were slaves whose testimony was thereby inadmissible, the case wasn't prosecuted by local magistrates or the satraps. (Orea ended up later marrying Juldaw's brother.)

Guile, Felia: Wife of Andross Guile. The mother of Gavin and Dazen, a cousin of the Atashian royal family, she is an orange drafter. Freed at Garriston just before the great battle. Her mother was courted by Ulbear Rathcore before he met Orea Pullawr.

Guile, Galatius: A Guile ancestor, a drunk and a gambler, important mainly because he married the woman who became known as Iron Ataea Guile.

Guile, Gavin: The Prism. Two years older than Dazen, he was appointed Prism at age thirteen.

Guile, Iron Ataea: Member of a small noble family that provided champion race horses for Ruthgar and Blood Forest. She stole Galatius Guile's heart and reshaped the Guile family's destiny.

Guile, Kip: The illegitimate Tyrean son of Gavin Guile and Katalina Delauria. He is a superchromat and a full-spectrum polychrome.

Guile, Sevastian: The youngest Guile brother. He was murdered by a blue wight when Gavin was thirteen and Dazen was eleven.

Guile, Zymun: A young drafter and member of the Omnichrome's army. Also known as Zymun White Oak, he claims to be the son of Karris White Oak and Gavin Guile.

Gunner: An Ilytian pirate. His first underdeck command was as cannoneer on the *Aved Barayah*. He later became captain of the *Bitter Cob*.

Hada: Handmaid to Tazerwalt, princess of the Tlaglanu.

Ham-haldita, Kata: Corregidor of Idoss before its fall. Ally of the Color Prince.

Harl, Pan: A Blackguard inductee. His ancestors were slaves for the last eight of ten generations.

Helel, Mistress: A member of the Order, she masqueraded as a teacher in the Chromeria and tried to murder Kip.

Hena: A magister at the Chromeria who teaches a class on luxin construction.

Hezik: A Blackguard whose mother commanded a pirate hunter in the Narrows. He can shoot cannons fairly accurately.

Holdfast: A Blackguard. His son is Cruxer and his widow is Inana, another Blackguard.

Holvar, Jin: A woman who entered the Blackguard the same year as Karris, though she is a few years younger.

Hrozak, Grath: A sadist who murdered hundreds personally, and was well known for his brutal military tactics.

Idus: A Blackguard scrub.

Inana: Cruxer's mother, and a Blackguard. Widow of Holdfast, a Blackguard.

Incaros: One of Lady Aglaia Crassos's room slaves.

Ironfist (birth name Harrdun): Commander of the Blackguard, thirty-eight years old, a blue drafter. Parian.

Isabel (Isa): A pretty young girl in Rekton. Deceased.

Izem Blue: A legendary drafter and a defender of Garriston under Gavin Guile.

Izem Red: A defender of Garriston under Gavin Guile. He fought for Gavin during the False Prism's War. A Parian drafter of red with incredible speed, he wears his ghotra in the shape of a cobra's hood.

Jalal: A Parian storekeeper who sells kopi.

Jarae: One of the Guile house slaves when Gavin and Dazen were children.

Jo'El, Seer: An ancient prophet, a Third Eye known for his promises of restoration following a coming devastation.

Jorvis, Ana: A superviolet/blue bichrome, student at the Chromeria, one of the women Andross Guile would have allowed Gavin to marry. Died in suspicious circumstances after she attempted to seduce Gavin by entering his rooms at night. The death was ruled a suicide, but the family claims it was murder.

Jorvis, Demnos: Ana Jorvis's father, and Arys Greenveil's brother-in-law, married to Ela Jorvis.

Jorvis, Ela: Sister of Arys Greenveil, wife of Demnos Jorvis, Blood Forester, mother to Ana Jorvis.

Jorvis, High Luxiat: One of the six High Luxiats during Gavin's first Freeing.

Jorvis, Jason: Brother to Ana, son of Ela and Demnos.

Jumber, Norl: A Blackguard, a casualty of the Omnichrome's War.

Jun: A Blackguard scrub.

Kadah: A magister at the Chromeria; a green drafter who teaches drafting basics.

Kalif: A Blackguard.

Kallea: Teia's sister; married to a butcher.

Kalligenaea, Lady Phoebe: A yellow superchromat with finer luxin control than even Gavin Guile.

Kallikrates: Teia's father. He ran the silk route as a trader before losing everything due to his wife's lavish lifestyle.

Keftar, Graystone: A green drafter and Blackguard scrub. He's an athletic, dark-skinned son of a rich family that paid for him to be trained before he came to the Chromeria.

Kerea: A Blackguard and an archer.

Klytos Blue: The Blue on the Spectrum. He represents Ilyta, though he is a Ruthgari. A coward and Andross's tool.

Kyros: Dazen Guile's tutor as a child.

Laya: A Blackguard who drafts red, present at the Battle of Garriston. Later killed in the Omnichrome's War.

Leelee: A pretty young kitchen slave in Andross Guile's household.

Lem (Will): A Blackguard, either simple or crazy, a blue drafter with incredible will.

Leo: A Blackguard inductee, hugely muscular, drafts red and sub-red. Often called Big Leo.

Lightbringer, the: A controversial figure in prophecy and mythology. Attributes that most agree on are that he is male, will slay or has slain gods and kings, is of mysterious birth, is a genius of magic, a warrior who will sweep, or has swept, all before him, a champion of the poor and downtrodden, great from his youth, He Who Shatters. That most of the prophecies were in Old Parian and the meanings have changed in ways that are difficult to trace hasn't helped. There are three basic camps: that the Lightbringer has yet to come; that the Lightbringer has already come and was Lucidonius (a view the Chromeria now holds, though it didn't always); and, among some academics, that the Lightbringer is a metaphor for what is best in all of us.

Lillyfield: Martial arts tutor to Sarai Lucigari and to Teia.

Little Piper: An orange/yellow bichrome Blackguard.

Lucia: A Blackguard scrub, she had a forbidden romantic relationship with Cruxer. Murdered by an assassin during a training exercise.

Lucidonius: The legendary founder of the Seven Satrapies and the Chromeria, the first Prism. He was married to Karris Shadowblinder and founded the Blackguards.

Lucigari, Lady: The mother of Sarai; a wealthy noblewoman of Abornea.

Lucigari, Sarai: Teia was her slave companion and training partner.

Lunna Green: The Green on the Spectrum until her death. Ruthgari, a cousin of Jia Tolver. Her brothers killed Arys Greenveil's parents during the war.

Lytos: A Blackguard, a lanky Ilytian eunuch. Partners with Buskin.

Malargos, Antonius: Cousin of Tisis and Eirene, a red drafter and devout follower of Orholam.

Malargos, Aristocles: Uncle of Eirene and Tisis Malargos; lost during the chaos in the aftermath of the Battle of Sundered Rock.

Malargos, High Luxiat Camileas: One of the High Luxiats during the False Prism's War. Sister of Dervani and Aristocles Malargos.

Malargos, Dervani: A Ruthgari nobleman, father of Eirene and Tisis Malargos, a friend and supporter of Dazen during the False Prism's War. A green drafter who was lost in the wilds of Tyrea for years. When he tried to return home, Felia Guile secretly hired pirates to kill him so that he wouldn't reveal Gavin's secrets. He survived the attempt and later became the Omnichrome's choice for Atirat.

Malargos, Eirene (Prism): The Prism before Alexander Spreading Oak (who preceded Gavin Guile). She lasted fourteen years.

Malargos, Eirene (the Younger): The older sister of Tisis Malargos. She took over the family's affairs when her father and uncle didn't come back from the war.

Malargos, Perakles: The brutal though cowardly head of the Malargos family prior to Eirene Malargos's ascension.

Malargos, Thera: Perakles Malargos's wife.

Malargos, Tisis: A stunningly beautiful Ruthgari green drafter. Her father and uncle fought for Dazen. Her older sister is Eirene Malargos, from whom she will likely inherit the wealth of a great trading empire, as Eirene has refused to bear children.

Maltheos: A Ruthgari noble family that fell before the False Prism's War.

Marae: One of Teia's younger sisters.

Marid Black: The Black during the False Prism's War.

Marissia: Gavin's room slave. A red-haired Blood Forester who was captured by the Ruthgari during the war between

Ruthgar and Blood forest, she has been with Gavin for over a decade, since she was eighteen.

Marta, Adan: An inhabitant of Rekton.

Martaens, Marta: A magister at the Chromeria. She is one of only a handful of living paryl drafters, and she instructs Teia.

Martaenus, Luzia: A young woman of Atan's town during Darjan's time.

Melanthes: The steward – and slave – of the Malargos family.

Mori: A soldier in the Omnichrome's army.

Mossbeard: The conn of a village on the Blood Forest coast near Ruic Bay.

Naelos: A Blackguard with whom Karris had a brief affair after the end of her engagement to Gavin Guile.

Naheed: Satrapah of Atash. She was murdered by General Gad Delmarta during the False Prism's War.

Naheed, Quentin: A young luxiat and genius polymath.

Nassos: A Ruthgari count in western Ruthgar. Liv Danavis's cousin serves him.

Navid, Payam: A good-looking magister at the Chromeria; Phips Navid is his cousin.

Navid, Phips: Cousin to Payam Navid. He grew up in Ru, and later joined the Omnichrome's army. His father and older brothers were all hanged after the False Prism's War when he was just twelve years old. Killed in the Battle of Ru.

Nerra: A Blackguard who invented great explosive luxin disks (hull wreckers) for sinking ships.

Niel, Amestan: Now the third largest exporter of wool in Paria, he knew Karris as a young man.

Niel, Baya: A green drafter and Blackguard.

Nuqaba, the: Keeper of the oral histories of Parians, a figure of unique and tremendous power due to her ancient office as both religious leader to the Parians, and as guardian of the great Library of Azûlay. Within her satrapy, she rivals both the satrap of Paria and the Prism in her influence.

Oakenshield, Taya: Known for extending the walls of what was once known as Oakenshield Fortress (now simply called the Castle).

Oakenshield, Zee: Andross Guile's great-great-grandmother, a green drafter.

Omnichrome, Lord (the Color Prince): The leader of a rebellion against the rule of the Chromeria. His true identity is known by few, as he has re-formed almost his entire body with luxin. A full-spectrum polychrome, he posits a faith in freedom and power, rather than in Lucidonius and Orholam. Also known as the Color Prince, the Crystal Prophet, the Polychrome Master, the Eldritch Enlightened, and derogatorily as Lord Rainbow. He was formerly Koios White Oak, one of Karris White Oak's brothers. He was horribly burned in the fire that triggered the False Prism's War.

One-Eye: A mercenary with the Cloven Shield company.

Onesto, Prestor: An Ilytian banker at Varig and Green.

Onesto, Turgal: The young scion of a great merchant banking family and Karris White Oak's spy.

Ora'lem: The legendary first drafter who used a Shimmercloak, literally meaning 'The Hidden'.

Orholam: From the Old Abornean, Or'holam, literally the 'Lord of Light.' Referred to by his/its titles rather than by a name as a sign of total respect. The deity of the monotheistic Seven Satrapies, also known as the Father of All. His worship was spread throughout the Seven Satrapies by Lucidonius, four hundred years before the reign of Prism Gavin Guile.

Orholam: A tongue-in-cheek nickname for a slave rower who once served Orholam as a prophet. Due to Gunner's superstitions, he is assigned to the seventh seat in the galley's ranks, seven being also the number of the deity.

Orlos, Maros: A very religious Ruthgari drafter. He fought in both the False Prism's War and as a defender of Garriston.

Or-mar-zel-atir: One of the original Blackguards who served Lucidonius. His name meant 'The Master Who Serves as [the goddess] Atirat's Spear' with the dual connotation that he was a master of the spear, and that he himself was lordly and used as Atirat's spear.

Oros brothers, the: Two Blackguard scrubs.

Param: A retired Blackguard. One of Karris's former lovers.

Payam, Parshan: A young drafter at the Chromeria who attempts to seduce Liv Danavis as part of a bet. After she learns of the bet, he fails in spectacular fashion.

Pevarc: He proved the world was round two hundred years before Gavin Guile, and he was later lynched for positing that light was the absence of darkness rather than a positive presence itself.

Philosopher, the: A foundational figure in both moral and natural philosophy.

Phyros: A member of the Omnichrome's army. He is seven feet tall and fights with two axes. Liv Danavis's protector and guardian.

Pip: A Blackguard scrub.

Pots: A Blackguard.

Presser: A Blackguard.

Ptolos, Euterpe: Satrapah of Ruthgar.

Ptolos, Croesos: Cousin to the Satrapah of Ruthgar, Euterpe Ptolos.

Pullawr, Orea: The White. A blue/green bichrome who refrained from drafting in order to prolong her life. She was married to Ulbear Rathcore before his death, twenty years ago.

Rados, Blessed Satrap: A Ruthgari satrap who fought the Blood Foresters although he was outnumbered two to one. He was famous for burning the Rozanos Bridge behind his army to keep it from retreating.

Ramir (Ram): A Rekton villager.

Rassad, Master Shayam: Completely blind in the visible spectrum, he allegedly could navigate with sub-red and paryl; taught Marta Martaens's teacher in paryl.

Rathcore, Ulbear: The late husband of the White, he has been dead for twenty years. An adroit player of Nine Kings.

Rig: A Blackguard legacy. He is a red/orange bichrome.

Roshan, Mahshid: A beautiful superviolet drafter, she serves as a greeter at the Crossroads tavern.

Rud: A Blackguard scrub. He is a squat coastal Parian who wears the ghotra.

Running Wolf: A general for Gavin during the False Prism's war. He was thrice bested by smaller forces commanded by Corvan Danavis.

Sadah Superviolet: The Parian representative, a superviolet drafter, often the swing vote on the Spectrum.

Samite: A Blackguard. She is one of Karris's best friends.

Sanson: A village boy from Rekton who grew up with Kip. Deceased.

Satrap of Atash: See Aravind, Lord.

Sayeh, Meena: Cousin to Samila Sayeh. She was just seven years old when she was killed in Gad Delmarta's purge of the royal family at Ru.

Sayeh, Samila: A blue drafter for Gavin's army. She fought in the defense of Garriston under Gavin Guile.

Selene, High Luxiat: One of the six High Luxiats. A close friend of Orea Pullawr.

Selene, Lady: A Tyrean blue/green bichrome. Not related to High Luxiat Selene (a relatively common name).

Sendinas, the: A Rekton family.

Shadowblinder, Karris: Lucidonius's wife and later widow. She was the second Prism. See also Atiriel, Karris.

Shala: Chosen by Felia Guile, Gavin's middle-aged room slave immediately following the False Prism's War. Her position was eventually permanently filled by Marissia.

Shales, Mongalt: A ship's captain.

Sharp, Master Murder: An assassin of the Order of the Broken Eye who has at times worked for Andross Guile when the Order endorsed the assignment.

Shayam, Lord: An influential follower of the Color Prince.

Shimmercloak, Gebalyn: Vox Shimmercloak's former partner. She seems to have died in a fire while on an assignment.

Shimmercloak, Niah: An assassin. Partner to Vox and a lightsplitter. Deceased.

Shimmercloak, Vox: A green drafter and assassin. He was kicked out of the Chromeria at thirteen. A devotee of Atirat.

Shining Spear: Originally called El-Anat, which means 'Anat is the Lord'. Once he converted to the Light, he became Forushalzmarish, then Shining Spear so the locals could pronounce it, beginning the tradition of Blackguards assuming new names upon joining.

Siana: One of Darjan's wives.

Siluz, Rea: Fourth undersecretary of the Chromeria library and a weak yellow drafter. She knows Janus Borig and directs Kip to meet her.

Small Bear: A huge archer with just one eye. He served Zee Oakenshield.

Spear: A commander of the Blackguards when Gavin first became Prism.

Spreading Oak, Alexander: The Prism before Gavin. Became a poppy addict shortly after becoming Prism. He spent most of his time hiding in his apartments. Son of Lord Bran Spreading Oak.

Spreading Oak, Gracchos: The youngest of Lord Bran Spreading Oak's six sons. Killed in the False Prism's War.

Spreading Oak, Bran: The head of an old noble family of Blood Forest, devout, an old classmate and friend of Orea Pullawr.

Stump: A Blackguard. Coastal Parian.

Sworrins, the: A Rekton family.

Takama, Mistress: Head of the Chromeria's binderies.

Tala: A drafter and warrior in the False Prism's War. She was also a defender of Garriston. Her grandson is Aheyyad Brightwater, and her sister is Tayri.

Tala (the Younger): A yellow/green bichrome. Named after the hero of the False Prism's War, she is an excellent drafter, though not yet an excellent fighter.

Talim, Sayid: A former Prism. He nearly got himself named promachos to face the nonexistent armada he claimed waited beyond the gates, forty-seven years ago.

Tamerah: A Blackguard scrub, a blue monochrome.

Tana: A Blackguard legacy, a scrub.

Tanner: A Blackguard scrub.

Tarkian: A polychrome drafter.

Tawleb, High Luxiat: One of the six High Luxiats.

Tayri: A Parian drafter and defender of Garriston. Her sister is Tala.

Tazerwalt: A princess of the Tlaglanu tribe of Paria. She married Hanishu, the dey of Aghbalu who later joined the Blackguard and took the name Tremblefist.

Temnos, Dalos the Younger: A drafter who fought in both the False Prism's War and the defense of Garriston under Gavin Guile.

Tempus: A Blackguard and a Watch Captain, he led the green drafters during the battle at Ruic Head.

Tensit: A Blackguard inductee.

Tep, Usef: A drafter who fought in the False Prism's War and later against the Omnichrome's armies at Garriston. He is also known as the Purple Bear, because he is a discontiguous bichrome in red and blue. After the war, he and Samila Sayeh became lovers, despite having fought on opposite sides.

Third Eye, the: A Seer, the leader of the original Seers Island inhabitants, and wife of Corvan Danavis, the new satrap.

Tiziri: A former student at the Chromeria. She has a birthmark over the left half of her face. Forced to leave when Kip failed to win a game of Nine Kings against his grandfather.

Tizrik: The son of the dey of Aghbalu. He fails the Blackguard testing, though not before Kip breaks his nose for being a bully.

Tlatig: One of the Blackguard's most skilled archers.

Tolver, Jia: The Yellow on the Spectrum. An Abornean drafter, she is a cousin of Arys Greenveil (the Sub-red).

Treg: A Blackguard who defended Garriston.

Tremblefist (birth name Hanishu): A Blackguard. He is Ironfist's younger brother and was once the dey of Aghbalu.

Tristaem: The author of *On the Fundaments of Reason*.

Tufayyur: A Blackguard scrub.

Tugertent: One of the Blackguard's most skilled archers.

Tychos: An extremely skilled orange drafter and hex-caster (a Chromeria-forbidden magic) in the Color Prince's army.

Ular: A Blackguard scrub, Jun's partner.

Usem the Wild: A drafter and defender of Garriston.

Utarkses, High Luxiat Daeron: One of the High Luxiats during the False Prism's War.

Valor: A Blackguard inductee.

Vanzer: A Blackguard and green drafter.

Varidos, Kerawon: A superchromat, magister and head tester of the Chromeria. He drafts orange and red.

Varigari, Lord: A scion of the Varigari family, originally fishermen before they were raised in the Blood Wars. He lost the family fortune and lands to his gambling habit.

Vecchio, Pash: The most powerful of the pirate kings. His flagship is the *Gargantua*, the best-armed ship in history.

Vena: Liv's friend and fellow student at the Chromeria; a super-violet.

Verangheti, Lucretia: Adrasteia's sponsor at the Chromeria. She is from the Smussato Veranghetis (an Ilytian branch of the family).

Vin, Taya: A mercenary with the Cloven Shield company.

Wanderer, the: A legendary figure, the subject of Gevison's poem *The Wanderer's Last Journey*.

Weir, Dravus: A spy with connections to the Blood Forest ambassador.

White Oak, Karris: A Blackguard; a red/green bichrome; the original cause of the False Prism's War.

White Oak, Koios: One of the seven White Oak brothers, brother to Karris White Oak. Though not originally believed to be a polychrome, after the disastrous fire that killed the majority of his family on the Jaspers, he disappeared and years later emerged as the Omnichrome in Tyrea.

White Oak, Kolos: One of the seven White Oak brothers, brother to Karris White Oak.

White Oak, Rissum: A luxlord, the father of Karris and her seven brothers; reputed to be hot-tempered, but a coward.

White Oak, Rodin: One of the seven White Oak brothers, brother to Karris White Oak.

White Oak, Tavos: One of the seven White Oak brothers, brother to Karris White Oak.

White, the: The head of the Chromeria and the Spectrum. She (a strong majority of Whites have been women, though it isn't a requirement) is in charge of all magical and historical education at the Chromeria (as opposed to purely religious instruction, which is the demesne of the High Luxiats). She is in charge of all discipulae, and matters political and social regarding the Chromeria (where the Black is in charge of matters mundane, practical, and martial, and is subordinate to her). She presides over the Chromeria, though her power is limited to casting tie-breaking votes – a rarity, as the Spectrum gives one vote to each of its seven Colors (the Black having no vote ever, though he is allowed to speak and attends meetings).

Wil: A green drafter, and a Blackguard.

Willow Bough, Briun: The satrap of Blood Forest.

Winsen: A mountain Parian, and a Blackguard scrub. An incredible archer.

Wit, Rondar: A blue drafter who becomes a color wight.

Young Bull: A blue drafter who fought with Zee Oakenshield.

Yugerten: A gangly Blackguard scrub, blue drafter.

Zid: Quartermaster of the Omnichrome's army.

Ziri: A Blackguard scrub.

Glossary

abaya: A robe-like dress, common in Paria.

Aghbalu: Both a Parian dey (city-state) and its capital city, this inland region is mountainous, its inhabitants known for their height and blue drafting, as well as a fierce independence from the coastal Parian deys.

ahdar qassis gwardjan: A green drafter-warrior-priest and servant of the green goddess/god Atirat.

alcaldesa: A Tyrean term, akin to village mayor or chief.

Am, Children of: Archaic term for the people of the Seven Satrapies.

Amitton: An Atashian city north of Sitara's Wells.

Anat: God of wrath, associated with sub-red. See Appendix, 'On the Old Gods.'

Angar: A country beyond the Seven Satrapies and the Everdark Gates. Its skilled sailors occasionally enter the Cerulean Sea. The Angari are matrilineal, remarkable for their blond hair and fair skin, their sailing skills, emphasis on hygiene, and their brewing of an alcohol from honey.

Ao River: A river on the border of Blood Forest and Atash.

Apple Grove: A small town in the interior of Blood Forest, a part of the White Oak patrimony for generations.

aristeia: A concept encompassing genius, purpose, and excellence, and often, the demonstration thereof.

Aslal: The capital city of Paria. The Eternal Flame, at the heart of the city, was lit by Lucidonius at his inauguration as Prism.

ataghan: A narrow, slightly forward-curving sword with a single edge for most of its length.

Atan's Teeth: Mountains to the east of Tyrea.

Atan's Town: An extinct village on the coast of what is now Tyrea. Legend holds that it was wiped out in a storm of fire. Some scholars believe this to be a symbolic interpretation of a massacre after Atan's Town resisted Lucidonius's forces. Others believe it was a literal magical storm, unconnected with politics or theology.

atasifusta: The widest tree in the world, believed extinct after the False Prism's War. Its sap has properties like concentrated red luxin, which, when allowed to drain slowly, can keep a flame lit for hundreds of years if the tree is large enough. The wood itself is ivory white, and when the trees are immature, a small amount of its wood, burning, can keep a home warm for months. Its usefulness and slow growth led to aggressive harvesting and extinction.

Atirat: God of lust, associated with green. See Appendix, 'On the Old Gods.'

Aved Barayah: A legendary ship. Its name means the Fire Breather. Gunner was its cannoneer for a time in his youth. It was during his service here that he is said to have killed a sea demon with a miraculous shot.

aventail: Usually made of chain mail, it is attached to the helmet and drapes over the neck, shoulders, and upper chest.

Azûlay: A coastal city in Paria; the Nuqaba lives there.

balance: The primary work of the Prism. When the Prism drafts at the top of the Chromeria, he alone can sense all the world's imbalances in magic and can draft enough of its opposite (i.e., balancing) color to stop the imbalance from getting any worse and leading to catastrophe. Frequent imbalances occurred throughout the world's history before Lucidonius came, and the resulting disasters of fire (see Atan's Town), famine, and sword killed thousands if not millions. Superviolet balances sub-red, blue balances red, and green balances orange. Yellow seems to exist in balance naturally.

bane: An old Ptarsu term, could be either singular or plural. It may have meant a temple or holy place, though Lucidonius's Parians believed they were abominations. The Parians acquired the word from the Ptarsu.

Barrenmoor: An expensive whiskey. Distilled by the same process as Crag Tooth, its rival, Barrenmoor evinces a smoky, medicinal, seaweedy nose with flavors of peat and salt.

beakhead: The protruding part of the foremost section of the ship.

beams: See Chromeria trained.

Belphegor: God of sloth, associated with yellow. See Appendix, 'On the Old Gods.'

belt-flange: A flattened hook attached to a pistol so it can be tucked securely into a belt.

belt knife: A blade small enough to be tucked in a belt, commonly used for eating, rarely for defense.

bich'hwa: A 'scorpion,' a weapon with a loop hilt and a narrow, undulating recurved blade. Sometimes made with a claw.

bichrome: A drafter who can draft two different colors.

Big Jasper (Island): The island on which the city of Big Jasper rests just opposite the Chromeria, and where the embassies of all the satrapies reside. At the time of the Lucidonian expansion, inhabited by the Ptarsu and enslaved Pygmies.

binocle: A double-barreled spyglass that allows the use of both eyes for viewing objects at a distance.

Blackguard, the: An elite guard at the top echelon of the Chromeria. The Blackguard was instituted after Lucidonius with a unique dual purpose: to guard the Prism, and to guard the Prism from him- or herself. Though commonly seen as bodyguards for the Prism (and at times the White, and at other times all of the Colors), the exact nature and extent of their duties is little known.

blindage: A screen for the open deck of a ship during battle.

Blood Plains, the: An older collective term for Ruthgar and Blood Forest, so called since Vician's Sin caused the Blood War between them.

Blood War, the: A series of battles that began after Vician's Sin tore apart the formerly close allies of Blood Forest and Ruthgar. The war was seemingly interminable, often starting and stopping, until Gavin Guile put a decisive end to it following the False Prism's War. It seems there will be no further hostilities. Also known as the Blood Wars among those who differentiate between the various chapters and campaigns of the long struggle.

Blue-Eyed Demons, the: A famed company of bandits whose king Gavin Guile killed after the False Prism's War.

blunderbuss: A musket with a bell-shaped muzzle that can be loaded with nails, musketballs, chain or even gravel. Devastating at short distances.

Braxos: A legendary city thousands of years old, cut off from the Seven Satrapies by the Cracked Lands, which were reputed to have been formed with magic during the Ptarsu expansion centuries before Lucidonius.

brightwater: Liquid yellow luxin. It is unstable and quickly releases its energy as light. Often used in lanterns.

Brightwater Wall: Its building was a feat to match the legends. This wall was designed by Aheyyad Brightwater and built by Prism Gavin Guile at Garriston in just days before and while the Omnichrome's army attacked.

Broken Man, the: A statue in a Tyrean orange grove. Likely a Ptarsu relic.

burnous: A long Parian cloak with hood.

Caleen/calun: A diminutive term of address for a girl or female slave/boy or male slave, used regardless of the slave's age.

Cannon Island: A small island with a minimal garrison between Big Jasper and Little Jasper. It houses artillery and, it's rumored, magical defenses.

Cerulean Sea, the: The sea the Seven Satrapies circle.

cherry glims: Slang for red-drafting second-year students.

chirurgeon: One who stitches up the wounded and studies anatomy.

Chosen, Orholam's: Another term for the Prism.

chromaturgy: Literally 'color working,' it usually refers to drafting, but technically also covers the study of luxins and Will.

Chromeria, the: The ruling body of the Seven Satrapies; also a term for the school where drafters are trained.

Chromeria trained: Those who have or are training at the Chromeria school for drafting on Little Jasper Island in the Cerulean Sea. The Chromeria's training system does not limit students based on age, but rather progresses them through each degree of training based on their ability and knowledge. So a thirteen- year-old who is extremely proficient in drafting might well be a gleam, or third-year student, while an eighteen-year-old who is just beginning work on her drafting could be a dim.

- darks: Technically known as 'supplicants,' these are would-be drafters who have yet to be tested for their abilities at the Chromeria or allowed full admission to the school.
- dims: The first-year (and therefore lowest) rank of the Chromeria's students.
- glims: Second-year students.
- gleams: Third-year students.
- beams: Fourth-year students.

cocca: A type of merchant ship, usually small.

Colors, the: The seven members of the Spectrum. Originally, each represented a single color of the seven sacred colors; each could draft that color, and each satrapy had one representative. Since the founding of the Spectrum, that practice has deteriorated as satrapies have maneuvered for power. Thus a satrapy's Color could be appointed to a color she doesn't actually draft. Likewise, some of the satrapies might lose their representative, and others could have two or even three representatives on the Spectrum at a time, depending on the politics of the day. A Color's term is for life. Impeachment is nearly impossible.

color matchers: A term for superchromats. Sometimes employed as satraps' gardeners.

color-sensitive: See superchromat.

color wight: A drafter who has broken the halo. They often remake their bodies with pure luxin, rejecting the Pact between drafter and society that is a foundation to all training at the Chromeria.

conn: A title for a mayor or leader of a village in far northern Atash; but more common in Blood Forest.

Corrath Springs: A small port city on the coast of Ruthgar.

Corbine Street: A street in Big Jasper that leads to the Great Fountain of Karris Shadowblinder.

corregidor: A Tyrean term for a chief magistrate; from when Tyrea encompassed eastern Atash. Now used for regional governors or even the leaders of larger cities.

corso: A title for the drummer on a galley.

Counselor to Kings, The: A manuscript, noted for its advocating ruthless treatment of opponents.

Cracked Lands, the: A region of broken land in the extreme west of Atash. Its treacherous terrain is only crossed by the most hardy and experienced traders.

Crag Tooth: A fine whiskey with a sublime nose hinting at rose and cinnamon made in distilleries at the edge of Blood Forest in the highlands above Green Haven. It evinces orange and raisin flavors under powerful chocolate.

Crater Lake: A large lake in southern Tyrea where the former capital of Tyrea, Kelfing, sits. The area is famous for its forests and the production of yew.

Crossroads, the: A kopi house, restaurant, tavern, the highest-priced inn on the Jaspers, and downstairs a similarly priced brothel. Located near the Lily's Stem, the Crossroads is housed in the former Tyrean embassy building, centrally located in the Embassies District for all the ambassadors, spies, and merchants trying to deal with various governments.

cubit: A unit of volume. One cubit is one foot high, one foot wide, and one foot deep.

culverin: A type of cannon, useful for firing long distances because of its heavily weighted cannonballs and long-bore tube.

Cwn y Wawr: A Blood Forest martial company of archers, tree climbers, green drafters and masters of camouflage. Found in the deep parts of Blood Forest. The name means the White Dawn.

dagger-pistols: Pistols with a blade attached, allowing the user to fire at distance and then use the blade at close range or if the weapon misfires.

Dagnu: God of gluttony, associated with red. See Appendix, 'On the Old Gods.'

danar: The currency of the Seven Satrapies. The average worker makes about a danar a day, while an unskilled laborer can expect to earn a half danar a day. The coins have a square hole in the middle, and are often carried on square-cut sticks. They can be cut in half and still hold their value.

tin danar: Worth eight regular danar coins. A stick of tin danars usually carries twenty-five coins, that is, two hundred danars.

silver quintar: Worth twenty danars, slightly wider than the tin danar, but only half as thick. A stick of silver quintars usually carries fifty coins, that is, one thousand danars.

den: One-tenth of a danar.

darks: See Chromeria trained.

Dark Forest: A region within Blood Forest where pygmies reside. Decimated by the diseases brought by invaders, their numbers have never recovered, and they remain insular and often hostile. Few Chromeria drafters have ever returned from trips to the Dark Forest.

darklight: Another term for paryl.

dawat: A Parian martial art: 'circling strike.'

Dazen's War: Another name for the False Prism's War, used by the victors. Dazen's defeated armies and disinterested observers sometimes call it simply the Prisms' War.

Deimachia, the: The War of/on the Gods. A theological term for Lucidonius's battle for supremacy against the pagan gods of the old world.

Demiurgos: Another term for a Mirror; literally a half-creator.

dey/deya: A Parian title, male and female respectively. A near-absolute ruler over a city and its surrounding territory. (Equivalent to the Atashian/Tyrea 'corregidor'.)

dims: See Chromeria trained.

discipulae: The feminine plural term (also applying to groups of mixed genders) for those who study both religious and magical arts, usually at the Chromeria.

drafter: One who can shape or harness light into physical form (luxin).

Elrahee, elishama, eliada, eliphalet: A Parian prayer meaning 'He sees, He hears, He cares, He saves.'

Embassies District: The Big Jasper neighborhood that is closest to the Lily's Stem, and thus is closest to the Chromeria itself. It also houses markets and kopi houses, taverns, and brothels.

epha: A unit of measurement for grain. (Approximately thirty-three liters.)

Ergion: An Atashian walled city a day's travel east of Idoss.

Everdark Gates, the: The strait connecting the Cerulean Sea to the oceans beyond. It was supposedly closed by Lucidonius, but Angari ships have been known to make it through from time to time.

evernight: Often a curse word, it refers to death and hell. A metaphysical or teleological reality, rather than a physical one, it represents that which will forever embrace and be embraced by void, full darkness, night in its purest and most evil form.

eye caps: A specialized kind of spectacles. These colored lenses fit directly over the eye sockets, glued to the skin. Like other spectacles, they enable a drafter to draft her color more easily.

False Prism, the: Another term for Dazen Guile, who claimed to be a Prism even after his older brother Gavin had already been rightly chosen by Orholam and installed as Prism.

False Prism's War, the: A common term for the war between Gavin and Dazen Guile, where the False Prism means Dazen.

Fásann Ár Gciorcal: The Greenveil family motto, meaning 'Our Circle Grows.'

Fealty to One: The Danavis motto.

Feast of Light and Darkness, the: A celebration of the equinox, when light and dark war over who will own the sky. Because the religious calendar is tied to the lunar calendar, the feast is sometimes as much as a month off the solar date of the equinox.

Ferrilux: God of pride, associated with superviolet. See Appendix, 'On the Old Gods.'

firecrystal: A term for sustainable sub-red, though a firecrystal doesn't last long when exposed to air.

firefriend: A term sub-red drafters use for each other.

Flame of Erebos, the: The symbolic pin all Blackguards receive: as a candle must be consumed to provide light, so too the Blackguards' lives require sacrifice to be of use to Orholam.

flashbomb: A weapon crafted by yellow drafters. It doesn't harm so much as dazzle and distract its victims by the blinding light of evaporating yellow luxin.

flechette: A tiny projectile (sometimes made of luxin), with a pointed end and a vaned tail to achieve stable flight.

foot: Once a varying measure based on the current Prism's foot length. Later standarized to twelve thumbs (the length of Prism Sayid Talim's foot, who decreed the standardization).

Free, the: (See disambiguation with the 'Freed' below.) Those drafters who reject the Pact of the Chromeria to join the Omnichrome's army, choosing to eventually break the halo and become wights. Also called the Unchained.

Freed, the: (See disambiguation with the 'Free' above.) Those drafters who accept the Pact of the Chromeria and choose to be ritually killed before they break the halo and go mad. (The closeness of this term with 'the Free' is part a deliberate linguistic war between the pagans and the Chromeria, with the pagans trying to seize terms that had long had other meanings.)

Freeing: The release of those about to break the halo from incipient madness; performed by the Prism every year as the culmination of the Sun Day rituals. A sensitive and holy time, it is accompanied with both mourning and celebration. Each drafter meets personally with the Prism for the ritual. Many refer to it as the holiest day of their lives. The pagans take a different view.

frizzen: On a flintlock, the L-shaped piece of metal against which the flint scrapes. The metal is on a hinge that opens upon firing to allow the sparks to reach the black powder in the chamber.

gada: A ball game that involves kicking and passing a ball of wrapped leather.

galleass: A large merchant ship powered by both oar and sail. The term later referred to ships modified for military purposes, which included adding castles at bow and stern and cannons that fire in all directions.

gaoler: One in charge of a prison or dungeon.

Gargantua, the: A veritable floating castle, it was Ilytian pirate king Pash Vecchio's flagship, with 141 light guns and 43 heavy cannons.

Garriston: The former commercial capital of Tyrea at the mouth of the Umber River on the Cerulean Sea. Prism Gavin Guile built Brightwater Wall to defend the city, but his defense failed, and the city was claimed by Lord Omnichrome, the Color Prince, later the White King, Koios White Oak.

Gatu, the: A Parian tribe, despised by other Parians for how they integrate their old religious customs into the worship of Orholam. Technically, their beliefs are heresy, but the

Chromeria has never moved to put the heresy down with anything more than strong words.

gemshorn: A musical instrument made from the tusk of a javelina, with finger-holes drilled into it to allow different notes to be played.

ghotra: A Parian headscarf, used by many Parian men to demonstrate their reverence for Orholam. In old Parian tradition, a man's hair is a sign of his virility and dominance and thereby his glory. In older times, however, age-related baldness was apparently unknown among Parians. In centuries of intermarriage with the other cultures of the Seven Satrapies, and baldness becoming more common, the ghotra has become less popular. Most wear it only while the sun is up, but some sects wear it even at nighttime.

giist: A colloquial name for a blue wight.

gladius: A short double-edged sword, useful for cutting or stabbing at close range.

Glass Lily, the: Another term for Little Jasper, or for the whole of the Chromeria as a collection of buildings. A reference to how the seven towers rise and turn to follow the sun.

gleams: See Chromeria trained.

glims: See Chromeria trained.

gold standard: The literal standard weights and measures, made of gold, against which all measures are judged. The originals are kept at the Chromeria, and certified copies are kept in every capital and major city for the adjudication of disputes. Merchants found using short measures and inaccurate weights are punished severely.

Great Chain (of being), the: A theological term for the order of creation. The first link is Orholam himself, and all the other links below (creation) derive from him.

great hall of the Chromeria, the: Located under the Prism's Tower, it is converted once a week into a place of worship, at which time mirrors from the other towers are turned to shine light in. It includes pillars of white marble and the largest display of stained glass in the world. Most of the time, though, it is filled with clerks, ambassadors, and those who have business with the Chromeria.

great hall of the Travertine Palace, the: The wonder of the great hall is its eight great pillars set in a star shape around the hall, all made of extinct atasifusta wood. Said to be the gift of an Atashian king, these trees were the widest in the world, and their sap allows fires to burn continually, even five hundred years after they were cut.

Great River, the: The river between Ruthgar and Blood Forest, the scene of many pitched battles between the two countries.

great yard, the: The yard at the base of the towers of the Chromeria.

Green Bridge: Less than a league upstream from Rekton, drafted by Gavin Guile in seconds while on his way to battle his brother at Sundered Rock.

green flash: A rare flash of color seen at the setting of the sun; its meaning is debated. Some believe it has theological significance, citing Karris Atiriel's sighting of it the evening before the battle in Hass Valley. The White calls it Orholam's wink.

Green Forest: A collective term for Blood Forest and Ruthgar during the hundred years of peace between the two territories, before Vician's Sin incited the Blood Wars.

Green Haven: The capital of Blood Forest.

grenado: A clay flagon full of black powder with a piece of wood shoved into the top, with a rag and bit of black powder as a fuse.

grenado, luxin: An explosive made of luxin that can be hurled at the enemy along an arc of luxin or in a cannon. Often filled with shot/ shrapnel, depending on the type of grenado used.

Guardian, the: A colossus that stands astride the entrance to Garriston's bay. She holds a spear in one hand and a torch in the other. A yellow drafter keeps the torch lit with yellow luxin, allowing it to dissolve slowly back into light, acting as a lighthouse. See also Ladies, the.

Guile palace: The Guile family palace on Big Jasper. Andross Guile rarely visits his home in the time Gavin is Prism, preferring to reside at the Chromeria. The Guile palace was one of the few buildings allowed to be constructed without regard to the working of the Thousand Stars, its height cutting off some of the light paths.

habia: A long man's garment, most common in Abornea.

Hag, the: An enormous statue that comprises Garriston's west gate. She is crowned and leans heavily on a staff; the crown and staff are also towers from which archers can shoot at invaders. See also Ladies, the.

Hag's Crown, the: A tower over the west gate into Garriston.

Hag's Staff, the: A tower over the west gate into Garriston.

haik: An outer garment that wraps around the body and head. Commonly worn in Paria.

Harbinger: Corvan Danavis's sword, inherited when his elder brothers died.

Hass Valley: Where the Ur trapped Lucidonius. Karris Atiriel (later Karris Shadowblinder) saved his army there, after climbing through the mountain passes at night to strike the Ur's camp from behind at dawn.

haze: A mind-altering drug. Often smoked with a pipe, it produces a sickly sweet odor.

Hellfang: A mysterious blade, also known as Marrow Sucker and the Blinder's Knife. It is white veined with black and bears seven colorless gems in its blade.

hellhounds: Dogs infused with red luxin and enough will to make them run at enemies, and then lit on fire.

hellstone: A superstitious term for obsidian, which is rarer than diamonds or rubies as few know where the extant obsidian in the world is created or mined. Obsidian is the only stone that can draw luxin directly out of a drafter if it touches her blood directly.

Hippodrome (Rath): A stadium dedicated primarily to horse and chariot races, the hippodrome in Rath occasionally operates as a public gathering place for executions and other important state functions.

hullwrecker: A luxin disk filled with shrapnel. It has a sticky side so that it will adhere to a ship's hull and a fuse to allow the attackers to flee before it explodes, often punching a hole in the ship's hull and spraying shrapnel in toward the crew.

Idoss: An Atashian city, now under the control of the Omnichrome's armies.

incarnitive: A term for luxin when it is incorporated directly into one's body. Forbidden by the Chromeria as debasing or defiling Orholam's work (the human body itself) with man's work, and often seen as a slippery slope to trying to fully remake the body and become immortal. In certain cases, the luxiats have turned a blind eye to more minor or prosthetic uses.

Inura, Mount: A mountain on Seers Island, at the base of which the Third Eye resides.

ironbeaks: A term for luxin- and will-infused birds, used to attack opponents at distance and then explode.

Ivor's Ridge, Battle of: A battle during the False Prism's War, which Dazen won primarily because of Corvan Danavis's brilliance.

Izîl-Udad: The Nuqaba's husband, the head of the family that had her mother assassinated. Now a cripple, rumored to have been pushed down the stairs by his own wife after he'd beaten her one too many times.

Jaks Hill: A large hill in the city of Rath overlooking the Great River, notable for its wealthy estates. The Guile Castle dominates the area.

jambu: A tree that produces pink fruit.

Jasper Islands/the Jaspers: Islands in the Cerulean Sea that hold the Chromeria. Legend has it that the Jaspers were chosen for the Chromeria by Karris Shadowblinder after the death of Lucidonius because they were part of no satrapy, and therefore they could be for all the satrapies.

javelinas: Animals in the pig family, often hunted. Giant javelinas are rare, but can reach the size of a cow. Extremely dangerous and destructive, giant javelinas are believed to have been hunted to extinction in all satrapies except Tyrea. Both species have tusks and hooves and are nocturnal.

jilbab: A long and loose-fitting coat, often with a hood. Often worn by Parians and occasionally Aborneans.

ka: A sequence of movements to train balance and flexibility and control in the martial arts. A form of focusing exercise or meditation.

kaptan: Ptarsu for head or leader. Possibly origin of 'captain'.

Karsos Mountains, the: Tyrean mountains running east and west that border the Cerulean Sea.

katar: A blade with a cross-grip and a hilt that extends up on either side of the hand and forearm. With this allowance for the fist and its reinforced tip, it is made for punching through armor.

Kazakdoon: A legendary city/land in the distant east, beyond the Everdark Gates.

Kelfing: The former capital of Tyrea, on the shores of Crater Lake.

khat: An addictive stimulant, a leaf that stains the teeth after chewing, used especially in Paria.

kiyah: A yell used while fighting to expel breath, tightening the trunk and empowering the body's movement.

kopi: A mild, addictive stimulant, a popular beverage. Bitter, dark-colored, and served hot.

kris: A wavy Parian blade.

Ladies, the: Four statues that comprise the gates into the city of Garriston. They are built into the wall, made of rare Parian marble and sealed in nearly invisible yellow luxin. They are thought to depict aspects of the goddess Anat and were spared by Lucidonius, who believed them to depict something true. They are the Hag, the Lover, the Mother, and the Guardian.

Laurion: A region in eastern Atash known for its silver ore and massive slave mines. Life expectancy for the enslaved miners is short, and the threat of being sent to the mines is used to keep slaves obedient and docile throughout the satrapies.

league: A unit of measurement, six thousand and seventy-six paces.

Library of Azûlay: An ancient library in Paria, the building itself is more than eight hundred years old, and built on the foundations of another library at least two hundred years older. The Nuqaba resides in Azûlay, in part due to her role as protector of the Library.

lightbane: See bane.

Lightguard, the: Andross Guile's personal army, nominally established to defend the Jaspers, answering only to him. Mercenaries, ruffians, veterans, and any others willing to fight for Andross Guile. Primarily washed-out Blackguards and the sons of poor nobles. Even their clothing is in contrast to the Blackguards: white jackets with big brass buttons and medals.

lightsickness: The after-effects of too much drafting. Only the Prism never gets lightsick.

lightwells: Holes positioned to allow light, with the use of mirrors, to reach into the interior of the towers or to sections of streets.

Lily's Stem, the: The luxin bridge between Big and Little Jasper. It is composed of blue and yellow luxin so that it appears green. Set below the high-water mark, it is remarkable for its endurance against the waves and storms that wash over it. Ahhana the Dextrous was responsible for designing and engineering its creation.

linstock: A staff for holding a slow match. Used in lighting cannons, it allows the cannoneer to stand out of the range of the cannon's recoil.

Little Jasper: The island on which the Chromeria resides. Became the site of the Chromeria after Vician's Sin.

Little Jasper Bay: A bay of Little Jasper Island. It is protected by a seawall that keeps its waters calm.

loci damnata: A temple to the false gods. The bane. Believed to have magical powers, especially over drafters.

longbow: A weapon that allows for the efficient (in speed, distance, and force) firing of arrows. Its construction and its user must both be extremely strong. The yew forests of Crater Lake provide the best wood available for longbows.

Lord Prism: A respectful term of address for a male Prism.

lords of the air: A term used by the Omnichrome for his most trusted blue-drafting officers.

Lover, the: A statue that comprises the eastern river gate at Garriston. She is depicted in her thirties, lying on her back arched over the river with her feet planted, her knees forming a tower on one bank, hands entwined in her hair, elbows rising to form a tower on the other bank. She is clad only in veils. Before the Prisms' War, a portcullis could be lowered from her arched body into the river, its iron and steel hammered into shape so that it looked like a continuation of her veils. She glows like bronze when the sun sets, and the entrance to the city comes through another gate in her hair.

luxiat: A priest of Orholam. A luxiat wears black as an acknowledgment that he needs Orholam's light most of all; thus he is sometimes called a blackrobe.

luxin: A material created by drafting from light. See Appendix.

luxlord: A term for a member of the ruling Spectrum.

Luxlords' Ball, the: An annual event on the open roof of the Prism's Tower.

luxors: Officials empowered by the Chromeria to bring the light of Orholam by almost any means necessary. They have at various times pursued paryl drafters and lightsplitter heretics, among others. Their theological rigidity and their prerogative to kill and torture have been hotly debated by followers of Orholam and dissidents alike.

magister: The term for a teacher of drafting, history, and religion at the Chromeria. It always retains its masculine ending: magister, not magister or magistra as appropriate. This is a relic from when all teachers were male; female drafters being considered too valuable for teaching.

mag torch: Often used by drafters to allow them access to light at night, it burns with a full spectrum of colors. Colored mag torches are also made at great expense, and give a drafter her exact spectrum of useful light, allowing her to eschew spectacles and draft instantly.

Mangrove Point: A village on the border between Blood Forest and Atash.

match-holder: The piece on a matchlock musket to which a slow match is affixed.

matchlock musket: A firearm that works by snapping a burning slow match into the flash pan, which ignites the gunpowder in the breech of the firearm, whose explosion propels a rock or lead ball out of the barrel at high speed. Matchlocks are accurate to fifty or a hundred paces, depending on the smith who made them and the ammunition used.

matériel: A military term for equipment or supplies.

merlon: The upraised portion of a parapet or battlement that protects soldiers from fire.

Midsummer: Another term for Sun Day, the longest day of the year.

Midsummer's Dance: A rural version of the Sun Day celebration.

Mirrormen: Soldiers in King Garadul's army who wear mirrored armor to protect themselves against luxin. The mirrors cause luxin to sheer off and disintegrate when it comes in contact with it.

Molokh: God of greed, associated with orange. See Appendix, 'On the Old Gods.'

monochromes: Drafters who can only draft one color. (See 'bichromes' and 'polychromes'.)

Mot: God of envy, associated with blue. See Appendix, 'On the Old Gods.'

Mother, the: A statue that guards the south gate into Garriston. She is depicted as a teenager, heavily pregnant, with a dagger bared in one hand and a spear in the other.

mund: An insulting term for a person who cannot draft.

murder hole: A hole in the ceiling of a passageway that allows soldiers to fire, drop, or throw weapons, projectiles, luxin, or fuel. Common in castles and city walls.

nao: A small vessel with a three-masted rig.

Narrows, the: A strait of the Cerulean Sea between Abornea and the Ruthgari mainland. Aborneans charge high tolls on merchants sailing the silk route, or simply between Paria and Ruthgar.

near-polychrome: One who can draft three colors, but can't stabilize the third color sufficiently to be a true polychrome.

non-drafter: One who cannot draft.

norm: Another term for a non-drafter. Insulting.

nunk: A half-derogatory term for a Blackguard inductee.

Oakenshield Fortress: The old, original fortress in Ruthgar on Jaks Hill, which eventually became Castle Guile, Corinth Castle, Rath Skuld and finally known simply as the Castle.

Odess: A city in Abornea that sits at the head of the Narrows.

old world: The world before Lucidonius united the Seven Satrapies and abolished worship of the pagan gods.

oralam: Another term for paryl, meaning hidden light.

Order of the Broken Eye, the: A secret guild of assassins. They specialize in killing drafters and have been rooted out and destroyed at least three times. They claim to have twenty-four paryl drafters who work in teams of two as invisible assassins with shimmercloaks. These assassins, also called Shimmercloaks, are the pride of the Order.

Overhill: A neighborhood in Big Jasper.

Ox Ford: A crossing on the Ao River border between Atash and Blood Forest.

Pact, the: Since Lucidonius, the Pact has governed all those trained by the Chromeria in the Seven Satrapies. Its essence is that drafters agree to serve their satrapy and receive all the benefits of status and sometimes wealth in exchange for their service and eventual death before they break the halo.

parry-stick: A primarily defensive weapon that blocks bladed attacks. It sometimes includes a punching dagger at the center of the stick to follow up on a deflected blow.

pathomancy: The reading of or the manipulation of emotions directly via orange drafting. Forbidden by the Chromeria.

Pericol: A city on the coast of Ilyta.

petasos: A broad-brimmed Ruthgari hat, usually made of straw, meant to keep the sun off the face, head, and neck.

pilum: A weighted throwing spear whose iron shank bends after it pierces a shield, preventing the opponent from reusing the weapon against the user and encumbering the shield. They are becoming more rare and ceremonial.

polychrome: A drafter who can draft three or more colors.

portmaster: A city official in charge of collecting tariffs and the organized exit and entrance of ships into his harbor.

Prism: There is only one Prism each generation. She senses the balance of the world's magic, balances it when necessary, and can split light within herself. Other than Balancing, her role is largely ceremonial and religious, with the Colors and the satraps all working hard to make sure that Prisms rarely turn their fame into political power.

Prism's Tower, the: The central tower in the Chromeria. It houses the Prism, the White, and superviolets (as they are not numerous enough to require their own tower). The great hall lies below the tower, and the top holds a great crystal for the Prism's use while he balances the colors of the world.

promachia: The institution of giving nearly absolute executive powers to a single person (The Promachos) during wartime.

promachos: Literally meaning 'he [or she] who fights before us', it is title that may be given during a war or other great crisis. A promachos may only be named by order of a super-majority of the Colors. Among other powers, the promachos has the right to command armies, seize property, and elevate commoners to the nobility.

Providence: A belief in the care of Orholam over the Seven Satrapies, and his intervention on behalf of its people.

psantria: A stringed musical instrument.

Pygmies [of Blood Forest]: A rare, fierce people of the Blood Forest interior, they claim common ancestry with the people of Braxos. Almost extinct. Their taxonomy is debated, with some saying they are only related to humans as horses and mules are related. They can interbreed with humans, though with great danger if the mother is pygmy, death in childbirth being the norm. Some Blood Forest chiefs and kings in the past claimed that pgymies were not human, and as they weren't, they deemed the killing of pygmies a morally neutral or even laudable act. The Chromeria declared pygmies human and such killing to be murder, but pygmy numbers have never recovered from a number of massacres and human diseases.

pyrejelly: Red luxin that, once set alight, will engulf whatever object it adheres to.

qassisin kuluri: Possibly an early incarnation of the Order, 'the color warriors (or assassins).' The exact provenance of the term is lost to history.

Rage of the Seas: An Ilytian galley.

rakka: A heavy insult, with the implication of both moral and intellectual idiocy.

Raptors of Kazakdoon, the: Flying reptiles from Angari myth.

Rath: The capital of Ruthgar, set on the confluence of the Great River and its delta into the Cerulean Sea.

Rathcaeson: A mythical city, on the drawings of which Gavin Guile based his Brightwater Wall design.

Rathcore Hill: A hill opposite (and somewhat smaller than) Jaks Hill in the city of Rath. The Hippodrome is carved into its side.

ratweed: A toxic plant whose leaves are often smoked for their strong stimulant properties. Addictive.

Red Cliff Uprising, the: A rebellion in Atash after the end of the False Prism's War. Without the support of the royal family (who had been purged), it was short-lived.

Rekton: A small Tyrean town on the Umber River, near the site of the Battle of Sundered Rock. An important trading post before the False Prism's War. Now uninhabited after a massacre by King Rask Garadul.

Rozanos Bridge, the: A bridge on the Great River between Ruthgar and the Blood Forest that Blessed Satrap Rados famously burned, so that his troops had no choice but to win or die.

Ru: The capital of Atash, once famous for its castle, still famous for its Great Pyramid.

Ru, Castle of: Once the pride of Ru, it was destroyed by fire during General Gad Delmarta's purge of the royal family in the Prisms' War.

Ruic Head: A peninsula dominated by towering cliffs that overlooks the Atashian city of Ru and its bay. A fort atop the peninsula's cliffs guards against invaders and pirates.

runt: An affably derogatory term for a new Blackguard inductee.

Salve: A common greeting, originally meaning 'Be of good health!'

Sapphire Bay: A bay off Little Jasper.

satrap/satrapah: The title of a ruler of one of the seven satrapies.

scrogger: A small rodent.

sev: A unit of measurement for weight, equal to one-seventh of a seven.

seven: A unit of measurement for weight, equal to a cubit of water's weight.

Shadow: Another term for a member of the Order of the Broken Eye.

Shadow Watch: A secretive martial drafting society based in Ruthgar.

Sharazan Mountains, the: Impassable mountains south of Tyrea.

shimmercloak: A cloak that makes the wearer mostly invisible, except in sub-red and superviolet.

Sitara's Wells: An Atashian town north of Ruic head. In otherwise arid land, its numerous artesian wells have made it a stop for traders and travellers for all of recorded history.

Skill, Will, Source, and Still/Movement: The four essential elements for drafting.

Skill: The most underrated of all the elements of drafting, acquired through practice. Includes knowing the properties and strengths of the luxin being drafted, being able to see and match precise wavelengths, etc.

Will: By imposing will, a drafter can draft and even cover flawed drafting if her will is powerful enough.

Source: Depending on what colors a drafter can use, she needs either that color of light or items that reflect that color of light in order to draft. Only a Prism can simply split white light within herself to draft any color.

Still: An ironic usage. Drafting requires movement, though more skilled drafters can use less.

slow fuse / slow match: A length of cord, often soaked in saltpeter, that can be lit to ignite the gunpowder of a weapon in the firing mechanism.

spectrum: A term for a range of light (for more information on the luxin spectrum, see the Appendix); or (capitalized) the council of the Chromeria that is one branch of the government of the Chromeria (see Colors, the).

spidersilk: Another term for paryl.

spina: The center line of a hippodrome, which often has a raised platform for announcements, demonstrations, and executions.

spyglass: A device using curved, clear lenses to bend light to aid in sighting distant objects.

star-keepers: Also known as tower monkeys, these are petite slaves (usually children) who work the ropes that control the mirrors in the Thousand Stars of Big Jasper to reflect the light throughout the city for drafters' use. Though well treated for slaves, they spend their days working in two-man teams from dawn till after dusk, frequently without reprieve except for switching with their partner.

Stony Field: A border town between Blood Forest and Atash.

Strang's Commentary: The authoritative work of theology, teleology, and epistemology (in that order) by Aldous Strang, the full opus fills one thousand scrolls.

Strong's Commentary: The authoritative work of epistemology, teleology, and theology (in that order) by Albus Strong, pupil and rumored illegitimate son of Aldous Strang, the full opus fills one thousand and one scrolls.

subchromats: Drafters who are color-blind, overwhelmingly male. A subchromat can function without loss of ability—if his handicap is not in the colors he can draft. A red-green color-blind subchromat could be an excellent blue or yellow drafter. See Appendix.

Sun Day: A holy day to followers of Orholam and pagans alike, the longest day of the year. For the Seven Satrapies, Sun Day is the day when the Prism Frees those drafters who are about to break the halo and go mad. The ceremonies usually take place on the Jaspers, when all of the Thousand Stars are trained onto the Prism, who can absorb and split the light, whereas other men burn or burst from drafting so much power.

Sun Day's Eve: An evening of festivities, both celebration and mourning, before the longest day of the year and the Freeing the next day.

Sundered Rock: Twin mountains in Tyrea, opposite each other and so alike that they look as if they were once one huge rock cut down the middle.

Sundered Rock, Battle of: The final battle between Gavin and Dazen near a small Tyrean town called Garriston on the Umber River.

superchromats: Extremely color-sensitive people. Luxin they seal will rarely fail. Far more common among female drafters.

Tafok Amagez: The Nuqaba's elite personal guard, composed entirely of drafters.

tainted: One who has broken the halo, also called a wight.

Tanner's Turn: A village on the border of Atash and Blood Forest.

Tellari separatists: Rebels behind the burning of the Great Library three hundred years prior to Prism Guile, they also attempted to destroy the Lily's Stem.

thobe: An ankle-length garment, usually with long sleeves.

Thorikos: A town below the Laurion mines on the river to Idoss. Serves as the center for arriving and departing slaves, the bureaucracy necessary for thirty thousand slaves, and the center for the trade goods and supplies necessary, as well as the shipping of the silver ore down the river.

Thorn Conspiracies, the: A series of intrigues that occurred after the False Prism's War.

Thousand Stars, the: The mirrors on Big Jasper Island that enable the light to reach into almost any part of the city for as long as possible during the day.

Threshing, the: The initiation test for candidates to the Chromeria. Through subjecting the initiates to things that instigate the most common fears and providing appropriate spectra of light, it usually reveals the initiates' range of drafting ability (with some uncertainty around the edges).

Threshing Chamber, the: The room where candidates for the Chromeria are summoned to test for their abilities to draft.

Tiru, the: A Parian tribe.

Tlaglanu, the: A Parian tribe, hated by other Parians, from whom Hanishu, the dey of Aghbalu, chose his bride, Tazerwalt.

torch: A red wight.

translucification, forced: See willjacking.

Travertine Palace, the: One of the wonders of the old world. Both a palace and a fortress, it is built of carved travertine (a mellow green stone) and white marble. Notable for its bulbous horseshoe arches, geometric wall patterns, Parian runes, and chessboard patterns on the floors. Its walls are incised with a crosshatched pattern to make the stone look woven rather than carved. The palace is a remnant of the days when half of Tyrea was a Parian province.

Tree People, the: Tribesmen who live (lived?) deep in the forests of the Blood Forest satrapy. They use zoomorphic designs, and can apparently shape living wood. Possibly related to the pygmies.

tromoturgy: 'fear working' or 'fear casting' banned by the Chromeria as are other forms of direct manipulation of emotions, man being created in the likeness of Orholam, any assault on the dignity of man's body (violence, murder) or his mind (emotion-casting, torture, slave-taking) are considered sinful – except as allowed by just-war theory and the rights of rule: a city can imprison a thief where citizens doing so would be kidnapped, et cetera. In general, the Chromeria takes a harder line towards things magical, especially manipulation of emotions and minds, as such things generate a natural terror and distrust among those they would rule. Luxors were a noted exception to this blanket prohibition, allowed 'a righteous fear-casting'.

Two Mills Junction: A small village in Blood Forest, not far from the border of Atash.

Two Hundred, the: Apochryphal. Two hundred of Orholam's progeny who rebelled and came to the world to rule over men and magic.

tygre striper: Also known as the sharana ru, said to be carved from sea demon bone, though others contest that the even rarer whalebone makes superior weapon. It is the only known mundane material that reacts to will: becoming hard or flexible depending at the user's will.

ulta: In the Order's religion, a man's highest goal, his life's purpose, and final test.

Umber River, the: The lifeblood of Tyrea. Its water allows the growth of every kind of plant in the hot climate; its locks fed trade throughout the country before the False Prism's War. Often besieged by bandits.

Unchained, the: A term for the followers of the Color Prince, those drafters who choose to break the Pact and continue living even after breaking the halo.

Unification, the: A term for Lucidonius's and Karris Shadowblinder's establishment of the Seven Satrapies four hundred years prior to Gavin Guile's rule as Prism.

Ur, the: A tribe that trapped Lucidonius in Hass Valley. He triumphed against great odds, primarily because of the heroics of El-Anat (who thereby became Forushalzmarish or Shining Spear) and Karris Atiriel (later Karris Shadowblinder).

urum: A three-tined dining implement.

vambrace: Plate armor to protect the forearm. Ceremonial versions made of cloth also exist.

Varig and Green: A bank with a branch on Big Jasper.

vechevoral: A sickle-shaped sword with a long handle like an ax and a crescent-moon-shaped blade at the end, with the inward bowl-shaped side being the cutting edge.

Verdant Plains, the: The dominant geographical feature of Ruthgar, enabling the farming and grazing that give Ruthgar its immense wealth. The Verdant Plains have been favored by green drafters since before Lucidonius.

Vician's Sin: The event that marked the end of the close alliance between Ruthgar and Blood Forest, and purportedly led to Orholam raising White Mist Reef and the mist itself at the center of the Cerulean Sea.

Wanderer, the: Andross Guile's flagship during the fight to save Ru.

warrior-drafters: Drafters whose primary work is fighting for various satrapies or the Chromeria. Usually far inferior in drafting from the Blackguard, who are the foremost warrior-drafters in the world.

water markets: Circular lakes connected to the Umber River at the center of the villages and cities of Tyrea, common throughout Tyrean towns. A water market is dredged routinely to maintain an even depth, allowing ships easy access to the interior of the city with their wares. The largest water market is in Garriston.

Weasel Rock: A neighborhood in Big Jasper dominated by narrow alleys.

Weedling: A small coastal village in Ru close to Ruic Head.

wheellock pistol: A pistol that uses a rotating wheel mechanism to cause the spark that ignites the firearm; the first mechanical attempt to ignite gunpowder. Some few smiths' versions are more reliable than a flintlock and allow repeated attempts to fire with repeated pulls of the trigger without manual cocking as flintlocks require. Most, however, are far less reliable than the already unreliable flintlocks.

Whiteguard, the: The term for the Omnichrome's personal bodyguard. Most likely a jab at the Blackguards whose black denotes humility in excellence.

widdershins: Counter-sunwise spinning.

willjacking/will-breaking: Once a drafter has contact with unsealed luxin that she is able to draft, she can use her will to break another drafter's control over the luxin and take it for herself.

will-blunting: A forbidden form of drafting used to directly attack another's will, connecting emotionally and intellectually with them and thereby forbidden as an assault on man's mind and dignity.

Wiwurgh: A Parian town that hosts many Blood Forest refugees from the Blood War.

wob: A term for a Blackguard inductee.

wyrthig: A Blood Forest term for a falsehood or tall tale.

zigarro: Rolled tobacco, a form useful for smoking. Ratweed is sometimes used as a wrapping to hold the loose tobacco to allow use of both substances at once.

Appendix

On Monochromes, Bichromes, and Polychromes

Most drafters are monochromes: they are able to draft only one color. Drafters who can draft two colors well enough to create stable luxin in both colors are called bichromes. Anyone who can draft solid luxin in three or more colors is called a polychrome. The more colors a polychrome can draft, the more powerful she is and the more sought after are her services. A full-spectrum polychrome is a polychrome who can draft every color in the spectrum. A Prism is always a full-spectrum polychrome.

Merely being able to draft a color, though, isn't the sole determining criterion in how valuable or skilled a drafter is. Some drafters are faster at drafting, some are more efficient, some have more will than others, some are better at crafting luxin that will be durable, some are smarter or more creative at how and when to apply luxin.

On Disjunctive Bichromes/Polychromes

On the light continuum, sub-red borders red, red borders orange, orange borders yellow, yellow borders green, green borders blue, blue borders superviolet. Most bichromes and polychromes simply draft a larger spectrum on the continuum than monochromes. That is, a bichrome is most likely to draft two colors that are adjacent to each other (blue and superviolet, red and sub-red, yellow and green, etc.). However, some few drafters are disjunctive bichromes. As could be surmised from the name, these are drafters whose colors do not border each other. Usef Tep was a famous example: he drafted red and blue. Karris White Oak is another, drafting green and red. It is unknown how or why disjunctive bichromes come to exist. It is only known that they are rare.

On Outer-Spectrum Colors

There is a small and controversial movement claiming that there are more than seven colors. Indeed, because colors exist on a continuum, one could argue that the number of colors is infinite. However, the argument that there are more than seven draftable colors is more theologically problematic for some. It is commonly accepted that there are other resonance points beyond the seven currently accepted ones, but those points are weaker and much more rarely drafted than the core seven. Among the contenders is one color far below the sub-red, called paryl. Another equally far above superviolet is called only chi.

But if colors are to be so broadly defined as to include colors only one drafter in a million can draft, then shouldn't yellow be split into liquid yellow and solid yellow? Where do the (mythical) black and white luxins fit? How could such (non) colors even fit on the spectrum?

The arguments, though bitter, are academic.

On Subchromacy and Superchromacy

A subchromat is one who has trouble differentiating between at least two colors, colloquially referred to as being color-blind. Subchromacy need not doom a drafter. For instance, a blue drafter who cannot distinguish between red and green will not be significantly handicapped in his work.

Superchromacy is having greater than usual ability to distinguish between fine variations of color. Superchromacy in any color will result in more stable drafting, but is most helpful in drafting yellow. Only superchromat yellow drafters can hope to draft solid yellow luxin.

On Luxin (with sections on physics, metaphysics, effects on personality, legendary colors, and colloquial terms)

The basis of magic is light. Those who use magic are called drafters. A drafter is able to transform a color of light into a physical substance. Each color has its own properties, but the uses of those building blocks are as boundless as a drafter's imagination and skill.

The magic in the Seven Satrapies functions roughly the

opposite of a candle burning. When a candle burns, a physical substance (wax) is transformed into light. With chromaturgy, light is transformed into a physical substance, luxin. Each color of luxin has its own properties. If drafted correctly (within a tight allowance), the resulting luxin will be stable, lasting for days or even years, depending on its color.

Most drafters (magic-users) can only use one color. A drafter must be exposed to the light of her color to be able to draft it (that is, a green drafter can look at grass and be able to draft, but if she's in a white-walled room, she can't). Each drafter usually carries spectacles so that if her color isn't available, she can still use magic.

PHYSICS

Luxin has weight. If a drafter drafts a luxin haycart over her head, the first thing it will do is crush her. From heaviest to lightest are: red, orange, yellow, green, blue, sub-red,* super-violet, sub-red. For reference, liquid yellow luxin is only slightly lighter than the same volume of water.

(*Sub-red is difficult to weigh accurately because it rapidly degenerates to fire when exposed to air. The ordering above was achieved by putting sub-red luxin in an airtight container and then weighing the result, minus the weight of the container. In real-world uses, sub-red crystals are often seen floating upward in the air before igniting.)

Luxin has tactility.

Sub-red: Again the hardest to describe due to its flammability, but often described as feeling like a hot wind.

Red: Gooey, sticky, clingy, depending on drafting; can be tarry and thick or more gel-like.

Orange: Lubricative, slippery, soapy, oily.

Yellow: In its liquid, more common state, like bubbly, effervescent water, cool to the touch, possibly a little thicker than seawater. In its solid state, it is perfectly slick, unyielding, smooth, and incredibly hard.

Green: Rough: depending on the skill and purposes of the drafter, ranges from merely having a grain like leather to feeling like tree bark. It is flexible, springy, often drawing comparisons to the green limbs of living trees.

Blue: Smooth, though poorly drafted blue will have a texture or can shed fragments easily, like chalk, but in crystals.

Superviolet: Like spidersilk, thin and light to the point of imperceptibility.

Luxin has scent. The base scent of luxin is resinous. The smells below are approximate, because each color of luxin smells like itself. Imagine trying to describe the smell of an orange. You'd say citrus and sharp, but that isn't it exactly. An orange smells like an orange. However, the below approximations are close.

Sub-red: Charcoal, smoke, burned.

Red: Tea leaves, tobacco, dry.

Orange: Almond.

Yellow: Eucalyptus and mint.

Green: Fresh cedar, resin.

Blue: Mineral, chalk, almost none.

Superviolet: Faintly like cloves.

Black: No smell/or smell of decaying flesh.

White: Honey, lilac.

(*Mythical; these are the smells as reported in stories.)

METAPHYSICS

Any drafting feels good to the drafter. Sensations of euphoria and invincibility are particularly strong among young drafters and those drafting for the first time. Generally, these pass with time, though drafters abstaining from magic for a time will often feel them again. For most drafters, the effect is similar to drinking a cup of kopi. Some drafters, strangely enough, seem to have allergic reactions to drafting. There are vigorous ongoing debates about whether the effects on personality should be described as metaphysical or physical.

Regardless of their correct categorization and whether they are the proper realm of study for the magister or the luxiat, the effects themselves are unquestioned.

LUXIN'S EFFECTS ON PERSONALITY

The benighted before Lucidonius believed that passionate men became reds, or that calculating women became yellows or blues. In truth, the causation flows the other way.

Every drafter, like every woman, has her own innate personality. The color she drafts then influences her toward the behaviors below. A person who is impulsive who drafts red for years is going to be more likely to be pushed farther into 'red' characteristics than a naturally cold and orderly person who drafts red for the same length of time.

The color a drafter uses will affect her personality over time. This, however, doesn't make her a prisoner of her color, or irresponsible for her actions under the influence of it. A green who continually cheats on his wife is still a lothario. A sub-red who murders an enemy in a fit of rage is still a murderer. Of course, a naturally angry woman who is also a red drafter will be even more susceptible to that color's effects, but there are many tales of calculating reds and fiery, intemperate blues.

A color isn't a substitute for a woman. Be careful in your application of generalities. That said, generalities can be useful: a group of green drafters is more likely to be wild and rowdy than a group of blues.

Given these generalities, there is also a virtue and a vice commonly associated with each color. (Virtue being understood by the early luxiats not as being free of temptation to do evil in a particular way, but as conquering one's own predilection toward that kind of evil. Thus, gluttony is paired with temperance, greed with charity, etc.)

> **Sub-red drafters:** Sub-reds are passionate in all ways, the most purely emotional of all drafters, the quickest to rage or to cry. Sub-reds love music, are often impulsive, fear the dark less than any other color, and are often insomniacs. Emotional, distractable, unpredictable, inconsistent, loving, bighearted. Sub-red men are often sterile.
>
> Associated vice: Wrath
>
> Associated virtue: Patience
>
> **Red drafters:** Reds are quick-tempered, lusty, and love destruction. They are also warm, inspiring, brash, larger than life, expansive, jovial, and powerful.
>
> Associated vice: Gluttony

Associated virtue: Temperance

Orange drafters: Oranges are often artists, brilliant in understanding other people's emotions and motivations. Some use this to defy or exceed expectations. Sensitive, manipulative, idiosyncratic, slippery, charismatic, empathetic.

Associated vice: Greed

Associated virtue: Charity

Yellow drafters: Yellows tend to be clear thinkers, with intellect and emotion in perfect balance. Cheerful, wise, bright, balanced, watchful, impassive, observant, brutally honest at times, excellent liars. Thinkers, not doers.

Associated vice: Sloth

Associated virtue: Diligence

Green drafters: Greens are wild, free, flexible, adaptable, nurturing, friendly. They don't so much disrespect authority as not even recognize it.

Associated vice: Lust

Associated virtue: Self-control

Blue drafters: Blues are orderly, inquisitive, rational, calm, cold, impartial, intelligent, musical. Structure, rules, and hierarchy are important to them. Blues are often mathematicians and composers. Ideas and ideology and correctness often matter more than people to blues.

Associated vice: Envy

Associated virtue: Kindness

Superviolet drafters: Superviolets tend to have a removed outlook; dispassionate, they appreciate irony and sarcasm and word games and are often cold, viewing people as puzzles to be solved or ciphers to be cracked. Irrationality outrages superviolets.

Associated vice: Pride

Associated virtue: Humility

LEGENDARY COLORS

Chi (pronounced KEY): The postulated upper-spectrum counter-part to paryl. (Often referred to in tales as 'far above superviolet as paryl is below sub-red.') Also called the revealer. Its main claimed use is nearly identical to paryl – seeing through things, though those who believe in chi say its powers far surpass paryl's in this regard, cutting through flesh and bone and even metal. The only thing the tales seem to agree on is that chi drafters have the shortest life expectancy of any drafters: five to fifteen years, almost without exception. If chi indeed exists, it would mostly be evidence that Orholam created light for the universe or for his own purposes, and not solely for the use of man, and would move theologians from their current anthropocentrism.

Black: Destruction, void, emptiness, that which is not and cannot be filled. Obsidian is said to be the bones of black luxin after it dies.

Paryl: Also called spidersilk, it is invisible to all but paryl drafters. It resides as far down the spectrum from sub-red as most sub-red does from the visible spectrum. Believed mythical because the lens of the human eye cannot contort to a shape that would allow seeing such a color. The alleged color of dark drafters and night weavers and assassins because this spectrum is (again, allegedly) available even at night. Uses unknown, but linked to murders. Poisonous?

White: The raw word of Orholam. The stuff of creation, from which all luxin and all life was formed. Descriptions of an earthly form of the stuff (as diminished from the original as obsidian supposedly is from black luxin) describe it as radiant ivory, or pure white opal, emitting light on the whole spectrum.

COLLOQUIAL TERMS

Students at the Chromeria are encouraged to use the proper names for each color, but the impetus to name seems unstoppable. In some cases, the names are used technically: pyrejelly is a thicker, longer-burning draft of red that will burn long enough to reduce a body to ash. In other cases, the reference becomes precisely the opposite of the technical definition: brightwater was first a name for liquid yellow luxin, but Brightwater Wall is solid yellow luxin.

A few of the more common colloquialisms:

Sub-red: Firecrystal
Red: Pyrejelly, burnglue
Orange: Noranjell
Yellow: Brightwater
Green: Godswood
Blue: Frostglass, glass
Superviolet: Skystring, soulstring, spidersilk
Black: Hellstone, nullstone, nightfiber, cinderstone, hadon
White: Truebright, starsblood, anachrome, luciton

On the Old Gods

Sub-red: Anat, goddess of wrath. Those who worshipped her are said to have had rituals that involved infant sacrifice. Also known as the Lady of the Desert, the Fiery Mistress. Her centers of worship were Tyrea, southernmost Paria, and southern Ilyta.

Red: Dagnu, god of gluttony. He was worshipped in eastern Atash.

Orange: Molokh, god of greed. Once worshipped in western Atash.

Yellow: Belphegor, god of sloth. Primarily worshipped in northern Atash and southern Blood Forest before Lucidonius's coming.

Green: Atirat, goddess of lust. Her center of worship was primarily in western Ruthgar and most of Blood Forest.

Blue: Mot, god of envy. His center of worship was in eastern Ruthgar, northeastern Paria, and Abornea.

Superviolet: Ferrilux, god of pride. His center of worship was in southern Paria and northern Ilyta.

On Technology and Weapons

The Seven Satrapies are in a time of great leaps in understanding. The peace since the Prisms' War and the following suppression of piracy has allowed the flow of goods and ideas freely through the satrapies. Cheap, high-quality iron and steel are available in every satrapy, leading to high-quality weapons, durable wagon wheels, and everything in between. Though traditional forms of weapons like Atashian bich'hwa or Parian parry-sticks continue, now they are rarely made of horn or hardened wood. Luxin is often used for improvised weapons, but most luxins' tendency to break down after long exposure to light, and the scarcity of yellow drafters who can make solid yellows (which don't break down in light), means that metal weapons predominate among mundane armies.

The greatest leaps are occurring in the improvement of firearms. In most cases, each musket is the product of a different smith. This means each man must be able to fix his own firearm, and that pieces must be crafted individually. A faulty hammer or flashpan can't be swapped out for a new one, but must be detached and reworked into appropriate shape. Some large-scale productions with hundreds of apprentice smiths have tried to tackle this problem in Rath by making parts as nearly identical as possible, but the resulting matchlocks tend to be low quality, trading accuracy and durability for consistency and simple repair. Elsewhere, the smiths of Ilyta have gone the other direction, making the highest-quality custom muskets in the world. Recently, they've pioneered a form they call the flintlock. Instead of affixing a burning slow match to ignite powder in the flashpan and thence into the breech of the rifle, they've affixed a flint that scrapes a frizzen to throw sparks directly into the breech. This approach means a musket or pistol is always ready to fire, without a soldier having to first light a slow match. Keeping it from widespread adoption is the high rate of misfires – if the flint doesn't scrape the frizzen correctly or throw sparks perfectly, the firearm doesn't fire.

Thus far, the combination of luxin with firearms has been largely unsuccessful. The casting of perfectly round yellow luxin musket balls was possible, but the small number of yellow drafters able to make solid yellow creates a bottleneck in production. Blue luxin musket balls often shatter from the force of the black powder explosion. An exploding shell made by filling a yellow luxin ball with red luxin (which would ignite explosively from the shattering yellow when the ball hit a target) was demonstrated to the Nuqaba, but the exact balance of making the yellow thick enough to not explode inside the musket, but thin enough to shatter when it hit its target, is so difficult that several smiths have died trying to replicate it, probably barring this technique from wide adoption.

Other experiments are doubtless being carried out all over the Seven Satrapies, and once high-quality, consistent, and somewhat accurate firearms are introduced, the ways of war will change forever. As it stands, a trained archer can shoot farther, far more quickly, and more accurately.

Coming soon!

The Blood Mirror

Lightbringer: Book 4

by

BRENT WEEKS

Stripped of both magical and political power, the people he once ruled told he's dead, and now imprisoned in his own magical dungeon, former Emperor Gavin Guile has no prospect of escape.

But the world faces a calamity greater than the Seven Satrapies has ever seen . . . and only he can save it.

As the armies of the White King defeat the Chromeria and old gods are born anew, the fate of worlds will come down to one question: who is the Lightbringer?

orbit

www.orbitbooks.net

extras

about the author

Brent Weeks was born and raised in Montana. After getting his paper keys from Hillsdale college, Brent had brief stints walking the earth like Caine from Kung Fu, tending bar, and corrupting the youth. (Not at the same time.) He started writing on bar napkins, then on lesson plans, then full time. Eventually, someone paid him for it. Brent lives in Oregon with his wife, Kristi. He doesn't own cats or wear a ponytail. Find out more about the author at www.brentweeks.com.

Find out more about Brent Weeks and other Orbit authors by registering for the free monthly newsletter at www.orbitbooks.net.

if you enjoyed

BROKEN EYE

look out for

SWORDS AND SCOUNDRELS

The Duellists: Book One

by

Julia Knight

Chapter One

They say that an ounce of blood is worth more than a pound of friendship. Vocho wasn't so sure about that. Probably depended on whose blood you were talking about, because blood seemed to have got him into nothing but trouble.

The wood Vocho and Kacha lurked in was a mean little thing, a straggle of trees and stunted bushes that fringed the muddy track between some two-cow town in the province of Reyes and a different two-cow, perhaps even three-cow town up towards the mountains and the border with Ikaras. A desolate and rain-sodden spot in the back of beyond, a far cry from the city of Reyes itself. Vocho sat and shivered and dripped as he watched his sister, atop her restless horse, wrestle with the clockwork gun.

'Are you certain you know what you're doing with that thing?' he said at last. In retrospect, it wasn't the best thing Vocho could have said to her just then.

Kacha stopped scowling at the gun and scowled at him instead before she raised a cool eyebrow and blew a drip of water off the end of her nose. 'Of course. Pretty sure I know where I went wrong last time.'

'You shot my horse's ear off.'

A curl of her lip from under her dripping tricorne. She was indistinct in the darkness under the sodden trees, her heavy black coat and that ridiculous hat fading into the shadows, leaving only the pale blur of her face.

'Anyone could have made that mistake,' she said airily. 'It's not like, oh, I don't know, killing the priest we were supposed to be guarding, right?'

'That was an accident!' Vocho was pretty sure anyway – the memories of that night were vague, and though they seemed vivid enough in his dreams, they soon faded to guesswork and ghosts when he woke up. Sadly the duellists' guild hadn't seen it as an accident when said priest had turned up with a sword hole in him. Worse, it was Vocho's sword, the hilt still in his hand. The guild, not to mention the prelate and his guards, tended to take a dim view of that sort of thing. Very dim.

'He was only a priest, and a bad one at that, and that was a good horse.' Vocho still smarted at the fact they'd had to sell the horse – for some reason it had got very nervy after that accident, and nervy horses weren't good in his new profession of highwayman.

'Maybe only a priest,' Kacha said. 'But he was the prelate's favourite. He was paying our wages, and the prelate's department and the guild get very upset about people killing priests they're being paid to guard.' Kacha hefted the gun, prodded the clockwork mechanism and scowled at it some more, like that would make it work properly. 'At least in the guild we didn't have to deal with these sodding things.'

Vocho subtly tried to edge his horse backwards, out of line of sight of the gun, but instead the beast barged sideways and knocked into Kacha's horse, making it shy and snap at the air, narrowly missing the feather stuck in the brim of Vocho's hat.

'Careful,' Kacha muttered, 'or it'll be your ear I take off, and not by accident.'

Vocho knew when it was time to stay quiet, and now was such a time. His older sister was mercurial in nature and none more so than when waiting in a dark and rain-drenched wood on the edge of cold mountains for some clocker or ex-noble to drive by so they could rob him, instead of being in a nice dry guild house in a nice hot city down by the coast. Especially when it was because of that dead priest they weren't in said dry guild house or hot city. Even more especially when Kacha had a new-fangled gun that was difficult to shoot right at best, and an accident waiting to happen at worst. Oh, how the mighty are fallen.

The rain intensified, bouncing from leaf to sodden leaf, shivering from cloud to ground in a constant litany of sound.

Confounded northern mountain weather. Vocho would have given a lot of money to be back in Reyes city. It'd be full-blown spring down there by now, and a Reyes spring tended not to include bucketloads of rain, but featured long hot lazy afternoons with a cool breeze coming in off the sea. The nightlife tended to be a little more refined than getting soaked to the skin in the muddy arse end of nowhere as well.

Raindrops plastered the jaunty feather on Vocho's hat into a tangled mess, ran down his neck, soaked through his heavy cloak and his fancy trousers, was utterly ruining the finish on his best coat and made his hands slip on the little crossbow. He didn't like crossbows any more than he liked guns, but they had a tendency to backfire less and sometimes you needed one, even if it was a coward's weapon. Not so long ago they'd have been drummed out of the guild for using one, or the gun, if they hadn't already been drummed out. He could hear his old sword master now. *A projectile weapon is only for those with no class or no balls.*

Three months ago he wouldn't have gone out on a night like this for any money. Three months ago he'd have had that choice. Now he had no money and no choice, so here he was, shrivelling in the rain like a sodding prune. He might be poor, more than poor now, but a man had to make an impression and right now all he was good for was looking like a rat drowned in a water butt.

One insignificant little mistake, and they never let you forget it.

Kacha sat up straight beside him, listening. The rain had soaked through her hat, turning it into a sopping mess, and her blonde hair was dark and lank, but she didn't seem to mind. Over the whisper of the wind and the rush of the rain came the faintest jingle, as of horse harness. A vague splashing rumble, as of carriage wheels negotiating a muddy road.

'Kacha . . .'

She shot him a lopsided grin, but it was wound tight as a bowstring. She always got twitchy before a fight, and always hid it with a grin.

'Mask,' she whispered. He pulled his soaking scarf over

his chin and nose and she did the same, making sure it was pulled up far enough to cover the telltale puckered scar under her eye. Between the scarf and hat, he'd have been hard pushed to recognise her if he didn't know her.

A carriage came in to view around the corner, mud splashing from its wheels. A lumbering coach and four, it looked promising – well kept with fancy harness, and the horses were all matched too, which boded well. The driver was a huddle of clothes bundled up in an overlarge shapeless hat and an oilskin cloak against the weather. One armed and lightly armoured man in front on a springy bay horse that looked like it'd jump out of its skin at the slightest provocation, one to the side on a steadier-looking grey. Both men looked thoroughly miserable even under large hooded cloaks. Vocho could sympathise.

A lamp either side of the driver gave Vocho and Kacha light to work with. They waited till the coach was almost on them, then Kacha dug her heels in and her horse leaped from behind the screen of bushes and in front of the carriage. Vocho wasn't far behind, aiming his horse to the rear of the carriage to stop it backing up. The bodyguard on the side didn't have a chance to do more than draw his sword before Vocho's bolt had his hand pinned to the side of the coach. Which was embarassing because he'd been aiming somewhere else, but he'd take what he could get.

In the hazy darkness at the front of the carriage the driver swore a blue streak and yanked on the horses, which protested at the treatment and managed to get themselves tangled in the traces. The carriage slewed to a stop, making the pinned bodyguard scream before his hand, bolt and all, came free. He knocked his head on the way down into the mud and slumped unconscious. Which at least saved Vocho a job.

By the time the horses had stopped, the fore bodyguard was down and out in the mud thanks to Kacha's bad-tempered horse lashing out at the bay and an expertly aimed smack in the head from the butt of Kacha's gun. The bay horse dumped its suddenly unresponsive rider and shot up the road, reins and stirrups flapping, like as not never to be seen again.

Like a well oiled machine, the two of them. When they worked together, nothing and no one could stop them. They hadn't been the best in the guild for nothing. At least it was earning them some money.

Muffled voices from inside the carriage, most with a hint of moneyed education about them, expressed varying amounts of surprise or drunken annoyance. Vocho heard a faint, 'I say! That was bit harsh. Need to discipline your driver, Eggy old lad, I almost spilt my wine.'

Kacha might have been wearing a mask, but her brother could see the flinch around her eyes at the name. Good and not so good. Ex-Lord Petri Egimont, ex-noble who liked to let everyone know it, first-rate duellist, currently a lowly clerk in the prelate's office, a pet, a symbol of the revolution the prelate liked to parade in front of his admirers more than anything, and yet of more than solvent means. He also knew both Vocho and Kacha, very well indeed in Kacha's case. Their little spy at the inn on the edge of the woods had neglected to mention who the owner of the carriage was, instead telling them how the man thought tales of highwaymen lately come to the woods were a crock of bollocks and how he was determined to reach his destination by morning. Not to mention how he didn't bother with many bodyguards, thinking he was above being robbed, or if he was, could beat them in a fair fight.

Sounded just like the pompous Eggy. More fool him.

A pale-haired head poked out of the carriage window. Not Egimont, but certainly once aristocratic if the quality of the chin, or lack thereof, was anything to go by. 'Driver? Driver!' His voice was strident and slurred. 'What the blazes do you think you're—'

Kacha shoved the barrel of the gun into the side of his nose. She made her voice a couple of octaves lower than it already was and slipped into a guttersnipe accent to avoid giving herself away to Eggy in the coach. 'Good evening. If it's all the same to you, I'd like to divest you of all your valuables, trinkets and trifles. Money or a hole in the head. I like to do things properly.'

'We'd prefer the money,' Vocho added from his end, affecting a noble accent. 'But sometimes a hole in the head is so satisfying, don't you think? And we haven't shot anyone for *days*.'

A click as Kacha did something menacing with the gun. A whispered conversation inside the carriage. Vocho caught sight of the driver, who waggled his eyebrows as though trying to say something. Sadly, Vocho didn't speak eyebrow.

'Oh,' said the pale-haired man, going cross-eyed as he tried to look at the barrel of the gun while not moving his head. 'Well. I'm sure we can come to some arrangement. Perhaps twenty bulls? I'm sure I've got enough change. That would seem fair . . . Oh.'

Kacha had nudged her horse up parallel to the carriage, and the evil-minded beast knew exactly what was wanted. It grabbed the pale man's hat off his head with a great show of teeth and for good measure at a signal from Kacha kicked hard enough to hole the carriage. That horse was more a highwayman than Vocho was, and made him mourn once again the loss of his old horse with its one ear. This new one was dancing under him like a ballerina.

'I think . . .' Kacha said with an air of contemplation. If she hadn't been wearing her mask, Vocho knew he'd see that lopsided grin again. 'I think everything you have would be fair. Those are our usual terms. I wouldn't like it said that we had favourites. As it's cold, I'll let you keep your underwear. Can't say fairer than that, can we?'

Just to underline her words, the horse snapped its teeth a hair's breadth from the pale man's nose. Between that and the gun barrel, it was looking like he'd have no nose left come sunup.

'Um, well yes, you have a point.' The pale man retreated into the carriage to a hurried and whispered conversation. Vocho caught, 'Damned cheek of it!' 'They've got a gun,' 'So have I, somewhere . . .' 'You can't even see straight, never mind shoot straight,' 'Being robbed by highwaymen is an extra, my lord' in a woman's voice and 'God's cogs, I was just starting to enjoy myself,' followed by a boozy-sounding burp.

Another head poked out. Dark rather than fair this time, long hair done in the latest foppish style, bound at the base of the neck so that it curled across one shoulder. The face less vacuous, with more of a chin. A trim little beard, a long haughty nose, sharp dark eyes and apparently at least slightly less drunk than Pale Hair. Egimont. Vocho had his sword out and ready, just in case. Just in case Kacha shot the ear off a horse by mistake, or Egimont in the face. Given their recent history, it wouldn't have surprised him. If she didn't, he might very well give it a try himself. He sneaked a look at her and was troubled to see her look stricken just for a moment. Like she was ready to drag down her mask and let the world know who they were. Let Eggy know who they were, which would be a disaster.

Time for action. 'Could we hurry this up?' Vocho asked. 'I'm getting sodding wet here.'

It was enough to get Kacha to pull herself together, and she gave him a brief nod to let him know.

'I'm sure we can negotiate, my good sir,' Egimont said to Kacha in the sort of deadpan drawl that made Vocho's shoulders itch. He said everything like that – when he spoke at all, which was rare enough – as though all was beneath his notice. He was just so effortlessly bloody *suave*, which was only the start of the things Vocho had against him.

He braced himself for Kacha's reply but she kept herself reined in. For now. Only the Clockwork God knew how long it would last.

'No, we may not,' she said in a voice thick with suppressed fury. 'Instead, I will shoot your gormless face off if I have to. We're good with cash though. And jewels, we like jewels, rings, necklaces, trinkets, trifles, baubles and bibelots. How much have you got?'

Egimont raised his eyebrows. Kacha had never got the hang of courtly manners though she could pretend well enough when she needed to. 'Not a lot as it happens. Temporarily embarrassed. You know how it is.' Egimont sounded odd – Vocho could only assume he was playing to the drunk ex-nobles in the carriage – which begged the question of why.

'Not really,' Kacha said. Vocho didn't like the way her finger was twitching on the what-d'you-call-it – trigger, was it? The thing that made the gun go bang anyway. 'Everything, that's what we're going for. Now out, all of you. And anyone looks like they're trying anything, this gun tends to go off at a moment's notice. So do I. And blood is such a trial to get out of silk, isn't it?'

Egimont sighed as though he was suffering a great trial for a mere triviality and feigned defeat, though knowing the preening mountebank Vocho didn't believe it for a moment. The door opened and they trooped out. Three men, one so drunk he could hardly stand, but not so drunk he couldn't be sick, which he managed to do all over the pale-haired fellow, who was pretty damned drunk himself. Two women not, how could Vocho put this? Not of the same class. Underfed, underdressed. Women who were most certainly of his own original station – wretched and plebeian, just trying to earn enough to eat the only way they could. Vocho leaned over the pommel of his saddle, sword out and ready in case these fools weren't as drunk as they looked.

'You ladies may go. If you're quick, the inn'll still be open.'

They didn't need telling twice – a quick glance of agreement between them and they hared up the muddy road without a backwards glance. Pale Hair looked after them forlornly. 'But I already *paid*!' he wailed to no one, or no one who cared anyway.

Kacha looked up at the driver, who silently spread his hands as if to say, *These posh sods deserve everything they get*. He was still waggling his eyebrows and mouthing something, but what with the dark and the rain, Vocho couldn't catch it.

'You keep an eye on him,' Kacha said to Vocho with a nod to the driver. Her horse grabbed at the ruffles on the front of Egimont's shirt and started to munch with much apparent delight and flashing of big teeth. Vocho would have sworn it understood the concept of intimidation, though good luck to it trying to get a rise out of the imperturbable Eggy.

'And now, gentlemen, if you'd like to empty your pockets.'

Kacha was enjoying this, Vocho could tell by the undertone in her voice even as she tried to disguise it. Payback for whatever had happened between her and Eggy, which had left her bad-tempered or alternately silent and dreaming for weeks.

A gun waved in front of them seemed to get them going. Eggy threw two purses into the mud, both clinking heavily. 'Go on, Berie,' he said. 'And get Flashy's too.'

Three more purses, all full. Not bad, not bad at all. At a signal from Kacha, Vocho leaped down from his horse, and that's where it all went wrong.

Kacha's evil sod of a horse took exception to Eggy's face and made a grab for it. Eggy wasn't as drunk as he looked, jumped back half a pace and snatched at the sword at his waist. Kacha wasn't drunk at all, but the horse's sudden lunge caught her off guard. The gun fired, there was a bang that seemed like it might take Vocho's ears off, followed by a brief, gurgling moan. Flashy held up a hand with a hole in it, and promptly stopped being drunk and started being passed out at about the same time he fell into the mud.

'Aw, shit,' Kacha said but she didn't get any further. Eggy had his sword out – despite the rest of his foppish appearance, it was a good if plain sword, well used – and went for her, smooth as well oiled gears, looking as effortless as ever. Berie tried the same with his flash and glitter sword, got it tangled up in his scabbard, tripped over his own feet and ended up face first in the mud next to Flashy, only less passed out.

Then things got really bad. A tinny feel to the air. The smell of burned blood. The two things together seemed very familiar, but Vocho couldn't place from where. The hairs on his neck and arms rose. Burned blood . . . what did that remind him of? And then it came to him that he was deep in the shit. Who burned blood? Magicians, that's who. What the hells was one doing here? There hadn't been one in the kingdom for years, not since the prelate gained power and had them killed or chased out for being against his careful, orderly new clockwork plan for the country. Which didn't explain why the smell seemed familiar.

Time for that later. He had to take out these men before the suspected magician still in the carriage caused carnage. He planted one foot on Berie's prone back, with a softish kick to the head to keep him there, and swivelled.

Kacha was off the horse by now – was it Vocho or was that evil thing grinning? – and stood, ready and waiting for Eggy to come on. The stupid gun was still in her off hand, and as Vocho turned she flung it at Eggy, catching him a great crack across the forehead that made him stagger back, feet slipping in the mud.

Even Vocho had to admit that Egimont was a fine duellist, but Kacha had the measure of him and a grudge besides. Vocho took half a heartbeat to see her slip under his guard and then left her to it. If there was one thing he was sure of, it was that his sister could take care of herself.

He wasn't so sure he could, not against a magician. About as rare as rocking-horse shit they were, or had been. Now they were non-existent in Reyes. Just about all he knew was they were as powerful as kings, which is perhaps why the prelate hated them so much. He'd heard of a man fried where he stood, turned to ash with not even the chance to flinch. Time to be seriously careful, but Vocho had never been a careful man. When he won, which was always, however he could, he did it with speed and above all *style*.

Only he'd never actually faced a magician. He'd never even seen one, only heard tales. Fuck it, you only lived once.

The inside of the carriage smelled of burned blood and infamy. It was no wonder Kacha hadn't seen the man, magician or not – he was in the far corner, dressed in flowing midnight blue, cloak, robe and hood fading into the shifting shadows of a dark and rainy night. His face was a pale, scarred smudge against the window and naggingly familiar. The faint suggestion of blood on his hands was the only new clue to what he was. Vocho's scant consolation was that if he was a magician, he needed blood to draw on to power his spells and there wasn't any handy. Except his own or Vocho's, but he had no intention of letting anyone get blood on his clothes.

During all the business outside – Vocho could hear the click and clang of blades, and Kacha flinging barbed insults that the stoic and ever-so-noble Egimont wouldn't deign to answer – the magician would have had time to prepare. He didn't seem drunk like the rest, in fact he seemed distressingly alert.

Vocho approached, blade ready in the Icthian style. Free form and ready for anything seemed best at this point, and besides it was his favourite. He advanced slowly but not especially carefully – his forte was the sudden, impulsive move that was frowned on in the guild but would also catch his opponent off guard.

The magician, if that's what he truly was, held up his bloodstained hands in a gesture that looked like a yield. Vocho didn't trust it for a second. Another step forward and his blade hovered over the man's throat.

'My money or a hole in my head, I understand,' the man said. Odd sort of accent, sort of hard and sibilant at the same time, the voice soft but with a crackling undertone that shivered all the hairs on Vocho's neck.

'That's the idea,' Vocho said and arranged his feet so he'd have the perfect balance should he need to thrust. He'd never been one for killing for killing's sake, but he'd not shy away if it was necessary. And a magician – it could be *very* necessary, if he wanted to live out the night. 'What have you got? No, no dipping in your own pockets, thanks. I'm a thief not an idiot.'

The magician inclined his head in agreement. 'So I see. I have nothing that would be any value to you, I assure you. A few papers, the clothes I wear. Quills and pens and scalpels for my work, you understand.'

A quick movement of his hand that drew Vocho's eye, a hand scarred beyond belief but in a bizarrely beautiful sort of way. Dark patterns flowed across knuckles, symbols etched there by who-knew-what sorcery. They seemed to move on their own, those patterns, a flow that took the eye and caught the brain, made him follow them like a starving dog following its master. An itch started between Vocho's shoulder blades, familiar and yet not, and turned to a burn.

'Nothing for you,' the magician said. 'Except I may have to kill you. With the utmost regret, of course.'

'Of course.' The patterns shifted, became scenes of blood and murder, of headless bodies and sightless skulls, of days of glory in the guild sparring arena that led Vocho's head off into odd, dark dreams. The voice sounded more and more familiar but he was past caring, too wrapped up in what the hands were showing him. The burning on his back grew worse, made sweat pop up all along his lip and his hand slick on the hilt of his blade. Frighteningly familiar, yet he couldn't remember – and did it matter, when those patterns were drawing him in?

A shout from outside, a curse from Kacha and then Eggy calling out an odd word, a name perhaps? A plea for help, certainly. The sounds snapped Vocho back to himself, just in time to see the magician dip a pen into a pot of . . . *of blood. Let's not be shy here, that's blood* . . . and begin a new pattern on his outstretched palm.

The magician was quick, but Vocho had made his name being the quickest man in the duelling guild, so fast he could stab a man and put away his sword before anyone had seen him move. Well, almost that quick. Maybe the magician wasn't expecting him to be so fast, maybe he thought Vocho was still hypnotised by the flowing patterns, maybe he didn't expect anyone to attack him at all – magicians were renowned for their arrogance. Whichever, he wasn't expecting a sword to run him through. Even so, he surprised Vocho by almost getting out of the way – so fast he blurred, but the point still caught him. Just not in the neck. Instead, the sword went straight through the meaty top part of the man's shoulder and pinned him to the side of the carriage.

The magician let lose a stream of words in a language Vocho didn't have a hope of understanding. Blood bubbled from the wound – Vocho needed to finish this and quick, before the magician used the blood to finish Vocho. Another thrust, quick as the first, and the magician was too busy grabbing something out of a pocket to move. The blade slid in, right into his windpipe. *Cast a spell now, bastard.* The magician's eyes flew wide and one hand scrabbled at his neck, at the blade. The other had hold of . . . *Oh shit.*

Vocho knew less than bugger all about magicians, but even he knew the scrap of paper with bloody shifting patterns on it wasn't good. A stored spell, that was all it could be, blood marking the paper like written death. There were tales of them that Vocho had never believed, but he did now. A spell to do what? He'd heard of some men vaporised . . .

He knew enough to get the fuck out of the way. He whipped his sword free of the man's neck in a gurgle of breath and blood and dived out of a window head first, rolling as he landed, screaming when the burning on his back caught on his shirt. Straight into the mud, but even he didn't care about getting mud on his nice coat now.

When nothing obvious happened, no explosions and he was still all there in one piece, he dared a look up. The carriage door flapped open. Inside, the only sign of the mage was blood on the seat and side of the carriage and a now burned and shrivelled piece of paper fluttering to the floor.

A lucky escape. *You're sitting in the mud, looking like an idiot while Kacha gets all the glory again.* He shoved himself up and took stock. He'd ended up on the other side of the carriage from where Kacha and Egimont were fighting. Hadn't she finished him off by now? When he thought on it, he realised how little time had elapsed from getting into the carriage and his rather ignoble exit.

He wriggled his shoulders – the burning had subsided as suddenly as it started – and made his way around the carriage to watch the show, maybe butt in and finish the job in case Kacha was having second thoughts. Flashy was still flat out in the mud, Berie either out cold next to him or pretending to be. Vocho rather thought the latter, but he wasn't fighting so that was all right.

Kacha had Egimont on the back foot – quicker even than Vocho when she was at her best, and against Egimont she would make damn sure she was at her best.

'Can we hurry up?' Vocho called. 'I'm freezing, soaked and

pissed off, and the rest are all dealt with. Stop playing with him and get on with it.'

Egimont was good, but he was never going to be good enough to beat Kacha, who could thrash every man and woman in the duelling guild except Vocho. And it was that 'except' that made her so deadly – she was always trying to up her game so she could beat him. Not to mention they weren't in the guild any more so no guild rules.

A wink from Kacha above her mask, a thrust that would have killed a lesser duellist. Egimont was quick though, Vocho had to give him that. He slipped in the mud as he parried, recovered like a guildsman, used the movement to come up under Kacha's guard in a classic action in the Ruffelo style that caught her off guard and made Vocho wonder whether she was going easy on him, then startled them both by not going for the thrust. He hesitated just a fraction, staring at Kacha like he'd never see her again, like all he wanted to see was her.

'Please, Kass.'

This was not good. Nor was the way Kacha hesitated at that 'please', the way she shook her head as though trying to shake some traitorous notion out of it. She'd lost her head over Petri bloody Egimont once before and got burned. Vocho wasn't going to let it happen again.

'Kass, we need to finish this. *Right now*.'

'Yes,' she said slowly. 'Yes, we do.'

With that, she spun behind Eggy, so quick he hadn't a hope. Took him out with a well practised wallop to the base of the neck that rolled his eyes up into his head before her other arm came up between his legs with an audible *whump*, a move that the gallant Ruffelo probably never even considered. Vocho caught Eggy before he fell into the mud with the rest – he'd some nice clothes on him, no sense ruining them.

Kacha blew out a ragged breath, wiped a hand across what he could see of her face and picked up the gun. 'Bloody things. Never will get the hang of them. Coward's thing, really. A good blade is where it's at, right?'

She threw the gun into the bushes by the side of the road. And good riddance.

'Better off sticking with swords,' Vocho agreed, knowing exactly why the subject had changed. 'Know where you are with a sword. Guns have no style anyway. No, no *panache*.'

She rolled her eyes but laughed anyway, a bit shaky but back to herself again. For now.

A peculiar noise reminded them of the driver, still up on his seat. Only just though, because he was bent over and wheezing like an old man, oilskin cloak flapping in the sodden wind like bat wings. On closer inspection, it seemed he was laughing fit to piss himself.

'Oh, that was a good one. Nice shot there.' He went off into gales of more laughter.

Kacha raised an eyebrow his way. 'Oh, do be quiet, Cospel. I didn't want to kill the stupid sod, just rob him. Now come and help me get his boots off.'

'Only good nob is a dead one, I always say, so it's all good to me.' Cospel wiped at his eyes, allowed himself one last chuckle and jumped down from the seat.

'You might have mentioned Petri was in the coach,' Kacha said.

'You might have mentioned the magician as well.' Vocho kept his voice light, but he could still feel the pained thud of his heart at the sight of that piece of paper, still remember the way the markings on the man's hands had tried to lead his brain astray.

'Magician?' Kacha asked in a weak voice.

'I tried!' Cospel said. 'Only couldn't *say* anything, could I? Not unless I want everyone to know I'm helping the robbers of Fusta Wood. Only turned up last minute. Didn't have a chance to let you know. Knew you two could deal with them though.'

Vocho yanked Eggy's boots off. A good make, soft leather to the knee, polished to a high shine under the mud. Probably even the right size. 'That's what the eyebrows were all about? Maybe you should teach them to do semaphore, then next time I'll have a hope understanding. Though I don't want there to be a next time, not to meet a magician.' Vocho shuddered.

Kacha looked down thoughtfully at Egimont and if there was a wistful look it soon vanished. 'What's *he* doing with a magician? He's only a clerk at the prelate's office. Not even a very important one. He's got some money as ex-nobles go, but not enough for that. Above that, his family has no power any more, and that's what I hear magicians crave. When I hear of them, which is just about never. Are you sure he was one?'

'Good question.' No, he wasn't sure, in fact he really hoped he was wrong, but if there was even a hint that it had been a magician they could all be very dead. It was probably just him being paranoid. He'd been twitchy ever since the whole thing with the priest. That must be it. Magicians were long gone. Paranoid. 'The answer is, I don't care as long as he isn't *here*. Now come on. Time we were on our way. Time to get paid.'

Between the three of them, they soon had everything of value off the men. Not a bad haul as things went. As well as the five purses, each of which would keep them fed and warm and drunk for a week or more, Vocho had a fine new pair of boots that didn't pinch too much, a splendid crimson silk jacket and matching short cape from Flashy that he would probably never wear, not in that crap sack of a village they were living in, and Berie's gilt and glitter sword, which looked good but on closer inspection bent like tallow when pressure was applied. Ah well, he could sell it anyway. Kacha made sure she got Eggy's sword – far better than Flashy's for all it was gilt-free – and stripped them of all their jewels.

They took all the clothes they didn't want and bundled them into a sack, leaving three almost naked gentlemen and two nearly naked guards. Who wouldn't care nearly so much as the gentlemen when they all arrived wherever they were headed, wearing nothing but underwear, with some rather suspicious damp staining around the crotch area in Berie's case.

On to the carriage, and their spy – Cospel – had been right. Under a seat was a trunk big enough to stash a dead body in, secured with no less than five impressive locks. Vocho almost drooled just looking at it. Whatever was in this chest, it was very valuable to someone – bodyguards, locks *and* a possible magician to guard it, a thought that made sweat prickle on Vocho's scalp. But they'd made it out of the debacle alive, the winners, and they had this too. That was the important thing.

He could hardly wait to open it. If they got away before that magician recovered from a sword through the throat, whoever owned it would never find it.

It took the three of them to get the chest up onto the back of Vocho's horse, which sank into the mud and groaned under the weight. Vocho gave him a pat and decided that seeing as his boots were covered in mud already, he could probably walk back. It wasn't like he wasn't already soaked.

Once they were done, Cospel too stripped off. Vocho tied him up on the driver's seat and left him to a shivering wet drive, with a 'We'll leave your share in the usual place.' He thought for a moment. 'Where were you headed anyway?'

Cospel shrugged. 'A town just along the valley – that's as far as this coach goes.'

Hmm. A long way from Reyes and Egimont's usual stamping grounds. Never mind, he could think on that later. Vocho and Kacha manhandled the limp and muddy men into the carriage and Cospel clucked the horses on.

They watched the carriage until it disappeared around a bend and all they could make out was a faint light through the rain. Kacha forced a laugh and took Vocho's arm as they led the horses off the road and into the darkness of the woods. Vocho wasn't fooled. Her hand shook, ever so slightly. He knew why too – she'd almost killed Flashy, and it had been a miracle she hadn't. She'd never say it, but she didn't like the killing part. Things happened in the heat of the moment, it was true – a slip, a stray thrust, an unexpected movement and she couldn't avoid that – but she avoided killing if she could. Too merciful, without that ruthless instinct. It was her one weakness as a duellist, as far as Vocho could make out, which meant obviously it was the one he ragged her about as often as he could. A duellist might have to kill, to protect whoever he was guarding, to finish the job, though they were expected to refrain whenever possible. Just as well he managed for them both when it was necessary, mostly.

That's what was making her edgy perhaps; not that Petri had popped up, like a bloody jack-in-the-box, just at the worst possible moment.

He sidled a look her way. No, it was Petri that had her rattled with that 'please', damn the suave bastard.

They stopped to watch the carriage light disappear behind another line of trees.

'The respected Egimont sent off in his drawers, displaying the only jewels he has left,' she said with a satisfied smile. 'Well, if that doesn't make you your precious new name, nothing will.'

'Bugger.'

'What?'

'I forgot to tell him our new names.'

Chapter Two

The next morning was cold still, though the rain had let up. This was small comfort to Vocho as he squelched across the yard.

Nights out robbing were all well and good, but the days were grey and boring lately. Ever since that accident with the priest, after which no one wanted to employ them. Not to mention the arrest warrant. He supposed they would have been unemployed sooner or later anyway – guns were the coming thing, no matter how long the guild tried to hold out against them. It'd taken a while for them to gain popularity because for a long time only the very rich or the clockers, men and women who owned the clockwork factories, could afford them. Then something – he didn't know what because he didn't pay much attention – had happened, and all of a sudden almost everyone in the capital, Reyes, had one. He'd heard all the guards, employed by the prelate's council and otherwise, used them now. Mostly they were cheap things, liable to spring apart into a thousand pieces the moment anyone tried to fire them, probably knocked up by some clocker looking to make a quick bull or ten, but still.

As Kacha had amply demonstrated last night, they were not cut out for guns. At least out here in the arse end of nowhere guns weren't so common. Yet they would be, and then he and Kacha would probably have to live like this, as *farmers* for fuck's sake, all the time. Unless they could start getting to grips with guns. Or get back into the guild. Or grow bloody wings, which had about the same probability.

Vocho hated farms. He hated the mud, the shit, the smell of pig pens, the beady little eyes of the chickens. He hated the hours too – up at the crack of sodding dawn, when any right-minded duellist should just be thinking of going to bed.

Especially a world-famous duellist like himself. Bloody priests getting mysteriously dead, buggering up his perfectly good life.

He and Kacha should practise, really. How hard could guns be if even the city watch – a band of men known more for their ability to be bribed than intellectual thought – could figure them out? But that would be like admitting defeat. Twenty years he'd trained at the blade, twenty years man and boy. And he was the *best*. He'd not been beaten since he was eighteen, and everyone knew his name, which was a byword for being fucking good with a sword. Only Kacha could come close. Privately he knew she was better at technique than he was, was certainly craftier, quicker at times, but, God's cogs, he had more style, more élan, more . . . well OK, more height and weight. But it was him they sang about, his name they called. He'd made bloody sure of it, and it rankled to have all that hard work thrown away.

Because everyone *had* called his name. Bards had sung of how he and Kacha had pulled themselves up by their bootstraps, out of the gutter and into the employ of kings and prelates and great men. They both had, but his was always the name that was sung the loudest. Because he paid the bards to, mostly, but even so. They'd sung of duels he'd fought and won, of great feats of heroism while guarding whoever was paying his wages via the guild that week. Most of it was a load of bollocks, naturally, but there had been one or two occasions where he'd been mildly heroic, like when he'd saved that child from falling out of a window at the change o' the clock, or he'd foiled that heist on the bank and the resulting swordplay had spread into the market before he'd nailed the ringleader, to a wall as it happened. Mostly it had just seemed like fun at the time, and a great way of showing everyone, particularly Kacha, how great he was.

The bards had sung about the romance of a guild that no one outside it really understood, about its history as sworn defenders of the old emperors before the Great Fall. They'd sung about how afterwards, when there were no emperors, the guildsmen had changed to swearing their lives to each other and how no man could break them from that swearing. They'd sung about how the empire had fractured into a thousand little kingdoms, and how the guild served them all on its own terms, and they'd sung about the nostalgia for a long-lost age it represented with Vocho as its most powerful icon, and how dashing he looked, which was only to be expected. And then . . . and then an evening that was vague in his mind, too much wine probably, and that priest. Now they sang about Vocho the priest murderer, who stabbed holy men in the back – only the second person, after the reviled Jokin, ever to be exiled from the guild after he'd taken his master's test and sworn his oath to be true.

He stamped across the yard and glared at the chickens. A fucking *farmer*. What style did a farmer have? Sackcloth trousers and perfume of pig shit. Vocho opened the gate to the coop and flung in the grain, not caring how it bounced off the heads of the hungry birds. The only bright spot in his day was going to be later, when he and Kacha would go through their haul from last night. Silks and jewels and bulls, lots of lovely bulls. Not enough to stop him being a farmer, though he had high hopes of the chest, which had been satisfyingly heavy. The locks looked tough but would yield with time. He'd always been good with locks.

The chest had been guarded by a magician too. Magicians were so rare they were almost legends, and they could command the ransom of kings as payment, or so the stories went. And what was anyone doing going to those lengths if what was inside wasn't worth a fortune? Our lad Eggy was an idiot only having the two bodyguards, even if he did have magic on his side. Not that it would have made much difference. They'd still have the chest; there'd just be more dead, or at least denuded, men.

Muffled exhortations to "Stand! Stand, you ruddy horse," leaked out of the stable, followed by a massive *thunk*, a *crack*, and a puff of splinters exploding into the yard as the horse took exception to Kacha's tone of voice or perhaps just the world being what it was, it was hard to tell.

Vocho finished his chores moodily and sloshed back across

the yard to the house. To the chest. It sat on the table like the world's biggest birthday present. He itched to get started on the locks, but Kacha had stropped and fretted and pulled the older sister trick, which made him even more determined to open the damned thing. She was the cautious one, compara-tively, and she'd said that if a magician had guarded it then they had to make sure there was no magic on the thing before they opened it. Which was all very well, but Vocho was dreaming of the things they could do with whatever money or precious items were inside. It was heavy enough to hold a bloody fortune in gold. Maybe . . . maybe enough to buy a pardon, get their old lives back. Maybe. Enough money and the good folks of Reyes would forget everything. The prelate's palace probably would, if he bribed the right person. Then perhaps Kacha would forgive him too. His life wasn't the only one he'd buggered up. He had things to make up for.

She caught him just as he was about to try the first of the locks.

"What in the hells are you doing?"

He jumped back, red faced and ready with a lie. "Just looking. To see if I could find any magic on it."

She snorted disbelief and came to the table, her recently cut ragged blonde hair bouncing indignantly. "And I'm the queen of the pig people. Honestly, Voch, do you think I can't tell when you're lying? Your left eye always twitches."

"Does not!"

She narrowed her eyes at him. "See, it's doing it again."

He studied her for a moment and wondered how far he could push it. Not far – he never could. She always saw through his bullshit, and it was why he loved her and why she drove him insane too. Kacha the wonderful, Kacha the perfect, Kacha, who could see when he was lying. Kacha, who always believed in him anyway, when no one else would.

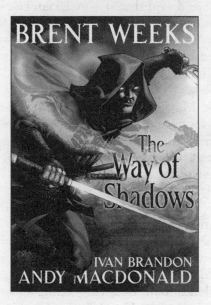

Enter the monthly

Orbit sweepstakes at

www.orbitloot.com

With a different prize every month,
from advance copies of books by
your favourite authors to exclusive
merchandise packs,
**we think you'll find something
you love.**

facebook.com/OrbitBooksUK

@OrbitBooks

www.orbitbooks.net